Escape to

Paradise

TRILOGY

MaryLu Tyndall

SHILOH RUN PRESS

An Imprint of Barbour Publishing, Inc.

Forsaken Dreams © 2013 by MaryLu Tyndall
Elusive Hope © 2013 by MaryLu Tyndall
Abandoned Memories © 2014 by MaryLu Tyndall

Print ISBN 978-1-63058-874-8

eBook Editions:
Adobe Digital Edition (.epub) 978-1-63409-377-4
Kindle and MobiPocket Edition (.prc) 978-1-63409-378-1

Cover Image from *Forsaken Dreams*, Faceout Studio, www.faceoutstudio.com

Published by Shiloh Run Press, an imprint of Barbour Publishing, Inc., P.O. Box 719, Uhrichsville, Ohio 44683, www.shilohrunpress.com.

Our mission is to publish and distribute inspirational products offering exceptional value and biblical encouragement to the masses.

Member of the
Evangelical Christian
Publishers Association

Printed in the United States of America.

Escape to
Paradise

TRILOGY

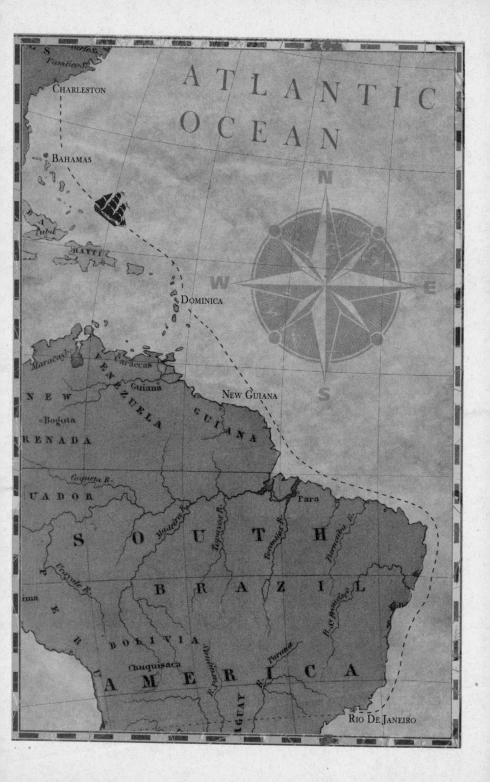

FORSAKEN Dreams

To obey is better than sacrifice.

1 SAMUEL 15:22

Dedicated to every Jonah running from God.

CAST OF CHARACTERS

Colonel Blake Wallace—leader and organizer of the expedition to Brazil and a decorated war hero wanted for war crimes by the Union. He suffers from post-traumatic stress disorder.

Eliza Crawford—widow and Confederate army nurse who signed on to nurse the colonists, married to a Yankee general, and disowned by her Southern, politician father.

James Callaway—Confederate army surgeon turned Baptist preacher who signed on as the colony's only doctor but who suffers from an extreme fear of blood.

Hayden Gale—con man who has been searching for his father to execute revenge for the death of his mother. Believing the man is heading toward Brazil, Hayden stows away on board the *New Hope.*

Angeline Moore—signed on as the colony's seamstress, Angeline is a broken woman who wants more than anything to put her past behind her. Unfortunately, there are a few passengers on board whom she recognizes from her prior life.

Magnolia Scott—Georgia plantation owner's pampered daughter who doesn't want to go to Brazil and will do anything to turn the ship around. Constantly belittled by her father, she is obsessed with her appearance.

Mr. and Mrs. Scott—once wealthy plantation owners who claim to have lost everything in the war, yet they still retain their haughty, patrician attitude toward others. They hope to regain their position and wealth in Brazil.

Sarah Jorden—seven months pregnant and a war widow, she signed on to teach the colony's children.

Wiley Dodd—ex-lawman from Richmond who is fond of the ladies and in possession of a treasure map that points to Brazil as the location of a vast amount of gold.

Harman Graves—senator's son and ex-politician from Maryland whose hopes to someday run for president were crushed when the South seceded from the Union.

Captain Barclay—old sea dog who was a blockade runner in the war and who captains and owns the ship *New Hope.*

Parson Bailey—signed on as the colony's pastor and spiritual guide.

Emory Lewis—the colony's carpenter who took to drink after losing his wife and child in the war.

Moses and Delia—a freed slave and his sister who, along with her two children, want to start over in a new land away from the memory of slavery.

Jesse and Rosa Jenkins—simple farmers who, with their young daughter, Henrietta, hope to have a chance at a good life away from the ravages of war.

Mable—slave to the Scotts.

Chapter 1

May 29, 1866
Somewhere in the Caribbean

We shall all be in heaven or hell by night's end!" Parson Bailey shouted above the din of the storm. "God save us. God save us." His pudgy face swelled with each fateful phrase, while his eyes as wide as beacons, skittered around the tiny storeroom with each pound of wave and wind.

Eliza Crawford extracted herself from her friends huddling in the corner and made her way to the parson, intending to beg his silence. It did no good for him to say such things. Why, a parson of all people should comfort others, not increase their fears.

Thunder shook the ship. The deck canted, and instead of reaching Parson Bailey, Eliza tumbled into the arms of the very man she'd been trying to avoid since she boarded the *New Hope* almost three weeks ago—Wiley Dodd. Though of obvious means, evident in the fine broadcloth coat he wore and the gold watch he so often flaunted, something in his eyes, the way he looked at the women, made her stomach sour.

"In need of male comfort, Mrs. Crawford?" he asked. That sourness now turned to nausea as his arms encircled her. Not that she needed much assistance in the squeamish department. Her stomach had been convulsing since the storm began a few hours ago. But the perfumed Macassar oil Mr. Dodd slicked through his hair threatened to destroy all her efforts to keep her lunch from reappearing over his posh attire.

"We are done for. Done for, I say." The parson continued his rambling as he clung to the mast pole.

"I beg your pardon, Mr. Dodd." Pushing against his chest, Eliza

13

snapped from his clawing grip.

The lizard-like smile on his lips belied their dire situation. "You're welcome to stay with me if you are frightened, my dear."

"Yesterday you called me a Yankee whore, sir!"

His smile remained though he gave a little shrug. "Desperate times and all that, you know."

Lightning flashed through the porthole, masking his face in a deathly gray.

"Why are you not frightened?" she asked him.

"Naught but a summer squall," he shouted over the ensuing roar of thunder. "I have experienced many such storms."

Eliza wondered how often a sheriff would have been to sea. Even so, he'd still chosen to remain below instead of help above with the other men. The ship careened upward as if it were but a toy in a child's hands. Eliza stumbled again and struck the bulkhead. A wall of water slammed against the porthole, creating a perverted dance of seething foam that lasted far longer than it should.

Was the ship sinking? Her lungs seized at the thought.

"The end is near. Near, I tell you!" the parson ranted.

The wave retreated. Leaden sky took its place, and Eliza scrambled on hands and knees back to her position beside a massive crate strapped to the bulkhead. Back to her only friends on this ill-fated ship. Mrs. Sarah Jorden and Miss Angeline Moore received her with open arms, neither one sobbing as one would expect of genteel ladies in such harrowing circumstances. Besides, there was sobbing enough coming from the other side of the room, where the wealthy plantation owners, Mr. and Mrs. Scott, and their pampered daughter, Magnolia, clung to each other in a desperate barbarism contrary to their elevated station. In fact, Mr. Scott had not opened his eyes in hours. Perhaps he attempted to drown out his wife's incessant howling, which elevated to a piercing level after each of the parson's decrees of doom. Tears streamed down Magnolia's fair cheeks, pricking Eliza's heart.

She should be angry at the young lady for exposing Eliza's ruse. But all she felt was pity.

Sitting beside the wealthy planters, Magnolia's personal slave hunched with folded hands and moving lips as if she were praying. Eliza hoped so. They needed all the prayers they could get. She had already lifted her petitions to the Almighty. Still, she whispered one more appeal, just in case, as she scanned the rest of the passengers crowded in the tiny storeroom—sent below by the captain when the seas had grown rough.

Farmers, merchants, lawyers, people of all classes and wealth. Jessie and Rosa Jenkins and their young daughter, Henrietta, had not uttered a peep since they'd tied themselves to a large table anchored to the deck. Mr. Harman Graves, a politician from Maryland, sat with his back against the bulkhead and a pleased look on his angular face, as if he knew something they did not. He rubbed an amulet between thumb and forefinger, lips moving as if in prayer, though Eliza doubted it was directed at God.

Next to him, Mr. Emory Lewis, a carpenter, if Eliza remembered correctly, kept plucking a flask from his pocket, taking a sip, and putting it back, only to repeat the ritual over again.

The eerie whistle of wind through rigging tore at Eliza's remaining courage. She shivered, and Sarah squeezed her arm, whispering something in her ear that was lost in the boom of another wave pounding the hull.

A child's whimper brought her gaze to her left, where Delia, a freed Negress, hugged her two young children close. A flash of lightning accentuated the fear tightening the woman's coffee-colored face. The fear of death—a fear they all felt at the moment. A fear that was no respecter of class or race. A fear that broke through all social barriers. For yesterday, the Scotts, as well as some of the others present, would not have agreed to be in the same room with a freed slave.

Or even with Eliza.

Thunder bellowed, barely audible above the explosion of wind and wave. How did this tiny brig withstand such a beating? Surely the timbers would burst any moment, splintering and filling the room with the mad gush of the sea. Locking her arms with the ladies on either side, she closed her eyes as the galloping ship tossed them like rag dolls over the hard deck.

"And the sea gave up the dead which were in it; and death and hell delivered up the dead which were in them: and they were judged every man according to their works." Parson Bailey had taken to quoting scripture, which only caused Mrs. Scott to howl even louder.

Eliza's thoughts shifted to Blake and the other men struggling to save the ship up on deck. Well, mainly to Blake, if she were honest. Which was something she hadn't been of late. But that was another matter altogether. *Oh fiddle, Colonel Blake Wallace,* she reproved herself. She shouldn't be calling him by his Christian name. Though the last nineteen days she'd spent in his company seemed a lifetime, in truth she hardly knew the man.

Then why, in her darkest hour as she faced a suffocating death in the middle of the Caribbean, was it Colonel Wallace who drew her thoughts? Not just her thoughts, but her concern—fear for his safety. Fear that she wouldn't have a chance to explain why she had lied, wouldn't have a chance to win back the affection that had so recently blossomed in both their hearts. She rubbed her tired eyes.

But what did it matter now? He hated her for who she was. No, for whom she had married. In fact, as she glanced over the terrified faces in the room, only loathing shot back at her. To them she was the enemy. An enemy they were risking their lives to escape. And now they were all going to die. Together in the middle of the sea. With no one to mourn them. No one who would know their fate. Not even Eliza's father or Uncle James and Aunt Sophia or little Alfred, Rachel, or Henry. Not that they would care. To them, she was already dead.

Disowned. Disinherited. Forsaken.

The brig twisted and spun around as if caught in a whirlpool. Angeline's trembling body crashed into Eliza on one side while Sarah's smashed into her from the other, making Eliza feel like a garment run through a clothespress. An explosion of thunder cracked the sky wide open, followed by an eerie silence, as if all of nature had been stunned by the angry shout of God. Or maybe they were all dead. But then the wind outside the hull and the whimpers of fear within resumed. Angeline pressed Stowy, her cat, tightly against her chest while Sarah's free hand clutched her belly swollen with child. Seven months along. How worried she must be for her wee one!

"Repent, for the end is at hand!" Parson Bailey's flashing eyes speared Eliza with a look of hatred. She knew what he was thinking. What they all were thinking.

That she was the reason for the storm.

Another thunderous blast and Eliza squeezed her eyes shut again, wishing—praying—this was only a bad dream. How did she get herself into this mess? Why, oh why, did she ever think she could start afresh in Brazil?

She opened her eyes and stared at the oscillating shadows: light and dark drifting over the bulkhead, crates, boxes, and tables. And over the hopeless faces. A torn piece of rope tumbled back and forth across the deck. Parson Bailey still glared at her. Something maniacal glinted in his eyes as he shared a glance with Mr. Dodd and Mr. Graves.

"It's you!" he raged, glancing over the others. "God told me this Yankee is the cause of the storm!"

Though all eyes shot toward the parson, no one said a word. Hopefully they were too busy holding on and too frightened for their lives to do anything about it. Mr. Graves, however, staggered to his feet, slipped the amulet into his pocket, and glanced at Eliza like a cougar eyeing a rabbit.

She tried to swallow, but her throat felt like sand.

Mr. Dodd grinned. "I say we toss her over!"

"Aye, she's our Jonah!" Mr. Graves added.

"Precisely." Parson Bailey nodded.

Though the freed Negress's eyes widened even farther, only the farmers, Mr. and Mrs. Jenkins, offered any protests. Protests that were lost in the thunderous boom of the storm.

"Don't be absurd, Parson!" Sarah added from beside Eliza. "God cares not a whit whether Eliza is a Yankee or a Rebel!" Yet, no sooner had the words fled her mouth than thunder exploded so loud it seemed God disagreed with the young teacher's pronouncement.

Eliza frowned. For goodness' sake, whose side was God on, anyway?

The ship bucked, and Eliza's bottom lifted from the deck then slammed back again. A rope snapped, and a crate slid across the room. Mr. Dodd halted it with his boot then glanced at Mr. Graves while jerking his head toward Eliza.

"Jonah must go overboard for the seas to calm!" The parson howled above the storm, though he seemed unwilling to let go of the mast pole to carry out his depraved decree.

Angeline squeezed Eliza's arm. "I won't let them take you!"

As much as she appreciated her friend's courageous stance, Eliza knew what she must do. She must leave, get out of this room, out from

17

under these incriminating eyes, before these men dragged her above and did just what they threatened.

Terror stole the breath from her lungs, but she tugged from her friends' arms nonetheless and lunged for the door. She was prepared for the angry slurs behind her when she opened it. She wasn't prepared for the blast of wind and slap of seawater that shoved her flat onto her derriere and sent her crinolette flailing about her face. Pain shot up her spine. Humiliation at her exposed petticoat and stockings reddened her face. But when she glanced around, everyone's eyes were closed against the wind and spray bursting into the room. Shaking the stinging water from her eyes, Eliza rose, braced against the torrent, gripped the handle with both hands, and heaved the door shut behind her. Then leaning her head into the wind, she forged down the narrow hall. She had no idea what she intended to do. Toss herself into the sea? She shivered at the thought. Yet if that was God's will, if He wanted her to throw herself into the raging waters, then so be it!

But then again, when had she ever obeyed God?

The burning prick of conscience was instantly doused by a cascade of seawater crashing down the companionway ladder. The mad surge grabbed her feet and swept them from beneath her. Gripping the railing, she hung on for dear life as she floated off the deck. Seawater filled her mouth. Thoughts of her imminent demise filled her mind. But then her body dropped to the sodden wood. Eliza gasped and spit the salty taste from her mouth.

Thunder roared, shaking the railing beneath her hand. The brig jerked and flung her against the ladder. Struggling to her feet, she dragged her dripping gown up the steps, unprepared for the sight that met her eyes.

Waves of towering heights surrounded the ship, their foamy tips scattering like spears in the wind. Rain fell in thick panels, making it nearly impossible to see anything except blurry, distorted shapes that surely must be the crew hard at work. Wind crashed into Eliza, stealing her breath and howling in her ears. Rain pelted her like hail. The ship pitched over a swell. Eliza toppled to the deck then rolled as if she weighed no more than a feather. She bumped into a small boat and gripped the slippery moorings anchoring it to the deck.

Salt! Salt everywhere. It filled her mouth. It filled her nose. It stung her eyes. It was all she could smell. And taste. That and fear. Not just her own. Fear saturated the air like the rain and waves. It boomed in the muffled shouts ricocheting across the ship. Buzzed in the electric charge of lightning. Clinging to the moorings, her gown flapping like a torn sail, she squinted and searched for the captain, hoping his calm expression would soothe her fears. Yet from his rigid stance on the quarterdeck and his viselike grip on the wheel, Eliza's hopes were swept away with the wind.

Which did nothing to ease her terror. A terror that numbed her heart as she accepted her fate. A wall of water slammed into her. She closed her eyes and hung on as the ship angled to port. Why did she always make bad decisions? Why did she never listen to her conscience? Stubborn, rebellious girl! If she hadn't married Stanton, if she had listened to her father and her uncle, she would be home now with a loving family. She wouldn't have been forced to become a nurse in the war, forced to witness things no lady should witness. Forced to take care of herself in a man's world.

Sailors, ropes tied about their waists, crisscrossed the deck in a tangled fury. By the foredeck, Hayden, their stowaway, his long dark hair thrashing around his face, held fast to a line that led up to the yards. In the distance, Eliza made out James Callaway clinging to the ratlines as he slowly made his way up to the tops. How could anyone hold on in this wind? Especially James, who was a doctor, not a sailor.

But where was Blake. . .Colonel Wallace? Fighting against the assault of seawater in her eyes, she scanned the deck, the tops. *Dear God, please. Please let him be all right.*

She must find him. Or discover his fate. She must talk to the captain. If they were going to sink, she'd rather know than cling to false hope. Bracing against the wind and rain, she rose to her knees, struggling against her multiple petticoats and crinolette. Inconvenient contraptions! If she stayed low, she may be able to crawl to the quarterdeck ladder and make her way up to the captain.

The ship rolled then plunged into a trough. The timbers creaked and groaned under the strain. Rain stabbed her back. Wind shrieked through the rigging like a death dirge. A massive wave rose before the ship. The bow leaped into it. Eliza dropped to the deck and dug her nails into the wood. *Oh God. No!* The ship lurched to near vertical. Lightning etched a jagged bolt across Eliza's eyelids.

She lost her grip. Tumbling, tumbling, like a weed driven before the wind. She threw her hands out, searching for something to grab onto. Anything. But the glassy wood slipped from her fingers, leaving splinters in her palms.

And terror in her heart.

Her body slammed into the railing. The ship canted. She rolled over the bulwarks, flung her hand out in one last effort to save herself. Her fingers met wood. She latched on. The salivating sea reached up to grab her legs, tugging her down.

Her fingers slipped. Pain radiated into her palms, her wrists. The brig heaved and canted again like a bucking horse.

God, is this how I am to die? Perhaps it was. She'd run from God long enough.

Rain slapped her face, filled her nose. She couldn't breathe. Her fingers slipped again. She couldn't hold on much longer.

A strong hand grabbed her wrist. A face appeared over the railing. "Hang on! I've got you."

CHAPTER 2

May 10, 1866
Nineteen days earlier
Charleston, South Carolina

The hand that gripped Eliza's was strong, firm, rough like a warrior's, yet gentle. He lifted her gloved fingers to his lips and kissed them while eyes as gray and tumultuous as a storm assessed her. "Welcome aboard, Mrs. Crawford." The voice equaled the strength that exuded from the man. No, not any man. A colonel, she had heard, a graduate of West Point. Though he was not broadcasting that fact to the Union authorities scouring Charleston.

"I'm"—he coughed into his hand—"Mr. Roberts, the overseer of this expedition. You are a nurse, if memory serves?" He assisted her from the plank onto the deck of the brig, where the scent of perspiration, tar, and aged wood swirled about her.

Mr. Roberts, indeed. She knew his true identity to be that of Colonel Blake Wallace, a decorated hero of the war, but his secret was safe with her. She smiled. "You are correct, sir." Thankful for his firm grip, Eliza steadied herself against the motion of the ship. Her heart needed steadying as well, as the colonel continued to gaze at her as if she'd sprouted angel wings. A flood of heat rose up her neck, and she tugged from his grip.

"Forgive me, Mrs. Crawford." He shook his head as if in a daze and turned to welcome another passenger on board, giving Eliza a chance to study the man who'd organized this daring adventure. In the early morning sunlight, his hair glistened in waves of onyx down to his stiff collar where the strands curled slightly. Drawn along the lines of a soldier, his body displayed a strength only hinted at by the pull of his white shirt

21

and black waistcoat across broad shoulders. Matching trousers stretched over firm thighs before disappearing inside tall leather boots. He turned and caught her staring at him. And then smiled—a glorious smile that was part rogue and part saint, if there was such a thing. Either way, it did terrible, marvelous things to her stomach. Or was that the rock of the ship?

Oh fiddle! He was heading her way. With a limp, she noticed. A slight limp that tugged at her heart.

"Do you have luggage, Mrs. Crawford?" Dark eyebrows rose over those stormy eyes, and Eliza thought it best not to stare at the man any longer. She was a widow, after all. A single woman. And she wouldn't want anyone getting the wrong impression of her character. "Over there." She pointed her gloved finger to a large trunk perched on the edge of the dock.

"Very well." Turning, he shouted to a man standing by the railing. "Mr. Mitchel. Would you bring that trunk to the master's cabin?"

"Aye, aye." The man darted across the plank.

The colonel nodded toward her and seemed about to say something when a burly man with a tablet stole his attention with a question.

Another man sped past Eliza, bumping into her and begging her pardon. Clutching her pocketbook, she stepped closer to the capstan, out of the way of sailors who scrambled across the deck of the two-masted brig, preparing the ship to sail and helping passengers and their luggage on board. The squawk of seagulls along with the thud of bare feet over the wooden planks accompanied the shouts of dockworkers and crewmen. Beyond the wharf, a group of citizens huddled on shore watching the goings-on from Bay Street.

Furniture, sewing machines, and a plethora of farming implements, along with trunks, lockers, and crates were soon hauled aboard. A pulley system, erected over the yards above, lowered a squealing pig through a hatch into the hold below.

Adjusting her bonnet to shade her eyes from the rising sun while fanning herself against the rising heat, Eliza studied the oncoming passengers. An elderly couple, dressed far too elegantly for sailing, boarded with a lady about Eliza's age whom she assumed to be their daughter. Wearing a pink taffeta gown with a low neckline trimmed in Chantilly lace, the young woman drew the attention of nearly every man on board, including several sailors who stopped to gape at her. Eliza couldn't blame them. With hair that rivaled the luster of ivory and skin as creamy as milk, she was the epitome of a Southern belle. Only her red-rimmed eyes marred an otherwise perfect face. That and her frown. She seemed oddly familiar to Eliza, as if they'd met before. Behind them, a young Negress, bent beneath the burden of a large valise, dragged a portmanteau as she struggled to keep up.

A tall man with light, wavy hair and wearing a gray three-piece suit, round-brimmed hat, and a pleasant smile on his face leaped from the walkway onto the deck and glanced over the ship, followed by a young couple with a small child, a foppish man all dressed in black with dark sideburns and a goatee, and finally a pregnant woman. Alone, with no husband at her side.

All strangers, yet soon they would become her bunkmates, her neighbors, her companions—perhaps even her friends.

That was, if she could keep her past a secret.

The colonel turned her way again, snapping his fingers at another man crossing the deck. "Forgive me, Mrs. Crawford. Max will see you to your cabin, where"—he scanned the deck—"I believe Mr. Mitchel has already taken your trunk. I trust we shall have a chance to become better acquainted after we set sail?"

She wanted to say she would enjoy that, but that would be too forward. Instead, she merely smiled and thanked him as the man led the way below deck. Standing at the companionway ladder, Eliza cast one last glance over her shoulder and found the colonel's eyes still on her. Ah, so he had taken note of her. As if reading her thoughts, he chuckled, coughed into his hand, and limped away.

Eliza had never been on a ship before. Born and raised in Marietta, Georgia, she had no reason to take to the sea. As a war nurse, she'd traveled on a train or a coach. Now as she descended below deck and the sunlight abandoned her and the halls squeezed her from both sides, her nerves spun into knots. And they weren't even out at sea yet! Her skirts swished against the sides of the narrow corridor, and she pressed them down, lest she snag the fabric on the rough wood. They passed another hatchway leading below, and the scent of something altogether unpleasant filled her nose. Thankful that the man didn't take her in that direction, Eliza followed him to an open door.

"Here ye go, miss. Used t' be the master's cabin, but the cap'n reserved it for the single ladies on board." Max pressed down springs of unruly red hair that circled an equally red face while he allowed liberties with his gaze on Eliza. She took a step back, unsure if it was safe to enter the room with this man in tow. His body odor alone threatened to stir her breakfast into disorder.

"That's very kind of him. Thank you, sir." She hoped her curt tone would drive him away. It did. But not before he winked above a grin that revealed a jagged row of gray teeth.

Sunlight filtered in from a small porthole, casting oscillating shafts of light over the cabin as small as a wardrobe. A woman, sitting on the only chair, looked up as Eliza stepped inside.

"Hello, I'm Angeline Moore."

"Eliza Crawford." Untying the ribbons beneath her chin, she eased off her bonnet. "Pleased to meet you. I suppose we shall be bunkmates?"

"Yes, and one other lady, I believe." Angeline stood. Copper curls quivered about her neck. Her smile was pleasant, her cheeks rosy, and her violet eyes alluring. And what Eliza wouldn't give for such feminine curves as hers. Or would she? Despite her dalliance with the colonel above, she had no interest in attracting men. She'd already tried her hand at marriage, and that had ended miserably.

"One more lady. . .in here?" Eliza glanced at her trunk, which took up nearly half the room. "With your luggage and the other lady's, we will be packed in here like apples in a crate." Her stomach tightened at the thought.

"I don't have a trunk. Everything I own is right in here." Angeline pointed to a small, embroidered valise on the table beside her.

Eliza thought it strange to have so little, but she didn't want to pry. Setting down her pocketbook, she planted her hands at her waist. "But where are the beds?"

Angeline pointed to three pairs of hooks on the deck head. "Hammocks, I believe." Her lips slanted.

"Oh my."

"We are better off than most." A voice coming from the hallway preceded a brown-haired woman with a belly ripe with child. A ray of sunlight speared the porthole and struck the gold cross hanging around her neck, causing Eliza to blink.

24

"Aside from those who can afford it, most passengers sleep together in the hold," the woman continued as she set down her case, pressed a hand on her back, and gave both of them a wide grin. "Good thing we are all single women. I'm Sarah Jorden."

Pleasantries were exchanged between the ladies whom Eliza hoped would soon become good friends.

"I am a nurse," Eliza offered, sitting down on her trunk. "And you, Mrs. Jorden? What brings you on this adventure?" She patted the spot beside her.

"Please call me Sarah. And I am the teacher." She smiled, sliding onto the seat. Brown hair drawn back in a bun circled an oval face with plain but pleasant features.

"Are there children coming aboard?" Angeline asked.

"I believe so. Several, in fact," Sarah said.

Angeline returned to her seat and began fingering the embroidery on her valise. "A teacher and a nurse." She sighed. "I fear I bring no such useful skills to our adventure. I am only a seamstress and not a very good one at that. In fact, it is unclear why I was even accepted for the journey."

"Oh rubbish, dear." Sarah tugged off her gloves. "We shall simply have to discover what talents God has given you."

A wave of red washed over Angeline's face. Odd. Perhaps she was just nervous about the journey—the unknown, the new beginning in a strange land. Certainly, being a single woman all alone made it all the more frightening. Or it should. Yet Eliza felt more excitement than fear. The sparkle in Sarah's eyes indicated she felt the same.

Reaching over, Eliza pulled the pamphlet out from her valise. The pamphlet she'd read so many times during the past two weeks, she knew it by heart. The pamphlet she had prayed over, thought about, agonized over.

Brazil! Brazil! Land of dreams. Land of hope. Land of beginnings! Fertile land available at only 22 cents an acre. Farmers, bring your tools; bring your implements, household items, and furniture; bring as many varieties of seeds as you can. People of every age and skill needed to recreate the Southern utopia stolen from us by the North. Become wealthy in a land of plenty, which Providence has blessed more than any land I have seen. Brazil welcomes you with open arms, a land of mild temperatures, rich soil, and perfect freedom. A land where dreams come true.

From the first time Eliza had read the pamphlet handed to her by a man on the street, three words continued to leap out at her, sealing her decision. *Dreams.* She'd had so many of those as a child. None of which had come true. *Hope.* Something she had lost during the past five years. *Beginnings.* A place she could go where people didn't know who she was—didn't know what she had done. A place where she wasn't shunned, hated, insulted, and rejected. Where she could start fresh with new people. A new society. A Southern utopia.

Was there such a thing outside of heaven?

Blake Wallace squeezed his eyes shut, not only to block out the sight of the port authority officer but to give himself a moment to think. He wanted another five hundred dollars?

That was nearly half of his remaining savings. He couldn't very well ask his passengers to pay more than the forty-two dollars he'd already charged them for the trip. Most of them were as poor or poorer than he was. In fact, many of the wealthiest families in the South had been stripped of their money, their belongings, even their property. Their homes had been ransacked and burned, their servants and slaves scattered, their dignity stolen. His jaw bunched at the memory of his own white-columned, two-story family home in Atlanta burned to nothing but ash and debris. And then two months ago, the land purchased by Yankees for pennies.

His family dead.

Most people had nowhere to live and little food to eat. They sought refuge under trees or in borrowed tents. Railroads were torn up, schools closed, banks insolvent, towns and cities reduced to rubble, and jobs nonexistent.

Now as he stood before this Yankee port authority officer in his fancy brass-buttoned jacket, it took all of Blake's strength, all his will, not to strangle him on the spot.

"There is the alternative. . . ." The man's voice was as slimy as his character.

Blake opened his eyes. A drop of tobacco perched in the corner of the man's mouth.

"And that is?"

"I could inform the new lieutenant colonel in town that you are a Rebel officer."

Though his stomach churned, Blake allowed no reaction to reach his stoic expression. Was it that obvious?

"Yeah, I can tell." The man spit a wad of tobacco to the side. "I can spot you Reb soldiers a mile away, and you officers give off a certain stink." He scrunched his nose for effect.

Blake narrowed his eyes, flexing his fingers at his sides to keep them from fisting the buffoon. A drop of sweat trickled down his back.

The port officer shrugged. "Have it your way. The new colonel in charge of Charleston won't rest till he ferrets out all you Rebs and either imprisons you or, better yet, hangs you."

Blake resisted the impulse to rub his throat. He didn't relish dangling at the end of a rope or rotting in a Union prison. And he knew if he stayed, that would be his fate. He'd been too visible in the war, had inflicted too much damage on the enemy. So it had been no surprise that a month ago, his name had appeared on the Union's most-wanted list for war crimes.

Which was why he changed his name, moved to Charleston, and decided to leave the States. Organizing and leading an expedition to Brazil, where he hoped to start and head a new colony, seemed the opportunity of a lifetime. And his last chance at a new life. At a good life. If such a thing even existed anymore.

Blake counted out the gold coins into the man's hand, clamping his jaw tight against a volcano of exploding anger.

"Where do you think you're going anyway, you and your pack of mindless Rebs? 'Specially in that old ship?" The port master jerked his head toward the brig. "You ain't even got steam power."

"Brazil," Blake said absently as he watched a dark-haired man hobble over the railing of the *New Hope* and drop below. Probably one of the passengers. Regardless of its age, the ship was a beauty. Fine-lined and sturdy, a square-sailed, two-masted brig of 213 tons, refitted with extra cabins for passengers, and owned and sailed by a seasoned mariner, Captain Barclay, an old sea dog to whom Blake had taken an immediate liking.

As he scanned the deck, Blake caught a flicker of brown hair the color of maple syrup. Mrs. Eliza Crawford stood against the larboard railing, the wind fluttering the ribbons of her bonnet.

"Brazil! I hear there's nothin' there but mosquitoes and malaria." The port officer's caustic voice drew Blake's gaze once again. "Not to mention everyone knows Brazilians are crossbred with Negroes!" He shook his head and chuckled. "Poisonous insects, scorching heat, too much rain, diseases like leprosy and elephantiasis—no wonder we won the war. You Rebs are dumber than a sack of horse manure."

Ignoring him, Blake finished counting the coins. "This is robbery, and you know it."

"You're the ones that robbed our country of her young men. Seems fittin' justice."

Sunlight glinted off something in the distance, temporarily blinding Blake. Two Yankee soldiers strolled down Bay Street, their dark blue uniforms crisp and tight, their brass buttons and buckles shining, and their service swords winking at Blake in the bright light. His heart lurched.

A nervous buzz skittered up his back. "Are we settled?"

"Yes, sail away, dear Rebel, sail away!" the man began to sing, but Blake didn't stay to hear the next chorus, though it haunted him down the wharf.

"Good riddance to ye, ye Rebel, sail away!"

Halfway to the ship, Blake sneaked a glance over his shoulder.

The soldiers had stopped to speak to the port authority officer. Would he turn Blake in? Of course he would. And keep the reward money as well as Blake's extortion fee.

Blake rubbed his neck again at the thought of his impending fate. He tried to swallow, but it felt like the rope had already tightened around his throat. Even so, hanging would be a kind sentence. The Union had done far worse to some of his fellow officers. Which was only one more reason for Blake to leave his Southern homeland.

That and the fact that everyone he knew and loved was dead.

The memory stabbed a part of his mind awake—the part he preferred to keep asleep. The part that, like an angry bear, tried to rip the flesh from his bones when disturbed. This bear, however, seemed more interested in tearing Blake's soul from his body as clips of deathly scenes flashed across his mind. Cannons thundered in his head, reverberating down his back. Men's tortured screams. Blood and fire everywhere.

No, not now! He gripped his throat, restricting his breath. He must jar himself out of the graveyard of memories. *Think. Think!* He had to think. He had to focus!

But his mind was awhirl with flashes of musket fire, mutilated body parts, the vacant look in a dead man's eyes. He stumbled. Shook his head. Not now. He could not pass out now. His passengers needed him. They'd put their trust in him to lead them to the promised land. Besides, he wasn't ready to die.

Blake thought about praying, but he'd given that up long ago. The day he'd received word that his baby brother had been killed at the Battle of Antietam. His only brother. The pride and joy of the entire family. He was only seventeen.

Blake drew in a deep breath and continued onward. The visions faded and his mind cleared. Perhaps God was looking out for him after all. He marched—limped—forward as nonchalantly as he could, trying to signal Captain Barclay on the quarterdeck to begin hoisting sail. But the old sea dog must've already assessed the situation, as sailors leaped to the tops to unfurl canvas. The plank had been removed, and men lined the railing, their stances and faces tight, their eyes suddenly widening at something behind Blake.

Only then did he hear the thumping of boots and feel the dock tremble beneath him.

A hand clutched Blake's arm and spun him around. Two Union solders stared him down. "And where do you think you're going, Johnny Reb?"

29

CHAPTER 3

Blake was sure the beat of his heart was visible through his chest. Yet with the control and experience gained from years in command, he faced his enemies with a look of authoritative aplomb. One, a mere sergeant, by the stripes on his coat, was busy gazing at a group of young ladies standing by the millinery shop across Bay Street. The other, a lieutenant, shifty-eyed, thickset, with a mustache that dripped down both sides of his mouth, stared at Blake as if he were a toad.

"Where are your papers, sir?" He jerked a thumb toward the *New Hope*. "You can't leave port without proper papers."

Blake's stomach churned as he reached into his waistcoat and handed them to the man. "Everything is in order. Surely the port master informed you."

"Port masters take bribes, Mr."—he examined the papers—"Roberts." He squinted as he glanced over the document. His friend finally lost interest in the ladies and faced Blake as well.

"Where are you heading?"

"As you can plainly see, Lieutenant, Brazil."

The sergeant chuckled. "I've seen the signs posted around town. You're starting a new colony, ain't ya?" He pointed a finger at Blake, nearly poking him in the chest. "'A Southern utopia,' the pamphlet said." He exchanged a look of disgust with his partner and continued laughing. "But what else should we expect from Rebs? Always running away like cowards."

Blake ground his fists together behind his back. Out of the corner of his eye, he saw the crew of the *New Hope* loose the lines that tied the ship to the wharf. Thankfully, the soldiers hadn't noticed. Blake's stomach tightened. Captain Barclay would leave without him. He'd instructed him to do just that should Blake be arrested. But he was so close. Just ten more yards and he'd be on board.

Just ten yards between him and freedom.

A dark cloud swallowed up the sun. A portend of bad things to come? Shifting weight off his bad leg, Blake scratched his neck, feeling the cinch of the noose already. A breeze coming off the bay brought the scent of rain and freedom, but it did nothing to cool the sheen of sweat covering his neck and arms.

The lieutenant slid fingers down his long mustache and thrust the papers back at Blake. "Prepare your ship to be searched, Mr. Roberts."

Blake's chest tightened. "For what purpose?"

"Slaves, Rebel soldiers, valuables that belong to the Union." He thrust his face into Blake's, dousing him with the smell of alcohol. "I'm sure we'll find plenty of contraband to confiscate." He faced his friend. "Go assemble a band of men. Tell them to arm themselves. We wouldn't want our Rebel friends to forget themselves, would we?"

"I assure you, Lieutenant, we aren't carrying anything illegal."

"Then you have nothing to fear." His gaze pierced Blake before he turned toward the sergeant ambling down the wharf. "Bart!" The man didn't turn. The lieutenant marched after him. "Sergeant Bart!" he yelled, finally getting his attention. "Bring me the list of war criminals again." He jerked a thumb toward Blake. "This one seems familiar. . . ."

But Blake didn't stay to hear the rest. The *New Hope* drifted from the quay, and the crew beckoned him on with anxious gestures, their faces pinched. He didn't have time to check how wide the expanse of sea had become between dock and hull. He didn't want to know. It mattered not anyway. He had no other choice.

Ignoring the pain shooting up his right leg, he bolted down the remainder of the dock and leaped into the air. His feet spiraled over murky water. His arms flailed through emptiness, scrambling to reach the rope the crew dangled down the side of the brig.

Curses and shots fired behind him. A bullet whizzed past his ear. The rope loomed in his vision as if it were at the end of a long tunnel. Larger and larger it grew. And yet farther and farther away it seemed. His lifeline. One scraggly rope that would either save him or hang him. The crew shouted encouragements, but their voices seemed muffled and distant. So did the pistol shots and the voice of the lieutenant damning him to hell from the wharf.

Pop! Pop! Pop! More shots exploded around him.

Tiny holes appeared in the hull of the ship, shattering the wood into chips. The brig drifted farther away. Blake's feet touched water. It was all over. He wasn't going to make it. Then his hand felt rough hemp. He closed his fingers. His shoulder snapped hard. His arm ached. He slammed into the hull with a jarring thud. Swinging his other arm up, he clutched the rope.

A shot zipped past his head. Its eerie whine catapulted him into action. He yanked his feet from the water and began to climb up the oaken hull. Someone pulled the rope from above.

A storm of boots thundered over the wharf, releasing a hail of bullets. A woman screamed. The wind snapped in the sails, and the water began a soft purl against the hull as the brig pulled out of port.

Almost there. Almost there. Blake released the rope and grabbed onto the bulwarks. Hands hauled him on board just as the soldiers on the dock unleashed hell.

Eliza backed away from the group of sailors as they dragged Colonel Wallace over the railing and onto the deck. She had not gone below as ordered. Not when a man's life was at stake. Not when their entire journey was at stake. She knew trouble was afoot when those soldiers had stopped the colonel. Nothing good ever came of a chat with Union officers. Certainly not in the past year since the war had ended. They were out for blood. Pure and simple. They wanted nothing but to punish the South for her sins. And as self-appointed judge and jury, they wielded the whip of revenge with the utmost cruelty.

Remorse and sorrow flooded her at the thought that she had once associated herself with the North. Quite intimately associated.

The colonel landed with a thump on the deck as a torrent of shots peppered the sky and the ship, and seemed to rain down on them from everywhere.

"In the name of the Army of the United States and by command of Lieutenant Colonel Milton Banks, I order you to stop and drop your anchor at once!"

Eliza glanced at the dock. At least twenty Union soldiers stood in line, some firing pistols and rifles at the *New Hope*, others furiously reloading their weapons.

So stunned by the sight, she could only stand and watch as sailors ducked and slumped to the deck all around her. Strong arms grabbed her shoulders and pulled her down just as a bullet struck the mast behind her. The acrid smell of gunpowder bit her nose. Still, the firestorm continued. But it was Colonel Wallace's body atop hers that caused her to tremble. Not any fear of death.

"Stay low, Mrs. Crawford." His hot breath wafted over her cheek as he cocooned her with his body—his muscles hard and hot from exertion.

Eliza couldn't breathe. Her skin buzzed. He smelled of man and sweat. Oh how she'd forgotten what it felt like to be held by a man. The shame of it! She must stop this at once. Here she was in the middle of a battle, her very life on the line, and all she could think of was how wonderful it felt to be in the colonel's arms. Sails flapped and thundered above her until, suddenly, they bloated with wind. The ship jerked, and the rush of water grew louder. Shots popped and cracked in the air, but they no longer struck the ship.

Colonel Wallace gazed down at her for a moment, uncertainty in his gray eyes, and something else. . . . He jumped off her as if she had a disease. A breeze swept his body heat away, leaving a chill behind. And the all-too-familiar feeling of being alone in the world.

He offered her his hand and helped her to her feet. "Forgive me, Mrs. Crawford."

But before she could thank him, he turned and hobbled to the railing where sailors lined up to watch the Union soldiers shake their fists in the air and growl at them from the quay. With a sweep of his hand, he gave a mock bow. "It's been a pleasure, gentlemen!" he yelled, eliciting chuckles from the crew.

Eliza could only stare at him like a silly schoolgirl. Such courage, this man. The way he had jumped across the wide gulf without hesitation beneath a barrage of bullets. Then the gallant way he protected her with his own body. Dare she admit that her skin still tingled from the encounter? And now, his lively sarcasm toward his enemy made her smile.

"Back to your stations!" Captain Barclay shouted from the quarterdeck. "We've still got to get past Fort Sumter and Fort Moultrie."

The sailors scattered like rats before light, some leaping into shrouds, others handling lines on deck.

"Praise God! Praise God!" A tall, gangly man with tiny eyes and thick sideburns emerged from the crowd, Bible clutched to his chest. "He has saved us!" He slapped Colonel Wallace on the back. "Excellent jump, my dear man. Excellent jump!"

Other passengers popped up from below to congratulate the colonel. He received all their accolades with a wave of his hand as if embarrassed at the attention. But there was one man not rejoicing. One man, dressed all in black, who leaned against the starboard railing, eyeing the proceedings as a scientist would a specimen beneath a microscope. His angular face nearly matched the odd-shaped stone he rubbed between two fingers. When his dark eyes latched on hers, he snorted and ambled away.

Eliza rubbed her arms against a sudden chill. Or maybe it was just the hearty breeze that now blew across the deck, filling sails and fluttering the hem of her gown. Making her way to the railing, she spotted the soldiers slogging down the wharf in defeat, far out of range now as the ship picked up speed. A kaleidoscope of tall ships anchored at wharfs and quays passed before her eyes. Warehouses and taverns cluttered the docks. Mills and shops stretched into Charleston, where citizens began to emerge from their homes. A loud horn startled her, drawing her gaze to the other side of the brig, where a steamship made its way into port, white smoke pouring from its stack. If only they had steam power, they'd make it to Brazil much quicker. The sooner the better, to her way of thinking.

She glanced back toward Charleston. A string of quaint homes stretched across East Bay Street, reminding Eliza of her family home in Marietta, a faint memory these past years.

Colonel Wallace slipped beside her, following her gaze to the city. Her heart skipped a beat as the wind showered her with his scent. "Take a good look, Mrs. Crawford. We shall not see Charleston in a long while, if ever again."

"Does it sadden you, Colonel?" She gave him a sly grin.

He blinked and raised his brows. "You know who I am?"

"I know *of* you, sir."

"No wonder those soldiers suspected me." He chuckled, his eyes sparkling. "It would appear my charade fooled no one."

"It is hard to hide the look of a warrior."

"Hmm. I wasn't aware there *was* a look."

Eliza dragged her eyes away from him to view Shutes' Folly Island off their port side.

Blake swung about, placing his elbows on the railing. The breeze toyed with the black hair at his collar. "Ah, Castle Pinckney." He pointed to a small masonry fortification on the island. "We used it as a prisoner-of-war camp during the war."

Eliza studied the crumbling structure and thought of all the Confederate soldiers still being held in prisons in the North. An ache weighed on her heart. Enough was enough. Why couldn't the Union forgive and forget? Build instead of destroy? What good would it do this great nation to foster even more hatred and bitterness? She sighed, squinting against the sun. Yet prejudices ran deep, fueled by the agony of loss. She, of all people, knew that firsthand. It would be years, maybe even decades, before the wounds of this horrid war healed. Which was why she must leave her beloved country, her beloved South forever. She swung back around as they passed the South Battery at the tip of Charleston. Charred, cold cannons lined the park like sleeping soldiers. Dormant until the next war woke them into action.

Colonel Wallace gripped the railing, lost in his own thoughts. Finally, he said, "No, I am not sad to leave what has become of the South. It will never be what it once was. The North has seen to that." Spite bit his tone, but he wiped it away with a smile. "And you, Mrs. Crawford? Are you sad to say good-bye to your homeland?"

"I have not belonged here for quite some time, Colonel." She cast a glance toward Fort Sumter up ahead, a sudden nervousness rising. "They won't fire upon us, will they?"

Following her gaze, he shook his head, but not before she saw a flicker of trepidation cross his eyes. "We are no longer at war. And, to them, the *New Hope* is but another merchant ship leaving Charleston. The soldiers would have no way to get word to them in time, for I see no telegraph wires connecting the mainland." He hesitated a moment, as if hoping to gain reassurance from his own words. Finally, he breathed a sigh then leaned one arm on the railing and assessed her with an intensity that caused a flush to rise up her neck. "You did not go below with the other women during the shooting."

"I don't fare well in cramped spaces."

His laughter bubbled over her, pulling a grin to her lips. "Then I fear you have chosen a rather uncomfortable voyage, Mrs. Crawford. There is no place on a brig that is not cramped."

"Except on deck," she said.

"Indeed. Then I shall be privileged to see you often."

She lowered her gaze.

"Forgive my boldness." His tone was contrite.

"No Colonel. It's simply been awhile since I've received a compliment."

Her comment brought a perplexed look to his face, but he smiled nonetheless. "Still, it was a rather brave thing to do. Staying above amidst the shooting."

Eliza gazed over the white-capped wavelets in the bay. The wind picked up, stirring the loose strands of her hair about her neck until they tickled her skin. She pressed a hand over them, suddenly embarrassed that she'd never been able to put up her own hair properly without a maid. "I must thank you for saving my life, Colonel. I'm not quite sure why I didn't duck like everyone else."

"Shock does odd things to people." He rubbed his jaw as sullenness overcame him. "I've seen that firsthand."

"I imagine you have, Colonel." Eliza had witnessed that as well. The shock of men who woke to amputated limbs and disfigured bodies. The shock of watching their friends and companions die beside them.

His gray eyes turned inquisitive and sad. "You no doubt endured much"—he seemed to be searching for a word—"unpleasantness, being a nurse on the battlefield."

"More than I cared to." More than she would ever forget. The ship bucked, and she grabbed the railing for support.

"You have my sincere admiration, madam, for volunteering for such gruesome service. Many of my own men would have died if not for the hard work and care of our nurses."

"It was the least I could do." The very least after what she'd done.

"And signing up to be part of a new colony in Brazil. A widow? I do believe your courage and tenacity surpasses many of the soldiers under my command."

"I fear I've always been too adventurous for my own good." Eliza laughed even while her heart swelled at the colonel's praise. Especially coming from a man like him. She'd done her research on him before joining his expedition. Hailing from a prominent family in Atlanta, he was a West Point graduate who rose to the rank of colonel within only a year after his first commission. Being a nurse, she'd had many contacts among soldiers, many of whom had served under the colonel. All had the same story. His men adored him and happily risked their lives for him, and all who knew him spoke of his honor and integrity.

"Still, Colonel. You flatter me too much. It is I who should sing your praises for the sacrifices you made on the battlefield."

He glanced across the deck, his lips tight. "We have all sacrificed."

His humility only added to her regard.

He faced her. "You sacrificed your husband to this horrid war."

Eliza nodded and shifted her gaze to the bay, suddenly feeling like she had no right even to speak to such a man.

"Forgive me. I'm far too blunt at times."

Eliza could now add kindness to his list of exemplary qualities.

"But let's talk of more pleasant things." He studied her. The tone and expression on his face made her wonder if he, too, felt the overwhelming attraction between them. Another flush heated her neck. Oh fiddle! She was behaving like an innocent girl, not a widow who knew the intimacies of marriage. But then again, men had not paid her much notice in the past three years when she'd been covered in blood and filth on the battlefield.

"What do you hope for in Brazil, if I may ask, Mrs. Crawford?"

"A new start, like most of us, I imagine. But most of all peace. I long for peace, and a place to nurse cuts and colds not amputations and bullet wounds."

He nodded his understanding.

"And you, Colonel? Aside from desiring any place where you aren't hunted by authorities, that is."

"You said it all so succinctly in that one word. *Peace.*" He gazed across the bay, such pain burning in his eyes, it nearly brought tears to her own. Pain and something else. A hint of hope, a longing. He faced her, snapping out of his daze. "Yes, peace. And to start a colony. Be there at the beginning of a new city, a new community, just like our forefathers. Very exciting!"

"And I have no doubt you'll find yourself as equal to the leadership of a colony as you were to the leadership of a regiment."

He looked down as if embarrassed by her compliment. How unusual and yet utterly charming for a man who was used to being in command.

"Now it is I who am flattered, madam. However, I'm quite pleased to have such an advocate on board."

"Then you can count on me, Colonel." Eliza smiled as they stared into each other's eyes a bit too long for being so newly introduced. Yet she couldn't seem to pull herself away.

Until thankfully, the snap of a sail broke the trance. With topsails spread to the rising wind, the *New Hope* approached the neck of the bay. Silence permeated every plank and timber as all gazes bounced between Fort Sumter on their right and Fort Moultrie on their left. Colonel Wallace stiffened. He slipped even closer to Eliza, as if he could actually protect her from a cannon blast. An endearing sentiment that brought a smile to her lips.

Though the American stars and stripes waved proudly above the fort, most of the buildings were nothing but crumbling ruins. Hammer and chisel echoed over the waters as soldiers worked to repair the once magnificent fort. Some of them stopped to gaze at the passing ship. One man even raised his hat to wave at them. Captain Barclay and a few sailors waved back, chuckling. As they sailed past, the remaining intact cannons merely winked at them in the sunlight.

Colonel Wallace released a breath. Captain Barclay ordered more sails raised, and within minutes, the unfurled canvas caught the wind in a jaunty snap, and the *New Hope* burst onto the open sea, free at last.

Other passengers emerged from below, among them the finely attired older couple Eliza had seen come aboard earlier.

"Mr. and Mrs. Scott," the colonel said in a low voice, following the direction of her gaze. "Wealthy plantation owners from Roswell, Georgia. Their daughter, Magnolia, must still be below. And behind them, there"— he pointed to a man in a striped shirt and suspenders. His rosy round face reminded Eliza of an aged apple. "Mr. Lewis, our carpenter."

The poor man's hands shook as he clasped them together and made his way to the foredeck. "He seems a bit unnerved," Eliza said.

"We are all unnerved, Mrs. Crawford. It is not easy leaving everything we know."

A gasp sounded from the Scotts' direction, and Eliza glanced to see Mrs. Scott, hand over her mouth, pointing across the deck at a Negro man and a woman with two small children.

"Ah yes." The colonel frowned. "The only freed Negroes coming on the journey. Moses; his sister, Delia; and her children, Joseph and Mariah."

Though many freed slaves had been wandering the streets since Eliza had come to Charleston, she'd never actually spoken to one. Her parents had kept a few house slaves in their home in Marietta, but Eliza had no idea whether freed slaves would be relieved, fearful, angry, or even hostile toward whites. Yet the kind look on Moses' face did much to ease her apprehension.

"And there is the doctor."

Eliza snapped her attention to a tall, brawny man with light brown hair and a scar angling down the side of his mouth. "Doctor?" She felt immediate relief that she wasn't the only medical person on board.

The colonel shifted his weight. "James Callaway. Well, at least he used to be a doctor in the war. He says he hasn't tended patients since. Became a preacher after that."

Eliza was about to comment on how odd a transition that must have been when a woman's scream blared from below.

All eyes shot toward the companionway hatch. Excusing himself, the colonel headed toward the sound when another scream pierced the air. Eliza followed him, fearing that her new roommates were somehow in trouble. Before they even reached the companionway, a man emerged. The wind caught his dark hair and blew it around him as he stumbled above, clutching his side. The plantation owner's daughter, Miss Magnolia, popped up behind him, her face awash with rage and fear. "He attacked me! That man attacked me in my cabin!" She dashed to her mother, who gathered her up in her arms and tried to console her daughter amid her hysterical sobs.

But the man didn't look as though he could attack anyone. Hand pressed to his side, he dropped to his knees before tumbling backward to the deck. Only then did Eliza see blood oozing in between his fingers.

She knelt beside him and studied the wound. "This man's been shot!"

CHAPTER 4

The night before

Hayden Gale sauntered into McCrady's Tavern, squinting as his eyes adjusted to the dim lighting. He scanned the mob of merchants, fishermen, gamblers, and ne'er-do-wells who frequented his favorite Charleston haunt, searching for the man he was to meet. Mr. Wilbur Ladson, Hayden's latest mark. Worth more than four thousand dollars a year and owner of more than five hundred acres of farmland in Ohio. The wealthy landowner had come to Charleston on a business deal, or so Hayden had heard. But Hayden's business with him had nothing to do with a deal and more to do with a sham—a sham that would make Hayden rich. Which was why he'd purposely made Mr. Ladson's acquaintance and, in the process, found him to be a man of oversized paunch and undersized intelligence. Add to that his excessive greed, and he was the perfect target. A target who would provide Hayden with both the means and the freedom to focus on a far more important goal.

Spotting the ill-bred, fatwit in the corner, Hayden headed his way, spiraling through tables laden with flickering lanterns, cards, and foamy mugs of beer, while waving off greetings tossed his way. It was good to be back in Charleston, the town of his birth, despite the memories that lurked in every corner, tugging at what was left of his heart. The heart he'd left behind when his mother had died and those same memories had banished him from town. But he was back now on a tip, a very reliable tip, that his father, Patrick Gale, had returned.

Hayden swept a gaze over the bawdy mob, looking for that face that was forever planted in his mind from a tintype of his mother's. He'd been searching for his father for fifteen years, and he wouldn't give up until he found him—and planted him six feet under for what he'd done. Even if it took the rest of his life. He scanned the faces one more time. His father wasn't here.

Just as well. Hayden had business to attend to. Besides, it was only a matter of time before he found the man. He'd nearly caught him in Galveston—had been in the same room with him, but the charlatan had slipped away. It was as if the man knew Hayden was looking for him. Which was impossible. Zooks, he probably didn't even remember he *had* a son.

Hayden stopped before Mr. Ladson, who was devouring a plate of shrimp and grits, grease sliding down his chin. A skinny man with spectacles perched atop a pointy nose sat beside him, sipping a drink. Odors of lard, alcohol, and tallow blended unpleasantness in Hayden's nose.

"Ah, Mr. Jones. Please join us." Mr. Ladson gestured toward a chair. "I'll order you a plate. Charleston excels herself in grits and seafood."

"No thank you." Hayden slipped comfortably into the phony name he'd given Mr. Ladson, as easily as he slipped onto the seat and gestured for the barmaid to bring him some port.

The three men drifted into conversation about the weather, the high price of goods in the South now that the war was over, the ease with which one could purchase Rebel land, all topics that conversely bored or angered Hayden. Though he'd spent some time during the past few years in the North, he was Southern bred through and through and hated what the "Reconstruction" was doing to his home. Reconstruction, indeed. More like destruction.

Mr. Ladson finished his feast, wiped his mouth with his napkin, and sat back in his chair. Someone began playing a piano on the other side of the room.

"We should get down to business, Mr. Jones." The skinny man, whom Hayden now remembered was Mr. Ladson's accountant, slid his spectacles up his nose. "Mr. Ladson and I have another business dealing later tonight."

"Another venture, sir?" Hayden smiled at Ladson. "It would seem your visit to Charleston has been quite lucrative."

"Indeed, Mr. Jones. First your deal involving a hundred acres of cultivated farmland and then another deal with Mr. Haley involving

41

a grand investment in a railroad. The South is indeed prime for the picking!"

Hayden ignored the man's ravenous glee. In fact, he ignored everything else but the name Haley—a name that sent his stomach into his throat. "Mr. Martin Haley?"

"The same. Do you know him?"

Hayden painted a nonchalant mask on his face to disguise the hatred roiling within, something he had grown quite adept at doing over the years. *Haley.* One of his father's aliases. "I've made his acquaintance." He tapped his fingers over the rough wood.

The skinny man's eyes lit up. "Do you vouch for his integrity, Mr. Jones?"

Hayden could barely restrain his laughter. As it was, he coughed into his hand to hide any telltale expression sneaking onto his face. "Of course. He's a fair man. In fact, I have some business with him myself."

The men exchanged a glance before Mr. Ladson said. "Well, you best hurry. I believe Mr. Haley said he was leaving town tomorrow."

"Leaving?" Hayden kept his tone nonchalant.

"Yes, headed for Brazil on some wild scheme to buy up land so the South can rise again"—he lifted his mug of ale in mock salute—"or some such nonsense."

Hayden sifted this new information through his mind, pondering the implications. It sounded just like his father to run off to Brazil on some harebrained enterprise. The barmaid returned with his port. After flipping her a coin and sending her a wink that made her giggle, he downed the drink in a single gulp.

The skinny man pulled out a leather satchel that Hayden hoped was full of money, while Hayden withdrew the writ of sale from his coat pocket along with a pen and ink and laid them on the table. Cultivated farmland, indeed. The property Mr. Ladson had toured was such, but the land he was purchasing was nothing but a swamp.

The accountant grabbed the document and scanned it in the lantern light, his beady eyes shifting back and forth. A drop of sweat slid from his slicked-back hair onto his forehead.

"I assure you everything is in order," Hayden said. Mr. Ladson picked up the pen, dipped it in ink, and anxiously awaited his friend's approval.

Just sign the paper and give me the money. Hayden hid his urgency behind a placid smile. Once this deal was completed, he would leave a far richer man than when he'd arrived. And just in the nick of time. He was down to his last twenty dollars. And the crème de la crème of this fortuitous night would be that afterward he would follow these slatterns to their meeting with his father. Finally, he would have his revenge.

He shoved down a pinch of regret over swindling Mr. Ladson. The man was a Northerner who hated the South. He certainly deserved far worse. Besides, he had plenty of money. Yet even those excuses did not stop the accusations that constantly rang in Hayden's ears day and night, the words that stabbed his conscience and haunted his dreams.

You're just like your father.

A shadow drifted over the table, causing the lantern flame to sputter and cower. Mr. Ladson hesitated, pen poised over the document that would free Hayden to pursue his father without any encumbrances.

A voice accompanied the shadow. "Hayden Gale?"

Hayden gazed up into a pair of seething eyes set deep in a pudgy face. Hair bristled on the back of his neck. "I'm afraid you are mistaken, sir. There is no one here by that name. Now if you don't mind." He batted him away. "We have personal business to discuss."

Gruff hands grabbed Hayden by the coat and hauled him from the chair, slamming him against the tavern wall. Dust showered him from above. Spitting it away, Hayden held up arms of surrender. "My name is Elias Jones, sir. You have the wrong man." He tried to make out the man's features in the shadows, but he couldn't recollect him from the many men he had swindled over the past years. How was Hayden supposed to remember each one?

"Do I now?" The man gritted his teeth and hissed like an angry cat. "You're the one, all right. You defiled my wife and swindled my family out of our last two hundred dollars. No, no, I'd know you anywhere." Releasing Hayden, he slugged him across the jaw.

Hayden's head whipped around. His cheek stung. Ah yes, now he remembered the man. Rubbing his face, he glanced over at Mr. Ladson, who had put down the pen and was frowning at Hayden. *Blast it all!* Hayden released a foul curse. "I have no idea what you are referring to, sir." Drawing back, Hayden slammed his fist into the man's rather large belly. "But I will not stand by while you attack me and my character

43

without cause." He shook his aching hand, but the man barely toppled over before he righted himself.

The music stopped, and a crowd formed around the altercation. Hayden wiped blood from his lip. He supposed he deserved the man's rage and worse for what he had done, but why did he have to find Hayden now when he was on the cusp of a huge deal?

Fist raised, the man charged Hayden again. This time Hayden blocked his blow with one hand while shoving the other across the man's jaw. Cheers erupted from the mob as more of the besotted gathered around to be entertained. But Hayden had no desire to provide said entertainment. He had no beef with this man, and he certainly didn't relish dying on the sticky floor of this hole-in-the-wall. Hayden's strike barely caused the burly man's head to swivel.

Shaking out the pain in his hand once again, Hayden backed away, studying the room for the best escape route. The man pulled out a pistol. Hayden barely heard the hammer snap into place over the raucous cheers, but the sound of it spelled certain doom.

"I'll kill you for what you've done, ye thievin' carp."

Hayden had no doubt he would do just that. "Now, calm yourself, sir. If you kill me, you'll go to jail, hang for murder. Then what would become of your lovely wife?"

The man seemed to be pondering that very thing as the shouts of the throng grew in intensity. *This can't be the end.* Hayden could not die for one night with a lady he barely remembered and a measly two hundred dollars. It just didn't seem fair. He'd done far worse than that in recent years. Several of those incidents now passed through his mind like a badly acted play—a play that would no doubt be performed before God on judgment day. Shame burned within him.

The ogre smacked his lips together. "Naw, killin' you will be worth it." He fired his pistol. Searing pain struck Hayden's side. Gunpowder stung his nose. The mob went wild, some rushing toward Hayden, others toward the man, while some broke into fistfights among themselves.

Gripping his side, Hayden ducked and wove a trail through the frenzied mob, finally blasting through the front door into the cool night air. He stumbled down the street, wincing at the pain and ignoring the horrified looks of passing citizens. He couldn't risk someone helping him. They would ask too many questions. Besides, his ruse was blown.

He must leave town as soon as possible. The pain of losing the fortune hurt nearly as much as his bullet wound. Nearly.

He slipped into a dark alleyway and slid to the ground by a rotting barrel. A rat sped across a shaft of moonlight. Hayden removed his hand. Blood poured from the wound. He peered into the shadows and grabbed a paper lying nearby. He intended to press it over his wound when a word at the top caught his eye. BRAZIL. He read further. A ship called the *New Hope* was leaving tomorrow at sunrise for Brazil to start a new Southern colony. Despite his pain, Hayden smiled. There could only be one ship leaving Charleston for Brazil tomorrow.

Perhaps fortune shone on Hayden after all.

Back to the present

Eliza glanced over the crowd of sailors and passengers closing around the wounded man. "Doctor, please help!" She addressed the man whom the colonel said was a physician, but he stood gaping at the patient as if he'd never seen blood before.

The colonel gripped the doctor's arm, drawing his gaze.

"That man assaulted me!" Magnolia Scott whined from across the deck.

"So you shot him?" the colonel barked.

"Of course not!" She huffed. "He was like that when he came in my cabin."

The crowd grew silent, their gazes shifting from Magnolia to the wounded man as if trying to imagine how he could have pulled off such a feat.

"I doubt he could assault anyone, Miss Scott." Eliza put voice to their thoughts as the captain barged through the mob and began spouting orders for the sailors to take the wounded man below.

"Do you have a sick bay, Captain?" Eliza stood.

"Aye, miss. But it's small and has few medicines. My man, Wilkes, will take you down."

"I'll show her," the colonel spoke up, dragging the doctor behind him.

Sinking down into the bowels of the ship once again, Eliza felt as though she were being smothered alive. At least the cabin in which the sailors put the wounded man was a bit larger than her own shared quarters, though not by much. They laid him in the center of the room on a wooden table that took up nearly the entire space, save for a cot, a work shelf, and a glass-enclosed cabinet sparsely stocked with bottles and vials. He groaned. Fear skittered across his green eyes. The doctor and the colonel entered behind her.

"I need a bowl of freshwater and some clean cloths," the doctor said to the sailors as they were leaving. "Remove his shirt, if you please, Miss, Miss. . ."

"Mrs. Crawford," the colonel interjected. "She's the nurse I told you about." He lit a lantern and hung it on a hook on the deckhead.

Eliza began unbuttoning the man's shirt. "Only a volunteer nurse. No formal training." The metallic odor of blood filled the air.

"The war?" the doctor asked.

She nodded, removing the soaked cloth.

"Then that's all the training you need."

"I did not. . .assault. . . ." The wounded man spoke, his voice strained and weak.

"Don't worry about that now." Eliza brushed strands of dark hair from his face. "We're going to remove the bullet and dress your wound."

"How did you get shot?" the colonel asked.

Oddly, the doctor remained at a distance. "And by whom?" he added.

The man had no answer.

"It didn't happen on board." Eliza examined the bloody opening. "Looks to be a day old at least."

The deck canted, and she gripped the table as the lantern sent waves of light over the patient. She didn't envy the doctor. It would not be easy to operate under these conditions. She faced him, awaiting his next command. He ran a hand through his brown hair streaked in gold and shifted his broad shoulders beneath a cutaway coat. The masculine lines of his chin quivered, stretching the scar angling down the right side of his mouth. But it was his eyes that drew her. The color of bronze. They would be striking except for the terror flashing across them at the moment.

"We must remove the bullet," the doctor said numbly as the sailors returned with the basin of water and cloths.

Eliza knew that much. Grabbing one of the cloths, she pressed it against the oozing gash. The man groaned, the sound joining the creak of timbers as the ship plowed through the sea.

The doctor gestured toward the wound, his eyes on the bulkhead. "You've dealt with these before, Mrs. Crawford, have you not?"

"I've assisted, but I've never extracted a bullet myself." It was then that she noticed his hands shaking. Which caused her pulse to rise.

"Then I will supervise," he said.

Colonel Wallace glared at him. "I agreed to your passage because you were a doctor, James."

"And I did not lie to you. I am a doctor. I simply haven't"—he halted and ground his teeth together—"I don't perform surgery anymore. Not since I left the battlefield. I told you I'm a preacher now. Been preaching the Word of God for the past two years."

"So, *Preacher*"—the colonel's tone was biting, his eyes raging— "you're telling me we have no doctor. No one to fix the broken bones and heal the diseases that will be inevitable in the jungles of Brazil?"

James took a deep breath in an effort to compose himself then flattened his lips. "I did not mean to mislead you, Colonel. I can instruct Mrs. Crawford. She can be my hands. But that is all I can offer you besides counsel in spiritual matters."

"What the dickens—I already have a parson aboard!" The colonel took up a pace while a look of contrition folded onto the doctor's face.

Eliza swallowed as the realization set in. She glanced at her patient. His fate rested in her hands and her hands alone.

CHAPTER 5

Blake ran a comb through his hair and studied his reflection in the cracked mirror hanging on the bulkhead of his cabin. A fleeting question regarding his sudden interest in appearances taunted his mind, but he already knew the answer. It was the lovely Mrs. Crawford and his expectation of seeing her within moments in the captain's cabin. It was why he had washed the grime from his face and donned a clean shirt and waistcoat. He only wished he had more fashionable attire and perhaps some of that bergamot or cedar cologne women seemed to love. But he had no such thing—he was a simple man with simple tastes.

Except, he realized with surprise, when it came to Mrs. Crawford.

There was nothing simple about her. After the good doctor had declared his inability to operate, she had gone to work, steady-handed and determined, moving like a fine-tuned instrument beneath the doctor's instructions. Only her trembling voice gave away her fear. Still, she had continued until the bullet was removed, the wound stitched, and the patient resting.

Where other women would have swooned at the horrors of digging through human flesh, she performed her duty with courage, a courage Blake had not often seen, even on the battlefield. That any woman could endure the nightmare she no doubt suffered as a war nurse only made him respect Mrs. Crawford all the more. That any woman who'd lost her husband, who was alone in the world, would venture to an unknown land to start a new life only increased that rising respect.

And did he mention she was also beautiful? Not in a Magnolia Scott stunning sort of way, but in the kind of beauty found in a field of flowers: delicate yet strong. Fresh, uncontainable, and wild.

His cabinmate, the good doctor—or should he say preacher—entered, hat in hand and hair tossed about his face, severing Blake's musings. James heaved a sigh. "I can't imagine what you must think of me, Blake." He tossed his hat onto the table. "I did not mean to deceive you. I knew you already had a parson and wouldn't sign another. So, once I discovered a nurse had joined the venture, I knew she could be my hands."

Blake stared at him through the mirror before turning around. The ship rolled over a wave, and he leveled himself against the shifting deck. "And what if there had been no nurse on board?"

"I wouldn't have signed up." James shrugged. "I would have sought another ship. One that needed a pastor." He dropped into a chair and leaned forward, elbows on his knees. "In truth, I didn't want to wait for the next ship. I wanted. . .no, *needed*, to leave everything behind."

A sentiment Blake could well understand. "Regardless"—he huffed—"you've left these colonists in a rather precarious situation."

"I still have the knowledge up here." James poked his head and gave a sheepish grin. "It's the hands that don't work anymore."

Blake rubbed his eyes and sighed, listening to the rush of seawater against the hull. It did much to soothe his nerves. "Well, I'm thankful Eliza could handle things." He studied his new friend for a moment, noting the way he clasped his hands together before him and stared at them as if they were foreign objects. "What's wrong with them?"

"I can't seem to stop them from shaking. Been like that since I left the assault on Petersburg in '64."

"Petersburg? I was there. Got a bullet in my leg to prove it."

James snorted. "Odd that it might have been me who tended your leg, but I don't remember."

"But you said you left?"

James nodded, his gaze still lowered.

"We won that battle," Blake said.

A moment passed in silence. "Still we lost nearly three thousand men that day." The trembling in James's hands increased. He clamped them together. "I couldn't stand it another minute. The blood, the agony, the mutilation of so many young men. Boys, really. I had to get away. So I ran away. Threw myself back into God's arms, into the preaching my father planned for me to do all along." He finally glanced up, a haunted look in his eyes, and rubbed the scar on his cheek. "But even that didn't help. Brazil is my last hope."

Emotion burned in Blake's throat. How many times had he felt like running away from the war, the stress and horror of battle after battle? But he was a colonel. His regiment depended on him. He had to do his duty. As a civilian doctor, James's situation was different. He'd dealt with amputated limbs and disgorged bowels and anguish and death all day and night with nothing but conscience to keep him at task. How could Blake blame him for leaving when he doubted conscience and duty would have been enough to keep him in such a hell?

He liked James. Straightforward, honest, humble. Blake had commanded enough men to recognize strength and goodness in a man's eyes. Besides, he could hardly fault James for trembling hands when Blake had his own visions and blackouts. "Brazil is the last hope for many of us," he finally said, his tone softening. Smiling, he gripped James's shoulder then grabbed his coat from a hook on the wall. "Come along, the captain will be waiting on us. I, for one, am looking forward to our first meal on board the ship."

James rose, straightened his string tie in the cracked mirror, and followed Blake down a long corridor and up a hatch where they emerged onto the main deck to a blast of wind and a magnificent starlit sky. Both stole Blake's breath away. Catching his balance on the rolling deck, he halted and gazed up at the million glittering diamonds spread across a black velvet curtain.

"Incredible, isn't it?" James said.

"Indeed."

All seemed quiet on deck. Most of the sails had been lowered and furled for the night, keeping only topsails faced to the wind. The first mate stood at the helm. Other passengers mulled about, but it was Mr. Graves, the ex-politician, who drew Blake's attention. He leaned over the starboard railing, cigar in hand, babbling something at the sea. Blake hoped the man wasn't mad. He had chosen him for his knowledge of government, which they would desperately need as their colony grew into a city. But it wouldn't do to have a lunatic organizing things.

It also wouldn't do to be pursued by a Union ship. The dark horizon offered Blake no glimpse of what dangers lurked beyond even as the smell of gunpowder still haunted his nose from his close encounter leaving Charleston. Still, the Union had better things to do than chase down one war criminal. And if Blake's memory served, there were no navy ships anchored in Charleston ready to depart at a moment's notice. The war was over, after all.

Shrugging off his worries, Blake hurried up the quarterdeck and down the companionway to the captain's cabin, where he was greeted by the fragrant scents of mutton stew, cheese, and buttered rice. His stomach growled. Far too loudly, for everyone in the room swept their gazes his way.

But it was only one gaze he was interested in. And her golden eyes sparkled when they met his.

Eliza hoped the captain had invited Colonel Wallace to dinner. She so wanted a chance to get to know him better. Now as he stood in the doorway, looking quite dashing in his suit of brown broadcloth, she could hardly take her eyes off him. He limped into the room with more authority than most did without disabilities to impede them. She lowered her gaze, hoping he hadn't noticed her staring at him, hoping he didn't find her too bold, and wondering if she hadn't lost her mind. After Stanton, Eliza wanted nothing more to do with marriage. She found the institution confining, restricting, and far too empty of the promises of love and romance she'd read about in Jane Austen novels. She had also found that she wasn't good at it. To even think of entertaining attentions from a man could only lead to disaster and heartache for them both. No, all she wanted was to escape her past and start over in a community in which she could use her nursing skills to help others. Then why, oh why, did Colonel Wallace affect her so? He was a Rebel officer! Of all the men on the ship, he was the one man she should avoid at all costs.

Introductions and greetings abounded between those in attendance: Mr. and Mrs. Scott, the wealthy plantation owners, and their daughter, Magnolia; Eliza's cabin mate Angeline Moore, whom she'd had to all but drag out of the cabin to attend; a man Eliza hadn't met, Mr. Dodd who was a sheriff from Richmond with an apparent problem keeping his eyes off the ladies. Then there was James Callaway, the doctor, of course, and Parson Bailey, who seemed too tiny a man to evoke fear of damnation from the pulpit.

A slave girl stood against the bulkhead behind the Scotts. Across from her, squeezed between a large chest and enclosed bookshelves stood two sailors awaiting commands.

Everyone took a seat around the table laden with bowls of stew, various cheeses, rice, and platters of biscuits and greens. Much to her delight, Colonel Wallace pulled a chair out for her right beside his own. The doctor, or should she say preacher, held out a chair for Angeline, placing her beside Eliza while he took the seat on her other side. Angeline thanked him and slid onto her chair, but her tone was strangled and her normally rosy cheeks had gone stark white as her gaze flitted between the doctor and Mr. Dodd.

Eliza laid a hand on her arm and gave her a concerned look, but the girl waved her off with an attempted smile.

The parson said grace in a rather loud and oversanctimonious tone that grated over Eliza, though she quickly reproved herself. She shouldn't think poorly of a man of God. Yet before he'd even intoned his lengthy "Aaaaaaaamen," the captain had already scooped a healthy portion of rice onto his plate.

"We won't be dinin' so well for the remainder of the trip, I'm afraid." Captain Barclay glanced across the table. Though his voice was as rough as rope and his face wore the age of the sea, his demeanor was pleasant and his eyes kind. "But I thought for our first night, it would do well to enjoy a hearty meal with some of my guests."

The ones paying for a cabin, from the looks of things. All except Sarah, who had begged off with an excuse of an unsettled stomach.

"How fares this stowaway of ours?" the captain asked.

"His name is Hayden Gale, Captain," Eliza offered, grabbing a biscuit from a passing platter. "At least that's the name he gave me in his delirium."

Through the stern windows behind the captain, moonlight cast sparkling pearls over the ocean, swinging in and out of Eliza's vision with the rock of the ship. How the plates and bowls managed to stay on the table was beyond her, but aside from a little shift here and there, they were as sturdy as sailors under heavy seas. Candles showered the linen tablecloth, pewter plates, mugs, and silverware with flickering light, creating a rather elegant dining table for being out to sea.

"And he isn't on the passenger list, Colonel?" the captain asked.

"No sir." The colonel took the plate of biscuits from Eliza. Their fingers touched, and a spark jolted up her arm. His eyes shot to hers, playful and inviting. She looked away. *Oh fiddle! He knows how he affects me!*

"Of course the miscreant isn't on the manifest!" Magnolia scowled and turned down a bowl of corn her mother passed. "I told you he attacked me in my cabin. He's nothing but a lecherous swine!" She sniffed, and Eliza got the sense the girl's histrionics were purely for show. Her mother threw an arm around her and drew her close. "There, there, now."

Mr. Dodd looked as though he wanted to hug the girl himself, though not for the same reasons, Eliza was sure.

"Well, we can't be turnin' the ship around now." The captain chomped on a biscuit, crumbs scattering across his full gray beard. "If he has money, he can pay. If not, he can work."

Eliza helped herself to some greens and handed the dish to Angeline, who passed it on, staring numbly at her plate as if in a trance.

"You can't seriously allow him to join us. He could be a criminal!" Magnolia twirled a lock of hair dangling at her neck, candlelight firing in her sapphire-blue eyes.

The brig canted, sending a brass candelabrum and several plates sliding over the white tablecloth. The creak and groan of wood seemed the only answer to the young lady's outburst.

Until the colonel spoke up. "Never fear, Miss Magnolia. I'll have a chat with him when he recovers. We will get to the bottom of this. I won't allow any harm to come to you"—he glanced at Eliza—"or anyone aboard this ship."

Eliza tore her gaze from his as the warmth of being cared for flooded her—a feeling she hadn't felt in years.

"Magnolia!" Mr. Scott all but shouted, startling Eliza. "Quit fiddling with your hair. It's a disgrace as it is." He glanced back at the slave girl as if Magnolia's coiffure were her fault, failing to notice that his daughter melted into her chair at his admonishment. Facing forward again, he adjusted the jeweled pin on his lapel as a scowl deepened the lines curving his mouth. "And speaking of harm, I had no idea I would be traveling with freed Negroes." His gaze shot to the captain. "I simply must protest."

The stew soured in Eliza's stomach. "They are freedmen now, Mr. Scott." She abhorred slavery, always had. Though her father had treated their slaves with kindness, her aunt and uncle, who had taken over the hotel after her father's law practice became successful, had not. Now that the war was over and the Negroes were free, she wondered if they were any better off, for she'd heard that nothing but lynch mobs and starvation awaited them.

"It is the law now." The captain shoved a spoonful of rice into his mouth, but Eliza got the impression his sentiments lay more with Mr. Scott's.

"They have a right to start over just as we do," Eliza added.

The colonel turned to her, but she couldn't tell if the expression on his face was shock or admiration.

Mr. Scott gave an incredulous snort. "Start over! What nonsense. Start over from what? For what purpose?"

"I couldn't agree more, sir." Mr. Dodd took a mouthful of stew then dabbed a napkin over his lips. Tall, well-dressed, with blond hair, a lopsided, pointy nose, and deep blue eyes, one could almost consider the sheriff handsome. Even his manners and speech indicated good breeding. But something about the man gave Eliza the quivers. And not in a good way.

Mr. Scott nodded his approval toward Dodd.

The colonel cleared his throat. "As much as it may unsettle some of us, Mrs. Crawford is right. They are free as we are and must be treated with respect."

"Respect? They were not created for respect." Mr. Scott's fork clinked a bit too loudly on his plate. "I say we drop them off at the nearest island."

His wife's gaze remained lowered, though a whimper escaped her lips. A breeze squeezed beneath the door, sputtering the candles and playing a symphony of lights and darks across the deckhead.

The colonel set down his glass. "We will do no such thing, Mr. Scott. And that is the end of it." His commanding tone brooked no argument, and Eliza could see why men obeyed him. Even Mr. Scott seemed momentarily speechless, though she was sure the pleasant reprieve wouldn't last.

Captain Barclay took a swig of wine, wiped his mouth with the tablecloth, and leaned back in his chair. "As much as I don't approve of freeing the beasts, it is the way of things now. They are hardworking and will no doubt be an asset to your colony."

Mr. Scott huffed his displeasure. Magnolia frowned and picked at her food.

Eliza wondered how the Scotts' servant felt about the conversation, but when she glanced her way, her face was as bland as the stew they were eating. Did she know she could be free? Why hadn't she left the Scotts? Eliza had heard that several slave owners had threatened to hunt down and kill any slaves who ran away. She hoped that wasn't the case with this sweet girl, who looked to be no more than fifteen.

Angeline pushed food around her plate, oddly keeping her face turned from James, who sat beside her. Finally, she joined the conversation. "And what is your opinion, Parson Bailey? Does God have something to say about slavery?"

The parson's scrawny shoulders rose. He set down his fork and took a drink, drawing out the moment. With a receding hairline, thick muttonchops, and tiny close-set eyes, he looked more like a mongoose than a man. A chuckle bubbled in Eliza's throat at the comparison, and she hid her smile behind a napkin.

"The Bible says much about slavery, Miss Angeline. Slavery was well accepted in biblical times, even encouraged."

James plopped a chunk of cheese into his mouth. "I beg to differ with you, Parson. Accepted, yes. Part of the culture of the day, indeed. But hardly encouraged. Not by God nor by Jesus. In fact"—he shot a glance over the table—"in the Jewish tradition, if a man was a slave to another, he was freed every forty-nine years during Jubilee."

The parson's face twisted in a knot. "And who are you, sir, to dare interpret scripture?"

"He is a preacher like yourself." The colonel smiled.

"Indeed." He turned condescending eyes on James. "From what church?

"My father pastored the Second Baptist Church in Knoxville, Tennessee. I took over the parish when I"—he coughed—"returned from the war."

"Humph." The parson wiggled his nose as if some unpleasant smell had invaded it. "Baptists, of course."

James was about to respond when Mr. Dodd leaned forward and addressed Angeline. "I know you from somewhere, Miss Moore."

Angeline choked on the first bite of food she had taken. She coughed into her napkin, not facing the man. "Mine is a common face, sir."

"I would hardly agree with that!" James said so emphatically a few of the men chuckled. A blush rose up his neck, and Eliza smiled.

55

Angeline was indeed a beauty. With hair the color of copper and violet eyes framed in thick lashes, she rivaled Magnolia in comely appearance. Yet unlike Magnolia, Angeline had a sweet demeanor about her and something else, a strength hidden by weakness.

Yet now, the poor girl seemed to be having trouble breathing. Eliza pressed a hand on her back.

"No, no, no." Mr. Dodd nodded, still studying her. "I'm sure we have met. It will come to me in time."

Angeline swallowed her meat and drew a deep shuddering breath as Eliza's gaze swept to Magnolia. She felt the same way about the Southern belle—as if she'd seen her before. But where?

"I don't see why we have to go to silly old Brazil anyway," Magnolia said, drawing her lips in a pout. "The South will eventually rise again, and all my friends are still in Roswell." Her eyes moistened as she glanced over the dinner guests, searching for an ally.

A growl emanated from Mr. Scott's direction.

Mrs. Scott bit her lip and laid a hand on her daughter's. "Now, dear, you know your father spoke to you about this."

"Brazil is the new Eden!" Mr. Dodd exclaimed. "A paradise waiting to be harvested." He leaned forward, a sly look in his eyes. "With plenty of gold, I hear."

"Gold, humph." James smirked, causing Dodd to go on rather forcefully. "Pirate gold, my good doctor, pirate gold. You'll see."

"Gold or not," the colonel interjected, "it is a land of freedom and new opportunities, and Lord knows, after what we have all endured, we need both."

"Here, here!" Captain Barclay slouched back in his chair and sipped his wine, assessing his guests. His gaze landed on Angeline who was still toying with her food. "Where are you from, Miss Moore?"

"Norfolk, Captain. My father was the owner of several shipyards there."

"Norfolk?" Mr. Dodd exclaimed. "Then that's where I've seen you. I was born in that fair city."

At his statement, some of the tightness seemed to leave Angeline's body.

"But you said *was*, Miss Moore," the captain pressed.

"Yes. He's deceased." She paused to collect herself.

The table grew silent for a moment. Not even the clink of a fork or the slosh of drink. Nothing but the rustle of the sea against the hull and the gentle creak of wood.

Eliza laid a hand on Angeline's arm. "I'm sorry for your loss." She wanted to ask her if his death was due to the war but thought it best not to dig any deeper into the lady's sorrow, especially in front of the others.

"The dear man is in heaven now." Parson Bailey offered the expected platitude.

The colonel finished his last bite of stew and set down his spoon. "I'm sure there is not a person at this table who has not lost someone close to them in this horrendous war."

Nods of affirmation and vacant eyes attested to the truth of his statement. All except Dodd, who cleared his throat and poured himself another glass of Madeira.

"Ah, Mr. Dodd," Captain Barclay said, "perhaps you knew Miss Moore's father?"

"No, I do not seem to recall a shipwright named Moore. However, I left town when I was but eighteen to pursue my profession."

"Which was?" Mrs. Scott asked.

"I was a sheriff in Richmond for several years." His shoulders rose.

Angeline broke into a fit of coughing. Her face turned red, and Eliza grabbed her arm and patted her back. "Hurry, something to drink," she said.

The carafe of wine was passed, and Eliza poured some into her friend's glass and held it to her lips. "Here, take a sip."

Magnolia licked her own lips and grabbed the carafe, filling her cup.

"What are you doing?" Mr. Scott snatched the glass from his daughter's hand. "Ladies do not drink. It is most unbecoming. And, for God's sake, sit up straight."

The poor girl straightened her spine immediately, placed both hands in her lap, and stared straight ahead as if she were a soldier.

Their eyes met, and Eliza saw an emptiness in them before they flashed in recognition. So the young woman remembered Eliza as well. A lump formed in her throat, and she prayed silently that her association with Magnolia had only been in passing. Otherwise, if the lady knew who Eliza had married, this trip would be over before it started.

At least for Eliza.

Chapter 6

Eliza was beyond exhausted. Many of the passengers had become seasick as the ship moved farther out to sea, and she'd done nothing but run back and forth from passenger to passenger, trying to ease their discomfort. Which of course she couldn't really do. Thank God she had not succumbed to the debilitating condition herself. Although being forced to traverse the cramped bowels of the ship like a gopher caused her stomach to clamp so tight, it forbade all passage of food anyway. It grew even worse when she had to visit the hold where most of the passengers were berthed. And where most of those who were still ill groaned and moaned and gripped their stomachs in agony. All she had on hand to help relieve their symptoms were mint tea and words of comfort. But that seemed trite in light of what they suffered.

Now, as she made her way to the captain's cabin to witness the stowaway's interrogation by the captain and Colonel Wallace, despite her exhaustion, despite her hunger, her heart fluttered in her chest. Rebellious traitorous heart! Of course she'd seen the colonel on deck during these past three days, busy helping the captain, but they'd not had an opportunity to speak. Which was for the best, of course. Yet something about him tugged on her, drawing her thoughts and heart like the needle of a compass to true north. And as with a compass, there seemed to be naught she could do to change its direction.

Maybe it was the sorrow that seemed to hover about him like thick, dark clouds gorged with rain. She'd seen many men afflicted in the same way during her years as a nurse. She'd also seen some of them find relief by simply sharing their horrors, their heartache and pain, with someone who cared. Perhaps she could be that someone for the colonel. Strictly as a friend, of course.

Pressing down her blue tarlatan skirts, she squeezed through the corridor, thankful recent fashions had flattened the wide crinolette and moved it around back, or she might get stuck like a fat mouse in a maze in these narrow hallways. After knocking and hearing a call to enter, she opened the door and slipped inside the captain's cabin. Her patient, the stowaway Hayden Gale, sat in a chair, looking none the worse for the pistol shot in his side. His long hair, the color of dark coffee, hung just below his collar, and though he pressed a hand over his wound, color had returned to his cheeks. Not an ounce of fear crossed his green eyes as he stared straight ahead at the captain.

To his left stood Colonel Wallace, arms crossed over his chest. His black string tie hung limp over his white shirt as if he'd done battle with it and lost. James was behind him, while two of the captain's officers guarded either side of the desk. Magnolia and her mother sat in the far corner, and Parson Bailey leaned against the bookshelves, nose in the air. Absent their coats—no doubt due to the rising heat—the bands tied around the men's arms appeared stark against their white shirts. Black bands that had become such a familiar, yet depressing, sight throughout the South this past year. Bands of mourning that represented a loved one lost in the war. Every man in the room had at least one, save Hayden. The colonel sported five as far as Eliza could tell. *Five.* Her heart went cold at the sight.

"Ah, there you are, Mrs. Crawford," the captain said, shifting her attention his way. "We thought you should be here since Hayden is your patient."

The colonel approached and gestured toward an empty chair by the Scotts, giving her a smile that sent her heart spinning again and making her wonder what he had looked like in his uniform. Quite handsome, she imagined.

"Now, Hayden, how did you come to be on my ship?" Captain Barclay leaned back in his chair, moving a pocket watch in between his fingers with astounding ease. Behind him, glittering shafts of morning sun bounced over the desk and the bulkheads, and over the stowaway, who snapped his hair from his face and huffed his displeasure at the question.

"As I told you, it was purely by accident. I got shot, became delirious, and wandered on board unwittingly."

"Crawled all the way up a swaying plank and onto a ship, did you?" James snorted. "You must have been quite out of your head!"

"I was, sir." Hayden gave the doctor a sardonic look then cocked his head in scrutiny. Seconds ticked by as the two men stared at each other, and Eliza began to wonder if perhaps they had met before. Although James seemed more annoyed than pleased. Then for no apparent reason, Hayden gave a hearty laugh and faced forward. "Yes *Doctor*. Quite delirious. And feverish, in fact."

Eliza didn't recall noting any fever, but she kept that to herself.

Magnolia stood and pointed a trembling finger his way. "I assure you, his assault on me was no accident!"

Hayden's interested gaze took her in. "Princess, though your beauty may warrant such an action from a desperate man, I, myself, have never had to beg, force, or steal affections from any woman."

A grin lifted the corner of Hayden's lips as he continued to gaze at Magnolia. Eliza agreed. He was far too charming to have to beg for feminine attention. Not only was the man appealing to look at but he had a dark, mysterious quality about him that, coupled with a roguish charm, made him quite alluring. Magnolia, apparently, was not of the same opinion, for the Southern belle stomped her tasseled boot on the deck, her eyes seething. "You have your proof! He is a beast!"

Mrs. Scott drew her daughter into an embrace. "Captain, you must do something to ensure my daughter's safety." The deck tilted, sending the ladies back down to their seats and the gentlemen bracing their boots.

Parson Bailey gave Hayden a look of pity. "God can forgive any sin, son. You have only to ask."

The colonel took a step toward Hayden. "What were you doing in Miss Scott's cabin, sir?"

"I was searching for something with which to bandage my wound. What else would I be doing?" Hayden stretched his broad shoulders beneath what had once been a fine, silk-lined, wool coat but was now torn and marred with blood.

"Mrs. Crawford and I can vouch for his condition, Captain," James offered, rubbing his chin. "He'd lost a significant amount of blood and could hardly stand."

"That doesn't mean he didn't have vile intentions." Mr. Scott's jowls quivered with his pronouncement.

"The heart is inherently evil," Parson Bailey added. A sail thundered overhead.

Hayden rolled his eyes. His jaw hardened beneath a sprinkling of dark stubble. "I did not mean to frighten the lady."

"Very well." Captain Barclay scratched his scraggly beard. "But there is the matter of why you were shot, sir."

Hayden hesitated, staring at the canvas rug beneath his boots. "Tavern brawl."

Magnolia huffed. "Mercy me. Does that not attest to his character?"

He gave her a sideways glance, a hint of a grin toying with his lips.

"That doesn't answer the question." The colonel's commanding tone had returned.

"A misunderstanding."

James rubbed the scar on his cheek. "Then why didn't you seek medical aid?"

"Like I told you, I was delirious. I don't even remember coming on board."

"Very well." Captain Barclay stood, opened and shut his pocket watch, then placed it on his desk. "There's naught to be done about it now. I'm afraid you're stuck with us, Hayden, all the way to Brazil. As soon as I drop off these fine people, I'll take you back to Charleston if that is your desire."

Hayden shifted in his seat and glanced over those present, his eyes softening for the first time since Eliza had entered. "I wouldn't mind trying my luck out in Brazil, seeing what she has to offer."

"She has nothing for you, I'm afraid." The colonel's gray eyes hardened around the edges. "You have not paid for your voyage, nor have you passed the criteria for joining our new society."

Hayden chuckled then clutched his side with a wince. "Zooks, what criteria? I'm strong and capable. You'd be fortunate to have me." The ship suddenly bucked over a wave, causing those standing to stumble. The parson struck the bulkhead with a thud.

"Not if you're a thief or murderer." Mr. Scott stiffened his jaw.

"Or a ravager of women," Magnolia spat.

Hayden snorted. "So what's it to be? Clapped in irons and locked below for the entire voyage?"

"That's for the captain to decide." The colonel deferred to Captain Barclay with a gesture.

The old sea dog circled his desk, stuffing his watch into a pocket. "When you've recovered from your wound, you may prove your strength and capability by joining my crew. That way you can at least pay for your passage."

Hayden flinched. "I know nothing about sailing."

"You'll learn quickly." The captain winked at his two officers, one of whom chuckled.

"I suppose I have no choice." Flattening his lips, he released a sigh. "Though, the work is beneath me." He tugged at his cravat, the lace of which was not only out of style but stained.

"And just what is your normal enterprise, Mr. Hayden?" Eliza spoke up, though she had yet to make up her mind about the man.

Eyes the color of jade assessed her. "Investments, Mrs. Crawford. I deal in land and commodities, foreign and domestic."

Something in the quirk of his lips and flash of his eyes made her wonder if he was being forthcoming.

Colonel Wallace shifted his boots over the deck and glared at the man. "If you so much as look at a lady for more than two seconds, or if I find anything missing on this voyage, I won't hesitate to feed you to the sharks."

Instead of cowering beneath the colonel's authority, Hayden gazed up at him, a playful sparkle in his eyes. "Such drastic measures, Colonel. Won't I even get a trial?"

"God sees all things done in the darkness," Parson Bailey interjected.

"I'm the law here," the colonel replied.

Hayden sat back in his chair with a huff. "You won't have any trouble from me."

This seemed to satisfy all present, except the Scotts, who approached the captain's desk spewing further complaints. The captain dismissed them with a wave and a hearty declaration that all would be well, sending them leaving in a stew of huffs and "I nevers." Just as quickly, he released Eliza, the parson, and Hayden with the excuse that he needed to discuss business with James and the colonel. The latter glanced forlornly at her as she left the cabin, his eyes full of promise. Was he as disappointed as she was at not having a chance to speak to each other? Or perhaps God was protecting her from her own foolish heart—a heart that had led her astray once before.

Just as Eliza was leaving, a sailor brushed past her and barreled into the cabin. "Captain, the compass is crushed. Broken clean through."

Her ears burning from the resultant curses behind her, Eliza headed toward the galley for some tea, wondering who would destroy a compass and why.

With a hot cup in hand, she finally entered her cabin to the moans and groans of Sarah, swinging in her hammock. The poor dear had also succumbed to the cruel whip of mal de mer, and Eliza hated that she couldn't do more to ease her suffering. Halting beside the pregnant woman, she wiped sweaty strands of hair from a face as white as the foamy wake off the stern. The foul stench of sickness emanated from the chamber pot on the table.

Slipping an arm behind Sarah's back, Eliza helped the woman sit, bunching pillows behind her and lifting the cup of mint tea to her lips. Her gaze wandered past the sunlight winking off Sarah's gold cross down to her distended belly, so round and firm with child, and a sad thought jarred Eliza. She would probably never have children.

When she'd first married Brigadier General Stanton Watts, she'd hoped to have a houseful. She could still see him standing at the altar the day of their wedding in his crisp blue uniform with sparkling brass buttons and the single gold star adorning his shoulder board, denoting his elevated rank. So handsome! At that moment, she'd believed she was the luckiest girl alive. That was until news of war interrupted their honeymoon.

After depositing her at his family home in Harrisburg, Pennsylvania, he'd thundered away on his horse to meet with a Union war council. During the next year, she'd only seen him twice when he'd made brief visits to their home and even briefer visits to their bed. Then he was gone forever, leaving her a widow at only nineteen.

She doubted she'd ever marry again.

Sarah sipped her tea, the sweet mint fragrance rising to sweep away Eliza's foul memories.

"Oh my, your face looks a fright!" Sarah breathed out between gulps. "The way you are staring at my stomach as if the child will burst through at any moment. I assure you"—she ran a hand over the bulge—"she isn't ready yet."

"Forgive me." Embarrassed, Eliza snapped from her daze and withdrew the cup. "It's just that I have always wanted children." She blinked. "Wait. You said, 'she.' How do you know?"

"I just know." Sarah caressed her belly with fingers born to love a child.

Eliza set down the cup. "Well, you needn't worry. I've delivered wee ones before. And the doctor is more than experienced, I should imagine."

Yet it was another voice that answered. "Yes indeed. James does seem more than competent." Angeline burst through the door, her face aglow with sun and wind, and her voice cheery.

When both ladies gaped at her, she lowered her lashes. "I meant to say, he seems highly intelligent. And kind." She brushed a curl from her forehead and frowned, her mood shifting as rapidly as the rays of sunlight through the porthole. "Which surprises me, actually."

Eliza and Sarah's stares turned into smiles, causing Angeline to continue babbling. "He makes a better doctor than a preacher, I think."

"How would you know such a thing? Are you acquainted with the man?" Eliza asked.

Angeline's eyes widened, and she let out a little laugh. "Of course not. No. I've never. . .no, no. Of course not."

Eliza helped Sarah lie back down, perplexed at Angeline's sudden nervousness.

Which abandoned the lady when she heard Sarah groan. Dashing to the hammock, Angeline squeezed her hand. "I'm so sorry you are sick. You must be miserable."

As though on cue, the deck seesawed, sending the hammock swinging and both Eliza and Angeline stumbling. Sarah threw a hand to her mouth, her face blanching, and Eliza quickly grabbed the chamber pot, but the woman waved it away.

Though Eliza had never been seasick, she knew from her experience these past three days how debilitating it must be. Men, far stronger than Sarah, had been reduced to whimpering sacks below decks, while she, on the other hand, put them all to shame with her kind smile and noncomplaining attitude. Even now she squeezed Angeline's hand and said, "Don't concern yourself with me. I'll be well soon enough."

Releasing Sarah's hand, Angeline stepped toward the porthole, where sunlight dusted her hair in waves of fiery copper.

Eliza was reminded of James's interest in the girl. Fiddle, if Eliza couldn't get married, she could certainly aid in finding agreeable matches for her friends. "Doctor or preacher, I do believe James has taken notice of you."

"Me?" Angeline gave a nervous chuckle. "No." She sank into a chair, her shoulders lowering. "He is simply kind to everyone."

Eliza raised a brow. She'd seen the way the doctor looked at Angeline at dinner and then several times on deck. "We shall see. And you"—she dabbed a moist cloth on Sarah's head—"I don't want you fretting over your upcoming delivery."

The woman gave a weak smile. "I'm not worried. God is with me, Eliza. He has never let me down."

Eliza nodded. God had been faithful to her as well, though she had not always been faithful to Him. Still, she wondered how this woman could say such a thing when she was about to bring a child into the world with no husband to care for them.

Sarah's gaze traveled between Eliza and Angeline. "Since I'm sure you are both wondering, my husband, Franklin, fought with the Sixth Georgia Volunteer Infantry." She paused and ran a hand over her extended belly, sorrow clouding her features. "After the war ended, he came home a different man. Wounded more on the inside than on the outside."

Eliza swallowed down a burst of angst at what the woman would say next. She reached for her hand.

"He hung himself in our barn just last Christmas."

Angeline gasped.

Moisture flooded Eliza's eyes.

Yet Sarah's expression was full of peace. "Don't look so sad. He's doing far better than we are now. I miss him, but I'll see him again."

Angeline's brows scrunched. "How can you know for sure?" When both Eliza and Sarah once again stared at her, she bit her lip. "Please forgive me, Sarah. I'm sure your husband is in heaven. It's just that. . .that"—she gazed out the porthole—"I fear my faith has slipped away over the years."

"We shall have to rectify that, shan't we, Eliza?" Sarah said.

Ignoring the woman's declaration, Angeline jumped to her feet. "Oh sweet saints, I almost forgot. Mr. Scott is reading portions of *Hunting a Home in Brazil* on deck. The air is clear and fresh, and it may do Sarah well to go above."

When they all agreed, Eliza and Angeline assisted Sarah out of the hammock, into a simple gown, and up the companionway ladder. A group of passengers huddled around Mr. Scott, who sat atop a barrel, reading from an open book. The constant bucking of the deck tried to disband the mob, but they clung as steadfastly to each other as they did to every word the old plantation owner uttered. Words that, through the sieve of wind, wave, and the thunder of sail, reached Eliza as naught but garbled grunts. The deck rose then dropped, nearly toppling the ladies and sending salty mist over their faces. Shaking it away, Eliza finally managed to settle Sarah against the railing closer to Mr. Scott, where they all could hear him better.

Wind gusted over them, sneaking beneath their skirts and puffing out the fabric until they appeared like three lacy bells dancing on the deck. In fact, as Eliza took in the scene, all the women's skirts were similarly bloated. Restraining a chuckle at the sight, she held her hat down and endeavored to hear Mr. Scott when she spotted the colonel on the quarterdeck beside Captain Barclay. He stood, hands clasped behind his back, with as much authority as if he were captain of the ship. His gaze shifted to her, and she thought she saw a smile touch his lips before the captain leaned to say something to him. No doubt the compass had either been repaired or replaced, for neither the captain nor the sailors seemed alarmed.

James, the good doctor, stood across the deck talking with a sailor, but his eyes had already found Angeline. Beside him, Mr. Graves, his ebony hair tossed in the wind, leaned against the starboard rail, puffing on a cigar and assessing the crew and passengers with the disinterested attachment of one watching a play.

"Have you been to Brazil?" one of the passengers asked Mr. Scott, drawing Eliza's gaze away from the distressing man.

"No, I haven't had the pleasure. But it says right here that Brazil is a Garden of Eden. A paradise of temperate weather, abundant fruit, and rich soil."

One of the women clapped her hands in delight.

"And the land's only twenty-two cents an acre!" another man shouted.

"An' there ain't no Yankees!" a man beside him said, eliciting a round of applause.

"Yes." Mr. Scott closed his book. "Rivers as wide as cities and filled with all manner of fish, and flowers as big as my hand that smell sweeter than a Georgia peach."

"May God bless our journey and our new colony." Parson Bailey, ever-present Bible clutched to his chest, gazed up at heaven as if the Almighty would shower him with good fortune at that very moment. Instead, the deck tilted and he staggered.

"And we can have slaves if we want," a man shouted, causing a few uncomfortable glances to find Moses and his sister standing up on the foredeck. Up until that point, the black man's face had been beaming at the descriptions of Brazil, but now he merely stared at the crowd without expression. Eliza found his courage admirable for a man who only a year ago would have been whipped for looking a white man in the eyes. Delia, his sister, however, lowered her gaze and gathered her children into her skirts.

"But you will *not* enslave Mr. Moses and his sister." Colonel Wallace's thunderous voice blared with authority as he leaped down the quarterdeck ladder and approached the group. Even with his limp, his gait reminded Eliza of the prowl of a lion. Mr. Scott scowled and dabbed a handkerchief over his brow.

"He has been freed and will remain free," the colonel added, fists on his waist. "However, I'm told you will be able to purchase slaves once we are on Brazilian soil if you have the intent and the coin. They allow no importation of slaves."

"What about Mr. Scott?" The blacksmith jerked a thumb toward the elderly plantation owner. "He has that slave girl with him."

Mr. Scott stuck out his chin. "She is my daughter's lady-in-waiting. Nothing more."

Eliza wondered if that was true. She'd not seen the girl do anything but shadow the spoiled woman since she'd come aboard.

One of the farmers removed his hat and dabbed the sweat on his brow. "What happens when we arrive, Colonel? How do we know where to buy land?"

The deck jerked to larboard, and Colonel Wallace shifted his weight from his bad leg. "We will sail into Rio de Janeiro, where we will meet with Brazilian authorities, perhaps even the emperor himself."

Gasps and glances sped through the crowd.

"I'm told," he continued, "they will assist us with scouts and interpreters to help us choose the best land."

"Oh, it all sounds so marvelous," Rosa Jenkins, one of the farmers' wives, exclaimed as she hugged her young daughter.

Dodd slunk through the crowd and stopped before the colonel. "I hear tell there's a hidden lake of gold guarded by monster crocodiles." His eyes flashed with excitement as he glanced over the mob. Some stared at him as if he'd lost his mind. Others ignored him, while interest lingered in a few gazes. In fact, more than one sailor stopped what he was doing and inched closer.

"Did you say a lake of gold?" a woman exclaimed.

"Just a myth, Mr. Dodd." James joined the group. "An old tale meant to fool the greedy."

Dodd looked him over with a sneer and patted his pocket. "Maybe the lake is a myth, but I have a map." His brows arched. "An old pirate map that describes the location of buried treasure."

The colonel chuckled. "If there were any treasure, I'm sure it's long gone by now, Mr. Dodd. Pirates don't tend to leave their gold for long."

"If they all got killed off, they do." Wind blew Dodd's blond hair into a frenzy and doused Eliza with the scent of his Macassar cologne. "Besides, I got this map from an old sailor who frequented pirate haunts in the Caribbean. Paid good money for it."

"I hope not too much." James chuckled, and several colonists joined him.

"Is that why you signed on with the colony?" The colonel's tone grew strained. "And here I brought you along for your experience as a sheriff."

"I'll be your law when the occasion calls for it." Dodd opened his pocket watch and gazed at the time as if he had an appointment. "But that won't stop me from looking for gold."

The colonel shook his head and snorted before returning to his post. Yet several passengers crowded around Dodd, wanting to know more about this mysterious treasure. Others continued prodding Mr. Scott for more information about Brazil, prompting from him further descriptions of exotic fruits, wild chickens that all but leaped into pots of boiling water, forests filled with mahogany and cherry, plenty of wild game for the taking, and sap as sweet as honey. But Eliza grew bored at the fanciful talk. For that was all it was. There was no paradise this side

68

of heaven. No utopia. She'd forsaken whimsical dreams when her family disowned her and left her to rot on the street. When she'd been forced to witness horrors no woman should see. Brazil was a new start for her. A place where people didn't know who she was. Nothing more. She raised her face to the sun, feeling its warm fingers caress her skin. A breeze tugged strands of hair from her chignon, but she didn't care. Though her father had forbidden her to wear it down, saying, "Only women of questionable morals wear their hair loose," Eliza had tossed aside her pins at every opportunity. Here in the relentless wind, she had the perfect excuse. She smiled as her curls tickled her neck and tumbled down her back. Free.

She was free at last.

No more loathing glances from the citizens of Marietta, no more being banned from shops, hotels, eating houses, and even from church. No more falling asleep hungry in tavern rooms not fit for pigs, selling her nursing skills for pennies to desperate souls who tolerated her presence. It had not mattered where she went or how far she ran, or even that she had changed her name, it seemed everyone knew the famous solicitor Seth Randal's traitorous daughter.

She drew in a deep breath of the briny air and smiled. The rush of water against the hull combined with the snap of sail and creak of timber into a soothing symphony that swept over Eliza, loosening her tight nerves. The ship lunged and sprayed her with salty mist.

Closing her eyes, she waited for the sun and wind to dry the moisture away when a voice crashed down on her from above. "A sail! A sail!"

"Where stands she?" Captain Barclay shouted as Eliza glanced across the horizon.

"Two points off our larboard stern, Captain!"

Spinning to face the back of the ship, Eliza spotted half-moons of snowy canvas floating over the azure sea about a mile astern.

Clutching her skirts, she crossed the deck to where the colonel stood, spyglass to his eye. "Who are they?"

"Unclear." He continued to study them. "I can't spot their flag."

Eliza's throat went dry. "You don't suppose the Union sent a ship after us."

He lowered the scope and gave her a reassuring smile. "They wouldn't waste their time. I'm the only contraband on board this brig."

Though the colonel's voice was strong and confident, his gray eyes held a hint of alarm. The wind flung Eliza's hair into her face. She swatted it away and glanced once again at the ship.

"Most likely a merchantman or a fishing vessel," he continued. "Nothing to trouble yourself over. See, even Captain Barclay isn't concerned." He pointed to the quarterdeck where the captain calmly studied the ship, his first mate by his side.

Eliza nodded, tension fleeing her as she drew a deep breath. However, that tension returned when off the bow of the ship, a wall of fog ascended from the sea, blocking their path.

Graves, the brooding ex-politician, caught the direction of her gaze and smiled at her from his spot by the foremast. But she hadn't time to wonder at the reason. Instead, she alerted the colonel, who upon seeing the fog, called to the captain. The sailors had been so intent on determining the origin of the other ship, they hadn't noticed the coming haze.

"Odd," the colonel said, shaking his head. "I've never seen a fog so thick when the sun shines."

"It seemed to come out of nowhere." Eliza gripped the railing.

"Still, it's just fog. If anything, it will keep us well hidden." Yet his tone seemed hollow and distant—unsure. She followed his gaze to the captain, who unleashed a string of orders for the crew to shorten sail. When she faced the colonel again, he assessed her with eyes as stormy and gray as the incoming fog. "But I perceive you are not a woman easily frightened. Neither plucking a bullet from a man's flesh nor traveling all alone to a new land seems to trouble you."

Warmed by his compliment, Eliza noted that James was assisting Angeline and Sarah below, out of the chilled mist. "I have never been accused of being timid, Colonel."

He shoved the telescope into this belt and leaned back on the railing, arms across his chest. His charcoal-colored hair danced over his collar in the wind. "War has a way of stealing one's innocence. As well as strengthening their character. However, in your case, this pluck of yours seems more something you were born with than something acquired."

She slipped a bit closer, allowing his large body to block the wind. Something about the man made her feel safe—a masculine assurance, confidence, and protectiveness that dripped from every pore and hovered in the air around him. And she hadn't felt safe in quite some time. Besides, she could stare into those piercing, gray eyes for hours—the ones that now looked at her with adoration. Adoration she didn't deserve. "I fear you may be right, Colonel. Though my fortitude has caused me much trouble through the years."

A mischievous twinkle crossed his eyes. "I should like to hear of your daunting adventures, someday, Mrs. Crawford."

Did any man have a deeper, more symphonic voice? It resonated through her in low, soothing tones that melted all her defenses. She backed away and lowered her gaze. "I would never want to disparage your good opinion of me, sir."

He took her hand in his. "You never could."

She tugged it away. What was she doing? She'd never been the flirtatious type. Perhaps three days of navigating wobbling decks and cleaning up vomit had warped her good senses. Senses that told her there could never be anything between a Southern colonel and a Yankee by marriage. Unless. . .after hearing her story, after hearing her reasons, perhaps there was a chance he would understand; a chance he could see beyond her past.

Another chill struck Eliza, and she hugged herself as the ship thrust into the fog bank. Gray roiling mist enveloped them, condensing in drops on the woodwork and lines.

"Stand by to take in royals and flying jib!" Captain Barclay's orders ricocheted over the deck. "And light the lanterns fore and aft!"

Colonel Wallace gripped the railing and gazed at the gray curtain. "Odd. Very odd."

Most of the passengers scrambled below out of the cold as deathly silence devoured the ship. Even the creak of wood and purl of water against the hull sounded hollow and distant. Above them, the tips of masts disappeared as they poked through the head of the vaporous beast.

Sailors stood on deck, wide-eyed. Some climbed aloft to adjust sails. Moses, Delia, and her two children hunkered together beneath the foredeck. Eliza couldn't blame them for not wanting to join the others below, considering their attitude toward the former slaves. Turning, she clutched the railing. Droplets bit her hands and spread a chill up her arms as white foam licked the hull beneath her.

Motion drew her gaze to Mr. Graves, who was still leaning against the foremast, one boot crossed over the other as if he hadn't a care in the world. A satisfied smirk sat upon his lips before he began to whistle. The eerie tune snaked over the deck, sending the hair on Eliza's neck bristling even as the mist thickened, obscuring him from her view.

Heavy moisture coated her lungs, making it hard to breathe. She felt the colonel stiffen beside her as his intent gaze took in the fog on both sides of the ship. He cocked his ear and closed his eyes as if listening for something. The lines on his forehead deepened.

Something was wrong. Eliza knew it. One glance at the colonel told her that whatever it was, he sensed it too.

He took her hand. "You should get below, Mrs. Crawford." His tone brooked no defiance. With a nod, she turned to leave when jets of yellow and red flashed in the distance.

"A shot! All hands down!"

CHAPTER 7

Once again Eliza felt the colonel's firm body against hers. This time, instead of landing on top of her, he'd forced her to the deck and pressed her head against his chest while he hovered over her like a human shield. Cocooned within a barrier of warm muscles, all she could hear was the *thump thump thump* of his heart.

Or was that the crew diving to the deck?

An ominous splash quivered the air around her. Curses flew. A blade of sunlight cut through the fog, piercing the wooden planks to Eliza's right. Pressing a hand on her shoulder—no doubt to prevent her from standing—the colonel rose and glanced over the ship. She felt the loss of his body heat immediately. Along with his masculine scent—both replaced by a chilled wind that smelled of fear and cigar smoke.

"Stay down," he ordered before marching to the quarterdeck, parting a fog that was already scattering beneath the sun's rays. Eliza peeked at Captain Barclay, his face a mass of angst as he raised the telescope to his eye.

"Lay aloft and loose fore topsails!" The captain's shout broke the eerie silence, startling Eliza. Immediately, sailors jumped up and dashed in all directions. Their bare feet thrummed over the wooden planks, sounding far too much like war drums on the battlefield.

"Man the weather halyards and topsail sheets!" Captain Barclay's booming tirade of orders continued. "Helm-a-starboard! Steady now!"

Rising to her feet, Eliza peered behind them, squinting as sunlight shoved away the mist. Off their larboard quarter, the ship they'd seen earlier burst out of the fog, foam flinging from her bow and the American flag flapping at her foremast.

She was heading straight for them.

"Bloody Yanks!" One sailor shouted as he passed Eliza and leaped into the ratlines.

The deck buzzed with sailors dashing here and there, clambering aloft or grabbing lines. Hayden, their resident stowaway, emerged from below, followed by James and a few other male passengers.

"Do you have shot for your guns, Captain?" The colonel's face had tightened like a drum, his eyes focused.

"Aye." The gruff seaman pointed forward where some men were removing canvas from two small guns on either side of the foredeck. "I only have these four-pounder swivels, as you can see." His hardened gaze swept to the oncoming ship. "We are a civilian ship, not a privateer. Those white-livered curs!" He slammed his fist on the quarter rail and barreled down the ladder.

Pressing his wounded side, Hayden led a group of men to the captain. "What can I do?"

In the mayhem, Eliza seemed to have been forgotten. She faced the oncoming ship as it rose and plunged through the sea, its ivory sails gorged with wind. Not a speck of fog remained anywhere. Instead, golden streams of sunlight poured upon the *New Hope* as if highlighting their position for all to see. For the Union ship to see. What did they want? More importantly *who* did they want? Fear curdled in her belly at the thought they were after the colonel.

Perspiration slid down Eliza's back. The ship pitched over a wave, and her feet skipped across the deck. Above her, sails caught the wind in a boom nearly as loud as a cannon. She'd heard more than her share of the monstrous beasts on the battlefield and seen the devastation they could wreak, but she had never been in the middle of a battle. Especially at sea.

The brig swung to port. Her timbers creaked and groaned as the ship tacked away from their enemy. The railing leaped toward the sky. Eliza clutched it lest she tumble across the deck. Her mouth went dry. *Why didn't the blasted Union leave them alone?* Hadn't they done enough damage?

The ship righted again. Wind whipped strands of Eliza's hair into her face. She brushed them aside just in time to see a yellow flame jet from the Union ship.

"Hands down!" the captain yelled, but Eliza had already anticipated the command and lowered herself to the deck planks. The smell of dank wood and tar filled her nose. A heavy body pressed against her back, barricading her from danger. The colonel again. She knew his scent, the feel of his steely muscles.

The snap and crack of wood split the air. Curses ricocheted over the brig. Captain Barclay loosed another string of orders, something about tacks and sheets and the helm. But Eliza was more concerned that someone may have been injured. Thankfully, she heard no screams.

"Go below, Mrs. Crawford." Colonel Wallace's breath wafted on her cheek before he jumped to his feet and assisted her up. Gone was the warmth in his gaze. Instead, steel coated his eyes, his mannerisms, even his voice. He'd slipped into command, ready for battle, as easily as one slipped on a coat.

"Can you manage a ship's gun, Colonel?" the captain asked, stealing the colonel's gaze from Eliza.

"I can."

"Then take command of one of them. My boys are bringing up shot, gunpowder, and a fire wick."

The colonel nodded, gestured with his head for Eliza to go below, and leaped up the foredeck ladder.

"I can handle a cannon as well." Hayden jerked hair from his face.

"And I can handle a pistol or sword." James joined him, standing before the captain.

"And us too!" several of the male passengers shouted.

Captain Barclay nodded in approval. "Very well, arm yourselves, men. I hope"—he stared at the Union ship—"we'll not be gettin' close enough to use them."

Sails thundered. The deck rose as the ship thrust boldly into the next roller, sending white spray aft. It swirled around Eliza's ankle boots before escaping through scuppers, joining a sea that roared against the hull as if it too had joined the fierce call to battle.

Clinging to the railing, Eliza faced the enemy ship. Closer now. She could make out the naval officers manning the gun at the bow.

"Get below, Mrs. Crawford!" Captain Barclay's voice startled her, and she swung around, nearly bumping into the beefy man. He sent her a warning glance before he charged across the deck, blaring orders as he went.

Eliza knew she should go below. But she had never been very good

75

at obeying authority. Besides, she'd rather be blown to bits on deck than die below cramped in the rank belly of the ship. Or worse, sink to the bottom of the sea with no way to escape.

Balancing herself on the heaving deck, she headed toward the companionway but slunk into the shadows beneath the quarterdeck instead. From there she had a good view of the front portion of the ship. The colonel included. With his shoulders stretched taut, his body stiff, and his face like flint, he commanded the men working on the cannon with authority, assurance, and determination. Wind flapped his shirt as he unbuttoned his cuffs and rolled up his sleeves, ready to do his duty. Here was a man accustomed to getting dirty in the trenches right beside his men. A rarity among other colonels Eliza had met.

Movement caught her eye, and she spotted Graves slinking around the foremast. Why hadn't he gone below with the other passengers? Or better yet, if he was going to stay on deck, why wasn't he helping, arming himself? Instead, he leaned against the mast and began to whistle as if he were taking a Sunday stroll.

"Fire as you bear, Colonel!" The captain bellowed, pacing across the oscillating deck, his hands clamped behind his great coat. How he maintained his balance was beyond Eliza. Sails roared as they sought the shifting wind then snapped their jaws upon finding it. The brig jerked and listed sideways. Foamy seawater clawed at her larboard bulwarks. Yet still the Union ship gained.

Eliza drew a shaky breath and clung to the wood of the quarterdeck. If they couldn't outsail the frigate, what was to become of them? Would they be sunk to the depths, or would the Union navy escort them back home? Where Eliza would face a lifetime of scorn and hatred. And what would become of Colonel Wallace? Surely his fate would be worse than hers. Even as he filled her thoughts, his voice drifted her way.

"Fire into her quarters. On the uprise, men!" he shouted. Raising spyglass to his eye, he studied the enemy. "Steady now. Steady." He lowered the scope. "Fire!"

One sailor tapped a wick to the gun's touchhole, and Eliza covered her ears. *Boom!* The deck quivered beneath her feet. Smoke swept over her. Coughing, she batted it away. "Oh Lord, please save us," she muttered, only now remembering to pray. Fiddle! Why did she always wait until things were beyond hopeless?

Blake peered through the gray smoke as the all-too-familiar blast of gunpowder assailed him. He squeezed his eyes shut against the sting as memories crept out from hiding. *No, not now!* He must maintain control. Shoving them back, he gazed toward the enemy as the *New Hope*'s shot plopped impotently into the sea just yards from the frigate's hull. Too short. But in line for a good hit. Blake frowned. He was an expert at cannons. But on solid land not on a heaving ship. How did the navy do it? Still, luck had smiled upon him, for his timing of the rise and fall of wave had not been too far off.

"Good shot, Colonel." One of the sailors turned, his face lined with soot.

"Not good enough. Reload!" Not that they had much chance against a U.S. frigate armed with what appeared to be Dahlgren guns and 32-pounder Parrott rifles. Besides speed, of course. Being smaller, the *New Hope* should be able to outrun a frigate. Blake shifted his gaze to the captain and his first mate leaning over a flapping chart held down by pistols. It would seem from the captain's expression, he was of the same mind.

"Max, Simmons," Captain Barclay shouted at two passing sailors. "Have you seen my sextant, protractor, and Gunter's scale?"

The men shrugged. "Last I saw, they was in your cabin."

"They aren't there." Captain Barclay scratched his beard, frowning. "Get below and search for them at once!" The two men dropped through a hatch while the captain returned to his chart.

The navigation instruments were missing? Along with the damage to the compass? Blake's gaze darted to the frigate as a cold fist slammed into his gut. The Union must suspect war criminals were on board. Otherwise, what reason would they have for so intent a pursuit? And if they caught and boarded them, they'd no doubt discover Blake's identity and haul him back to Charleston to be hanged. He'd never go to Brazil. Never have a chance to escape the memories of war. Never pursue the rising interest he had in Eliza.

Wind tore at his collar, tossing his necktie over his shoulder. The brig slid into a trough, and Blake braced his boots on the deck. He glanced back at the captain.

Orders, Captain! What are your orders? Urgency spun his heart into a knot. Oh how he longed to take command! But he knew nothing of sea battles. And he began to wonder whether Captain Barclay did either. Though the man appeared calm, he seemed trundled in uncertainty as his gaze sped from the charts to the Union frigate and then behind him to some distant spot on the horizon. Regardless, he must make a decision. And fast! On land, Blake would already be spouting orders. But he knew no such order to give here. Except to go faster!

The ship bounced, and he caught his balance. The sailors fumbled with powder bag and priming rod as they reloaded the gun. Amateurs. The men in his regiment would have had it loaded already.

Blake glanced over his shoulder where Hayden stood at the ready in command of the other swivel gun. They exchanged a nod. The stowaway's confident demeanor and his readiness to not only jump into the fray but take the lead elevated Blake's opinion of him. Clearly he'd served in the military. And then there was James, the doctor-preacher, standing before a group of brave passengers and sailors all armed with musket, swords, and pistols. Even Moses, the freed slave, stood among the pack, receiving no complaint from the others at his presence. Blake didn't have time to be amazed as a thunderous blast shook the sky. He ducked. The air sizzled. The shot zipped by his ear. Wood snapped. Splinters flew from the damaged foremast.

More explosions sounded. Distant and muted. Coming from everywhere, yet only coming from within him. Squeezing his eyes shut, he pressed his hands over his ears. *No!* Wails of agony pierced his skull. Flashes of light and dark traversed his eyelids, luring him into a nightmarish stupor. But he couldn't let them. Grinding his fists to his thighs, he punched to his feet, forced his eyes open, and inhaled a burst of salty spray. The cool seawater slapped him back to the present—slapped his gaze to the hole the last shot had torn in the foremast.

Too close. Far too close. Anger rippled up Blake's spine. He wiped the sweat from his face, leaving soot on his shirt. He would not allow one Yankee to set foot on board this ship! Not only for his sake but for the colony. The Yanks would steal all their goods, take him and probably others prisoner. And God knew what they'd do to the women. No, not on his watch.

"Loaded and ready, sir," one of the sailors said.

Blake swung about. The Union frigate dipped and bowed over the churning waves as if nodding its glee over an impending victory. Closer and closer she came. If only she'd present more than her narrow bow, Blake may be able to fire a shot that would do some damage.

Captain Barclay had abandoned his charts and marched across the deck, gazing aloft at the sails. A volley of orders spewed from his mouth. Sailors scampered above, and soon the *New Hope* veered to larboard, sending a curtain of spray into the air. Blake stumbled across the deck to the captain. "What is the plan?" he shouted over the roar of the sea just as a hail of grapeshot peppered the deck, punching holes in the sails above.

The men ducked. All except the captain. Instead, he frowned at his damaged sails then lowered his gaze to Blake. "The plan, Colonel?" He snorted. "Why, to tuck our scraggly tails and run!" His grin revealed a single missing tooth Blake had not noticed before. Yet at his lighthearted tone, armed sailors and passengers turned to listen. Hayden joined them from the foredeck.

Captain Barclay scanned the anxious faces. "We are faster than a frigate. If we fill all our sails, we can outrun them."

"But to where? They'll follow." Hayden cast a harried glance at the frigate as if he, too, had something to fear from the Union.

The captain's eyes flashed. "We are near the Bahamas, Mr. Hayden. There are hundreds of shoals off the windward islands. I expect our friends won't be followin' us, or they'll risk bein' grounded." He winked.

James quirked a brow. "How can you be sure?"

"Because I was a blockade runner in the war. Why, once I slipped through a fleet of Union war ships surroundin' New Orleans. Slunk right past them as if we were a ghost ship. By the time they saw us, we were too close to the shoals for them to follow. Never fear, gentlemen."

"But your instruments," Blake shouted into the wind. "Are we heading in the right direction?" He searched the captain's dark eyes for any hint of uncertainty but found only confidence.

"Never fear, Colonel. I know these seas like a pirate knows his booty." And without further ado, Captain Barclay turned away and cupped his mouth. "Sharpshooters to the tops. If they get any closer, fire at will!" He stormed toward the quarterdeck, muttering, "Those bedeviled muckrakers!"

James slung his musket over his shoulder and started for the ratlines when Blake clutched his arm. "But your hands."

"Only when I see blood." Grinning, he grabbed the rope and swung himself up. "I spent my childhood hunting. I'm actually a crack shot. Never miss," he yelled as he continued climbing above.

Several orange flashes drew Blake's gaze to the enemy frigate. Blood drained from his face. They had fired a broadside. *Boom! Boom! Boom! Boom!* He dove to the deck, hands over his head. Not that it would do any good. In battle, getting hit or not hit was a matter of chance. He'd seen men get their heads blown off on either side of him while he suffered not a scratch. After that, Blake had decided that either God did not exist or He simply didn't care about the affairs of men.

The crunch and snap of wood and chink of iron rang across the ship like death knells. Yet no screams sounded.

Blake would never forget the screams.

"Those blaggards!" The captain spat before marching across the deck to inspect the damage. A portion of the fore rigging hung in a tangle of slashed rope, and part of the gunwale was shattered. But the ship still sped onward. Jumping to his feet, Blake leaned over the railing where a smoking hole rent the hull.

"Above the waterline." The captain slapped his hands together. "Steady now, men. We'll be at the shoals soon! Martin, trim sails to the wind!"

Blake gazed at the oncoming frigate, angry foam exploding at her bow. Men lined her decks, hovering around cannons. Their captain stood on the foredeck, pompous arms crossed over his brass-buttoned blue coat. Blake could make out the gold band on the captain's hat, feel his determination span the sea to swallow up Blake's hope. He gazed at the sun now dropping in the western sky. He hoped the captain was right, for another expertly aimed shot might fell one of their masts.

And then all would be lost.

Shaking his head, Blake returned to man the swivel. The next few hours sped by in a chaotic jumble of cannon shots, shouts, maneuvering, veering, sails thundering, sea roaring, and muskets peppering until the muscles in Blake's legs felt like pudding and his heart sank like iron. The ache in his left leg joined the ever-present one in his right, which now felt like someone held a branding iron to it. At least he'd not had any episodes to add to the mayhem. Perhaps, as he had hoped, the more distance he put between him and the war, the more his memories would fade.

But what did it matter? The frigate was nearly upon them, and the islands were nowhere in sight. Captain Barclay's assured tone had faded to one of gloom as he paced the deck, uttering curse after curse. Even the most hardened sailors' faces paled in horror.

Clouds lined the horizon like gray-uniformed soldiers, fringed in red and gold by the setting sun. The frigate swept alongside the *New Hope*, not thirty yards away, giving the signal for them to put the helm down and heave to. Dark smoking muzzles of a dozen guns gaped at Blake from their main deck.

"Reload!" Blake urged his crew to hurry while they had a clear shot. He could not give up now! Not when his life was at stake. But Captain Barclay's loud "Belay all firing!" rang from the quarterdeck, freezing the sailors in place.

Wiping the sweat from his eyes, Blake stared at the captain, seeing on his face what he'd already heard in his voice. They were defeated. He swept his gaze to the Union frigate where one of the officers stood staunchly on the quarterdeck, a speaking cone raised to his mouth.

"Rebel ship, surrender or die!"

CHAPTER 8

Blake spun on his heels, his face hot and pinched. A flash of blue caught his eye, and he glanced to see Eliza standing against the quarterdeck. How long had she been there? Fear overtook his anger. Even now Union sailors were preparing to board and search the ship. Blake's fate was set in stone. Eliza's was not. Nor were the passengers'. Their future depended on the kindness and mercy of the Union captain. Something Blake hadn't much faith in at the moment.

Still, though his journey had come to an end, there might be a chance for the rest of the colonists. The thought of them thriving in freedom in Brazil would bring him a modicum of comfort when the rope cinched around his neck.

Terror clawed up his throat at the thought. He coughed and drew a deep breath. He must focus. He must do all he could to ensure the future success of the colony.

While the captain issued orders for the white flag to be raised and all sails to be lowered, Blake blasted out his own orders. "Parson Bailey." He approached the preacher, who had crept above when the firing ceased. The poor man stood against the main mast, face stricken and Bible clutched to his chest.

Blake wondered if he could trust anyone who had such tiny, shifting eyes. But the man was a preacher, after all. Reaching into his pocket, he handed the parson a key and leaned to whisper in his ear, "Go to my trunk. Find the four large leather pouches. We need to hide them." For within them lay the future of the colony—every cent and dollar each passenger had paid, along with Blake's own dwindling fortune.

Blake would gather the money himself, but the Yankees would be here any minute, and he could not ensure the safety of both money and passengers—the single ladies being his top priority at the moment. He'd seen firsthand the abuse they endured beneath the hands of angry Union soldiers.

Parson Bailey took the key in his trembling hand. Sweat dotted his forehead. "What do they contain?"

"The wealth of our colony. Our very future."

"Where should I hide them?" he asked, avoiding Blake's gaze.

Good question. Blake scanned the deck and hailed Captain Barclay, who immediately approached and stopped before them. Once Blake posed the question, the captain's understanding gaze shifted from the key in the parson's hand back to Blake. "I have a secret compartment in my cabin." He glanced at the frigate, where the sailors were lowering a boat. "Quickly, I'll show you, Parson."

The two men slipped down the companionway, giving Blake a chance to speak to Eliza. She stared at the frigate off their port side, the heaving of her chest the only indication of her fear.

Frowning, he approached her. "I told you to go below."

"Would it have made a difference?" Her voice was strong, controlled, as if being attacked by a Union frigate was an everyday occurrence.

Blake shook his head. What he wouldn't give to have more time with this astounding woman. He raised his hand, wanting to touch her, to remember the feel of her skin, but hesitated at the impropriety. When her eyes gave him no resistance, he gave in and caressed her jaw with his thumb. So soft. He would remember it forever.

She closed her eyes. Thick lashes fanned over her cheeks like silken threads floating on cream. "They'll take you back to hang, won't they?" she said on a sigh.

"Yes."

She sucked in a breath and gazed up at him, alarm tightening her features.

He wanted to tell her how astonishing she was. He wanted to tell her he'd never forget her, but Angeline dashed up to them in a flurry of gingham and angst. "What is happening?" Her voice emerged in a high-pitched squeak.

Easing an arm around her new friend, Eliza drew Angeline close. "It will be fine."

She exchanged a glance with Blake, prompting him to add, "Nothing to worry about. It will be over soon enough, and we shall be on our way."

However, their assurances seemed of no avail as the poor lady suddenly took to trembling. "But they fired upon us. Do you suppose they're after someone in particular?"

Yes, me. Blake offered a feeble smile. "Perhaps. Yet I'm sure you are safe in that regard, miss."

Still, the lady's face showed no relief. Even Eliza's whispers of comfort bore no effect on the poor woman as her fearful gaze locked on the frigate. Her behavior mimicked the terror raging through Blake's own gut—as if she, too, feared being arrested.

That same terror now threatened to blast away his resolve to remain in control—to ensure the safety of the colonists before he was hauled away in irons. His vision clouded. Flames shot toward him from all directions. He clenched his fists and shook them away. Across the deck, he spotted Hayden and called him over.

As the stowaway approached, his green eyes widened at the sight of Angeline then squinted in confusion. Soot blotched his skin in grays and blacks from his face down his neck and arms.

"Hayden," Blake said, drawing the man's gaze from the woman. "Find Sarah, the woman with child, and stay with her. If you are asked, you are her husband."

Hayden nodded, swung a musket over his shoulder, and after one last glance at Angeline, headed below.

"James!" Blake swung in the direction he'd last seen the doctor and nearly bumped into the man. James's bronze eyes burned with anxiety amid a face flushed and streaked. "Can you look after Miss Angeline? It would be best if she were married, if you get my meaning." Blake raised a brow.

Angeline turned her face from the doctor as if embarrassed. "No, that's quite all right. There's no need for that."

James nodded his understanding. "I'll take care of her." He took a spot beside her and extended his elbow. "Stay close to me, miss. There's nothing to worry about."

The lady uttered a trembling sigh but finally looped her arm through his.

Blake faced Eliza. "I'll be happy to step in as your husband if you have no objection."

He thought he saw a hint of a smile lift her lips before she nodded shyly. The entire scene would have been delightful if his head weren't thrumming like a drum.

And he weren't about to be captured and hanged.

The captain returned from below and nodded toward Blake before he faced the frigate and scowled. "In all my years as a blockade runner, I ne'er was caught. Until now, after the war is over. Blast them Yanks!"

Across the agitated sea, two jolly boats filled with Union sailors headed their way. The crew of the *New Hope* lined the deck, awaiting their guests, rifles and pistols in hand.

"I'm not letting those Yanks take us back!" one sailor shouted.

"We have no choice." Captain Barclay marched forward, hands on his waist. "Lower your weapons at once!"

A shot fired above them. All eyes snapped to the tops where a lone gunman straddled a yard, musket in hand.

"Stand down, Gibbs!" Captain Barclay bellowed, his alarmed gaze shifting to the frigate. "D'you want to get us all killed?"

The man swung through the shrouds and slid down the backstay to the deck with a thud. "Sorry, Cap'n. Was an accident."

But the men in the jolly boats had already stopped rowing, their muskets at the ready. Aboard the frigate, sailors loaded one of the Parrott rifles lining the deck.

Blake's world exploded. The sound of the sea and wind and shouts of men all faded into the background, replaced by the roar of explosions and the *pop pop pop* of hundreds of muskets. A scream curdled in his ears. Was someone hurt? He crouched, holding his head against the blaring noise. *Boom! Boom! Boom! Boom!* Cannon blast after cannon blast rocked the dirt beneath him. The crack of pistol and musket rained down on him. Why wouldn't they stop? He dared a glance over the deck, and instead of wooden planks and hatch combings and masts, a field of tall grass spread in every direction. Mist hovered over it like a death shroud. Lifeless bodies in twisted formations littered the mud. Something warm and wet dripped from Blake's fingers. He looked down. Blood pooled in his palms.

Somewhere in the distance a female voice called his name. That was the last thing he remembered.

The warning shot flew over their bow and plunged into the sea on the other side of the ship. Its deafening roar still vibrated in Eliza's ears when she noticed the colonel had collapsed to the deck, his hands over his ears. Kneeling beside him, she laid a hand on his back. He jolted and shouted, "No! Jeremy!" Sailors and passengers crowded around, confusion and fear mottling their faces. Beyond them, the captain shouted toward the frigate, attempting to persuade them that all was well.

The colonel moaned. His eyelids twitched, and his jaw was clenched so tight, Eliza feared it would burst.

James, the doctor, felt the colonel's face with the back of his hand.

"What's wrong with him?" One of the sailors who'd manned the gun with the colonel leaned forward, hands on his knees.

Captain Barclay shoved the crowd aside. "Clear away! Assume your positions! We are to have visitors soon." He spotted the colonel and halted. "What's the meaning of this? Odd's fish, is he shot?"

"No Captain." Eliza exchanged a glance with the doctor. She had a good idea what was happening to the colonel, and from the look in James's eyes, he agreed with her assessment.

"Jeremy! Jeremy!" the colonel shouted, planting his forehead on the deck.

"Let's get him below." The doctor rose and pointed to a few sailors, who grabbed the colonel by his feet and shoulders and carefully lowered him down the hatchway ladder.

No sooner had Eliza followed them into the sick bay than she heard the grinding thump of boats slamming against the hull, and soon after, the pounding of boots on the deck above.

"Take care of him, Mrs. Crawford." James gave her an unsettled look. "I must look after Angeline."

"Please do take care of her," Eliza said. "She seems quite out of sorts."

Nodding, he took off, leaving Eliza alone with a delirious man and her own nerves strangling her senses. Lowering herself into the chair beside the colonel, she took his hand in hers. "Oh God in heaven, please save us. Please don't allow the Yankees to do us harm or steal from us.

Enough of this war." She swatted a tear from her cheek and straightened her shoulders. "Enough!"

Leading an unusually calm Sarah up from below decks, Hayden ushered her to the starboard railing where the Yankee captain had ordered the passengers to line up for inspection. He'd found her in her cabin, kneeling awkwardly—due to her condition—before a chair, hands folded on the wooden seat. Though an admirable attempt to be sure, her appeal to God most likely vanished in the air above her, for Hayden believed the Almighty had wiped His hands of His creation long ago.

With a smile, the lady had taken his hand, expressing gratitude for his chivalry, and followed him above. Now she stood beside him, examining the proceedings with no trace of fear on her face.

"Never fear, God is with us," she whispered.

Hayden repressed a snort and scanned the pompous bluecoats strutting across the deck while their captain questioned Captain Barclay. Thank goodness he recognized none of them. It would not do well to cross paths with any navy officers he'd dealt with in his past. Nor would it do to cross paths with any civilians he'd done so-called *business* with either. But of course, what would they be doing on a navy frigate? He faced Sarah. "I am not afraid, madam. What astounds me is that you seem not to be as well."

"As I said, God is with us." She pressed a hand over her rounded belly. Plain brown hair held back in a bun framed an equally plain face. Yet her eyes, the color of the sea, exuded a serenity and kindness that made her almost attractive. For a woman bulging with child, that was. A bit too prissy for him, however, with her high-necked gown and continual chatter of God.

The doctor slid beside them, arm in arm with Miss Angeline, a woman whose comely face and copper curls were not easily forgotten. Even if the last time Hayden had seen them was on a WANTED poster in a police station in Virginia. Which would explain why her hands were now shaking and her breath came hard and fast. Whatever she'd done, it was none of Hayden's business. Besides, he'd probably done far worse. Still, he should inform her she had nothing to fear from the navy, but there was no reason to destroy her ruse. Along with his.

Just when these people were beginning to accept him.

Unfortunately, none of them was his father. Hayden had spent the last three days inspecting every inch of the brig, searching each passenger's face for the one that matched the tintype he'd carried in his pocket for fifteen years. He doubted Mr. Ladson had lied to him about his father heading to Brazil. The man's limited intellect and shoddy foresight forbade him the ability to swindle someone like Hayden. Besides, he had no reason to do so. Which meant Hayden's father either was taking a later ship or had changed his mind. Either way, Hayden was on the voyage for the long haul. Once at Rio de Janeiro, he would inquire with the authorities and discover if his father had already arrived. If not, Hayden would give him a month to show his face before he set sail for home.

His gaze shifted to the Scotts, who were hovering around their pretentious sprite, Magnolia. He'd never seen such silken, ivory curls. She was a stunner, he'd give her that. Until she opened her mouth.

The brig lopped over a wave as Union officers gathered weapons from grumbling sailors and began loading them into their boats.

"Wait. We will need those in Brazil." James stepped from the line, drawing attention his way.

A lieutenant approached, measuring him with disdain. "And you are?"

"James Callaway." He moved in front of Angeline as if he could hide such beauty from the man. The officer peered around the doctor, assessing the lady with hungry eyes. Clasping her hands together, she lowered her gaze.

"Did you serve in the Rebel army, sir?" The lieutenant addressed James, who was squinting at the sun's reflection off the two gold leaves and silver anchor on the officer's blue cap.

"I'm a preacher."

Hayden coughed, hiding a rising snicker. *Preacher, indeed.* Yes, he'd heard James preach before. And witnessed his hypocrisy shortly afterward—a hypocrisy that put the final straw in the haystack of Hayden's unbelief and set it ablaze. The good news was the man didn't seem to recognize Hayden from the one time he'd slipped into the back of his church on that cold night in January.

"Ah, two preachers on board." The lieutenant's gaze swerved in Parson Bailey's direction, but the man was hidden behind a group of farmers. "You Rebels are certainly religious sorts, but then you'll need the extra prayers of repentance, I expect."

Blood surged to Hayden's fists. And from the look on his face, the doctor's as well.

"Well, *Preacher*." The officer poked James in the chest. "I have found that weapons in the hands of Rebels are a danger to all that is good and free. Ergo, we will confiscate yours." He gave a caustic grin and spun on his heels.

"Then how will we hunt and defend ourselves?" Hayden knew he should keep his mouth shut, but his anger overcame his good judgment.

Halting, the man cast Hayden an impudent glance over his shoulder. "I don't have a care, sir. You should have thought of that before you tore our country apart." He continued onward.

"And you should—"

Sarah clutched Hayden's arm and drew him back. But thankfully the flap of loose sails above had drowned out his foolish outburst. The last thing he needed was to get into an altercation with a Union lieutenant.

Thunder grumbled in the distance where dark clouds amassed on the horizon. Captain Barclay handed the Yankee captain some papers. He leafed through them with a scowl as the *New Hope*'s sailors stood in haphazard rows on the main deck, some shifting their feet, some clenching and unclenching their hands as if anxious for a fight. Hayden would love nothing more than to get in a scrap with these feather-brained braggarts and put them in their place, but at the moment they held the advantage. And besides, there were innocent civilians to protect, farmers and teachers and blacksmiths—people far more innocent than he.

Most of whom now huddled on the foredeck, some shivering in fear, others staring straight ahead. Ever the politician, Mr. Graves leaned against the railing, a placid look on his face. Something about that man ate at Hayden's insides. Beside him, Mr. Lewis, the carpenter, sneaked swigs from a flask within his coat, reminding Hayden he could use a drink about now as well.

Two Union sailors hauled Moses, his sister, and the Scotts' slave before the frigate captain, who looked them up and down with so much disgust, Hayden wondered if the man realized he had fought a war to set them free. After ensuring they had, indeed, been released from their chains—a lie the Scotts' slave pronounced after repeated glares from her owner—the captain waved them off.

"Mr. Vane, Mr. Harkins," he barked at two sailors nearby. "Take a crew below and search every nook and cranny of this old bucket. I want everyone brought above. Even the rats. Do you hear me?"

"Aye, aye, Captain." Both men saluted and got to task.

"And Mr. Staves," the captain addressed the lieutenant who had recently spoken with James, "take ten men to the hold and haul up anything of value."

James leaned toward Hayden. "They are looking for someone in particular—a Rebel officer, no doubt."

"Where is the colonel?"

"In the sick bay with Eliza."

Hayden turned to Sarah. "If you're of a mind to pray, madam, now would be a good time."

90

CHAPTER 9

Every shuffle of boots, every shout, every pitch and inflection of a Northern accent, sent Eliza's heart into her throat as she paced the sick bay's narrow deck. She could hear the Yankee sailors searching the hold, the cabins. She could hear them rummaging in every corner and closet, and by the sound of their moans and grunts, hauling things above. She gazed at the colonel, envious of his unconscious bliss.

He'd been all but blissful up on deck when he'd crouched, hands to his ears, against phantom missiles, screaming the name Jeremy over and over.

She knew exactly what was happening to him. She'd seen it in military hospitals more times than she could count. Men reliving the horrors of war, reliving moments on the battlefield with such clarity it seemed they were still in the midst of the fighting. Hallucinations of brutality, death, terror. Usually the symptoms faded with time, but more often than not, these men ended up in asylums.

Tears pooled in her eyes at the thought of that happening to Colonel Wallace. She'd watched him through the entire chase—hadn't been able to keep her eyes off him. She'd met many officers in her years as a nurse, married one in fact. They were not all created equal. Stripes and pins and ribbons did not a warrior make. The true mettle of a soldier was measured on the battlefield. Eliza had seen officers knowingly send their men to their deaths while saving themselves. She'd seen others who froze and cowered when facing the full arsenal of an enemy advance. Even worse, there were those who gloated over heroic deeds not their own but performed by men of lower rank.

But not Colonel Wallace.

Though certainly unfamiliar with sea battles, he had taken immediate command of the gun crew, issuing orders as if they were second nature, staring down the enemy and facing death side by side with his men. No hesitation. No fear. Even when the frigate fired round after round at them, his concern had been for his men.

Now, lying on the cot, his nankeen trousers stretched tight over muscular thighs that still twitched from battle, his hair dark against the cream-colored pillow, his open shirt revealing a dusting of black hair, Eliza felt a stirring within her she'd never felt before. Not even with Stanton. She looked away. She shouldn't be staring at him while he slept.

Voices drilled down the halls. She could hear Captain Barclay bantering with the Union captain. She hoped Angeline and Sarah were safe. Water slapped against the hull, grating Eliza's nerves and making her stomach feel as though she'd swallowed a brick. Sinking into a chair, she gripped her belly and willed the terror to subside.

The colonel stirred, and she glanced his way.

She'd done all she could. The blotches on his cheeks and neck looked so real, she shivered in remembrance of the disease. And the moisture she'd dabbed on his skin did, indeed, appear like sweat from a fever. If only one didn't look too close. Which was what she was counting on. Close up, anyone could tell the marks were nothing but a paste of powder and a few drops of iodine. She sighed. Hopefully, Blake would remain unconscious and not disturb them. *Oh Lord, let him remain unconscious.* She wrung her hands together. The thud of boots approached, and she grabbed a cloth.

The door swung open, and two men entered. One a lieutenant and the other an unrated seaman.

"Well, look what we have here."

Settling her nerves, Eliza slowly rose and stared at the tall, lanky officer. "What can I do for you, Lieutenant?"

He laughed, took a step inside, and planted his hands at his waist. "In case you aren't aware, miss, your ship has been captured and boarded by the U.S.S. *Perilous.*"

Perilous, indeed. Eliza raised her chin. "In case you aren't aware, Lieutenant, we are no longer at war."

"In case you aren't aware, miss, we are searching for war criminals trying to escape their due justice."

"In case—" Eliza snapped her mouth shut. This was ridiculous. "As you can see, Lieutenant. There are no war criminals in here."

The man took another step inside, his lackey nipping at his heels. "Sir," the lieutenant shouted in the colonel's direction. "You are to go above at once!"

"Any fool can see this man is ill." Eliza huffed.

"Rather bold tongue for a defeated enemy, miss." His sordid gaze raked her. "However, ill or not, he must go above. Along with you." Snapping his fingers, he gestured toward the door.

"Very well." Eliza raised a brow and stepped aside, hoping they didn't notice her trembling legs. "If you want to be exposed to the pox, be my guest. Pick him up and take him above." She tossed the rag into a basin of water. "No doubt you've already been exposed just by coming aboard."

The lieutenant halted.

"Oh?" Eliza went on. "Captain Barclay didn't warn you?" She gave a sweet smile and clicked her tongue. "How uncivilized of him."

The man's mouth hung open, and he quickly drew a hand to his nose. The other sailor retreated toward the door, his face chalky white.

"Who is he?" The officer took a step back.

"Henry Crawford, a farmer from Savannah. I'm his wife, Eliza."

"A farmer? Did he serve in the military?" The ship rocked, and he pressed a hand to the bulkhead.

"No."

"Would youu swear to that?"

"I believe, sir"—Eliza raised her voice to cover the quaver in her voice—"I would know whether my own husband had been home the past four years."

His horrified gaze bounced between her and the colonel. "Very well," he coughed into his hand and glanced behind him, no doubt looking for the other sailor, but the man had already disappeared into the hallway. Rushing out the door, the officer slammed it behind him.

Boot steps faded down the hall. Eliza's breath fled her lungs as she slumped into the chair, willing her heart to return to a normal beat.

"Well done, Mrs. Crawford."

Eliza jumped at the sound of the colonel's voice. She threw a hand to her chest as his eyes popped open and a smile curved his lips.

"You were awake?"

"Not the whole time." His glance took in the room. Then swinging his feet over the cot, he sat and rubbed his face. "But long enough to know I should remain unconscious. What is this?" He stared at the paste on his fingers then swiped his cheek, depositing more of it on his hand.

"It's smallpox, and you should have left it in place should they return."

But they weren't returning. Even now, Eliza could hear the jolly boats hammering the hull as they grew heavy with goods and men. The colonel's gaze drifted above. "Very clever, Mrs. Crawford." He assessed her, admiration pouring from his eyes. "I imagine your ruse is the reason for their sudden departure."

But Eliza no longer cared. Nothing mattered but the way he was looking at her. And the way it caused a pleasurable eddy to swirl in her stomach. Retrieving the cloth from the basin, she turned her back to him as she wrung it out then handed it to him. "It was a simple trick."

"But not one that most would have considered." He wiped his hands and face. "I've never seen a lady so brave."

Eliza's insides buzzed at the compliment. "I am not easily intimidated."

He flashed a grin. "Indeed."

"I fear it has oft gotten me into trouble in the past."

"But this time your bravado saved me from certain hanging." He released a breath and ran a hand through his hair. Lantern light swayed back and forth over him as if it were dancing to the creak and groan of the ship. He stared at the rag in his hands. "Because I collapsed like a weakling."

Anguish lined his face, coupled with a flush of embarrassment.

"Not a weakling, Colonel. A witness of horrors unimaginable." Paste smeared his left cheek where he'd missed a spot. Giving in to an urge, Eliza took the cloth and knelt before him. Their eyes met, just inches apart. She could smell his scent, strong and musky, could feel his breath on her cheek. A storm brewed in those gray eyes, so vibrant, so intense, it seemed she could dive in and swirl among the tempest. If only she could. She would do everything in her power to calm the storm within him.

"I am familiar with your symptoms, Colonel." She wiped his cheek.

He merely stared at her in wonder as if she had descended from heaven.

"Many soldiers suffer as you do," she continued. "There," she added, "no more pox." She rose, but his frown had returned.

"I am not *many soldiers*." He pushed to his feet, avoiding her gaze. "Sounds like the Yanks have left. I should go above to see if I can help."

Eliza didn't want him to leave.

He found his coat hanging on a hook and grabbed it as shame weighed heavy in the air between them. His shame. Unnecessary shame.

"You really ought to sit and have some tea before you leave."

He glanced at her then—an apologetic glance. "You are a kind woman, Mrs. Crawford." Then weaving around the operating table, he headed for the door.

"Who is Jeremy?"

He froze. The deck tilted. Eliza grabbed the table for balance.

"Where did you hear that name?"

Eliza nearly cried at the sorrow in his voice, the anger. "You spoke it in your delirium."

He turned. His Adam's apple slid down his neck as he studied her, assessing her—assessing her worthiness, perhaps. "My brother," he finally said.

"I'm sorry."

Tossing his coat on the table, he said, "Perhaps I will have that tea, after all, Mrs. Crawford."

❦

Her smile swept the gloom from the cabin. Her understanding touched a place deep in his heart he thought long since extinct. She brushed past him to retrieve the pot of tea, making apologies for her wide skirts and saying something about how ships were not made for women's fashions. It brought a much-needed chuckle to his lips and stole away a smidgeon of the embarrassment from his episode. Episode. For he knew not what else to call them. They'd started after the Battle of the Wilderness in '64 and had only gotten worse when the war ended. He hated that Mrs. Crawford had witnessed his weakness, hated that anyone had. He was the leader of this expedition and must be in control at all times. But, heaven help him, he could use a friend on board. And Mrs. Crawford filled a void he'd long since assumed was dead and buried.

She handed him a cup and squeezed past him to take her seat in

95

the chair once again, apologizing for the cold, stale tea. But Blake could not care less. Heat trailed his skin where their arms had touched ever so briefly. He was starting to enjoy the ship's tight quarters.

He leaned back against the wooden slab that served as an operating table. His leg ached, and he rubbed the familiar pain.

"I can have a look at your leg, Colonel."

He sipped his tea, examining her. "It's nothing. Old bullet wound."

"But it pains you." Eyes as golden and glistening as topaz showered him with concern.

"Now and then." Blake reached for his coat on the table, plucked out the belt plate he'd been carrying around for four years, and handed it to her.

She examined it. "A military belt buckle. Georgia, if I'm not mistaken." She flipped it over, no doubt noting the initials *JSW* etched in the metal.

"Jeremy Steven Wallace."

She swallowed and cupped it in her hands as if it were precious. "What happened?"

He shrugged, fighting back the pain, not wanting it to show. "The same thing that happened to thousands of other young men—he died in battle."

She said nothing, only gazed at him with as much pain in her eyes as he felt in his gut.

"He was only seventeen." He set his cup down on the table with a *clank*, feeling the familiar anger scorching his belly. "Wounded at Antietam, then finished off by a Union officer while he lay on the field. Or so I heard."

Her eyes glassed with tears, causing his own to rise. Standing, he turned away and crossed his arms over his chest, seeking anger instead of sorrow. Anger was much easier.

"And the rest of your family?" she asked.

He clenched his jaw. "Died in our home in Atlanta when Sherman burned it to the ground. My sisters were only five and twelve." He stared at the shadows of light and dark oscillating over the divots marring the deck. He heard her stand, heard the swish of her skirts, felt her touch on his arm where all that remained of his family were five black bands.

She leaned her head on his back as if she were trying to absorb his pain. The gesture eroded the fortress around his heart. He wanted to embrace her, run his fingers through her hair, cry until the pain ceased, but instead he stepped away. "I'm sorry," he said. "I shouldn't have burdened you with my sad tale."

"It helps to talk about it."

"Not for me." His temple throbbed. "The Yankees took everything: my family, my home, my leg. And as you saw earlier, my sanity." He gripped the edge of the table until his fingers hurt. "I hate them. Loathe them, in fact. All Union officers and their families should be hanged. No, worse. Quartered and then hanged. And anyone who had anything to do with them."

⟡

Eliza shrank back. The hatred spewing from Blake's mouth filled the room, sending its venom into every crack and crevice. She'd seen plenty of anger during the war, and plenty more hatred over the past years, but she'd never seen such malevolent contempt. The man's eye even began to twitch. She wanted to tell him that forgiveness was the only way to peace. But that hadn't worked with her own family, why would it work with this raging beast before her? For that was what he'd transformed into. A beast with the gleam of murder in his eye.

But then he drew a breath, lowered his shoulders, pried his fingers from the table, and the old colonel was back. "Forgive me, Mrs. Crawford, I've distressed you."

"I don't distress any easier than I frighten, Colonel." She offered him a smile.

One which he returned. "But I've gone on and on about myself. I know you lost a husband in the war, probably other family members as well. I've met very few who haven't."

Eliza clasped her hands before her. "No, my family still lives. My father and an uncle and aunt. My father is Se—" She slammed her mouth shut, shocked that she'd almost given his name. A name any military officer who had dealt with President Davis would know. A name that had been tainted by his traitorous daughter. "A. . .good man. He and my aunt and uncle"—she babbled on in order to cover her stutter—"own a grand hotel in Marietta." Fiddle! She was giving him too much information.

"Hmm. I hear the town was occupied in '64." Lines deepened on his forehead. "Lots of destruction."

Eliza had heard as much as well. And although she'd not been allowed home, she had prayed for her family daily. "We suffered through it." She looked away.

"And your mother?"

"Died when I was twelve." That much was true. The words still stung as if it happened yesterday. She pressed a finger on the locket hidden beneath her bodice and tugged on the chain to pull it out. "My mother," she said, opening it to reveal the portrait and the lock of hair that were all she had left of the woman who had meant the world to her.

Leaning forward until she felt his body heat, Blake studied the picture. "She's beautiful." His eyes shifted to the lock of hair attached to the inside of the lid. "And your hair is the same color."

Eliza swept back a tear. "Thank you. My father gave the locket to me on my sixteenth birthday." She snapped it shut and allowed it to dangle down the front of her gown. "I haven't taken it off since." Her life had changed drastically the day her mother died. "After Mother's passing, Father became quite obsessed with my safety. Barely let me out of his sight." Smothered her was more like it.

"Odd that he allowed you to run off to the front lines as a nurse."

Eliza realized her mistake too late as skepticism flickered across his face. "I fear when I get something in my mind, it is hard to stop me." She gave a nervous giggle. Oh how she hated bending the truth to this man.

He smiled. His gray eyes studied hers. The air between them heated, and Eliza swallowed at his intense perusal. He was so close, she could smell him, hear his breath, see the pulse throbbing in his taut neck. "And your husband. May I ask what happened to him?"

"Killed in action." She wouldn't tell him for which side. Could never tell him. The past few days, she'd harbored a small hope that perhaps he wouldn't fault her for her marriage, that perhaps they had a chance at building on what was obviously a strong mutual attraction and admiration, but after hearing his rage at Yankees and everyone associated with them, that hope was crushed. She pressed down the folds of her skirt and took a step back, if only to break the spell he cast on her. Regardless of the way this man made her feel, regardless of her admiration for him, there could never be anything between them. Ever.

She would be his friend. Help him with his condition if he allowed her. That was it.

Blake took her hand in his. His warm strength folded around her fingers, and she hadn't the will to pull away. "I'm sure he was a hero. What is his name?"

CHAPTER 10

Eliza bit her lip, trying to think of a name, any name but the one the colonel asked of her. But in her fear, her mind became a vacant hole with only one name filling it: Brigadier General Stanton Watts, commander of the 106th Harrisburg brigade—Union army. So loud did it ring in her thoughts, she feared it would slip past her lips and her guise would crumble, leaving her an enemy to all on board the ship.

But God took pity on her yet again in the form of a knock on the door and the cheery face of James, who eyed their locked hands with upraised brows and a slight smile. "Ah, you're on your feet, Colonel. The captain wishes to speak to you. If you're up to it."

The colonel released her hands, cleared his throat, and took a step back. "The frigate?"

"Gone. Along with half of our weapons, a good portion of our rice and fresh produce, and all of our pigs."

"The passengers and crew?" The colonel grabbed his coat.

"All present and accounted for. Thank God." The doctor scratched his chin. "However did you elude them? They seemed quite intent on finding any Rebel officers on board."

The colonel and Eliza shared a glance and a smile that caused a tingle all the way down to her toes. "It would seem I had a guardian angel," he said, his eyes remaining on hers as if held there by some invisible force. Finally, he cleared his throat, thanked her for the tea, and sped out the door. Without his masculine presence, the cabin grew large and cold. And it felt less safe somehow.

Picking up his cup, she ran her fingers over the brim where his lips had been, remembering his pain, the agony in his voice when he spoke of his family. All of them gone. *Lord, why? How could You allow so much*

100

suffering? It was too much to bear. Too much for one man. No wonder he hated the Yankees. And anyone associated with them. Which meant her, of course. No, even if her past was never revealed, it would be unjust, even cruel to befriend him, let alone consider anything beyond friendship. She must put the colonel out of her thoughts.

Setting the cup on the tray, she began to tidy up the cabin when a knock on the open door turned her around to see Magnolia, an anxious look on her face.

"Magnolia. You startled me. Are you ill?" Eliza started toward her, only then noticing that the young woman's hands trembled.

Pressing down her skirts, Magnolia floated into the cabin, her sapphire-blue eyes skittering over the sideboard containing medicines and surgical implements. "It's my nerves, Eliza," she said in that accentuated Southern drawl that was as sweet as warm molasses. "I cannot seem to relax."

"Understandable." Eliza studied the young woman as she squeezed her own skirts through the narrow space between table and bulkhead. "It was a most harrowing day. I trust you've not been in a battle at sea before."

This drew a smile from Magnolia as she shook her head, sending flaxen curls bouncing over her neck. "I was wondering if you had something to soothe my nerves." Her gaze sped to the medical cabinet once again before her face crumpled. "I simply cannot tolerate another moment on this ship."

"You don't have seasickness, do you?" Eliza took her hand in hers.

"No." She tugged from Eliza's grasp and plopped down in the chair. Then dropping her face into her hands, she began to sob.

Eliza knelt before her. "Oh dear, there's no need to cry. Everything will be all right. The Union ship is gone, and we are on our way to our new home." Evidenced by the flap of sails above and the increasing purl of the sea against the hull.

"It's not that." Magnolia raised her gaze to Eliza, tears spilling down her cheeks. "I want to go home!" Her pout turned into a scowl as a streak of defiance scored her eyes. "I'm engaged to marry Samuel Wimberly." She swiped the remaining moisture from her face and raised her chin. "He's a prominent lawyer from Atlanta. Why, he was even an adviser to President Jefferson Davis."

Eliza flinched. No doubt he knew her father, then, both being solicitors and both working with the president. But she could never mention the connection. "I'm sure he's a wonderful man." Eliza handed her a handkerchief.

"Of course he is. And he adores me." She sniffed and drew the handkerchief to her nose. "We were supposed to wed before this horrendous war began, but then Samuel thought it best to delay the ceremony until the hostilities were over." Another tear wound its way down her creamy cheek. "And now my parents have dragged me away from everything. From Samuel, from our home, from. . ." She hesitated, looking perplexed. "Well, from simply everything!" She gazed down at her pink petticoat peeking from behind cream-colored skirts fringed in Spanish lace. "Look at me. I'm a mess! I look like a street urchin. Or so Daddy told me this morning."

Eliza didn't know whether to feel sorry for the lady or chastise her for her spoiled attitude. She could find no flaw in the woman's appearance. In fact, she could pass for any Southern lady ready to receive guests for afternoon tea. Still, it had not escaped Eliza's attention that Mr. Scott rarely had a kind word for his daughter. Though Eliza's own father had been stern, he'd never berated her. And never in public. What would it be like to grow up with a father like Magnolia's? And then to be dragged away from her entire world, and worse, the man she loved? The poor girl. "I'm sure your parents are doing what is best for you. No doubt your plantation was ruined as many were by the Northerners."

Magnolia looked down, hesitating. "We could have stayed and recovered our losses. But Daddy was so angry—angrier than I've ever seen him—at the Yankees. He's been that way ever since my brother Allen was killed at Chancellorsville. He said we needed to get as far away from them as we could and start over. But I don't want to start over." She began to whine again, an ear-shattering whine that set Eliza's nerves on edge. She poured the girl a cup of tea, hoping it would keep her mouth—and vocal chords—quiet.

Thanking Eliza, she took it, but her hands shook so violently, tea spilled over the edge. "Don't you have something for my nerves?" Blue eyes that held a deviant twinkle gazed at Eliza. "You *do* look so familiar to me."

Ignoring her, Eliza grabbed the cup to settle it. "This is chamomile tea. I know it's cold, but it will help calm you."

Magnolia bit her lip. "Mercy me, I was hoping for something a bit stronger."

Eliza cocked her head. Shaking hands, nervous twitch at the corner of her mouth, desperation in her striking eyes—Eliza had seen those symptoms before. But never in a lady. Nor one of such high breeding. Eliza wondered if her parents knew. "I have nothing stronger. But never fear, the trembling will subside in a few days."

Magnolia set the tea down, spilling it on the table, then stormed to her feet. "I don't know what you are referring to! Oh why did I ever come to you? You're merely a war nurse."

Yet the girl made no move to leave. Instead, she clasped her hands together and glanced toward the medicines.

Eliza wanted to be angry at her, but she looked so pathetic and sad. "I'm sorry, Magnolia. I wish I could help you." She laid a hand on her arm. "Believe me, your discomfort will pass."

Magnolia huffed, assessing Eliza as if she were a wayward servant. But then something flickered in her eyes before they narrowed into malicious slits. "I *do* remember you now."

Eliza's heart cinched. Turning away, she mopped up the spilled tea. "I fear you are mistaken. We have never met."

"No. You're Seth Randal's daughter. Your aunt and uncle are acquainted with my parents. They run that fancy hotel in Marietta. . . . What was the name? Oh yes, the Randal Inn."

A chill bit Eliza. "I'm sorry, but you have the wrong lady."

"No, I never forget a face. But your name isn't Eliza Crawford. . . ." Magnolia laid a shaky finger on her chin before her eyes lit up with malevolent glee. "Ah yes, Flora. Miss Flora Randal, isn't it? Your father knows my Samuel."

Eliza's blood ran cold. "I know no one by that name." She picked up the teacup and placed it on the tray, fiddling with the spoons so as not to show that her insides had twisted into a hopeless knot. She hadn't heard her given name in a long time. Five years to be exact. Not since she had married Stanton. Not since her father had told her Flora Randal was dead to him.

Suddenly, memories of Magnolia flooded her. Two years before the war, Eliza's aunt and uncle had hosted a party at their hotel for some passing dignitaries. The Scotts had been invited because of their familial relation to the governor of Georgia, who was also in attendance. Though Eliza had not met Magnolia's parents, she and Magnolia had exchanged brief pleasantries. At the time, they had both been girls just coming of age, Magnolia only sixteen and Eliza a year younger. Though Magnolia had changed quite a bit in seven years, Eliza remembered envying her for the way all the men in the hotel had fawned over her. And in the midst of the festivities, she had commented thus to Magnolia. A morbid realization now crawled up Eliza's throat. It was after that playful admission that Magnolia, in what was surely a kind gesture, had introduced Eliza to Stanton, an acquaintance of the family's.

Magnolia gasped and drew a hand to her mouth. "Mercy me! You married Stanton Watts!"

"Shhh." Dashing to the door, Eliza shut it then leaned back against the wood. "Please, Magnolia." Her tone and eyes pleaded with the young woman to keep her secret, but Magnolia only chuckled in return.

"Oh my. The wife of a Yankee general right here in the middle of all these angry Rebels! It is simply too much!"

"That was a long time ago. My husband is dead. I spent the last three years nursing Rebel soldiers on the battlefield." Eliza felt all hope draining from her.

"Never fear. I will keep your little secret, Mrs. *Crawford*." Magnolia adjusted her flowing skirts as a coy smile flitted upon her lips. "If you will do me just one little ole favor."

Eliza narrowed her eyes.

"I believe you *do* have something that would ease my nerves, after all, do you not?"

"You are blackmailing me?"

She pouted. "That's such a nasty word. Let's just say we have an understanding."

Forcing down her anger, Eliza brushed past Magnolia, opened the drawer of the desk, and pulled out a half-empty bottle of rum.

The smile Magnolia offered her could have brightened the darkest cave. Greedily, she snagged the bottle from Eliza's hand like a child after candy.

"That isn't good for you, Magnolia. It will ruin your health and your life."

She pressed the bottle against her chest as if it were the most precious thing in the world. "I don't care. I need it."

Eliza should grab it back from her and shatter it on the deck. She was a nurse, after all. It was her job to look out for the health of others. But what choice did she have? "You know what will happen to me if you tell the others."

A flicker of concern, dare Eliza say, even care, appeared on the girl's face. "I shan't say a word." Hiding the rum in the folds of her skirt, she flung open the door. "As long as you continue to treat my nerves."

"That is the only bottle I have."

"Well, I suppose you'll have to find more, won't you?" She gave Eliza the sweetest smile before sashaying away, flinging the words over her shoulder, "Thank you Mrs. *Crawford*. You've been most helpful."

When the younger woman was gone, Eliza's legs gave out. She leaned on the operating table. Her fate—her very life—was now in the hands of a spoiled, pompous tosspot.

⚜

Blake hobbled across the deck of the *New Hope*, drawing in a breath of the briny air. The sun reigned over the seas from its position high in the sky, its bright golden robes fluttering over ship and water. Hammering drew his gaze to a group of sailors working to repair the foremast rigging and the rents in the bulwarks. Yesterday Blake had assisted in plugging up the hole in the hull above the waterline. Thankfully all minor repairs. The frigate's attack could have been so much worse.

Sailors stopped to glance his way, as did Mr. Graves, who puffed on his cigar on the foredeck, along with a group of passengers sitting atop crates, eating their morning biscuits. Whispers sizzled past his ears from behind upraised hands. He knew they spoke about his episode. Shame doused him as he made his way toward the railing. He'd wanted so much to present himself as a strong leader to this group. But he had already failed.

If only the nightmares would stop, maybe the blackouts would as well. He gripped the railing and gazed at the azure sea, sparkling like a bed of dancing diamonds. A hearty breeze spun around him, cooling the sweat on the back of his neck. Every mile south brought them warmer weather and heavier air.

He nodded at Captain Barclay, who stood by the binnacle, and the man returned his greeting. They'd developed a mutual respect for each other these past days. More than once the captain had thanked Blake for his help manning the guns and commanding the crew during the chase. And more than once, Blake had thanked him and his men for not giving away his identity.

Scanning the deck, he found Sarah sitting atop a crate, her skirts spread around her, instructing a group of children at her feet, their sweet laughter a compliment to the creak of the ship and rush of water that had become so familiar to Blake's ears.

Mr. and Mrs. Jenkins, the young farmers, stood behind their daughter, Henrietta, as she listened intently to the story Sarah was telling. The freed slave woman's children stood at a distance, their feet itching to join the other young ones, but Delia's firm hand on each shoulder kept them in place. That and the scowl on Mr. Scott's face as he leaned against the railing beside his wife and daughter. On Miss Magnolia's other side, Dodd attempted to engage her in conversation, but from the young lady's pursed lips and raised nose, Blake doubted the ex-lawman was gaining any ground.

Mr. Lewis, the carpenter, seemed already three sheets to the wind as he clung to the capstan, rolling with each sway of the ship. Parson Bailey strolled around the deck with James, their heads bent in conversation, no doubt regarding some deep theological argument. A call from above shifted Blake's glance to the sailors working the sails. Barefooted, they skittered across the yards as if they preferred balancing on a teetering strip of wood to walking on dry land. The first mate stood on the deck beneath them, shouting up orders. Beside him, Moses, the freed slave, assisted a group of sailors in carrying a barrel of water on deck for the passengers.

They plunked it down beside Hayden, who was polishing the brass fitting atop the foredeck railing. Yesterday Blake had seen him scrub the deck and assist sailors hauling lines. Despite his intrusion on their voyage, the man did not shy from hard work. He'd also proven himself brave and competent during their battle with the Union frigate. In fact, the man had charmed his way so far into everyone's graces that the suspicious circumstances that brought him on board seemed all but forgotten. If he decided to stay on with them in Brazil, Blake could use another strong man to help lead the colony.

Yet still no sign of Mrs. Crawford—Eliza. Her Christian name floated through his mind, longing to appear on his lips, longing for the familiarity it would signify between them. Perhaps all the excitement from yesterday kept her in bed. Or perhaps she was avoiding him. Yes, perhaps he'd been too forward, too open with his thoughts and sentiments. And he'd gone and frightened her away. He couldn't blame her. What would any woman want with a lame man who was obviously going mad?

Speaking of mad, Mr. Graves's dark, piercing eyes assessed Blake from afar. Dressed in his usual black suit, and with his equally black hair, whiskers, and mustache, the man presented a rather somber figure. Spooky was more like it. Yet that impression haled more from his attitude, the way he stood at a distance and stared at people—like he was staring at Blake now—as if he could read his thoughts. A frisson of unease settled in Blake's gut. Mr. Graves smiled, and Blake tore his gaze away. No sense in offering the man any encouragement.

Leaping up the quarterdeck stairs, he made his way to the stern, wincing at the pain radiating through his leg. Which seemed to be getting worse, not better. He guessed that was to be expected with all the heaving and careening and the extra effort it took just to keep upright on the ship. Nevertheless, he would be glad to settle on dry land again.

Leaning over the taffrail, he watched the foamy wake bubble off the stern and dissolve in the deep waters. Just like everything good in his life.

He plucked his brother's belt plate from his pocket and fingered it, shifting it in the sunlight, examining all the facets, the engraving, squinting when it reflected light in his eyes. Which only reminded him of Jeremy's smile, so bright and warm.

Perhaps in a new place, a new country, where no memories of the war or his past existed, Blake would find freedom from his nightmares. In a place where no Yankee roamed, his soul could rest, forget, and find peace.

It was his only hope.

A loud twang crackled over the ship, followed by a snap. Blake spun around. Sailors shouted and rushed across the brig. Rigging parted. The brace on the weather side began to split. One of the yards swung free.

Beneath the urgent shouts of the captain, the first mate joined a group of sailors in the ratlines, scrambling aloft to capture the wayward yard.

Blake started toward them. The ship canted. The yard shifted and struck the first mate.

He fell to the deck with a soul-crunching thud.

On the captain's heels, Blake dashed down to the main deck as men circled the fallen man. But it was the look on Mr. Graves's face that halted Blake in his tracks.

A look of sheer joy.

CHAPTER 11

Sink me for a pirate if this voyage ain't under a jinx!" Captain Barclay slammed his fist on his desk, overturning a bottle of ink and sending Eliza's heart into her throat. He righted the bottle before too much of the black liquid spilled on his charts. At least the ones he had left. For in addition to smashing the main compass in the binnacle and stealing the captain's sextant and scales, the thief had also absconded with several of his maps.

Eliza suddenly wished she had not been summoned to the captain's cabin, along with James, to give a report on the first mate's condition. She'd spent enough years enduring her father's temper to last a lifetime. Yet the other men in the room—the colonel, the parson, and two sailors—seemed unaffected by both the captain's outburst and by the furious pace he now took up before the stern windows, growling like a bear.

"Your first mate suffered quite a blow to his head," James stated. "I'm afraid, he's slipped into a coma. There's no telling when he will wake up. Weeks perhaps."

"But he will wake up?" the captain asked, looking concerned.

"I believe so, Captain. In time."

The news did not improve Captain Barclay's mood. He halted, his face hard as quartz. "We are chased and boarded by a Union frigate, my rigging splits and nearly kills my first mate, and"—he tossed the rest of a drink to the back of this throat then slammed the glass down on his desk—"where in Neptune's sea have my instruments and charts gone off to?"

At the man's enraged tone, Eliza took a step back, her ears ringing at the string of curses that followed his statement. The colonel, noting her unease, came to stand by her side.

Always the gentleman. He cleared his throat, drawing the captain's gaze.

"Forgive me, Mrs. Crawford." Captain Barclay said before he poured himself another drink.

"If I may, Cap'n." One of the sailors, the boatswain, whom Eliza believed was named Max, stepped forward. "I might know who took yer instruments."

The deck heaved. Water hissed against the hull. The colonel steadied Eliza with a touch. But the captain only gaped at Max in consternation. "Well, spit it out, man, I haven't all day! Whoever it is, they'll be slurpin' bilgewater by morning!"

"That fine-lookin'"—Max cleared his throat—"the Scotts' daughter, I meant to say." He fidgeted with his hat. "I saw her enter yer cabin yesterday morn."

"And you said nothing!"

The captain's bark sent Max back a step. "How was I to know what the tart was up to?" He shrugged, and his tanned face turned a deep shade of scarlet. "Figured it was none of me business why the lady came to yer cabin alone."

James's eyes widened.

"Oh my." Parson Bailey opened his Bible and began flipping through the pages.

"Oh for the love of. . ." Captain Barclay huffed. "Bring her here immediately. And her parents!"

Within minutes, the Scotts arrived, acting as indignant as if they'd been whisked away from a royal ball.

"What is the meaning of this, Captain?" Mr. Scott grabbed the lapels of his fancy coat.

But the captain's eyes were on Magnolia, who had slipped behind her father's large frame. "I would like a word with your daughter, sir."

"My daughter?" Mr. Scott flinched then turned to find Magnolia cowering beside her mother. With a huff, he dragged her forward. "What could you possibly wish to discuss with her?"

"Miss Scott." Circling the desk, the captain crossed his meaty arms over his chest. Sunlight angled through the window, jouncing over his indigo coat. "Do you have somethin' to say to me?"

Magnolia's eyes widened. Her gaze skittered about the room before

110

landing back on the captain. "I don't believe I do."

"About the cap'n's instruments." Max jerked a thumb toward Captain Barclay. "How ye stole them from his desk."

"An' smashed the compass," the other sailor chimed in.

"Oh dear." Mrs. Scott sank into a chair.

Magnolia's eyes turned to shimmering pools. Her bottom lip quivered, and she stumbled over the deck. Eliza rushed to slip an arm around her back for support.

A real tremble *did* course through the lady, but she jerked from Eliza's embrace and glared at her parents. "I want to go home." Tears trickled down her cheeks. "I didn't mean to hurt anyone. I only wanted the ship to turn around and head back to Charleston!"

Wind pounded against the stern windows.

Mr. Scott gawked in horror at his daughter. "What have you done?"

"There is no place in the kingdom of heaven for thieves and liars," Parson Bailey said, causing Mrs. Scott to whimper.

And red fury to course across Mr. Scott's face. "You stole the captain's instruments?" His voice rose with each word as he glared at his daughter. "What were you thinking?" He grabbed her arm until tears spilled from her cheeks, his jaw tight above quivering jowls. But then his eyes wandered over the group, and composing himself, he faced Captain Barclay. "Do tell me that wasn't the reason we were captured and boarded."

"No, not entirely," the captain said. The ship creaked and groaned as it tumbled over a wave.

Magnolia tripped, never taking her gaze off the deck. "I just wanted to go home," she mumbled. "I just wanted to go home."

"Miss Scott," Captain Barclay said, "you put the entire brig and everyone on board in grave danger." He gripped the edge of his desk behind him and leaned back with a sigh. "Thank God I have a hand compass and an extra sextant. But my charts. What did you do with them?"

"I tossed everything overboard," she said without looking up.

Mrs. Scott's whimpering transformed into wailing, reminding Eliza of a sick cow.

Which seemed somehow fitting, since Mr. Scott, at the moment, resembled a bull penned in a cage. "Of course we will pay for the damages, Captain. Please accept our apology." His tone was one of restrained fury. Then turning, he clutched Magnolia's arm in a pinch and dragged her out the door. "You have embarrassed me to no end, young lady. Incorrigible behavior. Simply incorrigible!" When his wife didn't follow, he shouted over his shoulder. "Come along, Mrs. Scott." As if waking from a stupor, the woman rose, face to the floor, and shuffled out the door.

The parson sped after them, muttering something about repentance and restitution.

Despite Magnolia's actions, Eliza felt sorry for her. She knew what it was like to live with an overbearing parent who insisted on managing every detail of her life. No doubt that was the reason Magnolia had turned to drink. In truth, she and Eliza were not so different after all. Eliza had been no less rebellious against her own father. In fact, she'd been more. She could still picture him standing in his study the day she told him she wanted to marry Stanton.

"You will not marry that man! He is from Pennsylvania of all places. He is not one of us. Besides, it has already been arranged. You are to marry Miles Grisham."

Miles Grisham, the heir to the Grisham railroad fortune. And a mealymouthed weasel of the worst kind. "But, Papa, please. I don't love him."

With a snort, her father strode to the window. Dressed in a fine cutaway coat of gray broadcloth with silver braid trim shimmering in the afternoon sun, he presented such a handsome, commanding figure. "Love only causes pain." He huffed. She knew he was thinking of her mother. Her death when Eliza was only twelve had robbed her father of his youth, his zest for life—his heart.

As if confirming where his thoughts had taken him, he said, "Your mother would approve of Mr. Grisham."

"Mother would want me happy."

He spun around. "And you think I don't? This is for your own good. You'll see."

When Eliza opened her mouth to protest further, he held up a hand. His signal that the discussion had come to an end.

And Eliza's signal to resort to drastic measures—to disobey him and run away with Stanton. Like Magnolia, she had not considered the implications of her actions that day. Now, looking back, she wondered if she'd only married Stanton to get out from under her father's thumb.

The captain's voice jarred her from her thoughts.

"Colonel, I'd like to make you my acting first mate if you'll accept the job."

Colonel Wallace stretched his broad shoulders, which seemed to rise beneath the man's question. "Me? I hardly know what to do."

"The men respect you." The captain sipped his drink then pointed it toward the colonel. "Besides, I've been watching you. You learn fast."

James nodded his approval.

"Very well," the colonel said. "I'll do my best."

Eliza's heart nearly burst with happiness for him. He'd more than proven that he was a leader of men and quite capable of the position.

After the captain dismissed them with a wave of his hand, Max brushed past Eliza, touching her arm as his eyes roved over her, giving her an unpleasant chill—a chill that instantly warmed when the colonel proffered his elbow with a smile. But Eliza begged off with the excuse that she needed to check on her patient. She'd love nothing more than to spend time with the colonel, but it was better this way. Better for them both.

⚓

Two uneventful weeks passed. Uneventfully delightful in the sense that they'd not seen another ship, nor had the weather been overly uncomfortable, though it had rained consistently each afternoon. But also uneventful in that most of the passengers had settled into a daily routine and were now complaining of the monotony of company and scenery. And of the food! Porridge and biscuits for breakfast, chicken and biscuits for lunch, and chicken and biscuits for supper. Eliza wouldn't care if she never tasted chicken again. Besides, she couldn't stand the sound of the poor creatures being butchered each morning and evening. Since the Yanks had stolen their rice, cheese, pigs, and most of their produce, the meals had become something to endure rather than enjoy.

Nevertheless, they'd also had a pleasant lapse of medical emergencies. Aside from the first mate, whom Eliza checked daily, there were no other catastrophes except a few rashes and one case of diarrhea. Well, unless running into the colonel every time she turned around was a catastrophe: by the forecastle; on the main deck; by the stern; in the galley, the hold, the sick bay. Wherever she went to try to avoid him, there he was with that hypnotic grin on his face and a request on his lips to join him for a stroll.

What was a lady supposed to do? She could hardly ignore someone on board a tiny brig. And if she dared to admit it, she enjoyed every minute she spent in his company. Minutes in which she'd grown to know and admire him even more.

Sunlight angled across the cabin as Eliza put the final pin in her hair and slipped on her bonnet. Behind her, Sarah's gentle snores filled the tiny space as she swung in her hammock to the movements of the ship. So far along with child, she must be quite uncomfortable and tired. Yet every day she gathered the children together to teach them their lessons. Angeline had already risen and left the cabin sometime in the night, as she often did. Eliza suspected some tragedy ran deep within the poor lady. If only she could get her to talk about it. Perhaps Eliza should pray. Oh fiddle! Of course. Why hadn't she thought of that?

Lifting up a quick prayer for Angeline, she slid a few pins on her hat to keep it in place, took one last glance in the mirror, and turned to leave, looking forward to her daily stroll on the deck. And hoping, against her own good sense, that the colonel would seek her out.

Closing the door as quietly as possible, Eliza made her way down the hall, stopping when a macabre tune floated up from the hold. No, not a tune. A chant of some kind. She'd heard it before in the wee hours of the night. It had slithered down her spine and sent a shiver through her exactly like it was doing now. But who would be uttering such a direful chant?

Shaking it off, she climbed the ladder to the main deck, squinting at the sun, now a hand's breadth above the horizon. Wind tumbled over her, dislodging her hair from its pins and loosening her hat, making her wonder why she bothered to attempt the fashionable coiffeur at all.

Gripping the brim, she proceeded across the deck and spotted Magnolia battling her parasol. Eliza had managed to find another bottle of brandy in the sick bay to lock the woman's tongue, but with the Union frigate absconding with most of their rum, she didn't know how much longer she could appease the girl. Surely Magnolia wasn't cruel enough to ruin Eliza's life when there was no alcohol to be found on board?

A gust of wind tore the parasol from Magnolia's hands, sending it bouncing in the air on its way out to sea. Mable, her slave, dropped the load of books she carried and caught the parasol just in time, handing it to her disgruntled owner, who snagged it from her with a scowl. Moses darted toward them, picking up the books for Mable and handing them to her. Her cheeks reddened like raspberries on chocolate as she nodded her thanks.

Eliza couldn't help but smile at the budding romance. The thought of which drew her gaze to Blake at his usual spot on the quarterdeck. He'd filled the role of first mate as if he'd been born on a ship. How he'd learned all the names and positions of the sails and when they should be raised or lowered, furled or unfurled, she had no idea, but the crew leaped to task whenever he shouted an order. Wind swept over him as he stood conferring with the captain, flapping his white shirt. His dark eyebrows knit together at something the captain was saying, but then he saw her, and his forehead relaxed into soft lines.

Chastising herself for being caught staring at him—yet again—Eliza positioned herself at the starboard railing and gazed out over the blue expanse of sky and sea. She'd never realized how many shades of blue there were: azure, cobalt, indigo, navy, turquoise, cerulean, teal, beryl. And each so beautiful and unique, appearing at the whim of sun, cloud, and wind. As well as the depth of the sea, Captain Barclay had told her.

Closing her eyes, she drew in a breath of briny air tainted with the odor of fish. She fingered the locket hanging around her neck. Thoughts of her mother were interrupted by the clipped gait of the colonel's boots coming her way. Her heart leaped.

"Another fine day, is it not, Mrs. Crawford?"

"It is indeed, Colonel. The ocean grows more magnificent each day."

"I hear it's even more beautiful off the coast of Brazil." The brig flopped over a wave, showering them with salty spray and causing them both to laugh.

Eliza brushed the moisture from her skirts as the colonel's expression sobered. "May I join you, or do you prefer to be alone?" he asked.

If ever there had been a time for her to deny his request, it had been two weeks ago when he'd first asked the same question. But too much time had passed, too many strolls around the deck, too many conversations of happier times in the South before the war, and now Eliza could not imagine denying herself the only thing she looked forward to on the journey. Even though she knew it was unfair to them both. Oh what a weak woman she was! Always led by feelings and not by reason. She should make an excuse that she needed to think, to pray—to do the right thing for once in her life! Instead, she faced him. "I would love the company, but surely you have duties to attend?"

"Ah, you won't get rid of me that easily, Mrs. Crawford. Besides, with a clear sky and a steady wind, there's not much to be done at the moment."

That moment turned into several minutes as the colonel shared with her the reason he started this venture to Brazil. Eliza found herself mesmerized by his words; the inflection of his voice when he spoke; his confident, resonant tone; how the sunlight reflected the ocean's blue in his gray eyes; and the way the wind batted the tips of his coal-colored hair.

"Forgive me, I've gone on and on about my hopes for Brazil," he said.

"There's nothing wrong with wanting a simple life, Colonel. Not after what you've endured. What we've all endured." Eliza sighed and held down her bonnet against a burst of wind. "To work hard, reap the fruit of your labors, raise children, and live in peace. Peace from others lording it over you, peace from oppression and hatred." Yes, Eliza could well understand that. She longed for that kind of life, herself, as well.

"So, you *were* listening to me." He smiled.

"Always, Colonel."

His eyes sparkled pleasure at her response as he leaned on the railing and cocked his head. "Now, what of your dreams, Mrs. Crawford? I would love to hear them."

But she couldn't tell him that her only real dream was to escape the scorn, the hatred toward her in the South. The sun spread sparkling ribbons over waves, and she lowered the brim of her hat against its brightness. "Like you, I simply wish to put my past behind me and start over."

"But you still have family in the States. Why have they not come with you?"

Eliza bit her lip. "We have become estranged, I'm afraid."

"Ah." Understanding flashed across his eyes. "No doubt your father did not wish you to become a war nurse."

Though that was not the reason for the estrangement, it was true enough to allow Eliza to nod in agreement.

The brig rose over a swell, and he touched her elbow to keep her steady. "I'm sure he had your best interests at heart."

She wouldn't tell him that it was her father's own interests, his own reputation, that led his heart. A fact that still weighed heavily on Eliza. Had he ever really loved her? Or was all his meddling, his smothering, his guiding merely a way for him to control her, mold her into the perfect daughter of a prominent solicitor?

❦

Blake hated that he'd somehow caused the sorrow burning in Eliza's golden eyes. Gold like the sun with flecks of silver that sparkled when she laughed. He must bring back her smile. Scanning the deck, he spotted Mr. Dodd pointing to his treasure map and spouting off to a group of passengers. "Well at least you've not got your heart set on a chest of gold like Mr. Dodd."

Clutching the brim of her hat, whereupon ribbons and feathers hopelessly flailed about, she glanced toward the ex-lawman and rewarded Blake with a grin. "Indeed. I am not one for fanciful tales. Can you believe it? Treasure maps and pirates!" She chuckled.

Blake scratched his chin. "And apparently they buried their chest of gold right outside of Rio de Janeiro."

"I hope he didn't pay overmuch for such a forgery." She gave him a sly look. "Though it is rather amusing."

"Then, I take it, you don't believe him?" Blake's attempt at lightness fell flat when, still staring at Dodd, the lady's face tightened. "I find him uncomfortable to be around. But if he does find gold, the better for him. Perhaps then he will keep his eyes off the ladies."

"Yes indeed." The man's obsession with women had not gone unnoticed by Blake. "Let me know if he bothers you, and I will handle it."

She smiled at him shyly and lowered her gaze. Such innocence from a married lady. He enjoyed every moment spent in her company. More than any of the ladies he had courted before the war. When he had thought himself too wounded, too damaged, for any possibility of finding a wife, Eliza Crawford had rekindled hope within him for the first time in years. If only she could overlook his weakness.

Yet the look in her eyes at the moment exuded more respect than pity. And he felt her admiration straight down to his boots. Wind gusted over them. Loose strands of her hair danced over her shoulders in a wildness that was so much like the lady herself. Brave, free, uninhibited. He'd never met anyone like her.

A shout drew his gaze to Miss Magnolia, who was scolding her slave—for some minor infraction, no doubt. After her tirade, she settled onto one of the heavy crates the captain had brought on deck for the passengers. The young lady's gaze drifted above and remained there so long, Blake followed it to find Hayden, stripped to his trousers, his chest gleaming with sweat, working on one of the halyards.

"Odd that she stares at a man she claims to despise," Eliza offered with a chuckle.

Blake cocked a brow at her, noting her eyes were fastened on the man as well. A spike of jealousy caused his annoyance to rise. "Our stowaway is a handsome figure, is he not?"

A coy grin toyed on her lips. "He is no match for you, Colonel." She immediately swept her gaze to sea. "Forgive me. That was far too bold. I fear my thoughts have escaped my mouth again!"

Another endearing quality of hers. "I'm afraid I cannot forgive you, madam." For it meant that, despite his limp, despite his mad episodes, she found him agreeable. And that alone gave him the impetus to ask her to receive his courtship. He wanted to know her better. Wanted to have an understanding between them that excluded all others. She was, after all, only one of four unmarried women aboard, and he saw the way the other men looked at her.

Yet, was it fair of him to pursue her when he had the responsibility of the entire colony on his shoulders? Yes, he'd be busy, especially after arriving at Brazil, but she'd proven herself more than capable of handling any situation. And with her by his side, with her wisdom, skill, bravery, and kind heart, Blake knew he could tackle anything.

After glancing around to ensure they weren't going to be interrupted, he took her hand in his, heart thundering in his chest more than it had on any battlefield. "Mrs. Crawford, I know this is sudden. I know you may think me completely mad, but I would be so honored"—he hesitated, shifting his stance—"you would make me so happy"—he cleared his throat—"if you would allow me to court you."

Instead of the expected smile, the joyful glimmer in her eyes, horror glazed over them then eased onto her face, tightening her features and parting her mouth. Tugging her hand from his, she backed away as if he'd just asked her to climb to the top yard.

CHAPTER 12

Stripped to her petticoats, Eliza ran a damp cloth over her face and arms in an attempt to rid herself of the salty film that seemed permanently glued to her skin. Though she tried, she could not get the colonel's request to court her out of her mind, out of her thoughts. Or out of her heart. Thank God one of the sailors had interrupted them with a complaint of a rash, which was soon followed by a string of infirmities from others that had kept her in the sick bay the rest of the day. Safe from having to answer the question to which her heart screamed, *Yes!* but to which her mind screamed, *No!*

Yet. . .was a courtship possible? Could one tiny mistake several years in the past ruin her chances for happiness? She had thought so. "Oh Lord, I don't know what to do," she said out loud, not really expecting an answer. Not really wanting to know the answer if it meant the colonel was not a part of her future. Which was probably why she wouldn't hear one. She dipped the rag back into the basin of water. The door opened, and she swerved about, covering herself.

"Oh, forgive me, Eliza." Angeline entered the tiny cabin and quickly closed the door. "It's terribly hard to find privacy aboard this ship."

But Eliza had lost all thoughts of modesty when her eyes latched onto the fluffy bundle in Angeline's arms. "Oh my." She stepped toward Angeline and ran her fingers over the black fur. The cat gazed up at her with amber-colored eyes. "Where did you find it?"

Angeline eased into the single chair and set the feline on her lap. "Below in the hold. I went to get some flour for Cook, and I found this wee one pouncing on a rat. A rather large rat, I might add." She chuckled, and Eliza thought how comely she was when she smiled. Which the lady didn't do very often.

"Most women would have swooned at the sight of a rat. You impress me." Eliza knelt to caress the cat, who began purring under so much attention.

"I've been exposed to much worse." Angeline's tone was far too nonchalant for such a statement.

Eliza squeezed her hand. "We've all been exposed to things these past few years that no lady should have to endure." Though Eliza had a feeling Angeline wasn't talking about the war at all. There was something in her demeanor, a sorrow, a worldly knowledge that had stolen the innocence from her eyes. Eyes that now bore shadows beneath them.

"I notice you don't sleep well," Eliza said, bringing the lady's surprised gaze to hers.

"Forgive me for waking you. I try to be quiet."

"I'm a light sleeper." Eliza sat on the trunk beside Angeline. "But that isn't why I mentioned it. Perhaps I can find some medicine to help you rest?"

"Nothing helps. I've been this way since. . .well, since the war."

Eliza nodded her understanding. The dreadful war had changed a lot of people—for the worse. "It must have been horrible to lose your father. Who took care of you?"

"My uncle." The woman seemed to choke on the word. "Then I was on my own."

Eliza wondered what happened but kept silent.

"I did many things I'm not proud of," Angeline added numbly, as if to no one in particular.

"You are not the only one." Eliza sighed.

Angeline's brow wrinkled, and she looked at Eliza, first with curiosity and then with shame. Finally, she gazed down and stroked the cat.

"What will you call her?" Eliza attempted to lighten the mood.

"It's a he, I believe. And he's quite skinny. I fear he hasn't been eating well." The cat leaped from her lap and slinked around the cabin. "I'm going to call him Stowy since he's our stowaway cat."

Eliza chuckled and rose. "Excellent choice. If we keep him in here with us, at least we shan't have to worry about rats crawling on us during our sleep."

Angeline trembled. "At least not the rodent kind."

Her words gave Eliza pause. "Has someone been bothering you?" she asked. "I can have the colonel speak to them." She nearly laughed at her own statement. Did she think the man was her personal bodyguard to share as she desired?

"No. Nothing like that." Angeline's violet eyes swept to the porthole where the setting sun bounced in and out of view. "It's just Mr. Dodd. He keeps staring at me."

"You are a beautiful woman. I fear you'll have to manage the attention. Especially when there are so few single women on this journey."

"Perhaps you are right." She offered Eliza a curt smile then brushed a lock of copper-colored hair from her forehead.

The cat wove around Eliza's feet and then pounced on a shaft of sunlight shifting over the floor.

"Besides"—Eliza turned back to the small mirror, attempting to pin up her unruly locks—"I hear there is a celebration on deck tonight. Apparently some of the passengers and sailors brought along their fiddles and have agreed to play. I insist you join me above. After all we've been through on this voyage, we could use some gaiety."

"Oh, I couldn't possibly." Angeline rubbed her arms as if a chill had come over her.

"Why not?" Eliza gave up on her hair and opened her trunk, seeking her only formal gown, an emerald percale over a bodice of white muslin, trimmed in Chantilly lace. Her fingers touched something hard and cold, and she pulled out the gold pocket watch Stanton had given her. The last thing he had given her. The only thing he'd given her of a personal nature. She flipped it over to see her initials engraved on the back in fine filigree. *FEW*. Flora Eliza Watts. Folding it inside a handkerchief, she placed it back in the trunk and retrieved her gown.

Angeline sat back in her chair with a sigh. "I've never cared for parties or dancing."

"Do say you'll come listen to the music at least. It's better than sitting here alone with a cat."

"Is it?" Stowy leaped at one of the hammock ropes and began gnawing the twines. Angeline smiled. "I'm rather fond of him already."

Yet after much persuasion, Eliza finally convinced her friend to accompany her. Sarah soon returned, begging off from the party with an excuse of exhaustion and promising to watch Stowy while they were above.

So, within an hour and dressed in their finest, Eliza and Angeline emerged onto the deck just in time to see the sun splash ripples of saffron and maroon across the horizon. A jaunty wind held the sails full and stirred the seas into frolicking waves. Everyone was in high spirits as passengers and sailors alike assembled to enjoy the festivities.

Across the deck, the colonel, with one boot propped on the gunwale, was deep in a conversation with James. His gaze traveled her way more than once, and she thought she saw him smile. Which did nothing to becalm the flutter of her heart. She knew she'd have to answer his question sooner or later, but for the life of her, she still had no idea what to say. Perhaps she could avoid him until she did. After all, there were plenty of other men to dance with. Though once the sun had set and the music began, she found her traitorous gaze wandering repeatedly toward him, hoping he would finish his conversation and approach her.

Fiddle, flute, and harmonica joined in a mellifluous melody that swirled like steam into the black bowl circling the ship. Clusters of twinkling stars spanned the inky curtain as if God himself had flung handfuls of diamonds into the sky. The main deck cleared, and couples moved in a country dance. Their efforts to maintain their balance on the shifting wood while performing the steps brought a chuckle to Eliza's lips.

On the quarterdeck, Captain Barclay smoked a pipe and watched the proceedings. Beside him, Parson Bailey prattled on about the evils of dancing. When nobody paid him any mind, he dropped below. The Scotts joined the dancing couples, and Magnolia made her way to stand beside Eliza and Angeline. The smell of alcohol clung to her as tightly as her low-cut bodice.

"Good evening, ladies." She greeted them with a smile. "Seems we are the only single women of any station on board."

Eliza's face grew hot. The audacity of the woman to attempt a friendship with her when she had threatened to destroy her life— continued to threaten her!

Though there was a hearty evening breeze, Magnolia drew out

her fan, waving it flirtatiously over her face. "I find the colonel quite handsome, don't you?"

Eliza ignored the twinge spiraling through her gut.

"However, he *does* have that limp." She sighed. "And then there's James, the doctor or preacher or whatever he is. Oh mercy me, what does it matter? Those devilish bronze eyes could make any woman swoon."

Angeline smiled as her gaze reached across the deck to the good doctor. "I don't believe the doctor is all that he seems to be," she mumbled.

The ship rose, and Eliza clipped her arm through Angeline's. "Indeed, why would you say such a thing?"

"No reason." Her tone carried an intrigue that piqued Eliza's curiosity.

Yet when both ladies glanced at Magnolia, it wasn't the colonel or James her eyes were fixed on, but Hayden Gale, standing beside the aforementioned men, one boot on the bulwarks, one arm on the railing, returning her gaze.

"But you forget our roguish stowaway," Angeline added.

"He's a pig," Magnolia spat.

Eliza restrained a smile. "I believe the pig is heading this way."

Emerging from the crowd like a prince scattering his subjects, Hayden, dressed in a suit of brown broadcloth with silk-lined lapels—no doubt borrowed from one of the colonists—presented quite the dashing gentleman. Especially with his dark hair slicked back and tied in a queue and that devilish grin on his face. To Eliza's surprise, he halted before Magnolia.

"Would you care to dance, Miss Scott?"

Magnolia stared at him as if he'd asked her to walk the plank. "I would not, Mr. Gale." She raised her pert little nose. "Not if you were the last man on board."

Eliza cringed at the girl's rude behavior.

Yet Hayden only grinned as one brow rose over moss-green eyes. "Since it appears no one else will dance with you, it was only charity I had in mind."

"Of all the nerve!" Magnolia blurted. "I have no need to beg for a dance."

"And yet you turn away one freely offered."

"I do not dance with ruffians."

"And I do not dance with swaggering shrews. On board a ship, we can hardly afford to be finicky."

Angeline gasped. Eliza hid a smile.

Magnolia fumed and stomped her foot. "How dare you?" He caught her raised hand—the one aiming for his face—in midair. And after placing a kiss on it, he bowed to them all and left.

"Of all the. . ." Magnolia's chest rose and fell as her gaze followed Hayden across the deck, but thankfully she stewed in silence.

The couples began a quadrille. A sailor sheepishly asked Angeline to dance, his eyes firing with delight when she agreed. Magnolia turned down the next man and the man after that before she huffed away to join her parents.

The ship seemed to sway with the music as water purled against the hull in a soothing accompaniment. Light from lanterns hanging from masts spun dizzying circles over the deck as Eliza strained to see through the miasma of twirling skirts and bobbing crinolettes. Several sailors looked her way, but it was Mr. Graves who finally approached, dressed in his usual black and looking even more sinister in the shadows of night. To make matters worse, Dodd joined him, his eyes aglow with desire. They both asked her to dance at the same time.

To which Mr. Graves frowned and waved the man off. "I was here first."

"First or not," Dodd replied, "it should be the lady's choice."

Eliza closed her eyes and prayed for a solution.

"Mrs. Crawford, I believe you promised me this dance."

That voice—that baritone voice of assurance that caused her stomach to flip and her eyes to open. She placed her hand in his. "Indeed, Colonel. If you will excuse me, gentlemen."

❧

Blake led Eliza onto the makeshift dance floor, thrilled she had accepted his offer to dance. After her reaction to his question earlier, insecurity had swamped him. Perhaps he had misread her affections for him. Perhaps he had been too bold. Spoken too soon. Perhaps she bore no feelings for him outside of friendship.

"It seems you have saved me once again, Colonel." She smiled, and the lantern light danced in her golden eyes. "First from the hail of Yankee bullets in Charleston, then from the frigate's guns, and now from a fate far worse than both."

Blake chuckled. "It is nothing. I excelled at West Point's training to rescue fair maidens." He hobbled in step, hoping his awkwardness didn't offend her.

She smiled. "Obviously. And a valuable skill it is. Along with commanding troops, organizing expeditions, manning ship's guns, and assuming the role of first mate?" Her approving tone did much to sweep away his insecurities.

"I am at your service." He dipped his head playfully.

She smiled and looked away, her face darkening as if the comment made her sad.

From the moment she'd come on deck, he'd been watching her every move, anxious to end his conversation with James about the price of land in Brazil and the viability of growing corn and cotton, meanwhile hoping she refused any offers to dance. However, when Mr. Graves and Mr. Dodd approached her, Blake excused himself abruptly.

Not that he thought she'd accept their offers, but because both men tended to make the women on board uncomfortable. Mr. Graves because of his unsociable demeanor and the sinister way he stared at everyone from afar and Dodd for his mad gold-hunting dreams and prurient glances toward the ladies.

Placing her gloved hand atop his, he twirled her about the deck. Between the music and laughter and all the spinning and stepping, conversation became impossible. He longed to speak with her in private. He must know her feelings. Though at the moment, Blake was the happiest of all men simply to be near her—to be the one touching her, the one to whom she cast her smiles. They danced a cotillion, a country dance, and then a quadrille. And when the musicians took a break, she stood by his side chatting with the other passengers.

Finally, he could stand it no longer. Begging everyone's pardon, he led her to the larboard railing away from the crowd and fetched her a drink of whiskey-tainted water. Thank goodness, Eliza's smallpox ruse had sent the Union sailors scrambling for the safety of their frigate before they absconded with every ounce of spirits on board, or the *New Hope*'s passengers and crew wouldn't be able to drink the stale water at all. A night breeze wafted over them, cooling the perspiration on Blake's neck, as he strained to see Eliza's features in the shifting lantern light. Why did his chest feel as though an army marched across it?

Eliza scanned the crowd. "Look, Hayden and Angeline are dancing. I'm so glad. I all but dragged her above. I do hope she has a good time." Eliza prattled on as if she were nervous about something. Or worse, as if she were trying to avoid bringing up their earlier conversation.

She cast Blake a sly look. "I'm afraid Hayden received quite a tongue-lashing from Magnolia earlier."

"Yes, I believe the entire ship heard." Blake had actually felt sorry for the man. But he didn't want to talk about Hayden or Angeline or Magnolia. He shifted his stance and gazed over the ebony sea. What was wrong with him? He'd commanded hundreds of men without batting an eye, but he couldn't ask one woman to accept his courtship. Squaring his shoulders, he faced her and opened his mouth to speak when Eliza pointed upward.

A shooting star sped across the black expanse like a fiery rocket, drawing "oohs" and "ahhs" from the crowd. The brig jolted, and Blake took the opportunity to slip his arm around Eliza's waist. To keep her from stumbling, of course. The promise of rain tinged the air, and the musicians packed up their instruments. Some of the passengers and crew went below. Blake's throat went dry. He must ask her before she retired for the evening and it was too late. Before he had to live another moment in this agony. "Eliza." He took her hands in his. "You never answered the question I posed earlier today."

⚜

Eliza drew a nervous breath and glanced across the deck where only a dozen or so people remained. When had the music stopped? When had the couples gone below? She hadn't noticed—she hadn't noticed anything but the man before her.

He caressed her fingers, gently, expectantly. The wind rustled his coal-black hair. Lantern light speckled the stubble on his chin. His eyes found hers. She wished she could see them better in the darkness.

"You have me quite beguiled, Eliza. Tell me you feel something for me."

Eliza squeezed her eyes shut, trying to sort through the jumble in her mind, trying to make the right decision. For once. She had only been married to a Yankee for a year. And she had never been accepted in his circle. Born and raised in Georgia, she was a Southern girl through and through. Did Blake need to know about that one short year? Couldn't she just pretend it never happened? Oh how she longed to erase it from her memory. And her past!

Opening her eyes, she met Blake's gaze, tinged with disappointment, no doubt at her delay in answering him. She hated to see him pained. Longed for joy to fill those wondrous gray eyes. "You know that I do, Blake. How could I not? Any woman would be thrilled to receive your affections."

He blinked as if startled by her declaration. Then a wide grin split his lips, and he lifted her hand for a kiss. "I could never have hoped—" He swallowed. "Then you agree to a formal courtship?"

Against all sense, against everything within her screaming to tell him the truth, Eliza replied, "Yes."

The joy, the hope returned to his eyes. He caressed her jaw with his thumb, gazing at her as if she were a precious jewel. Never had Stanton looked at her that way. Ever. Tremors of heat swept through her, igniting every sense, bringing back to life places in her heart long since dead. His thumb eased to her lips. And finally he moved in for a kiss.

A scream etched across the ship. Eliza jerked to see Magnolia slap a sailor across the cheek. The sharp crack of her hand on his faced shifted all eyes toward the altercation.

Excusing himself, Blake rushed to Magnolia's side, as did several other gentlemen, including Hayden.

Eliza followed. The sailor backed away, rubbing his face. Anger pinched his weatherworn features as he pointed a finger at Magnolia. "She promised me."

"She promised you what?" Captain Barclay stomped into the crowd, scattering it like buzzards on a carcass.

"A kiss," the sailor said.

"I did. . .no such thing." Magnolia wobbled and held her hands out, though the seas were mild.

Hayden clutched the man's arm and jerked him aside. "How dare you assault a lady! He should be locked up below, Captain."

"Wait." Blake stepped forward. "Let's find out what happened first before we go passing sentence."

Magnolia's eyes drifted hazily over the forming crowd.

"She said if I gave her a drink"—the sailor pulled a flask from his pocket and shook it—"she'd give me a kiss. She's been bribin' all the sailors out of their spirits tonight."

"You, sir, are a scamp." Magnolia pointed a finger in his direction, but her hand teetered back and forth. Giggling, she covered up her mouth and started to fall.

Releasing the sailor, Hayden reached out for her, but Eliza got there first. Better to get the lady below to her parents before she made a total fool of herself.

Chuckles filtered through the remaining crowd. Some of the passengers left, shaking their heads.

"Come now, Magnolia." Eliza tugged her arm. "I'll help you below."

"I don't want to go below!" She stomped her foot and swayed in the other direction.

James hooked her arm with his to keep her from falling as he gave Eliza a look of understanding. "But you must, miss. There's a storm on the way." He glanced above as light sprinkles fell.

"Aye, see that she sleeps it off." The captain gave a hearty chuckle then faced the sailor. "Mr. Lenn, don't be makin' bargains for kisses again, or you'll answer to me." The sailor nodded as the captain barged back through the crowd, his pipe smoke filtering behind him.

Eliza and James tugged on Magnolia, but she stood her ground and began singing.

Blake heaved a sigh. "You may have to hoist her over your shoulder, James."

"You will do no such thing. Do you know who I am? I am Magnolia Scott, daughter of Benjamin Scott, owner of the largest plantation in Georgia!" Her eyes slithered over the crowd and landed on Eliza as if she'd just realized she held her arm.

"You." She tugged from her grasp and raised a finger to her lips, smiling. "I know who you are."

Eliza's eyes widened, and she shook her head in warning.

Magnolia's head bobbed atop her neck as if it sat on a spring. "Want to know a secret?" She laughed, first eyeing James beside her and then scanning the few people still on deck.

"No they do not. Now, come along." Eliza grabbed her arm again.

"Mrs. Crawford is not her real name." Magnolia gave a silly smile. "No no no."

Eliza swept her desperate gaze to James. "She's becoming delirious. It may be best to carry her below."

James nodded and bent to gather her up when Magnolia took a step back. "She's Flora Randal Watts"—she hiccuped—"wife of Brigadier General Stanton Watts of the Union army."

CHAPTER 13

Eliza's blood abandoned her heart. It sped away in a mad dash that left her cold and empty. She couldn't move. Could barely breathe as everyone's eyes snapped in her direction. Some of them registering shock. Others sparking with disdain.

Thunder cracked a fierce whip across the sky, and it began to sprinkle—drops tap, tap, tapping Eliza's doom on the wooden planks of the deck. Three lines as deep as trenches split Blake's forehead. "Is this true?"

Silence tiptoed around the raindrops as everyone held their breath, awaiting her answer. The ship heaved, and Magnolia stumbled. Hayden caught her before she toppled to the deck. She began to sing a ditty as if nothing were amiss and she hadn't just destroyed Eliza's life.

"I wish I was in the land of cotton,
Old times, they are not forgotten. . . ."

Wiping rain from her face, Eliza scanned the eyes locked on her like cannons on an enemy. The seas grew rough. Lantern light shifted over them in bands of silver and black—black like the bands on their arms, honoring lost loved ones. The blame for their deaths now cast at Eliza's feet. Then suddenly rain pounded the deck. It slid down Eliza's cheeks and pooled in her lashes until everything grew blurry. She wished they would all disappear. She wished she could melt into the deck. Anything but answer the question toiling on Blake's face.

Magnolia continued to belt out her tune,

"Look away! Look away! Look away! Dixie Land.
In Dixie Land where I was born,
Early on one frosty morning. . ."

Of all the songs to sing now!

Eliza shifted her gaze to the edge of the crowd, where Angeline gave her a sympathetic look. The only one. She swallowed. Better to get it over with. Better to tell the truth, come what may. Wiping rain from her eyes, Eliza squared her shoulders. "Yes, it is true."

"*Look away! Look away! Look away! Dixie Land,*" Magnolia continued, instantly silenced by Hayden's hand on her mouth.

Gasps sped through the crowd.

"Well, I'll be. . ."

"I don't believe it," one woman exclaimed.

"A bloody Yankee in our midst!"

Max spit a brownish glob onto the deck near her feet.

Eliza lowered her gaze, not wanting to see the fury, the hatred in their eyes. Not wanting to see it in Blake's.

Captain Barclay shoved through the crowd. "You best all get out of the rain. Looks to be a"—he froze when he saw their faces—"wet night." He uttered the last words slowly as his gaze shifted to Eliza.

Mr. Dodd rushed toward her, eyes blazing. Eliza cringed, fearing he intended to push her overboard. Instead, he pointed a finger so close to her face she could smell the chicken stew he'd had for dinner. "Yankee whore. I say we toss her overboard."

"I agree," one of the farmers shouted. "The Yanks murdered my brother, stole our land! She deserves to die."

"I lost everybody and everything in the war!" Max seethed.

Thunder boomed, confirming their assessment as "ayes" fired into the air.

"I don't want no Yankee going to Brazil with us. Dash it! I'm going there to get away from them!"

Swallowing down the hard lump in her throat, Eliza finally dared a glance at Blake. He hadn't moved. He still stared at her. Rain slid down his face and dripped from the tips of his hair onto his coat, melting away all the affection, the adoration of only moments ago. Replaced by a hatred so intense, she could feel it crackle in the air between them.

Magnolia slouched onto a barrel and lifted a hand to her head.

James and Hayden gaped at Eliza with disgust. A tear trickled down Angeline's cheek. Or was it rain? Graves grinned at her from beyond the crowd.

Lightning flashed silver across the sky, distorting the men's faces into demonic masks.

The blacksmith grabbed her arm and began dragging her to the railing. Others mobbed around her, pushing her from behind, nudging and shoving.

"No!" Angeline screamed. With elbows extended, the lady attempted to plow through the crowd, but they pushed her aside with ease.

Eliza's mind spun. Terror seized her breath. She had expected anger, hatred even, but not this. Not being tossed into the sea. She didn't even know how to swim. Not that it would matter in the middle of the ocean. Closing her eyes, she ceased struggling against the meaty grips, ceased listening to the hate-filled curses. Rain lashed across her back as if God Himself were punishing her. Perhaps He was.

"That's quite enough!" Blake's stern voice opened Eliza's eyes. He shoved his way to the front of the mob and spread out his arms as if he could contain their advancing fury. "We aren't murderers."

"No, but she is!" one man yelled as the seething crowd halted. Rain did an angry dance on the deck and over the shoulders and heads of the venom-dripping throng—pelting and striking and spitting. It stung Eliza's bare skin and soaked through her gown. She shivered. But not from the cold.

Captain Barclay took a spot beside Blake. "No one on my ship is tossing anyone overboard!"

Eliza tried to settle her thrashing heart. *What had taken the man so long?*

"Now what's this about you bein' a Yankee, Mrs. Crawford?"

Eliza tugged from the clawlike grips and rubbed her sore arms. Groans of disappointment ricocheted over her as the mob retreated, oscillating with the sway of the ship like a band of cannibalistic warriors dancing before a feast. Hugging herself, she drew a shredded breath. A mask of determination, of duty, had covered Blake's face, hiding all emotion. But she knew he hated her. The loss of his affection extinguished her last spark of hope.

She raised her chin and met the captain's gaze. "I am not Eliza Crawford. My name is Flora Watts."

More curses punctured the air, followed by renewed admonitions to toss her overboard, but all were quickly silenced by a single shout from Blake.

The ship pitched over a wave, and Eliza nearly slipped. Water soaked through her only decent pair of satin slippers. When the mob grew silent, she continued. "However, I am not a Yankee. I was born and raised in Marietta, Georgia. My father is Seth Randal, a prominent lawyer. Our family owns the Randal Inn."

Rain fell in buckets now. Most of the women ducked below. Yet the men remained, surrounding her like a lynch mob, water pouring off their hats in rivulets that pounded the deck like judges' gavels pronouncing her guilt. They waited, stone faced and determined, for her to put the final nail in her own coffin.

So she did.

"But it is true that I married Stanton Watts, Brigadier General Stanton Watts, from Harrisburg, Pennsylvania."

Thunder shook the sky, sending a tremble through the ship.

"See! She's a Yankee lover. A traitor to the Confederate states!"

One man spit on her, followed by another and another. Eliza squeezed her eyes shut. She supposed she deserved it. She had married a Union officer against her father's wishes, against her family's urgings. But Eliza always did what Eliza wanted to do. She always allowed her feelings to guide her—to toss and turn her like the waves were now doing to the ship.

"Where is your Yankee husband now?" one of the farmers demanded.

"He's dead." Eliza shouted over the roar of the rain and wind. "Died four years ago in the Battle of Fredericksburg."

"And she *did* volunteer as a nurse in the war." That was Blake's voice. He was sticking up for her. It brought her gaze to him, but he still refused to look her way.

"Yeah, but for what side?" Dodd shouted.

"For the South, of course." James gave her a nod.

The captain heaved a sigh, drew off his hat, and smacked it on his knee, splattering rainwater.

"I say we lock her up below," Max, the ship's boatswain, growled. "A prisoner of war."

"We are not at war." The hint of kindness in James's tone sent a ribbon of warmth through her—just a tiny ribbon. At least they all didn't hate her.

The rain worsened. More passengers scurried away, shaking their heads and muttering under their breath. Eliza wished they would all leave, for if she had to endure their hateful stares for another moment, her heart would surely crumble in her chest.

Angeline eased beside Eliza and wove her arm through hers. "It doesn't matter who she married. She's a good woman, a healer, and she's as much a Southern lady as I or any of the other ladies on board are."

James's brow rose at the lady's bold declaration. A declaration that seemed to stun the rest of them into silence. The deck teetered. Eliza's legs turned to mush, and she leaned on her friend for support. But it was the care in Angeline's eyes that renewed her strength.

Until Mr. Dodd sauntered to stand before her, his blond hair slicked back, rain dripping off his pointy nose and licking the gold chain hanging from his coat pocket. "We can't just let her go. She's the enemy!"

Angeline's grip on Eliza tightened. "She's no such thing!"

Blake stepped forward. "She will remain free until we reach Rio de Janeiro. Then we will send her back to Charleston with Captain Barclay." He glanced at the captain. "If that's agreeable to you, sir."

Captain Barclay nodded, slapping his hat back atop his head and holding up a hand against Dodd's further protests.

"Then it's settled." Blake gestured for the crowd to disperse. "Now go on, get below out of the rain."

Grunts of disappointment followed the remaining colonists as they slowly obeyed. Hayden helped a swaying Magnolia toward the stairs. Eliza knew she should feel hatred toward the woman, but at the moment she felt nothing at all.

Nothing but agony.

Without a single glance her way, Blake hobbled toward the hatch and dropped out of sight.

Only Angeline remained by Eliza's side.

Lightning flashed. The ship heaved, and the women clung to each other to keep from falling. But Eliza no longer cared. In fact, she wished she would fall over the railing into the churning sea. Tears spilled freely down her cheeks as Angeline swung an arm around her, holding her against the wind and the rain, saying nothing, until finally she led Eliza below.

The next morning, as dawn broke, a flicker of promise, of hope, teased Blake's groggy mind. Memories of dancing with Eliza, of her agreeing to a courtship paraded through his thoughts, scattering joy like confetti. Until reality came crashing down on him, treading those glittering scraps underfoot. She had betrayed him. Used him. Lied to him. Even worse, she had nearly caused him to betray everything and everyone dear to him. Especially his brother. Anger chased his sorrow back into the dark corners where it belonged. Where it would stay. He would not defile the memories of his family by spending a second mourning the loss of Eliza.

He would not.

After climbing out of his hammock and getting dressed, Blake dragged himself onto the main deck. If only to get away from James's constant badgering. Blake would have expected the doctor to share his fury about Eliza's deception, about her relation to a man who had issued orders that murdered so many young Southern men. Especially after the doctor had witnessed the result of those orders firsthand. But perhaps James was more preacher than doctor as he proclaimed, for his forgiveness had come swiftly on the heels of Eliza's confession.

A confession she would not have offered had her ruse not been uncovered by Miss Magnolia.

And Blake would still be pursuing a courtship with a woman who was his enemy.

Fisting his hands, he emerged to a shaft of bright sunlight that was quickly gobbled up by a dark cloud. One sweep of the horizon revealed seas as agitated as his stomach. Foamy sheets of dark water soared then sank as they raced across the wide expanse as if trying to escape some upcoming disaster. Black clouds roiled on the horizon, sparking with lightning, like witches' cauldrons. The ship plunged into a trough, and Blake hung on to the companionway railing.

Only a few passengers braved the weather. Some huddled beside the capstan while sailors hauled lines, scrubbed the deck, and attended their duties. Mr. Graves leaned against the foredeck railing, his black hair blowing behind him, face lifted to the breeze as if he rather enjoyed the menacing weather.

After the deck leveled, Blake started toward the quarterdeck to take his post. That's when he saw her, standing at the larboard bulwarks. Her loose curls tumbled in the wind down to her skirts. Lacy gloves covered her hands as they gripped the railing. Her eyes were closed, and her lips moved as if she prayed.

Prayed indeed. For forgiveness, he hoped.

Or did he? If there was a God, surely He wouldn't grant this traitor absolution so quickly. She must pay for her crimes—for her betrayal to him and to the South.

And for breaking his heart.

She *knew* what the Union had done to him. What he had lost. Yet still she had received his attentions, even encouraged them! What sort of person did that? A heartless, cruel one.

Brigadier General Stanton Watts! Yes, he knew the name. Had heard of his atrocities, his brazen orders that had cost so many lives on both sides. Her association with that madman made her as culpable as he in those acts.

He could never forgive her. Never. She was the enemy, and the sooner they got to Brazil, the sooner he could rid himself of her.

Eliza *felt* Blake behind her. The *thu-ump thu-ump* that marked his hobbled gait scored a groove across her heart. She held her breath. Was he coming to speak to her? Coming to say he'd behaved horribly last night, that he'd thought things over and her past didn't matter? But then the *thu-ump* passed, hastening in both pace and tempo until, out of the corner of her eye, she saw him climb the quarterdeck ladder.

Releasing her breath, she gripped the railing. The seas blurred in her vision. Gray, riotous seas this morning, not the usual smooth turquoise of the Caribbean. Above, clouds swarmed like a flock of predatory birds seeking victims, blocking out the sun that had ascended from its throne only a few hours earlier. After spending a fitful night crying and tossing—if one can toss in a hammock—she'd come above at dawn to pray, to think.

To cry alone.

She knew she took a great risk standing at the railing where some spiteful passenger or sailor could grab her legs and fling her into the sea, but somehow in her dizzying anguish she didn't care. Perhaps she deserved it.

Thoughts of Brazil, of its golden shores, lush jungles, and fertile soil, caused tears to flood her eyes once again. She would never live there, would never be a part of the new world these colonists were building, never have a chance at a new life, a new beginning.

Wiping the moisture from her face, she breathed in the salty air tainted with the sting of rain. No, she would be forced back to a land that writhed beneath the cruel boot of the North, a land where she didn't belong. To either side. Ostracized by her own family as well as her husband's, with no friends, she had nowhere to go. No way to survive.

Angeline slid beside her and placed her hand atop Eliza's, jarring her from her misery. Sarah appeared on her other side. "How are you this morning?" The compassion in Angeline's voice nearly caused a fresh outburst of tears.

"We know you didn't sleep well," Sarah said.

"I'm sorry if I disturbed you." Eliza gazed out at sea. "Be careful ladies, I'm not sure you wish to be seen with me."

"Don't be silly." Sarah gave an unladylike snort. "God has no preference for Rebel or Yankee. He loves everyone equally."

Eliza knew that. She remembered that from her years at church. Yet hearing it now, in a tone that was ripe with sincerity and love, helped settle its truth in her heart.

"Besides." Angeline batted a strand of hair from her eyes. "They had no right to be so cruel to you last night. It matters not that you were once married to a Yankee general. It's not like you were on the battlefield fighting our troops."

"You are both kind," Eliza said. "But I wouldn't want the other passengers to hate you on my account."

"God asks us to befriend the downtrodden, Eliza." Sarah's tone offered room for no other possibility.

Angeline pursed her lips. "I don't give a care what the others think." She grew pensive, almost sad, before she continued, "We all have our secrets, do we not?"

"Indeed." Sarah wove her arm through Eliza's, making her wonder what secrets these two wonderful women could possibly possess that were as bad as Eliza's.

A man cleared his throat behind them, swerving them around to see James. Drawing a deep breath, Eliza braced herself for the doctor's chastisement.

Yet only sympathy gleamed in his eyes.

Wind tossed his sun-glinted hair and rustled the collar of his shirt as he greeted the ladies with a smile that angled the scar alongside his mouth. He faced Eliza. "Mrs. Crawford. . .or Watts, is it?"

"Eliza will do, James."

"Eliza, I want to apologize for the barbaric behavior of the other passengers last night. A ferocious, shocking display."

Not shocking to Eliza. She had become more accustomed to such brutality over the past three years than she cared to admit. Still, she didn't know quite how to react to the man's kindness.

He studied her. "Do I surprise you?"

"It's just that after all you saw on the battlefield, I wouldn't expect. . ."

"Ah, but God commands us to forgive."

Eliza's gaze found Parson Bailey sitting on the foredeck reading his Bible. When he'd come above earlier, he'd cast a loathing glance her way before choosing a spot on the other side of the ship. "It seems Parson Bailey does not share your view."

James chuckled. "The good parson and I do not agree on many things." With that, he tipped his hat and bade them good day. Angeline stared after him as he left. "Such an agreeable man."

"Indeed." Eliza said.

"Blue-coated harpy!" one of the passengers shouted from the starboard railing where a small group had clustered.

"Traitorous fink!" another added.

"Baudy turncoat!"

"Pay them no mind, Eliza." Angeline tugged her around to face the sea. A sea that now heaved and throbbed, flinging foam onto the bulwarks. The ship bolted, and Eliza gripped the railing. Seawater soaked through her gloves. The light of day retreated behind clouds as dark as coal.

"Oh dear." Sarah squeezed Eliza's hand. "I believe a storm is coming."

No sooner had she uttered the words, than the captain's voice bellowed across the ship. "Everyone, below deck, if you please!" Turning, Eliza watched as the captain spoke to Blake, who immediately barked a list of commands: "Hands by the topgallant halyards! Shorten sail! Reef topsails! Set storm mizzen!"

The crew scrambled to do his bidding while passengers hurried below. Looped arm in arm with Sarah and Angeline, Eliza made her way to the hatch, hearing the captain say just before she dropped below, "We are in for a wild ride with this one."

CHAPTER 14

Twenty-four hours later

Eliza's fingers burned. Her lungs filled with water. Yet she hung on to the railing of the brig with all her remaining strength. If these were the last minutes of her life, she wouldn't give up. She would fight to the bitter end. Lightning notched the black sky in silver. Thunder bellowed for her to release her grip. *No! I will not!* The brig flopped back and forth like a child's toy in a pond, plunging Eliza into the sea one minute and flinging her into the air the next. She wanted to cry. She wanted to scream. But the wind tore her voice from her mouth. What did it matter? She was about to die. If she didn't fall, her fellow passengers would toss her over anyway. At least that's what they threatened to do when Eliza was below decks with them only moments before. Those threats had forced her above into the belly of the beastly storm.

Maybe she *was* a Jonah after all.

Her fingers slipped. Pain radiated into her palms, her wrists. The brig heaved and canted like a bucking horse.

God, is this how I am to die? Perhaps it was. She'd run from God long enough.

Rain slapped her face, filled her nose. She couldn't breathe. Her fingers slipped again.

A strong hand grabbed her wrist. A face appeared over the railing. "Hang on! I've got you."

He gripped her other hand just as her fingers slid from the railing. The ship teetered, dunking her into the raging sea. Water enveloped her, sloshing and gurgling and pulling her down. But whoever held her did not let go. Then just as quickly as it had tipped to the side, the brig lifted

140

from the water, slinging her upward. The man hauled her on board. They landed like two sacks of sodden rice on the slippery deck, his body atop hers.

It was Blake. He lifted from her, water dripping from his anxious face before the deck lunged again. Grabbing her, he clung to the hatch combing. "Foolish woman!" was all she heard as the bow tilted so far up, she thought the ship would topple over backward.

Once the deck leveled, Blake took her arm, yanked her to her feet, and dragged her to the companionway. "Get below!" Rain streamed down his face. His hair hung in strands of ink.

"I can't go back down there!" she shouted. "They want to toss me overboard."

Grimacing, he untied the rope from around his waist and handed it to her. "Go to your cabin and tie yourself to something."

"But you—"

"Now!" He thrust the rope into her hand and turned to leave.

Clinging to the railing, Eliza made her way below, unsure whether to be happy or sad that she was still among the living.

⚓

Grabbing another lifeline, Blake tied himself to the capstan. On the quarterdeck, Captain Barclay gripped the wheel beside the helmsman, their expressions strung tight as they strained to control the ship. Tension constricted the captain's voice and lined his face, causing Blake's terror to rise. If the hardened seaman was so worried, they must be in real danger.

Strands of hair stung Blake's cheek. He jerked them back and dove into the wind, making his way to his post alongside Hayden, where Moses and a group of sailors battled lines attached to yards above. *Foolish, mad woman!* She'd almost gotten herself killed! He hadn't noticed her until a flash of violet skirts tumbling over the deck caught his eye. He'd darted toward her as fast as the heaving ship would allow, but he was too late. She had gone over.

And his heart had gone overboard with her.

He'd thought he'd lost her. And in that brief moment, his life lost all meaning. His anger fled him, and he'd dashed to the railing. When he'd seen her dangling there barely able to breathe, wave after wave slamming her, terror had taken over all reason. And he knew he'd do anything to save her.

But he didn't have time to ponder that now as a wall of water slammed into him, sweeping his feet out from beneath him and sending him careening over the deck. Gripping his rope, he shut his mouth against the torrent and hung on. The waters subsided. He struggled to rise. The captain brayed orders that were quickly stolen by the roar of the storm. Above him, sailors clung to yards and masts that swung back and forth like demonic pendulums. How much more could the brig take before it split in two? Sailors appeared from below, dragging trunks, crates, and barrels to the railing. Blake helped them hoist them over the side, knowing they were losing what was left of their food, their water, their tools, and other necessities for the new world, wondering how they would get by without them.

If they survived the storm.

Eliza didn't like being told what to do. She would have rather stayed above with a lifeline tied around her than be tossed back and forth like a bale of hay in a wagon—a wagon that felt like it was tumbling over a cliff. But after Blake had so graciously offered his own rope, leaving himself in temporary peril, what else could she do? So she tied herself to the table in her cabin and curled into a ball on the deck, praying for God to save them. Now two hours later, the roar of the storm lessened, the crash of waves against the hull subsided, and the thunder retreated.

Either she had died and this was her own personal hell—being on board a ship full of people who hated her—or they had survived and were still afloat.

Untying herself, she crept from the cabin to emerge onto a sodden deck with equally sodden crewmen slouching in various positions of exhaustion—looking much like the remaining sails: drenched, torn, and tattered. Soon passengers popped above. With white faces and open mouths, they gazed around at the bare-masted ship. Though only hours before, some of them had demanded they toss Eliza overboard, now they paid her no mind.

Captain Barclay remained on the quarterdeck. Water dripped from his blue coat, which was angling off one shoulder. His hair, stiff with salt, stuck out in every direction, making him look like a drenched porcupine. A very angry porcupine. He growled orders, sending some men to assess damage and others below to assist with the pumps.

Were they taking on water?

Water dripped from yards and spars, plopping on the waterlogged deck. Electricity crackled in the air as a brisk breeze chilled Eliza. She hugged herself. Angeline and Sarah sped toward her, and together they surveyed the storm retreating on the horizon. Like a monster tucking its tail between its legs, it rumbled away, baring angry teeth of lightning as it went.

Blake, his shirt plastered to his chest, molding every muscle and sinew, gave her a cursory glance before he assisted the sailors in cleaning up the shards of wood and torn lines that littered the deck.

His disregard stung her, destroyed the hope that had sprung when he'd risked himself to save her. But that was the kind of man he was. A noble man who would risk his own life. . .

Even for an enemy.

After all were present and accounted for, the parson, at James's urging, said a prayer of thanks for God's rescue and that no lives had been lost. As all heads bowed, the *drip-drop* of water from the rigging above was the only reminder of the terror they had endured. Eliza said her own prayer of thanks. She didn't know why God had saved her, but she had to admit she was glad to be alive.

The damage report of torn sails, a cracked mast, one split yard, and a hold full of water etched a deeper frown on Captain Barclay's face, but his subsequent decision to set sail for one of the nearby islands seemed to encourage everyone after their near watery grave. There they could restock their food and water supplies and allow the crew a few days to make the necessary repairs.

The next day the *New Hope* hobbled into the bay of an island so lush and beautiful, Eliza wondered if they hadn't found the paradise they were seeking. Emerald water caressed glistening ebony sand that led to a canvas of mossy forest in every possible shade of green. As they drifted closer to shore, the air filled with the melody of a myriad of birds chirping and singing their greeting.

The island of Dominica, the captain had announced, though how he could be sure of their location after the storm, Eliza had no idea. But he had his remaining charts and some instruments and the sky to guide him. Not to mention his vast experience on the sea.

After being confined to the tiny brig for three weeks, everyone declared the sight was more precious than gold. Well, everyone except for Mr. Dodd. And perhaps Mr. Graves, who seemed impervious to joy.

As Eliza made her way through the crowd to the railing for a better look, people scattered as if she had malaria. Spiteful glances and foul words shot her way, but she did her best to ignore them. Swallowing the emotion burning in her throat, she drew a deep breath of air filled with life and tropical flowers, while the captain issued orders for the crew to begin repairs.

"It should take no more than two days," he shouted to the passengers. "Two days to stretch your legs upon the shores and replenish our water supply."

This turned everyone around to face him, including Eliza. Her gaze immediately shifted to Blake standing beside the captain. No longer looking like a drowned rat from the storm or even a military man, he appeared more like a hardened sailor as he stood, boots spread apart, on the swaying deck, black hair in wild disarray, arms crossed over his chest, and necktie flapping in the wind. His eyes grazed over her for a second. A mere second in which she no longer saw hatred. Dare she hope?

"We need everyone's help," the captain continued, "to search for edible fruits, coconuts, and freshwater."

"I know this island well." Parson Bailey's voice rose in excitement. "I was sent here as a missionary several years ago." His beady eyes shifted over the crowd as if seeking approval. "I can find water and food. Just send me ashore with some men and barrels. I know where to look. There's also a settlement across the island. Roseau, I believe. We can buy supplies there."

"We must save our money to purchase land and tools in Brazil," Blake said, his tone begging no argument.

The parson shrugged.

James nodded his agreement. "We'll have to live off what we have left in the hold and whatever we can scavenge from the island for the remainder of the journey."

Mr. Jenkins, one of the farmers, placed an arm around his wife and their young daughter and held them close. "But you tossed over my crate of farming implements."

"And my trunk of pots and pans," a rather robust lady declared.

"And my chest of gowns!" Magnolia sobbed from the edge of the crowd where she stood between her parents. Gazes shot her way, whispers hissing through the air. Ever since she'd made a besotted spectacle of herself, her parents had kept her close.

"What am I to do without them?" she continued to wail.

"Zooks, how will you survive with only *five* gowns?" Hayden chuckled, drawing her viper stare.

"I only have two left, if you must know." She gave him a petulant look.

"You won't have much need for them in Brazil." Angeline wove through the crowd to stand beside Eliza.

Hayden's and James's gazes followed her as did most of the men's, including Mr. Dodd's.

The captain cleared his throat. "My apologies for bein' forced to lighten the load, but it couldn't be helped."

"No apologies necessary, Captain." Blake gave the man an approving nod. "We owe you our lives."

One of the men jerked a thumb at Eliza. "I say we leave the Yankee on the island."

Words of agreement rang from both passengers and crew. All except Angeline, James, and thankfully, Blake.

"Aye," Max, the boatswain, added. "She can catch the next ship back to the States."

"The parson said there's a settlement on the other side of the island," a woman offered.

The blacksmith stepped forward. "We can return her money, and she can purchase passage home."

Their words twisted a cord around Eliza's stomach until she worried the breakfast she'd consumed earlier would reappear.

More agreements zipped through the air. Angeline squeezed Eliza's hand and tried to shout above the clamor, but it was James's voice that stopped them. "We cannot leave a woman alone in the midst of untold dangers."

"It's more than she deserves." Dodd gave her a malignant grin.

Moses, his sister, and her children clung to each other on the other side of the ship, their wide eyes blaring a concern for Eliza that their lips dared not voice.

Her gaze shot to Blake. She wondered if he would say anything. But he simply stood there, eyeing the mob and rubbing his chin. Finally, he spoke. "She stays with us. No matter what she's done, we cannot abandon her to die."

Eliza released a breath.

"Why not?" a sailor spoke up. "We should let God decide, shouldn't we, Parson?"

Parson Bailey gripped his Bible and forced piety onto his face. " 'Vengeance is mine. . .sayeth the Lord.' "

"I say she's bad luck!" one of the farmers shouted. "Ever since she came on board, we been attacked by a frigate, the first mate got injured, and now we been hit by a storm."

Mr. Lewis teetered through the mob, swirling the scent of alcohol in his wake. "Ah, let her stay. She's a good woman. We all need a fresh start." Clipping his thumbs in his suspenders, his kind eyes met hers. She smiled in return, wondering if the drunken carpenter would be the only man to speak up for her.

"Leave her here!" the blacksmith yelled.

"But she's our nurse!" Sarah spoke from the hatchway, where she emerged onto the deck. "We need her." Her eyes locked with Eliza's.

"James can handle things. He's a doctor."

Eliza's harried gaze sped to Blake. As leader of the expedition, wasn't the decision his? Surely, he would demand that she stay and order the mob to silence. Instead, he faced the captain and uttered the words that sealed her fate. "This is your ship and your decision."

Her heart plummeted.

Captain Barclay scratched his salt-encrusted hair. "In truth, I ain't so sure that she didn't bring all this bad luck on us. Besides, her presence here only causes trouble. And I don't need no more trouble, if you know what I mean."

Blake studied the captain, a stunned look on his face as if that was the last thing he expected the man to say. "How can a woman traipse through the jungle alone to Roseau without getting mauled by some animal, attacked by natives, or dying from exposure?"

"I'll send a sailor with her. Max"—Captain Barclay pointed to the boatswain—"you can get Mrs. Crawford to Roseau in a day and get back before we sail, can't you?"

"Aye. Gladly." He grinned as his eyes absorbed her.

"No. You can't do this." Angeline's tone bordered on hysterical.

"I agree." Sarah gazed up at the captain. "It's inhuman."

"I protest too," James added. "Even if she makes it, even if she manages to barter voyage on a ship, she'll still be in danger sailing unescorted."

Blake shook his head and clenched the railing until his knuckles whitened.

"You gave me the decision, Colonel," the captain said, "and this is what I say. For the good of the voyage and all aboard."

Blake's eyes met hers. "Then allow me to escort her."

The captain waved a hand. "I need you here to organize your people to search for food. Max will do."

"But Captain"—Blake's suspicious gaze took in Max—"you might as well sentence her to death."

Captain Barclay's jaw stiffened as he surveyed the mob and then glanced at Eliza. "Very well. Let's put it to a vote then. Those in favor of leaving Mrs. Crawford, or whatever her name is, on Dominica with provisions and money, say, 'Aye.'"

Ayes blared across the ship like trumpets.

CHAPTER 15

Eliza dug her toes into the black sand, allowing the grains to cover her feet, enclosing them in a warm cocoon. She wished she could do the same with her entire body—bury herself right there on the beach, hide away from everyone on board the *New Hope*, everyone who hated her. Everyone who would rather see her dead than spend another minute with her.

New Hope, indeed.

New hope for everyone but her.

Gentle waves the color of glistening turquoise stroked the shore as a myriad of brightly plumed birds warbled happy melodies from waving palm and plumeria trees. A balmy breeze soothed her face and frolicked among her curls. All traitors to the angst roiling within her. As soon as Max finished his duties, he would escort her through the jungle to the city of Roseau, where she would supposedly barter passage aboard a merchant ship heading to the United States.

Alone.

Alone, ostracized, forsaken. Once again.

Tugging the chain around her neck, she pulled out the locket her father had given her on her sixteenth birthday and opened it. Her mother's face stared back at her, so graceful, so beautiful. Eliza ran a finger over the lock of hair. "Oh Mama, I miss you so. I need you. If only you hadn't died, maybe Papa would have been more reasonable. Maybe he wouldn't have suffocated me with his rules. You always had a way of soothing his dour moods." Yet the more she stared at the tiny portrait, the more it reflected her own image. Not only did Eliza look like her mother, but she'd been told they were alike in many other ways. No wonder her father sought so desperately to protect her. He couldn't

148

bear to lose her mother all over again. But in the end, Eliza had caused his worst nightmare to come true.

A wayward tear coursed down her cheek, cooled by the wind. She wiped it away. She would not give these people the satisfaction of seeing her sorrow. Her devastation. Not that anyone paid her any mind.

Laughter drew her gaze down shore where several passengers gathered coconuts while the children played tag with the crashing waves. Dark sand—formed by a volcano, one of the sailors had told her—spread a blanket of shimmering onyx across the beach. Dodd sat on a fallen tree, speaking to one of the farmer's wives. Mr. and Mrs. Scott, Magnolia between them, sat beneath the shade of a mango tree while Mable waved a palm frond above their heads. After their sorrowful parting, Angeline had joined a group scouring the jungle for bananas and other fruit. Sarah wasn't feeling well and had stayed on board. And true to his word, Parson Bailey and six sailors had headed off into the jungle, barrels hoisted on their shoulders, in search of freshwater.

Blake, James, Hayden, and some of the other men had grabbed axes and swords and disappeared into the tangle of green looking for wild boar the parson said inhabited the island.

"Blake," she whispered. Despite her aching heart, just saying his name made her smile. He had stood up for her. And James had as well. She was grateful for that, even though now they seemed to have all but forgotten her.

But how could she blame them?

"Oh Lord, I've made a mess of things again." Snapping her locket shut, she let it dangle down the front of her bodice then picked up a shell and tossed it in the water. "I should have asked whether it was Your will that I join this venture. Instead, I just forged ahead, giving no thought to the consequences." As usual.

"Praying, Mrs. Crawford?"

Eliza jumped at the voice and turned to see Moses, Delia, and her two children approaching. The young man—about twenty years of age—towered over his sister by at least a foot, but the woman made up for the discrepancy in the width of her hips. Hips that had born the precious boy and girl now grinning at Eliza as if she were a princess. Joe and Mariah, if she remembered correctly. She looked into Moses' kind eyes. "Yes, it seems the only recourse left to me."

"An' a good recourse it be, missus. God loves t' answer His children's prayers."

"Let's hope so, Moses."

"Hope you don't mind de interruption." Moses tore off his hat. "But Delia an' I want to say good-bye proper an' thank you for your kindness to us on board de ship."

Delia smiled. "You ne'er had a bad word to say 'bout us, missus, an' you heped my Joey when he got sick."

Eliza struggled to rise against her confounded crinolette, but finally stood and shielded her eyes from the sun. "There's been far too much damage, far too much heartache inflicted on your people. It is enough. You are free and should be treated as equals."

" 'Fraid dat's gonna take some time to come about, missus." Moses fumbled with his floppy hat.

Eliza sighed. "I fear you are right."

Giggles from the other children drew the longing gazes of both Mariah and Joseph. Moses frowned and released a sigh. "Seems to me, you be getting a taste of how we feel."

Eliza glanced at the people gathering food downshore and then over at the ship where the cadence of hammer and saw filled the air. Mr. Graves, in his usual black attire, stood at the railing. Even from a distance, she could feel his dark gaze boring into her.

Outcast. Ignored. Belittled. Yes, she did have an inkling of how it felt to be a Negro. All except for the shackles, of course. "I'm so sorry," was all she could think to say.

Moses nodded and slapped his hat atop his head. "Godspeed to you, missus."

"We wish you well," Delia added, lowering her gaze.

"And you." Eliza knelt before young Joe. "Now, you take care of your mama, young man, and your sister here."

The little boy smiled.

After they left, Eliza scanned the beach for any sign of Max, but he was nowhere in sight. She glanced at the sun nearing its zenith. Surely he hadn't forgotten her. Not by the way his lecherous grin had raked over her when the captain had assigned him the task of taking her across the island. Despite the heat of the day, Eliza shivered at the memory. Perhaps God was giving her a chance to escape the clutches of the unsavory sailor. Oh fiddle! Why had she not thought of that? She should leave now, head out without him. Surely it would be better to die alone in the jungle than take her chances with a man she hardly knew. Swinging about, she slipped on her shoes, plopped her bonnet atop her head, and gathered her valise.

She cast one last glance at the passengers on the beach, the children playing in the surf. No sign of Blake. She had hoped he would come to say good-bye—that despite the captain's orders, he would insist on taking her to Roseau himself. But she'd clung to silly dreams her entire life. Perhaps it was time to forsake them and grow up. Turning, she raised her chin and plunged into the web of green.

⌘

Blake hacked a trail through the thick greenery, thankful the Yankees hadn't taken his service sword. He and this sword had fought many a battle together, and it had saved his life more than once. He couldn't imagine wrestling against a foe, or these tangled vines, without it.

Ahead of him Hayden trounced through the forest, hefting a machete. The other men had separated in order to cover more space. All except James whose heavy breaths sounded from behind Blake. Entering the jungle from the breezy beach had been akin to flinging oneself into a fiery furnace. The deeper they went, the hotter that furnace became. Moisture dripped from leaves and branches and puddled around shallow, snaking roots. The air, quiet and dank, barely stirred by their passing. Yet the jungle was anything but silent. Life teemed in buzzing and chirping and croaking all around them. It saturated the air with the smell of damp earth and sweet flowers. But Blake didn't care. He was thirsty, hot, and his leg burned. None of which was the reason for his foul mood.

Raising his sword, he sliced through a thick vine, releasing the anger that burned a hole in his heart. Sending a lady alone on a sea voyage. It was unheard of. It was cruel! With no one to stand up for her and protect her, anything could happen. He'd heard how most sailors talked. He knew how lonely they were after months at sea. The presence of a beautiful woman on board could cause them to do things they'd never consider otherwise.

James came alongside him. Stripped to the waist, sweat glistened on his chest and dampened his hair. His gaze scoured the ground, looking for pig droppings. Whatever *they* looked like. Yet, James seemed to know. He'd borrowed a pistol from one of the passengers, ready to shoot a boar as soon as they spotted one. Blake doubted they would. They'd been searching for two hours and had seen nothing but monkeys and parrots and iguanas. In front of them, Hayden halted, drank from a canteen, then passed it their way.

Blake took a swig. "There must be something we can do." He wiped his mouth on his sleeve.

"Eliza?" James dragged a handkerchief across his neck and tipped the canteen to his mouth.

Blake nodded as squawking drew his gaze upward. A green parrot, with a red band around his neck, paced back and forth across a branch as if trying to tell them something.

Taking back the jug from James, Hayden grunted.

"I understand people's anger, I do." Blake planted the tip of his sword in the dirt. "Blast it, I'm angry at her too. My entire family was killed by Yankees. We've all lost someone. But this. It's wrong."

"She'll be all right." Hayden stared at him with eyes the same color as their surroundings, eyes that harbored no sympathy. "She's bad luck. The sooner she's gone the better."

"Bosh! It's murder, pure and simple." Blake ground his teeth together. "We can't know that she will arrive safely in Charleston. What difference does it make if she spends another month with us and then returns safely with Captain Barclay?" By the way Max looked at Eliza, Blake couldn't be sure she'd even arrive in Roseau unscathed. Though the captain had reassured him of such.

"She's not bad to look at, I'll give her that." Hayden corked the canteen and swung it around his shoulder. "But she is a Yankee by marriage, and has no business coming on this journey."

"She shouldn't have deceived us." James gazed up at the parrot that was still squawking above them. "But in truth, her sympathies don't lie with the North."

"Once a Yankee, always a Yankee." Hayden hefted his machete and stomped away.

Blake shook his head. He should let her go. Eliza had brought this on herself. But something inside him refused to loosen the knot she had on his heart. A knot that had formed during moments they had shared these past weeks, the things he'd told her that he'd told no one else, the care he'd seen in her eyes. Was it all a ruse? Had she used him for comfort, for companionship, all the while knowing she was his mortal enemy? Anger simmered in his belly at her deception. Still, Yankee or not, she didn't deserve this.

"All we need do is convince everyone else that her nursing skills are indispensable," James said, mischief twinkling in the corner of his eyes. "If their own safety is at risk, they'll allow her to stay—I guarantee it."

Blake couldn't help but smile at his friend. "But how do we orchestrate a medical emergency? Aside from shooting one of the passengers, that is." He chuckled and shifted his weight off his bad leg. "Not that there aren't a few I wouldn't mind shooting."

"I am in agreement with you there." James snorted. "Whatever we decide, we must hurry before she travels too far away."

Blake grinned at the devious look on the doctor's face. His scheming was unexpected, to be sure. But welcomed with exuberance. "An injury of some sort." Swinging about, he darted back down the path. "Not life-threatening, of course. But one requiring her attention."

"Something quite bloody, which would preclude me from assisting." James hastened behind him.

Blake lifted his sword. A ray of sunlight broke through the canopy and glinted on the metal. "I know just the thing."

CHAPTER 16

Misery. A fitting word to describe Eliza's present predicament. Perspiration coated her from head to toe and glued her underthings so tightly to her skin that she doubted she'd ever pry them asunder. Sharp branches clawed at the lace on her sleeves and tore her gown. A monkey had absconded with her hat. Mosquitoes and God-knew-what-other flying pests dove at her from all directions. Twigs and leaves twisted her hair into knots. Her throat gasped for water; her legs ached, and she was lost and alone in the jungle.

And she'd only been walking for a few minutes!

The idea of making it to Roseau on her own, the idea that had fired her determination to cross the tiny island without aid from man nor beast—or even permission from God—crumbled into nonsensical pieces in her mind. What had she been thinking? She hadn't even brought along food or water.

Halting, Eliza drew a handkerchief from her sleeve and dabbed it on her forehead. She gazed up at the greenery crisscrossing the sky where dozens of colorful birds flitted about and laughed at her foolishness. Oh fiddle! Let them laugh. No doubt once the passengers of the *New Hope* discovered she'd ventured out on her own, they'd all be laughing at her.

Holding her valise before her like a shield, she forged ahead. Unable to take her trunk, she'd been forced to select only a few of her things: a clean chemise, petticoats, an extra pair of stockings, one other gown, two books, her journal, and the pocket watch Stanton had given her. The rest she'd given to Sarah and Angeline.

A faint sound met her ears. Not the sound of a bird or insect, but the shout of a human.

"Help! Help!" Muffled but desperate, the voice spun her about.

Nothing but flora met her gaze. Still the sound continued. Wait. She recognized that voice. James. He sounded frantic. And that was enough to send her barreling back the way she had come. As she did, the voice grew louder, more defined, until within minutes, the shore appeared in shifting glimpses through the foliage. She halted and brushed aside a fern for a better view.

Several yards down shore, Hayden and James emerged from the jungle, carrying Blake between them. Blood coated one of his legs. Or at least she thought it was blood. Passengers darted toward the men. Eliza spotted Max among them. If she showed herself, no doubt the beastly sailor would drag her back into the jungle to begin their journey, and her situation would disintegrate even further. Yet. . .

The doctor broke from the crowd and leaned forward on his knees. He shook his head and turned away, clearly unable to bear the sight of so much blood. Several people tried to tug him toward the patient, but he resisted them and backed farther away. If he couldn't treat Blake's wound, Blake may be in danger of bleeding to death or infection.

Alarm charged Eliza's legs into action. Hoisting her skirts with one hand and her valise in the other, she swatted aside the leaves and dashed toward them. The crowd parted, surprise at her presence registering on their faces. But Eliza didn't care. Trying to settle her thumping heart, she searched Blake's prostrate form. The trousers on his left leg were ripped to the knee. A handkerchief, soaked in blood, covered the wound.

"What happened?" She dropped to the sand beside him and gazed at Hayden.

"Apparently, a sword accident." Hayden's tone carried an odd cynicism.

"It's nothing." Blake groaned. "Help me up."

"We will do no such thing," Eliza snapped. Her gaze traveled to the blood dripping on the sand beneath his leg. A shiver coiled around her. She peered beneath the cloth. "I must stop the bleeding. You're going to need stitches."

"Oh my." One woman sounded as though she would faint. Another drew her away from the crowd. Still the men huddled closer, staring at Blake as if he were performing a circus act. James pushed his way past them. Beads of sweat lined his face. His eyes locked on Eliza, avoiding the bloody leg. She knew from the terror flashing within them that he would be of no help.

155

Drawing a deep breath, Eliza scanned the mob. "Give me your neckerchiefs, ties, anything you have to press on the wound." The men stared at her numbly at first but finally began tossing her sashes, handkerchiefs, and neckties. She pressed them onto Blake's leg. He moaned.

"We need to get him to the ship."

"The doc can take care of him." One man jerked his head toward James.

"I quite agree. Let the doctor perform his duties," Mr. Scott added. "You should be well on your way, Mrs. Crawford."

James's gaze skittered over the crowd, at the sky, the trees, the shore, anywhere but on the blood oozing from Blake's leg. "I fear I cannot, gentlemen." He gripped his belly, dashed for the trees, and emptied the contents of his stomach.

Dodd studied him, his brow wrinkling. "Well, I'll be. I heard you were afraid of blood. I just didn't believe it!" He burst out laughing and slapped his hat on his thigh.

James ran a sleeve over his mouth and faced the crowd. "I told you I'm not a doctor anymore. Mrs. Crawford is all you have."

"If I don't treat him properly, he could die," Eliza said.

The ship's helmsman shoved through the throng, assessed the situation, then gestured toward the small boat. "Aye, we'll allow the lady to tend to him."

⚓

Leg propped on a stool, Blake leaned back in the chair and watched Eliza tend his wound. He was pleased his ploy had gotten her back on the ship, not so pleased at the pain that coursed through his leg. Blast it, he hadn't meant to slice so deep. He'd only meant to nick a bleeder so it would look far worse than it was. After all, he was accustomed to injuries such as this on the battlefield. What was one more if it saved Eliza's life? Still, with the depth of the cut, he'd put himself in danger. Now, being so close to her made him wonder if it was worth it, for her presence only caused him more pain. Not the physical kind, but the kind that came from longing for her so desperately while hating her so intensely.

James stood on the other side of the sick bay, guiding Eliza with words, eyes on anything but the bloody mess.

Tenderly, she removed all the sashes and kerchiefs, now stained beyond use, and stared at the gash Blake had painstakingly made across his skin. The bloody gush had reduced to a dribble. She dabbed it with a clean cloth.

"Ouch."

"Don't be such a baby." She smiled. "I'm sure you've endured far worse than this in battle." She tossed the cloths into a basin and began peering and poking at the wound.

Wincing, but duly chastised, Blake kept his outbursts to himself. Of course he had suffered worse injuries. That was expected in battle. But not expected from one's own hand. Somehow, it made the pain far worse.

Eliza wiped her hands on her apron and addressed James, who had taken to picking at a splinter in the bulkhead. "Stitches and a nettle poultice, Doctor? Is that what you would recommend?"

"Precisely. Though a rinse of spirits would aid greatly as well." He continued plucking the wood while Eliza opened the cupboard and then slammed it with a frown. "I seem to be fresh out of alcohol at the moment."

"Not to worry," James said. "The nettle will do. Well"—he rubbed his hands together—"I can see that I am not needed here. I believe I'll get some fresh air." And before Blake could protest, the doctor fled the room.

Leaving him alone with the traitor.

Eliza's gaze sped over Blake. Long enough for him to see the anguish in her eyes. The light that had sparkled so brilliantly in them the past three weeks had been doused by the hatred and anger from the crew. From him.

"This will only take a minute." She opened the glass case filled with medicines. "I know how difficult it must be for you to be in the same room with me." Her voice carried no bitterness, only despair.

Blake bit back the measure of sympathy that kept trying to rise. He had only done this to save her life, nothing more. Any honorable man would have done the same. Then why couldn't he keep his eyes off her? With her back to him, she drew instruments and vials from the cabinet and arranged them on a tray. Her hair fell in spirals the color of maple syrup, dripping over her tiny waist. Even though it was embedded with twigs, Blake longed to run his fingers through the silky threads. Small tears littered her gown, and an abrasion marred her left arm, reminding him of what he'd heard while the sailors rowed him to the brig. Max accused her of leaving without him, of forging into the jungle alone, to which Eliza had responded that she'd rather be eaten by a panther than travel with him. Even in his pain, Blake had smiled. He swallowed. What was he thinking? He must not allow any sentiments to rise for this woman who had betrayed her countrymen—who had betrayed him.

If his scheme worked and the passengers and captain allowed her to stay, he would tolerate her presence on board, but other than this single necessary moment, he would avoid her at all costs. He had done the honorable thing. Saved her from probable death.

That was where his duty ended.

Swerving around, she knelt before him and placed a tray on the cot. "This will hurt a bit, Colonel. Would you care to bite down on a piece of wood?"

"I'll manage, thank you."

She drew a deep breath and threaded the needle. "How did this happen? Seems an odd thing to occur while looking for pigs."

"Boar." Her scent filled his nose, tantalizing his senses. Blake cleared his throat. "I was hacking through the jungle when my blade slipped."

"Hmm." She slid the needle through his flesh.

It felt like she'd set his skin on fire. Blake closed his eyes, listening to the slap of water on the hull, the hammering and shouts from above, the screech of pelicans. Anything to distract him from the searing pain.

She must have noticed his discomfort, for she uttered a "sorry" that sounded genuine.

Yet the pain was nothing compared to the suffering she had already caused him. "Pains of the flesh I can handle," he muttered.

She met his gaze and swallowed before continuing her work. "I never meant to deceive you."

Blake had never seen such lustrous eyes. "You didn't even tell me your real name. How can that be unintentional?"

She slipped the needle through and tugged on the thread. Her lower lip trembled. "You are right. I should have been truthful." She continued stitching his wound, but Blake could no longer feel the pain for the agony in his heart. He'd hardened himself to it.

"But then you wouldn't have let me join your venture, would you?" she asked.

Lantern light crowned her head and glistened on her moist lips—lips he had almost kissed. He licked his own. "No."

"I had to get away." She clipped the thread and tied it. Then dipping her fingers into a poultice, she spread it over the stitches.

"We all needed to get away." Blake couldn't tear his eyes from the way her delicate fingers caressed his skin. "From Yankees." He sighed. "You betrayed everyone on board." Good, now the anger returned.

She cut a swath of bandage and wrapped it around his leg. "I was born and raised a Southerner just like everyone else on this ship." She looked up at him. Her breath filled the air between them, her eyes just inches from his face.

Blake looked away from the pain he saw in her gaze. He offered a caustic snort. "At least some of your story was true."

"It was all true." Her eyes narrowed. "Everything I told you about my past. I simply changed the names and omitted one year of my life."

"A year in which you betrayed your country."

She jerked the bandage tight. Blake hid the pain from his face. With a huff, she gathered her tray and stood, turning her back to him. "Doesn't my service as a war nurse count for anything?"

"Ah, so you hoped to make restitution."

She spun around, her skirts knocking a tin cup to the deck with a clank. "No, that's not why I served in the war."

"Why didn't you just stay with your husband's family? I hear the Yanks love Southern traitors."

"They tossed me out, if you must know." She stooped to pick up the cup, her skirts billowing around her. "Although I wouldn't have stayed anyway. They hated me for my Southern ties as much as you hate me for my Northern."

Emotion clambered up Blake's throat at the agony in her voice. No. He would not allow any compassion to form for this traitor. His gaze dropped to the locket dangling against her bodice. She'd mentioned strained relations with her family in Georgia. Now he knew why. Still, why had they not taken her in after her husband died? "And your doting father? Was he the one who forced you into nursing? To recover the family name, perhaps?" He hated the sting of sarcasm in his voice.

"My father is Seth Randal III, adviser to Jefferson Davis," she announced, rising to her feet.

Aghast, Blake stared at her. An adviser to the president of the Confederate States. With a traitorous daughter!

"So, surely you see how a Yankee daughter would have ruined his career. He had no choice but to disown me the minute war was declared." She swallowed and looked away. "I had no home to come back to."

Blake tore his gaze from her, clenching his jaw against his rising sympathy, despite his best efforts to push it down.

She set the cup on the table. "I hope someday you'll find it in your heart to forgive me."

Forgive her? Blake fingered the five black bands circling his arm. How could he forgive any Yankee for what they'd done?

His thoughts drifted to Lieutenant Harkins, who had rushed to him from the battle of Antietam—blood splattered across his uniform, eyes wild from the insanities of war—to tell Blake of his brother's death. Wounded, Jeremy had lain on the battlefield after the hostilities had ended while Union soldiers scavenged for valuables among the dead. Rebel doctors also wove among the injured, attending to those who could be saved. But they hadn't made it to Jeremy in time before one particularly vile Union officer ran his injured brother through with his sword.

All for a gold pocket watch the lad refused to give him.

Blake knew that watch. Their father had given it to Jeremy when he enlisted. It had been their grandfather's, who'd fought in the War of 1812, and his father's before him, who'd fought in the Revolutionary War. A good luck piece, since neither had died in battle.

Oh Jeremy, why didn't you just give it to him?

The thud of a boat against the hull jarred Blake from his nightmare. Orders and commotion filtered down from above. Hayden poked his head inside the cabin. "Parson Bailey's gone missing."

Setting his injured leg on the deck, Blake rose, ignored the pain, and headed for the door. "I will never forgive you, Mrs. Crawford. Or any Yankee."

CHAPTER 17

Blake stormed out of the sick bay, leaving a trail of loathing in his wake that sent Eliza reeling backward. Fighting back tears, she picked up the basin of bloody rags and placed it on the table. She would prefer to stay below and clean up, away from the scorn and hatred of everyone above, but Hayden's statement that something had happened to Parson Bailey spurred her to wash her hands and follow Blake.

The arc of a golden sun dipped behind palms, flinging glistening jewels over the bay. A breeze cooled the perspiration on Eliza's brow and neck as she emerged from below. Passengers and crew mobbed the deck, encircling something in the center. Hayden and Blake shoved through them, and Eliza followed to find the sailors who had accompanied Parson Bailey in search of water. One of them leaned against the mast, holding a bloody rag to his head. Clutching her skirts, she started toward him, but his eyes, as sharp as black darts, halted her.

"What is she still doing here?" Mr. Scott straightened the jeweled pin on his embroidered waistcoat, his voice incredulous. "The colonel appears well enough to me."

"Aye, I thought she was long gone," a sailor said.

Blake limped to stand beside the captain. "She tended my wound. And now she'll tend Mr. Simmons." He leveled a pointed gaze at the man in question. "Unless he prefers his injury to putrefy and rot his brain."

The sailor's face blanched, and he beckoned Eliza forward with his eyes.

"What happened?" Blake asked.

Captain Barclay scratched his gray beard. "Seems our parson struck Simmons over the head and took off."

161

"Yep, that's what he did," another sailor added. He pointed to the man standing beside him. "George and I was"—he cleared his throat—"well, we was relievin' ourselves when we heard Simmons yell out. When we found him, he was on the ground moaning, and the parson was gone."

Eliza inched toward Mr. Simmons, making no sense of their story. Lifting the bloody cloth, she peered at the swollen knot atop his head. Nothing too serious, though she should clean it and apply a poultice as soon as possible.

"Is that true, Simmons?" the captain asked.

"Aye, Cap'n. I sat down on a tree trunk to rest a spell, and the next thing I know, I'm waking up to these two ugly mugs swirling in me vision." He gestured toward the other sailors with a chuckle. "And the parson is nowheres to be found."

"Perhaps he was taken by natives," Hayden offered.

"But why wouldn't they take all of us? And they didn't take our barrels or weapons. Don't make sense."

"No, it doesn't." Blake shifted his weight. Pain clouded his features, but at least no blood appeared on the bandage around his leg.

James huffed. "And we still have no water."

"We found a creek." The sailor's eyes lit up beneath a brow furrowed with sweat and sand. "We can get water tomorrow."

"Aye." Captain Barclay planted his hands at his waist and squinted at the setting sun. "At first light, we'll search for the parson and gather water." He glanced toward the men still hammering in the yards. "Repairs will be finished tomorrow, and we need to get sailin'. I've wasted enough time as it is. There's cargo in New Orleans waitin' for me to pick it up after I drop your colony off in Brazil."

"We can't just leave the parson here." Angeline spoke from her spot across the deck, drawing curious gazes her way.

"Yes we can, miss." Captain Barclay's tone bore neither rancor nor sympathy. "Especially if he struck my man here."

"We don't know that for sure." Sunlight glinted gold in Dodd's wavy hair—most likely the only gold he'd ever find. "He could have been kidnapped. Why, when I was a sheriff in Richmond, I dealt with many a kidnapping. There was one in par—"

"We didn't hear no struggle or no screamin'." The sailor crossed his beefy arms over his chest.

"An' we saw no one else there," the first sailor said.

"What about *her?*" Graves stroked his black goatee and gestured toward Eliza.

Her breath caught in her throat as all eyes speared her with a scorn so real, she felt its punctures in her chest.

"I need to bandage this man's wound," she squeaked out, frustrated that terror revealed itself in her voice.

Blake stepped forward. "We need her. She's the only person on board who can tend to our sick and injured." He pointed to his wounded leg. "Are you willing to risk your lives for your blasted pride?" Though Eliza knew the only reason he stood up for her was for the benefit of his precious venture, his words warmed her.

"And we'll need her when Sarah's baby arrives," Blake added.

"That's not for another two months," Dodd said. "We'll be in Brazil by then and can find someone there."

"Besides, we have the good doctor." Mr. Scott declared. "He'll get over his fear of blood soon enough."

But James shook his head. "I doubt it. I've been like this for over two years."

"What good is a doctor who's afraid of blood?" one of the soldiers spat with disdain.

"But you can tell one o' us what to do, Doc," one of the farmers added.

The statement fired a plethora of comments into the air like grapeshot, most of which hit their mark in Eliza's heart, and one that sank deep. "Her husband probably killed some of our kin!"

"Aye, she's bad luck to be sure," one sailor shouted. "And now, the parson's gone missing."

"Don't be silly." Angeline moved to stand beside Eliza. "There's no such thing as bad luck."

"But there's such a thing as God's curse, ain't there, Doc?" Max asked. "Aren't you a preacher too?"

James rubbed the back of his neck. "There are curses in the Bible. But not for—"

"There you have it!" Mr. Scott huffed. "The woman is cursed."

"It doesn't matter," Blake shouted. "We would be cursed far worse if we lost her."

Captain Barclay finally raised his hands in a gesture that silenced the mob. "I, for one, have had my fill of bad luck." He faced Blake. "Beggin' your pardon, Colonel, but it's still my decision, and I say the Yankee goes. Max will escort her halfway to Roseau first thing in the morning. She can find her way from there." With eyes like a hawk, he scanned the crowd, daring any to disagree. "I've been at sea long enough to know there *is* such a thing as bad luck. We'll put her ashore, get water, and search for the parson, but we will set sail tomorrow afternoon, and that's my final say on it."

Not wanting anyone to see her fear, Eliza had been successful at keeping her tears at bay, but now, hours later in her cabin, she could not stop them from trickling down her cheeks. Nor could she stop from trembling like a palm frond in the wind. She'd accepted her fate that morning, but to have her hopes revived only to be dashed again had wreaked havoc on her emotions. Darkness slithered outside the porthole of her cabin, teasing her with its temporary reign as every minute ticked by until the sun would rise and she'd be put ashore.

"What shall I do, Stowy?" She kissed the top of the feline's head and snuggled against his furry cheek, but the only answer she received was the contented rumble of a purr.

Unable to eat, she'd refused dinner and instead had paced her cabin, pleading with God for another chance. Sarah had joined her shortly after sunset. But after praying with Eliza and encouraging her to trust her fate to the Almighty, she had retired, complaining of a sore back. Poor food, the constant movement of the ship, and the oppressive heat did little to ease the discomfort of the woman's condition. Yet thankfully, she now swayed calmly in her hammock, sound asleep. In a way, Eliza had much in common with Sarah. They were both alone in the world, and both had huge obstacles to overcome. Yet while Sarah slept peacefully, believing God would take care of her, Eliza's restless soul drove her mad with worry.

The door creaked, and Angeline entered. "I thought you'd be asleep," she whispered after glancing at Sarah.

"I can't." Eliza hugged herself and plopped down in the only chair.

Skirts swished. Angeline sat on the trunk beside her and took her hand.

"It isn't fair." Stowy leaped onto Angeline's lap and curled into a ball. She stroked his fur as if he were her only friend in the world. "Why don't I go with you?" Her voice lifted in excitement. "Two are better than one."

"Don't be absurd. Why should both of us suffer? You haven't done anything wrong."

Nothing but the creak of the ship and Stowy's purrs replied. "You don't know that," Angeline finally whispered.

Eliza squeezed her hand. "Surely nothing that would warrant them hating you as much as they hate me."

"I'm not so sure." Angeline's voice weighed heavy with regret. "I don't even know why they hate you. I mean, you're not really a Yankee."

"They are hurting. They need someone to blame."

Rising, Angeline bundled Stowy in her arms.

"Thank you, Angeline. It's nice to have friends on board." Even if Eliza could count them all on one hand.

Moonlight swayed over Angeline with the rock of the ship. Silver, black, silver, black. Much like the woman's moods. Happy then sad, bold then timid. Eliza could not forget how Angeline had nearly fainted when the frigate captured them. Or, alternatively, how she boldly stood beside Eliza when the passengers threatened to toss her overboard. Eliza longed to know Angeline's story. She longed to help her. But now she'd never have the chance.

"Won't you try to get some sleep?" Angeline asked.

"I don't think I can. You go ahead. I'll just sit here awhile."

Within minutes of undressing and crawling into her hammock—with Stowy curled by her side—Angeline's breathing deepened, leaving Eliza alone again. A loneliness that cloaked her in a familiar, heavy drape. Minutes passed. The muffled sounds of voices echoing through the ship faded one by one until nothing remained but the lap of waves against the hull. Nothing save the frantic thump of her heart and the horrifying visions of her future. She tried to pray, but out of her hopelessness, no words formed. Instead, she crept out of the cabin and made her way above to the starboard railing. Perhaps some fresh air would clear her head and give her a new perspective.

A quarter moon flung silver and blue braids across the choppy bay as a breeze stirred the palms ashore in a gentle swishing cadence. Bowing her head, she clasped her shaky hands and began to pray.

Against the rolling of the ship, Magnolia clung to the ladder and made her way above deck. Her parents snoring away in their stifling cabin afforded her the perfect opportunity to slip from their watchful gazes and steal a few moments alone. She hadn't slept in four nights—not since she'd made a spectacle of herself at the dance and revealed Eliza's secret to all. Slipping her hand into the pocket of her gown, she withdrew a peppermint leaf and plopped it in her mouth. Just in case she came across anyone on deck. She'd tried to control her drinking after that night but found the incident had only increased her need for the vile liquor. Vile, wonderful elixir that took away the pain and made life bearable.

A night breeze, laden with the scent of wild orchids and sweet mangoes, swirled about her, nearly wiping away the stench of the ship and its filthy crew—an odor that seemed permanently lodged in her lungs. She peered into the darkness, seeking Mr. Lewis. The aged carpenter always carried a flask of brandy on him. And Magnolia always managed to talk him out of a sip. Or two. But he was nowhere in sight. Only a few slouching shadows loomed on the fore- and quarterdeck that were most likely watchmen fast asleep.

Another figure stood at the starboard railing, just outside the light from the lantern hanging from the mainmast. Magnolia took a step forward, squinting into the darkness. Mercy, it was Eliza. She was the last person Magnolia wished to see! She imagined the feeling was mutual. No doubt the woman hated her for what she'd done. Turning, Magnolia intended to return to her cabin when an alarming and utterly foreign idea halted her. *Perhaps I should apologize.* That would be the right thing to do, wouldn't it? After all, Magnolia hadn't meant to say anything. In fact, she hardly remembered saying anything at all. But, for goodness' sake, since Eliza was to be cast off on the morrow, an apology was the least Magnolia could offer her for the trouble she'd caused. Bracing herself for the lady's rage, Magnolia crossed the deck and slipped beside her. Eliza's lips moved beneath closed eyes.

Praying? *How quaint.* Yet Magnolia supposed she might be reduced to prayer if she were being stranded on an island in the morning. She leaned toward her, longing to hear how laypeople prayed. All she'd ever heard were the prayers recited in church.

Eliza's eyes shot open. She reeled backward with a start. "Magnolia, you frightened me."

"Forgive me. I didn't mean to."

Eliza's gaze scoured her from head to toe. "Do you need medical attention?"

The true concern in her voice only heightened Magnolia's guilt. "No. I'm quite all right." She sighed and glanced over the inky sea. Inky and dark like her soul.

Eliza's brow knitted. "As you know, I won't be around after tonight, so if you have a question or a complaint I can help you with. . ."

Magnolia swept a shocked gaze her way. "You would help *me*?"

Moonlight trickled over Eliza's smile as she glanced toward the island.

"After what I did?" Magnolia leaned on the railing. Across the bay, dark shadows churned and swayed, making the island look like a breathing, living entity. A monkey howled. Or at least Magnolia thought it was a monkey. She shivered at the thought of being in the jungle alone.

"I came to tell you how sorry I am." Tears burned behind Magnolia's eyes. "I never meant to break my promise. I was. . .well, I was. . ."

Eliza covered Magnolia's hand with hers. "I know." She gave a tiny smile of understanding. "You weren't yourself."

Though Magnolia heard the words, she could not process them. All she could do was stare at the woman whose life she had ruined.

"We all make mistakes, Magnolia. Believe me, I know how it feels to be punished for something you can't take back."

Magnolia swallowed.

Eliza patted her hand then gripped the railing again. "You are forgiven."

A tear slid down Magnolia's cheek. "Just like that. You could die because of me."

"My life is in God's hands, not yours. Here," she said, handing her a handkerchief. "What's done is done."

Magnolia dabbed her face. "But I blackmailed you."

"Alcohol does strange things to people."

Magnolia sniffed, wondering why she smelled smoke all of a sudden.

"I suppose you must think me a spoiled tart, a spoiled, besotted tart."

Eliza turned toward her. "No, I don't. I think you are hurting. I think you drink to cover something up. Something deep inside."

Indignation flamed up Magnolia's spine. "Mercy me, of all the nerve! You don't know me." How dare the woman gaze at Magnolia as if she were somehow beneath her? "What could possibly be wrong with my life? Aside from being forced on this despicable journey, that is. I'm wealthy and beautiful and educated. I can play the piano and paint a masterpiece, and I speak French and Italian. Men adore me, vie for my hand in marriage."

Eliza's lips folded, but still the look of pity remained. "I meant no offense."

"I wish you the best, Eliza. Good night." Magnolia spun around. She needed a drink, and she needed one badly.

<hr />

Eliza stared after the beauty as she flounced across the deck and disappeared below. What an odd conversation. What an odd woman. One minute apologetic, the next riding her high horse. Yet Eliza found no anger within her toward the woman. Regardless of her list of accomplishments and abilities, Magnolia seemed haunted by something, desperate even, and a bit broken inside. Despite the airs she put on to impress others.

Something Eliza need not worry about. She knew where she stood—with these people, with her family back home. With the entire country, in fact.

The smell of smoke curled her nose. She scanned the ship. A white haze floated over the deck. A shadow shifted to her left. Blake dropped from the quarterdeck and darted to the main hatch where a misty vapor pumped into the air.

"Fire!"

CHAPTER 18

Grabbing the bucket, Blake tossed the seawater on the last dying embers in the hold. The coals sputtered, closing their red, glowing eyes with the final hiss of their demise. The line of exhausted men that extended up the ladder cheered. Faces creased with soot shone with glee in the lantern light as the crowd broke up and headed above.

Hayden slapped Blake on the back. "Good thing you saw the smoke in time." With his dark hair, soot-covered face, and wide eyes, the man looked more like a startled owl at midnight than their tenacious stowaway.

Running a sleeve over his forehead, Blake chuckled at the sight.

Hayden gave him a knowing grin. "You're quite a mess yourself, mate."

Captain Barclay, sweat dripping from his beard, stared at smoking ashes. "Souse me for a gurnet, I can't figure what started the fire. Especially in the hold. My men know better than to leave a lantern lit down here."

"Perhaps a passenger. . ." James spoke from the ladder as he descended to join them.

Moses emerged from the shadows, ashes blotching his meaty arms. "No sir. No passengers down this far. We was all asleep above."

James stared at the smoking remains of what had been a pile of old sailcloth. "Thank God the flames were put out easily."

"Aye," Captain Barclay said. "Or we'd *all* be marooned on this island."

Like Eliza. The smell of smoke and bilge bit Blake's nose as the thought bit his heart.

"This trip be cursed, says I," one of the sailors said, his voice heightened with fear. "We'll be lucky to make it to Brazil alive."

The captain huffed his response and waved toward the man. "Gather some men and get this mess cleaned up and the water pumped out. Then inspect the hold for damage." As the sailor sped off, Captain Barclay faced Blake. "We should question Miss Magnolia. If she's desperate enough to toss my instruments overboard, who's to say she wouldn't start a fire?"

Blake shifted his boots in the sludge and winced at the ache in both legs. Though he'd love to draw suspicion toward the spoon-fed tart and away from Eliza as the source of their bad luck, he could not do so in good conscience. "Don't think it was her. I saw her above with Eliza when the fire started."

"Ah yes, Mrs. Crawford. Lenn!" The captain shouted at the sailor, who poked his head back down the hatchway. "Tell Max to get ashore with Mrs. Crawford straightaway. I want to set sail in a few hours." Then turning, he headed toward the ladder muttering, "Cursed woman."

Blake hung his head. Why had he gone and reminded the captain of Eliza?

An hour later, washed and wearing fresh clothes, Blake stood at the railing watching a boatload of sailors row Eliza ashore. She hadn't pleaded or groveled or begged or cried. She'd merely stared straight ahead. All except one glance. One glance at Blake before she climbed down the rope ladder. It was enough to see the remorse, the anguish, the fear in her eyes. Not hatred. Not anger as he'd expected.

He hadn't meant to eavesdrop that morning. Another restless night had driven him above, seeking solace in the gentle waters of the bay—seeking solace for a mind not only tortured with recurring battles, but swamped with thoughts of Eliza's perilous future. Then she had appeared, as if his dreams had taken form. He watched as she gazed over the sea, wistful and morose, before she clasped her trembling hands together and bowed her head in prayer. He watched her for several minutes from his position in the shadows of the quarterdeck, feeling like a muckraker for intruding on her privacy. He watched her because he could do nothing else. Then when Miss Magnolia had joined her, his curiosity got the better of him. All right. So he *had been* eavesdropping.

But what he'd heard sent his mind reeling. She'd forgiven Magnolia! She'd forgiven the pretentious, spoiled lush without so much as a blink of her eye. The woman who had ruined her life and shoved her into a future riddled with uncertainty and danger. Astounding!

Now as the men rowed Eliza to that treacherous future, she cast one last glance over her shoulder at him. If he were a praying man, he'd petition God for her safety, but he'd given up on prayer long ago. Instead, he ran a hand through his wet hair and cursed.

Blast it! He could not reconcile a lying Yankee with the woman he saw last night. How could he keep his anger toward her blazing when her honor, kindness, and generosity doused the flames at every turn? Sunlight sliced swords of silver across the bay as if angry at Eliza's fate. Steam rose from the jungle, blurring the island. Yet no breeze stirred to offer comfort to those witnessing the lady's judgment. Blake dabbed the sweat from his forehead, resisting the urge to follow her. To escort her to Roseau himself. Forfeit his journey to Brazil. His dreams. But his brother's howl as a Yankee sword plunged into his gut, his family's screams as they burned to death, haunted him with voices that had been silenced far too young, voices demanding justice.

And he couldn't do it.

James appeared beside him, his gaze following Blake's. "You did your best to save her."

"It wasn't good enough."

"God will take care of her. I've been praying, and I sense He's already answered."

Blake snorted and shifted his weight.

"How's your leg?" James asked.

"Healing." Blake stretched it out. Even after standing on it for hours, no blood stained the bandage she'd applied.

"She's a good nurse," James said.

Blake was about to agree when Angeline dashed to his side, her face twisted in fear. "It's Sarah." Her gaze shifted to Eliza nearly on shore then back to Blake.

"What about her?" James stepped forward.

"She's having her baby. And something is terribly wrong,"

⸎

James assisted Eliza over the railing. "How is she?"

"In a lot of pain and bleeding heavily. She's asking for you." James

171

took her arm and swept her past the onlooking passengers and crew and down the companionway ladder. A scream that sounded as though Sarah's limbs were being ripped off one by one filtered from below.

"Have you ever delivered a baby, James?"

"No." He stopped at the door to the sick bay, fear skittering across his eyes. "I did most of my doctoring on the battlefield. Regardless, I can't do this. Not with all that blood."

Eliza nodded and grabbed the handle. "Hot water, clean rags. Lots of them, please. Oh, and rum if you can find it."

"Already got them. I'm sorry I can't be of more help." Another ear-piercing howl split the air. Eliza's heart raced. "Not to worry, Doctor, I understand. Besides, I'd rather be here than out in the jungle."

He smiled and opened the door, ushering her inside. Sarah lay on the cot gripping her belly, terror contorting her features. Angeline sat beside her holding her hand. Both ladies' expressions softened when they saw Eliza.

There was so much blood. Eliza withheld the shriek that jumped to her throat as she moved toward Sarah. "So, your little one decided to make an early appearance? Doesn't she know she's not due for another two months?"

She smiled, and Sarah's breathing seemed to steady.

"I need to examine you, all right?"

"I'll be waiting in the hallway." James started to close the door when Magnolia pressed through, her slave, Mable, in tow.

"You shouldn't be here," Eliza snapped, washing her hands in a basin of water.

"I want to help."

"Neither you nor Angeline should be here, being unwed."

"We can hardly stand on propriety at a time like this." Angeline dabbed a rag over Sarah's face.

"Besides," Magnolia leaned in to whisper, "my slave has delivered babies before."

Eliza spun around. "Why didn't you tell anyone?"

"If I had, you wouldn't be here, would you?" Magnolia's cultured brow rose above her knowing smile.

Confusion tumbled through Eliza at the woman's kindness. "Thank you, Magnolia." She faced Mable. "Is this true?"

The girl lowered her gaze. "Yes'm. I's delivered a few babies."

"In that case, I would love your help."

But the examination revealed Eliza's worse fears. Forcing a look of composure, she stood, washed her hands again, and took Mable aside. "Have you delivered a breech baby?"

❦

Every scream, every agonizing wail sent hot needles down Blake's back. He'd never been this close to a birthing, and he never wanted to be this close again. At least not within earshot. It reminded him far too much of the screams of agony on the battlefield. And they said women weren't courageous enough for battle. From the sounds of what Sarah was going through, he'd bet her bravery and endurance would surpass most of the men he'd commanded.

The captain paced before the wheel, hands locked behind his back. Blake knew he was anxious to get under way. So was Blake. Several passengers mulled about the deck in the blaring, afternoon sun. Mr. Graves, cigar in hand, stood at the bow of the ship overlooking the bay as if he were in charge of the entire expedition. The Scotts huddled beneath the shade of an awning erected for their benefit. Mr. Lewis nursed a flask while playing a game of whist with a group of ex-soldiers. Moses and his sister and her children kept to themselves by the capstan. Dodd smiled and tipped his hat at every passing lady. And sailors scattered about, whittling wood or tying ropes as they awaited their captain's orders.

Soon the men emerged from the jungle, kegs of water propped on their shoulders. Blake released a breath. Finally, something to divert his mind from the incessant screams. Within minutes they rowed to the brig, and with the help of the other sailors, they hoisted the kegs aboard. The captain met them. "No sign of Parson Bailey?"

"No Cap'n. We looked everywhere. He didn't leave a mark, footprint, nothin'." The man jerked his head toward another sailor. "You know old hound nose here can track anyone." A torturing wail filtered through the ship. "Is someone dyin'?" the sailor asked.

"No. Just deliverin' a baby." The captain's voice was matter-of-fact, but his mind seemed elsewhere. "I have no choice then. I have a schedule to keep and can't hold it up for one man. We must set sail if I am to make it to New Orleans in time."

The sailor removed his tarred straw hat and wiped the sweat from his brow. "Don't make no sense. The man couldn't just disappear."

Disappear. An idea sprang into Blake's mind like a predator on prey, an idea that chilled him to the bone. Hobbling across the deck, he leaped down the ladder, hoping with everything in him that he was wrong.

"What's got into you, Colonel?" Captain Barclay followed him down the companionway.

He halted at the door to the captain's cabin. "Parson Bailey was the last person to handle the funds for our colony."

Understanding flickered across the old man's eyes. The men barreled into the cabin behind the captain, who darted to his desk. Kneeling, he felt for a latch beneath the bottom drawer. A click echoed through the cabin. Blake's breath caught in this throat. A secret lever swung open. The captain pulled out a tray. Empty.

All their money was gone.

CHAPTER 19

Eliza cringed as Sarah let out another deafening scream.

"What's happening?" The poor woman panted. A sheen of perspiration covered her face and neck and glued her brown curls to her skin. Fear sparked from her eyes. "Why does it hurt so much?"

"All birthing hurts. Nothing to worry about." Eliza feigned a calm tone and pressed her hands on Sarah's womb, feeling for the position of the child. Still upside down. But the pains were coming closer now, within minutes. Eliza's palms grew damp. Her mind spun in terror. Women often died in childbirth. Especially when the baby was not in the correct position. What was she to do?

Calm. Remain calm. Eliza drew in a deep breath and lifted up a prayer. The same thing she'd done during the war when men's lives were in her hands. But back then, she'd had a bevy of doctors to call to her aid. Here she was alone.

"It be best if she squats," Mable said in a timid voice, her gaze barely meeting Eliza's. "It will hep de baby come out."

"Then let's get her up." Eliza stood and gestured to Magnolia, who'd been pacing the tiny room, and to Angeline beside the bed. "Ladies, the baby is coming. Grab Sarah's arms and assist her to a sitting position."

They complied, though alarm pinched their expressions, an alarm Eliza felt strangling every nerve. Sarah moaned as they maneuvered her. Grabbing a stack of blankets, Eliza laid them on the deck beneath the woman and rubbed her hands together to settle the trembling.

Lifting her face, Sarah wailed for what seemed minutes. The sound of her pain sliced a hole in Eliza's heart as the metallic smell of blood filled her nose.

"Mercy me, is she going to die?" Magnolia whimpered, her lip trembling. "I can't stay here if she's going to die."

Angeline shot her a seething look.

"Then go," Eliza spat. She had no time for weakness. "But no one is going to die."

Sarah's face reddened. Her grunts and groans joined the creaking of the ship.

Mable knelt. "Don't push, ma'am. Try t' not push."

Sarah's eyes flashed. "Are you mad?" she ground out, her face so mottled in agony, Eliza barely recognized her.

The slave girl cowered beneath the woman's chastisement, and Eliza laid a hand on her shoulder for comfort.

Sarah panted. "Forgive me, Mable." Her chest rose and fell. Angeline dabbed the sweat on her forehead. Magnolia's face had gone bone white.

Amazed that, in her pain, Sarah still considered the young slave's feelings, Eliza clasped her sweaty hands. "When you feel like pushing, squeeze my hands instead."

Sarah nodded. Angeline rubbed her back and whispered in her ear. "It will be all right, Sarah. All women go through this. It's perfectly normal."

Eliza didn't have time to wonder where an unmarried woman like Angeline would have witnessed a birthing, for another pain soon hit. Sarah slammed her eyes shut until tears streamed from their corners. She squeezed Eliza's hands. They grew numb with pain. Eliza bit her lip, tasting blood.

Mable held Sarah's skirts out of the way.

The woman howled for what seemed an eternity, not stopping to catch her breath.

Finally one tiny foot appeared.

Then the other.

"Wrap his legs in de blanket," Mable instructed. "Or he'll get too cold before the rest comes out."

Eliza grabbed a clean spread and covered the baby's legs, holding him in her hands. He or she wasn't moving. Neither did any more of the babe appear. Sarah's wail turned savage. All color drained from her face.

No Lord, no. Please don't let them die!

Blake couldn't believe his eyes.

"Gone! What do you mean gone?" James shoved his way through the crowd mobbing the captain's cabin and peered into the tray. He exchanged a harried glance with Blake.

Rising, Captain Barclay slammed the empty tray atop his desk, grabbed a bottle of brandy from his cabinet, and poured himself a glass.

"The good parson stole our money." Blake voiced what his mind refused to accept.

"Parson Bailey?" Dodd exclaimed.

"It makes sense now." The sailor pressed the bandage wrapped around his head. "That's why he hit me."

"Zooks. The parson. Who would've guessed?" Hayden snapped hair from his face.

"This is preposterous!" Mr. Scott stormed forward, his jowls quivering. "I cannot believe it!" His wife seemed ready to faint beside him.

"How will we buy land? Food? Building materials?" One of the farmers, Mr. Jenkins, held his young daughter close.

"That was all I had left in the world," the blacksmith said.

"We trusted you with our money!" one man pointed a finger at Blake.

"You shouldn't have allowed the parson to know where it was!" the baker's wife shouted.

James lifted his hands. "It's not the colonel's fault. Every one of us trusted Parson Bailey."

"I agree." Hayden rubbed the back of his neck and scowled. "What's done is done. The man was a thief. He fooled us all."

"Quite easy for you to say, sir." Mr. Scott fumed. "None of the money was yours. Most of it was ours." He glanced at his wife, whose expression had frozen in shock, then over to Blake. "Isn't that true, Colonel?"

"You were quite generous," Blake mumbled, still too shocked and angry with the parson to deal with Mr. Scott's concerns. Still, since the war had stripped most of the colonists of their wealth, the Scott's contribution, meager as it was, had constituted over half of their combined funds.

"So, we have lost more than anyone else." Mr. Scott all but growled.

Blake wondered what difference it made. "Once you gave me your money, sir, it became part of our colony's combined wealth to be used for land and supplies. Besides, there is naught to do about it now."

Captain Barclay refilled his glass.

Blake wanted to slam his fist on the bulkhead, wanted to grab his pistol and shoot someone. But he'd learned on the battlefield to set an example for his men. And now as he glanced over the passengers, all eyes looking to him for answers, he swallowed his fury and slipped into his role as leader and provider. "Money can be earned again."

"We should go back home." Mr. Graves slithered into the room. "Better to be in a familiar place with nothing than a foreign country destitute."

"Aye, aye," some expressed their agreement.

But Blake didn't want to go home. Going home meant failure, defeat. Going home meant his death. He'd invested all he had in this venture, and he wasn't about to give up now. But these people had also invested their fortunes. They had entrusted him with their money. And he had let them down. Blake had failed at war. He had failed to save his brother. Failed to save his family. Now this. Though Blake's father had always loved him, he'd held both his sons to a high standard. Failure was never an option. Failure was for the mediocre, the riffraff of society. Never for a Wallace.

"Why don't we go lookin' for the parson?" Max tugged on his red neckerchief.

"Where?" the sailor whom the parson had struck asked. "He's probably already at Roseau by now or some other port where he can catch a ship."

Graves stroked his goatee. "Agreed. We'll never see that money again. All the more reason to go back to Charleston."

"We should put it to a vote," the captain said.

Blake squeezed the bridge of his nose. He didn't want a vote. A vote meant the possibility of returning. But the captain was right. After the loss of most of their cargo and now their money, it wasn't Blake's decision to make.

"Very well," he conceded. "Gather all the passengers on deck."

Minutes later, Blake took a spot beside the captain on the quarterdeck and gazed down at the passengers crowding below. Beyond the ship, the island of Dominica waved like a mirage upon the turquoise bay, taunting him with the loss of their money. Somewhere amid its teeming jungles and coal-black shores, Parson Bailey strolled, his pockets heavy with gold. Or perhaps the sailor was right, and the thieving barracuda had already set sail for home.

Per the captain's orders, sailors eased across yards, untying furled canvas in preparation to leave. Others loitered on the deck, casting interested gazes at the proceedings. Blake swallowed. His fate, his very life, lay in the decision of these people he'd handpicked to come on this voyage.

He gestured the crowd to silence then cleared his throat. "I'll not deny that we have suffered many losses. But there is still hope. I've heard the emperor of Brazil is willing to sell land on credit, as well as provide food and supplies to help new colonies until their first harvest."

"I don't want to be beholding to some foreign emperor!" one man shouted.

"What if we can't pay up and he throws us in jail?"

Hayden braced his boots on the rolling deck. "I say we continue. Most of us have nothing to go back to anyway."

"A stowaway doesn't have a say!" Mr. Scott bellowed. Hayden sent the man a scathing glance.

"Say or not, the man is right," James piped in. "We all left because our homeland wasn't our homeland anymore. The Yankees stripped us of everything we loved dear. Why would anyone want to return to that?"

"I lost my wife and only child." Mr. Lewis's hopeless tone stifled Blake's disdain for the drunk carpenter.

Graves sauntered to the front of the crowd, brushing imaginary dust from his black coat. "We should return because it is still a better choice than starving or being eaten by a wild animal in the jungle."

"Oh ye of little faith, Mr. Graves." Blake planted fists at his waist. "You insult the competence of this fine group. I chose each of you for your exceptional skills. Why such dire predictions?"

"Because I am a pragmatist, sir." He gave a slanted smile. "And I know when we are beaten."

Grunts of agreement chipped away at Blake's patience. He wiped the sweat from the back of his neck and squinted at the sun high in the sky.

James leaped onto the quarterdeck ladder, clung to a backstay, and addressed the crowd as a breeze flapped his open shirt. "Our forefathers came to America long ago with much less than we have here. They fought the elements and the natives, and forged a living in an untamed wilderness. Why should we do any less?"

"I quite agree." Dodd clipped his thumbs into his belt. "Besides, there's gold to be found in this new land. I have the maps to prove it." He surveyed the mob, his eyes twinkling. "And I'll cut a share to anyone who helps me find it."

Some of the men's eyes widened.

"I'll drink to that." Mr. Lewis lifted his flask in the air and took a sip.

"Rubbish." Mr. Scott chortled.

"I couldn't agree more," Graves snickered, sounding like the politician he was. "Chasing dreams and fantasies is not for grown men and women. We created successful lives in America once. We can do it again!"

Nods of affirmation bobbed across the deck.

Blake studied the odd man. "Why did you sign on for this voyage if you are so intent on going back?"

"I am a politician, Colonel. I don't vote for risky ventures doomed to fail. And this venture has become far too risky for my tastes."

"Life is full of risk." Hayden crossed his arms over his chest. "Returning home would hold as much a risk as sailing ahead."

James gave him a nod, and Blake followed with an approving glance. "Let's put it to a vote, then," the captain intervened.

"Agreed." Blake drew a deep breath. "All in favor of returning raise your hand and say, 'Aye.'"

"Ayes" echoed across the ship, piercing Blake's heart like musket shot as he counted the hands. Twenty.

"All those against returning, say *nay*."

Nays in equal volume and number filled the air.

Blake scanned the deck. His stomach constricted with the count of each hand. "Twenty." He sighed. "We are equal." Yet there were forty-four colonists in all. Yes, of course. The women below. Since the screams had ceased, he'd all but forgotten them.

"What'll we do now?" one of the farmers asked.

"I vote with the ayes." Magnolia emerged from the companionway, blood on her gown and a grin on her face.

"Hush up, girl!" Her father seethed. "You don't know your own mind. And what in the tarnation is all over your gown? Good heavens,

Mrs. Scott, look at your daughter." Covering her mouth, the lady sped to Magnolia and dragged her below.

"Twenty-one to twenty." Blake felt as if a piece of rope had lodged in his throat. Four additional votes could seal his fate. Eliza would no doubt vote to return, since she was to be sent back anyway. Miss Angeline might as well, considering the bond the two women had formed. That left only Sarah. And her one vote wouldn't be enough.

CHAPTER 20

Nothing happened aboard a ship that was not soon privy to all who had ears. Which was why Eliza knew, from the shouts and the tapping of feet above her, that something important was taking place on the main deck. Something that, no doubt, had some bearing on her future. Yet even though Sarah had delivered a healthy baby girl, Eliza hesitated to leave her until mother and child were resting comfortably. Instead, she sent Magnolia to see what was happening and report back immediately. But when the lady did not return, Eliza settled the baby in Sarah's arms, gave Angeline final instructions, and headed above.

Even before she reached the top of the hatch, she deduced the reason for the gathering from the heated discussion. "I vote with the nays," she said, popping onto the main deck. Eyes darted her way, some scanning her with contempt, some blinking at the blood splattered across her apron, others shifting their gazes away as if she were a leper.

Blake grinned. Or at least Eliza thought it was a grin—hoped it was a grin.

"She doesn't get to vote," the baker said. "She's a Yankee."

"Aye, that's right! She shouldn't even be here," one of the ex-soldiers shouted.

Blake's jaw flexed. "She paid the same as the rest of you."

"I simply refuse to accept the vote of a Yankee." Mr. Graves's tone was incredulous. "I doubt any *true* Southerner would."

"This Yankee just saved Sarah's life." Angeline's voice spun Eliza around to see the lady emerging from below. Lifting her chin, she cast a stalwart glance over the passengers. "Saved her life and the life of her baby through a difficult delivery. A healthy baby girl." She smiled at Eliza and squeezed her hand. "So if you won't accept her vote, surely

182

you'll accept mine. I vote we continue to Brazil. And so does Sarah."

Batting hair from her face, Eliza looked up at Blake, wondering what the final count was. Relief reflected in his gray eyes before he looked away. "That makes twenty-three to twenty-one in favor of continuing on to Brazil."

Some shouted in victory. Others moaned. Mr. Graves skulked away.

"Never fear. We will survive," Blake shouted, gripping the quarterdeck railing and halting the retreating mob in their tracks. "We will create a new land, a land where we can keep our freedom, our honor, our integrity, and our Southern ways. A land where no one can tell us how to live."

The confident tone of his voice, the determined assurance lining his features, and the commanding spread of his shoulders all combined to create an aura of ability, of trust, that drew people to follow him. He must have been magnificent on the battlefield. Even now all eyes latched on him and all grumbling ceased.

"Here, here." Dodd thrust his fist into the air, followed by Mr. Jenkins, Mr. Scott, and several other men.

Captain Barclay gave Blake an approving nod before bellowing orders that raised sails, weighed anchor, and set their course. As the crowd dispersed, Blake assumed his duties as first mate with ease. Leaping to the main deck, he brushed past Eliza. Drawing in a deep breath of his masculine scent, she remained in place, stunned. Afraid to move. Afraid that if she did, someone would remember that she wasn't supposed to be on board at all—that she was supposed to be marooned on the island, whose waving palms now taunted her from beyond the starboard quarter.

Shouts echoed across the ship. Sails lowered and flapped in the breeze as men heaved on the capstan to raise the anchor.

James approached, a mischievous twinkle in his eyes. "Good work, Eliza. Shall we check on your patient?" He proffered his elbow with a wink. "Out of sight, out of mind, eh?"

With a grin, Eliza placed her hand on his arm and allowed him to lead her below.

⚜

Eliza woke with a start. Darkness saturated the cabin. Grabbing the hammock rope, she pulled herself to sit and listened. Nothing but the creak of the ship and deep breathing of her friends met her ears. But she thought she heard. . .well, it didn't matter. She was no doubt dreaming. Lying down, she closed her eyes and tried to fall back asleep. Much needed sleep ever since Sarah's baby was born. Little Lydia woke up hungry two or three times a night. Yet once Sarah started feeding her, she slipped back asleep in no time. Eliza wished she could do the same. But more often than not, she lay awake for hours pondering her fate.

Wondering if it wouldn't have been better to have remained on Dominica. At least there no one knew who she was. Here, on board the brig, almost everyone hated her. They ignored her, avoided her, and cast disdainful glances her way. To make matters worse, Blake had not said a single word to her in a week, nor even graced her with a glance. His rejection hurt her the most. At least Angeline and Sarah still spoke to her, as did Magnolia, James, and a few of the farmers' wives. She should be thankful for that.

An eerie song filtered through the bulkhead, raising the hairs on Eliza's arms. So she *had* heard something. Sliding from her hammock, she nearly tumbled to the deck. What she wouldn't give to sleep in a bed again. After slipping into a blouse and settling a skirt over her nightdress, she left the cabin and inched up the companionway ladder. Ribbons of light and dark swept over the deck from a lantern hanging at the mainmast. A warm breeze, ripe with brine and a hint of dawn, toyed among the strands of her loose hair.

The chanting stopped. She peered into the darkness but could not find its source. Odd. Probably one of the sailors, embarrassed at seeing her at this hour. Grabbing her skirts, she braced herself on the heaving deck and made her way to the railing. Dawn would break soon, and with each mile they sailed southward, the sun's ascension grew more and more beautiful. She knew because she had often been up at this hour— the perfect time to enjoy fresh air without being assailed by reproachful glances and bitter comments.

Gripping the railing, she drew a deep breath of the sea and prayed for strength to endure another day. Inky water bubbled and churned beneath a sky lit by a thousand twinkling stars, so incredibly beautiful. It was hard to remain morose for long. The warm air suddenly chilled. She glanced behind her. A dark shadow slithered across the deck and disappeared into the shadows. Eliza's skin crawled. "Who's there?"

When no answer came, she faced the sea again and nearly bumped into Mr. Graves. He eyed her with a predatory look that sent her leaping backward. "Mr. Graves, you frightened me."

"Sorry, my dear. Unintended, I'm sure." A burst of wind blew his dark hair behind him. "What are you doing up on deck this time of night?"

"I could ask you the same thing." Eliza gripped the railing and took a step away from the strange man.

"I don't sleep, Mrs. Crawford."

"At all? Or just tonight?"

"Rarely."

"I seem to be having the same trouble lately," she muttered, more to herself than to him.

"I would expect so."

His features were lost to her in the shadows, yet she sensed a hostility—no, something deeper—a malevolence that chilled the air around him.

She rubbed her arms and took another step away, thankful the roar of rushing water drowned out her thumping heart, lest he sense her fear. Leaning one arm on the railing, he turned toward her. The smell of tobacco bit her nose as silence made the passage of time unbearable.

Eliza stepped back yet again. "Why do you tarnish your reputation by speaking to a traitor?"

"When I saw you here alone, I thought you might be in some sort of trouble."

"As you can see, I am quite well." She used a dismissive tone, hoping he'd let her be.

He paused. "There are many people who would not wish that so, Mrs. Crawford."

"Are you one of them, sir?"

He chuckled. The first time she'd ever heard the man chuckle. "For instance"—he waved a hand through the air—"with you standing alone at the railing, anyone could come along and toss you overboard."

Eliza gulped.

"All they need do is grab your feet, and *voila*"—he flicked his wrist and gazed at the churning foam below—"over you go." He sighed. "Who's to stop them?"

"I would." Blake emerged from the darkness like a leviathan from the deep.

Eliza's heart lurched into her throat. Mr. Graves plucked a cigar from his coat pocket. "Never fear, my good colonel. I was merely warning the lady of the possibility, not advocating the action."

Blake crossed his arms over his chest, inflicting Graves with his silent stare.

Finally, the man dipped his head to the two of them. "Well, I suppose. . . Good evening. Or should I say good morning to you both." Then turning, he strode away, whistling a disjointed tune.

Eliza's legs gave out, and she gripped the railing. "Thank you, Blake."

"Colonel." His jaw tightened. Yet he made no move to leave.

"Of course. We are back to formalities."

"Do you blame me?"

Eliza flattened her lips. "Then why not allow Mr. Graves to toss me overboard?"

"Because I am not a murderer, Mrs. Crawford. . .or Watts."

Eliza drew in a ragged breath, trying to settle her nerves. Still he stayed, taunting her with his presence. As agonizing as it was, she wanted him to stay. She wanted to talk to him. Make him see how sorry she was. "Why are you awake so early?"

A hint of gray circled the horizon. "Nightmares. I can't seem to rid myself of them." He approached the railing, sorrow weighing his tone.

Eliza longed to touch him, longed to smooth the lines on his forehead. "Quite normal for men suffering from the war."

He cleared his throat as if embarrassed about his malady. "How is the baby? I have not seen Sarah above deck."

"Lydia. She is small but healthy. The difficult birth taxed them both."

"I doubt either would be alive without you."

Eliza gobbled up the compliment like a starving woman would a scrap of bread. Yet just like a scrap, it did nothing to ease her hunger. "Mable, Magnolia's slave, was a great help."

"Hmm. Regardless of what the crew thinks, they are fortunate to have you on board for the journey."

Another compliment? Dare she hope he was softening toward her? "And you? What do you think, Colonel?"

He faced her. His eyes as hard and unyielding as steel. "I wish I had never met you, Mrs. Crawford. That is what I think."

⚓

Blake regretted both his words and his tone the minute they left his lips. Not because he didn't mean them, but because Eliza's sweet face melted into a puddle of despair. Yet it couldn't be helped. When he saw Mr. Graves harassing the lady, as an officer and a gentleman, Blake was obligated to step forth. It was his duty and the only reason he had broken his vow of silence to the lady.

But that was all it was. She was still a liar and a traitor. Two things he could never forget.

Or forgive.

Then why had he stayed?

It was as if some invisible force had kept his feet fastened to the deck, some rebellious need to hear her voice, to look into those golden eyes once more. Eyes that now flooded with pain and turned away. Excusing himself, Blake mounted the steps to the foredeck, seeking solace at the bow where the crash of waves drowned out his conflicting thoughts. In the east, the sun peeked over the horizon, but instead of tossing golden spires across the water, a strange darkness immediately stole the light. A gray mass, thick and black—like storm clouds, yet not storm clouds—appeared in the sky. It settled on the water and began to grow and tumble toward them like a dust storm on an open prairie. Yet this dust storm soon spanned the entire horizon and rose into the sky, shoving back the sun and obscuring all stars in its path. The helmsman eased beside him, his eyes wide.

"What is it?" Blake asked.

"I dunno, Colonel. I ain't seen nothin' like it."

"Wake Captain Barclay."

Within minutes, the captain and most of the crew flooded the deck, along with some passengers who had woken during the commotion. Telescope pressed to his eye, Captain Barclay examined the approaching monster, his body stiffening. He lowered the glass. The lines on his face deepened.

"There's no thunder," he said. "No lightning. No rain. It's not a squall. But what is it?" He tapped the telescope into the palm of his

187

hand then turned and bellowed orders to the crew to lower sail.

James slipped beside them.

More people came above, rubbing their eyes and turning to look at the hungry cloud churning and swirling and moving toward them, eating up the ocean in its path. The air fled Blake's lungs. He glanced over his shoulder to see Eliza, staring at the foggy beast, hugging herself. Angeline stood beside her. Concern for their safety, for *her* safety, bit at his conscience. Before Blake could act, James headed toward them, but Hayden leaped in front of him and beat him to the ladies, leading them beside the quarterdeck.

Then it hit. The gray mass swallowed up the brig without so much as flapping a sail or stirring a lock of hair. No breeze. No wind. No sight. Nothing but gray covered everything: the sea, the sky, and the ship. It was as if a bowl had been dropped on them by the spoiled child of some unearthly giant. Eerie silence reigned. An odd smell, like sulfur, burned Blake's nose. Sailors lit lanterns. Passengers huddled together as voices shot through the fog calling to friends and family.

Blake groped his way toward the main deck, looking for Eliza, but he couldn't see a soul in the thick smoke. Voices sounded hollow as if coming from within a deep well. "Eliza!" His voice bounced across the deck and returned to him, ringing in his ears. Sails flapped above. The sea dashed against the creaking hull, telling him that at least the ship still sailed.

Then the coughing began. At first a few coughs pumped into the fog from all around, then more and more until they coalesced into a crescendo that reminded him of corn popping in a kettle.

"All hands stay where you are. No one move." Captain Barclay's shout muffled through the fog. "Stay calm." Yet his voice was far from calm.

Shadowy figures drifted in the haze. Fearful muttering tickled Blake's ears. What in the blazes was going on? Heart seizing, he found the railing and slid his fingers along the damp wood, thrusting into the smoke toward the spot where he'd last seen Eliza.

Crackling sounded. Light speared the darkness. A single ray at first, striking the deck and scattering the mysterious vapor. Then another shaft and another until the deck, railing, wheel, the masts, the entire brig took form and shape and the mysterious gray shroud disappeared, leaving the ship in full sunlight. Scanning the horizon, Blake squinted at the brightness but found no trace of the gray mass. How could it have dissipated so suddenly? His stomach tightened. The last time they'd been cloaked in fog, the Union frigate had fired on them. This time he wasn't even sure the strange cloud *was* fog. Whatever it was, he shivered at the possibility that it brought an even worse disaster.

He glanced over the brig, making sure no one was hurt. Dodd toppled to the deck. Then two other passengers. Mrs. Scott fainted in her husband's arms. Mr. Jenkins coughed then slouched over the railing. Hayden collapsed beside Eliza.

Captain Barclay opened his mouth to speak, but only garbled words emerged before he fell to the deck with a thud.

CHAPTER 21

Thunder bellowed in the distance. Eliza gazed at the dark, roiling clouds—dark and heavy like her heart. She hugged herself against a sudden chill and forced her attention to the two canvas-bound forms lying lifeless on the plank: Mr. Milner, one of the ship's seamen, and the baker's wife, Mrs. Flanders, with her husband crouching over her body, tears streaming from his eyes.

James opened his Bible and began to read:

" 'And as we have borne the image of the earthy, we shall also bear the image of the heavenly. . . . So when this corruptible shall have put on incorruption, and this mortal shall have put on immortality, then shall be brought to pass the saying that is written, Death is swallowed up in victory.' "

The words sounded hollow in Eliza's ears. Hollow like the empty threat of thunder in the distance. After all the catastrophes they'd thus endured, what damage could any storm do to them now? What curse could be worse than the deadly disease that had plagued them ever since the strange, ethereal mist had enveloped the ship? *Was* it a curse? Were there such things? Yet three days later, with over half the passengers and crew sick, and these two precious lives gone, what else could Eliza think?

Worst of all, though Eliza and James had tried every cure and medicine at their disposal, nothing seemed to work. Tears blurred her vision as she glanced over the morbid assembly, faces filled with shock, despair, and, in some, contempt as they met her gaze. Nearly everyone on board had a loved one or friend sick or dying below in the hold. And now, these deaths stole any hope that they'd ever see their loved ones returned to health.

Frantic as any caring doctor could be, James had searched through all his medical books, staying up long into the night until his eyes were red and his face haggard. Now, as he stood reading the scriptures, even his voice bled frustration. Over his shoulder, Mr. Graves leaned casually on the foredeck railing, watching the proceedings with a detachment that sent unease slithering all the way to Eliza's toes.

"O death, where is thy sting? O grave, where is thy victory? The sting of death is sin; and the strength of sin is the law. But thanks be to God, which giveth us the victory through our Lord Jesus Christ."

Eliza shifted her gaze away from Mr. Graves only to land on Blake, beside James, his face a mask of control that defied the outrage in his eyes. He would not look at her. Hadn't looked at her all day.

James closed the Bible, said a quick prayer, and nodded to the sailors standing at the end of the plank. They lifted the wood. The bodies slid over the railing and plunged into the agitated sea with a resounding splash.

Lightning carved a jagged knife across the sky.

The crowd scuffled away, all save Mr. Flanders, who stood at the railing staring at the last remnants of his wife's body before she sank to the bottom of the sea. Eliza longed to comfort him, but the hatred she'd seen earlier in his eyes kept her in place.

Hatred that now spewed toward her from the friends of the dead seaman.

"It's her fault!" one of them shouted. "She's bad luck!"

"Aye, she's the cause of this," another sailor said, darts of malice firing from eyes red with grief.

People turned to stare at her. Thunder rumbled.

James marched forward, Bible pressed to his chest. "Now, gentlemen. No one can cause an illness."

"The devil can!" one of the passengers shouted.

Eliza glanced over the mob, seeking a friendly face—any friendly face. But she found none, save James. Wind blasted over them, whipping her hair onto her cheek. She brushed the strands aside. She was so tired. Tired of being hated. Tired of being threatened. Tired of tending the hopelessly sick. So tired in every way possible. A detached numbness overtook her.

Mr. Graves stared at her from the foredeck, his lips sliding into a grin. Blake, who had been gazing out to sea, finally turned toward the ruckus. A battlefield of emotions stormed across his face. He opened his mouth to say something when James continued, "This woman has been helping your loved ones get better. She's been up for three days straight with no sleep and little food tending their every need."

Lightning cast their faces in a deathly gray. Rain drops splattered on the deck. Women and children darted below. The men lowered their gazes and shuffled off, from the rain or from the doctor's speech, Eliza couldn't be sure. And she didn't care. Wiping water from her face, she smiled at James and headed below deck. His footsteps followed her.

The sour stench of illness nearly sent her back above, but she pressed on, determined to do what she could to ease the suffering. She sat on the stool beside the first hammock and rubbed her aching legs, thankful for the temporary relief. Settling the swinging bed with one hand, she pressed a damp rag over the feverish face that sank deeper among the canvas folds with each passing day. Poor Mrs. Jenkins hadn't woken in two days. Eliza had barely been able to get enough broth down her throat to keep her alive. Her husband looked up from the chair at the end of the hammock, their young daughter, Henrietta, in his lap. His brows teetered in anticipation of good news but quickly sank when Eliza shook her head.

Rising, she moved to the next patient. Raindrops tapped a death march on the deck above. Swaying lanterns cast undulating shadows across the sick—light and dark, light and dark—as if trying to decide which ones would live and which ones would die.

Eliza's gaze met James's across the way. He attempted a smile, but she could see from his face that hope was slipping away, replaced by a brewing frustration and anger. Beside him, Angeline held a cup of water to Hayden's lips. At least he was still conscious and hadn't slipped into delirium as some of the sick had done. Beyond her, Magnolia flitted from patient to patient like a hummingbird, hovering over each one long enough to offer a kind word or a sip of broth. She split her time between those below and her mother in their state cabin above. Still, the sight astounded Eliza. She never would have thought such charity existed in the self-absorbed woman.

The ship dove, and Eliza clung to a mast to keep from falling. Patients' groans and grunts rose to join the creak of wood and pounding of water against the hull. Though the captain lay ailing in his cabin, with the first mate recovered from his injury and Blake's assistance, the ship sped heartily on its way. She only prayed they wouldn't arrive in Brazil a ghost ship, with not a living soul left on board.

Eliza shivered at the thought.

She lifted a mug of broth to a young ex-soldier and, once he'd taken a sip, wiped the dribbles from his chin. He mouthed a "thank you" before closing his eyes once again. In the next hammock, Sarah, with Lydia strapped to her chest, read the Bible to the blacksmith's wife. Though Eliza had told her she should rest and avoid contact with the illness, she insisted on helping, stating that if it was God's will for her to get sick, she'd get sick no matter what.

As Eliza made her way to a table to fetch a fresh rag and some more broth, Moses glanced at her from his spot beside his ailing sister, his eyes filled with anguish. Little Joseph and Mariah, one on each knee, stared at their mother with longing. Eliza looked away before tears spilled down her cheeks. So much agony. So much pain.

A man groaned and held out his hand to her. Stopping, she clasped it and offered him a smile.

"Am I going to die, Mrs. Crawford?"

⸎

Holding a hand to his nose, Blake hobbled down the ladder, deeper and deeper into the bowels of the ship, into the darkness and death that lurked below. With each inch of descent, his heart sank lower in his chest. Lower where no shreds of hope remained. At the bottom, hammocks swayed with the movement of the brig, looking more like a school of ghostly sardines than humans. He scanned the precious passengers who'd volunteered to care for the ill, and his traitorous eyes landed on Eliza—forever drawn to her like a ship to a lighthouse. She leaned over the blacksmith, one arm behind his shoulders, as she pressed a cup to his lips.

Blake inched closer.

"There, there, Mr. Murray. Get some rest now." She smiled and lowered him to the hammock then wiped his mouth.

"But am I going to die?" Terror etched his pale face.

She dabbed the cloth over his forehead and took his hand in hers. "Of course not. You're far too ornery to die." She smiled, and the man's chuckle turned into a cough. But it was the look in her eyes that set Blake aback. Concern and kindness. Not an ounce of resentment or malice for the man who, two weeks ago, had insisted she be fed to the sharks.

In fact, as Blake watched her move to the next patient, it occurred to him that most of the people she tended had demanded that she be left on Dominica to die. Each had said hateful, vile things to her. Yet here she was sacrificing sleep and her own health, wandering among the filth and stench, to bring them a modicum of comfort.

Tearing his gaze from her, he headed for James, the man he'd come down here to see in the first place. Blake had to know if any progress was being made in determining the cause or cure of the illness.

"Cure?" James rubbed the scar on his cheek and blew out a long sigh. "I have no idea." I've studied every book I have, tried every medicine. Nothing." He gestured toward someone over Blake's shoulder and then turned to call Sarah before facing Blake again. "Now as to the cause, I have my suspicions."

Just then Eliza appeared beside them, followed by Sarah and baby Lydia.

Motioning them to follow, James led the group deeper into the shadows, away from patients' ears. Blake ducked beneath a beam and took a spot as far from Eliza as he could.

Rubbing the sweat on his neck, James shifted his stance as if unsure how to proceed. Several seconds passed before he leaned toward the group and raised his brows. "I believe this is a demonic curse."

⚜

Mrs. Swanson finally drifted off to sleep. Releasing a sigh, Angeline pressed a hand to the base of her aching back and stretched her shoulders. Even though she was accustomed to hard work and little sleep, caring for the sick and dying was taking its toll on her physically—and emotionally. She hated that there was nothing she could do but offer broth and comforting words. Words that, in truth, brought no comfort at all. They all knew they were dying. She could see the fear, the agony, in their eyes. Some took it well, almost submitting to the angel of death who lurked in the shadows of the hold. Others fought, thrashing in their hammocks and screaming in delirium. It was to those patients

Angeline went. She'd had much experience with angry, maniacal men. She knew how to handle people who were out of their wits.

And besides, she deserved the worst they gave her.

Easing strands of hair from her face, she walked down the narrow path between rows of hammocks, looking for someone else in need and avoiding the one person she could never face, Mr. Dodd. Thank goodness, James didn't seem to recognize her. It had been dark the night she'd met him a year ago, and he was. . .well, he was. . .a very different man back then.

Dodd was another story. As she passed him, one glance told her his fever had increased. Blond hair matted to a forehead and cheeks that were moist and red. Feeling a pinch of guilt, she stopped and slid beside him. What harm could he do to her now? In his delirium, he probably wouldn't recognize his own mother, let alone Angeline.

Pulling a clean cloth from her apron pocket, she wiped his face and eased hair from his brow. Yes, she remembered that pointy chin and crooked nose. Too well, in fact. The sight of it so close brought back memories she'd sooner forget.

Music from a pianoforte drowned out the rush of the sea against the hull. Hammocks disappeared, replaced by tables laden with cards and mugs of ale all surrounded by patrons and doxies instead of those tending the sick. His puckered lips swooped down on hers. Angeline turned her face away as she forced a playful giggle.

"Come on, sweet pea, you shouldn't tease ole Dodd." He pinched her chin and forced her mouth to his. He tasted of sour fish and ale, and she struggled to be free. But he clamped his arms around her waist and shoved her against him. The other men surrounding the table chuckled and whistled their encouragement. Angeline pushed against his chest, but he only laughed and fell into a chair, drawing her onto his lap.

"Ah, ah, ah, miss. You're far too comely a catch to toss back into the pond. Far too comely." He took a long draught of ale and grinned her way, foam lacing his mustache.

"You best be obeying the man, miss," one of his friends said. "He's the law here in town."

Angeline's repulsion turned to terror. "Law." She gulped.

He opened the flap of his coat, and candlelight flashed on a badge.

A sheriff's badge. "So, you see, you're in good hands, miss." He nibbled on her neck.

Angeline allowed him. Allowed him because she could barely breathe.

Mr. Dodd moaned, tearing her from the horrid memories. She dabbed his forehead again. He hadn't recognized her back then. Perhaps he'd been too drunk. Perhaps he hadn't seen the posters. Whatever the reason, she'd earned a reprieve that night.

That long, despicable night.

Now, with her unpainted face and more modest clothing, perhaps she'd earn another reprieve. Especially if he died. Oh sweet saints, shame on her! What a horrible thing to think. Truly she wished that fate on no one.

Dodd groaned again. He drew in a breath, and for a few long seconds, it seemed he stopped breathing. Angeline leaned her ear toward his mouth.

He clutched her wrist. Pain shot into her fingers.

Shrieking, she tried to pry her hand free, but his clamp on it was as strong as it'd been two years ago.

His eyes popped open and snapped toward her. "I know who you are," he hissed. "I know who you are!"

⚜

"That's absurd!" Blake huffed and turned to leave.

James grabbed his arm. "Hear me out. We all believe in God, right?"

The ladies nodded. Blake remained silent.

"Then we must also believe in the devil. The good Word says he roams around like a roaring lion, seeking to kill and destroy us."

"Yes, that is true," Eliza said.

Sarah nodded. "I see where you are heading, Doctor."

But Blake did not. "What has this got to do with anything?"

"It has to do with healing these people and stopping this nonsense." James's voice grew determined. "I've never seen anything like that gray mist, have you?" Before Blake could answer, James continued. "There's something evil about this sickness. I can feel it in my spirit."

"All you feel is discouragement like the rest of us." Blake snorted.

"Demonic or not, what can *we* do about it?" Eliza sounded as wilted as a lily in the desert.

"I propose we fast and pray. Gather whoever wishes to join us to fight this evil force."

That was his plan? His great, marvelous plan? Blake couldn't help the chortle of disbelief that tumbled from his lips. "Go ahead and pray. With the captain sick, I have a ship to run." He turned to leave when Angeline screamed, tore her hand from one of the patients, and fled up the ladder.

Blake released a heavy sigh. "Now what?"

CHAPTER 22

Excusing herself from James and Sarah, Eliza hurried after Angeline. She glanced at Mr. Dodd in passing. He appeared to be sound asleep. Even if he wasn't, what could he have done in his condition to upset her to the point of screaming and dashing from the hold?

Eliza found her in their cabin, sitting on the chair, head in her hands, sobbing. Stowy circled her feet and rubbed against her ankles, omitting a pathetic *merow* at being ignored.

At the intrusion, Angeline turned her face away and wiped her tears. "Forgive me, Eliza. I didn't mean to alarm you." Stowy leaped into her lap and plopped down as if he owned it, drawing a tiny smile from Angeline as she stroked his fur.

Sliding onto the trunk, Eliza handed her a handkerchief. "What happened?"

Two shimmering pools of violet swept her way. "It's nothing."

"Did Dodd say something to you?"

Was it Eliza's imagination, or had the sound of his name sent a tremor through the lady? Angeline straightened her shoulders and glanced toward the porthole where gray skies spread a gloomy sheen through the cabin. Minutes passed with only Stowy's purrs and the dash of water against the hull to tantalize their ears. Angeline blew her nose. "I thought I could escape my past. I thought I could start over."

"Of course you can." Eliza squeezed her hand. "We all can. That's what this voyage is about."

"It hasn't turned out that way for you." Sharp eyes assessed Eliza.

"No." Eliza stared at the nicks and scratches marring the wooden floor.

Angeline sighed and eased a copper curl behind her ear. "I fear it won't be a new start for me either."

"I don't see why not." Eliza reached over to pet Stowy. "Unless you married a Yankee general we don't know about."

Angeline gave a sob-laden chuckle. "No." She scratched Stowy beneath the chin, and the cat's purrs rumbled through the cabin. "Far worse, I'm afraid."

Eliza shivered at the look of despair on her friend's face. "I don't see what could be—"

"He knows me." Angeline's lip trembled. She gathered Stowy in her arms and stood. "He remembers me."

"Mr. Dodd?" Rising, Eliza wrapped an arm around her shoulder, pulling her close, desperate to comfort the lady but not knowing how.

But Angeline stiffened and pulled away. She batted tears from her cheeks as if they were rebellious imps.

"It's okay to cry, you know," Eliza said.

"I've cried too many tears already." Angeline sniffed and drew the handkerchief to her nose as she took up a pace, her skirts swishing. Two steps forward. Two steps back. That's all the space the tiny cabin afforded. "And a lot of good my tears have done me." Her breathing steadied, and the next time she looked at Eliza, a shield covered her eyes. But a shield from what?

"So what if Dodd knows you? He can do nothing to you here." Eliza said. "You have friends. You are protected."

"What he knows about me would destroy those friendships."

"Not with me." What could this poor woman have done? "Whatever your past holds, you can start fresh in Brazil. It's a new land with unlimited possibilities."

"You don't understand. Once my secret is known. . ." Angeline set Stowy down and hugged herself. "Let's just say no one will want me around."

Eliza sighed. "I certainly wouldn't wish that pain on anyone."

Stowy leaped into a hammock and reached a paw out to touch Angeline when she passed, but the lady was so deep in thought, she didn't notice. Halting, she raised remorseful eyes to Eliza. "I'm so sorry, Eliza. I'm being insensitive to your predicament."

Eliza shrugged. "What's done is done. Your worst fears are my reality. But I've survived, and you will too." She plucked Stowy from the hammock and nuzzled the feline against her neck. Though she longed to know what horrible thing Angeline had done, it wouldn't be proper to ask. If she wished Eliza to know, she would tell her. "We've all made mistakes, done things we've regretted. People may not forgive us, but God does. He has taken care of me, and He will do the same for you."

Angeline gave a unladylike snort. "I'm afraid there are some things even God does not overlook." She fingered the lace fringing her neckline and gazed out the porthole.

"That's not true. There is nothing He cannot forgive. But He will have to reveal that to you in His time."

"You've been very kind to me, Eliza." Angeline's tone had the tenor of a farewell. Stowy reached for her from Eliza's arms, and she gathered him up and drew him to her chest.

"Seems you've made another friend, as well," Eliza said.

Angeline smiled and kissed Stowy on the head.

"Whatever happens"—Eliza touched her friend's arm—"you will always be welcome wherever I am." Though with no home, no family, and no prospects, she wouldn't tell the lady that might be the poorhouse.

"Thank you, Eliza." Angeline sniffed and waved her away. "Now, you go on. There are people who need you far more than I."

After hugging the lady, Eliza left and headed down the hall. Fear clambered up her throat—fear for Angeline, fear for the sick people below.

Fear for them all.

❧

Eliza's stomach grumbled. Embarrassed, she pressed a hand over her belly and glanced over the assembled group: the doctor, Sarah with Lydia strapped to her chest, and two other passengers. That was everyone the doctor could find who was willing to fast their evening meal and come together to pray against the evil that had invaded the ship. Eliza had been disappointed not to see Blake. His quick dismissal of the power of prayer broke her heart. She knew the war had wounded his faith. What she hadn't realized was that it had ripped it from his soul.

The small group joined hands when a knock on the storage room preceded Moses who entered, floppy hat in hand. "D'you mind if I pray wid you?"

An uncomfortable silence was the man's only answer. One passenger, a farmer named Gresham, coughed and shifted his stance.

Moses turned to leave when Sarah stretched out her hand. "Of course, Moses. We'd love to have you."

James shifted a pointed gaze over the group. "Yes, we would."

"I ain't praying with no colored." Mr. Gresham's tone hardened, along with his jaw.

Moses froze. James closed his eyes. "God accepts all of His children, Mr. Gresham. If you do not, I suggest you leave."

Eliza raised her brows, pleased with the doctor's strong conviction and a bit embarrassed at her own hesitation. Most people had been raised to believe that Negroes were a lower breed of humanity, less capable, less intelligent. It would take some time for that mind-set to change. Yet she, of all people, should understand what it felt like to be judged for something that had nothing to do with who she really was on the inside.

Scowling, Mr. Gresham stomped out.

"And you, Mr. Bronson?" James asked.

"A prayer's a prayer. I don't suppose it matters who it comes from."

Moses hesitated, but at James's prompting, he finally joined the circle.

"Very well, let's pray, shall we?"

James proceeded to deliver the most eloquent yet powerful prayer Eliza had ever heard. He went on for at least twenty minutes, expounding the mercies and grace of God and praising Him for His goodness and love. He continued by thanking God for His power to answer prayer and His presence among them. Standing beside Eliza, Moses, filled the air with "amens," confirming the word James spoke and bringing a smile to Eliza's lips at the man's faithful exuberance.

Finally, James brought the prayer to a close. "And now, Father, we speak to the evil on board this ship, the evil that has caused so many to fall ill. And we command that evil, that sickness, to depart and never return, in the powerful name of Your Son, Jesus."

"Yes Lord!" Moses shouted, startling Eliza.

"We thank you for hearing our prayer, Father," James concluded. "Let Your will be done."

"Amens" parroted around the group as eyes opened. Eliza and Sarah wiped tears from their cheeks. The men nodded, smiling.

A heaviness seemed to lift. Eliza couldn't explain it, but the room, the air, seemed lighter, the heat less oppressive, the smell less offensive. Even the light from the single lantern seemed to glow brighter.

"God is here among us." James scanned the deckhead.

"I sense Him too, Mister James," Moses said.

Sarah seemed equally delighted, thanking God for making Himself known. Yet aside from the airy feeling, Eliza felt nothing. Oh how she envied their closeness to the Almighty.

Mr. Bronson clapped James on the back. "Never heard such a good prayer."

James smiled. "We know God heard us. Let us pray His answer comes swiftly."

And that it did! The very next day, Eliza noticed slight changes in most of the patients: their fevers were reduced, their breathing was steady, and some of the sick were able to eat. In the corner of the dark hold, the prayer team reassembled to thank God for His healing, lifting words of praise and worship. Overcome with joy, Eliza slipped away to see how the captain fared.

Now as she sat by his side in the big cabin, she noted that he, too, seemed much improved over yesterday. Color had returned to his weathered face, and he slept so peacefully, he hadn't heard her enter.

"Father, You healed everyone on board. Just like we asked." Eliza could hardly believe it. Yes, she believed in God, believed He could do whatever He wished, but she'd also seen so many prayers go unanswered. Her own, as well as a multitude of soldiers' prayers as they lay dying in a hospital.

Taking advantage of a moment alone, Eliza caressed the back of her neck and rubbed her tired eyes. She'd hardly slept in four nights, and her eyelids felt as if cannonballs sat atop them. Every movement renewed aches throughout her body, resurrecting memories of her time nursing the wounded right after a major battle. With the distant sound of cannons and muskets peppering the sky and the stench of blood and gun smoke saturating the air, bodies had poured into the tent hospital like some macabre theater of horrors. So many of them, Eliza had no idea where to start. Screams and moans and pleas for help assailed her from all around. Outstretched bloodied arms reached for her as she hurried past. She couldn't get to them all. She could never get to them all.

Blake halted and gazed at Eliza as she sat on the stool beside the captain's bed. With her head in her hands, rebellious trickles of silken hair dribbled about her face. Was she sleeping? Praying? He took a step toward her. She didn't move. The poor lady was no doubt beyond exhaustion, yet here she was checking on the captain, tending to a man who would have marooned her on an island without so much as a "by-your-leave."

Sunlight angled in from the stern windows, shifting over the captain's desk with each sway of the ship. Thank God they'd had good weather these past days and no ship sightings. Nothing Blake and the first mate couldn't handle alone. And now that they'd passed the fourteenth parallel, Blake had been sent down to inform the captain of their progress.

But he couldn't keep his gaze off Eliza. Sunlight sprinkled her hair with glittering amber and shimmered over the green sash tied about her coral-colored gown. He swallowed. She must be asleep, poor girl. Blake took another step forward, unable to resist staring at her when she was unaware, unguarded. With her face anchored in her hands, her lashes fluttered over her cheeks like dark ribbons on ivory sand.

He knelt beside her, studying her, wondering how such a caring lady could have betrayed her country, her family, her friends. Him. The planks creaked beneath his boot.

Her eyes popped open. "Oh!" She leaped from the stool and threw a hand to her throat, her chest heaving.

"I didn't mean to startle you." Blake stood.

She rubbed eyes that were firing with anger. "You have the audacity to stare at me inches from my face while I am asleep, and you didn't mean to startle me?"

"I was merely curious as to whether you had stopped breathing." He bit down the lie, for he could never reveal the truth. Nor could he reveal his overwhelming urge to take her in his arms and kiss away the pain and stress on her face.

"Sorry to disappoint you, Colonel." Her shoulders lowered, and she widened her eyes as if straining to keep them open. "I must have fallen asleep." She gathered an empty teacup and then leaned over to lay the back of her hand against the captain's cheek. Her locket dangled in the air—back and forth, back and forth—hypnotizing Blake. Or maybe it was her feminine scent.

"His fever has broken," she said.

"I hear everyone is recovering."

"Yes. God chased away the evil on board. It truly is a miracle."

Blake huffed and crossed arms over his chest. "If you say so, Mrs. Craw. . .Watts."

His use of her real name sent a rod through her spine. She raised her chin. "I do say so, Colonel. There is no other explanation." Zeal burned in her golden eyes.

"There is always another explanation," Blake said, regretting his combative tone. Blast it, he hadn't wanted to fight with her. Quite the opposite in fact. These past two weeks, his mind had been at war with both his emotions and his mouth. And though he had commanded a regiment, he seemed incapable of ordering them to task. He ran a hand through his hair and sighed. "You should go. Get some rest."

"Yes, I'm sure you find my presence bothersome." Clutching her skirts, she turned to leave.

Blake blinked at the woman's change in demeanor. Ever since her secret came to light, she'd been remorseful, sad. Now she had turned defiant, angry. For some reason, instead of igniting his anger, it brought a smile to his lips.

"Regardless, I thank you for caring for the sick these past few days. You've sacrificed much for people who wished you ill." He wanted to say something, anything to keep her from leaving.

Halting, she faced him, her eyes searching his. "I'm a nurse. It's what I do." She started to leave again but stopped. Her eyes dipped to his recently injured leg. "However, I owe you a great debt for wounding yourself on my account."

Blake blinked, studying her, his mind spinning. "How did you know?"

"I didn't." One corner of her lips raised in a delightful grin. "But it was quite a noble act."

Blake resisted the smile pushing against his lips. "No matter what you've done, I couldn't allow a woman to be in danger."

"It does seem that God wishes me to remain on your precious voyage." Anger laced her tone.

If her words were true, then Blake owed God a debt, for despite himself, despite his fury, despite his pain, he was glad Eliza was on board. He wanted her to stay on board. And he hated himself for it.

"Perhaps God wishes me to stay on at Brazil? Surely you will need a nurse."

His right leg ached, reminding him of the bullet wound he'd received at the siege of Petersburg. Reminding him that the lady's husband—the man with whom she'd shared a name, a home, a bed—was responsible for many of his soldiers' deaths, his friends' deaths, even his brother's. Guilt tore his recent sentiments for the lady to shreds.

Steeling himself against those luminous gold eyes, he stared at her. "God has no say in that, Mrs. Watts. You will head back to the States as soon as we reach Rio. And that's final."

She spun around and slammed out the door, but not before he saw her eyes moisten. Fisting his hands, Blake hung his head.

CHAPTER 23

Steadying the hammock with one hand, Magnolia wiped a cool cloth over Hayden's head with her other. Hair the color of dark coffee fell away from his moist face, once tanned and healthy, now pale and blotched in red. Most of the other patients had awakened and were recovering from the terrible illness that had plagued half the ship's passengers.

All except Hayden Gale.

Why Magnolia cared, she had no idea. The man was obnoxious beyond all toleration. Obviously of low birth and morals. Uneducated. Uncouth. Mercy me, he was a stowaway! Probably a thief and murderer. Or worse, a ravisher of innocent women. Which she was still certain was the reason for his presence in her cabin when they'd first set out from Charleston. It mattered not that he had a bullet in his side; his kind didn't allow such trivial matters to keep them from their lecherous desires. She dabbed his cheeks as her gaze took in his masculine features. Dark stubble circled his mouth and sped a trail up his jaw where sideburns reached just below his ears. A strong Roman nose, prominent cheeks, and brows and lashes as dark as night completed the noble visage.

"I suppose you *are* handsome in a provincial, boorish sort of way," she breathed out. Actually, now that the man was asleep and not assailing her with his sarcastic quips, he did remind her of someone. A man equally as handsome but with a heart as dark and fiery as Hades itself. She gulped the memory away.

Her association with that man had cost her everything.

The ship canted, and Magnolia clung to the hammock. Cheery voices rose around her from recovering passengers as they ate their noon meal of hardtack soaked in chicken broth. But why not Hayden?

Dipping the cloth into a bucket, she wrung it out and pressed it on his chapped lips. Something about the man intrigued her. His mysterious past, his wolfish good looks, or was it the way he looked at her when he thought she took no note?

"Yes, you are quite a fascinating man, Hayden Gale. What brought you to our ship? What secrets do you hold in that handsome head of yours?"

"Wouldn't you like to know?"

Magnolia gasped and snapped her hand back.

One eye open, he peered at her as a grin quirked the edge of his lips.

"How dare you? How long have you been awake?" Magnolia stomped her foot on the moist deck, the hollow thud muffling the impact she intended.

Hayden opened his other eye. "Long enough to know that you find me handsome and fascinating."

"Ohhhhhh!" Magnolia tossed the cloth on his face. He snatched it away, but his grin remained.

She narrowed her eyes. "It isn't polite to listen in on other people's thoughts. And besides, I was just being nice. They say people can hear things even when they are delirious with fever, and since you hadn't woken up like the others, I thought saying something nice—though it carried not a speck of truth—would help you recover quicker. That's all. Oh mercy me, don't look at me like that! I'm telling the truth. You are a true cad, you know." She planted her hands on her hips. "What do you have to say for yourself? Stop smiling at me!"

Hayden instantly forced a frown, though laughter twinkled in his eyes. "How can I get a word in with all your blabbering?"

"Uhhhh!" Magnolia grabbed the rag and dropped it into the bucket. "You are the most infuriating man."

"Yet you are still here."

"Magnolia Scott!" The commanding voice filled the hold, drawing all gazes to Magnolia's father as he stormed down the middle aisle, handkerchief over his nose. "Your mother and I forbade you to tend to the sick in this cesspool." His outraged glance took in the hammocks then the crates and barrels lining the hold. "This is beneath your station. Simply beneath you!"

Magnolia closed her eyes, wishing she could disappear, mortified that her father continued to berate her in front of everyone.

"And look at you! You're a mess. Stains on your dress, hair jumbled like a bird's nest, and what is that?" She could feel his breath on her neck. "Perspiration!" He said the word as if it weren't a natural condition, as if she'd purposely bathed herself in sweat to offend him.

She opened her eyes to see Hayden gazing at her with pity.

She hated pity. Especially from someone like him. "Papa, I like helping the sick. It makes me feel useful."

"Useful, humph." He grabbed her arm. "Come with me. Your mother is feeling better and is asking for you. If you want to feel useful, attend to your own."

Magnolia glanced over the myriad eyes staring at her with sympathy—eyes of the patients, Eliza, Sarah, and the doctor—as her father dragged her like a ragamuffin up the ladder. Would she ever be free of her debt to him?

⚓

Within three days, nearly all the sick on board had fully recovered and everyone was back to their normal routines. Though shipboard life could be incredibly dull, Eliza discovered that after all they'd endured, she quite enjoyed the mundane pace. Now, at the starboard railing, she looked in awe of the most beautiful sky she'd ever seen. A pearly ribbon circumscribed the horizon. On it rested a broad belt of vermilion, interspersed with streaks of gold, followed by a swath of bright cream that extended to a delicate pale blue. Another day had dawned, and Eliza thanked God that the horizon was not only stunning but clear. No storms, no weird mist, and no pursuing ships. At this rate, they should sight the coast of Brazil within a day or two. A warm breeze flowed over her, fluttering her hair and casting a pinkish hue into the air. She glanced up to see red powder dusting the windward side of the sails and rigging.

"African sand, Mrs. Crawford," Captain Barclay said as he joined her. "At least that's what I've heard it called." Sunlight accentuated the lines on his face and sparkled silver in his beard. "Always see it at this latitude sailing windward of the islands."

"What causes it?" Eliza feigned a casual tone, though she was glad the man actually spoke to her.

He shrugged. "Just dust saturatin' the atmosphere. All the way from

Africa they say."

"Well, it is very pretty. It's as if God were painting us with vibrant color."

He scratched his whiskers then dropped his gaze to his boots. "I wanted to thank you, Mrs. Crawford, for helpin' the sick on board, and for tendin' to me as well. The doc told me what you did."

"It was my pleasure, Captain."

She had barely finished her sentence when Captain Barclay turned and charged back across the deck. Despite his abrupt departure, Eliza was warmed by his attention. In fact, as she glanced over the ship, several passengers met her gaze with a nod or a smile, not with the loathing glances of before. James stood by the foredeck talking with Angeline and Sarah. The Scotts sat together on chairs beneath a sailcloth while Mable attended to their every need. Mr. Dodd, thumbs stuck in his waistcoat pocket, talked to a group of passengers about his favorite subject—gold. At the far end of the foredeck, Delia and Moses laughed as Delia's children dashed across the deck. The Jenkins's little girl, Henrietta, gazed up at them from the main deck as if she wished to join them. And Mr. Graves stood at the stern smoking a cigar and staring into the frothy water bubbling off the back of the ship.

Even Hayden smiled at Eliza as he made his way to Angeline. Halting before the lady, he said something and proffered his elbow. She hesitated, glanced at James and Sarah as if obtaining their permission, then slipped her arm through his. Both Magnolia's and the doctor's gazes followed them as they took a turn around the deck.

Blake stood at the bow of the ship staring straight ahead as if he could make Brazil rise from the ocean by sheer will. If anyone could move continents purely by resolve, it was him. She'd never met a more bullheaded man. He glanced over his shoulder, and their eyes met, but he quickly turned back around. If only his heart would soften like the others' hearts, perhaps she could convince him to allow her to stay in Brazil.

"Oh Lord, let it be Your will." For she didn't know how she'd survive back home. Yet wasn't it like her to ask God to conform to what she wanted? Or worse, to go ahead and do what she wanted and then ask God to bless it? Oh fiddle. She would try to change. She truly would.

Closing her eyes, she tilted her face to the sun, basking in its warmth.

It was far too pleasant a day to think of past mistakes. There had been no ill tidings since the deadly mist, no freak accidents, no inclement weather. Perhaps their luck was about to change. She felt rather than heard someone slip beside her. The spicy scent of cigar smoke swept past her nose, and she tensed, knowing she would find Mr. Graves close by. Sure enough, when she opened her eyes, the politician stood not a foot away. His smile lacked the warmth of most people's. In fact, it chilled her to the bone.

"Good morning, Mr. Graves."

He leaned an elbow on the railing. Pink dusted his black hair, giving it a mahogany sheen. "You astound me, madam."

"How so?"

"You care for people who would just as soon throw you to the sharks as look at you." Yet his tone was not one of astonishment but more of disappointment.

"Regardless of their sentiments or intentions," Eliza said, "it isn't right to allow them to suffer."

He cocked his head and studied her as if she were an anomaly. Yet his frown remained. In fact, his intense perusal forced her gaze back out to sea. Perhaps if she got to know him a bit better, he wouldn't frighten her so.

"Where are you from, Mr. Graves?"

"Northern Maryland." He puffed on his cigar.

"Do you still have family there?"

Wind tore puffs of smoke from his lips before he'd had a chance to exhale. "My mother and father are dead, if that's what you're asking, madam." His tone was one of annoyance. "Murdered in their beds by Yankee soldiers."

Wonderful. Someone else on board who had every reason to hate her. "I'm sorry." The words fell impotent from her lips.

"My father was a senator from Maryland, only recently retired," he continued. "I was to take his place, you see. I'd been trained to do so my entire life."

"You were running for the Senate?"

"Yes." His black eyes brightened for the first time since she'd known him. "And doing quite well, I might add." But then his expression soured, and he peered down his nose at her. "That is until the South ceded from the Union and all my dreams were obliterated."

He stroked his black goatee and stared out to sea. "I was to eventually run for president, you see. It was all planned from my birth. Every moment, every second of my life was spent working toward that single endeavor."

The ship rose on a swell, and Eliza gripped the railing, thinking how strict and disciplined and terribly unhappy his childhood would have been. Even now, a dour cloak seemed to cling to the man.

"Why did you not remain behind, Mr. Graves? Surely you can still run for president."

Eyebrows as thick and dark as night bent together as his chortle filled the air. "A Southerner as president? That will not happen in my lifetime. No, the war changed everything."

"Then perhaps you need a new dream, Mr. Graves."

Taking one last puff on his cigar, he flicked it into the sea. "There is no other dream." The veins in his neck pulsed. "But I do have plans to rectify my reputation." He twisted a gaudy ring on his finger, drawing Eliza's gaze to the tiny golden snakes that formed the band.

Her blood ran cold. Part of her wanted to ask him what plans. Part of her didn't want to know. "I do hope they are good plans, Mr. Graves. For the good of the colony. Perhaps you can run for office once we get established."

"Ah yes, it is all about power, isn't it?"

Eliza flinched at the insinuation. "I beg to differ, sir. It's about service to one's community."

"Bah. That's what they tell you, but it's the power most politicians are after."

"Is that what you are after?"

He shrugged. "Of course. But one can use power for good."

True. But too often those who yearned for power weren't good at heart. Eliza remained silent, wishing the disturbing man would leave.

A few moments of silence passed, ushered by with the rustle of water against the hull.

"I sense in you a rebellion against authority, Mrs. Crawford."

Eliza swallowed. How could he know that? "I have had my problems obeying orders."

His smile was brighter than she'd ever seen it. "Perhaps we are more alike than you think."

Not wanting to consider that option, Eliza asked, "How can one so obsessed with power approve of rebellion?"

"Only by rebellion can you obtain power, no? Look at Lucifer. Once he was merely an archangel. Now, he rules an entire kingdom."

A shiver coiled down her back. "A dark, evil kingdom."

"A kingdom, nonetheless."

CHAPTER 24

Blake woke to the ominous *rat-tat-tat* of drums. War drums. Drums that signaled his troops were on the march. Drums that meant they were about to face the enemy. Scrambling from his hammock, he nearly toppled to the deck in a frenzy to find his sword and pistol. Shadows leaped at him from all around. He batted them away, groping for his weapons. His men needed him. Were they already on the field? How had he overslept? A moan sounded. He swerved. Shapes formed in the darkness. A hammock swung to the rhythm of creaking wood.

"Another nightmare, my friend?" James's groggy voice carved a trail of reason through Blake's delirium. He rubbed his eyes as the bulkhead, the hammocks, the tiny desk and chair took shape and form. Drawing a deep breath, he ran a hand through his sleep-tousled hair.

"Sorry for waking you yet again."

Thump thump thump sounded from above. Voices blared. One glance out the porthole told Blake it was still dark. Something wasn't right. Jumping into his trousers, he hefted suspenders over his shoulders, grabbed his pistol, and flew out the door. Ignoring the pain in his leg, he sprang up the ladder and emerged on deck to a warm breeze and a starlit sky. Instead of harried screams, spirited laughter met his ears as the crew darted back and forth gathering something off the deck. Fish. Blake tried to focus in the dim light of a single lantern. An object flew over the railing. He leaped out of the way. It landed by his feet with a thud. A fish. But no. A bird. No. A fish with wings. Blake closed his eyes. He must still be in his nightmare. Either that or he'd gone completely mad.

"Well, I'll be." The astonishment in James's voice reassured Blake of his sanity. He opened his eyes to see his friend, loose shirt suspended over his chest, sword at the ready, gaping at the odd scene.

"You see them too?" Blake had to be sure.

James slapped him on the back. "God is raining fish, my friend!" Then setting his sword aside, he rushed to join the melee.

Stooping, Blake picked up the wriggling fish by its tail and examined it.

"Flying fish. They're attracted to the lanterns at night," Captain Barclay shouted from the quarterdeck. He rubbed his hands together. "We'll be eatin' well for supper."

Blake laughed and shook his head, depositing the fish into a bucket one of the sailors held out to him.

"Ain't it a miracle, Colonel?" the man said.

"Indeed." Though Blake would hardly label it so. A freak of nature perhaps, but a miracle? Why would God send fish when clearly all the disasters He'd allowed proved He intended them nothing but harm?

After helping the crew gather the suicidal fish, Blake went below and finished dressing then spent the day assisting the captain and his officers with the sailing of the brig. Now, as evening descended, he took a position at the side rail, enjoying the unusually fair weather they'd been having recently. Temperatures ranged in the seventies to eighties from day to night. And with a fair wind and calm sea, Blake hoped their troubles were behind them.

His troubles, however, did not seem to be at an end, for he could not get Eliza out of his mind. It didn't help that she recently came above looking beyond lovely in her cream-colored gown, its skirt split at the front and back to reveal a lavender petticoat beneath. Nor that her complexion glowed fresh and healthy from sea and sun. Neither did it help to hear her sweet voice as she giggled in glee watching the flying fish that were still swimming around the brig. Though they no longer jumped aboard, schools of fifty to one hundred kept pace with the ship on either side of the bow, skipping over surface like swallows looking for flies. Fascinating creatures, to be sure.

"I can hardly believe they are not birds," Eliza said to Angeline and Sarah as others gathered around to watch.

Pushing from the railing, Blake made his way to the other side of the ship as far away from Eliza as possible. The smell of roasting fish sent his empty stomach convulsing, and he had to admit that as interesting as the creatures were, he was rather looking forward to having one for supper. The deck heaved. He staggered and gathered a steady grip on the railing. Salty spray covered his face, leaving a touch of cool refreshment as he gazed at the stunning sunset. Above him, blue sky bled into swirling emerald and maroon at the horizon where the sun spanned its golden wings over a cobalt sea.

"No one can deny the existence of God when looking at such beauty." James joined him.

Blake grew tired of the man's constant talk of God. "And what can one deny when they gaze upon severed limbs and spilt entrails upon the battlefield?" His tone was caustic, and he regretted speaking.

James merely smiled. "One cannot deny that mankind is fallen and in desperate need of salvation."

"Then why didn't God save us? Why didn't He stop the war, all the killing?"

"Because He gave mankind a wonderful yet dangerous gift." James leaned on the railing and gazed at the foam riding high on the hull, his mood somber. "Free will. We are the ones who start wars, not God."

Blake shook his head. "But God could still intervene if He wanted to."

James rubbed the scar on his cheek and shrugged. "Yes, He could. But then we would be nothing but puppets in His hand with no will of our own. No choices to make. Like the North inflicting their will on us, telling us how to live our lives, stripping us of our power, our freedom to decide. Is that the kind of God you want to serve?"

In truth, Blake didn't want to serve any God. Yet James's last description was exactly how Blake had always thought of the Almighty—a strict ruler in the heavens toying with mankind for His own pleasure. It stunned him to consider He might be a more benign sovereign who actually cared enough to give man his freedom. "Still, God could stop us from making bad choices and just allow us to make good ones."

James's lips slanted in skepticism.

Blake sighed. "But that wouldn't be free will either, I suppose."

"I believe it hurts God a great deal to see us suffer from our bad decisions. Which is why He sent His Son to endure all the consequences, the punishment due us for our sinful choices. But love isn't love if it's forced. That's true slavery." James stared out to sea. "Someday He will set all things right. In the meantime, we should try to choose more wisely."

Blake huffed. "I should have brought you along as preacher, not doctor."

"If you are offering me the position, I gladly accept." James held up his hands. "Especially since these are useless for doctoring." He gripped the rail with those hands that were now steady as solid oak. "Thank God, Eliza is still with us."

Blake cringed at the sound of her name. "Don't get used to having her skills. I still intend to send her back."

"And have no nurse or doctor?"

"We have your knowledge. Someone else can follow your instructions until I can find a replacement."

"Not if I can't watch the surgery."

Voices drew Blake around to see the lady in question strolling across the deck with Sarah and Angeline. No longer did people steer clear of her. In fact, several spoke directly to her, including a few of the farmers' wives, and the blacksmith's wife. Even Mrs. Scott acknowledged her in passing.

James arched one eyebrow, his eyes twinkling. "Perhaps we should put her fate to another vote?"

Eliza took a seat on one of the chairs the sailors had brought above for the ladies. She smiled at Angeline perched on one side and Sarah and baby Lydia on the other and then glanced over the happy group, chatting and laughing as children wove to and fro among people, barrels, and chairs strewn across the deck. Platters of fish were passed among the throng, along with bowls of biscuits and dried bananas. For the first time in two weeks, Eliza's heart felt a pinch lighter. Dare she say, even hopeful?

Even the enigmatic Mr. Graves, who normally stood afar watching everyone, joined the festive crowd, smoking his cigar and piling food on his plate. Beside him, the liquor-loving carpenter, Mr. Lewis, consumed his meal with exuberance. His fiddle lay at his feet ready to serenade the passengers and crew after dinner. Moses gathered several plates in hand and returned to the foredeck where his sister and her children ate by themselves. Eliza wondered how long it would be before the group accepted him. Or if they ever would. Yet despite the possibility that nothing might change for him in Brazil, the man always wore a smile and gave glory to God.

Eliza's eye caught Max's, gaping at her from the quarterdeck, a hungry look on his face that she surmised had nothing to do with the food. Shifting her gaze away, she found the baker whose wife had died of the mysterious illness, standing at the starboard railing, staring blankly into the darkening shadows. Eliza longed to comfort him but knew she was the last person he wished to see. Besides, she'd seen James speaking with him earlier, perhaps even praying with him, as she'd noted their heads dipped together.

Lanterns hanging on the main and foremasts cast shifting braids of light over the scene with each movement of the ship. Above them a curtain of clouds hid the usual parade of sparkling stars from view. Speaking of hiding, Blake stood across the deck, as far away from Eliza as he could get without falling overboard, James at his side. After a few moments, the doctor stepped forward and tapped his spoon on a mug, stifling the chatter and drawing all eyes toward him. "Bow for the blessing, if you please."

Mr. Lewis covered his mouthful of food in shame, drawing chuckles from the crowd as all eyes closed. James proceeded to bless the food and thank God for the bounty and the good weather and for God's healing and His careful watch over them.

"Amens" rang across the deck, along with the clank of spoon and fork on tin plates.

"I've never had flying fish before." Angeline nibbled on a piece. "It's quite good."

"I'm sure to love it as long as it isn't chicken." Eliza giggled and sampled a bite, delighting in the subtle nutty flavor as a heavy gust flung strands of hair into her face. Brushing them aside, she wondered where the wind had come from. Only moments before, the air had been so calm. Even the dash of water against the hull seemed to heighten in tone and volume. Yet no one appeared to notice.

"A veritable feast!" Mr. Dodd exclaimed from across the main deck. "And a sign of good fortune to come." He raised his glass.

To which others raised their glasses and shouted in agreement.

Sarah gazed lovingly at Lydia snuggled against her breast.

MaryLu Tyndall

"She's a good baby." Eliza sipped her water. "She hardly cries at night anymore."

"She's a happy baby." Sarah smiled. "I am thankful she doesn't disturb your sleep too much." She ran a finger over Lydia's plump cheek. "She looks so much like her father."

It was only the second time Sarah had spoken of him. But the sorrow in her voice forbade Eliza to question her further. Instead, she bit into a piece of hard banana. The sweet crunchy flavor burst in her mouth, reminding her of Mrs. Tom's peach pie back home. She wondered if the woman still cooked for her family's hotel in Marietta. And if she still made those delectable pies and cakes Eliza enjoyed so much. The ones Papa and she had shared so often together. The one and only thing they had in common. Memories both sweet and sour flooded her much like the sweet and salty taste filling her mouth. She would never enjoy those pies again. Nor ever see her father.

"Magnolia Scott!" Mr. Scott's bellow brought all eyes to the overbearing plantation owner as he drew his daughter aside with a stiff hand and bent his head toward hers, eyes aflame.

"Poor girl," Sarah said.

"Cruel father," Angeline added with such spite, it jarred Eliza.

"Did you have a difficult father?" Sarah asked her.

"No, my parents were wonderful." She glanced down at the plate in her lap. "My father was. I never knew my mother. She died giving birth to me."

"I'm sorry." The deck canted, and Eliza clutched the edge of her plate to keep it from falling off her lap. Others did not fare so well as clanks and clinks followed by groans bounced over the deck. She glanced up to assess the damage and found Hayden staring at Angeline from his position by the starboard railing. Not just staring, seemingly mesmerized by her. Eliza leaned toward her friend. "I believe you have an admirer."

Angeline followed her gaze to the handsome man, her face pinking. "I hope not. He's agreeable enough, albeit a bit mysterious, but I didn't come on this voyage to find a husband." In defiance of her statement, her eyes searched the ship as if looking for someone. But then her smile instantly snapped into a tight line, and she lowered her chin. Eliza looked up to see Dodd staring at her with neither the same attraction

218

nor the interest of Hayden. But rather a look of puzzlement, coupled with a hint of contempt.

Angeline coughed and drew in a shredded breath.

"Whatever is wrong, Angeline?" Eliza handed her a cup of water. "Here, drink this."

"Nothing. It's nothing." She took a sip, her quivering hand nearly spilling the fluid. She set her plate and cup on the deck and pressed fingers on her forehead. "I'm not feeling well."

"So sudden?" Eliza stared at her quizzically then back at Dodd, whose gaze had not left the lady. Whether he recognized her from somewhere or not, it wasn't polite to stare. Setting down her own plate, Eliza intended to march over there and tell him just that when Angeline stayed her with a touch. More like a tight grip on her arm. Fear blazed in her eyes as she shook her head. "Please don't."

"I don't know why you fear him or what happened between you," Eliza said. "But at the very least, he should be instructed on proper decorum. I can have the colonel speak to him if you'd like."

Angeline swallowed. "No, please. Let it be."

"Very well." Eliza sat back, noting that Dodd had the audacity to continue staring at the lady, though her discomfort was obvious to all. Tearing her gaze from him, Eliza turned to tell Angeline that if she'd only confide in her, maybe Eliza could help, but a large crack, like the snapping of a giant whip, split the sky above. Then without warning, rain gushed on them as if they'd sailed under a faucet. Eliza assisted Sarah and her baby toward the main hatch, where people, hunched over, fled in mass. She only hoped this new storm wasn't a portent of another coming disaster.

Chapter 25

Blake darted across the sodden deck to the railing as fast as his wounded leg would allow. Screening his eyes from the sun, he peered into the distant haze, looking for any sign that the "Land ho" he'd just heard from the crosstrees was indeed true. He glanced over his shoulder to see the captain raise a telescope to his eye and peer through it for what seemed an eternity before he shouted, "Land indeed. We have reached Brazil, gentlemen!"

Clapping and cheering ensued as passengers and crew alike sped to the railings vying for a glimpse of their new home. Blake couldn't help but give his own cheer. After the downpour last night, he had his doubts they'd ever find Brazil. And though they still had several miles to traverse to get to Rio, just the sight of land helped ease his spirit that they were going to make it after all.

◈

Eliza threw a hand to her aching head. She'd heard the cries of land an hour ago and should have risen from her bed—hammock—along with Angeline and Sarah, but she hadn't slept a wink last night. Instead, she'd done nothing but wrestle with the itchy canvas and tangle her sheets into a hopeless knot. Tossing that knot aside, she climbed out of her hammock, her bare feet landing on the deck with a thump. Though she had no interest in viewing a land she would never enjoy, perhaps it was better to go above than to lie here and feel her frustration rise along with the heat.

Ah, what she wouldn't give for a proper toilette: a basin of freshwater scented with lavender, a bar of soap, cucumber cream for her dry skin, her favorite heliotrope perfume, powder to scrub her teeth, a proper

220

mirror, and a maid to comb the tangles out of her hair. Ah yes, and a bath! But all she had was a simple comb, a small mirror, and a bowl of stale water that smelled worse than she did. After doing her best to freshen up and pin up her hair, Eliza dressed and rose onto the main deck to the glare of a full sun and fresh morning breeze.

The first thing she saw nearly sent her scrambling back below.

Blake cradled Lydia in his arms. The tiny baby appeared no bigger than a mouse against his rounded biceps and wide chest. Yet the adoring look in his eyes as he glanced down at her, and the awkwardness in his stance, as if the babe were made of porcelain made Eliza weak in the knees. He gently eased Lydia back to her mother, and Eliza turned lest he see her staring at him.

Making her way to the foredeck, she stopped to glimpse Brazil. There it was. Naught but a flea on the ocean's back, yet the passengers pointed and "oohed" and "ahhed" as if it were Shangri-la itself. All but two of them—Angeline, who stood off by herself, and Mr. Graves, who leaned on the capstan looking as morose as if a relative had died. Eliza was just about to join Angeline when she saw James slip beside the girl and offer her a smile.

Good. If anyone could cheer her up, it would be the doctor. Gripping the railing, Eliza allowed the stiff breeze to wash over her, wishing it would wash away her troubles as well. Above, the sun flung glitter over the earth, turning the sea into silvery ribbons and the distant land into shimmering emeralds.

"Beautiful, isn't it?" Blake's voice sent her heart leaping and plunging at the same time.

She drew a deep breath and gave him a sly glance. "Do be careful, Colonel, fraternizing with the enemy will not look good on your record."

A slight grin tugged at his lips. "I fear my record is already tarnished beyond repair."

"I doubt that. I would guess you served with distinction."

"It depends which side you were on." His melancholy tone defied the humor of his words.

A gust of wind brought his scent to her nose. All spice and male. Unable to resist, she drew in a deep breath, trying to implant the memory of it on her senses. "And no, I do not find the land beautiful, since I am forbidden to set foot upon it."

"You have no one to blame but yourself, Mrs. *Watts*." The lines on his forehead deepened.

Tired of his blatant hostility, Eliza faced him, planting a hand at her waist. "Have you come to torture me, Blake, or is there a reason you suffer my presence?"

A shimmer of amusement crossed his gray eyes before he frowned. "I came to tell you that you are not to disembark in Rio de Janeiro. I will lead the colonists ashore to a hotel the emperor has prepared for us where I will sign the appropriate paperwork and inquire about a loan for the land. Then, if all goes well, we will return to the ship, and Barclay will sail us to our new home before you leave for the States."

"And what if it doesn't go well? What if the emperor won't lend you the money for land? Then what?"

"Then we take a vote on whether to stay and work for the money or head home." Blake said. "Either way, you will return to the States. Is that clear?"

The ship slid down the trough of a wave, and Eliza felt her heart sink with it. She knew he hated her. But she had hoped that hatred had softened a bit. "Never fear, I will not tarnish your paradise with one touch of my traitorous toe."

"Good." He clipped out and stiffened his jaw.

Eliza turned her back to him, not wanting him to see the moisture clouding her eyes. A dark blotch appeared in her blurry vision. Blinking, she focused on a strange mass that rose from the land lining the horizon. At first only a dot, it grew larger and larger as it headed their way. Blake saw it too. Lengthening his stance, he gripped the railing and stared at the anomaly. Several of the crew and passengers joined him, some pointing, some questioning, others heading below.

"What is it?" Eliza asked.

Blake didn't answer. Instead, he glanced at the captain and his officers on the quarterdeck, who seemed equally puzzled. Captain Barclay pressed a telescope to his eye. "Birds!" he shouted. "Birds!"

Eliza spun back around to see that the cloud had separated into distinct dots—flying dots. Birds, yes. She could make them out now. They looked like seagulls. Thousands of them. Sailors stared wide-eyed. Some crossed themselves.

"Grab your muskets and pistols!" the captain bellowed.

Muskets and pistols? Eliza wondered what all the fuss was about. They were just birds after all. . .

But then the flock rushed the ship like an army at battle. The beating of their wings thundered overhead. *Thwump thwump thwump.* Alarm rippled through her. Her breath stuck in her throat. Sunlight fled as the birds landed on yards and stays and railings, squawking and cawing as if scolding the ship for daring to come so close to land.

Sailors scrambled down from aloft and darted across the deck in such a frenzy one would think they were being attacked by pirates. Others came above, pistols in hand.

Blake pulled a man aside. "What's going on?"

"Spirits of departed sailors come for revenge." The sailor's wide eyes skittered to and fro.

"Rubbish," Blake snapped, but the man tore from his grasp and jumped down an open hatch.

"They'll sink us, they will," Max yelled, his face redder than usual. "They're jealous of our life and will try to take it from us."

The remaining passengers fled below. Eliza should join them, but her feet appeared to be melded to the deck. Still more birds came. Their squawking grew louder, the flap of their wings more chaotic. Eliza covered her ears against the thunderous sound.

"Fire at will!" Captain Barclay shouted.

A huge bird landed on the railing beside her, spreading its wings and emitting a heinous screech from a triangular beak nearly as large as its body. Shrieking, Eliza jumped back with a start and bumped into Blake.

His arms encircled her. Two birds dove for them. She cringed as Blake pulled her to the deck and hunched his body atop hers.

She didn't have time to consider his protective actions. The air crackled with the *pop pop pop* of musket fire. *Pop pop pop!* Shrieks spiraled across the sky, followed by thuds and splashes as birds fell to deck and water.

Blake's arms tightened around Eliza. The rough stubble on his chin scratched her cheek. His breath filled the space between them. His tight muscles encased her in a protective cocoon, spinning her heart and mind into a jumble of confusion and ecstasy. Despite the fear, despite the birds, she never wanted to leave.

Then he stiffened. He gripped her shoulders and groaned. Eliza turned to peer at him. His eyes were clamped shut, his lips moving. His chest rose and fell like storm swells. He squeezed her arms. "No! No! No! To the ground, men. Drop to the ground!" he shouted, his expression twisting. Sweat broke out on his forehead as he tightened his hold on Eliza.

"It's all right, Blake. You're on a ship. Not in battle."

Yet the incessant cracking of pistols and thump of dead birds defied her statement. One of the feral beasts landed right beside them. A single vacant eye stared up at Eliza.

Releasing her, Blake began to thrash. "Retreat! Retreat!" Eliza threw her arms around him and held on tight. It was the only thing she could think to do. "Shhh, shhh. Wake up, Blake. It's over now. The war is over."

His eyes popped open. Horror sprang from their depths. "They're dead. They are all dead!" He palmed his forehead and growled in agony. Eliza clutched his arms, trying to get him to look at her. But he fell to the deck in a heap.

⁂

Angeline stood at the stern railing. The eye of a full moon stared at her from just above the horizon, watching her, assessing her with a detached curiosity born to those beings that existed beyond the vain, hollow condition of man. Or woman. Satisfying its curiosity, or perhaps just growing bored in the attempt, it continued to rise upon its nightly throne, flinging silvery lace on the ebony sea and over the wake bubbling off the back of the ship.

Wind whipped over the railing, flapping her collar and sending loose strands of hair flailing about her head. She shivered and hugged herself, ignoring the single tear that broke free from her eyes.

Memories she could not escape seeped into her blurred vision. Male faces, young and old, their eyes filled with desire. Drunken laughter, salacious grunts and groans, hands groping, touching places no one should. Pain, shame, waking to the smell of stale alcohol and bad breath.

Wanting to die.

Then do it. End the pain.

The whisper floated on the wind, swirling around her. Wiping her face, she glanced over her shoulder. No one was there. No one save the quartermaster at the wheel, the night watchman on the foredeck, and Mr. Graves shrouded in a cloud of gloom and cigar smoke at the larboard railing. She faced the sea.

She was alone. So alone.

"Oh Papa, why did you have to die? You were all I had in the world." More tears fell, cooled by a wind that pushed them across her cheeks to dampen her hair. "Why did you have to leave me with Uncle John?"

But what good did it do to think of the past? It was over. Finished. She couldn't change it any more than she could change what she had done.

Or what she had become.

The only question that remained was could she live with the shame—with the pain—anymore? A question that had repeatedly driven her from her hammock in the middle of the night. A question that must now be answered once and for all, lest the uncertainty of it slowly eat away at her until there was nothing left of her soul.

It was only a matter of time before Mr. Dodd told someone about her. And the illusion of her virtue would disappear, along with all her newfound friends. Then the looks would begin—the looks of scorn from the women and lust from the men. And the innuendos would start, the winks and suggestive glances, the nighttime visits. And if they ever discovered the rest of her tale, they'd lock her up below. Or cast her from the colony like they'd done to Eliza.

All hope drained from her and washed away with the foamy wake trailing behind the ship.

She'd been a fool to think she could run away from her past. That she could leave it behind in the States. Like a ball and chain fettered to her ankle, she had dragged it on board with her. She would never be free.

Unless. . .

Yes, end it all. It's the only way to find peace.

Glistening onyx waves beckoned her from another world. A watery world where all was tranquil. Where the voices would not taunt her. Where no one would point accusing fingers her way. Where no one would lock her behind bars. Peace. Freedom.

Come. . .come to me and be free!

A cool mist moistened her skin and sent goose bumps skittering up her arms. She balanced herself over the heaving deck and gazed over the sea. Dark clouds had swallowed up the gleam of the moon and the shimmer of waves, making everything dull and lifeless.

Slipping off her shoes, she sat on the railing and eased her legs over the side. Twenty feet below, froth seethed off the back of the ship and disappeared into the dark waters. Just like she would do. She trembled. It was better this way.

Do it!

Her pain would end. No one need know.

"God, forgive me." She drew one last breath and slipped off the bulwark.

CHAPTER 26

A line of defeated troops trudged across Blake's brain. He raised an arm to rub his temples, but his head felt as heavy as a cannon, and he dropped to the bed again, mission thwarted. The creak of wood and gush of water reminded him he was on a ship. The feel of the lumpy cot beneath him told him he must be in the sick bay.

The troops in his head fired another round of humiliation into his memory. Ah yes, he'd had one of his episodes. And once again in front of Eliza and God knew who else. No doubt the entire crew. He moaned, more from shame than pain. Pain he could deal with.

Soft fingers slipped through his. Like threads of silk against burlap, they eased over his rough skin, bringing him more comfort than he cared to admit.

Eliza.

He peeked at her through slits. Waves of maple-colored hair tumbled over her shoulders and down the front of her gown. She squeezed his hand and cradled it between her own; then lifting it to her lips, she placed a gentle kiss on his fingers.

Blake swallowed at her tender display.

Releasing a heavy sigh, she gazed at him, her golden eyes filled with concern, even fear.

Fear. The birds! The shots. Had she been hurt?

He snapped his eyes open. She jerked back, releasing his hand.

"The birds. Are you injured?" he asked.

She shook her head. "They are gone. Those that weren't killed, the sailors chased away." She dropped a rag into a basin. "It's nearly midnight. You slept a long while."

Blake's body relaxed as his gaze took in the room. At least they were alone. No one else was here to witness his weakness. No one but the one person he least wanted to see him in this feeble condition.

"Who else saw?"

"Only one of the sailors." Her voice was tender, reassuring. "He helped bring you below after you blacked out."

Blast it! Renewed pounding assailed his head, and Blake squeezed the bridge of his nose. "What kind of a leader can I be when I swoon like some limp-hearted female?"

She quirked a brow.

"No offense meant, Eliza."

She gave a tiny smile, no doubt at his use of her common name. A slip on his part. "You're suffering from the war," she said. "It will pass in time."

Blake tried to rise but thought better of it when dizziness struck him. "My last battle was over a year ago. Have you seen other soldiers recover?"

"No."

"Then don't shower me with your empty platitudes, Mrs. Watts."

She swallowed and fingered the locket around her neck. Blake felt like a louse. He remembered the tender way she had kissed his hand while she thought he was asleep. The way she'd gazed at him like no woman ever had. The way it sent an unwelcome thrill through him. "You are kind to tend to me."

"You protected me from the birds." She smiled.

"So, we are even."

"That's not why I'm here, and you know it."

He didn't want to think about why she was here, caring for him, loving him with her eyes. "Ah yes, your obligation to tend to the sick and injured."

She rose and picked up the basin of water sitting beside the bed. "Of course. What else?" Her jaw tightened, and she moved to the side table. "You should rest, Colonel. These episodes tax you, I'm sure."

She was going to leave. He couldn't blame her. But despite his anger, he didn't want her to go. Straining against the throb in his head, he sat and swung his legs over the side of the cot. "Regardless, I thank you."

"As you pointed out so succinctly, there is no need." Her tone was curt.

"Yet you care for a man who is determined to send you home." And who had earlier made a point of telling her just that in rather harsh and certain terms.

She swung to face him. Her skirts swished and bumped the examining table. A tiny smile graced those luscious pink lips—the ones he'd almost kissed the night of the dance—but then sorrow drew them down. "I cannot help caring. As you no doubt cannot help sending me home. I only hope we can part as friends and not enemies."

Her statement jarred him. If they were friends, he would not want them to part. Ever. That she still considered him a friend sent a wave of astonishment through him.

She poured water from a pitcher into a cup and handed it to him.

He sipped it. She started to leave. The pain in his head mounted like a rising storm.

"Don't." His voice came out barely a scratch. "Don't leave."

Halting, she spun around, hair dancing around her waist, and stared at him quizzically.

"Why did you marry Stanton Watts?" He could think of nothing else to say, nothing that would keep her here with him.

She blinked and then searched his eyes. "Why do you wish to know?"

Blake sipped his water and set down the cup, forcing anger from his tone. "I want to understand why you became a traitor to your country. How anyone could do such a thing."

"I married him before the war."

"But things were already tense between the North and South. You knew that."

"I did." She lowered her chin and began picking at the wooden operating table. "I don't know why I married him. He was handsome, charming, intelligent. He promised me a lavish life filled with adventure. Vowed to take me traveling with him to exotic lands. But most of all, it was a chance to be free from my father's control." She released a bitter chuckle. "In truth, I ended up in a far worse prison."

"Did you love him?" Blake knew he didn't have a right to ask, but he had to know. He had to know whether the emotion he now saw in her eyes was for the loss of her husband or because she regretted the marriage.

"That's rather bold, Colonel." She tossed her hair over her shoulder as if she could toss aside his question. But then she blew out a sigh. "I don't know. I suppose I thought I loved him in the beginning. But in truth, the news of his death did not overwhelm me with sorrow. I'd only seen him a few times during our year of marriage."

Her words broke through a hard place in Blake's heart. He studied her, the defiant lift of her chin, the way she held herself with confidence, the depth of sorrow and loss in her eyes. And all his anger fled away. Shaking off the ache in his head, he stood with one thought in mind. To take her in his arms.

Halting just inches before her, he brushed a wayward lock of hair from her face then eased a hand down her arm. Warm and soft beneath the cotton sleeve. She looked up, her eyes shifting between his in wonder, in hope. Vulnerability lingered in her gaze. A trust he didn't deserve.

He rubbed his thumb over her cheek. A tiny moan escaped her lips.

"Man overboard! Man overboard!" The frenzied call threaded through the deckhead, snapping Blake's senses alert.

"Man overboard!" The thunder of footsteps rumbled down the hall.

Blake exchanged a look of terror with Eliza before he barreled out the door.

⚜

Eliza leaped onto the main deck to the sound of the captain ordering sails furled and the sight of sailors rushing in a frenzy across the brig.

"What's happening?" Blake shouted, making a beeline to the captain, who stood on the quarterdeck.

"Woman overboard!" Captain Barclay gestured with his head behind him before he continued bellowing orders, "Hurry it up there, lads. Ease off jib sheet! Helms-a-lee! Bring her about, Mr. Simmons!"

Eliza's heart felt as though it would burst through her chest as shock transformed into panic. She darted to the starboard railing and scanned the sea. Nothing but inky blackness met her gaze.

James popped on deck, his shirt askew, his hair like a porcupine's. He gazed about wildly then took the quarterdeck ladder in a single leap and met Blake above. Eliza followed them to the stern where several sailors stood gaping at the churning sea.

"I heard the splash," one of them said. "She was standin' right here one minute, and the next she was gone." He shook his head and rubbed his whiskered chin.

"Who was it?"

"The pretty lady with the reddish brown hair."

"Angeline?" Panic clamped Eliza's throat, forbidding further words. She gripped the railing and stared at the dark waters. A tremble punched from her heart down her back into her limbs until she could hardly stand. "We have to do something!"

"Can we lower a boat?" Blake stormed toward the captain as he tore off his boots, one by one.

"Not till we tack. Thank God we weren't sailin' fast."

Spinning around, Blake's eyes met hers, and she knew what he intended to do. He started toward the railing when James muttered "I'll get her" as he tore off his shirt. And before anyone could protest, he took a running leap off the stern of the ship, leaving Blake behind.

⟡

James had no idea what he was doing. Not until he plunged into the cool water did the realization hit him that he'd actually dived off a perfectly sturdy brig into the vast ocean. When he'd first heard that a woman had fallen overboard, he'd darted above to offer his assistance. But after he'd learned it was Angeline, he didn't remember a thing. He must have taken off his shirt, because now as his head popped above the waves, salty water thrashed his bare chest. He glanced behind him at the *New Hope* beginning its turn into the wind.

"Angeline!" he shouted, scanning the dark sea from his vantage point atop a swell. "Angeline!"

He'd been fascinated with the woman ever since she'd come aboard. There was a sweet yet somber spirit about her that tugged on his heart, and though he'd engaged her in conversation as often as she would allow, she'd been hesitant to share much of her past. He only knew that she'd lost her parents and had lived with an uncle. And that something terrible had happened to her. The last part he surmised. Yet she'd bravely stood up for Eliza more than once, putting herself in danger for her friend. And she'd worked tirelessly to aid the sick stricken with the mysterious illness.

Regardless, she was a human being. And after James's fall from grace, he had vowed to God to save as many as he could from death—both physical and spiritual.

Something caught his eye in the distance, but then the wave passed, and he sank into the trough. He started in that direction, happy his father had taught him to swim in the lakes back in Tennessee. Still nothing had prepared him for such huge waves. What appeared like mere ripples from the deck of the brig now became giant swells rising like monsters from the deep. He hesitated as another wave swept him up toward the starlit sky. Focusing his gaze in the direction where he'd last seen something, he shouted, "Angeline!"

"Help!" A tiny squeak, barely audible, bounced over the sea.

Heart thundering in his chest, James pounded his arms through the water. "Lord, please don't let her die."

As the crest of each wave propelled James toward the sky, Angeline came more clearly into view before she disappeared behind the next ebony wall. James's arms ached. His legs felt like rubber, but still he pressed on. Water filled his mouth with brine. Coughing, he spit it out only to take in more.

Angeline's arms flailed as she bobbed in the churning water. One minute her drenched copper hair popped above the waves, the next she vanished below the surface. James didn't have much time. Groaning, he plowed forward. The water became sand, his limbs weak as noodles.

One more wave. Just one more wave, and he would reach her. Gathering his remaining strength, he ground his teeth together and punched through the sea then slid down the final trough. There she was! Her head sank beneath the water. He gulped in a deep breath and dove. Feet pounding, he swept his arms about in a frantic search. Water that felt as thick as molasses oozed between his fingers.

Lord, help.

His lungs begged for air. He touched something. An arm. He grabbed it and dragged her above. Limp and heavy like a sodden sack of rice, her dead weight nearly forced them both back below.

Treading water with one arm, he held her with the other and leaned his ear to her mouth.

She wasn't breathing.

Stripped to the waist, Blake clung to the lifeline. His bare feet dragged through the sea while foam licked his legs and spray blinded his eyes.

Above him at the quarterdeck railing, the crew and a few passengers stared across the sea. Their shouts and hysterics had faded to whispered prayers and anxious pauses as all eyes were on James swimming their way, towing Angeline behind him.

Captain Barclay issued orders to the helmsman and topmen to make adjustments that would halt the ship as close to James as possible.

Finally, James's heaving breaths could be heard above the slap of water as he and Angeline slipped down the side of a particularly large wave. Cheered on by those above, Blake reached toward them, bracing his feet against the hull. But the sea shoved them farther away, and they disappeared again behind an obsidian swell. Blake groaned, squinting to see in the dim moonlight. There! They reappeared, this time nearly within reach. James's single arm rose and fell in the water like an anchor. Methodical. Determined. As if moved by a strength not his own. His head dipped beneath the surface. Stretching as far as he could, Blake fisted the water and grabbed the man's arm. He pulled with all his might and finally drew James and Angeline to his side. He handed one of the lines to James, who barely managed to grab hold.

"Get her above. She's not bre—breathing." James clung to the rope, mouth open and breath coming hard.

Blake nodded and removed his own rope, tying it beneath Angeline's arms. "Haul up!" he shouted. Then grabbing the rope with one hand and Angeline with the other, he planted his feet on the hull and inched up as sailors pulled from above. Hayden grabbed the woman from Blake and laid her on the deck.

"Let me see her." Eliza pushed the crowd aside and fell by her friend, leaning her ear toward the lady's mouth.

Blake hoisted himself onto the railing and glanced down to see if James needed help, but the man was right behind him on a second rope. Still breathing hard, he leaped onto the deck and dashed toward Angeline, shoving Hayden aside.

Eliza lifted hollow eyes to his. "She's gone. I'm sorry."

"No!" Dropping to his knees, James placed an arm behind Angeline's neck, and angled her head to the side. Water spilled from her lips. "Blankets! Lots of blankets!"

Sailors sped off, returning in seconds with coverlets and spreads, which James quickly wrapped around her, placing some under her feet to lift them from the deck. Then gently yet firmly, he applied pressure to her abdomen. More water spewed from her mouth.

Everyone stared aghast, including Blake. Only the flap of loose sails echoed through the night, along with James's groans as he attempted to empty the woman's lungs. Eliza sat numbly watching. Tears streamed down her cheeks and dropped into her lap. Finally, when no more water came, James leaned down, placed his lips on Angeline's, and breathed into her mouth.

Blake had never seen such a thing. He raked his wet hair, hoping the doctor knew what he was doing. Yet how had the lady slipped overboard in the first place? She would have to have been sitting on the railing in this mild weather. But why would she do that? He glanced over the horrified faces of the sailors, the captain, Eliza, and Hayden, his gaze finally landing on the lady's shoes sitting neatly on the deck.

Coughing and sputtering drew his gaze back to Angeline. James turned her over, and more water spewed from her mouth onto the deck. She gagged and coughed. Eliza threw her hands to her chest and squealed with glee.

"Sweet, merciful Heaven!" Captain Barclay said with a smile.

Sailors cheered. James leaned back on his legs and breathed out a "Praise God!" Then leaning over, he scooped Angeline into his arms and rose.

Eliza, coming out of her shock, leaped to her feet and followed the doctor below. Blake shared a glance with the captain, who gave him a nod before turning and spitting a trail of orders to get the brig back on course.

❦

Angeline wasn't dead. She knew, because as the doctor carried her to the sick bay, his touch sent warmth tingling over her skin. Certainly one didn't tingle in hell, and certainly not in the pleasurable way she was tingling at the moment. His light hair hung in strands, dripping on his bare shoulders. His breath came heavy. He smelled salty and fresh like the sea. Had he dived in after her?

Kicking the door open, he laid her on the cot then bent to brush saturated strands of hair from her face. Concern sped across his eyes, those bronze-colored eyes that seemed so wise, so full of kindness.

"You're going to be all right now." He attempted a smile, but in that small grin, Angeline found a hope that made her almost believe him. Almost. Unlike Dodd, James didn't seem to recognize her from their brief exchange nearly a year ago. At least that was one thing to be thankful for.

Hayden stormed into the cabin, Eliza on his heels. He moved to the edge of the bed, squeezing James aside, and took Angeline's hand, caressing her fingers. "Angeline. . .Zooks. Thank God James found you." He seemed genuinely distraught.

Angeline tried to respond, but her throat felt like sandpaper.

"All right, gentlemen," Eliza said, her skirts swishing as she moved forward. "I must ask you to leave. I need to get her out of her wet clothes, and she needs to rest."

Hayden stood, but James seemed hesitant to leave. In fact, he continued to stare at her as if he'd almost lost a prized possession. "I'll come back to check on you later."

Angeline stared at him, confused. Why was he acting so oddly? She was anything but prized. Sculpted arms and a firm, molded chest sprinkled with light-colored hair filled her vision. Arms strong enough to swim out to save her and bring her back to the ship. Water dripped from his breeches onto the floor. He shoved back his wet hair, and she had a vision of his lips on hers, his breath inside of her. "You saved me." Her voice sounded like rough rope.

He merely smiled in return.

"Thank you."

Still, he said nothing, but instead followed Hayden out the door. After they left, Eliza took Angeline's hands in hers. "Thank God you are safe."

But Angeline knew God had nothing to do with it. And if He did, her being alive was only further punishment for her crimes.

235

CHAPTER 27

After the incident with Angeline, Hayden headed up on deck, too frustrated to go back to sleep. Dawn would be upon them in a couple of hours, and he could use the time to think. Think about what he was doing on this crazy, ill-begotten venture with these befuddling passengers. And especially how was he going to find his father once he got to Brazil. A vision of Angeline's lifeless form lying on the deck caused his fists to clench as he made his way to the port railing. Aside from a possible friendship with the colonel—as odd as that would be—his few brief moments with Angeline had been the only thing to stir his interest on this otherwise dismal journey. Well, besides his time with Magnolia. He rather enjoyed teasing the spoiled sprite. But Angeline was different. There was something about her that went far beyond appearance: a meekness he'd rarely seen in other women, a deeply imbedded sorrow he could well understand, and a fiery spirit that enthralled him. Of course there was also the fact that her comely face had stared at him from a WANTED poster in Norfolk, Virginia. Five hundred dollars was a lot of money for the capture and arrest of such a stunning woman. If he hadn't been so anxious to leave town before the constable discovered who he really was, he would have searched for her himself. The lady intrigued him, and he longed to discover her secrets. But a certain someone kept getting in the way.

"James," he spat out the name as he reached the railing, striking the wood with his fists. The righteous doctor had to go and play the hero. But a hero he was not. More like a liar and a hypocrite from what Hayden remembered. Hayden would have happily jumped in after Angeline if he'd been there in time. As it was, he arrived on deck after the good doctor had already disappeared into the sea.

Moonlight spread a silvery sheen over the inky water as the brig plunged through a wave, showering Hayden with spray. It did nothing to cool his humors. Pushing from the railing, he crossed his arms over his chest and snapped hair from his face. Wealthy, learned, privileged men like James thought they had the upper hand in everything. Life, business, women. But Hayden had spent a lifetime proving them wrong, and when it came to Angeline, he wasn't about to forfeit her to the likes of him.

A hiccup tickled his ear, and he turned to see a lady sitting atop a barrel by the foremast. Her shimmering gown clued him to her identity long before he was close enough to see her face. That angelic face of creamy skin, plump lips, pert little nose, and catlike eyes.

She stared blankly out to sea, lost in her thoughts, and Hayden found her nearly tolerable in her silence.

"Miss Magnolia."

She leaped. "You frightened me."

He gave a mock bow. "My apologies."

The smell of alcohol—brandy, if he wasn't mistaken—filtered to his nose and caused his lips to curve.

"What do you want?" She rubbed a hand beneath her nose.

"A sip of whatever you're having."

Eyes as hard as silver met his. "Whatever are you referring to, sir?" Her voice lifted in a sweet Southern drawl.

Hayden chuckled and leaned on the railing beside her. "You can cease the coquettish theatrics, princess. I'm not one of your fawning beaus back home."

She flattened her lips. "That is an understatement, Mr. Gale."

"Call me Hayden." He extended his open palm. "Since we'll be drinking mates now."

"Drinking—ahhhh," she ground out through clenched teeth, then reached within the folds of her skirt and handed him a flask.

He took a sip. The spicy liquor with a hint of orange slid down his throat with ease. Yes, brandy, indeed. "And just where does a lady find alcohol on board a ship?"

"Hard as it may be for you to believe, some people like me and wish to give me gifts."

Hayden snorted. "By that you mean you've been flirting with lonely sailors again."

Her eyes narrowed before she swept her gaze out to sea. "You won't tell my parents?"

"Not as long as you're sharing." He grinned.

"Petulant cur."

Hayden took another drink and handed it back to her. "I've been called worse."

"No doubt."

Sails flapped above as the brig hefted over a wave. Peering into the darkness, Hayden longed to see her expression. "Pray tell, princess, why is such a cultured and lovely lady as yourself drinking spirits on deck in the middle of the night?"

She wiped the lip of the flask with her handkerchief, tipped it to her mouth, and gulped down the pungent liquor like a hardened sailor. Then shoving the hardwood stopper into the spout, she set the flask aside. "After all the commotion caused by that woman, Angeline, I couldn't sleep."

"That *woman* nearly drowned." Hayden's anger flared.

"I'm not"—she hiccupped—"without sympathy, Mr. Gale." Magnolia pressed fingers to her temple. "But word among the sailors is she jumped."

Jumped? He flinched. "Perhaps she loathes being on this ship even more than you," he said.

"If you are suggesting I throw myself overboard"—poison laced her tone—"prepare to be disappointed."

"Too late."

The brig tilted. She shifted on the barrel, and Hayden reached for her, but she slapped him away. "If you find my company so distasteful, then leave."

"Not until you tell me why you need to saturate your senses with alcohol."

"I don't want to be on thissss horrid, ill-fated ship. I want to go back home where I belong." Though her words slurred, her despondency rang clear, eliciting a speck of sympathy for the lady. But only a speck.

"Hmm." Hayden fingered his chin, studying the way the moonlight sprinkled silver dust over her hair. Lovely. Too bad she was such a priggy shrew. Priggy, yes, but belittled by her father. "And what is waiting for you back home that you cannot live without?"

Wind tore a flaxen curl from her pins. She stuffed it back with a huff. "My fiancé, if you must know. He's a wealthy lawyer from Atlanta, Samuel Wimberly."

"Indeed?"

"Yes *indeed*. Do you doubt me?"

"I only wonder why he isn't here with you, that's all."

"Because he is a very impotent man. He worked side by side with Jefferson Davis through the entire war."

With difficulty, Hayden restrained a chuckle at her slip of tongue. "That still doesn't answer my question."

Magnolia blew out an exasperated huff. "Audacious brute!" She stood, stumbled, batted him way, and staggered to the railing. "You shouldn't even be on this voyage. I don't believe your story, by the way."

Hayden slid beside her, hovering his hand over her back to prevent her from toppling with the next wave. "So you have informed me."

She turned to him, her eyes swirling over his face as if looking for a place to land. "Why didn't you leave us in Dominica, Hayden? Just what do you hope to accompliss in the middle of an uncivilized jingle? I mean, jungle."

He cocked his head, quite enjoying her inebriation and noting the way the moonlight made her skin look like porcelain. "I'm looking for someone."

"In Brazil?" She giggled then hiccuped and covered her mouth.

He wouldn't tell her of course. Wouldn't let anyone know his true purpose. Stepping closer, he leaned toward her. "Perhaps I am looking for you."

She backed away, brow furrowing. "Leave me be. I shouldn't even be talking to you. You are nothing but a—"

"Handsome rogue, if I remember." He grinned.

Was that pink blossoming on her cheeks? "You prove my point, sir." She jutted her chin. "A gentleman would not remind a lady of such a thing."

He eased closer, his gaze unavoidably dropping to her moist lips. "I have never been accused of being a gentleman."

She gave an unladylike snort. "No doubt you have been acoosed of much worse."

He ran a finger down her arm. "Aren't you afraid to be alone with such a scoundrel?" He gave her his most mischievous grin, enjoying the opportunity to put this pompous brat in her place.

Instead of shrinking back from him or dashing away in fear, she studied him with. . .*interest*? Moonlight glossed her eyes in sapphire as her brandy-drenched breath filled the air between them.

She shoved her lips onto his.

Hayden was so shocked, it took him a second to react. Well, less than a second if he was truthful. Reaching his arms around her waist, he pressed her curves against him and caressed her lips with his own. Her passionate moan encouraged him to trail further kisses up her jaw to her earlobe then down her neck. She quivered in his arms. He brought his lips back to hers, hovering, tempting, as their heavy breaths mingled in the air around them. Heat soared through him. Unexpected. Mounting. Fiery. Passion crackled in the air. She swallowed his lips with hers. He tasted brandy on her tongue. She moaned again.

Then stiffened.

Jerking from his embrace, she gaped at him in horror before gathering her skirts and dashing across the deck like a cream puff sliding over a wooden plate.

<hr />

After one last peek at Angeline sound asleep in sick bay, Eliza eased the door shut and started toward her cabin, deep in thought over the events of the night. Intermittent lanterns created wavering spheres of light on the bulkhead, making the hallway seem even narrower and more compressed than it was. It didn't help, of course, that her crinolette bounced off the sides with each jerk of the ship. She felt like a fat mouse squeezing through a tiny maze, and the sensation did nothing for her already taut nerves. The ship canted to larboard. She braced a hand on the rough wood as thoughts of Angeline filled her mind, resurging the terror of nearly losing her friend, of the horrible death she would have suffered. And most of all, the question of how she could have possibly fallen overboard.

Lost in her musings, Eliza barreled into something solid. Rock solid. And warm.

Leaping back, she turned to run, thoughts of the lecherous Max spinning her mind into a frenzy, when a familiar voice stopped her.

"Forgive me. I didn't mean to startle you."

Blake. She spun around to see his head bent beneath the low deckhead, his body filling the hallway, his presence sucking the air from every corner—from her lungs. The memory of their near kiss in sick bay sent her heart into wild thumping. Or had the affection she'd seen in his eyes been her own wishful thinking?

"If you'll excuse me," she said, trying to control the quiver in her voice, "I was heading to my cabin."

"I came to inquire about Angeline."

"She is sleeping. James is with her."

"James? Is that proper?"

She huffed. "He's a doctor, Colonel. And he insisted."

He grew serious. "What did she tell you about. . .about what happened?"

Lantern light angled over his firm jaw, shadowed by morning stubble. But his eyes remained in darkness.

Eliza stared at the bulkhead, the staggering light, anywhere but at him. "She said she slipped."

"Hmm." He shifted his stance, still not moving to let her pass.

"You don't believe her?"

He scratched his jaw, suddenly bunched in tension. "She would have had to have been sitting on the railing to have accidentally fallen overboard, no?"

Eliza hugged herself and leaned on the bulkhead, giving up hope that he would allow her to pass and not sure she wanted to go anymore. Mainly because his tone no longer harbored hatred, just as it hadn't in those precious moments they'd shared in the sick bay earlier. "Perhaps. I don't know."

"Her shoes were on the deck."

"They were?" Eliza's heart twisted in her chest. "Then that must mean. . . Oh, I cannot consider what that means."

The lantern shifted, and she saw the deep lines on his forehead and the way his eyebrows nearly melted together when he was frustrated. "I'm concerned for her," he said. "If she attempted it once, she may try again."

"I agree. I'll talk with her tomorrow. Perhaps Sarah can help. She has a comforting way about her that makes people want to confide in her."

He seemed pleased with her answer, yet still he did not move. His scent saturated the air around her, shoving aside the stench below deck.

"Did the captain have an explanation for those odd birds?" She regretted bringing up a topic that might cause him stress, but she longed to extend their time together.

"No." His tone indicated neither offense nor burden. "He's never seen anything like it. At least not so many birds at once."

She felt his eyes search her in the darkness. She would give a fortune for a peek into their gray depths, if only to assess what he might be thinking.

"Was there something else, Colonel?"

Something else? Blake stifled a chuckle. Yes, there was something else—he didn't want her to leave. He couldn't get her out of his mind. He thought she was the most astounding, amazing woman he'd ever met. He cleared his throat. "No," he said and turned crossways to allow her to pass when Magnolia's voice stormed down the companionway.

"Stay away from me, you. . .you. . .wanton reprobate!"

Hayden sauntered behind her. "I'm not following you, princess. I'm heading below to get some sleep."

Blake faced the intruders. Magnolia halted when she saw him. Her eyes shifted to Eliza and filled with tears before she tore down the hallway, stumbled, and toppled to the deck, petticoats and lace bobbing in the air. "Now look what you've done," she sobbed.

"Me?" Hayden knelt to assist her, but she swatted him away, instead allowing Eliza to help her to her feet. Then after flinging a spiteful glance his way, Magnolia fell into Eliza's arms and unleashed a torrent of tears. "That man assaulted me. Again." She pointed at Hayden, who huffed in frustration and rolled his eyes as if she'd said he had two heads.

Brushing past the ladies, Blake stepped toward him. "What happened?"

Hayden folded his arms over his chest. "She kissed me."

"I did no such thing!" Magnolia stomped her foot, took the handkerchief Eliza handed her, and drew it to her nose. "I have no need to steal kisses from disgusting men."

"Apparently you do," Hayden quipped.

Blake rubbed his jaw and speared Hayden with a look that had sent lesser men cowering. "This is the second time the lady has accused you of assault, Hayden. I'm starting to wonder if there isn't some merit to her claims."

"Blake, a word, if you please," Eliza said from behind him.

Hayden's eyes narrowed. "I may be many things, but I've never harmed a lady."

The man's honest, indignant tone lent truth to his statement. Besides, why would he do such a thing on a ship where there was no place to run? "Until we sort this out, perhaps I should lock you below," Blake said.

"Yes. Yesss. . .Lock him up! No woman is safe with him raining loose," Magnolia wailed.

"Blake," Eliza called again. Blake clenched his jaw. Couldn't the woman see he was dealing with a potentially volatile man? He faced her. She tipped an invisible glass to her lips and gestured toward Magnolia, who seemed to have fallen asleep on her shoulder.

"Now, let's get you to bed, dear," Eliza said as she led the young lady away.

Blake scratched his head and faced Hayden. "Did you give her the spirits?"

"Quite the contrary," Hayden said. "I found her above like that. We spoke. She kissed me. That's that."

Blake rubbed his temples where a slow, dull ache began. "Do me a favor and just stay away from her." He didn't give Hayden time to answer before he brushed past him with a growl. Two more weeks until they reached Rio. He couldn't wait to get off this mad ship!

CHAPTER 28

I've brought you some breakfast." Eliza squished through the narrow space between the operating table and bulkhead while trying to balance a tray laden with coffee, some sort of odd-smelling porridge, and a biscuit.

Angeline offered her a languid smile, tossed her legs over the cot, and rubbed her eyes. "Thank you, Eliza. I'm not hungry." Salt-encrusted curls hung limp around her face.

"After your swim in the sea, I should think you would be." Eliza set the tray down, hoping her jovial tone would lighten the lady's mood.

It didn't.

"At least have some coffee. Cook brewed some up just for you." Eliza handed her the cup and slid onto a chair beside her. The chair James had occupied until just an hour ago. The poor man must be exhausted after keeping vigil over Angeline all night.

Though the heat in the sick bay had significantly risen since dawn three hours ago, Angeline warmed her hands on the cup as if it were winter. She took a sip.

"What happened?" Eliza asked. "We were so worried."

Angeline stared at the black coffee in her cup oscillating with the movement of the ship. "I guess I slipped."

Eliza gave a sigh that held more doubt than frustration. Leaning forward, she took one of Angeline's hands in hers. "I wish you'd tell me. Maybe I can help."

Angeline set the cup down. "No one can help."

"Is it Dodd? Is he threatening you? One of the sailors? You must know you are not alone."

Her eyes grew misty, and she squeezed Eliza's hand. "Oh Eliza.

You've been so nice to me. Thank you for being my friend."

"I'll always be your friend. No matter what."

"I'm sorry I worried you all so much. And James, risking his life to save me."

"Hayden was about to jump in as well. And Blake. That's three men willing to die for you, Angeline."

"I'm truly humbled by everyone's concern." She released a heavy sigh and picked up the coffee again. "I'm much better now, Eliza." Violet eyes swung to hers, brimming with sincerity. "I truly am."

Eliza had never had so much trouble getting anyone to open up to her before. Oh the stories she would hear in the battlefield hospitals—the secrets soldiers would share with her during the long hours of the night. They'd said she was a good listener. Someone who cared. She'd prided herself on not only being able to tend the wounds on their bodies, but the wounds on their hearts as well.

But Angeline was an iron chest. With a thick iron lock. And there was no key in sight. "I only hope that you will come to me if you need to talk or if you have a problem. Will you promise me that?"

She nodded. "Honestly, I don't know what came over me." She shook her head and swallowed. "I didn't mean to put anyone else at risk."

So, she *had* jumped. The truth bore a hole in Eliza's heart. She brushed hair from Angeline's face. "Nothing can be so bad that you forfeit your life. Whatever it is, you can count on me to always stick by your side."

Angeline gave a halfhearted smile. "Thank you."

"Very well." Eliza rose. "Eat your breakfast, and I'll go fetch some water to rinse that hair of yours." Yet, as Eliza made her way down the hall, she couldn't shake the feeling the poor lady's troubles were only just beginning. And the worst of it was, once they got off in Brazil, Eliza wouldn't be around to help her.

Twelve days later, Eliza peered into the darkness, trying to make out the features of the continent just a half mile off their starboard side. Nothing but murky shadows met her gaze. Shadows that had snaked around her hammock, strangling her and jarring her awake. In fact, the closer they sailed toward their destination, the more agitated her sleep had become, as if Brazil toyed with her emotions, taunting her with the fact that she'd never set foot on its shores. Or perhaps she was merely depressed because in a few days, everyone she'd grown to know and care for would abandon her for their new home, leaving her all alone once again.

Forsaken. For one mistake.

Myriad stars reflected off a sea as slick as polished onyx, creating a mirror image of sky on water, while a half-moon smiled down on her as if trying to reassure her all would be well. But she knew it was a lie. With most sails furled, the ship barely whisked through the liquid pitch that seemed as thick as the coating around her heart. Eerily peaceful. She guessed it to be around midnight, though she couldn't be sure. The helmsman paid her no mind, and the only night watchman snored from the foredeck.

Not that she minded the company of other passengers. They no longer shunned her or insulted her or even cast disparaging looks her way. In fact, most of them were quite courteous. She supposed it had much to do with her willingness to treat their complaints without hesitation. Everything from the ague, to corns, earaches, sore gums, and diarrhea to heartburn.

"Love does conquer all, Lord." She gazed into the dark void, allowing the night breeze to trickle through her hair, warm and soothing. "And good does conquer evil." For some people anyway. Aside from those few precious moments nearly two weeks ago, Blake had remained at a distance, speaking to her only when forced. She couldn't make heads nor tails of his behavior. Hadn't he almost kissed her in the sick bay? He'd seemed so kind then, so interested in hearing her side of things. Then, as quickly as donning a uniform, he had switched from warm, loving Blake to cold, impervious Colonel Wallace.

Even so, during the past weeks, she'd caught him looking at her more than once from across the deck. Sometimes he gazed at her with such intense admiration it seemed they were the only two people on board. Other times, anger—no, confusion—shadowed his stormy eyes before he looked away.

Frustration soured in her belly. If he wished to hate her, then hate her, but the occasional moments of interest, the glimpses of affection, and the flickers of hope they lit in her heart would be her undoing.

No doubt that was another reason she stood staring into the darkness instead of lying fast asleep in her hammock.

Yet she was the one who had married a Yankee general. Against her father's wishes. Against her entire family's wishes. And if she admitted it, against her own conscience. She hadn't loved Stanton. Not really. She'd been enamored with him. With his position, his power, his commanding presence. The way he made her feel like an adult, not like the child her father always reduced her to. Under her father's roof, she was told what to wear, what to eat, whom to associate with, where to go. But with Stanton, she'd been given the run of her own house. Stanton was her ticket to freedom, her road to living life by her own rules. That was, until the war began and he was called away and she moved into his family's home in Pennsylvania with his parents and siblings. They had never accepted Stanton's marriage to Eliza and made no excuse for their cold behavior. Nor did they hesitate to monitor her every word, correspondence, and movement. As if she were a Southern spy!

The brig rose over a swell, and Eliza braced her slippers on the deck. She'd gotten so used to the rolling of the ship, she hardly had to think about steadying herself anymore. In fact, she'd grown to love the sea for all its wildness and passion and unpredictability. She felt free on these waters—more than she had anywhere else. Her chest grew heavy at the thought of being forced to disembark back in Charleston—back to a land where she didn't belong.

Clutching her locket, she rubbed a thumb over the fine silver. "Why am I so rebellious, God? I'm so sorry. Why don't I ask for Your wisdom before I jump into things? Why don't I listen to Your voice and obey?"

No answer came, save the rush of water against the hull and flap of sail. She breathed in the warm, briny air and then released it in a long sigh. Her rebellion had cost her everything. And now it would cost her the chance at a new life and the love of a man she adored.

Closing her eyes, she gripped the railing. When would she ever learn?

"Well lookee what we gots here." The male voice gave Eliza a start, and she looked up to find Max leaning on the railing beside her, a gleam in his eyes that sent terror slithering up her spine.

"What do you want?" Eliza inched away from him, casting a glance over her shoulder at the helmsman. He was no longer at the wheel.

Max snorted, a maniacal, lethal sort of snort that tightened the noose around her heart. "I'm thinkin' you should be nicer to yer enemies, Mrs. Watts."

"I've been more than polite to you, Max. Now if you please." She clutched her skirts and turned to leave.

He yanked her arm. Pain spiked into her fingers, numbing them beneath his squeeze. "Yankees like you killed me wife and me only son. Took everything from me."

"You're hurting me." She attempted a calm tone. He gripped her harder, drawing her close until his mouth hovered over her ear.

"Yer goin' to pay for what your husband did, Yankee whore. An' when I'm done with you, I'll feed you to the sharks."

A line of bluecoats emerged from the trees like garish devils. Another row appeared behind them. Then another and another as the first line spread out and took their positions, rifles at the ready. At the sight of so many troops, gasps and moans spilled from Blake's men while others merely stared in numb horror. The young private standing next to Blake swallowed hard, his Adam's apple bobbing with each nervous swallow. Henry Swanson had just turned seventeen last week. The camp cook had made him a small cake of cornmeal and molasses, and his company had thrown a celebration, complete with fiddle and harmonica. He was the same age Jeremy would have been. Had he lived. Which made Blake's need to protect Henry all the more desperate. Blake gave the lad a reassuring nod, which had no effect on the terror flashing in the boy's eyes.

The *rat-tat-tat* of drums and the eerie sound of a flute filled the air. Why were battles always accompanied by music? As if a patriotic tune could somehow rebuild the morale of a troop of dejected, defeated boys. Boys who should be back home on their farms helping with chores and courting pretty girls instead of facing an early death.

Grabbing the saddle horn, Blake planted his boot in the stirrup and mounted his thoroughbred. He stroked the horse's sweaty neck. "That a boy, Reliance." The steed pawed the muddy ground. Steam blasted from his nostrils. In over twenty major battles and thrice as many skirmishes, Blake had not once been injured while he rode atop Reliance.

Sensing the upcoming battle, horses pawed the ground and snorted while men muttered prayers. Officers bellowed commands. Cannons fired, shaking the ground. Smoke filled the air. Blake drew his sword, leveled it before him, and gave the order to charge.

If there was a hell, it surfaced on that field near Richmond, Virginia, on that cold October day in 1864. A barrage of smoke and fire and terrifying screams surrounded Blake. He slashed his way through the enemy ranks, dispatching Union soldiers left and right. Cannon fire pounded his ears—sent tremors through his body. Sparks from muskets lit up the smoke-filled air like fireflies at dusk. Blake gasped for a breath. Sweat stung his eyes. He swerved Reliance around to check on his men when fire ignited his leg. Reliance let out a pain-filled screech and started to fall. Blake tried to jump from the tumbling beast, but a Yankee soldier thrust a blade into Blake's side. Gripping the wound, he toppled to the ground. Reliance dropped on top of his leg.

Sounds of battle faded into the distance as his own heartbeat thumped in his chest. *Thump, thuuump thuuuump.* The beat slowed, grew dimmer. He was going to die. He could no longer feel his leg. One glance told him that Reliance was dead. Pressing a hand over the blood oozing from his side, Blake turned his head in search of help. The vacant eyes of Henry Swanson stared back at him, a bullet in his forehead.

"No!" Blake screamed, unable to stop the tears flooding his eyes—unable to stop the vision of his brother, Jeremy, lying in a field like this poor lad, dying all alone.

"No! Jeremy! Jeremy!" Blake leaped from his hammock and landed on the deck on all fours. The brig rocked gently beneath his hands. Sweat dripped onto his fingers. He gasped for a breath. An ache rose in his leg. He rubbed it, struggling to rise. The bullet had struck an artery. If not for Reliance's weight upon it, Blake would have bled out on that field.

"Jeremy?" James's groggy voice sifted through the air.

Blake rose and leaned his hands on his legs, gathering his breath and settling his heart. "Go back to sleep." Rubbing grief from his eyes, he pulled on his trousers, tossed a shirt over his head, and left the cabin before James could say another word. Blake didn't feel like talking. He didn't feel like thinking. All he wanted was some peace. Yet before he even made it above, thoughts of Eliza flooded his mind. After a nightmare like the one he'd just had, he would expect to feel nothing but fury toward her, yet all he found was an affection that, if she returned, promised to soothe away his bad dreams forever.

He'd been avoiding her for just that reason. After the incident with the birds and the tender moments they'd shared in the sick bay, Blake's mind and heart had taken up arms and once again engaged in a fierce battle on the field of confusion. The worst of it was they often switched sides. One minute his mind wanted her to stay, but his heart demanded justice for his family. The next, his heart ached to be with her, but his mind refused entrance to a Yankee. At one point, the fighting became so intense, Blake believed he was going mad. Still, he had no idea what to do. But he did know one thing. Every day he spent on this brig, watching her care for everyone and forgive everyone who'd wanted her dead, both his heart and mind seemed ready to forfeit the battle.

He climbed on deck to a gentle night breeze and the smell of salt and damp wood. Scents he'd grown quite fond of these past months. A muffled squeal brought his gaze toward the foredeck. He peered into the darkness, but nothing seemed out of the ordinary. *Thump. Groan.* Blake limped toward the sound.

A woman's moan made him charge around the capstan. "Who's there?"

A bulky shadow spun around. Lantern light reflected off the blade of a knife. "None of yer business, Colonel." Max spit to the side.

"Blake." The voice emerged as a pleading squeak, barely audible above the rush of the sea, but it grabbed his heart and wouldn't let go.

The brig shifted and moonlight shimmered over maple-colored hair. *Eliza.*

Fury tightened every nerve, every muscle within Blake. "What is the meaning of this?"

"Run along, now, Colonel." Max pointed the knife at Blake. "The Yankee strumpet's gettin' what's comin' to her, that's all."

Blake studied the lecherous fool, weighing his choices. He could reason with the man, threaten to tell the captain, and have him locked below. Or. . .

With lightning speed, he clutched Max's wrist and tightened his grip like a vise. Surprise turned to anger and then fear and finally pain in the sailor's eyes. Blake squeezed harder, feeling the crack of bone.

Max released the knife. It clanked to the deck by Blake's bare feet. Before Max could react, Blake slammed a fist across his jaw then slugged him in the gut. The sailor bent over with a groan. One final pounding of Blake's fists on Max's back sent him toppling to the deck.

Eliza stepped into the light. A cascade of hair tumbled around a pale face and trembling lips. Her gaze took in Max lying on the deck then shifted to Blake as if she didn't believe he was real.

"Are you all right, Eliza? Did he hurt you?" Blake reached for her. She hesitated. Not waiting for her to respond, Blake gathered her in his arms.

∽⊶✧⊷∾

Eliza sat on the cot in the sick bay, already missing the feel of Blake's arms around her. Like steel bands of armor, they did much to assuage her trembling. A trembling that still racked her body.

Sitting on a chair beside her, he handed her a glass of stale water. The mug quivered in her hand, spilling water over the side. He cupped his hands around hers and helped her take a sip. That was when Eliza knew she must be dreaming. The tender way he held her hands, the lines of concern furrowing his brow, the look of adoration in his eyes. Yes, she was surely dreaming. No man who had ignored her for nearly two weeks would be looking at her like that. "Thank you."

Setting down the cup, he eased strands of hair from her face. His eyes widened, and horror claimed his expression. "You're cut."

"I am?" Eliza pressed fingers over her neck. She touched something warm and wet. And painful.

Blake headed for the side table, returning in a moment with a damp cloth.

"Here, let me." He tugged her hand away and dabbed the wound, his warm breath filling the air between them.

"I didn't feel the knife."

"You were in shock."

In truth, she felt like she still was.

She reached up to stop him. "No need to do that."

"Let me care for you. Lord knows you've tended to me enough times." His commanding tone stopped her from further complaints. It had been a long time since someone had cared for her.

After he cleaned and bandaged her wound, he retrieved a blanket from a drawer and flung it over her shoulders. Her breath heightened as memories of the attack assailed her. "Thank God you came when you did."

Blake's jaw knotted. He leaned forward, elbows on his knees, and gave her a look of reprimand. "What were you doing on deck alone at night?"

She lowered her gaze. "I couldn't sleep."

"Couldn't sl—" He stood and took up a pace. "There are still those on board who wish you harm."

Eliza kept silent—both elated and confused at his display of emotion on her behalf. "Why should you care?"

He halted and studied her. "I do not wish you harm, Mrs. Watts."

"Then stop calling me that. It hurts me every time you do."

He huffed. "Would you prefer, Mrs. *Crawford*?"

Ah, there was the bitterness she'd come to expect. Eliza drew a shuddering breath.

He knelt beside her. "Forgive me, Eliza. You're trembling." Thick, rough fingers swallowed her hands. His eyes never left hers, searching, caressing her with his gaze. "You've been so kind to everyone on board, even those who have been cruel to you. Why?"

"God commands us to love our enemies." At least that was one thing in which she'd been obedient. "Besides, I truly do care for them."

"I've never met anyone with such a kind heart."

"Have a care, Colonel." She gave him a coy smile. "You speak blasphemy of a Yankee."

His eyes twinkled in amusement.

An uncontrollable shudder waved through her. No doubt mistaking it for fear, he drew her close, encasing her in the shield of his arms. "You're safe now."

The words dissolved in her heart like honey in tea, erasing all the pain, the rejection of the past months. She began to sob.

Nudging her back, he wiped tears from her cheeks with his thumbs—hard and calloused but they felt so wonderful against her skin. His gray eyes swirled like gentle storm clouds, not churning in their usual tempest. He cupped her face in his hands, his gaze shifting between hers. His chest rose and fell. His masculine scent filled her lungs. He brushed his thumb over her lips and licked his own. Eliza's breath caught in her throat. He was going to kiss her.

CHAPTER 29

Blake's lips met hers.

Eliza's heart sputtered like the flame of a candle, flooding her belly with heat. He caressed her cheeks with his fingers. His lips brushed over hers as if afraid to land.

"Eliza, sweet Eliza."

His mouth melded with hers. He tasted of salt and man. Meaty arms swaddled her with protection and strength.

Eliza submitted, allowing him to kiss her fully, all caution, all sense, tossed overboard. How could she do anything else? She'd never been kissed with such need, such urgency, such tender yearning. Such love. She never wanted this moment to end.

❦

The kiss was like none Blake had ever experienced. His body reacted. His mind spun with delight. He felt Eliza's hunger, her affection in every touch of her lips across his. Pressing her close, he relished the way her curves molded against him.

But no. He withdrew. Passion glazed her eyes. She moved to kiss him again. Grabbing her arms, he pushed her back.

"Blake." His name emerged breathless on her lips. "If that is the kiss of an enemy, then I fear I am captured."

He chuckled. The woman never ceased to amaze him. Pulling her close, he pressed her head against his shoulder and ran his fingers through her hair. "It is I who am defeated." Something he should have accepted a month ago.

She peered up at him with a trust he did not deserve. "I do not wish to defeat you, not ever."

"Shhh now, get some rest. We'll discuss terms of surrender in the morning."

She released a heavy sigh and snuggled against him. It took every ounce of his remaining strength to resist the soft morsel in his arms, but thankfully, she fell asleep within minutes. Easing her down onto the cot, he covered her with a blanket and slipped from the room before he tarnished her reputation forever.

Four hours later, as dawn broke in an array of glorious color, Blake stood at the bow of the brig, watching a school of dolphins play tag with the *New Hope. New Hope*, indeed. For the first time in weeks, he felt new hope springing within him. Not only because they were to arrive in Rio within a few days, but because he'd made up his mind about Mrs. Watts—Eliza.

Shame pinched him. He shouldn't have kissed her without an understanding between them. He shouldn't have kissed her at all! But she had been so sweet, so frightened, so trusting, he'd been unable to resist. He'd gotten caught up in the moment, severing the string between his heart and mind. Sighing, he raked a hand through his hair. Now that he *had* kissed her, what was he to do? Could he truly consider a courtship with a woman whose husband had killed his countrymen?

Moving to the starboard railing, he crossed his arms over his chest and gazed at the Brazilian landscape as the sun lured sand and trees out from hiding. Coconut groves and plantains popped into existence, shading lazy fishing villages—all set against a background of ominous blue mountains.

"Have you ever seen a more beautiful morning?" James appeared beside him, faced the opposite direction, and lifted a hand toward the rising sun. "With water as smooth as glass, the sun rises upon its glorious throne, trailing robes of crimson and gold." He smiled.

"Doctor, preacher, and now poet as well. Is there no end to your talents?" Blake said.

Splashes drew their gazes to dolphins and bonitos playing in the foam coming off the bow.

"Aha, a good sign! Dolphins leading us straight to Rio's harbor." James rubbed the back of his neck. "Though, I must say, if it's already this warm, I fear we are in for a searing afternoon."

"Get used to it, my friend. I hear it's even more scorching on land."

"You'll get no complaints from me. Reminds me of Tennessee summers."

Blake had heard that Brazil mimicked their familiar Southern climate, minus the cold winters, of course. He hoped that would aid the colonists in acclimating to the new land, for they would have problems enough just surviving. But he wouldn't think of that now. For now he would enjoy the panorama of green lowlands passing by the brig as hundreds of small gulls whirled above a forest of palm trees. If all of Brazil was this beautiful and lush, their new home would be a paradise, indeed.

James's yawn reminded Blake of his nightmare. "Sorry to wake you last night. And all the other nights." He gave a sheepish grin.

"Don't trouble yourself over it." James spun around and gripped the railing. The lines at the corners of his eyes grew taut as he gazed at the sea. "It was another dream about your brother? Jeremy, was it?"

Blake nodded. "Killed at Antietam."

"I was at that battle."

Blake snapped his gaze to James as agony weighed down his heart. Surely the doctor wouldn't have crossed paths with Jeremy. And yet hope surged within him, hope for any tiny morsel about his last moments on this earth. "Private Jeremy Wallace of the 7th Georgia Infantry. He died on the battlefield." The brig pitched over a wave, shifting his brother's ever-present belt plate in Blake's pocket. Pulling it out, he ran fingers over the initials, *JSW*, picturing his brother standing in the parlor of their Atlanta home, dressed in his fresh uniform, excitement bursting from his brown eyes. He'd looked far too young to be dressed like a soldier. Far too young to be heading into rising hostilities that would become war. Hadn't it just been a year earlier that he'd roamed the city streets playing pranks on the neighbors and flirting with pretty girls? Blake's mother had cried. His father had embraced the young lad with pride. And Blake had felt sick to his stomach. None of them ever saw him again.

"I'm sorry," James said. "Is that his?"

"All I have left of him." Blake slipped it back into his pocket as shame burned a hole in his heart. How could he have tossed his brother's memory aside so flippantly, defiled it so vehemently, by kissing Eliza? Or had he? Perhaps her brief marriage to Stanton did not make her a traitor at all. Ugh, the confusion was driving him mad! But he did know one thing. He would not kiss her again until he was sure they had a future. Until he was sure a relationship with her would not betray everything he held dear.

"I tended some of the wounded after the battle. Perhaps I came across him." James loosened his necktie, as if the memory of that day stole his breath.

"I doubt it. He was sliced through by a Union officer on the field after the battle was done, or so I was told." Blake clenched his fists until they ached. "For a pocket watch."

James froze. His mouth hung open.

"What is it?" Blake asked.

"Nothing."

"You remember something."

James snapped his gaze toward the mainland as pain tightened the corners of his mouth. His long silence threatened to unravel Blake's carefully wound control.

"It was a horrible battle," the doctor finally said, rubbing his eyes. "We lost thousands that day. I don't remember specific soldiers. Though I do recall that many of our wounded were finished off by Union troops scouring for treasure."

Blake huffed his frustration. "Brutal savages."

"We were no better." James rubbed the scar on his cheek.

Perhaps. Blake drew a deep breath of morning air, hoping to sweep away the foul memories. Slapping his palms on the railing, he lifted his face to the breeze. "Let's talk of brighter things, shall we? Like arriving at our new home soon."

"Hard to believe we are almost there."

"Especially with all the bad fortune that has come our way." Voices brought Blake's gaze to a few passengers emerging from below. On the foredeck, Mr. Graves stared at Brazil, rubbing something between his fingers. When had he come above?

"I'd say." James chuckled. "Chased and boarded by a Union frigate, nearly sunk in that horrendous storm, the strange illness, the rigging splitting and injuring the first mate."

"The fire," Blake added.

"Parson Bailey stealing our money." James shook his head.

"And that baffling bird attack."

James stretched his shoulders and sighed. "It almost seems like someone or something is trying to keep us from our destination."

Blake's gaze unavoidably swept once again to Mr. Graves. "Yet they have not succeeded, have they?"

James cocked a brow, a twinkle in his eye. "We aren't at Rio yet."

Eliza woke to the smell of Blake on her skin and the memory of his lips on hers. She smiled and stretched her hands above her head. What a wonderful, incredible night. Well, all except Max's attack. But even that had brought Blake to her rescue and lowered the shield around his heart. She only hoped it remained lowered and didn't lift again with the rising of the sun. Swinging her legs over the cot, all the sweet sounds she'd grown to love cascaded over her: the thumping of feet above, the creak and groan of the ship, the purl of water against the hull, the shouts of sailors. She listened for one particular voice, the one that sent her heart crashing against her chest. There it was. That commanding, confident shout calling for everyone's attention.

Rising, she examined the scratch on her neck in the mirror and did her best to pin up her hair and smooth the wrinkles from her gown before heading above. From Blake's tone, whatever he wished to tell the passengers sounded important.

Weaving through the mob amassing on deck, Eliza spotted Sarah, Lydia in her arms, standing beside Angeline. Thank goodness Angeline seemed to have recovered from her leap into the sea nearly two weeks ago, though she still refused to discuss the reason she'd wanted to end her life.

Now as she looped her arm through Eliza's, she leaned toward her and whispered, "Where were you last night?"

"I slept in the sick bay." At Sarah's concerned look, Eliza added. "I'll tell you both later."

"Your attention, please." Blake's voice drew all gazes toward him as he stood on the quarterdeck beside the captain. Since she'd seen him last, he'd shaved and donned a proper vest over his shirt, a necktie, and a pair of tall, leather cavalry boots. Eliza thought him the handsomest man in the world.

A breeze tore at her hair, cooling the perspiration forming on her brow, and flapping the sails overhead. The ship rose on a swell, and everyone braced their feet against the canting deck.

"I'd like to take a vote on a rather important question." Blake's tone carried a hint of nervousness. "It concerns Mrs. Crawford." His gaze sought hers and remained there for several seconds as if no one else existed on board the ship. The remembrance of their kiss sent heat flushing through her. She tried to ignore the lingering sensation and focus on the matter at hand, hoping beyond hope that the vote he spoke about had to do with her future on this venture. As if confirming her thoughts, he smiled, and her heart felt as though it were pounding a hole in her chest.

"What about her?" someone yelled, jerking Blake's gaze from her.

He drew a deep breath. "I believe the lady has more than proven how valuable she is to our group. In fact, she has been nothing but kind to all of you, even those who would have abandoned her on Dominica."

Eliza's heart beat even faster.

"Aye, she healed my earache," one man shouted.

"And she delivered my baby," Sarah added.

"And stitched up my cut," a sailor said.

Affirmations of all she'd done flipped into the air like huzzahs after a victory until the captain finally called for silence.

"I realize she married a Yankee officer," Blake continued. "But she is still a true-blooded Southern lady. And let's face it, we have all made mistakes."

Nods of affirmation bobbed through the group.

"Raise your hand if you agree to allow Mrs. Crawford—Eliza—to continue with us."

Eliza couldn't believe her ears. She wanted to rush into Blake's arms and shower him with kisses. Instead, she gripped Angeline's and Sarah's hands and said a silent prayer.

Arms went up all across the deck.

Eliza closed her eyes, afraid to count them, afraid they weren't the majority. Seconds passed like hours. The roar of the sea pounded in her ears. The rumble of sails thrummed on her heart. She squeezed her friends' hands as a trickle of perspiration made its way down her back.

Finally, Blake's voice boomed over the ship. "It's settled then. Eliza stays."

Groans and grunts from those who disagreed buffeted her ears—and her heart—like pistol shots. Yet when she opened her eyes, she found Blake gazing at her once again. The intensity of his look weakened her knees and opened her heart to the possibility that maybe dreams did come true.

Sarah and Angeline squealed in delight and tugged on her arms, dragging her gaze from Blake's. Batting a wayward tear, she hugged them both and allowed herself a moment of bittersweet victory.

Bittersweet because there were still many who wanted nothing to do with her. Mr. Dodd among them, as he snapped his pocket watch shut, gave her a snide look, and strolled away.

Some of the passengers crowded around, offering their congratulations. The Scotts raised their noses and dropped below, while Magnolia gave Eliza a sincere hug. Even Mr. Graves offered his best wishes, though from his tone and demeanor she couldn't be sure that was a good thing. From across the deck, James nodded and smiled. Hayden approached and placed a gentlemanly kiss on her hand and then gave her a mischievous wink that no doubt had charmed a thousand women. A thousand and one from the look on Magnolia's face.

However, a dozen or so people scattered away, scowling at her as if she were the devil himself. How could she settle into a new colony when so many still hated her?

When the crowd dissipated, Moses and Delia, children in tow, approached Eliza, beaming smiles on their faces. "We's so glad you can come wid us."

Mariah, Delia's youngest girl, dashed toward Eliza. Horrified, Delia tried to extricate her daughter from Eliza's skirts, apologizing profusely and cowering as if she expected to be chastised. But Eliza knelt to take Mariah in her arms. "No need to apologize, Delia. I love children." Though Eliza's father would probably die on the spot if he saw her embracing a black child. Surprise dashed across Delia's eyes before she smiled and took young Mariah from Eliza's arms.

The family soon left, and Eliza turned to see Blake standing a short distance away, watching her with interest. "No need to try and impress me further with your extraordinary kindness, Eliza," he said as he approached. "I said you could stay." His grin was sly and charming.

She gazed up at him, her body temperature rising with each step he took toward her. "I don't know how to thank you, Blake. I. . .I. . ."

He placed a finger on her lips. Her pulse raced. "No need," he said, offering her his arm. "It was the right thing to do."

Slipping her hand into the crook of his elbow, Eliza allowed him to lead her to the railing. "And is that the *only* reason you took a vote?" Her tone was teasing. But instead of bolstering her hopes with an amorous response, his silence pounded them into dust. Those stubborn lines on his forehead appeared again. Which meant he was either frustrated or confused.

"About those terms of surrender, Colonel?" She made another attempt to revive the Blake that had made an appearance in sick bay the night before. But he remained hidden beneath a somber exterior.

Leaning one arm on the railing, he faced her. "Eliza, I want to apologize for kissing you. It was wrong of me to take advantage of your frightened condition."

A stone sank in Eliza's stomach. "I wasn't frightened. Well, not then. And you didn't take advantage of me. I wanted to kiss you. I know that is improper of me to say and you must think me far too forward, but it's the truth, nonetheless."

A hint of a smile touched his lips then faded. "Still, I promise you it will not happen again."

"Colonel!" Captain Barclay bellowed from the quarterdeck. "A moment, if you please."

Without another word, Blake excused himself and left. A chill settled on Eliza in his absence. Facing the sea, she pounded her fists on the railing.

What a fool she'd been! Blake didn't love her. The kiss had meant nothing to him. Eliza was no innocent. She understood men. The passion she'd felt in his kiss was just that. Passion. Physical passion in a moment of weakness. If not, he would have made his intentions clear. He would have professed his love to her, asked to court her. Instead, his contrite tone gave her no room for hope. All the blood drained from her heart. Bowing her head, she fought to keep tears from her eyes.

She loved Blake. She loved him so much it hurt. And she knew one thing. It would be impossible to live side by side with him, see him and talk to him every day, perhaps even watch him love another, and know she would never be his.

CHAPTER 30

Anticipation crackled across the ship. It sizzled in every creak and moan of wood, every thunder of sail, every dash of water against the hull. It buzzed in the excited murmurs of the passengers as they stood at the railing in breathless anticipation of their first glimpse of Rio de Janeiro.

Pressed between Sarah and Angeline, Eliza stood among the excited throng, most of whom had been awakened by Captain Barclay's shouts announcing their soon arrival. How the man knew they were so close, Eliza had no idea. The passing vista was much of the same glistening white beaches and luxuriant greenery they'd been seeing for days.

At the bow, Mr. Dodd kept rubbing his hands together and pacing back and forth, shifting his gaze over the mainland. Did he actually believe he would simply set foot on land and forthwith find the illusive pirate treasure? If it even existed. Eliza smiled and glanced at Mrs. Scott, sitting atop a barrel, an expression of abject misery twisting her face as Mable fanned her profusely. Mr. Scott stood by her side, not a speck of enthusiasm peeking from behind his austere expression, while Magnolia leaned against the foremast, looking more bored than usual. That was, until Hayden sauntered by and gave her a roguish grin before tipping his hat at her parents and joining James at the railing. Magnolia's gaze followed him, a pout on her lips and her creamy skin pinking, making Eliza wonder what, if anything, had happened between them.

Moses, Delia, and her children stood on the other side of the ship, but Moses' gaze was on poor Mable, whose arms must surely be aching from so much fanning. The children's gazes, however, were on little Henrietta Jenkins and two other youngsters playing a game of cup and ball on the main deck. A few feet beyond the young ones,

Mr. Lewis sat atop the capstan, face down and hunched over, most likely from overindulgence in alcohol last night. The man must have brought along his own stash, since the ship's meager supply was dwindling fast. And at his usual spot at the larboard railing, Mr. Graves stood apart from the others, dressed in black from head to toe, with an equally dark aura hovering around him. Thank goodness Max was nowhere in sight. Locked below, Eliza had heard, by the Captain's orders after Blake told him what the man had done.

Lydia's gurgles brought Eliza's attention back to Sarah, who adjusted the baby's blanket to cover her eyes from the sun. Dabbing the perspiration forming on her neck, Eliza wondered how the child endured a blanket in this heat. Yet she seemed quite content as she smiled at her mother and reached for the shiny cross hanging around her neck. The love sparkling in the child's eyes brought back memories of Eliza's own mother. She felt the loss in the pit of her stomach. How different her life would have been if her mother hadn't died of fever when Eliza was only twelve. Most likely, Eliza never would have married Stanton, nor would she be on this voyage. Nor would she have met Blake. And while his commanding voice continually bounced over the deck, causing her heart to skip a beat with each deep intonation, she almost wished she *had* never met him. She hadn't spoken to him since he'd apologized for their kiss and dashed off to attend his duties yesterday. And she wasn't altogether sure she wished to speak to him. As painful as it was, she knew now what she had to do. There was no other option.

Straightening her shoulders to give an appearance of an inner strength she didn't feel, she stared at the passing web of greenery. Water the color of emeralds caressed golden sands leading to patches of foliage interspersed with tall cliffs and boulders that seemed to grow out of nowhere.

Something moved in the jungle. At first Eliza thought it must be an animal, but then the rustling leaves parted and a person emerged onto the beach. A man dressed in Union blues. His gaze locked on Eliza's. Her blood ran cold. She rubbed her eyes then peered at the spot again. Alarm sped through her. It couldn't be. *Stanton?* It was Stanton! She'd know him anywhere. His thick brown beard. The way he clasped his hands behind his back. The gold winking at her in the sun from his shoulder straps. She closed her eyes again and shook her head, trying to dislodge the vision. Her breath cluttered in her throat, nearly suffocating her. When she opened them again, he was gone.

"Did you see him?" Eliza asked her friends, hearing the quiver in her voice.

"See who?" Following the tip of Eliza's pointed finger, Angeline stared at the passing spot.

"I don't know. I saw someone in the trees. A soldier. A Union soldier." Eliza threw a hand to her throat.

"Impossible." Sarah laid a hand on Eliza's arm. "Oh, my dear. You've gone pale. I'm sure it was an animal of some sort. Do you wish to sit down?"

"No." Eliza tried to settle her heart. "Thank you. I am sure you are right." Her attempted smile felt tight on her lips. She was going mad. There was no other explanation. Stanton was dead. She'd seen his dead body lying in a casket. Of course he wasn't standing on a beach in Brazil. In the agony of her recent decision, her mind must've conjured him up—to torture her for all her bad choices. That was all. *Lord, how many times must I repent? When am I to be free of the guilt?* She lowered her chin and stared into the foam swirling and crashing off the hull.

"There she is!" Captain Barclay shouted. "Sugar Loaf. You can't miss her!"

All eyes shot off the bow where a black mass jutted toward the sky. The excitement rippling through Eliza erased all memory of Stanton. Men returned to their posts, everyone "oohing" and "ahhing" at the gorgeous view. Beyond Sugar Loaf, mountain ranges appeared through the morning mist, their rounded summits covered with verdure and tropical forest, while the faint outline of a much larger range loomed in the distance, rising above a heavy belt of snow-white clouds.

Eliza felt Blake's overpowering presence behind her long before he spoke.

Overpowering, thrilling, and. . .unsettling.

"Sugar Loaf is a huge slab of black granite, ladies," he began. "Towering over us by some thirteen hundred feet. Isn't she magnificent?"

"Indeed, she is." Angeline craned her neck as the monstrosity rose before them. "See how the sunlight washes her in purple."

Shielding her eyes from the reflection, Eliza admired the beauty as Blake swept his hand toward the mountains surrounding the bay.

"The square tower of the Gavia, the crested Corcovado, the pinnacle of Tijuca. All the familiar mountain faces which stand like sentinels looking down upon the loveliest expanse of water in the world. The bay of Rio de Janeiro."

Eliza had never heard such excitement in his voice. "How do you know their names?"

"I've been studying Brazil for months. Ever since I first decided to gather a group of colonists to come here."

Captain Barclay shouted orders to lower sail and set course toward a fort perched on a large rock in front of Sugar Loaf. The Fort of St. Cruz, Blake informed them. Uniformed men scurried from the gate to spread across the front of the large building. One of them raised a speaking cone to his mouth and uttered a string of words in a language unknown to Eliza. Yet Captain Barclay seemed to understand fully as he replied through his own cone.

"What are they saying, Colonel?" Sarah asked.

"I have no idea, though I imagine they are asking who we are and where we are from."

Eliza raised a brow at him. "You mean to say you didn't learn Portuguese as well?"

His grin sent her heart racing again, and she faced forward. Perhaps it was better not to look at the man.

Finally, the signal for them to pass was given, and the *New Hope* skated into the bay. Like jagged teeth, the surrounding coast jutted into the water, forming innumerable smaller lagoons. Charming islets dotted the bay, their borders filled with orange and banana trees, the lush greenery interrupted only by small villas. A sky of the most superb blue spanned overheard while myriad kingfishers dove beneath the water, only to emerge seconds later with fish in their beaks. Catamarans and fishing boats, as well as a few larger ships drifted over the aquamarine water, which was as calm as a lake. Rio de Janeiro itself extended from the bay upward. Several hills sat in its midst, layered in small houses, while in the valleys, countless fine homes, churches, and public buildings sprawled out in all directions. Beyond the city loomed a lofty chain of mountains, their peaks lost in the mist.

Aside from a few gasps and murmurs, most of the passengers stood in stunned awe of the beauty before them. But Eliza felt only sorrow.

Though she should be happy to at least witness such an exotic place, her insides grieved already at the loss. She had made her decision.

Excusing himself, Blake went to assist the crew in lowering sails and anchoring the ship. A small boat soon arrived carrying the port physician, or so the lithe, dark-skinned man claimed to be. After inquiring whether anyone on board was sick and casting a cursory glance over the passengers, he told the captain to wait for the customs house boat and promptly left, dabbing the perspiration on his neck with his handkerchief.

And wait they did. For an hour. The rising heat soon leeched all enthusiasm from the passengers and crew. Some went below. Others sought out shade on the deck, while still others endured the heat at the railing, unable to pull away from the splendid view of the city.

"I cannot believe we are finally here," Angeline said, her tone a mixture of excitement and sorrow. A breeze flirted with her copper curls, and Eliza's heart went out to the lady. She wished she could stay and help her with whatever troubled her, but that was not possible. She would, however, entrust her to Sarah's capable care. And of course Eliza would pray for her daily. For all these people she'd come to love.

Finally, the dockmaster arrived—a short man with a corpulent belly and a wide straw hat. He leaped on board from a small boat rowed out by Negroes, who were stripped to the waist, their ebony skin shimmering in the sun. After inspecting the hold, he, Captain Barclay, the first mate, James, and Blake disappeared into the captain's cabin for what seemed an eternity. An eternity in which the sun became even more oppressive, boiling the pitch out of the deck seams and extracting an equal amount of sweat from each passenger. Eliza went below to gather a few things to go ashore but found her cabin akin to an oven and quickly returned to the breezes above.

Since they were only to stay in Rio a short while before they set sail for their new land, Eliza saw no reason not to join the others ashore. It would give her time to explain her decision to her friends. To Blake. Besides, she longed to set foot on dry land again and to see more of this wondrous city.

Soon the men emerged from the captain's cabin. And after shaking hands, the dockmaster whistled to a group of men waiting at the docks alongside boats, sending them leaping to task and rowing out to retrieve the passengers. Within an hour, Eliza, along with Angeline, Sarah, and several other passengers bumped against the wharf pilings and were assisted onto land by several Negroes, who seemed none too inhibited to stare straight into Eliza's eyes. Other people, some white, some black, and some in all shades in between came to greet them. The men wore white trousers, broadcloth frock coats, and black silk hats, while the women, all with black hair and fine eyes, wore brightly colored skirts and blouses. And all of them strode about barefooted. They chattered in Portuguese and other languages Eliza couldn't place and extended hands to shake in greeting and fingers to stroke the newcomers' arms and clothing.

Unsure of the proper response and uncomfortable with their familiar touches, Eliza thanked them, grabbed her valise, and hobbled down the dock toward dry land, not used to walking on the unshifting surface. She planted her foot on the sandy soil, raised her face to the sun, and drew a deep breath of tropical air. She was in Brazil. The land of new beginnings.

Unfortunately, those new beginnings were not for her.

❦

Hefting a duffel bag over his shoulder, Blake headed down the cobblestone street, wishing more than anything he could spend time with Eliza alone. Was it his imagination, or had she been avoiding him since the vote yesterday morning? Even today she seemed aloof, reserved. He couldn't imagine why. He thought she'd be thrilled to stay with the colonists—with him. Or at the very least, more appreciative. But perhaps he hadn't given her enough time for the good news to settle firmly in her mind. Then with the dock mate's arrival, he'd been too busy with paperwork to seek her out. And now there were far too many citizens and workers crowding the streets and threading through the throng, all gawking at the newcomers.

Negroes and mulattoes—men, women, and children of every shade, from the deepest black to the palest white—carried sugarcane, bananas, oranges, and other fruits and vegetables in huge baskets across their backs, and they thought nothing of bumping into others as they went along.

The smell of fish, sweat, and waste pricked Blake's nose. He coughed, and his legs wobbled. James gripped his arm. "Steady there, mate. After being on the brig for nearly two months, it will take awhile to get our land legs again. I can hardly walk a straight line myself."

Blake thanked him and ran a sleeve over his forehead. "That isn't the only thing that will take some getting used to. This heat is unbearable."

James glanced across the sky, which was devoid of clouds save for a dark patch on the horizon. "It's still early in the afternoon. No doubt it will cool down later."

"It's not so much the heat as the humidity." Blake leaped out of the way of a mule-drawn cart.

"Humidity or not, I'll be glad to sleep in a bed tonight," Hayden said from Blake's other side.

"Let us pray this immigrants' hotel has enough beds for us all." Though Blake would be surprised if that were the case. The lodging was, after all, provided by the Brazilian government at no expense to the colonists until they signed all necessary papers and were deeded their new land.

"I doubt we'll have anything but a straw tick." James chuckled and rubbed his neck.

"Ah, come now." Blake smiled. "The city seems quite civilized to me." At least more civilized than he'd expected. He scanned the narrow street. Houses on either side sported brightly colored stucco and red-tiled roofs. Inhabitants sat on glassless window ledges while others peered around the corners at them. Gardens filled with colorful trellises and gilded, flower-strewn screens surrounded each building.

"See, look." Blake pointed to a line of tramcars clacking over a track. "They even have a tramway."

"But these roads are a disgrace." Hayden squeezed between a passing wagon and the front of a house as thunder rumbled in the distance.

"My biggest concern"—Blake felt his jaw tighten—"is being able to convince the Brazilian immigration authorities to lend us money for land and supplies. At least until we can bring our first crops to market."

"Thank God we still have some farm implements and seed left," James said.

"But not enough," Hayden added. "Do you think they'll be generous? From the notices I read, it seemed they really wanted us here."

"I hope so." Blake ran a hand over his forehead with a sigh. "I've heard nothing but how benevolent the Brazilian government is. Now that we *are* here, let's pray they see us as a worthwhile investment."

James smiled. "Pray?"

"Figure of speech." Blake snorted. "You pray. I'll hope."

"Peixe! Camaroes!" The cries brought Blake's gaze to Chinamen standing beside open carts filled with fresh fish and prawns. Beside them every imaginable fruit bounded from baskets lining thatched stands: bananas, mangoes, watermelons, pineapples, lemons, pears, and pomegranates. The sweet smell permeated the air, and Blake licked his lips. He hadn't had fresh fruit in weeks. Other peddlers, bearing long bamboo poles over their shoulders with huge baskets filled with fruits and vegetables, wove through the mob with an ease that belied the enormous weight they carried. Hawkers conveyed clothing and jewelry in brightly painted trunks strapped to their backs. Naked children by their side, Negresses, wearing turbans, squatted on mats, selling fruit and vegetables. And in the midst of all the chaos, tiny monkeys and parrots of every color and plume squawked and chattered and flitted from stand to stand.

Blake couldn't help but glance repeatedly behind him at the group of women. And in particular, to the luxurious maple-colored head bobbing among the crowd. Surely, with all their petticoats, the heat was getting to them, yet they seemed so enamored with their surroundings, they didn't utter a single complaint. In fact, most of the colonists hobbled along, gazing at everything with wonder, offering no protests about the heat or the long walk, all except the Scotts, who seemed quite miserable, especially once the road began to ascend.

Hayden seemed equally oblivious to the city's charms. In fact, he appeared to be searching for someone—or something—as his gaze stretched down the street.

"I'm surprised you decided to stay with us, Hayden." Blake transferred his duffel bag to his other shoulder.

"I thought I'd investigate what Brazil has to offer. Besides, just like the rest of you, there's nothing for me back home."

The sun disappeared, offering them a reprieve, and Blake looked up to see a mass of dark clouds. Where had they come from? A breeze tore in from the bay, cooling the sweat on his skin.

They turned down Rua de Direita. Fine shade trees lined a broad paved road edged with flagstone shops, restaurants, and stores. Scents of fresh-baked bread, garlic, and oranges swept away the stink of the city. Blake halted and rubbed his sore leg. "This could be any street in America."

"Indeed," James said. "I am quite astonished."

Hayden stretched his neck to see over the crowd. "If you'll excuse me, gentlemen." And without another word, he sped off as if he had a pressing appointment.

"But you won't know where to find us," James called after him.

"I'll find you; don't worry." He shouted over his shoulder before disappearing into the crowd.

As if nature was unhappy with the man's curious departure, thunder cracked the sky and released a violent deluge. One minute, all was dry as a bone. The next, sheets of rain fell on them as if they stood beneath a waterfall. Though some citizens ducked into shops and houses, most of the workers continued onward as if nothing was out of the ordinary.

"Keep going!" Blake shouted to the colonists behind him. "We are almost there!" Yet he could no longer make out their faces through the wall of water. He longed to backtrack and ensure Eliza was well, but he was the only one who knew how to get to the immigrants' hotel. Raising his duffel bag against the rain, Blake plunged forward. Lightning scored the sky. Thunder shook the sodden ground beneath his boots, and within minutes, water flooded the streets and gushed down gullies and alleyways like a raging river. Blake had never seen so much water rise so quickly. It covered his boots and stormed around his ankles, making his feet sink into the mud like anchors. He glanced at James beside him, who, with head down and breath heaving, forged through the torrent as best he could. Then just when Blake thought they might be in danger of being washed away, the rain ceased and the hotel appeared before him.

What he expected was a large shack or a small stucco house at best. What he saw before him was quite the palatial setting. Rain dripped from the eaves of a grand, white, two-story building that would rival any hotel in Charleston. In front, rows of imperial palms lined a walkway that led from the gate to the steps while marble fountains and benches dotted a garden rich with beautiful flowers. Sunlight chased the clouds away, transforming puddles into shimmering pools and sending steam rising on the marble steps. Setting down his duffel, Blake shook the water from his hair and turned to find Eliza.

Clutching Blake's hand, Eliza allowed him to help her up the slick porch stairs. With her legs still wobbling from the sea and the rain making everything slippery, she could imagine tumbling onto the walkway in a heap of stockings and petticoats. His chuckle brought her gaze to his, and she wondered if he was reading her thoughts. Water pooled on his lashes, dripped from the tips of his dark hair, and covered his skin and clothes with a slick sheen that brought a musky smell to her nose. She couldn't help but smile. "You look like a drowned raccoon."

"And you, a beautiful mermaid." He brushed a saturated lock from her cheek. The tender gesture only further befuddled her mind. Oh fiddle, but she would miss him. At the thought, she lowered her gaze.

His finger on her chin brought her eyes back to his. He cocked his head, studying her. "Why the frown? I much prefer your smile."

Laughter emanated from within the hotel as the colonists congregated in the lobby for further instructions. The men who brought up the rear leaped onto the porch, drew off their hats, and slapped them against their legs. After nodding toward her and Blake, they slipped inside.

Eliza swallowed. She might as well get it over with and tell him now. Turning, she gazed over the gardens where sunlight transformed raindrops into diamonds, and then beyond to the odd city with its hilly streets and brightly colored houses. The *drip-drip* of water tapped a nervous cadence on her heart. "I cannot stay, Blake."

His eyebrows collided. "What are you talking about? The vote was in your favor."

"Barely." She bit her lip, still not meeting his gaze. "I came on this voyage to get away from the hatred. At least back home I have a chance to change my name, move somewhere where nobody knows me. Perhaps Kansas."

"They will grow to love you in time. As the rest have." Gray, pleading eyes swung her way.

As you have? She waited for words that never came. "Perhaps." A breeze chilled Eliza's damp gown, and she hugged herself. "Perhaps not." She wouldn't tell him the truth. That it was her love for him that drove her away. Instead, she fought back tears and forced a smile. "Thank you for wanting me to stay. That means more to me than anything."

"Then stay." He grabbed her arms and turned her to face him. "We need you."

But did *he* need her? Want her? She nearly crumpled beneath the pain in his eyes, the desperation—desperation for her as a nurse or for her as a woman? His breath warmed the air between them and filled her with memories of their kiss. She tried to tug from him, but he wouldn't let go. "The doctor can handle things," she said.

"I cannot believe you're giving up so quickly. After all we've been through."

Eliza met his gaze, those stormy eyes filled with angst. "Don't you see it's because of what you've been through, what they've all been through, the pain and loss of the war, that I must leave?" She stared at his necktie and the way the hollow of his throat rose and fell with each breath. "My presence will only be a reminder of your loss."

If only he'd say he forgave her. That he loved her. If only he'd take her in his arms and beg her to stay, she would. For him. Instead, he just stood there, the muscles in his jaw bunching as if engaged in battle. Then releasing her, he took a step back, leaving her cold and shivering.

She faced the yard, which was even blurrier beneath her tears. "After Captain Barclay deposits you on shore near your new home, I intend to sail with him back to America," she finished.

Blake only stared at her in silence. Though she wanted to look at him—to see if there was anything else besides anger in his eyes, she couldn't bring herself to do it. Finally, he spun around, marched into the hotel, and slammed the door behind him.

CHAPTER 31

Blake's newfound joy washed away with the last remnants of rain from the storm. Stubborn, independent woman! After he'd set aside his misgivings about her allegiances, set aside his animosity, his anger. After he'd called for a vote and all but begged her to stay! No doubt she had more Yankee blood in her than she admitted.

The man standing behind a massive mahogany desk stuffed his thumbs into his lapels and shouted over the din in a Southern accent that Blake found comforting. "Ladies and gentlemen! Ladies and gentleman!" Within a few moments, the chattering ceased and all eyes swept his way.

"I am Colonel James Broome, formerly of the 14th Alabama Infantry, and currently manager of this fine establishment. Welcome to Brazil!"

Excitement buzzed through the saturated crowd once again as Blake spotted Eliza slipping through the door to stand in the back. This should be the happiest moment of his life. They had made it to Brazil! Despite all the countless struggles and tragedies, Blake had successfully led these colonists to the promised land. And from the looks of the abundance in town, it was indeed a land flowing with milk and honey.

Then why did his heart feel as though it had been rolled over by a howitzer? Shaking off his grief, he made his way to the front and introduced himself as the expedition leader. Colonel Broome welcomed him adamantly and then began the business of showing the new arrivals to their chambers.

Blake found his room neat and clean, the walls beautifully papered and the ceiling gilded and frescoed. Two iron-framed beds, a washstand,

and a table and chairs—all painted green—bordered the southern wall. After the tight, dirty confines of the brig, Blake felt as though he'd entered a palace. James followed on his heels, throwing his pack onto one of the beds and whistling. "Look at these lavish accommodations. I never would have expected this." The sparkle in his eyes vanished when he looked at Blake's face. "Perchance has the rain soured your mood? We have made it, Blake." He slapped him on the back, the action sending spray over them both.

"Eliza's not staying."

James flinched. "Why not?"

Slipping out of his saturated coat, Blake tossed it on the bed and began unbuttoning his shirt. "Apparently not enough people voted in her favor to suit her."

James walked to the window, his boots squishing over the wooden floor. A breeze ruffled the plain cotton curtains, bringing the scent of flowers and rain-freshened air. "I can't blame her, really. Did you see some of the looks the nays gave her? The Scotts, Mr. Dodd, and those soldiers, Wood and Adams?" He shook his head. "Hard to live so close to people who wish you dead."

Blake tore off his shirt and grabbed a towel from the washstand. "You're supposed to be on my side."

"Which is?" James spun around and struggled to remove his drenched coat.

"For her to stay, of course."

"Stay for you or for her?"

"Why does everything have to be so black-and-white?" Blake sat and tugged off his boots.

"Life is black-and-white. Good and evil. There is no middle ground."

Blake rolled his eyes. Of course there was middle ground—a thousand different shades of gray between black and white. Grays such as killing your fellow American on the battlefield in a nonsensical war, lying to protect a neighbor, stealing to avoid starvation. . .

And courting the enemy that murdered your family.

Standing, he opened his duffel bag and pulled out his best suit. "We need her skills."

James grinned.

Blake shoved his legs into a dry pair of trousers, pulled them to his waist, and sat back on his bed with a sigh.

"It's obvious you adore her." James leaned back on the window ledge. "Yankee husband or not."

Blake stared at his friend but found no mirth, no mockery in his eyes. In fact, he found none within himself. Instead, the words "adore her" settled in a comfortable place in his heart.

"Come now, are you going to deny it?" James arched a brow.

Blake leaned forward on his knees. "Truth is, I can't imagine life without her."

"Then why not ask her to marry you?"

"Marry?" Blake punched to his feet. "Ridiculous notion," he mumbled. Grabbing a shirt, he flung it over his head and fumbled with the buttons—anything to keep his mind off the thought of Eliza as his wife. A thought that was both alarming and thrilling. "Marrying her won't change the way the others feel about her."

"No, but it will change the way *she* feels. The others will come around when she is your wife."

Wife. After the war, Blake had never thought to take a wife. What woman would want a broken shell of a man? Without family, fortune, or name, what did he have to offer a lady?

"If you don't do something soon, it will be too late." James's voice sent turmoil into Blake's already churning gut. "We set sail again tomorrow and will be at our new land by sunset."

Blake tucked in his shirt and reached for his belt.

"Do you love her or not?"

Why didn't the blasted man stop talking? "It's not that simple." Blake eased on his vest and turned to look in the mirror. Yet all he saw staring back at him was a bitter, damaged, used-up ex-colonel whose mind was so tortured from the past, he didn't know what to think anymore.

"It isn't as complicated as you make it, Blake. Come now, you two are made for each other. Anyone can see that." James tugged his wet shirt over his head and tossed it in the corner.

Blake ground his teeth together. But it *was* complicated. More complicated than devising battle plans. More complicated than following orders that sent young boys to their death. More complicated than anything Blake had thus endured.

Even the luxury of a steaming bath had not soothed away the pain in Eliza's heart. Neither had Angeline's noble attempts to cheer her up, nor—once Eliza had told the lady her plans—her vain pleadings for Eliza to remain with the colonists. Not even Stowy balancing on the edge of the porcelain tub and slipping accidentally into the water had lightened Eliza's mood. Though he had looked rather comical with his sopping fur flattened against his lanky body. Why Angeline hadn't left the cat on board the ship, Eliza couldn't guess. Yet when she'd watched the lady gently dry Stowy with a towel and saw the way the cat nuzzled against her and purred, Eliza supposed the two were inseparable.

If only that were true of Eliza and Blake.

Regardless, as Eliza now descended the stairs to the main lobby, she had to admit it felt good to have her skin and hair free of the sticky, salty sheen that had clung to her since she'd boarded the *New Hope*. She wished she could do the same for her gowns, but there'd be no time to wash them here.

The foyer was abuzz with the news that Emperor Dom Pedro intended to visit that afternoon. Several of the colonists sped past Eliza, retreating to their rooms to dress in their finest attire, only to descend within minutes embellished in lace, satin, and beads. Like a flock of colorful parrots, they flitted about the lobby, spilling onto the front porch and stairs, peering down the long drive and chattering excitedly among themselves. As they waited, Eliza gazed at the city from the window, entertaining the idea of perhaps staying in Rio instead of returning to the States, but thoughts of not knowing anyone or the language or culture promptly squashed that plan. Along with the idea of joining another expedition. No doubt another group of colonists would discover her secret just like this one had, and she'd end up in the same position.

Shortly after three o'clock, the royal coach entered the main drive. Everyone clapped in glee as the emperor emerged and ascended the steps. Having never seen a man of such rank before, Eliza stood on tiptoes for a good look at him. Dressed in a plain black suit, with dark hair and a beard streaked with gray, Eliza guessed him to be in his late forties. Stark blue eyes scanned the crowd above a prominent nose. Only a single star on his left breast indicated his royal position. As soon as he entered the building, aides in tow, a shout went up from the crowd. "Viva! Viva! Dom Pedro Segundo!" Hats flew into the air as everyone cheered and celebrated his arrival, offering their thanks to the emperor for taking them in.

Eliza couldn't help but get caught up in the exuberance, if only for a moment. But as soon as she spotted Blake leaning against a doorframe, arms crossed over his chest, staring numbly at the proceedings, Eliza remembered the celebration was not hers.

Blake entered the small room where the leaders of the individual expeditions met briefly with the emperor. Apparently two other groups of colonists were staying at the hotel. One, under the command of an adventurer named Bails, had sailed all the way from Galveston. The other, led by an former naval lieutenant, hailed from Savannah. At the request of one of the emperor's aides, the three men took seats at one end of a long table while the emperor lowered himself into a large ornate chair at the other, two attendants flanking him. An interpreter welcomed them once again. Dom Pedro informed them they could stay in the immigrants' hotel for up to thirty days, during which time food and water would be provided. He also mentioned he would send a band of musicians and a feast to the main gallery that night to help them celebrate their new beginning.

The man's generosity budded hope for Blake's upcoming request, but his mind kept drifting back to what James had said. *Marry her.* At first Blake had thought the idea ludicrous, absurd. Marry a Yankee widow? What would his family think? What would his brother say? What about all the men he'd served beside, those who'd been maimed and disfigured in the war, the men who'd died at the hands of Yankees? Men whose faces still haunted him every night. What would they say?

No. It was ridiculous.

Then why did the idea still float about his thoughts? Prodding him, teasing him—delighting him?

"I am well pleased with the appearance of your people," the emperor's interpreter continued. "My country is here to help you in any way we can."

With that, the leader of Brazil waved them away with a brush of his hand. As the other men exited, Blake approached the emperor with caution, begging a few words of his majesty's time. Twenty minutes later he left the room bearing a much lighter load. True to his word, Dom Pedro, after hearing Blake's sad tale of the loss of their fortune and most of their tools, not only agreed to loan them the money to purchase land, but also to send along donkeys and carts stocked with supplies, as well as a guide to help them acclimate to the Brazilian jungle.

If not for the ache in his heart, Blake would utter a shout of victory—perhaps even thank God for this unexpected blessing. Instead, he wandered onto the porch for some fresh air and found Sarah rocking her baby in a chair. He started to turn, seeking privacy for his thoughts, when her greeting brought him back.

"Exciting day, isn't it, Colonel?" Her knowing eyes assessed him.

He smiled. "Exciting and profitable. I have just procured a loan from the emperor for our land."

"God be praised! That is good news, indeed."

Little Lydia gurgled as if equally pleased.

"Eliza informed me she won't be joining us, after all." Her voice was tinged with sorrow as she gazed at the garden steaming beneath the blazing sun.

"So, I have heard."

"She seems quite distraught."

Blake released a sigh of frustration. The woman would be the death of him yet. "She is welcome to stay if she wishes."

"It must be hard for her to be so hated."

"That, too, is her own doing." Blake cringed at his harsh tone.

Sarah, however, swept eyes as blue and calm as the bay toward him. "Yet you have forgiven her, haven't you, Colonel?"

Blake squirmed and looked away. "For the foolishness of youth in marrying a Yankee? Yes, I suppose."

"It is a good start."

Colorful birds squawked overhead. One landed on the fence post, cocked its head, and stared at them with one curious eye. Blake took a deep breath. There was a smell to the city he couldn't describe. A mixture of sweet, salt, and spice that was rather pleasing. They were indeed in a new land. He faced Sarah, remembering that she had lost her husband in the war. "You had no qualms about befriending Eliza after you discovered her. . .her"—he cleared his throat—"affiliations."

"Of course not. I do not hold my husband's death to her account, or anyone's. That is merely the nature of war. Even if I did, I would forgive her."

"So quickly?" Blake shifted the weight off his sore leg, his ire rising at the woman's ridiculous piety. "And would you forgive the man who pulled the trigger?"

A shadow rolled over her face, and Blake immediately regretted his words.

"My apologies, madam. I'm afraid too much time in the company of soldiers has stolen my manners."

Sincere eyes met his. "Yes, I would forgive him. When God has forgiven me for everything, how can I not forgive others?" Lydia began fussing, and Sarah rose. "Unforgiveness will only make you bitter and sick, Colonel. You came here for freedom, did you not? Then forgive and be free."

⸎

Eliza didn't want to attend the party. Why should she? She wasn't staying in this new land. She had nothing to celebrate. But Angeline and Sarah would not relent with their pleadings, even going so far as to threaten to stay with her in the room and pout all night if she did not attend. Hence, the reason she now descended the stairs between the two aforementioned ladies dressed in her finest, albeit a bit crusty, gown of emerald percale over a bodice of white muslin trimmed in Chantilly lace. Which wasn't nearly as fine as Magnolia's gown of pink silk looped with sprinkles of golden beads. The raving beauty flitted about the guests, flirting with all the young gentlemen from other expeditions as music that sounded very much like a band from back home floated through the room.

Squished between her friends like a petticoat in a clothespress, Eliza followed the crowd into the back gallery, a large magnificent room lit by a hundred candles and overflowing with a profusion of flowers and plants. Along one side of the room stretched a table laden with all sorts of odd-looking food. Chairs and tables framed the rest of the room, surrounding a black-and-white marble floor. Mulattoes and slaves, barefoot and dressed in white trousers and shirts and sporting blue caps, skittered about with drinks on trays. People from the three expeditions filled every crack and crevice, the crescendo of their voices overpowering even the band, which Eliza could now see consisted of three french horns, three drums, a clarinet, and a fife—all played by Negroes.

Eliza hated hotels. She'd practically grown up in a hotel after her mother died, helping her aunt and uncle. In fact, it was at such a gathering at their hotel in Marietta that she'd met Stanton. He was on his way to Atlanta on a military matter and had stopped for the night. She pictured him standing in his brigadier general's uniform with its dark blue tails, its line of gold buttons down the front, and two gleaming shoulder straps. She was only sixteen at the time, and he'd taken her breath away. And even though he'd been speaking to several men who appeared intent on his every word, he'd frozen when she entered the room. In fact, his eyes never left her—though she'd slipped through the crowd, uncomfortable under his scrutiny—until Magnolia had dragged her over for an introduction.

Eliza could remember her feelings even now. Excited, enamored, flattered that a man of his station and reputation would be interested in her.

"I'm starving. Let's see what Brazilian fare is like." Angeline tugged on Eliza's arm, pulling her from the past and dragging her to the oblong table.

"Ladies, I'll join you in a moment," Sarah said, looking very pretty in a red-and-white-striped gown and fringed lacy shawl. "I'm afraid Lydia needs changing again."

A quadrille began, and couples lined the floor as Angeline and Eliza wove through the crowd to examine the feast. Much of the food was familiar: bowls of rice, whole chickens, bananas, guavas, grapes, strawberries, peaches, some sort of cooked pork that omitted a garlicky smell, other indescribable entrees, and coffee and wine aplenty.

"Miss Angeline." Hayden's voice turned them around. In a borrowed suit of black broadcloth—which was a bit short in both sleeve and trouser—clean-shaven with his dark hair tied behind him, he looked nothing like the bleeding stowaway on the deck of the brig two months ago. After giving a gentlemanly bow and proffering his elbow, he raised an eyebrow and asked Angeline to dance. The smile he sent her was dazzling. Angeline shot a questioning look at Eliza, but at Eliza's urging, the two swept onto the dance floor, leaving Eliza to sample the food alone. Or perhaps make her escape back to her room. With just that thought in mind, she turned to see Blake, looking more dashing than ever, making a beeline in her direction.

CHAPTER 32

I hear the *carne seca* is quite good." Blake's presence consumed the space beside her as he pointed to a platter of meat. His eyes, full of sorrow and anger the last time she'd seen him, held a new light. Perhaps he had finally accepted her decision. Still, she had hoped to avoid him tonight, fearing her own heart could not bear the pain. In fact, after his angry exit earlier that day, she wondered why he would speak to her at all.

But none of that seemed to matter now that he stood so close to her— all male and strength. "Carne seca"—she attempted the pronunciation— "what is it?"

"Sun-dried beef."

"And this." He spooned a chunk of what looked like soggy bread from a bowl, placed it on a plate, and handed it to her. "Corn bread soaked in cream and sugar."

"Hmm." Eliza obliged him by taking a bite and was instantly rewarded with a burst of succulent sweetness.

"And this is *biscoito de polvilho*." He pointed toward another dish. "Cakes made from the mandioca root. Very good and nutritious, I'm told."

"And here we have *palmita*." He continued gesturing to different dishes and enlightening her with his knowledge of Brazilian cuisine.

But Eliza wasn't listening anymore. She was so enamored with his lively manner and his presence, she could hardly put two thoughts together. Wearing a single-breasted waistcoat over a white shirt, black trousers, and his usual tall boots, he towered over her by at least a foot. Had he always been this tall? Or perhaps she had shrunk with her recent sorrow. He smelled of soap and shaving balm, and she drew a deep breath of him.

"And this, believe it or not is *tatu*, or armadillos." He chuckled and offered her a smile that reminded her of the days they'd shared before he'd discovered her identity.

She shook her head, trying to dislodge what was surely a fabrication of her desperate heart. "And how do you know all of this?"

"The man who is to be our guide, Thiago Silva Melo"—he gestured to a tall man with a tanned complexion standing by the door—"informed me of each dish when they first set the table." He stared down the line. Plucking a small piece of cake from a platter, he plopped it in his mouth then served her a piece.

Eliza took a bite. Sugar and almonds filled her senses. Their eyes met, his warmly glazed, hers searching for the reason behind his attentions, daring to hope.

"There's a"—he gestured toward her mouth—"a. . ." He brushed her lips with his thumb. "Crumb."

"Oh." Embarrassed, Eliza dabbed a napkin over her mouth still tingling from his touch.

He leaned toward her ear. His breath warmed her neck. "Lucky crumb."

Eliza's heart sped. Her toes tingled. Even as her anger began to simmer. What cruelty was this? Did he wish to torture her into changing her mind about staying? He lengthened his stance. His gray eyes churned like a turbulent sea. He hesitated, opening his lips as if he wished to say something, before flattening them again.

The quadrille ended, and people crowded around them seeking refreshments, but Eliza barely noticed. Blake took her gloved hand in his. "Would you care to dance?"

"No thank you." She didn't want to dance. She wanted to stare into those eyes for as long as she could. She wanted him to keep looking at her as if she were Dodd's lost pirate treasure.

He frowned and glanced across the people lining up for a reel. His fingers loosened on her hand, and for a terrifying moment, she thought he might leave. Her heart braced for the impact. Instead, he tightened his grip. "Perhaps a stroll in the garden?"

Though her insides screamed to run away, to leave, lest her heart suffer a wound beyond repair, she could do nothing but allow him to lead her around the dancers and out the side door. Moonlight dusted the landscape in sparkling silver. Lofty palms swayed above dancing ferns and graceful orchids of every shape and color. Eliza slipped her hand in his elbow as they walked in silence. Lanterns hanging from trees spread snowflake patterns over the grass beneath their feet. Water bubbling from a fountain blended with the fading gaiety coming from the hotel as he led her away from the crowd. She gazed at him, memorizing every detail, every movement, his hobbled gait that was more a march than a casual stroll, the tightness of his jaw, as if he bore all the problems of the entire world, the three lines creasing his forehead, his adorable awkwardness in these social situations. Who would help him when he had one of his episodes? Who would hold him until it had run its course? Who would comfort him?

Sorrow threatened to overwhelm her.

He stopped and faced her, taking both her hands in his. Eliza's pulse raced. He shifted his stance and gazed across the garden.

"Is something wrong?" she asked.

He smiled and released a tiny snort. "I fear I'm not very good at this."

Eliza waited. Her breath retreated back into her lungs.

He kissed her hands then bowed on one knee and gazed up at her.

Eliza's heart stopped beating.

"Will you marry me, Eliza?"

Blake braced himself for her rejection. Aghast, she stared at him, her tiny brows bowing together as if he'd asked her to align herself with the devil. Perhaps he had. What was he thinking? He'd done nothing but show her his disdain most of the voyage. And now, without an explanation, he begged for her hand?

Her breath released in short bursts as if she had trouble breathing. Her eyes searched his, confused and conflicted.

"I'm sorry." Blake rose. "Forget I ever—"

Her lips were on his. She flung her arms around his neck, pulling him near. He lost himself in her taste, in her passion, in the beat of her heart against his. He cupped her face and drank her in, desperate for more of her. His mind reeled at the impossibility. His body thrilled at her response. A little too thrilled at the moment. Withdrawing, he nudged her back, but she snuggled close and leaned her head on his shoulder.

"If you're trying to soften me for your rejection," he said, "please don't stop."

She looked up at him. "Rejection? I never kiss a man out of pity, sir." Her voice was teasing, but then she grew sad and took a step back. "Have you forgiven me for marrying Stanton?"

"Yes." Lifting her hand to his lips, he kissed it. "I'm sorry it took me so long to understand, to let go of my bitterness."

She eased her fingers over his jaw. "You suffered so much. I hated it that my marriage caused you more pain." Then a teasing look claimed her face. "Wait. You're only marrying me for my nursing skills, aren't you?"

He gave her a mischievous grin.

She turned her back to him, her skirts bouncing like lilies on a pond. "I won't be married for charity." Her tone was playful.

Blake stepped toward her, longing to bury his face in her hair. Instead, he leaned and whispered in her ear. "It isn't your nursing skills that captivate me." She smelled of gardenias and jasmine. "Eliza, you are the most. . . You are the most. . . Oh blast it all, you enchant me. I can't imagine my life without you." He slipped his arms around her waist and drew her back against him. "It is I who should worry that your yes is but an act of charity."

"Nonsense." She spun around, her golden eyes shimmering with tears. "I love you, Blake. I have loved you from the first moment you took my hand and welcomed me aboard the *New Hope*."

"My heart was lost then as well." He caressed her cheek. He couldn't believe she loved him! "So, you'll marry me?"

"Yes." She embraced him. "Yes. Yes. Yes!"

Gently, he pushed her back and gripped her shoulders. "Some of the colonists may never accept you. Can you handle that?"

"With you by my side, I can handle anything."

Blake wrapped his arms around her. He felt the same way. Nothing would ever come between them again.

⤖⬥⤙

Eliza woke to the sound of dozens of birds chirping congratulatory tunes outside her window. Joy! Joy everywhere! In her heart, in her spirit, buzzing over her skin, in the sweet tropical air, in the sounds of life filtering through the halls of the immigrants' hotel. She was engaged to Colonel Blake Wallace! Could it be true? Was it only a dream? Yet when she turned and opened her eyes to see Angeline staring at her, she knew from the twinkle in the woman's eyes, it was no dream.

"Good morning, Mrs. Soon-to-Be Eliza Wallace." She smiled. Stowy leaped on Eliza's cot and performed a balancing act up her side and onto her shoulders before nuzzling his face in Eliza's hair.

"Come here, you little beastie." Eliza grabbed the cat and sat up, placing him in her lap. "I can hardly believe it." She touched her lips where Blake had kissed her over and over again in the garden before escorting her back to the party lest people began to talk. There they had announced the news, much to the delight of many and to the horror of some. But Eliza didn't care what people thought anymore. She didn't care about anything but becoming Blake's wife.

Two hours later, after a light breakfast of mangoes, some sort of bread soaked in milk and cinnamon, and the best coffee she'd ever tasted, Eliza joined the *New Hope* colonists as they made the long trek back to the bay, into boats, and back onto the ship that had been their home for the past two months. Aside from a few compliments over breakfast, Blake had been too busy organizing everyone, checking maps, and signing final papers to speak to her. Still his occasional smiles and knowing glances filled with love were enough to warm her inside as much as the rising heat of the day did to her outside.

Once on board she positioned herself at the railing and gazed at the beautiful city, not sure when she'd be back. With God's help, in a few years their new colony would thrive and they would have no need of constant supplies from the city. Their new colony! Eliza held back a shout for joy as Angeline and Sarah joined her. A colony she would now be a part of creating. A new life in a new world. She glanced over her shoulder at Blake and their new Brazilian guide, both men leaning over a map spread atop the capstan. Her heart leaped. A new life with a man she adored.

"He is quite a catch, Eliza. I'm so happy for you," Angeline said.

"He *is* wonderful, isn't he?" Eliza giggled, surprising herself. Giggling was not something she'd done for quite some time.

"Now we have a wedding to plan, ladies." Sarah laid Lydia over her shoulder and patted the infant's back.

"Yes indeed." Mrs. Scott, Magnolia by her side, approached the group. "I've orchestrated many wedding parties before. Of course they were elaborate affairs, and we have nothing to work with here, but we shall make do. We'll need an archway and lots of flowers and some sweet punch and cakes, and of course some of the ladies can stitch a veil from the lace in our old shawls. Oh it will be such fun!" Eliza wondered at the sudden change in the woman. Hadn't she been one of the more vocal *nays*, alongside her husband? Yet weddings had a way of bringing women together, she supposed.

While the lady continued chattering with the other women, Magnolia gave Eliza a sincere smile. "I wish you every happiness, Eliza."

Other ladies soon joined them, all aflutter about plans for a wedding on the beach, going on and on about what a wonderful way it was to start the colony and how it would bring them all good fortune. They continued to prattle, most completely unaware that the ship had struck sails and headed out of the bay to the open sea. Regardless, Eliza couldn't help but relish in the acceptance of a few ladies who heretofore had done nothing but cast her looks of disdain. Perhaps the rest would accept her in time, after all. Soon a stiff breeze drove the women below, leaving Eliza alone.

"You want to stay near to your beau, I suppose." One elderly lady winked at her before joining the others.

Eliza's glance took in said beau—all six feet of steely muscle—assisting Hayden and a sailor as they heaved a line that led above to the sails. She longed to spend time alone with him, talking about their love and their plans for the future, but she knew that despite the first mate's return, the captain had come to depend on Blake. Instead, she would gladly settle for a lifetime with him.

With a huge smile on her face, she turned to gaze out over the azure sea, bubbling in frothy waves as if it held the same excitement she felt within. The wind tore her hair from its pins once again, but she was thankful for its cooling caress after the oppressive heat of land. She wondered if their new home would be as hot as Rio. No matter. She would grow accustomed to it.

Several minutes passed while she gazed at the lush greenery passing by the ship. She felt, rather than heard, Mr. Graves slip beside her. With him came an outward chill, a shrinking in her soul. She couldn't quite explain it. He stared at the passing shore, the lines on his face drawn and unyielding.

"Good day, Mr. Graves." Eliza forced down her unease.

He nodded but said nothing.

"You do not seem as overjoyed as the rest of the colonists at our arrival in Brazil," she said.

"Quite perceptive, madam." He gripped the railing, still gazing at the land passing by them in an artistic blend of greens, browns, and gold.

"I don't understand, sir. Why did you join the colony if you did not wish to come here?"

Breaking his trance, he turned to face her, leaning his elbow on the railing. "Forgive me, Mrs. Crawford." He smiled. "I meant only to say that now that we *are* here, I am unsure whether the colony will be a success."

"Where is your faith, sir? We will succeed because we must succeed." She would not allow this sullen man to spoil her newfound joy.

"Faith?" He gave a repugnant snort. "Faith in what? Faith in people? Faith in *God*." The Almighty's name spewed from his lips. "No. I have faith in something else."

Anger tightened her jaw. "And what is that, Mr. Graves? Yourself?"

"No madam." He faced the land again, and a smile coiled his lips. "In power. And the pursuit of that power."

"As you have told me." She followed his gaze to the shore, her emotions running the gambit from fear to anger to sorrow for the man.

"There is something here in Brazil I had not anticipated." The snake ring on his finger winked at her in the sunlight.

From the intense longing in his eyes, Eliza sensed his anticipation wasn't sparked by the same thing that had delighted her—the land's lush beauty.

"Can't you feel it?" He gestured toward the land. "An energy, a preeminent, living force that supersedes our limited understanding."

She glanced at the man curiously before he went on.

"I had thought to have my revenge, but I see now that if I had, I would have missed out."

Now, she knew he'd gone mad. Eliza's breath caught in her throat. The man's words had spilled numbly, almost unbidden from his twisted mind. "Revenge, sir? On us?" She remembered that the South's seceding from the Union had ruined his political aspirations.

He flinched and fingered his black goatee. "What does it matter now?"

She thought of all the disasters that had befallen them on their journey. Could Mr. Graves have been responsible somehow? "What are you saying, sir? That you are the cause of our troubles?"

"Me?" An incredulous brow rose above dark eyes burning with victorious glee. "How could I have caused those things? I'm simply a man."

Indeed. She eyed him. "Why are you telling me this?"

"Because out of all the simpletons on board, I thought you might understand. You have a rare sense about you, Eliza. You are familiar with rebellion. And you've seen something, haven't you?" He leaned toward her. "I thought perhaps to find a kindred spirit."

Familiar with rebellion? Yet it was his last words that caused the vision of Stanton standing on the beach to reappear in her mind. But that had just been a figment of her troubled imagination, hadn't it? "Mr. Graves, if your intent is to ruin our colony, then, sir, I am most definitely not a kindred spirit."

"Ah." He glanced over his shoulder at Blake. "Your recent engagement has no doubt settled your alliances."

"My alliances have always been with the colony. Where are yours, Mr. Graves?"

"Where they should be, madam. Where they should be." He gave her a malignant smile, tipped his hat, and strolled away.

And the feeling of uneasiness left with him. Eliza drew a deep breath. She would have to inform Blake of her odd conversation with Graves. If he was responsible for any of the disasters that had plagued their journey and if he had any nefarious plans for the future of the colony, Blake should know so he could stop him.

She glanced behind her, noting that she was finally alone. Now was the perfect time to do what she'd set her mind to do. Slipping her hand into the pocket of her gown, she pulled out the watch Stanton had given her. The initials *FEW* sparkled in the sunlight in beautiful scripted letters. Though the watch appeared a bit masculine for a lady, it was the only thing Stanton had ever given her that had a personal touch. He hadn't even picked out the wedding ring he'd placed on her finger, but rather it was an heirloom that had been passed down through his family. One she'd been forced to return after Stanton's death. Why she'd kept the watch, she didn't know. Perhaps, deep in her heart, she mourned the loss of her first love, or what she had thought was love. Perhaps it gave her comfort that Stanton might have truly loved her after all. She sighed and flipped it over, allowing the chain to dangle over the churning waters. She'd retrieved it from her luggage for one purpose. To toss it into the sea. For she wanted no reminders of her past when she married Blake.

James slid beside her and gripped the railing. Hair the color of wheat tossed behind him as his bronze eyes found hers. "Congratulations, Eliza."

"Thank you, James. I am very happy." Perhaps she should tell the doctor what Mr. Graves had said. But no. It was too happy a day to ruin anyone's mood. Even hers. She would put all thoughts of the odd man out of her mind for now.

"God's plans always work out for the best." He slapped the moist railing and lifted his chin to the sun.

"I see that now." She paused and flattened her lips. "It's amazing to see God turn my blunder into a blessing."

"I'm sure most of us have secrets we'd prefer to keep hidden." The way he said the words and the glimmer of shame in his eyes made Eliza wonder just what nefarious secrets an honorable man like the doctor could possibly have.

"I have no excuse for what I did save my stupidity and rebellion." Eliza gazed at the Brazilian coast speeding by in a kaleidoscope of vibrant greens and creamy beaches. "I always jump into things without thinking, without consulting God. Even if I do consult Him, I still do as I please."

"A common human frailty. Submission is no easy feat for any of us." He snapped hair from his face. "But I've discovered it is well worth it, for God always knows what's best for us." He chuckled. "How arrogant we are to assume we know better than our Creator. His ways are perfect while ours are so flawed."

"I'm starting to see that. I could have saved myself much pain if I'd only obeyed."

The air suddenly stiffened as if an invisible wall rose between them. When Eliza looked at James, she found him staring at the pocket watch in her hand.

"You've gone pale, James. What is it?" She laid a hand on his arm.

"Where did you get that watch?" His voice sounded hollow.

Eliza held it up. "From my husband. It was the last thing he gave me."

James's breath gusted from his chest as his dazed look never left the watch. "Your husband? What was his rank again?"

"Brigadier general."

"Do you know if he fought at Antietam?"

She stared at him, her mind spinning with his questions. "I believe so, yes. He was killed only a few months later."

"And when did he give you the watch?"

"You're scaring me. What is this about?"

"Answer the question, please." She'd never seen him so serious.

"I received it in the mail a week before we received news of his death."

"May I?" He held out his palm, and she slid it onto his hand. "These initials. They are yours?"

"Yes. Flora Eliza Watts."

A cloud covered the sun. James lowered his head.

"What is it, James?"

He fisted the watch until his knuckles turned white. "I met your husband on the battlefield."

"You did? Pray tell, where?"

"Antietam."

James finally faced her, and what she saw in his eyes sent the blood retreating from her heart. She swallowed the burst of angst threatening to destroy her joy.

"After the battle, we suffered major losses. Over ten thousand wounded—so many we couldn't count. I went out on the field to assess the injured before we transported them back to the hospital. Body parts and organs were strewn over the field. But it's the screaming I'll never forget."

Eliza's eyes misted at his pain, even as she feared what he would say next.

"Union soldiers canvassed the dead, stripping them of their effects."

Nausea bubbled in her stomach.

"I approached a young boy no more than seventeen. He had a leg wound. Not fatal from the looks of it. A Yankee soldier, a brigadier general, appeared out of nowhere. I noticed him because it was rare to see a man of his rank combing the field after a battle. He never glanced my way but instead knelt by the lad and yanked on a chain around the boy's neck. At the end of it hung a pocket watch."

Eliza felt the blood drain from her face. "You think he was my Stanton?"

"Let me finish." The lines on the doctor's face dipped in sorrow. "The boy gripped the Yankee officer's arm and shook his head, pleading with him not to take it. Instead, the man pulled out his sword and thrust it in the boy's heart then yanked the watch from his neck. Afterward, he stared at his new trinket for a minute, smiled, and stuffed it in his pocket."

Eliza's legs turned to mush, and she grabbed the railing. James took her elbow to steady her. "How can you be sure it was Stanton?" she asked.

"This is the watch he took." James opened his palm. "I'm sure of it. I'd recognize this silver etching anywhere. Besides, I saw the initials. See how big the letters are and the way they glitter in the sun? It was a bright afternoon that day."

A sour, putrid taste filled her mouth. Eliza knew Stanton had been cruel, she just didn't know how much of a monster he truly was. She pressed a hand to her belly, forcing her breakfast to remain. "So, he didn't have it engraved just for me. He murdered a boy for it and was pleased when the initials matched mine." And all this time, she'd been carrying it around, admiring it, dreaming that Stanton had harbored a modicum of love for her.

"But that's not the worst of it."

The doctor's tone sent Eliza's heart into her throat.

"The watch was an heirloom passed down through the military men in the boy's family as a good luck charm."

"How do you know this?"

"Because that boy was Jeremy Wallace, Blake's little brother."

CHAPTER 33

As the *New Hope* drifted to a halt and the anchor was cast, Blake sought out Eliza through the crowd amassing on deck. He'd been so busy with his duties, he hadn't been able to speak to her all day. During the one break he'd had, she had gone below, no doubt to rest in her cabin. Now, spotting her at the railing, he shoved through the mob, pleased to hear the exclamations of excitement at the sight of their new home. It was beautiful indeed.

But even more beautiful was the sight of Eliza, her hair springing from her pins in the breeze and tumbling down her back over her small waist. He slid beside her and covered her hand with his.

"It's exquisite, Blake." Her eyes remained locked on the coast, just twenty yards from the brig. Water the color of aquamarine spread fans of ivory filigree on golden beaches that stretched for miles in either direction. A lush tropical jungle in every shade of green fringed the beach and grew taller as it receded on hills that ended in distant mountains capped with creamy clouds. To their left, a wide river reached emerald fingers laced in foam toward the sea.

Blake swallowed. "It is, isn't it? I can't believe we are finally here." He drew her hand to his lips for a kiss then ran a finger over her cheek.

Still Eliza would not look his way.

Captain Barclay spit a string of orders to the crew to lower boats, open hatches, and prepare the blocks and tackles to hoist the cargo above deck. Passengers scrambled to get out of the way and go below for their things.

Still Eliza did not move.

"Are you all right?" Blake finally asked. He felt a quiver run through her, and he settled his arm over her shoulder drawing her near.

"Something has frightened you."

"Me?" She looked up at him then, her eyes red and puffy. "Frightened of a new adventure?" Her laugh faltered on her lips.

Taking her shoulders, Blake turned her to face him. "You've been crying. Did someone hurt you? Say something to you?"

She lowered her chin. "No. Nothing like that."

"Then what?"

She brought her gaze back to his, her eyes flitting across his face, as if too frightened to land. Pain or perhaps sorrow weighed heavy on her features. Then she smiled, and her body seemed to relax. "I suppose I'm far too excited about our new life, that's all. So much has happened."

"You aren't having second thoughts about us, are you?"

She caressed his jaw. "Never"

He drew her close and kissed her forehead, his fears abandoning him. Together, they faced the shore. "James has agreed to wed us on that very beach tomorrow."

"He has?" She flinched as if this news surprised her, but then uttered a sigh that seemed to relieve her of some burden. "I can hardly believe it, Blake. I'm so happy. I pray nothing will ever separate us." A shadow rolled across her face as she gazed up at him. "Tell me nothing will ever separate us."

Confused, Blake brushed a lock of hair from her forehead. "What could ever do that?"

A breeze blew in from the shore, ripe with the sweet smell of life, tropical flowers, and hope. Blake smiled and stared into the jungle that would soon become their new home. Something shifted in the greenery. A shadow sped through the trees then disappeared. "What was that?"

"What?" Eliza followed his gaze.

"I thought I saw someone in the trees. . . .a shadow." Blake rubbed his eyes, but when he looked again, nothing but oversized vines and palm fronds met his gaze.

Eliza stared at the spot for a moment, seemingly deep in thought, but then she gave him a placating smile. "You are no doubt tired. As we all are." She leaned her head on his shoulder. "Besides, this place is far too beautiful to harbor anything dangerous."

Eliza couldn't tell him. She simply couldn't. She knew Blake too well. It had taken him weeks, months, to forgive her for marrying a Yankee. He would never forgive her when he discovered that Yankee had murdered his brother. And for a pocket watch, no less.

Eliza clutched her skirts and stepped from the wobbling boat onto the shore. Sand squished beneath her shoes as waves caressed her stockinged legs. Holding her valise in one hand and her skirts in the other, she waded the short distance to the beach where passengers who had already arrived waited. Turning, she shielded her eyes from the sun and watched as Blake helped sailors hoist supplies from the hold using a series of pulleys strung over the yards.

Bare-chested, his back—now bronze from the sun—glistened in the bright light. Beside him, Moses, also bare-backed, and Hayden lowered smaller crates and barrels into the waiting boats. No, she couldn't tell him. She wouldn't. What good would it do? The past was the past. She couldn't change it. Nor could she change what Stanton had done.

She glanced over the other colonists. Angeline, Stowy in her arms, assisted Sarah and Lydia into the shade of a banana tree. Magnolia, along with her parents, perched on a crate beneath a palm, the ever-present Mable fanning them all as best she could. Mr. Dodd's excited gaze shifted from his map to the jungle then back to his map again. Children played tag with the incoming waves, while most of the men assisted in offloading crates and barrels from the incoming boats. Even Mr. Lewis, in his normal sponged condition, hefted a large sack onto his shoulder and hauled it ashore in an effort to help. Graves, however, stood off to the side smoking one of his cigars and staring at the jungle with a most peculiar look on his face. She'd meant to tell Blake about her conversation with the strange man, but the revelation about the pocket watch had pushed all other thoughts from her mind.

Slipping off her wet shoes, Eliza wandered down the beach, watching as her stockinged toes sank into the sand, wishing she could bury her past just as easily. *Why, Lord? Why do you place this truth on me now? When I've finally found happiness? Oh what am I to do?*

"You have to tell him." Though Eliza had not spoken her prayer out loud, the answering voice was as audible as if God were standing right beside her. Heart seizing, she turned to see James looking at her like a schoolmaster with a pupil. Oh how she hated that look! She'd seen it enough on her father's face to last a lifetime.

"What good would it do?" She swung about and continued walking.

He slid beside her. "It may do no good at all, but that doesn't matter. It's the right thing to do."

"He will hate me."

"Possibly."

Eliza kicked a wave, sending foam into the air. "I could not bear it. Not again."

James halted her with a touch, stuffed his hands into his pockets, and stared at her with that look again.

Shielding her eyes from the sun, she forced pleading into her tone as she met his gaze. "You won't tell him, will you?"

"Not my place."

"And you'll still marry us?"

He nodded. "But you must do one thing for me in return."

Eliza's breath huddled in her throat.

"Pray," James said. "Ask God what you should do, and then do it. If you do that, I'll never say another word about it. I promise."

Sounded simple enough. God wanted her to be happy, didn't He? God was a God of mercy. Surely He wouldn't punish her for something Stanton had done.

She barely had time to nod her agreement when Angeline, Sarah, Magnolia, and several other ladies descended on her with excited voices and giddy smiles, all agog with plans for her wedding.

As the ladies drew her away, Eliza cast one last glance over her shoulder at James, who gave her a nod. The praying she could do. The obeying she'd never been very good at.

◈

"You did good work today, Moses." Blake laid the final hewn log on the pile and turned to see the black man's features in the darkness.

"Yessir. Thank you." Moses wiped a cloth over his brow and stopped to catch his breath.

Blake did the same. They had worked side by side all day. First on the brig, hoisting goods into boats and then on land, chopping wood for fires. And Blake had learned one thing about the large Negro. Well, maybe two. He was a hard worker. He didn't complain. And he was kind. Three then. Yet there was one thing that had troubled Blake all day, ever since Moses had taken off his shirt.

"Moses, the stripes on your back. Where did you get them?" The words had barely left Blake's mouth before he silently chastised himself for his boldness.

But Moses seemed unaffected. "I don't mind, sir." The large man stretched his back. "Dem stripes are the compliment of my former master. Dat man loved his whip." He chuckled.

Blake found nothing amusing about it. "You're such a hard worker. I can't imagine anyone ever being displeased with you."

"He was displeased with everything, sir. Didn't matter so much what any of us slaves did."

"How did you get free from him?"

"We didn't. After de war, he threatened to shoot any of us who tried to run away." He kicked the sand, the first indication of any anger within him. "He shot my wife. My wife in God's eyes, since they wouldn't let us get married proper."

Shock sped through Blake along with a sinking feeling that twisted his gut into a knot.

Moses lowered his gaze. "Shot 'er right in de back."

"I'm sorry." Blake knew the words were meaningless, but he didn't have any others to offer.

"I ran away after dat." Moses lifted his gaze to the dark sky strewn with clusters of stars. "My wife be in glory now. An' I forgive him." He shrugged as if he were forgiving a slap on the face or the theft of a small object, not the stripes marring his back and the death of his wife.

Confusion ripped Blake's reason to threads. "How can you do that? Forgive so easily?"

"Not up to me, sir. I ain't de judge. That be God's place. Besides, He's forgiven us more than we deserve."

Blake wanted to ask him what kind of judge allowed such injustice, but Captain Barclay marched toward him and slapped him on the back. "Excellent work today, Colonel!"

"Thank you, Captain." Blake turned back to see Moses' dark figure fading into the shadows.

"Are you sure you ain't interested in becomin' my first mate?" the captain continued. "You not only learned to handle a ship in two months better'n any seaman I seen, but you've organized this disorderly group into a civilized camp in a single afternoon. I could use a man like you."

Blake glanced down the beach. Flickering light from two massive fires spread a glowing sphere over the sand and pushed back the encroaching shadows of the night. Around them colonists sat on logs and trunks, chattering excitedly about the days ahead. A massive tent for the ladies stood stark against the dark forest. The men would sleep on the sand. He'd already assigned three shifts of two watchmen to stand guard throughout the night.

"I appreciate the offer, Captain, but I believe I owe it to myself and these people to give this colony my best shot."

"Well, if anyone can do it, you can."

Hayden, cup in hand, slogged in the sand toward them, followed by James. "Captain, when do you set sail?" James asked.

Captain Barclay scratched his beard. "Was goin' to leave tomorrow, but I believe I'll stay for the weddin' and festivities and leave the day after. My men could use a good party."

At the mention of the wedding, Blake realized he hadn't seen where had Eliza gone off to. He had left her after dinner over an hour ago. Now she was nowhere in sight.

James slapped a bug on his arm. "We will miss you, Captain. It's been a pleasure sailing with you and your crew."

"Agreed," Hayden added with a quick nod. "Thank you for taking me on board."

"You are a good worker, Hayden. We were glad to have you." Captain Barclay gazed at the *New Hope*, nothing but a dark silhouette against a smoky horizon, and chuckled. "Though 'twas quite a voyage, I'd say. Ne'er had so much bad luck on one trip before."

"But God saw us through," James added with a smile.

Hayden grunted and sipped his drink.

"Indeed," Captain Barclay said.

"What are our plans, Blake?" Hayden asked. "After the wedding, of course." He winked.

Other than the wedding night? Blake couldn't help but smile—and warm at the thought—but he quickly rubbed his mouth before the others noticed. "The emperor said the donkeys and wagons should be here in five or six days. We wait for them to show up and—"

A loud screech blared from the jungle, sounding half human, half beast. The hair on Blake's arms stood at attention as all eyes shot toward the sound. The colonists grew silent. Blake peered into the dark maze so full of life that it undulated and billowed as if it were alive. "I was told there were no longer any natives here, but I thought I saw something earlier. A person."

"Probably a trick o' the sun is all." Captain Barclay spat to the side. "An' that there was probably just a monkey. For such tiny creatures, they sure make quite a clatter."

Blake loosened his tie. That didn't sound like any monkey he'd ever heard. But then again, he hadn't heard that many monkeys in his lifetime. "After the donkeys arrive," he continued, "we pack up and hack our way inland. The emperor told me there is some prime farming land just a mile or two upriver."

James rubbed his hands together. "I can't wait to get started."

Hayden glanced toward the colonists around the fire, his eyes alighting on Angeline—or was it Magnolia?—Blake wasn't sure.

"It will be hard on the ladies," Hayden said. "Going through the jungle."

James followed his gaze and frowned. "They survived a precarious sea journey. They will survive this."

"What of the lady who tossed herself into the sea?" Captain Barclay asked.

"She seems quite recovered," James said, his eyes, too, on Angeline.

Hayden tossed the rest of his drink into the sand.

"Her mood does seem much improved," Blake offered even as the lady's laughter echoed over the sand. "Speaking of moods, mine would be much improved if I could find my fiancée. She seems to have disappeared yet again."

Hayden cocked a brow. "You've got quite a handful in her."

Smiling, Blake started down the beach, turning to face the men as he walked backward. "I commanded a regiment of over a thousand men, how hard can it be to handle one small woman?"

Eliza knelt in the sand and stared across the dark sea. A half-moon rose on the horizon, frosting the tips of ebony swells. The crash of waves joined the buzz and chirp of a myriad night creatures singing in the forest behind her as the smell of salt and smoke and moist earth filled her nose. She breathed it in like an elixir. This beautiful place was her new home, would be her new home, and she would be Blake's wife tomorrow.

If everything worked out as she hoped. As she dreamed.

She fingered the locket around her neck. "Oh Mother. I wish you could meet him." A shooting star caught her eye, drawing it to the thousands—no, millions—of stars flickering against the dark sky. "Lord, You said all things work together for good." At least she thought she remembered a verse like that. When was the last time she'd even read her Bible? Sarah had been so faithful to read hers every day, even offering to read passages out loud to Eliza, but Eliza had never had time.

"I'm sorry I haven't spoken to You very much, Father. You know I believe in You and I love You. There's just been so much going on. Please forgive me." She bit her lip, waiting for a burst of thunder or maybe lightning to strike, but instead a light breeze whisked over her as if God, Himself, were caressing her face. She smiled, emboldened to continue. "I love Blake. He's everything I've ever wanted in a man. Strong, protective, smart, kind, honorable, and good. And he loves me—can you believe it?" She chuckled. "Me?" Poking a finger into the sand, she began sliding it through the warm grains. "But there's this thing, this unimaginably horrible thing that Stanton did. Well, You know." Even now she felt the weight of the pocket watch in her skirt. She had wanted to toss it into the sea. Should have tossed it. But something held her back. It wasn't hers to throw away. In truth, it didn't belong to her at all.

It belonged to Blake.

A tiny crab skittered up to her leg, stopped, and then dashed away. She glanced down the shore where lights from the two fires flickered in the distance. "I don't know what to do. What good would it do to tell him?"

A tear spilled down her cheek, instantly cooled by the breeze. "I can't lose him. Please." She swallowed the burning in her throat. "But what is Your will? What would You have me do?"

There, she had asked. Now she would wait a few minutes, give God a chance to answer, and if she heard nothing, she'd do what she felt was right. Which was not telling Blake.

A wavelet crashed ashore, spreading a circle of bubbling foam over the sand. Palm fronds stirred by the wind sounded like gentle rain. It was so peaceful here. Yet out of that peacefulness came a voice.

You must tell him, child.

A voice that did not come from within or without. Neither was it a shout or a whisper. But Eliza had heard it, nonetheless. And her heart sank into the sand beneath her.

"Father? Was that You?"

You must tell him.

Tears poured down her cheeks. She dropped her head into her hands. "I can't."

Trust Me. . .for once.

Eliza sat up and looked around. No one was there. Nothing but the crabs and the surf. Yet *"for once"* kept ringing in her ears. No one would know that but God. No one would know that she'd been disobedient her entire life. Gone her own way. Done whatever she wanted. And she'd gotten herself into mess after mess.

If you love Me, you will obey Me.

"I do love You, Father. You've always been there for me, no matter the mess I've made of things. You've always helped me, forgiven me."

Then stop fighting Me.

Eliza wiped the moisture from her face. Who could fight God? Yet, as she thought over her life, she had indeed fought Him. Just as she'd fought her own father. And anyone else who tried to control her, smother her. She'd always thought that if she obeyed God, she'd be restricted, imprisoned, unhappy with choices that were not her own, when in reality, the choices she'd made had stolen away her freedoms even more. Stuffed her in a cage from which there was no escape.

In fact, God had neither smothered her nor reprimanded her. He was the perfect Father, the perfect gentleman. Almost too perfect, for He had allowed her too long a leash. Her rebellion had caused so much pain, not only for herself, but for her father, her aunt and uncle, even Stanton. And now Blake.

"I've been such a fool!" The tears came again, this time sliding down her cheeks in abandon. "I'm so sorry. If I'd only listened to You."

I love you, precious daughter.

Eliza closed her eyes, sensing the caress of God on her face in the gentle breeze. "I love You, too, Father."

Moments later the crunch of sand sounded, breaking Eliza from her trance. Batting tears from her face, she stood and turned to see the shadow of a man coming her way.

"What on earth are you doing out here by yourself, Eliza? It isn't safe." Blake's voice reached her ears. Before she could protest, he took her in his arms, surrounding her with his strength, breaking her resolve to do the right thing.

She pushed away from him. "I must tell you something, Blake."

CHAPTER 34

Air seized in Eliza's throat. She drew a shaky breath. "I must tell you now, Blake, or I never will," she rasped out.

He kissed her forehead. "Whatever it is, it doesn't matter. This time tomorrow we will be wed." The desire dripping from his sultry voice was nearly her undoing. As were his lips touching hers.

Pushing against his chest, she backed away. "Hear me out, please."

He must have sensed her dismay, for he took her hand in his. "What is it, Eliza?"

Waves stroked the shore in a soothing pulse that defied the one thundering within her. She searched for his eyes in the darkness, glad when she couldn't find them. At least she wouldn't see the pain, the anger that would burn within them when she told him the truth.

A wavelet tickled her foot, and he led her aside. "If someone has upset you, tell me, and I'll speak to—"

"It's about my husband."

He caressed her fingers. "Whatever it is, I don't care. I'll be your husband tomorrow." He leaned down to kiss her, but she laid a finger on his lips.

"You're scaring me now," he said. "What is it?"

"Something I learned only yesterday. But something you must know." Her heart pounded so forcefully against her ribs, she worried it would break through. Reaching into her pocket, she felt the watch and slowly pulled it out. Then turning toward the moonlight, she held it out to him.

He stared at it but made no move to touch it. The buzz of the teeming jungle, the crash of waves, and the distant crackle of fire and chatter of the colonists all combined to scrape against Eliza's nerves.

302

Furrows appeared on Blake's brow, slight at first, then deepening with each passing second. Seconds that ticked out Eliza's last moments with him in an agonizing slowness. Finally, he reached for it, held it to the light, flipped it over. And gasped.

His chest rose and fell like a sail snapping in the wind. He stumbled.

Eliza gripped his hand to steady him. His eyes met hers. Or at least she felt them meet hers—dark, gaping holes staring at her in shock, in confusion so thick she could feel it thicken the air between them.

"Where did you get this?"

She'd found it. She'd bought it. She'd stolen it. A dozen lies forced their way onto her tongue, vying for preeminence. "Stanton."

He released her hand. It fell to her side, empty and cold. "Your husband gave this to you?" His voice rose, etched in pain.

Eliza nodded, fighting back tears.

"This is my family's." He pointed to the engraving. "These letters stand for Frederick Evan Wallace, my great-grandfather." He closed a fist over the watch and glanced at the dark sea, where waves churned and frothed as if heightened by his anger. "The last person to have this was my brother, Jeremy."

"I know."

He snapped his gaze to her. His silence stole the remainder of her hope. She knew James had told him what he'd seen that day in Antietam. She knew Blake was putting the pieces together—laying the bricks one atop the other to form an impenetrable wall between them. "Your husband murdered my brother."

The words hung in the air like a massive judge's gavel ready to pound Eliza into the sand.

"I didn't know, Blake. I didn't know any of this until James saw the watch yesterday. It was a gift from Stanton. I thought he'd had my initials engraved on it. Flora Eliza Watts. I'm so sorry, Blake. I'm so very sorry."

He pulled away from her as if she had a disease. "Your husband killed Jeremy," he repeated numbly. Then, enclosing the watch in his fist, he thrust it in the air, chain spinning about his arm. "For this watch!" he shouted.

Tears coursed down her cheeks. She hugged herself as Blake's breath came out heavy and hard. A breeze flapped the collar of his shirt and the ends of his necktie but did nothing to cool the anger steaming off him. His face grew dark, indistinguishable with the night.

"I'm so sorry, Blake, I didn't know." She laid a tentative hand on his arm.

He shrugged her off and backed away.

"Blake?"

"I never want to see you again." His voice was hard as steel and cold as the chill darting down Eliza's back. Then turning, he stormed back to camp.

Eliza crumbled to the sand in a puddle of agony. Minutes later, or maybe it was hours, Angeline and Sarah surrounded her with loving arms and useless words of comfort before leading her back to the tent, where they tucked her into bed. But her mind and heart refused her sleep. Instead, she watched tree branches cast eerie shadows on the canvas roof, like giant claws reaching for her, trying to pull her into the abyss of despair. Was Blake asleep, or was he as upset as she was? Oh what did it matter? He never wanted to see her again. She would leave with Captain Barclay as soon as he readied the ship to set sail. There was no other choice. Tears slid onto her pillow. Angeline murmured a name in her sleep, and Eliza reached out and grabbed her hand, hoping to comfort her in the midst of her dream. She would miss her terribly. And Sarah. And even Magnolia. And all the friends she'd made among these people.

"Lord, why?" she whispered. "Why, when I obeyed You? When I did what You asked?" Wind flapped the tent, sweeping beneath the canvas and wafting over her.

I love you, precious one.

Despite her agony, despite her pain, Eliza found her anger dissipating. God was with her, and He loved her. In fact, she spent the remainder of the night talking with Him. About her life, her father, Stanton, her bad choices, and her good ones. She prayed for each of her new friends: for Angeline to find peace, for Sarah to find love again, for Magnolia to. . .well, just for Magnolia. For James to find healing from the internal wounds he seemed to carry around, for Hayden's agitated spirit to settle, for Dodd to find a treasure far better than gold, for Mr. Lewis's bitterness and drinking to ease, for Mr. Graves to let go of his quest for revenge and power, and for all the rest to find what they were looking for in this new land.

And finally for Blake. For him to forgive all those who had hurt him in the war, for his nightmares and episodes to stop, and for him to find a woman to love him.

The last prayer was the hardest of all, but once Eliza had uttered the words, she realized what true love was. It was selfless and pure and sought only the best for the object of its devotion.

By the time the first rays of the sun set the tent aglow in pinks and saffron, Eliza felt at peace for the first time in her life. She had done the right thing. Against her own wishes, she had told the truth. She had done the hard thing. She had obeyed God. And though the outcome was worse than she could have imagined, the guilt, the burden of fighting her Creator, of trying to run her life on her own terms, was gone, lifted from her shoulders in the same way the pulley had lifted the cargo from the hold. She had spent the night with God and found Him to be a loving, caring, wise, compassionate Father. Never again would she forge out on her own. Never again would she decide her own fate. Why would anyone do such a thing when there was a God who created them, who knew the past, present, and future? And who always knew the right choice to make, the right path to choose.

⊱⊰

Noises from camp drew Blake's gaze to James sitting by the fire, stirring the red coals to life. Men stood and stretched while a few ladies emerged from the tent. Rising to sit from the place in the sand where he'd dropped from exhaustion, Blake rubbed his eyes. The arc of the sun peered over the horizon, the train of its royal robes fluttering over sea and sky in an array of vermilion, gold, and coral. Such beauty should have been prohibited on a day like today. It should be dark and gloomy and stormy, not bright and cheery. Picking up a shell, Blake tossed it into the sea, feeling as empty and devastated as he always had after fighting a major battle. Only this battle had been on the inside, not on the outside. Somehow, it seemed much harder.

People pointed and glanced his way, leaning their heads in gossipy prattle. No doubt word had spread throughout camp of what had happened. He wanted neither their pity nor their advice. Advice he was sure to receive now as James headed toward him bearing a steaming mug.

305

Leaping to his feet, Blake dusted sand from his trousers and met him halfway—passed him, actually—holding up a hand against the outstretched mug.

"Coffee. You look like you need it."

"Not if there's a price." Blake huffed, continuing onward.

"It's free." James kept pace beside him.

"I don't want to hear it."

"What?"

"Your opinion."

"Good, 'cause I wasn't going to give it."

Ignoring the stares shot his way, Blake wove through the camp, kicking sand as he went, and retrieved the machete from its spot wedged in a tree stump.

"If you intend to hack Eliza to pieces, I'm afraid I *do* have an opinion on that." James gave a wry smile.

"Don't give me any ideas." Blake spun about and marched toward the jungle.

Still James followed. "Telling you the truth was hard for her to do."

Blake spun around. "You knew, didn't you? You knew that soldier was her husband."

Planting his fists at his waist, James glanced downshore. "Not until I saw the watch."

Blake grunted and started on his way again.

"Unforgiveness will destroy you, Blake."

Ignoring him, Blake plunged into the tangled web and began hacking his way through the vines and branches, releasing his fury on the plants. Yet after several minutes, rather than appease his anger, every strike seemed to add fuel to the flames. One glance over his shoulder told him James had not followed him. Good. He faced forward and slashed left and right, back and forth, focusing on the vision in his mind. The one that had been there all night. The one he couldn't shake— Eliza's husband plunging his blade into Jeremy's chest. And her, the adoring wife, sitting at home waiting for him to return. Blake raised the machete. *Slash!* Receiving his family's watch as a love gift from Stanton. Sure, she hadn't known what he'd done, wouldn't have approved, but how could she have married such a monster? *Hack!*

In a frenzied rush, he slashed his way forward. Sweat streamed down his face, dripping off his chin. The smell of musk and earth and life battled against the sense of death invading his soul. Stopping, he wiped his sleeve over his forehead and gazed at the canopy forming an impenetrable roof over the jungle. Birds flitted from branch to branch. The sounds of the ocean faded behind him, replaced by the buzz of insects and warble of parrots.

And a still, small voice. . .

Sarah forgave.

Blake spun around. No one was there. Shaking his head, he forged ahead. *Slash! Hack! Whack!*

Moses forgave.

Halting, Blake scanned the jungle. He must be having another episode. Or worse, he was going mad. Yes, Moses had forgiven the man who had beaten him, killed his wife. And Sarah had forgiven those who had killed her husband. They were better people than Blake. Stronger, with good hearts.

Whack! His fury exploded on an innocent vine. Fury that fueled him. Fury that had kept him going during the war, after the war. And after he'd found his entire family dead.

Slash! Hack! Branches and vines flew in every direction. His chest heaved. His shirt clung to his skin. Thirst clawed at his throat. But he didn't care. He would beat down this jungle until the pain subsided. Until the grief left him. Even if he had to beat a trail to the other side of Brazil.

Stopping, he yanked the black bands from his arm and stuffed them in his pocket then tore off his moist shirt and continued. A spiky vine caught his skin and ripped through flesh. Blood trickled onto his belly.

Sarah and Moses have peace.

Yes, they did. They were happy, not tormented like Blake. He pictured Sarah's kind face and Moses' wide, blinding smile.

Something moved to Blake's left. A dark flicker. A shadow. Blake hacked in that direction. A breeze cooled his sweaty skin. The sound of a crackling fire filled the air. Coming from nowhere yet everywhere. Chilled air twisted around him. Shivering, Blake halted and squeezed the bridge of his nose. He was definitely going mad. The crackling turned into groans, low and guttural.

Ignoring them, Blake raised his machete and continued. How

could he marry a woman whose husband had so brutally murdered his brother? He would be defiling Jeremy's memory—his entire family's memory. They would never forgive him.

He would never forgive himself.

Hack! Thwack! Blake halted to catch his breath. A shadow drifted among the greenery ahead of him. It moved slowly, methodically, the gray mist coalescing into a single shape, solidifying, until the leaves parted and out stepped. . .

Jeremy.

His brother, in his Rebel uniform with gray kepi atop his head, stared at Blake, a blank look on his face. Blake closed his eyes, his heart racing. The episodes had never produced anything so real before. Yet when he peered at the sight again, Jeremy remained.

Blake stumbled forward, reaching out. "Jeremy." But the boy turned and ran into—no through—the tangled shrubbery, stirring not a leaf. A shiver bolted across Blake's shoulders. His hands began to tingle. Raising his machete, he darted after his brother, slashing away the branches as he went.

He burst into a clearing. Jeremy lay on the ground. Blood bubbled from a wound on his chest and trickled to the dirt at his side. His vacant eyes stared into nothing.

"No!" Blake headed for him, his mind spinning at the impossibility. But then Jeremy faded into black smoke and disappeared. The crackling began again, and Blake fell to his knees. "No!"

He choked on his own breath. His leg burned.

"God help me!" he shouted.

I am here, son.

Jumping to his feet, Blake swept his blade across the clearing. The crackling ceased. Sunlight broke through the canopy in shafts of glittering light.

"God?" Blake breathed out the question.

The shafts danced and twirled, growing larger and wider until they spilled over him with warmth, chasing away his chill and forcing the shadows back into the jungle. "You're real?"

Yet what other explanation was there for the intense sensation that now poured down on him? Blake's mind twisted. If there was a God and He was here. . . He raised the machete. "Why did you allow my family to be killed? My brother?"

James's words returned to fill his mind: *"God gave mankind a wonderful yet dangerous gift—free will."*

"But You could have stopped it. All of it." Blake fell to his knees again and hung his head. "But then we would all be puppets without free choice." He tried to recall James's words. "And love given without choice is nothing but empty servitude." Finally, Blake understood why God allowed man to have a will of his own. He lifted his gaze to the canopy. Dozens of tiny white butterflies danced in the light.

A sensation struck him, a flash, a flicker, a vision, and suddenly he knew that Jeremy and his parents were happy and well. He couldn't say how he knew, but he knew—could sense them smiling down on him. Along with God. A sense of belonging, of family, filled his chest till he thought he would burst. There was life after this world, and God would set things straight in the end.

"I'm so sorry I doubted You. I'm so sorry I blamed You." Leaning forward, Blake touched the spot where Jeremy's blood had spilled. But there was nothing there.

His thoughts sped to Eliza.

Sarah had told him unforgiveness would make Blake bitter and sick. That it was a prison. Blake bowed his head, trying to force the picture of Jeremy's bloodied and bruised body from his mind. Yes, he could forgive Eliza. She'd been young and impetuous when she'd married Stanton. How could Blake blame her for the actions of her husband? Still. Would Blake's family forgive him for marrying her? Reaching into his pocket, he pulled out the five bands and gazed up at the rays of sun piercing the canopy. Somehow, he knew they would. Knew they no longer cared about such things. He laid the bands on the spot where Jeremy's body had lain, an offering of his sincerity. "I forgive her, Lord."

Then forgive him as well.

Stanton? Blake swallowed as he realized the man was probably in a very bad place right now. A place Blake wouldn't wish on anybody. Yet anger still burned in Blake's gut. He felt no forgiveness in his heart toward the horrid man, but he could say the words. He could do that one thing. Take that small step. "I forgive him, Lord." Nothing changed after his declaration, yet he'd obeyed. "I suppose I have some work to do on that one." He shrugged as Eliza's beautiful face filled his thoughts.

Eliza!

Blast it, she might already be sailing away with Captain Barclay.

Rising, Blake shouted his thanks to God, grabbed his machete, and raced into the jungle.

CHAPTER 35

Eliza stood on the beach, arm in arm with Angeline and Sarah. Their support and love had sustained her through many a dark moment on board the ship. And now it sustained her in her darkest moment as she waited to leave Brazil—forever. Above them, the merciless sun hurled fiery blades on sand and sea. Perspiration beaded her neck and brow. But she didn't care. These were her last moments with her friends. Her last moments as part of the colony.

Lydia cooed, and Sarah spread a lacy shawl over the baby's head, rocking her back and forth. Eliza ran a finger over the child's soft cheek, wondering if she'd ever have a baby of her own. Most likely not. Who would marry a traitor?

Shouts drew their gazes to Captain Barclay storming across the deck of the *New Hope*, issuing orders that sent some of his crew skittering up shrouds and others dropping below. Upon discovering there would be no wedding, he'd decided to leave forthwith. Thankfully, he'd allowed Eliza to remain ashore to say her good-byes while he prepared the ship. Yet now as Eliza and her friends watched in silence, those preparations seemed to be coming to an end. Soon he would signal the final boat to bring her on board.

Stowy circled Eliza's feet and rubbed the fringe of her gown as if saying good-bye. Bending over, Angeline bundled the cat in her arms and stroked his fur. From several yards down the beach, where the colonists loitered about camp, wind brought the scent of cooking fish to Eliza's nose. Her stomach grumbled, but she had no appetite. She'd already said good-bye to most of them. Several had expressed their sorrow at the way things had turned out, which gave Eliza a measure of comfort.

However, aside from Angeline and Sarah, James seemed the most distraught. Even now he paced through the camp, glancing occasionally at the jungle as if he expected some miracle to occur and Blake to appear. Over her shoulder, Eliza studied the thick greenery where she'd been told the colonel had disappeared earlier that morning, but there was no sign of him. She hoped—no prayed—he was all right. She would have loved to have had one more chance to apologize, one more chance to gaze into those stormy, gray eyes. But perhaps God was sparing her that pain.

"The captain's signaling the boat." Sarah's voice was solemn, bringing Eliza's gaze to the sailor waiting by the small craft down shore. He gestured for her to come.

Straightening her shoulders, she drew a breath for strength and fought back the burning in her eyes. "I pray you both find the happiness you seek in this grand new world," she addressed her friends, forcing a smile.

Angeline sniffed and raised a hand to her mouth. "It will seem so empty without you."

Eliza squeezed her arm, but no words of comfort formed on her lips. She'd already said them all.

The trio began walking down the beach. Eliza's feet felt like anvils, her heart like a stone. A tear broke free and slid down her cheek. They halted before the boat, and the sailor held out a hand to assist her on board where her valise awaited her.

"I will pray for you every day, Eliza," Sarah said, shifting teary eyes her way.

"And I shall pray for you both as well." Eliza drew her friends into an embrace.

"Finally!" James's voice thundered across the beach. Swiping tears away, Eliza looked up to see Blake hobbling out from the jungle. He scanned the beach, his eyes latching on hers. Raising a hand to ward off James's approach, he started toward her. Stripped to the waist, the muscles in his chest and belly surged and rippled with each step. Sweat glistened on his skin. His dark hair, normally combed, was now ruffled by the wind. Like a cannon to its target, he sped her way. Eliza's heart lurched into her throat. Did he intend to push her into the sea?

"Oh my," Angeline said.

Sarah tugged on the lady's arm. "Come, Angeline, it appears the colonel has something to say to Eliza."

Eliza cast a pleading look at her friends. She opened her mouth to ask them to stay, but a mere squeak emerged from her lips. Sarah offered her a comforting smile and a wink before dragging Angeline and Stowy away.

Blake halted before her. He smelled of sweat and forest musk, and she was afraid to look into his eyes. Afraid of what she'd see. Instead, she stared at his bare chest, raw muscle flexing from exertion.

"Eliza," he breathed. Placing a finger beneath her chin, he raised her gaze to his. Remorse and affection burned in his eyes. Her legs wobbled. He took her hand and led her down the beach, away from prying eyes and ears.

"I've been a complete fool." He halted and stared at their locked hands.

She opened her mouth to speak, but he placed a finger over it and smiled. "Let me finish." He dropped to one knee—his bad leg—and grimaced. "I love you, Eliza. It was wrong of me to hold you responsible for Stanton's actions."

The words trickled over her mind like water over a rock. Cooling, soothing, yet not remaining. Not making sense. It must be a dream. But then that dream spoke again.

"I'm sorry for the way I behaved. I love you, Eliza. I don't deserve your forgiveness, but please say you'll forgive me, and that you'll still marry me."

His voice, the sincere urgency in his eyes, sparked her heart to life like a match to kindling. If this *was* only a dream, Eliza must give it a happy ending. She knelt in front of him and took his hand and placed it over her heart. "Yes. Now and forever, I am yours."

He smiled and gathered her in his arms. And together they laughed and cried and kissed, oblivious to all around them. Until clapping and cheering sounded from down shore.

Eliza's face warmed. "Does this mean I'm staying?" She gestured to the sailor waiting by the boat, a confused expression on his face.

Blake waved him off before facing her again and helping her to her feet. "By my side forever." He picked her up and swung her around and around, their laughter mingling in the air above them.

Within minutes, the sailor rowed back to the *New Hope* where the boat was hoisted on board, and Captain Barclay waved his farewell to all of them. Soon, with all canvas spread to the wind, the brig drifted away.

✦

Three hours later, Blake, bathed and in his best suit, stood beside Eliza beneath a bamboo arbor festooned with passionflowers and seashells. James, open Bible in hand, stood before them. The sound of waves kissing the shore and an orchestra of birds provided the music.

"Charity suffereth long, and is kind; Charity envieth not; Charity vaunteth not itself. . ." James read from the Bible, but all Blake could think of was how glad he was that the beautiful lady beside him would soon become his wife. "Charity. . .beareth all things, believeth all things, hopeth all things, endureth all things. Charity never faileth." Closing the Holy Book, James looked up. "You may face your bride."

Finally. Blake turned and took Eliza's trembling hands in his. Dressed in a creamy silk gown she'd borrowed from Magnolia, she glistened like an angel dropped from heaven. The locket she cherished so much hung about her neck. Sunlight glimmered in the maple ringlets dangling about her shoulders. A violet and pink orchid adorned her hair. She smelled of gardenias and sweet fruit, and Blake licked his lips in anticipation. Not just of their night together. But of their life together. Of making her his.

James opened the Book of Common Prayer. "Repeat after me. Do you, Blake Wallace take Eliza Watts to be thy wedded wife. . . ?" As James continued, Blake focused on each precious word, eager to promise her anything. Finally, the man concluded.

"I do," Blake said emphatically, smiling at Eliza and silently thanking God for revealing Himself to Blake, for forgiving him and helping him to forgive others, and for this amazing woman before him.

Eliza repeated her part, barely audible over the crash of waves, her tone timid and quavering. Nervous? The dauntless Eliza Watts? Blake couldn't help but smile.

". . .till death do us part, according to God's holy ordinance." She finished and gazed up at him, her eyes glossy with happiness.

Blake slid the green band one of the ladies had woven from vines onto her finger. He would buy her a better ring in Rio when he had the chance. And the money.

Yet she glanced down with such pride in her face it may as well have been covered with diamonds.

"I now pronounce you man and wife. You may kiss your bride."

But Blake didn't need an invitation. He swooped Eliza into his arms and pressed his lips against hers.

Cheers and laughter filled the air around them, along with the sound of a fiddle and a harmonica. Eliza pulled away from him, seemingly embarrassed, yet the promise in her eyes spoke of the night to come.

⚜

Sunlight brushed Eliza's eyelids like the gentle caress of a wave. Back and forth, warm and inviting, luring her from her sleep. The crash of the sea, the warble of birds, the chatter of people, and deep male breathing swirled in an eclectic symphony over her ears.

Male breathing?

Eliza moved her fingers. Warm, firm—and hairy—flesh met her touch! Flesh that rose and fell like a bellows. Memories flooded her sleepy mind. Wonderful, glorious memories! Rising on her elbow, she propped her head in her hand and stared at the man beside her, still not believing what her eyes beheld.

Blake. Her husband.

Thank You, Father. Thank You. You have blessed me far beyond anything I could have hoped for. And deserved. Wind tore at their tiny shelter of bamboo and palm fronds—a wedding gift from the men to give them privacy. The leaves fluttered, allowing the morning sun to dapple patches of gold over Blake's body.

A magnificent body that reminded her of the night they'd spent in each other's arms. A night that far surpassed her wildest dreams—far surpassed any moment she'd spent with Stanton. She ran her fingers over Blake's bare chest. He moved. Groaned. Opened one eye. And smiled.

He drew her near. "Is that my wife I see?" His voice was groggy with sleep.

"Pray tell, sir, who else would be in your bed?"

He grew serious. "Only you, forever." He kissed her forehead and brushed his hand down her back. "Hmm. Methinks the lady forgot her clothing this morning."

315

His touch gliding down her bare skin sent a shiver to her belly. "Does it offend you?" She gave him a coy smile. "If so, I can be dressed within a minute."

"Don't you dare." He gently flipped her onto her back and planted his arms around her, pinning her in. "We still haven't finished discussing your terms of surrender."

Five days later, after the donkeys and wagons had arrived, the colonists stood before the jungle, all packed and ready to go. Excitement and uneasiness crackled in the air as everyone waited for Blake's command to forge ahead. And if he admitted it, Blake's own nerves were tight as a drum. He felt as though he were leading troops into battle, not farmers into the forest. Yet just like a battle, the outcome was unknown. They were entering a new land, creating a new world of their own, trekking into a jungle few had even seen. Who knew what struggles, what trials, what triumphs, and pleasures awaited them?

Thiago, their guide—a man Blake found to be both intelligent and kind—stood to Blake's left while Eliza stood on his right. Her sweet scent was driving him mad, but there was nothing to be done about it now. She slid her hand in his and gave him such a look of approval, of love, he had to whisper another thanks to God for allowing this precious woman to be his wife.

In front of them, Hayden, James, and several men held machetes, ready to hack a path through the jungle. Angeline, carrying a cat of all things, and Sarah with Lydia strapped to her chest, joined them, while Magnolia and her parents stood off to the side, looking none too pleased at having to enter the steaming knot of greenery. Nor had they, along with a few other colonists, been pleased to discover the wagons were not meant to carry them, but to haul what remained of their supplies.

Blake glanced across the crowd. Renewed zeal flickered in Mr. Dodd's eyes, causing Blake to chuckle. He truly hoped the man found his blasted gold. Even Mr. Graves seemed unusually excited as he gazed at the jungle like a scientist studying a specimen. Mr. Lewis folded his hands over his corpulent belly as if he hadn't a care in the world, while Moses, Delia, and her children brought up the rear.

Blake faced the jungle again. Waves thundered behind him. Birds and insects chirped and buzzed before him, luring him onward.

Something moved among the leaves. A shadow.

Blake's vision of Jeremy rose stark in his mind. It had seemed so real.

"Are you ready, Blake?" James glanced over his shoulder.

But Blake was still looking at the forest. A chill traversed his back.

"What is it?" Eliza stared at him quizzically.

"We should go before it gets too hot," Hayden urged.

"I thought I saw something in the jungle," Blake said.

"What?" Angeline followed his gaze.

"I don't know. A darkness. A shadow. It's probably nothing." Blake shook his head, feeling silly. Yet the sense of foreboding remained.

James cocked one brow. "Never fear, God is with us, my friend."

Blake nodded and slapped him on the back before facing the colonists. "Move out!" he shouted. Then hefting a sack onto his shoulder, he squeezed Eliza's hand and led her and the band of colonists into the thicket.

James was right. Whatever was in this jungle, they would not face it alone. They had God on their side.

Author's Historical Note

Disillusioned by the loss and devastation of war and persecuted under the vengeful thumb of the North, nearly three million Southerners migrated from the former Confederate States in the years following the Civil War. Many of them remained in the United States, moving out west or to larger cities of the North. A great majority traveled to Canada and Mexico. Exactly how many immigrated to Brazil is unknown due to poor record keeping at the time. Southerners were not even required to have passports. They simply boarded ships and sailed away!

Despite much opposition from newspapers, politicians, and even some war heroes, thousands of Southerners risked the long, dangerous voyage to Brazil for the benefit of maintaining their way of life in peace. Conservative estimates derived from newspapers, available numbers, and descendants tell us that perhaps close to twenty thousand Southerners came to Brazil to resettle after the war. It is believed that today more than a hundred thousand of their descendants still inhabit the fair country. But why Brazil? Brazil offered a similar climate to that found in the Southern states, had plenty of land good for growing sugarcane and cotton, had cheap labor, and boasted religious and political tolerance. Also, though the importation of slaves had been outlawed in 1850, slavery within the country was still allowed.

The following letter from Frank Shippey, one of the early Confederados (as they soon came to be called) conveys the sentiment of the day:

> Since the surrender of our armies, I have roamed in exile over the fairest portions of the globe. But it has been reserved for me to find in Brazil that peace which we all, from sad experience, know so well to appreciate. Here, the war-worn soldier, the bereaved parent, the oppressed patriot, the homeless and despoiled, can find a refuge from the trials which beset them and a home not haunted by eternal remembrance of harrowing scenes of sorrow and death.

Elusive
Hope

"For man looks at the outward appearance,
but the LORD looks at the heart."
1 SAMUEL 16:7 NKJV

Dedicated to all those who feel they never measure up.

ACKNOWLEDGMENTS

First and foremost, I thank God for giving me the opportunity and ideas to continue writing novels for Him. I am nothing without Him. He is the Father I never had, a more loving father than I could have ever hoped for. I also owe my deepest thanks to everyone at Barbour Publishing for believing in me and continuing to publish my books! For all the extra effort every one of you puts into each novel, I thank you from the bottom of my heart!

I could not write without the support and love of my dear author friends: Laurie Alice Eakes, Louise M. Gouge, Debbie Lynne Costello, Ramona Cecil, Patty Hall, Julie Lessman, Laura Frantz, Ronie Kendig, Dineen Miller, Camy Tang, and Rita Gerlach. There are so many more I don't have room to list here, but thank you all so much for your encouragement, prayers, and love!

Special thanks to Michelle Griep, who read this manuscript when it was raw and unpolished and loved it anyway!

And to my Motley Crew, the best crew who ever sailed the high seas! Your Captain loves you!

Last but not least, thank you, Traci DePree, for your continued expert editing and for making this book shine in places I didn't know it could.

CAST OF CHARACTERS

Magnolia Scott—Spoiled plantation owner's daughter who hates her new life in Brazil and longs to return to Georgia to marry her fiancé. Constantly belittled by an unloving, domineering father, she believes her only value is in her appearance.

Hayden Gale—Con man who is searching for his father whom he believes is responsible for the death of his mother. Bent on revenge, he'll do anything to punish the man who ruined his life, even becoming as much of a liar and cheat as his father was himself.

Colonel Blake Wallace—leader and organizer of the expedition to Brazil. A decorated war hero, Blake suffers from an old wound that causes him to limp. Blake is serious, commanding, and disciplined and feels the weight of responsibility for the colony's success. He recently married Eliza Crawford.

Eliza Crawford Wallace—Blake's wife and Confederate Army nurse who runs the colony's clinic. Once married to a Yankee general, she was disowned by her Southern family. Eliza is impulsive, stubborn, courageous, and kind.

James Callaway—Confederate Army surgeon turned Baptist preacher who signed on as the Colony's only doctor, but who suffers from a fear of blood. Feeling as much a failure at preaching as he does at doctoring, James nevertheless still pursues a higher purpose for the colony.

Angeline Moore—signed on as the colony's seamstress, Angeline is a broken woman with a sordid past that she prefers to remain hidden. Unfortunately there are a few colonists who seem to recognize her from her prior life.

Mr. and Mrs. Scott—once wealthy plantation owners who claim to have lost everything in the war, they hope to regain their position and wealth in Brazil by marrying off their comely daughter to a Brazilian with money and title.

Wiley Dodd—ex-lawmen from Richmond who is fond of the ladies and in possession of a treasure map that points to Brazil as the location of a vast amount of gold.

Harmen Graves—Senator's son and ex-politician from Maryland whose hopes to someday run for President were crushed when the South seceded from the Union. Hungry to rule over others, Graves slowly goes mad when he encounters a supernatural entity beneath an ancient temple that promises him riches and power.

Sarah Jordan—war widow who gave birth to her daughter Lydia on the ship that took them to Brazil, and who signed on to teach the colony's children.

Thiago—personal interpreter and Brazilian liaison assigned to New Hope to assist the colonists settle in their new land.

Moses and Delia—a freed slave and his sister, along with her two children, who want to start over in a new land away from the memory of slavery.

Mable—slave to the Scotts.

CHAPTER 1

September 20, 1866
Colony of New Hope, the jungles of Brazil

Magnolia tumbled backward and fell, bottom first, into a mud puddle. Uttering an unladylike curse, she scowled at the black sludge splattered over her skirts. Footsteps pounded. Boots appeared in her vision. She knew whom they belonged to before she looked up. "Now, look what you've done!" Warm moisture soaked into her petticoats and undergarments. Chuckling sounded in the distance. A blistered, scraped hand extended toward her. "I've come to rescue you, fair maiden." The voice strained to withhold laughter.

She glared up at the buffoon, Hayden Gale, a stowaway on their ship to this desolate place. Her gaze took in the sweat shining on his brow, the mischief twinkling in his green eyes, the dark stubble on his chin, then lowered to his bare chest visible through his open shirt—which was what had gotten her into trouble in the first place. His lips quirked into a grin.

"I believe you've assisted me quite enough." Sinking her hands into the puddle, she struggled to rise, but her ridiculous crinoline prevented her from doing so in a ladylike fashion. She would have to accept his help. But that didn't mean she couldn't have a little fun in the process. Gathering a handful of the black ooze Brazil was so famous for, she reached up and gripped his hand, smashing the mud against his palm until it trickled out between their fingers. Not a flinch, not a tick, altered his grin. Not a flicker of surprise or anger crossed his eyes.

Only a single eyebrow arched toward the sky. He pulled her to her feet then released her hand and shook off the offending slime. "I fail to see how your clumsiness is my fault."

Plucking a handkerchief from her sleeve, Magnolia wiped the muck from her hands and arms as best as she could. In all her twenty-three years, she'd never been as dirty as she had been the past three months in Brazil. No matter how often she washed, there was always a smudge here, a stain there, a bit of perspiration where it ought not to appear on a lady. And forget trying to maintain a decent coiffeur. Lifting her chin, she started walking down the path. "You called my name, distracted me. And I tripped over a root."

"You were staring at me for so long, I thought you might be in some sort of trouble." He slid beside her, his knee-high boots sloshing in the mud.

"Staring at you? I was doing no such thing." Magnolia halted, met his gaze, but then thought better of it, and instead scanned the large field where Hayden had been only moments before. Men picked and dug and hoed the earth in preparation for planting coffee and sugar. To the left of the field stood the thatched huts that formed the city of New Hope, their new colony in Brazil.

Hayden raked a hand through his dark brown hair, slicking it back. "I'm not blind, Princess. You were staring at me for several minutes. More like ogling, if you ask me. See something you like?" He grinned.

"Ogling! I was not—" Magnolia bit down her fury before she gave the insolent plebeian more reason to taunt her. "You, sir, are a cad. And my name is not Princess." Uncomfortable at his closeness, she took a step back and nearly fell again. He reached for her, but she jerked to the side, trying with all her strength not to stare at his brick-firm chest peeking at her from within his shirt. A shirt he must have hastily donned when he'd seen her topple into the puddle.

It was that brick-firm chest, billowing with corded muscle and gleaming in the sun, that had stopped her in her tracks on her way back to camp. She'd become further mesmerized by his rounded biceps and the way his dark hair hung around his face while he dug furrows in the field. Mercy me, what was wrong with her? She'd never stared so boldly at a man before. Not even at Samuel, her fiancé. Yet, she'd never seen him with his shirt off. Yes, that must have been it. Surely that was it.

Hayden leaned toward her again and sniffed.

Magnolia flinched. "Whatever are you doing?"

"Just investigating the cause of your sudden clumsiness."

Heat raged through her veins. He referred to her occasional need for spirits, of course. She glanced around to make sure no one was within earshot. "How dare you mention that in public. Besides, it's not yet noon."

"Ah." His tone was sarcastic. "Then I shall be on the lookout after dinner in case you topple to the ground again."

"I don't drink every day, you fool. Oh, never mind. Why am I talking to you?"

"I don't know. Why are you?" He cocked his head and studied her. He smelled of sweat and man.

"Because you will not leave." Her gaze lowered to his lips and the remembrance of the kiss they'd shared on the ship that brought them to Brazil sent her belly spinning. Why couldn't she forget about the silly incident? It had been nothing, really. Surely a rake like Hayden hadn't given it a second thought.

"If you'll excuse, me, sir. I must get back to camp." She skirted around him, but he fell in beside her. "I'll escort you."

"No need. I'm in no danger." *Except from you, perhaps.*

"I beg to differ, Princess. You never know when a root might leap out and trip you again."

"Very amusing," she hissed. Choosing to ignore Hayden, but very aware of his presence beside her, Magnolia forged ahead, batting aside insects as she went. There certainly hadn't been so many carnivorous, flying pests in Georgia, had there? *Georgia.* The name of her homeland soothed her nerves like honeyed tea. They'd told her Brazil was a paradise, a Garden of Eden, but instead she found it to be a seething maze of vermin-infested vines compared to Georgia's gentle rolling hills and sweet honeysuckle trees.

Why, oh why, had her parents forced her from their plantation in

Roswell, Georgia, from her servants and slaves and balls and gowns and friends and—well, if she were honest, they really had lost most of those things in the war. But regardless, why had they forced her from all she knew and dragged her into the jungles of Brazil?

And then there was the heat. Not just any heat, but a heat that was visible in spirals of steam rising from the greenery around them. She dabbed the perspiration on her neck and face and drew in a breath of humid air that weighed down her lungs, making them as heavy as her heart. She must return home. She could not spend the rest of her life in this primordial wasteland, slaving and sweating and working like a commoner. Wasting her beauty on men who were far beneath her.

Like the man beside her. A working man, a stowaway on their ship. Why, he hadn't even planned on joining the colony. And though he'd stayed and helped them clear the fields and set up camp, she sensed a restlessness in him. As if he were waiting for something, looking for something—which would explain his many long absences from the colony. No, Hayden was not the type of man to plant roots in a shoddy outpost. She sensed a kindred spirit in him—a need for wealth and success—which was why she tolerated his presence. When he found what he was looking for here in Brazil, perhaps she could convince him to take her back home.

She batted aside a tangled mass of lichen hanging from one of the trees as the sound of rushing water met her ears. The mighty river beside their new colony had lulled her to sleep many a night when her tears would not cease. It had been her only comfort as her parents snored on the other side of their hut, oblivious to her agony.

Always oblivious to her agony. Or perhaps they believed she deserved it. For the things she'd done.

"You should not venture so far away from camp," Hayden offered as he plodded along beside her. "Thiago tells me there are wolves and jaguars in these jungles."

"I was seeking fruit for our noon meal."

"And yet you return empty-handed." He smiled.

Magnolia huffed. "I couldn't find any." None she could reach, anyway. Besides, she was unaccustomed to work. Her family once owned the largest cotton plantation in Roswell. Her father even owned part of the famous Roswell Manufacturing Company—until the Yankees burned it to the ground. And he was also a member of the city council. She'd grown up with a bevy of slaves caring for her every whim. What did she know of menial work? She stared at the scrapes and mud marring what once had been white, silky skin on her hands and arms.

Hayden swept aside an oversized fern and gestured for her to proceed into the camp as if he were escorting her to a ball. Tightening her lips, she grabbed her skirts and brushed past him into the town of New Hope. Well, it wasn't really a town. Not yet. It was just two rows of thatched huts of various sizes lining a wide sandy path. Nine buildings on the left, nine on the right, and three on the end that served as the clinic, town hall, and meeting shelter, complete with tables, chairs, and a large brick oven and fireplace. Not exactly the Southern utopia they'd hoped to build, but it was better than sleeping on the ground in a tent as they'd done when they'd first arrived on the shores of Brazil. In fact, they'd found these huts already built and filled with crude furniture— or rather, Hayden had found them—just a week after they entered the jungle, apparently abandoned by whoever had made them. James, their doctor turned preacher, had declared it a gift from God.

Magnolia was not so sure.

To the south of town, the river bubbled and gurgled as it made the two-mile journey down to the sea. Eventually, it would be their easiest means to transport their crops to the ocean where ships would then take them to market. That was, if they ever managed to work the tender soil and keep the encroaching jungle at bay long enough to bring the coffee and sugar to harvest. *And* if they built the cane press and mill they needed to process those crops with only twenty-eight men to do the work. Some of whom were unaccustomed to getting their hands dirty at all. They could have purchased slaves in Rio de Janeiro if Parson Bailey hadn't absconded with all their money. Magnolia sighed, thinking of all the hardships they'd endured on the trip here and how many more were still to come.

If they didn't make a success of the colony, they'd have to return home to the devastation of the war-torn South. Fine by her since she had a fiancé waiting for her, but most of the people had nothing to return to. Even worse, they faced persecution by the North.

As she headed down the path, women skittered about carrying pails of water and baskets of fruit. Sarah Jordan, the town's teacher, lifted her gaze from where she knelt working in her vegetable garden and waved at Magnolia. The sound of hammers peppered the air as men reinforced the huts with cut branches and palm slats. Only temporary shelters, their leader Colonel Blake had said, until they could build proper homes. A luxury for which Magnolia's father was not willing to wait.

"A Scott has never lived in a hut and never will live in a hut," he had proclaimed with his usual aplomb.

Shielding her eyes, she peered into the distance beyond the town where Moses's bronze back shimmered in the sun as he erected the frame of a large house. Her father had hired the ex-slave to build them a home "away from the riffraff of town." How he intended to pay the man, Magnolia had no idea, since they hadn't much money left to their name. But she had a feeling Moses was more than happy to do the work if it placed him closer to Mable, Magnolia's personal slave. She had not missed the coy glances drifting between the two. Most unusual, for Magnolia had not assumed Negros capable of deep, abiding relationships.

But at least someone was enjoying their stay in this godforsaken place.

The home, however, was a sign her parents intended to stay. She never truly believed they would subject themselves to live like savages, but poverty did strange things to people. Poverty. She refused to accept that brand in life. If only she could return to Atlanta and marry Samuel, she'd never have to worry about money again.

Or bugs, or heat—her stomach growled—or hunger.

"You may go back to the fields now, Hayden." She dismissed him with a wave, knowing full well both her tone and gesture would annoy him to distraction.

His subsequent groan—akin to an angry bear's—brought a satisfied smirk to her lips.

"I'm not one of your slaves, Princess," he said with more frustration than anger. "We are all equal here. There are no bluebloods who plant their soft bottoms in plush carriages and spew mud on all those they pass."

Magnolia was about to kick some of that mud on his trousers when her mother's shrill voice stiffened her.

"What in heaven's name! Miss Magnolia Scott. You are covered in dirt."

"I am?" Magnolia gazed at her gown in mock horror. "Oh, mercy me, however did that happen?" She smiled at Hayden, who winked at her before he excused himself and walked away.

Her father, following close on her mother's heels, scrunched up his nose, scanned her from head to toe, and shook his head. "I realize we live in the jungle but that doesn't mean we are to behave like wild beasts."

Magnolia sighed. She started to tell him what happened—wanted to tell him that it didn't matter what she looked like here in the middle of the jungle—but decided it was no use.

"Go wash that mud off and put on something presentable!"

"Yes, Papa," Magnolia said numbly as she made her way down the street with one overpowering thought in mind. The sooner she left Brazil, the better.

CHAPTER 2

M agnolia poured fresh water into the basin, set the bucket down, and pressed a hand on her aching back. She couldn't even carry water from the river without causing herself pain. She was completely useless. Back home on the plantation, she'd kept busy with her cotillions and soirees and calling on her friends for tea, keeping up with the latest gossip, and playing the coquette with the town's eligible bachelors. But here in the Brazilian jungle, life was hard. Even though the sun was just peering over the horizon, most of the men had been up for an hour tilling the fields, chopping wood, and building a barn. The women were up as well, preparing breakfast, hauling water, and gathering fruit. No one was idle. Well, except Magnolia's parents, who spent most of their day complaining of the heat and overseeing Moses as he built their new house. Magnolia so wanted to help the colony. She truly did. But she didn't know how.

So, she came to the one place where she felt of any use at all. The clinic. Even the smells permeating the tiny hut—a mixture of pungent herbs and lye and beeswax—brought her a smidgeon of comfort.

"Good morning." Eliza's cheerful voice preceded the lady into the hut. "You're up early, Magnolia." The ex-war nurse and wife of the leader of the colony, Colonel Blake, never failed to have a positive outlook on life.

"I couldn't sleep. My father snores."

Eliza gave her a knowing glance. "Ah, yes, my husband made quite a racket last night as well." Magnolia grinned. Pink blossomed on Eliza's cheeks as she set down a bundle of clean cloths. "But, honestly, I couldn't care if he sang Dixie all night at the top of his lungs, as long as he's by my side."

Now it was Magnolia's turn to blush. Yet her heart grew heavy at the same time. Would anyone ever love her like that? Had Samuel, her fiancé? Obviously not or he would have sought her out after the war—would have come to Brazil looking for her by now, begging her to return. "Marriage becomes you, Eliza. You are fortunate to have such a wonderful man love you so much."

"God has been good to me." Eliza began folding the cloths, but her beaming smile began to fade. "My first marriage was different. Stanton was a beast. Cruel and heartless. And selfish." She shot a somber glance at Magnolia. "It's so important, Magnolia, whom you choose to marry. And sometimes, it's the least likely person you would ever consider."

Magnolia knew she spoke about the troubles that had almost kept Eliza and the colonel apart. In fact, it was a miracle they'd been able to overcome the obstacles and marry at all. Moving toward the cupboard, Magnolia grabbed a damp cloth to wipe down the examining table in preparation for their first patient. Had Samuel been the least likely person for Magnolia to marry? No, he had been the most likely. Young, handsome, wealthy, from a prominent family, educated, and on the path to success, who else would be more suited to become her husband? He was the perfect choice.

"You should never choose a husband based on a list of requirements," Eliza continued as if she read Magnolia's mind. "Only God knows the man for you."

A breeze blew in and rustled the loose strands of Eliza's brown hair. The woman never seemed able to keep her coiffure pinned up properly. Magnolia patted her own bun and dangling curls, ensuring all was in place as she pondered the woman's words. Samuel would make a great husband. She would never have to worry about money again, and if his political aspirations succeeded, he would usher her upward through society's ranks. Of course she loved him. Who wouldn't love a man like that?

By the time their first patient arrived, a myriad of birds, kissed awake by the sun's ascent, began their orchestra outside the tiny hut, adding a cheerful tone to the morning. Sarah, a war widow and the colony's teacher, entered the hut, greeted them both, and laid her baby, Lydia, nearly four months old now, on the examining table. Magnolia kept the child busy by making funny faces while Eliza examined her, pressing her abdomen, looking in her mouth, nose, and ears, listening to her heart and lungs with the stethoscope and asking Sarah dozens of questions.

"You're good with children, Magnolia," Sarah said after the examination was complete. "You should help me out in the school."

"Oh no, I couldn't possibly." Magnolia shook her head. "Truly, I don't care for children at all." She leaned over and blubbered her lips at Lydia, making the baby giggle. "But I make an exception for your sweet girl."

Eliza washed her hands. "Do you never wish to have children of your own, Magnolia?"

Magnolia ran a hand over her tiny waist that had been the envy of all of Roswell, maybe even all of Georgia. "And ruin this figure?" She laughed.

"There are some things more important than a good figure." Sarah's smile softened the censure in her blue eyes. Magnolia bit down her retort. Though a lovely lady and pleasant in all respects, Sarah was no raving beauty. How could she possibly understand losing the only thing that made Magnolia stand above the other ladies in her class?

"Is that why you still wear your crinoline? And all those petticoats?" Eliza asked while Sarah dressed little Lydia. "Most of the women have given up on such cumbersome underthings in this insipid heat."

"My father forbids it. It isn't proper. A lady should dress like a lady wherever she is."

Sarah hoisted Lydia in her arms. "I believe we should always be modest and look our best, but I also believe in comfort. Most of the women in Rio de Janeiro didn't wear these contraptions."

Most of the *commoners*, she meant. But Magnolia wouldn't say such a thing. She also wouldn't tell them that just because they were in a savage country that didn't mean they had to dress like savages. Mercy me, that thought sounded so much like her father, it caused her stomach to sour.

Several more patients came in with minor complaints: a cut, a sore back, indigestion, and a rash. Magnolia did her best to assist Eliza while trying to learn as much as she could about tending the sick and wounded. She would never tell her father, but she found the profession fascinating and enjoyed the rewards of healing those in need.

"You make an excellent nurse, Magnolia," Eliza said after the last patient left.

"I do?" Magnolia bent over to pick up the bandage scraps. The statement both shocked and sent a spiral of elation through her. She'd never been good at anything. Except—according to her father—being beautiful.

"Of course. You aren't squeamish. You are efficient, professional, and kind."

Magnolia almost dropped the bowl of bloody water she held. She stared at Eliza as the woman dried her hands on a towel, waiting for her to chuckle or offer a playful grin.

But it never came.

At least not before Mr. Dodd wandered into the clinic, gripping his injured hand. With a wild mop of blond hair, side burns that crawled down to his chin, a sculpted nose, and sharp blue eyes, the ex-lawman from Virginia was not entirely unappealing. Unless you were a woman and he happened to be in a gawking mood.

"What a busy morning," Eliza exclaimed, ushering him to the examining table. "How did this happen?"

"Digging. Ran into a sharp root."

"For gold?" Magnolia's mocking tone drew his gaze—a gaze that absorbed her like a sponge. The man fancied himself not only a Don Juan, but a fortune hunter as well. He'd been searching for treasure ever since they hit the Brazilian shore—*pirate treasure*, he said. And he had a map to prove it. Foolish quest if you asked her.

"And I'll find it one day too," he said. "You'll see."

Eliza handed a basin of fresh water to Magnolia. "Hold your hand over this, Mr. Dodd."

He did so, and Magnolia focused on the twig embedded in his bloody flesh rather than face the lecherous look in his eyes. "Will you share your gold, Mr. Dodd, with those who have fed and housed you during your search?"

He chuckled and reached his other hand up to scratch his blond whiskers. "I like a woman with pluck, Miss Magnolia. I do." The sharp tang of blood rose to join his smell of dirt and sweat. "But I do my fair share. I look for gold on my own time."

Magnolia wasn't sure about that and, from Eliza's grunt, neither was she.

"Now, this will hurt a bit." Eliza yanked the twig from Mr. Dodd's hand and immediately pressed a cloth on top.

To his credit, the man uttered no cry.

He *did* utter a moan of delight, however, when Angeline entered the clinic. The town's seamstress, and one of the few single ladies in the colony, froze at the sight of him. Unease. No, more like fear skittered across her striking violet eyes. Shifting her gaze away, she hastened to put a cluster of thick, fleshy leaves down on the sideboard. "Some aloe for you, Eliza." Her voice broke, and Magnolia's sympathies rose for the woman who always seemed eager to leave Mr. Dodd's presence.

"Thank you, Angeline," Eliza said.

"Good morning to you, Miss Angeline." Dodd's sultry tone stiffened her spine. "When I'm done here, I'll gladly walk you back to your hut."

Frowning, Eliza grabbed a bottle of alcohol and poured it on his wound.

"Ouch!" He leapt off the examining table. "What'ya do that for?"

Magnolia and Eliza shared a smile, but Angeline had already dashed out the door.

❧❦❧

Raising his machete, Hayden slashed through a thick copse and shoved the branches aside, the first time he'd used the blade today. "The jungle isn't as dense as I thought it would be this far inland."

He could hear the rustle of Thiago's sandals stomping through the dried leaves that covered the forest floor. The Brazilian guide, assigned to their colony by the emperor to help acclimate them to the country, had been an invaluable aid to Hayden as he searched for his father. "No, *senhor*, much of the jungle inland has no *arbusto*. . .brush."

"Just tall, thin trees." Hayden glanced up at the trunks thrusting into the sky some sixty to a hundred feet above them. Birds, plumed in colors that would shame a rainbow, flitted from branch to branch, warbling their happy tunes. "And these." He grabbed a vine of vegetable cordage suspended from a branch, then gestured to the dozens of others hanging all around them and running along the leaf-strewn ground before climbing up the trees again. "What are these again?"

"*Sijpos,*" Thiago said as he stopped beside him. "We use them to tie wood together for buildings and fences and many other things. Some call them nails of Brazil."

"Indeed." Hayden tugged on it. "As thick and strong as ship cordage. Amazing. We should use these in the construction of New Hope."

"A good idea."

Hayden dabbed the sweat on his brow, noting the Brazilian never seemed to perspire or even breathe hard. In fact, he quite resembled a Spanish conquistador of old with his olive complexion, black hair, and strong noble features.

"What are we looking for again, senhor?" The man's dark eyes sparked in playfulness.

"A camp. Or any sign of colonists like us." Hayden uncorked his canteen and took a long draught.

Thiago nodded.

When the heat had become too oppressive to work in the fields, Hayden had grabbed the Brazilian guide and stole away for a few hours of exploring. As he'd been doing since they'd arrived at the abandoned settlement over two months ago. Trouble was, he wasn't finding anything—not a footprint, not a scrap of clothing, not a discarded bowl or pot. Nothing that would indicate humans had inhabited these forests for years. So, where could his father have gone?

The immigration officer in Rio had given Hayden the exact location of the clearing and huts that now made up their colony of New Hope. Though the colonists had been overjoyed to find fields already cleared for planting and shelters already erected, Hayden's disappointment couldn't have been more devastating. He'd come so close to ending his fifteen-year hunt for the man who had ruined his life—to finally receive the satisfaction of watching his father pay for what he'd done—that to have missed him by only a month gnawed away at Hayden's soul. A soul that seemed to grow more empty with each passing day.

He started forward again, asking Thiago about the many plants and trees that surrounded them. So far they'd seen tree ferns, bamboos, lofty palms, acacia, cassia, mango trees, and breadfruit and lemon trees. A green lizard scrambled over Hayden's boot. A thick black spider skittered up a tree trunk, while monkeys howled in the distance. The smell of sweet blossoms and rich earth wafted beneath his nose. A paradise teeming with life.

Yet, paradise or not, if Hayden didn't find any sign of a settlement in his next two trips, his best bet would be to go to Rio and ask the immigration agent if he'd heard from Hayden's father. Perhaps the man had returned to the city for supplies or to change his colony's location. Or, even worse, to book passage on a ship back home.

Perhaps Hayden could take Thiago along to Rio. Especially since Hayden wasn't altogether sure how to find the city over land. And the guide had been more than willing to accompany him on most of his treks into the jungle. In fact, Hayden had enjoyed his companionship.

"Thiago, how is it you know English so well?"

"My father is an American dentist." He chuckled.

"A dentist?"

"Yes. Much needed in Brazil. We have few dentists." He tapped Hayden on the shoulder and spread his mouth wide, proudly displaying rows of strong, glistening teeth.

Hayden grinned and stomped onward, scanning the ground for any sign of human footprints. "I see the advantage in having a dentist for a father."

"Yes, senhor. Not the least is I learn English. Though we not speak it much at home. Father want to only speak Portuguese."

"And your mother?"

"A native of Brazil. From long line of Portuguese royalty. I have royal blood in my veins. But it is nothing here. The emperor rules all."

A band of monkeys swung through the vines overhead, some stopping to chastise the humans below, no doubt for some jungle infraction, before they scampered off to join their friends. Hayden wondered about the emperor. He had seemed a nice enough fellow, but just how much freedom would they have if their new colony became a successful, burgeoning town?

"Instead of becoming dentist like my father," Thiago continued, "or working at a trade, I become interpreter for English-speaking immigrants. It is good job. I meet many interesting people."

Hayden chuckled to himself. More like the easiest vocation in the world. Thiago got free food and lodging just for talking with people and making sure they weren't stealing the emperor's lands. Hayden should have thought of that years ago. It would have settled on his conscience better than swindling people out of their money.

"Like Mrs. Sarah," Thiago added.

Good thing the man talked for a living. He was certainly good at it. "What of her?" Hayden nudged aside a thicket of vines then ran a hand over the sweat lining the back of his neck.

"She very pretty. And nice. Is she not?"

"I suppose." Hayden hadn't really noticed. The teacher was far too prudish for his tastes. Besides, she just had a baby, and he had no interest in being a father. He would probably end up being just as bad a one as his own had been.

"What happened to her husband?"

"He died in the war." Hayden slapped a mosquito on his arm and turned to study Thiago. "You have an interest in her." It wasn't a question. More an observation. And one that was confirmed by the way the man squirmed and dug his hands into his pockets.

"She nice to me."

Hayden swung around. "She is nice to everyone." Still, he smiled.

Perhaps the poor widow would find love after all.

As he passed a large tree, Hayden eyed a beetle the size of his palm clinging to its trunk. Butterflies and other more annoying pests buzzed around his ears and face. A shriek sounded in the distance. A monkey? A bird? Hard to tell above the cacophony of croaks, buzzes, and squawks surrounding him. The living jungle swayed like gentle waves at sea, and Hayden sensed a thousand eyes on him.

Then the crackling began. Barely audible at first, but heightening with each step he took. He glanced around, saw nothing, and continued. Still the sound increased like the spit and crack of a large fire. Raising his machete, Hayden scanned the foliage. "Do you hear that?"

"Yes, senhor, but I do not know what it is." Thiago's dark brows collided as he froze and stared into the jungle.

A shadow—no, more like a dark cloud—sped through a cluster of trees to their right.

Hayden pivoted in that direction. Thiago pulled a pistol from his belt and cocked it. The sound echoed in the moist air. The crackling halted.

The dark shadow sped to their left.

Hayden's chest tightened. "Who's there?" he shouted.

The leaves rustled. A large fern parted. Hayden raised his blade.

CHAPTER 3

Clutching her skirts, Angeline darted from the clinic, eyes on the ground, trying to get as far away as she could from Mr. Wiley Dodd. All the while, chastising herself for not staying in Rio de Janeiro when she had the chance. But how could she have made a living? She didn't speak the language. Or have any skills. Except one. And that particular one she refused to use ever again. Which brought her back to Mr. Wiley Dodd. Wiley. The perfect name for the man, for he was as wily as a fox. Surely he recognized her. He had to. Then why hadn't he told anyone else? Did he intend to blackmail her? If so, she wished he'd get on with it.

To make matters worse, he'd been a lawman back in the States! From Norfolk of all places. Sweet saints, if he were to connect her to the woman the Norfolk police had been looking for, it would all be over. Her new beginning. Her second chance here in Brazil.

Her life.

Hugging herself, she hurried down the main street, forcing tears from her eyes, and barreled into a chest as firm and wide as a tree trunk. She brought her gaze up to see a thin cotton shirt plastered against muscles bulging from exertion. Oddly, the sight brought her no alarm. Just the opposite, in fact. She gasped and took a step back, raising her gaze at least a foot to the sprinkling of dark stubble on a rounded chin, the slant of steady lips, and finally to the bronze eyes of the doctor turned preacher. "Pardon me, James. I didn't see you."

343

The corners of those bronze eyes now crinkled in concern. "Are you all right, Miss Angeline?" He cocked his head and touched her arm. "You've been crying."

"It's nothing."

"Something wrong at the clinic?"

"No. nothing like that." She slipped from his touch. Not because it bothered her. But because it didn't. In fact, she rather liked it. She dropped her gaze to see mud sprinkled over his Jefferson boots and splattered on his brown trousers held up by a thick belt into which a pistol was stuffed. So odd for a preacher, but then again the jungle wasn't exactly Jackson Avenue in Knoxville, Tennessee, where the man had grown up. And where she'd met him that dark, bleak night over a year ago. He'd claimed to be a preacher then as well, though he'd behaved like nothing of the sort. Thankfully, he didn't seem to recognize her from their brief encounter. She refused to ponder the odds of having met, prior to their journey to Brazil, two of the twenty-eight men in a colony of strangers. If there was a God, He was definitely not on her side.

Yet, now, standing so close to James and seeing the way he glanced around ensuring no one was bothering her, all thoughts of that conundrum, along with fears of Wiley Dodd, fled like bats in the sun. And she felt safe. As she always did in the doctor's presence.

As she had that night on the ship when he'd risked his life to pull her from the sea. The night she'd tried to end her misery once and for all. Despite her agony, despite her wish to die, she'd felt safe in his arms as he carried her, dripping wet, across the deck. He'd been bare-chested then. Why was she, now, having so much trouble keeping her eyes off him with his shirt on? *Sweet saints, Angeline. He's a man of God!*

As if possessing an uncanny ability to read her thoughts, his face reddened and he shifted his stance. A breeze tossed the tips of wheat-colored hair across his collar. "I was coming to get some water for the men working the field." He glanced toward the open stretch of land beyond the town. "Forgive me for my slovenly attire, Miss Angeline."

His sudden nervousness brought a smile to her lips. "No need to apologize, Doctor. None of us can keep up appearances like we used to."

The blacksmith's wife passed them with a nod, a basket of oranges in hand.

James swept his gaze back to Angeline and smiled. His expression grew sober. "If there is something or *someone* bothering you, I hope you know you can come to me."

"I do." But she wouldn't. How could someone like her ever think to approach a preacher with her problems?

"Well, then, I must get back. Good-day to you, Miss Angeline." He had the most genuine sounding voice she'd ever heard. As if he meant every word he said. She nodded as he skirted around her on his way to the river. And she felt the loss of him immediately.

"I expect to see you at Sunday Services," he called over his shoulder.

Sunday services. So far she'd been able to avoid them with one excuse or another. Not that she didn't believe in God. But simply because she was sure He no longer believed in her.

⚜

"I almost killed you, Graves!" Hayden lowered his machete while Thiago uncocked his pistol and stuffed it back into his belt. "What in the Sam Hill are you doing out here, anyway?"

"Just exploring like you." Graves gave a sly grin that angled one half of his black mustache down to his chin. "Difference is"—he glanced at the web of greenery above them and sighed—"I found something for my trouble."

Hayden raised his brows, his interest piqued, along with his annoyance. The mysterious Mr. Graves had kept his distance from the others throughout the entire sea voyage and now in their new town as well. He hailed himself as a politician who once ran for the senate until the war killed his plans, along with his family. And just like a politician, he refused to do any real work, preferring instead to wander the jungles in search of food and supplies. Or so he claimed. Hayden had yet to see him return with anything of value.

"Do tell, Graves, what did you find?" Hayden plucked a cloth from his pocket and wiped the sweat from his head and neck, trying to mask his irritation.

"Come and see." Without waiting for a reply, Graves swerved about and disappeared into the shrubbery. Hayden should have ignored the cantankerous man. He should have continued with his own search, but his curiosity got the better of him and he started after him, Thiago in his wake.

Graves was easy to track. Dressed in his usual black trousers, black shirt, and waistcoat, he reminded Hayden of the dark shadow he'd just seen flitting through the greenery. Or had he seen anything at all? He thought to ask Thiago about the odd mist, but didn't want to sound foolish. Probably just an illusion brought on by the heat and humidity, which seemed to rise with each step he took. He longed to take off his boots, but he'd seen too many snakes and insects to risk tromping around barefooted. Sweat slid down his back and covered his neck. Slicing a piece of twine from a nearby plant, he tied his hair behind him. What a sight he must be. He certainly looked nothing like the gallant gentleman he presented himself as whenever he'd been working a scam. His thoughts drifted to Mrs. Henley, the charming, beautiful Katherine Henley. How her face would light up when Hayden sauntered into a room wearing his silk-lined suit of black broadcloth and stylish top hat. He knew the first time he'd met her at the horse races in Louisville that he would soon have her swooning at his feet, willing to do anything he asked. He grinned. He'd made at least two thousand dollars off her. Not bad for only a few week's work. But, of course, the lady's husband was none too pleased when he discovered she'd purchased an empty, useless cave instead of a silver mine. Hayden hoped the man hadn't been too hard on her. He shrugged off a twinge of guilt before halting and glancing up at the canopy.

Thiago bumped into him from behind. "What is it, senhor?"

"Do you hear that?"

"No."

"Exactly. The birds have stopped chirping. And where is the incessant drone of insects?"

Thiago ran a hand through his dark hair and looked around. "You are right. They are gone."

"Over here!" Graves's shout lured Hayden onward, the crunch of leaves beneath their feet the only sound filtering through the trees. Despite the heat, a chill slithered down his back. He hoped he wasn't walking into a trap. The thought caused a curse to emerge from his lips as he plunged through one final thicket and nearly bounced off a massive stone wall that was at least ten feet high.

"Holy Mary, mother of God." Thiago crossed himself.

"What is this place?" Hayden shifted his shoulders beneath a palpable heaviness in the air.

"This way." Graves gestured. Hayden had never seen the man so exuberant. Which made him feel even more uneasy. They followed the wall as it curved around the clearing, no doubt enclosing something within. A fort, perhaps? But out in the middle of the jungle?

"I do not like this." Thiago moaned from behind as they came to an opening that must have been the entrance but was now merely a rotted wooden gate strangled by green vines.

"Isn't it incredible?" Graves slapped the stones with his hand. "Looks to be quite old. Perhaps built by natives."

Incredible? A different word came to Hayden's mind—*disturbing*. Though covered with moss and vines, the stone structure stood as a firm reminder that whoever built it had been trying to keep something out. "If natives erected this, it makes one wonder what they were afraid of." Hayden shifted his stance and glanced from Graves to Thiago. Didn't they feel the heaviness in the air?

"Perhaps, they feared *Lobisón*," Thiago said as he gazed up at the wall's height and then peered around the corners of the broken gate to examine the thickness of the wood. "Or something far worse."

Hayden wondered what could be worse than a man that turned into a wolf but thought it wise not to ask. He already had the urge to turn and run and never come back, to trust his instincts—the ones he'd honed living on the streets. They had saved his life more than once and now they were telling him to scurry out of there as fast as he could.

Yet, what if his father had come this way, stayed here, left a clue?

Without a word, Graves slid through the opening and disappeared within.

Hayden started after him when Thiago clutched his arm. Wide

eyes met his. "I do not think we should go in, senhor."

"Stay here if you wish, but I must see what's inside." Turning, Hayden entered and halted beside Graves. Across a courtyard infested with weeds and vines and broken pottery, at least twenty stone obelisks rose from the ground like mummies from a mass grave. Hayden made his way to the closest one and brushed aside the vines to find an engraved collage of gnarled faces in various postures of agony. His stomach clenched. He backed away, shifting his gaze to two rectangular slabs of stone, lying prostrate upon blocks of granite. A massive fire pit rose from the center of the clearing. Scattered around it lay broken wooden idols and stained blades whose handles had long since rotted off. Beyond the clearing, a crumbling building rose from the greenery like a monster from a swamp. Columns that reminded Hayden of a plantation house held up a flat roof and formed an open air portico that faded into darkness.

"Looks to be a temple of some sort." Graves remarked as he tromped across the courtyard, his tone one of enthusiasm.

Shaking his head, Hayden slowly moved toward one of the tables. In between the moss and vines, dark stains peered up at him from the light stone. His stomach convulsed. "If this is a temple, I don't think it's a Christian one."

"No." Thiago's tremulous voice came from just inside the gate where he stood frozen. "These are ruins of Tupi. They were cannibals."

Hayden's glance returned to the fire pit, shifted to the ancient blades, then moved to the stains on the table. Bile rose in his throat. Gagging, he bent over, praying he wouldn't vomit and embarrass himself in front of these men.

"Cannibals?" Graves's dark eyes flashed.

Hayden took a deep breath and rose to his full height.

Pulling an amulet from his pocket, Thiago crossed himself again. "I wait outside."

Hayden longed to go with him, but he couldn't seem to move. Instead he stared at the ghastly scene, imagining what horrors must have occurred within its walls.

A *caw caw* drew his gaze upward to a black bird with the wingspan

ELUSIVE *Hope*

as wide as a man was tall. The odd sight kept Hayden riveted as the beastly bird crossed the clearing and disappeared. Something about the bird, its size, the loneliness in its cry, caused air to seize in his lungs.

Graves headed toward the temple where he plucked a torch from a holder on the wall, struck a match, and lit it. "I'm going in to explore. Join me?"

"I'll wait here," Hayden said. If his father had come this way, Hayden should find some evidence in the courtyard. There was no reason to subject himself to further horrors.

Graves gave him a taunting snort before he mounted the steps and entered the building with the exuberance of a child at Christmas.

As disturbing as his presence was, Graves's absence left Hayden alone with the dark foreboding he'd felt upon entering this fiendish site. He ran his sleeve over the sweat on his brow and started his search of the area, careful not to touch anything. He'd grown so accustomed to hearing the chatter of the jungle that the absence of it spiked his nerves. Perhaps that was the reason for his discomfort. He prayed that was the *only* reason.

He circled one of the obelisks, cringing at the tormented faces carved into the stone and wondered if these were the faces of those who'd been killed by the Tupi. His chest tightened. He backed away. The crackling returned. Soft like the sound of waves, yet harsh as if a thousand fires were lit all around him. Hayden drew his machete and swerved around. No one was there.

Then she appeared. Materialized out of the torrid air like a mirage in the desert. Yet unlike a mirage, she stood before him as real and vibrant as he remembered her. Mrs. Katherine Henley, hair cascading around her head in a bouquet of golden curls. Striking emerald eyes, now swimming in tears.

Hayden rubbed his own eyes, hoping to sweep away the vision, but still she remained. He reached for her. She retreated.

"Why?" she asked. "Why did you do it?"

Hayden swallowed. *This can't be happening*. It's the heat. His thirst, this evil place playing tricks on his mind.

"I thought you loved me. You told me you loved me." Tears

streamed down her cheeks, glistening in the bright sun.

"You're not here. You're not real." Hayden clenched his jaw.

"Is that what you think? That I don't feel the pain you caused me?" Her sorrowful expression turned as hard as the stone obelisk they stood beside. Rosy lips drew into a cracked gray line. Her eyes turned to slate. "You think you can't hurt people simply because, to you, they aren't real. I know who you are, Hayden Gale. I know who you are!"

Hayden's heart thundered in his chest. He was going to be sick. Tearing away from her, he ran up the stairs of the temple and plunged into the darkness after Graves. Thoughts dashed in his mind, racing past impossibility. Someone had to be playing a trick on him. But nobody knew about Katherine. Nobody but him.

Darkness enveloped him and with it came another kind of heaviness. It pressed on his shoulders as if the air weighed more inside the building than without. A light fluttered from a dark corner.

"Ah, you've gained your courage, I see." Graves's voice echoed over the stone walls. "Come here. I've found something quite interesting."

Hayden squinted as his eyes grew accustomed to the gloom. The room extended so far back he couldn't see the end. Rotting chairs, tables, and bowls littered the cold, stone floor, along with dirt and dried weeds. A collection of handmade axes and swords hung on one wall. Hayden glanced over his shoulder and scanned the courtyard but Katherine was gone. Just an illusion. Of course. Hadn't he just been thinking of her? No doubt his guilt had gotten the better of him. He drew a deep breath of dank air that smelled of mold and agony.

The flicker of Graves's torch drew Hayden's gaze, and he headed toward him with one thought in mind—to drag the madman out of here and leave this place posthaste. A rancid smell much like rotten fruit assailed him as he passed a large pond circled in stone. Steam spiraled off the dark water like misty fingers rising from the grave. Apprehension twisted his gut and he hurried along, his gaze drawn to metallic engravings that decorated the entire back wall. Torch light glinted off a golden crescent moon surrounded by stars that hung above what appeared to be a stone altar. Thinking this must be what drew Graves's attention, Hayden faced him, intending to make a joke that they shouldn't tell Dodd about the temple or he'd strip the place of all its gold. But Graves wasn't looking at the golden moon. He was staring at words etched into the stone above an opening to the side of the altar.

"Do you know what this says, my friend?" Graves held the torch up to the lintel.

Hayden glanced at the words. Latin? How had Latin words come to be written in the middle of a Brazilian jungle? "No."

"It says 'Beware, the Catacomb of the Four.'"

CHAPTER 4

Back in New Hope, Hayden slid his knife across the bark and watched the mahogany curl beneath his blade. One of the many wonderful things this jungle possessed was a variety of rare, exotic wood. His good friend, a furniture maker from Savannah, would be happier than a beaver in a woodshed with such abundance. Smiling at the thought, Hayden carved another slice, carefully shaping the wood like a potter molding clay. The smell of roasted fish and fried bananas stirred his stomach to life, and he looked up to see several of the farmer's wives hovering about the massive brick fire pit at the edge of the meeting shelter. At least that was what the colonists were calling the large pavilion left by the previous settlers. Based on the table and several chairs scattered beneath the palm-frond roof, Hayden assumed the area must have been used for meetings, for sharing meals, and perhaps even for the occasional party. But why had his father's colony left after working so hard to erect the huts and build all the furniture? Not to mention felling trees and clearing away part of the jungle for planting crops?

Something had driven them away. Something frightening.

His thoughts scattered to the eerie temple Graves had found earlier: the stark silence surrounding the area, the heaviness in the air, the odd Latin phrase about catacombs. Could something from that unholy place have caused the last colonists to leave? But no. From the looks of it, no one had set foot there in years.

The setting sun speared golden rays through the web of green, casting a bluish hue over the jungle, before sinking beneath the tree tops. And just as quickly, the warble of birds transformed into the buzz of crickets and croak of frogs. Though Hayden ought to have been accustomed to it by now, the sudden onset of night took him by surprise. Rising, he struck a match and lit one of the many lanterns hanging on posts throughout the camp while other men did the same. The golden cones lit the street at intervals and made the camp look almost civilized. Almost. Settling on a bench beneath one of the lights, Hayden resumed his whittling as James Callaway, the doctor-preacher approached and eased beside him.

"What are you making?"

Hayden studied the long piece of wood he'd formed into what could pass for a table or chair leg. "Not quite sure."

"You've got talent, Hayden. We could use some decent furniture around here." James shifted on the bench, causing it to wobble. "Whoever made these didn't know what he was doing."

Hayden nodded his agreement. The ramshackle furniture had been shabbily assembled and would no doubt fall apart within a year. And though Hayden would love to put his skills to use, he had no plans to remain with the colony. He had to leave, find his father, and make him pay. But he couldn't tell James that.

"Where did you learn woodworking?" James asked.

"I spent a summer working in my friend's furniture shop in Savannah."

"It shows." Groaning, James stretched his back and gazed over the darkness that now inhabited the field they'd been plowing all day. "I tell you, I've never worked as hard as I have these past two months." He chuckled.

Hayden had no doubt James was unaccustomed to hard work, except, perhaps, for his years as a battlefield doctor. Before the war, the man had been a preacher. And a hypocrite. But then no one knew about that except Hayden from the one time he'd seen him in Tennessee back in '60. Regardless, the doctor's family came from big money. Not like Hayden's. No, Hayden had been forced to scrape and beg just for scraps to eat. Until he figured out how easy it was to swindle the rich.

Too easy, as it turned out.

Angeline's sweet laughter drew both men's gazes to the comely russet-haired seamstress carrying a platter of food to the table in the meeting house. She not only drew their gazes, but those of several of the other single men, including Mr. Dodd, who took a seat on a stump across from Hayden. Hayden hated the way the man ogled her, and he wasn't altogether pleased at James's interest in her either. Yet, what did it matter? Hayden wasn't staying long. But if he was. . .well, the woman intrigued him. He was sure he'd seen her face on a wanted poster in the Norfolk, Virginia, jail. He never forgot a face, especially a beautiful one like hers. And now that he'd discovered she had a sweet disposition and a kind heart, the dichotomy of her brush with the law fascinated him all the more.

Setting the platter on the table, she returned to the fire and began stirring a kettle. Though she claimed her family were wealthy shipwrights, she did not shy away from hard work.

So unlike Magnolia. Who now entered the clearing, flanked by her pretentious parents and followed by their slave, Mable. Wearing a lilac taffeta gown and with her flaxen hair pinned up in a waterfall of curls about her neck, the spoiled plantation owner's daughter presented a rather alluring picture.

As long as she kept her mouth shut.

Her gaze brushed over him with a dismissal that pricked his ire. He shrugged it off. He'd been engaged in verbal battle with the shrew ever since he'd wandered into her cabin on board the *New Hope* with a bullet in his side. Since then, the only time she'd been quiet was when he'd kissed her on board the ship. But oh, what a kiss! He reacted even now at the remembrance, and his knife slipped over the wood, slicing his finger. A thin line of blood rose from his skin.

"Let me see that." As if the war nurse could smell blood on the wind, Eliza appeared out of nowhere.

The doctor, sitting beside Hayden, had the same ability but the opposite reaction. Coughing, he turned his face away, and Hayden had the sudden urge to shove his bloody hand into the man's vision just to see him squirm. But that wouldn't be nice. And Hayden *did* like the doc, even if he was a bit preachy.

"It's nothing," Hayden said.

Eliza knelt to examine his hand. Reaching into a pouch clipped to her belt, she opened a jar and spread salve over Hayden's wound as a night breeze swirled around them, cooling the perspiration on his neck.

"Ouch." Pain brought his gaze down to Eliza pressing against his cut. "It felt better before you touched it."

"Don't be such a baby, Hayden," she chided him. "You don't want it getting infected, do you?"

The spicy scent of the food drew more people from their huts in anticipation of supper. The blacksmith and his wife, the baker, the cooper, several farmers, another plantation owner, and several ex-soldiers, forty-two in all. Most of whom got along just fine.

Eliza wrapped a bandage around his finger. "I believe you'll live."

Hayden grinned as she rose and looped her arm through her husband's, who had just joined them. For all his sternness, the colonel, and leader of their ragtag southern outpost, melted like wax whenever he looked at his wife. Ever since their wedding on the beach the day after the ship set them ashore, the two hadn't kept their eyes—or their hands—off each other.

Hayden averted his gaze from the look that now passed between them. A private look of promised love and intimacy.

Sarah, the teacher, announced dinner and the group moved to sit in the meeting shelter, the women at the table and the men scattered about on chairs and stools. After James said a prayer of thanks to bless the food, Thiago educated them on their Brazilian fare for the night.

"Rice, beans, *carne seca* or dried beef, boiled cabbage with garlic, fried bananas, roasted *bacalhau* or cod, and mandioca cakes." The guide smiled broadly. "Mandioca is a root that grows here in Brazil," he continued in his Portuguese accent. "It is poisonous if you eat it raw but once cooked it is safe. Known as the bread of Brazil. Very good." He rubbed his tummy and smiled, eliciting a few chuckles from the colonists. "Eat and enjoy!"

Hayden gathered a plateful, anxious to appease his hunger after a long day's work. The food tasted as good as it smelled, and he couldn't shovel it into his mouth fast enough to satisfy his aching belly. While they ate, James and Blake discussed what else needed to be done before they planted the fields, as well as the best way to organize the men and gather materials to build a sugar press, mill, and barn. With each spark of enthusiasm in their voices and each glimpse of excitement on their expressions, Hayden's heart sank. He couldn't join them. No matter how much he longed to be a part of recreating a Southern utopia in this strange new land, he couldn't stay. He'd come for a different reason, and he must keep his focus.

His gaze landed on Magnolia, who seemed as miserable as he was. Scowling, she picked at the food Mable had brought her as if it were poison. Her father leaned toward her and said something that further deepened her frown and sent her dashing down the main street in a riot of taffeta and lace. Her abrupt and over-dramatized departure, however, did nothing to dampen the jovial mood of the colonists, who continued to converse and laugh while the children giggled and played in the center of the square. Hayden shook his head at her childish behavior even as pity stung him for the way her father treated her. As no father should treat a daughter.

The soothing rush of the river harmonized with the buzz of nighttime insects to create a pleasant tune that, combined with the scent of orange blossoms in the gentle breeze, settled an unusual peace over Hayden. Despite the hard work involved in tilling the farmland and building the colony, Brazil was indeed a paradise: green and lush and teeming with life, and with more wild fruit and fresh water than a person could want. What Hayden wouldn't have given to have spent his childhood here instead of begging and stealing on the streets of Charleston. At least he would have had plenty of food and not been surrounded by hooligans and drunks intent on taking advantage of a young, innocent boy.

As if reading his thoughts, a predatory growl echoed through the trees, causing the hairs on his arm to stand at attention. Silence descended on the camp as all eyes shifted toward the dark jungle surrounding them. They'd heard beastly howls before but this one seemed closer, more intent. Thiago hopped up from his seat beside Sarah, yanked four polished stones from his pocket and headed toward Blake.

"Colonel, put these rocks at four corners of camp, they will keep out the *Lobisón*." Fear sparked in his dark eyes as he cast a wary glance over the jungle. "The man-wolf. That is his call."

"Man-wolf?" Blake stood. "What nonsense is this?"

"No nonsense, Colonel. He is part man, part wolf. Legend says if he attacks you and you live, you become Lobisón too."

James closed the man's hand over the charms as if the sight of them repulsed him. "We have no need of these, Thiago. God is far more powerful than any wolf. He will protect us."

Thiago narrowed his eyes. "You do not know what Lobisón can do, Mr. James. These rocks are part of the *Penha*, a mountain rock consecrated to Virgin, our Lady of the Rock. Very powerful against evil."

Hayden was about to remark on the foolishness of such a notion when a woman's scream split the night.

CHAPTER 5

Magnolia batted tears from her face and stormed toward the edge of camp. Could her father not cease his harsh censure of her for one meal? Just one meal when she wasn't castigated for her appearance or the improper way she was eating her food? She could almost understand, almost, if they were seated at an elegant linen-clad table, dining with British royalty or even with the upper-crust of Georgia—rich, eligible men of substance and power—but they were sitting on stumps in the middle of a primordial jungle eating with commoners! She was tired of being told what to wear and how to fix her hair and how to sit and walk and speak. And behave. It wasn't like she had to impress anyone except snails and toads and oh—something cracked beneath her shoe. She froze, cringed, and slowly lifted her foot, not daring to glance down. A squishy sound met her ears, sending the few bites of supper she'd consumed into her throat.

"Oh. . . I hate this place!" she squealed and glanced back at the glow of the campfire flickering between leaves. She'd been so distraught, she'd passed her parent's hut and plunged into the jungle unaware. Buzzing and chirping and croaking surrounded her like a living, breathing entity—a dark, breathing entity made up of quivering shadows and pulsating greenery. She grabbed her skirts, intending to head back to camp when the soothing sound of water beckoned her onward. Perhaps she could wash her face and have a moment's peace before she faced the colonists, who were no doubt entertaining themselves this very moment with gossip about her sudden departure.

Glancing around at the dark foliage, she took a tentative step toward the bubbling sound. Truth be told, she seemed to provide the citizens of New Hope with much entertainment of late. Just because she was different: educated, more attentive to her appearance, genteel, and refined while most of them were nothing but farmers, soldiers, and tradesmen. Why, oh why, had her father subjected her and her mother to such plebian rabble! She swept aside a branch and moved forward.

Something buzzed by her ear. "Oh, shoo!" She batted it away, hoping the insect wouldn't get caught in her hair. The hair Mable had spent nearly an hour curling and pinning before supper. Just to please Magnolia's father.

Moonlight penetrated the canopy in a clearing up ahead and sparkled over a rippling creek. The scene appeared so serene, it was hard to believe there were dangers in the jungle like the jaguars and wolves Hayden had told her about. Over her shoulder, she could still see the lights of New Hope through the foliage. Perhaps it would be safe enough to sit for a while and clear her thoughts.

Gathering her skirts and adjusting her crinoline, she lowered onto a flat boulder, allowing her billowing gown to settle around her. Moonlight transformed the tiny creek into silvery braids that rose in a mist of fairy dust across the clearing. The beautiful sight did much to calm her spirits. But she had something else that would help even more. After one last glance at the camp, she withdrew a flask from the secret pocket she'd sewn in her petticoat, uncorked it, and took a long draught of the port she'd stolen from her father. The smooth, tawny liquid eased down her throat, unwinding her tight nerves with each warm embrace. She drew in a deep breath of the moist jungle air, fragrant with passion flowers, and tried to forget her father's reprimand for the slouching manner in which she sat. "So unlike a lady," he had said.

Another sip of port and the disappointment blaring in his tone began to fade. Her shoulders lowered, and the rod that held up her spine melted. Leaning over, she untied her ankle boots and kicked them off, not caring if her stockings became soiled. Hiking up her skirts, she wiggled her toes, took another sip, and giggled as she dipped them, stockings and all, in the cool water. If her father could see her now.

A crackling sound joined the nightly hum of the jungle. Low at first, gentle like the hiss of a dying fire. But then it grew in intensity and sharpness. Magnolia sat up and scanned the foliage but the oscillating shadows of dark and gray revealed nothing. No fire. No torch. "Hello?" The crackling stopped.

Shaking her head, she took another sip. It was almost gone. And the way her father kept track of his precious liquor, she doubted she'd be able to steal more any time soon. At least not enough to benumb her mind and heart against her horrid circumstances. Not enough to make it bearable to rise each morning and face the heat and insects and back-breaking labor. Or at least her attempt at labor. No, she would have to find another source of liquor. Mr. Lewis, the old carpenter, seemed to have an unending supply. Perhaps she could cajole him into sharing.

The crackling began again. Or was it simply the wind quivering the leaves? But, there *was* no wind. At least not enough to cool her skin. Perspiration moistened her forehead and neck, and she leaned toward the creek to splash water on her face when she caught her reflection.

Moonlight silhouetted curls the color of the morning sun that fell from her chignon about her shoulders. Only one errant strand was out of place in an otherwise perfect coiffeur. Oval eyes that were almost catlike in shape reflected blue from the silvery water. High cheekbones, a refined chin, a small perfectly shaped nose, and rosy lips completed the visage that had brought so many gentlemen to their knees. One of whom had destroyed her family. And another whose suit she would have accepted—whose family and reputation could have restored her own family's name—if only her parents had not dragged her off to Brazil.

If her father hadn't been so proud and stubborn and allowed them to wed before the war, they'd all be sitting in a comfortable parlor in Atlanta sipping tea from china cups instead of drinking river water from pewter mugs.

As if reading her thoughts, the crackling turned to laughter, soft, malicious laughter. Magnolia corked her flask and put it away. No more port for now. She was starting to hear things. A shadow slithered through the greenery. And apparently see things, as well. "Hello?"

A growl rumbled through the trees. Close, but yet, not close. Magnolia froze. Her heart thundered in her chest. Her fingers grew numb. She scanned the forest, afraid to move. Something flickered in the water. Leaning over, she gazed at her reflection again.

Her beautiful golden hair began to shrivel. Like old twine left too long in the sun, it shrank and grew brittle until, strand by strand, it slid off her head, landed on the water, and floated away. Leaving her bald. Completely bald!

Flinging her hands to her head, she did the only thing she could think to do. She screamed at the top of her lungs.

Hayden was the first one to burst into the clearing, James and Colonel Blake on his heels. What he expected to see—what his worst fears imagined—was Magnolia being mauled by some wild animal. What he saw instead was the lady gripping her head and screaming, "My hair! My hair!" After scanning the clearing for a wolf, he dashed toward her, forced her hands to her sides, and led her into the moonlight to see if she'd been bitten or injured. But aside from her hair being hopelessly torn from its pins, she seemed unscathed.

Yet her eyes told a different story. They were wide and etched with fear. No, not fear—absolute, excruciating horror. They searched his as if looking for an answer. "My hair," she sobbed.

"Your hair? What about it?" Hayden wondered if she'd either gone mad or—he dipped his nose toward her mouth—had too much to drink. Obviously the latter due to the pungent scent of alcohol hovering around her. Angry, he released her.

"What happened? Are you all right?" James approached and drew her into an embrace. She fell against him and started to cry. Of course she did. Hayden couldn't believe he'd been so gullible. That was exactly what she wanted—attention.

And everyone fell for it. Blake, pistol in hand, surveyed the edge of the clearing, while Eliza rushed to Magnolia and took James's place by her side.

"My hair," Magnolia whined.

"What about your hair, dearest?" Eliza brushed a lock from Magnolia's face.

"Don't coddle her. Nothing happened." Hayden huffed as James circled the camp, examining bushes and sweeping aside leaves.

"It was gone. All gone." Magnolia's gaze shot to the small creek. "When I looked at my reflection"—she drew in a shredded breath— "my hair fell out. I was bald!" she whimpered, tears spilling from her eyes. "I was completely bald."

"Well, you aren't bald now." Eliza held one of Magnolia's long strands in front of her. After touching it, Magnolia released a shuddering sigh.

"Nothing here." Blake joined them.

"No animal tracks at all," James added.

"But the crackling." Magnolia stared into the jungle, wiping her face. "The voices. Did you hear them?"

Blake's gaze snapped to Magnolia.

"No. We didn't hear anything," Elisa said.

Hayden rubbed his eyes, angry that this woman's insecurity and propensity to drink caused so much unnecessary trouble. Yet hadn't he heard crackling at the temple right before Katherine Henley appeared? How strange that Magnolia heard the same sound before seeing something that wasn't there. But no, it was only Hayden's guilt and Magnolia's insecurity that caused these illusions. Nothing more. Then why did Blake continue to stare at Magnolia as if her ramblings made sense?

"Let's get back to camp, shall we?" he finally said.

Hayden agreed. He'd left a half-eaten supper he intended to finish. They all started back when Magnolia halted, tugged from Eliza's grip, and darted back toward the creek mumbling something about shoes.

"I'll watch over her," Hayden offered. No sense in the foolish girl keeping them all from their food. With a nod, Eliza looped her arm through her husband's as they joined James on his way back to camp.

"Where are my shoes?" Magnolia pointed toward the sand. "They were right there."

"Drop the charade, Princess. Everyone is gone, and I'm not buying it."

"Not buying wha—" She spun to face him with what looked like real tears in her eyes. Hayden grinned. Ah, yes. She was good. He'd give her that. But she had no idea who she was dealing with.

Those eyes turned to glaciers as she planted hands on her hips. "You think I'm lying? You think I made up the crackling sound and the baldness. Why would I do that?"

He crossed his arms over his chest. "For attention. Or because you've had too much to drink."

"I'm not drunk." She stomped her foot. "I know what I saw." She gazed down at the mud dripping from the hem of her gown and groaned. "And I don't care what you think. Where are my parents? Didn't they hear me scream?" Her gaze darted toward the camp.

So that was it. She'd staged this to test her parents' love for her. But Hayden knew they weren't coming. Her father had risen from his seat, seen Hayden and the others speeding by, and then sat back down to finish his meal. Did he not care for his daughter at all or was he so accustomed to allowing others to do his work, that he left the safety of his own family in their hands?

Poor girl. A wave of sympathy flooded him as a breeze swept the ivory tips of her loose hair across her waist. Standing there—silent—a look of innocence and desperation on her face, she looked like a sad forest sprite, all glitter and beauty. And something within Hayden stirred.

She swung her gaze to his and huffed, breaking the spell. "Stop looking at me like that."

"Like what?"

"Like you want to kiss me again."

"Again?" he toyed with her.

Her lips drew tight. "I know you remember." He caught a glimpse of her glassy eyes in the moonlight before she turned and began stomping back to camp, mumbling, "Incorrigible man."

But she was right about one thing.

He did want to kiss her.

CHAPTER 6

eave?" Blake looked up from his desk in the large hut that served as New Hope's town hall, looking more like the army colonel he used to be, rather than the leader of a meager colony in Brazil. A stack of papers, a gold pocket watch, a set of quill pens and ink, a tilting pile of books, and a telescope from the ship spread across the top in a haphazard manner that was at odds with the colonel's regimented style. Setting down his pen, Blake sighed as he eyed the ledger he'd been writing in then leaned back in his chair.

Hayden didn't envy the task of keeping accounts for the colony. Though he'd always been good at making money, he'd never been good at managing it properly. Or holding on to it.

Shifting his boots over the tamped dirt floor, he drew a deep breath of sweat, coffee, and gunpowder. He knew this wasn't going to be easy. So instead of facing Blake, he glanced over the shelves housing their dwindling supplies: sacks of rice, beans, flour, coffee, and dried beef. Extra shovels, picks, axes, and rakes were propped against the wall, ready to be moved to the barn when it was built. Lanterns and candles lined shelves behind Hayden, along with whale oil, extra canvas, and tar. Finally, he faced forward and glanced at James, who sat on a chair beside Blake's desk. Rays from the setting sun floated in through the window and hallowed his body in gold, making him look like the preacher he claimed to be.

Angling his shoulders, Hayden stretched his back and gazed at his two friends. Though their skin was tanned a golden brown from hours in the sun, and dirt smudged their tattered clothes, both looked more robust and healthy than when he'd first met them on board the ship over four months ago. He wondered if the same were true for himself, for he'd never felt better, except for the sorrow welling in his gut at the thought of leaving them. His friends. He'd never really had friends before.

James stood. "You can't be serious. We are going to plant within the week. You've put so much work into this town."

Hayden stared at the ground. "It cannot be helped. I belong in a city, not a jungle," he lied. Truthfully, he had loved his time here in Brazil, away from the filth and crime that always encroached where large groups of humans inhabited, here out in the fresh air, perfumed with the sweet smells of the jungle, where fruit was plentiful and life was simple. Where everyone worked together—well, almost everyone—to build a new world. Where, for the first time in his life, he had put in a hard day's work and been rewarded for it. With muscle aches, yes. But aches he was proud of. Aches that came from honest work. Aches that caused a twinge of something foreign inside him, something he'd never expected to feel—self-respect. Not only that, but he had earned the respect of the two men who stood before him—men who wouldn't have given him a moment of their time back in the States. And that had been worth all the money he'd ever swindled.

But he couldn't stay. He had a man to find. A debt to pay. He'd promised his mother on her death bed.

Blake hobbled around the desk. His uneven gait from an old war wound did nothing to detract from his commanding presence, nor from the frustration masking his face. "I realize you were a stowaway on this journey, but you have fit in with the colony so nicely. You're a hard worker and an honorable man."

Hayden stifled the chuckle in his throat.

"And I've come to depend on you," Blake continued. "We all have."

"Indeed." The doctor's brow wrinkled. "You've taken on a leadership role among us. The town needs men like you."

Hayden crossed his arms over his chest and gazed out the window. He had expected opposition. He had expected frustration, even anger.

He hadn't expected to be cloaked in praise. Especially from the two men he admired most in the world. He cleared his throat. "I appreciate that. I truly do. But there is something I must do."

"Here in Brazil?" Blake asked.

"Perhaps. Perhaps not. But I must go to Rio to find out." Hayden silently chastised himself for saying far too much already, but the look of sorrow and concern in his friends' eyes was chipping away at his wall of resolve. "I cannot tell you any more than that."

Blake nodded and leaned back on his desk with a sigh. "It will be difficult without you."

James rubbed the scar angling down the side of his mouth. "Then there's a chance you will return?"

"A slight chance." Hayden shrugged. "Time will tell."

"When are you leaving?" Blake asked.

"Tomorrow."

"On foot?" James asked.

"Yes, Thiago gave me directions. It shouldn't take more than five days if I travel quickly."

"All alone in the jungle?" Blake asked.

"I can take care of myself."

Blake nodded. "Since you'll be in Rio, would you inform Mr. Santos that we've moved our location a mile west and that once we have planted our crops and started building the town, we will send Thiago back with the exact acreage we intend to purchase as stated on our provisional title?"

"Of course," Hayden said. He needed to speak to the immigration officer anyway.

Rising, Blake clutched Hayden's shoulders, his gray eyes pointed and somber. "We will miss you, Hayden. Be safe and God speed." He released him and sighed heavily.

Thankfully, before Hayden's eyes grew moist and he embarrassed himself.

"I will pray for you every day, my friend." James gave a sad smile. "And in particular that you will return to us soon. You always have a home in New Hope."

Hayden extended his hand to the doctor, but the man drew him into an embrace instead, slapping his back before releasing him and turning away.

Hayden shifted his face from their view. Clearing his throat, he nodded and grunted his thanks to both men before hurrying out the door. He'd never had a home. At least none he remembered with fondness. After his mother had been killed, he'd never had a family either. He'd been a gypsy, a drifter. He should be used to it. Then why was it so hard to leave this silly town?

✦

Brushing aside leaves, Magnolia crept up to two men circling a fire just outside of town. Unable to sleep, she'd left her parents' hut, thinking some fresh air and listening to anything but her father's snoring would help settle her nerves. But the distant flicker of flames soon lured her to the outskirts of town. She wouldn't have ventured any farther except that she could make out Mr. Lewis's and Thiago's faces in the firelight. Harmless enough men. And she'd been meaning to speak to Mr. Lewis anyway. The friendly old carpenter, who reminded her of the bumbling overseer on their plantation back home, had a mind that dwarfed the size of his heart. All she had to do was smile and plant a kiss on his bristly cheek and he happily shared whatever spirits he had on his person.

And she sure could use a drink tonight.

So intent on whatever they were doing over the flames, the two men didn't hear her approach—didn't hear the leaves rustle or the twig snap beneath her boots. Didn't even turn until she said, "Whatever are you doing, gentlemen?" The teasing reprimand in her voice sent fear skittering across their faces.

"Oh, mercy me, don't trouble yourselves. Whatever it is, I won't tell a soul." She curled a hand on her hip. "As long as you let me in on it." Her grin disarmed them, and they both smiled in return.

Mr. Lewis returned his attention to the contraption sitting atop the flames, while Thiago rose to usher her close. "We make rum— Brazilian rum."

367

Delight filtered through her. "Oh, I knew I smelled something delicious." Adjusting her crinoline and multiple petticoats, she lowered herself onto a stump while Mr. Lewis checked a thermometer that was perched inside an iron pot hanging over the fire. Tubes sprang from holes in the container's sides and ran down to another kettle sitting in a bowl of water off to the side.

The old carpenter looked up, flames flickering over his pudgy face. "It's a distiller, miss."

"We distill sugarcane juice," Thiago added. "Make *pinga,* or rum. Very good." His handsome eyes sparkled as he took a seat beside her. Tall, lithe, tanned, with dark features, the interpreter's exotic looks were not without appeal, though he possessed a boyish impetuousness that prevented a more serious look. Besides, he had no wealth nor prominent position in Brazilian society.

"I should have known you'd be up to mischief, Mr. Lewis." She teased the old carpenter.

He chuckled. "Well, miss, our drinking supplies are rapidly shrinking. So when Thiago, here, informed me he knew how to make this pinga, so famous here in Brazil, what was a man to do?" He winked.

Thiago's brow wrinkled. "You will not tell anyone."

"She won't." Mr. Lewis answered with a sly smile. "Not if she wants us to share."

The fire crackled, shooting sparks into the air as the smell of smoke and night-blooming orchids battled for preeminence.

Magnolia placed a finger over her lips. "On my honor, my lips are sealed. Now"—she glanced around—"do you have any of this ping. . . pinga for sampling?"

"Ah, sim. . .yes." Thiago pulled a flask from his shirt pocket. "We made some last week." He uncorked it and handed it to her.

"Good thing 'cause I only have one more bottle of rum from the ship." Mr. Lewis scowled. "That is, unless Hayden can bring some back from Rio."

Hayden? Rio? Magnolia batted away a bug and took a sip. The pungent liquid stung her tongue, filling her mouth with a spicy orange taste. She coughed and struggled to breathe. "Mercy"—her voice sounded like an old woman's—"but this is strong."

Both men chuckled. The buzz of cicadas intensified around them, reminding Magnolia of the odd crackling she'd heard the other night. "But what is this about Hayden and Rio?"

"He leaves tomorrow." A breeze tossed Thiago's shoulder-length hair behind him as he stared at the fire. "I tell him best way to walk to Rio from here. I will miss him. We travel jungle together much."

"Tomorrow?" Magnolia took another sip of pinga, wondering why her heart suddenly cinched in her chest. "Why is he going? For supplies?"

"He say he not happy here. Did not find what he look for."

"He's not coming back?" Magnolia felt like she weighed a thousand pounds. She took another drink to ease the pain and was pleased when her mind began to numb.

That numbness, however, did not reach her heart. Not even after several more sips.

Three hours later, with valise stuffed and swung over her shoulder, Magnolia shoved aside the canvas door of Hayden's hut and entered the dark room. She had never been in a man's bedchamber before, and her heart did a hard tumble in her chest as she stood there frozen, focusing on the sound of male snoring, seeing nothing but shadows. She hated disturbing his sleep—had paced in front of his hut for hours—but she had no choice. What if he left before she'd had a chance to speak to him? Then she'd be stuck in this bug-infested jungle forever.

Hayden was her last chance.

She took a step toward his cot, the edge of which was visible now in a stream of moonlight drifting through the window. A dove cooed outside and somewhere in the distance a growl rumbled through the jungle, reminding her why she needed this man's protection on the way to Rio. If only he would agree to take her.

Another step and she could smell him. All musk and man. Not an offensive smell, but a scent that brought delight to her heart, much like the smell of peach pie brought a flood of good memories from her childhood. He stirred and shifted position, his arm landing in the moonlight. His hand—twice the size of hers—bore scrapes and calluses from his work in the fields. She hoped he wouldn't get the wrong idea upon finding her at his bedside in the middle of the night. But she was desperate. And desperate times called for desperate ways, or measures, or whatever it was they said.

She took another step and knelt beside his cot. His breathing was deep and rough like the man himself, and she wished she could see his face in the shadows. Now, how to wake the sleeping beast? A gentle touch, perhaps. That always worked with her father. She lifted her hand to lay it on his arm.

When his fingers gripped her wrist like iron shackles.

Before she could react, he leapt, flung her onto the cot, flipped her over, and pinned her arms down with his own. Magnolia would have screamed, but she didn't want to alert anyone. Instead, she struggled against his tight grip. "Get off of me this instant!"

He released her, disappearing into the shadows. A match struck and the flame sped through the air to light a candle, illuminating the petulant fiend.

⚜

"Magnolia?" Hayden blinked, trying to clear the sleepy haze from his eyes. "Zooks, Princess, what are you doing sneaking around my hut in the middle of the night?" He'd heard her—and smelled the alcohol on her breath—the moment she'd entered. He hadn't survived on the street for eight years without learning to sleep with one eye open. Of course, he hadn't known it was Magnolia. Or a lady, for that matter. Not until he'd tossed her, as light as a feather, onto the cot and felt her soft skin beneath his fingers—heard her quiet sob. Now as she sat up and rubbed her arms where he'd clutched them, guilt assailed him for hurting her.

"I came to speak to you. Why else would I be here?" She fixed him with a pointed gaze that dropped to his bare chest then quickly looked away.

He grinned. "In the middle of the night?" She looked delicious with her flaxen hair tumbling over her shoulders, cheeks flushed pink, and eyes sparking in anger. He licked his lips, wishing she had come here for a tryst, rather than for whatever reason put that scowl on her face.

"I heard you were leaving in the morning."

"Ah." He pressed a hand over his heart. "And overcome with sorrow, you came to tell me how much you're going to miss me."

"Don't be absurd!" Pressing down her billowing skirts, she struggled to rise, but instead plopped back hopelessly onto the cot with a growl. Hayden should help her, but he was rather enjoying watching her expression contort into cute little folds with the effort. Finally, she managed to stand. Stuffing strands of hair into their pins, she straightened her posture along with her skirts as if she hadn't just crawled off a man's bed. "Now, look what you've done to my hair."

"I've done?" Hayden snorted. "You're lucky that's *all* I did." Grabbing a shirt from the back of a chair, he tossed it over his head. "Do you always sneak up, besotted, on men in their beds? Not wise if you wish to keep your virtue, Princess."

"My name is Mag—" Her eyes speared him. "I am not besotted, and my virtue is none of your affair."

"And it won't be as long as you behave like a dissolute minx."

"Grrrrrr." She bared her teeth like a she-wolf. "How predictable that a man like you would have no care for a woman's virtue."

Hayden closed his eyes, trying to make sense of the woman's ramblings. An impossible feat, he finally decided. Sinking into a chair, he scrubbed his face with his hands. "What is it you want, Princess? I was rather enjoying my sleep." Only then did he see her valise lying on the floor with something lacy spilling onto the dirt.

She scrambled to retrieve it, stuffing the item back inside as a pink hue crept up her neck.

"Going on a trip?" he asked.

"Yes. With you." She lifted her pert nose in the air but then instantly lowered it, frowned, and formed a pout with those luscious lips. "Oh, please say you'll take me with you to Rio?"

Hayden would have laughed if he hadn't been so shocked. As it was, all he could do was stare at the candlelight flickering in her blue eyes. He searched those eyes that now looked at him with such innocence and pleading—searched for the shrew that had been there only moments before. But she hid the hellion well. When she wanted something. He raked a hand through his hair. "No."

"What do you mean, no?" Her tone was incredulous, as if no man had ever denied her request.

"I believe the word speaks for itself, Princess. I have business in Rio, and it's unclear whether I will return. The last thing I need is a woman, and a coddled one at that, to slow me down."

The corners of her mouth tightened. Her fists clenched. She seemed to be having difficulty restraining that inner hellion at the moment. Finally she said, "I will not slow you down, Hayden, you have my word. And once we get to Rio, you can wash your hands of me."

Hayden opened his mouth to respond, but she continued her tirade. "I only need an escort to Rio, where I intend to book passage on a ship back to Charleston. Then you'll never see me again. What is so difficult about that? Upon my word, I can keep up with you in the jungle. And you won't have to do anything for me except lead the way. In fact, you'll hardly notice me at all."

Hardly notice her? Hayden groaned inwardly. He'd have to be deaf not to hear the woman's interminable chattering and blind not to notice her stunning face and curvaceous figure. No, the woman would definitely be a distraction.

As well as a major aggravation.

"What of your parents?"

"They don't know. I'm twenty-three. I can take care of myself!" She patted her hair in place then took a step toward him. "I beg you, I can't stay in this savage backcountry another day. I'll simply go mad."

Hayden wasn't altogether sure that hadn't already occurred. After all, the woman had been hysterical over thinking she was bald just two days ago. "How will you afford to book passage on a ship?"

"I have money. You need not worry about me."

Of course he would worry about her. Was the woman daft? If she came with him, she would be under his protection. He would be responsible for her welfare and safety. And *that* he couldn't have.

He needed no complications, no obstacles, no temptations to keep him from his goal.

Temptations. . .ah, he knew just the way to be rid of her. Curling his lips in a sultry grin, he moved toward her, scanning her with his gaze. "What of your reputation? All alone in the jungle with a man for five days. And nights." He raised his brows. "What will people think?"

She looked away. Moonlight sprinkled glitter dust on her hair and cast shadowy arcs beneath her lashes. "No one need know. Especially not back home."

Hayden closed the gap between them. The scent of alcohol vied for dominion over her sweet, feminine scent—a scent that reminded him of citrus and cedar. He rubbed the stubble on his chin and drew a deep breath, leaning to whisper, "And would you risk arriving in Rio with your virtue shattered?"

Drawing a jagged breath, she retreated. Her leg struck the cot. She winced. "I assure you, there is no risk of that!"

He continued to stare at her.

Her eyes became flames. "You wouldn't dare!"

He fingered a lock of her hair. As soft as he'd expected. "You don't know what I would or wouldn't do, Princess." Of course he would never force himself on a woman, but she didn't need to know that. Besides, he quite enjoyed playing the cad. One of his many roles.

And a role that, apparently, she bought, lock, stock, and barrel. Eyes round, she swallowed hard and clutched her valise to her chest like a shield. "You are a vile toad, Mr. Hayden Gale!" she spat before storming out of the hut.

Hayden chuckled, a sudden emptiness settling on him at her departure. Perhaps he shouldn't have teased her so, but it was for the best. Releasing a heavy breath, he gathered his things as dawn's first glow slid over the wooden window frame. He should get going. The sooner he left, the better.

Chapter 7

With the tip of her parasol, Magnolia brushed aside a particularly slimy-looking vine upon which a family of monstrous beetles had taken residence. Not only residence, but they appeared to be procreating at lightning speed and in astounding numbers! She cringed as she held the vine out of her way and ducked beneath. Her parasol slipped. The vine descended like a dragon with gaping beetle jaws. It slapped her in the face, showering her with bugs.

She screamed. Then quickly slammed her palm over her mouth. Dropping her valise, she sprang back and furiously batted the foul creatures scrambling over her skirts and bodice. Her stomach leapt into her throat as she hopped about the clearing like a frog on hot coals, shaking out the folds of her gown. After several agonizing minutes—and when she could find no more of the black multilegged beasties—she drew a handkerchief from her pocket and fluttered it about her face, waiting for her heart to settle. Then, swearing under her breath, she grabbed her valise and forged ahead, scanning the endless canvas of green.

Mercy me, she'd lost Hayden again! Why did that infernal man have to walk so fast? Good thing he left boot prints in the mud large enough to belong to a bear as well as broken branches and leaves so she could follow his trail or she'd be hopelessly lost. She shivered at the thought and glanced around at the thousands of birds and insects abuzz in the tangled canopy. Chirping and croaking and warbling and hissing and droning. Could they never stop and give her a moment's peace? She would go mad with the incessant hum!

And the heat! Never should a lady perspire this much. With each step, her damp petticoats rubbed against her corset, which rubbed against her chemise, which of course was glued to her skin. Soon her petticoats would be stuck to her as well, and next her over-skirts and bodice, until finally she would be completely drenched.

And smelling nothing like a lady.

Her skirts caught on something. The sound of fabric tearing grated her ears before she had the good sense to stop and free herself. "Oh, bah!" She stared at the rent in her beautiful dimity gown as tears filled her eyes.

How was she to endure five days of this torture? Perhaps it hadn't been such a good idea to follow Hayden, after all. She had thought it wouldn't be too difficult to keep hidden among the brush of the jungle nor to follow the odious man's trail. After all, she'd gained some stamina these past months. She'd grown accustomed to the bugs and the heat and to walking more than usual. Hadn't she? Then why did she feel as though she slogged through molasses—hot, prickly molasses?

But what else was she to do when the man refused to escort her to Rio? And even if he had, after his provocative insinuations, she wasn't sure she trusted him. This way was better. He would lead her to Rio and never be the wiser. Of course, she hadn't thought what she would do at night. And for food beyond the fruit the jungle offered. But she couldn't think about that now.

Using her valise as a shield and her parasol as a sword, she forged ahead, searching the trail for boot prints. There. A huge one. And over there, another. My word, but the man had a hearty stride. Perspiration stung her eyes, and she swiped it away, looking for the next print. Nothing but mud and leaves met her gaze. Lowering her valise, she inched ahead, batting aside vines and scouring the ground in all directions. Nothing. No prints, no flattened leaves, no broken branches. It was as if he had been taken up by God on this very spot like Enoch or Elijah. But she knew that couldn't have happened to the stowaway rogue. How she remembered her Bible stories, she had no idea. She hadn't opened the book in years, nor had she truly listened to the sermons her parents had dragged her to each Sunday.

She swirled around, peering through the greenery, looking for a flash of his dark blue coat, a hint of his hair, the color of roasted almonds. But all she saw was a labyrinth of green spinning around and around until dizziness jumbled her thoughts and sent her breath huddling in her throat. Her heart seized. What would happen to her now?

"Looking for me?"

Magnolia shrieked as Hayden emerged from the jungle looking at her with that patronizing I'm-in-control-and-you're-a-dolt look.

"How dare you sneak up on me!" She poked him with her parasol.

Without even a flinch, Hayden snagged it and tossed it to the ground. "Me? Sneak up on you?" He snorted. "You're the one who's been following me."

"I have not. We just happen to be going in the same direction."

"Is that so? And what direction is that? North, south, east, or west? How can you tell when you can't see the sun?"

"How can you tell?" She placed a hand on her hip.

"Because I'm used to living on my own, finding my way, not relying on a footman and a carriage to take me wherever I want at the snap of my fingers."

Why was his voice so sharp with spite? And his eyes like green thorns? "It is not my fault that you were not born to privilege, Hayden."

He hung his head and sighed, his jaw bunching then expanding as if it were going to explode any minute. She took a step back, studying him: shirt plastered to his sculpted chest, coat in hand, tight trousers stuffed within boots. An extra belt was strapped around his waist that held a long knife, a pistol, and a canteen. Was that all he'd brought? Dark hair hung to his shoulders over a chin grizzled with stubble. When he lifted his gaze to hers, the look in his eyes sent an icicle down her spine. He wouldn't hurt her. . .would he?

"I heard you the minute you started following me, Princess. I figured if I gave you enough time, you'd quit and go home. This isn't exactly a stroll through Battery Park."

"Well, you're right about that. It's an absolute oven. Or hell. I can't decide which. A rather large insect has decided I'm his next meal"—she batted the air around her—"and, apparently, he's invited all his relatives to the feast. I have blisters on my feet." She pouted. "And my shoulders ache from carrying my valise and shoving aside these interminable leaves."

The right side of his lips quirked. "We've only been walking for an hour."

She frowned, withdrew a handkerchief, and dabbed at the perspiration on her neck. "An hour? Are you sure? It seems much longer. How can you tell the time when you can't even see the sky?" She glanced up. "I feel like I'm trapped in some maniacal green web. And no doubt the spider will return soon to devour me." She gave him a victorious grin. "And you, as well."

"No, just you." He crossed his arms over his chest. "Especially if you don't return to New Hope this minute." He jerked his head in the direction from which they'd come. "If you start now, you can reach camp before noon."

Magnolia gripped his arm, surprised at the rock-hard muscle twitching beneath her fingers. She offered him her most I'm-just-a-dainty-desperate-woman-who-needs-a-strong-man look—the one that always brought men to their knees. "Please take me with you, Hayden. I shan't be any trouble. I promise." She inched out her bottom lip and forced moisture into her eyes. There, that should do it. She'd lowered herself far enough in front of this plebian. In a matter of moments, even the hardened Mr. Hayden would crack beneath her feminine wiles and beg her to accompany him.

Instead he narrowed his eyes as if deciding what to do. "Nicely done, Princess." He pried her fingers from his arm. "A bit over the top for my tastes. But I'm still not taking you to Rio. Not now and not ever. I don't need a clingy, whiney female to take care of."

"Clingy?" She picked up her parasol and leveled it at him. "I cling to no man. And I don't whine either." She lifted her chin. "I softly protest."

He snorted and shook his head. "Run along, little one." He gestured toward the trail. "I haven't time for this foolishness."

"You would send me back alone?" She'd expected his defiance if he discovered her, but what man could resist a damsel in distress? "It's not safe."

"Then you shouldn't have followed me." He strode off. "Good day, Princess."

Magnolia started after him. "Why do you keep calling me that?"

"Because you behave as though your class and fortune make you queen of all." He waved a hand through the air in dismissal.

"I do no such thing!" She stomped her foot. "Come back here this instant. What sort of gentleman leaves a lady alone in the jungle? You will escort me to Rio at once, Hayden Gale."

He chuckled. "You prove my point, Princess. Now hurry along before it gets too late."

Fuming, Magnolia swatted a bug and watched as Hayden marched away with that swaggering gait of his.

She felt like screaming. She felt like crying. But she hadn't the energy for either.

⚜

At the sight of Thiago entering the hut, James punched to his feet, grabbed the letter off Blake's desk, and glanced at Magnolia's parents huddling in the corner. Finally they would get to the bottom of this. Mr. Scott's usual bombastic expression was absent, replaced by fear and shock as he held his sobbing wife by his side. Light from two lanterns attempted to wash away the early morning gloom that had saturated the town hall ever since the Scotts had dragged Colonel Blake and James from their beds just minutes before, waving a piece of foolscap through the air and rambling some nonsense about a kidnapping.

James rubbed his sleepy eyes and glanced out the window where the rising sun painted a verdant green over the dark canvas of the jungle. The scrape of the colonel's chair sounded, pulling James's attention back to the matter at hand. He cleared his throat. "What I'm about to say must remain within this group. Is that clear?"

Thiago raised his dark brows.

"It would seem that Miss Magnolia has run away."

Mrs. Scott burst into sobs.

"Apparently with Hayden Gale," Blake added.

Mr. Scott patted his wife's back in an attempt to calm the poor woman. "I am not convinced that she went willingly, I tell you! She loathed the scoundrel. Told me so herself on many occasions."

"But you can vouch this is her handwriting?" James asked, holding up the paper.

Mr. Scott nodded. "No doubt forged under duress."

"Perhaps," Blake said with a frown. "Yet I'm having a difficult time believing Hayden would kidnap Magnolia."

Mrs. Scott lifted moist, red-rimmed eyes. "Surely you remember that this man was a stowaway. He made advances on my precious girl before."

James tightened his jaw. Accusations that were never proven, but he wouldn't upset the poor woman further.

Releasing his wife, Mr. Scott thundered forward. "I demand you send out a search party at once."

Blake raised a hand. "Yet you do not want the lady's reputation besmirched, do you?"

"Yes, yes, that's right. Which is why we must tell everyone she has been kidnapped."

"I will not do that, sir," Blake said. "I will not ruin a man's reputation on pure speculation."

"But you'll ruin my daughter's on it?" Mr. Scott raised his voice, his jowls quivering.

"Not speculation. . .her own words," James said.

"Preposterous! She would never run away with a man." Mr. Scott's face reddened. "She's a good girl."

Not a girl at all, James thought. *A grown woman.* Even if it was the first kind word he'd heard Mr. Scott say about his daughter in all the time he'd known the man. Still, he doubted Hayden had anything to do with this. From what James could tell, the disdain between Hayden and Magnolia was mutual. The more likely scenario was that Magnolia had followed Hayden, hoping to get to Rio to make her escape. In fact, if James knew Hayden, the man was probably dragging her back to New Hope as they spoke.

"That charlatan has taken her. Kidnapped our baby!" Mrs. Scott wailed.

The colonel circled his desk. "Magnolia did not hide her hatred for Brazil or her desire to go home. Is it possible she saw this as her chance to do just that?"

"Alone with that. . .that rogue? No, no. Not my Magnolia." Mr. Scott gazed out the window where a breeze brought in the smell of rice cakes and mangos being prepared for breakfast. Yet something in his eyes, a flicker of apprehension, told James the man wasn't altogether sure of his statement.

"Hayden is no rogue," James said. "He has more than proven his good character over the past few months. Besides, I agree with Colonel Blake. Until we know the facts, we should stick to what we *do* know."

"Humph." Mr. Scott took up a pace across the hut. "Very well, then, at least send Thiago to bring her back." He waved at the Brazilian guide as if he were a fly on the wall. "He will suffice."

Blake's brow furrowed. "But a larger party would cover more territory, find her quicker. Surely that would be better if she is truly in danger."

Mrs. Scott slumped into a chair and dropped her head into her hands.

"No, I will not see our good name destroyed aga—" Mr. Scott halted midsentence, alarm rolling over his expression. "I will not risk her reputation."

"Very well." Colonel Blake faced Thiago. "Are you willing to go after the lady and ensure no foul play is afoot?"

"And bring her home." Mrs. Scott lifted her tear-filled gaze.

James raised a brow. "Only if she wishes."

Thiago stuffed hands in his pockets. "I cannot go, senhor. The emperor pays me to stay with colonists. I cannot abandon my work or there will be huge punishment. I will instruct someone else which way to go."

Blake faced the Scotts. "Will you compensate her rescuer? Offer some incentive?"

Mr. Scott's gaze skittered over the men in the room before he grabbed the lapels of his coat. "Whoever goes will have my undying gratitude, sir, as well as the satisfaction of saving my daughter's life."

James shook his head. Had Mr. Scott's grief, his desperation, of only a moment ago been merely an act? When the Scotts often bragged of their wealth, were they not willing to part with anything to see their daughter safely home?

Later that morning, James stood before the assembled colonists, open Bible in hand, ready to give the Sunday message—a sermon on love and self-sacrifice, a last-minute change in light of the Scotts' behavior toward their daughter. While the old carpenter, Mr. Lewis, played his fiddle and led them in the hymn, James tried to shake off the feeling of foreboding that had cloaked him since early that morning— since the middle of the night, in truth. Ever since he'd woken in a chilled sweat from a nightmare he couldn't remember. He only recalled that it was terrifying and grotesque, and that it had draped a heaviness on him that had been accentuated by Magnolia's foolish escapades. It was a heaviness he'd felt building ever since they'd arrived in this new land. Like an ominous cloud in the distance drifting ever nearer, blotting out the sun ray by ray by ray.

Gazing across the faces, he caught a glimpse of russet hair glowing like polished mahogany in the morning sun. *Angeline.* He shifted his stance for a better view of the petite woman who always seemed dwarfed by the other colonists. Of course, it didn't help that she'd sat all the way in the back, though he should be happy she'd accepted his invitation at all. If anything could improve his mood, it would be that charming lady. In fact, all the ladies of New Hope were present, Bibles in hand and faces alight with eager expectation of hearing God's Word. What a welcome change from the women he'd been accustomed to dealing with back in Knoxville, both in church and out. *As a jewel of gold in a swine's snout, so is a fair woman which is without discretion.* The verse from Proverbs rose in his mind, reminding him of women he'd known who had lured men to destruction. Who had lured him to destruction. He'd made it his life's goal not only to avoid such women but to clean the streets of them. Difficult to do in Knoxville, but much easier to accomplish in a new town, in a new utopia based on the Word of God.

Opening his Bible, James began reading from 1 Corinthians 13. He'd been officiating the services ever since Parson Bailey had run off with their money on Dominica. Yet he still felt unequal to the task. Worse, he felt like a hypocrite. He wondered if God looked down on him, shaking His head in disgust that James dared to preach after his many failings on both the battle and mission field.

His voice broke. Clearing his throat, he looked across the crowd. A shadow to the right caught his gaze. Dark mist rose on an empty stump like steam from a cauldron, spinning and curling and thickening until it took the form and shape of a soldier. A corporal, he could tell, from the two stripes on the arm of his coat. He looked familiar. That innocent face. That tawny mop of hair. Yes, James remembered him from a battle—the Seven Days Battle, if he wasn't mistaken. But the boy had been killed, hadn't he? Confusion twisted James's thoughts as he scanned the faces staring at him, waiting for him to continue. He shifted his gaze back to the corporal, who was really just a boy dressed like a soldier. So many of them had been.

A few colonists turned to see what he was looking at. Their brows furrowed and they shook their heads. Clearly they didn't see the young man.

The boy smiled at James, but his smile slowly faded as his eyes took on a vacant stare. Blood stains pooled on his gray coat, expanding in a circular death march. His uniform tore as if by an invisible blade. The boy's chest ripped open, riddled with bullets. Sunlight winked off specks of metal embedded in bloody flesh. Still he stared at James, not a shred of emotion on his pale, placid face.

"Why did you let me die, Doctor? Why?"

CHAPTER 8

Hayden poked the fire, urging the flames to rise, then threw another log on the embers. If he kept the coals hot enough and sat close enough, the mosquitoes kept their distance. There was a price, however—the sensation of roasting like a pig on a spit. Being eaten alive or roasted alive. Great choice. Something pricked the back of his neck. Swatting the offending insect, he eased up the collar of his coat, which only enhanced his discomfort. But at least his arms and chest were covered. More importantly, at least he suffered alone.

Retrieving a long strip of carne secca from his pocket, he shoved it into his mouth and tore off a bite as his thoughts drifted to Magnolia. He grinned. The audacity of that woman following him into the jungle! A bold move for the primped lady. She must have been desperate, indeed, to venture into such dangerous terrain without being assured of protection and proper escort. Desperate or stupid. Or brave. No matter. She could be whatever she wished as long as she did it somewhere else.

As tempting a morsel as she was, Hayden didn't need the extra trouble of forging through the jungle with a prima donna in tow, nor the trouble he would have facing her parents if he ever returned to camp. No doubt they would place the blame on him for their daughter's disappearance. Though he did feel a slight twinge of guilt for leaving her alone. He probably should have escorted her back to New Hope, but she'd been so close to town, and he'd wasted enough time in his life on empty-headed harridans.

383

He bit off another chunk of dried pork, savoring the spicy flavor. He'd only brought enough for two days. After that, he hoped fruit and small critters would suffice to keep him going until he arrived in Rio, where he was sure he could *convince* someone to offer him a meal or two and a change of clothes. Then he would proceed with his business—questioning the immigration officer about his father's whereabouts. If the man had changed locations, he would have to report his whereabouts to the proper authorities. Though the land was cheap at only twenty-two cents an acre, the Emperor certainly couldn't have immigrants swarming around, settling wherever they wished and on whatever sized plots they wished.

Reaching into his waistcoat pocket, Hayden pulled out a small leather-bound tintype. Flipping the latch with his thumb, he opened it and held it to the firelight, studying the photograph he'd stared at a thousand times. He'd memorized every feature of the man: his black hair, slicked back and curled at his collar; the cultured whiskers that covered his angular jaw; his gray satin waistcoat; the sparkling gem pinned to his tight cravat; the chain dangling from his pocket; the round-brimmed hat in one hand while the other rested arrogantly on his waist. But it was the man's eyes that drew Hayden. Always his eyes. Even in the fading picture, Hayden detected the smug gleam of a swindler.

Like father, like son.

The fire crackled and spit. Sparks danced like fireflies into the darkness. Around him, the jungle played a nightly orchestra that was so different from its daytime melody. More peaceful, secretive, almost sinister. Not a breeze stirred the leaves. Sweat dotted his forehead. A distant growl set his hairs on end. Whatever it was, it wouldn't come near the fire. He was safe for now. A twig snapped. Leaves rustled. Closing the tintype, he dropped it back into his pocket, grabbed his pistol, cocked it, and scanned the darkness as memories of his vision of Katherine Henley knotted his nerves.

Crackles that didn't come from the fire sizzled in the air, or was it merely the sound of crickets? Movement caught Hayden's eye. He slowly rose. Sweat slid down his back. A man formed out of the darkness, tall with stylish dark hair and cultured sideburns. Green eyes flashed at Hayden, followed by the hint of a sardonic smile.

Hayden's breath fled his lungs.

Father?

A woman shrieked, drawing his gaze. When he looked back, the man was gone.

Another scream.

Plucking a burning stick from the fire, Hayden darted into the brush, sweeping the torch before him, pistol at the ready. Something moved in the shrubbery. He leveled his weapon and thrust the flame forward to keep the creature at bay. A piece of torn lace flashed in his view. A glimmer of blond hair. His heart stopped. *Please, not another vision.* Another vision would only mean one thing—that he'd gone completely and utterly mad.

The lady whimpered. One hand emerged from the bush and flattened onto the dirt, followed by another. Then a face pushed through the leaves as terrified eyes glanced upward. Hayden swept the torch aside but before he took another step, the woman leapt to her feet and barreled into his chest.

"Oh, thank God, it's you, Hayden." Her breathless words escaped with a groan. "There were bats! Bats everywhere! Diving at me, attacking me! Trying to bite me and drain my blood."

Hayden couldn't help but chuckle as he braced one arm around the trembling lady.

"It was horrible! Just horrible! I thought they were. . ."—her grip on him loosened—"I thought I was. . ."—her voice faded—"done for." She went limp in his arms.

"Dash it!" Tossing the torch into a puddle, Hayden grabbed her before she fell. "Magnolia!" Her name shot from his lips with the hissing of the flame. Yes, it was her. He knew by the soft feel of her skin, the embellished hysterics in her voice. But not by her smell. The scent that filled his nose was most definitely not sweet citrus and cedar.

Releasing the hammer on his gun, he shoved it into his belt and hoisted her into his arms. Anger simmered the food in his gut. Anger followed by concern, for she felt as light as cotton and just as weak.

A dozen thoughts peppered his conscience. Was she injured? Had an animal bitten her? Had she encountered a poisonous snake or frog? He laid her down by the fire, tore off his coat, bunched it up, and placed it beneath her head. Whatever contraption women wore beneath their gowns made her skirts flare up like a balloon. Even so, with all her petticoats, he couldn't find her legs to inspect them for injuries. Not that he should be looking at her legs. Still, she bore no marks or bruises on her face, neck, and arms except scrapes from traversing the jungle and bites from insects. He poured water on his handkerchief and dabbed her face. She moaned. Ebony lashes fluttered over pearly cheeks.

"I thought I'd lost you," she whispered, her voice scratchy like wool.

"Are you injured?" Helping her to sit, Hayden dipped the canteen to her lips.

She gulped down the liquid as if she hadn't had a sip all day.

"Easy now." He withdrew while she caught her breath.

She pushed him away, her eyes regaining their clarity. "Injured? Of course I am." Her shrill voice returned, and he instantly regretted giving her the water. "My feet are covered in blisters, my arms with scratches"—she brushed fingers over her cheeks, horror claiming her features—"My face. Oh, my face. There are bites all over it. And my hair." Fingering errant strands, she attempted to tuck them into the rat's nest that used to be her coiffeur. "Everything aches and I'm dreadfully hungry. And frightened. And I was attacked by a flock of bats!" Her blue eyes became a misty sea.

And Hayden's anger returned. "A colony."

"What?" She sniffed.

"A colony of bats. Not a flock."

"Oh. Who cares?"

"I told you not to follow me." Hayden growled and rose to his feet, chastising himself for not hearing her behind him all day. For believing she'd obeyed him and relaxing his vigilance.

"I stayed farther behind this time." She gave him a satisfied smirk. "It's not easy to track a man from such a distance, you know. I did quite well. Well, except for this horrendous state I find myself in." Her gaze swept over her torn, stained gown, and misery shoved her pride aside once again.

Zooks, the woman's fickle moods! Hayden's jaw tightened to near bursting. "Too bad you wasted all that suffering. You are still not coming with me."

"You wouldn't leave me out here alone!" A look of innocent incredulity appeared on her face. "I'll never find my way back from this distance."

Hayden ran a hand through his hair and marched away from her lest he do something he regretted.

"I can pay you."

The words turned him around.

"My parents are wealthy."

"How wealthy?"

"We owned the largest cotton plantation in Roswell." Planting her hands on the ground, she struggled to rise, her skirts ballooning in her face. "Grr," she squealed in exasperation and flopped back down.

Despite his anger, Hayden took pity on her and extended his hand, helping her to her feet. "*Owned* does me no good. Especially since the North confiscated your land, did they not?"

She took a few tentative steps, her delicate features knotting in pain. Hayden kept his grip on her hand firm until she settled. "What pains you?"

"My feet. I can hardly walk."

"Yet you managed to follow me all day." He released her with a huff, refusing to fall for her charade. This coddled woman knew exactly how to get others to fawn over her every need.

Pressing down her skirts, she attempted to wipe dirt from the once pristine fabric, her brow and lips twisting into odd shapes in the process. Finally she gave up and turned her back to him in a swish of creamy cotton. "We sold everything as soon as those infuriating Yankees marched into town. That was long before the war ended, as you know." She affected a nearly believable sob. "We lived under occupation for months and months. It was simply"—she threw a hand to her chest and cast a despairing look at him over her shoulder—"well, it was simply unbearable."

Hayden snorted. Though he'd heard the news about Roswell, and it was quite possible her parents had cashed out what they could of their holdings in time, she was playing him. But for what? Sympathy?

Her chest rose and fell. "I believe I'm growing faint."

An owl hooted as if laughing at her declaration. Hayden folded his arms over his chest. "Then you'd better sit down."

Frowning, she fiddled with her skirts and lowered herself onto a tree stump. "Turn your face, I must remove my shoes."

For some reason he didn't feel safe turning his back on this vixen. Nor did he like being ordered about like some servant. "You may remove your shoes, Princess, but I'm not removing my eyes from you."

She scowled and began fumbling beneath her skirts. "How could I forget? You are no gentleman."

"Indeed. And now you have all but handed yourself to me on a platter." He'd intended his tone to be threatening, even sultry, but it came out laced with anger and disgust. Finally a breeze fluttered the leaves and cooled the sweat on Hayden's neck and arms. But it did nothing to cool his irritation.

She froze, her face paling. A growl in the distance drew her gaze and a visible tremble ran across her shoulders. Perhaps not everything was an act. Hayden took a step toward her. "You are safe by the fire."

She looked at him as if he'd been the one to just emit a feral growl.

"*And* with me." No sense in toying with the woman any further. As much as he hated to accept it, he was stuck with her.

She bit her lip and began fumbling for her shoes again but said nothing. A definite first for her. The fire crackled and spit. Turning, Hayden added another log and tried to shake off his anger. The prospect of being paid would certainly make the trouble of bringing her along worthwhile. "Do tell me of this vast estate." He snapped a branch with his boot and tossed it into the flames. Smoked curled into the darkness, biting his nose.

"It was to be my dowry," she said, her voice strained. "My parents sent it to my aunt and uncle in Ohio for safekeeping with the provision that upon my parents' death or my return to America, the money would be handed over to me at my wedding."

"And why didn't your parents simply bring the money along with them to Brazil?"

"As insurance. Provision for me in case something happened to them."

Hayden scratched his jaw. It sounded believable enough but something wasn't right. "Being the astute businessman your father claims to be, surely he would have preferred to invest that money here in Brazil and see a hearty return, rather than leave it so far out of reach languishing in a jar somewhere."

"There was no guarantee of any return here." Firelight etched lightning across her eyes. "We knew nothing about Brazil and saw no need to bring additional monies besides the amount required. As it turns out, it was a wise choice since the parson would be in possession of our fortune now." She gave him a smug look as her hands continued to grope beneath her skirts.

One muddy red shoe emerged from the flurry of soiled lace like a dragon from a cloud.

Plucking the pistol from his belt, Hayden laid it on the log and sat down. "So, you have a dowry. What is that to me? We are here and it is there." Zooks, he could have used that money. He needed supplies. Badly. And a tracker to find his father.

"You aren't going back to the States?"

"What I seek is in Brazil."

Another shoe emerged. Along with a wince and a frown. "Then, why are you going to Rio?"

He shuffled his boot in the dirt. "If you have no means to pay me, we have no deal." A final test to see if she had any money at all.

Cultured brows folded over eyes brimming with fear. "A gentleman requires no compensation to help a lady."

"Yet, we have already established I am no gentleman." He grinned, though his insides broiled at the predicament she placed him in. Of course he wouldn't leave her in the jungle.

A frog—no, more like a toad—hopped along the edge of the

small clearing. Magnolia gasped and drew her knees up to her chest, scouring the ground around her.

Hayden rose. "Why would I want to endure your feminine theatrics for four more days? Especially without payment."

"Feminine theatrics, mercy me!" She huffed. "Of course there are feminine theatrics. I'm a woman, after all."

She certainly was. Even covered in dirt and bug bites, she presented quite an alluring sight. One which he allowed his gaze to rove over at the moment. If only to taunt her.

"You are no better than that toad." She squinted and tilted her head toward the bush where the creature had disappeared.

"A toad who will take you back to New Hope tomorrow," he said. Perhaps Hayden should do just that. He hadn't been with a woman in over a year and this one was far too distracting. Far too distracting and far too infuriating.

"No, wait, please." Her voice pleaded. "I do have some money with me. I need some of it to purchase passage home, but you're certainly welcome to the rest. If that's not enough, I promise to send you more when I arrive at my aunt and uncle's."

"I thought the money would only be delivered upon your marriage."

"I have no doubt I'll be married soon enough. My fiancé waits for me even now."

A slight intonation, a slight hesitation in her voice, gave Hayden pause. She was lying about something. But was it the money, her fortune, or the fiancé? "So, where is this money of yours?"

Turning aside, she stretched out her legs until slender toes peeked out from beneath her skirts. Slender, blistered, bloody toes, laced in frayed stockings.

Hayden swallowed. Loathing the guilt that swamped him, he rose, tore off several leaves from a nearby plant and knelt before her. "May I?"

She hesitated, her eyes shifting between his. Finally she nodded and inched her skirts up to her ankles. Blisters and raw skin peered at him through what was left of her mangled stockings, and he cursed under his breath. Picking at the hose, he removed the silken scraps, grabbed his canteen, and poured water over her feet. She jerked but didn't cry out.

"All this from walking?"

"I suppose I'm not accustomed to being on my feet all day."

Hayden glanced at her ankle boots. Not really ankle boots but tall, fancy red-leather boots scrolled in velvet designs with silk ribbons and heels at least two inches high. "Not exactly the best choice of footwear for a long trek."

"I had nothing else."

He didn't doubt that. "Why didn't you tell me about your feet?" He poured more water on the wounds.

"I did." She pulled them back. "Wait, I brought some of Eliza's salve." Opening her valise, she waded through its disheveled belongings.

Hayden took the jar from her hand. Their fingers touched. Their gazes met. She was distracting him with those beguiling eyes. Eyes that shifted between his—unsure, fearful, needy. They did funny things to his stomach. And to his breath, which seemed to have vacated his lungs. He looked away, opened the jar, and began applying the ointment. He'd never seen such delicate feet. Nor such blisters. He concentrated on them, not on the creamy skin that wasn't marred, nor on the sweet puffs of her breath wafting over him as she tried not to cry out at his touch.

The jungle sang a chorus around them as a breeze spun a cluster of dried leaves across the clearing. The tattered lace at her hem stirred. There. There was her sweet scent beneath the sweat and mud, a scent unique to her, a scent that caused his pulse to rise. Especially now when she was so close. And so quiet. . .and vulnerable.

"Thank you, Hayden." For once her voice held no sarcasm or spite.

It weakened his resolve. And he couldn't have that. "And just how do you plan to walk tomorrow?" He kept his tone sharp.

"So, you *will* take me?"

Against his better judgment, yes. "First, show me this money you speak of." He finished applying the ointment and sat back, wondering at the sensation in his fingers where he'd touched her. The lady was comely, to be sure. More comely than most. Yet he'd never suffered a shortage of attention from alluring women. Why did this one affect him so?

Reaching once more into her valise, she sifted through the contents and pulled out a velvet drawstring bag. "Gold coins. At least three hundred dollars worth."

He shielded his excitement. Three hundred dollars would buy him a wagon full of supplies and a good tracker. Picking up the leaves he'd gathered, he pressed them onto her feet.

"All I need"—her voice came out shredded like her stockings as he continued wrapping her wounds—"all I need is enough to buy passage back home and then purchase conveyance to my aunt and uncle's and the rest is yours."

Searching the vines hanging from trees for the right size twine, he sliced a piece with his knife and tied the leaves in place around her feet. She thanked him again. He avoided her gaze. Avoided seeing the appreciation in her eyes that he heard in her voice. Avoided anything that would soften him toward her, make him weak. He took the bag, opened it, and held it to the firelight. Gold coins winked back at him. Gold that made his head spin with delight and his brows arch in surprise at her honesty. He bobbed it in his hands, measuring the weight.

She slapped a bug on her arm and glanced around the camp as if she weren't the least bit interested.

Tying the pouch, he handed it back to her as a wonderful idea formed in his mind. "You have a deal, Princess."

"So you'll escort me to Rio and see me safely on a ship back to America?" She eased her skirts down over her feet.

Hayden strangled a chuckle. Who was she fooling? She wouldn't make it alone on a ship to the States. Not surrounded by sailors who'd been out to sea for months. Not unless he could find a ship of monks! She would be a Magnolia blossom ripe for the picking. And he could never allow that to happen. He was a swindler, not a monster. "Yes, of course."

"A good ship with a good captain who will ensure my safety?"

He nodded. But he had other plans for the enchanting Southern belle. Plans that would aid him greatly in discovering the whereabouts of his father. For Hayden relied solely on the information provided by Brazil's immigration officer, Mr. Eduardo Santos. And the man was not forthcoming with information unless his palms were greased with gold. Gold Hayden needed for supplies and a tracker. Yet if there was one thing Hayden had noticed about the man—besides the fact that he was as crooked as a bent twig—it was that he had an eye for the ladies. And a woman of Magnolia's beauty and charm would have no trouble extracting the information Hayden needed. All she had to do was flutter her lashes, give him a coy smile, flatter him in that dainty, Southern, I'm-a-helpless-woman-in-need-of-a-real-man-accent, and Mr. Santos would tell her the location of Midas's treasure if he knew it. How did Hayden know? Because if he were not a stronger man, if he were not privy to feminine devices and the tricks of skullduggery, he would, no doubt, himself, be bewitched by the siren.

Besides, he wasn't being completely dishonest with her. If Mr. Santos informed Hayden that his father had left for the States, he would accompany Magnolia home. However, if not, he would return her to New Hope to her parents where she belonged. Maybe they would even offer him a reward. And, of course, he would keep the money she paid him to escort her. All in all, it promised to be a lucrative venture.

For him, that was.

He gestured toward her feet. "I won't carry you through the jungle."

Her satisfied smirk faded into anger. "I'll be quite all right in the morning. Besides, I can wear extra stockings." She glanced around. "Now, where can I freshen up before supper?"

Hayden rubbed the back of his neck. "Supper?" He chuckled. "I do apologize, Princess, but food was not part of our bargain."

"But. . ." Her brows crumpled. "What will I eat?"

"The jungle is teeming with edibles."

She scanned the dark, oscillating greenery as if expecting a platter of roast beef to emerge through the leaves. Hayden couldn't take his eyes off her. With her skin flushed and moist, her flaxen curls tumbling over her shoulders, her chest rising and falling beneath her bedraggled bodice, she'd never looked more beautiful.

CHAPTER 9

The trail widened, giving Colonel Blake a chance to catch up to James on their way to the temple. "How are you faring today, Doc?"

"Well enough." James flicked a glance at him, hoping his friend would take the hint that he didn't feel like talking. In fact, he'd hardly spoken to anyone since his strange episode at the beginning of his sermon yesterday. Until he figured out what happened, he planned on keeping it to himself. He'd even skipped lunch and supper in order to avoid conversation with the colonists. Which didn't make him a very good spiritual mentor, but if he was going crazy, he wouldn't be much use in that area anyway.

Batting aside a huge fern, he trudged forward as the group followed Thiago to some strange temple the man kept going on about.

"What happened yesterday?" the colonel asked.

James ran a sleeve over his forehead. "Isn't it obvious? I made a fool of myself." Worse than a fool. He'd shouted and trembled like a leaf in the wind before he made his apologies and dashed from the dais.

"Not in my eyes, you didn't. Obviously, something upset you enough that you couldn't continue your sermon." Blake shrugged, rubbed the old war wound on his leg, and continued limping beside James. "You are human, not some supernatural creature, unscathed by life."

James ground his teeth. Wasn't it shameful enough his fear of blood prevented him from using his doctoring skills? Would God

395

now send another unfounded fear to keep him from his spiritual duties as well? "As the town preacher, I should at least appear to have my emotions under control." But once again he'd let everyone down, including Miss Angeline, who had finally made an appearance at Sunday services. Most likely her last.

He gripped the musket so tightly his fingers ached as countless colorful birds flitted overhead, mocking his sullen mood. Stepping over a craggy root, he hoped Blake would continue on in silence as they made their way to this mysterious temple. Though Eliza, Miss Angeline, and some of the women had wanted to come along, the colonel forbade them. James agreed. No sense in putting the ladies in unnecessary danger. Hopefully, there would be no danger at all. Perhaps they would even find something useful for the colony.

Mr. Graves certainly seemed intrigued, for ever since he'd found the place, the man had spent all his waking hours in the ancient structure, or so Thiago had said. Yet for all Thiago's chattering about the place, once Blake decided to go, the Brazilian guide had warned them to stay away. And when Blake refused to listen, Thiago pleaded to remain at camp.

"You saw something. When you were starting your sermon." Blake's statement drew James out of his musing and back to a topic he didn't wish to discuss. He glanced over his shoulder at Dodd and a few other men following behind, and then forward to Thiago leading the way. "How did you know?"

Blake heaved a sigh. "What was it?"

"A boy I operated on at the battlefield. A young corporal." James swallowed. He squashed a bug on his arm and wished he could squash the memory as easily. "He died under my knife." His hand trembled, and he switched the musket to his other one.

"I saw my brother." Blake said the words so matter-of-factly, James thought he hadn't heard correctly. Blake's younger brother had died a vicious death at the battle of Antietam—a battle James had witnessed.

"When?"

"When we first arrived. I went into the jungle to sort things out about Eliza." He brushed aside a fern. "And there he stood, plain as these trees around us, in his private's uniform, staring at me."

James's mind spun, trying to make sense of the story.

"Then he took off," Blake said. "Darted into the jungle."

"What did you do?"

"I ran after him. Found him lying on the ground in a clearing, blood gurgling from his chest." The colonel's voice cracked.

James halted and stared at his friend. The others wove around them, casting curious glances their way.

"We'll catch up," Blake said before he faced James and whispered, "And Eliza saw her dead husband."

Heart tightening in his chest, James gazed up at the knotted canopy. "What is going on?"

"You're the preacher. I figured I'd ask you."

James wouldn't tell him he was no better preacher than he was a doctor. "You think this is something spiritual?"

"What else could it be?"

Planting the barrel of his musket in the dirt, James leaned on the butt. "When we stood on the beach right before we entered the jungle, you said you felt something strange. I've felt the same thing since we arrived. A heaviness. Something oppressive...dark."

"Indeed." The lines on Blake's forehead deepened as he squeezed the bridge of his nose. "And Eliza has sensed the same."

A lizard scrambled up a tree trunk. Sunlight shimmered a rainbow of colors on its slick skin as it stared at James with one eye. "Perhaps this ancient temple will give us some answers."

But all the temple did was cause James's stomach to convulse. While Thiago stood guard at the entrance, refusing to enter, and Dodd, with a glimmer in his eyes, went in search of gold, sounds from within the building drew Blake, James, and the rest up the stairs and through the front porch.

James covered his nose against an unidentifiable stench as they passed broken tables, chairs, pottery, and a steaming pool of water on their way to the back of the large open room. A glimmer drew his gaze to a golden crescent moon and stars embedded in the back wall above a stone altar. To their left, the sounds of digging and a man's grunt lured them through an opening into a tunnel that led downward to the distant flicker of a torch. Bracing against stone walls on either side, James groped his way over the uneven ground. By the grunts and moans coming from in front and behind, the others seemed to be having the same trouble keeping firm footing.

Finally they reached stairs that descended with ease to a place where the tunnel widened. Two lit torches hung on the wall. A pile of rocks and dirt sat off to the side.

Graves emerged from a hole to their left, a shovel full of pebbles in his hand. At least James thought it was Graves. His normally stylish shirt was torn. Sweat-caked mud splattered over his arms and face. Dust speckled his waistcoat and grayed his black hair, making him look older than his nearly thirty years. James had never seen the posh politician so out of sorts. Nor had he ever seen him smile.

"Ah, you've come to see for yourselves." Torchlight glimmered over rows of white teeth that stood out against his filthy face.

"See what? What are you doing down here?" James asked, wiping sweat from his neck. "It's hot as Hades."

"Digging." Tossing the pebbles onto a pile, Graves set down his shovel—the one that had been missing from camp for days.

"For what?" Mr. Lewis finally caught up to them, the smell of alcohol following the old carpenter in his wake. "Gold?"

Graves snorted and ran a finger over his once cultured mustache that now hung in muddy strands. "Nothing so meager. I assure you." He leaned toward them, his tone spiked with glee. "Can you feel it? Can you hear it?"

All James felt were a thousand invisible spiders crawling on his skin.

"I don't hear anything," the colonel said.

Graves gave an exaggerated sigh before his brows lifted and he held up a finger. "*Shh.*"

Nothing but the drip of water and the moan of wind sounded through the dank tunnel.

"There! Did you hear them?" Graves said.

James shook his head. Colonel Blake crossed his arms over his chest. They shared a look of agreement that the man had gone mad.

"You still can't hear them?" Disgust weighted his voice as Graves's thick eyebrows dipped together. "Of course not." He waved a grimy, bruised hand through the air. "Go back to your farming, gentleman. I will find them. I will dig them out. And then you will see."

"What are you talking about? Find who?"

"The glorious ones. They are trapped." Graves started back toward the opening.

"There's nothing here but ruins, Graves." Blake reached for the man. "Come back to New Hope. Help us build something new, not dig up something old."

Graves swung around and stared at the colonel as if he'd asked him to strip naked and dance a jig. "I want nothing to do with your New Hope. Now, leave me be."

James almost felt sorry for him. But hadn't they all thought his behavior on the journey to Brazil a bit strange? On board the ship, the politician had always kept to himself, more like an observer than a part of their group. He'd even seemed happy when misfortune after misfortune had befallen them. Now James worried how long he could stay at this ghastly temple without food and water. The colonel seemed to be of the same mind when they emerged onto the front courtyard, unable to convince Graves to return. "What are we to do with him? He's obviously lost his mind."

"It's so quiet." Removing his hat, the old carpenter wiped sweat from his brow and glanced up. Tufts of cotton-like clouds drifted across a cerulean sky they normally didn't see much of through the canopy. But it *was* quiet. Unusually quiet.

Eerily quiet.

James lowered his gaze to the haunting images on a nearby obelisk. Despite the sweat moistening his skin, a shiver coursed through him.

Mr. Dodd charged through the broken gate. "I found something you should see, Colonel."

Wondering what, besides gold, could have put the ex-lawman into such a dither, James and the rest of the men followed him back through the front entrance and then around the broken wall until they stopped behind the enclosed structure. A vast, open field stretched out from the temple. Huge black circles of what once must have been charred grass or shrubbery were scattered haphazardly across the brown—no, gray, deathly gray—terrain. Whatever had seared the ovals into the ground must have happened long ago, yet nothing grew at all in the wide space. No moss; no seedlings; no grass, trees, or bushes. Not a single speck of green. Heat waves spiraled from a ground that appeared as dry as bones—as dry as a grave.

"What happened here?" The colonel shifted weight off his bad leg.

"It looks like a battlefield." Dodd scratched his head. "Don't it?"

"Not like any I've ever seen," Lewis offered.

James swallowed down a burst of dread. He didn't know how he knew. But he knew. He could feel it in his gut. Sense it in his spirit. "Something horrible happened here. Something far worse than we could ever imagine."

CHAPTER 10

$\mathbf{M}$agnolia folded the coverlet she'd slept on—or rather had lain awake on—and put it back into her valise. After they had forged their bargain last night, Hayden had begun to act strange, getting that look in his eye she'd seen among so many suitors back in Roswell—as if he were starving and she was a sweetmeat. She couldn't blame him, really. Even in her disheveled state, she was rather alluring. But really, the rogue! So, announcing her intention to retire for the evening, she waited for him to erect some sort of shelter or prepare a soft place for her to lay her head. Instead, he had shrugged, lain down on the ground by the fire, and promptly fallen asleep.

Of all the nerve! Did he actually expect her to sleep in the dirt with all the bugs and snakes and other mucus-oozing critters? And shouldn't he be keeping watch over her? Protecting her from beasts and intruders? But from the snores that soon filtered her way, she'd surmised that was the last thing on his mind. She'd been so furious, she considered sticking a hot coal inside his shirt or—she grinned at the thought—down his trousers, but thought better of it. No need to rouse his temper—or worse. And since she depended on him to get to Rio De Janeiro, she needed to stay in his good graces. If he even had any.

So, she'd done all she knew to do. She'd sat by the fire, huddled beneath her coverlet with a knife in hand should a predator happen by. And not just predators, but any of the innumerable crawly things that overran the jungle. One of them, a particularly gruesome beast of a spider had ventured within a few feet of her. Hairy and black and as large as a man's open hand, it had stared at her as if it intended to nibble her flesh. In her exhaustion, she'd thought she'd seen it lick its prickly lips. If spiders had lips. So, she did what she did best.

She screamed.

Hayden never stirred. She'd poked the ghastly creature with a burning stick. The spider, that was, not Hayden. Regardless, the entire incident had been far too much for a lady with such a delicate constitution! Though she'd hoped to ration herself, she'd even partaken of a few sips of the Brazilian rum she'd brought along for comfort. And comfort her it did. Sometime in the middle of the night, she must have fallen asleep for she woke up lying on her side, her cheek glued to the mud, and ants crawling on her nose.

The man in question, her supposed escort, her protector. . .was still fast asleep.

How could he sleep with the morning clamor blaring down at them from the canopy? An unholy cacophony that had begun before the first gray mist chased away the darkness and now continued in both intensity and volume as the heat rose with the sun. Plucking her French hand mirror from her valise, she eased her fingers over the elaborate gold gilding and smiled at the delicate violets painted on the back. A gift from her father on her fifteenth birthday. But like everything from her father, it came with an admonition. *Only the finest, fairest ladies in Paris have one of these, my dear. Keep it near to ensure you always look your best.* Magnolia could still feel the sense of unworthiness that flooded her at that moment, the fear of not being able to live up to her father's standard. A fear that had become her everyday reality since. Still, she had loved the mirror. And the ivory comb that came with it, which she now pulled from her valise and began sifting through the hopeless tangles in her hair, all the while keeping an eye on the sleeping hero.

"Humph." Some hero he was. What sort of man took payment to assist a helpless lady? What sort of man cared not a whit for that lady's comfort in the middle of the jungle? Her comb struck a particularly thick snarl, and she struggled to loosen it without breaking her hair. A man as stubborn and thickheaded and twisted as this knot, that's who!

Exasperated, she growled, and switched to another section of her hair, wishing Mable were here to make her presentable as the slave always did in the morning, but the girl would have just gotten in the way. Besides, Magnolia's mother needed her. All their other slaves had run off after the war, leaving Mable to be lady's maid to both Magnolia *and* her mother. The absolute shame.

She raised her mirror to examine her face and began to sob at the sight of dirt smudged on her cheek and bite marks rising like volcanoes across her creamy skin.

The hero moaned and turned on his side. Sculpted arms folded across his chest. Dark stubble peppered his chin and jaw, while equally dark hair dangled over his neck. Mercy me, but the man was handsome. When he was asleep. When he was awake, his brutish personality all but masked his natural good looks. Yet hadn't he displayed moments of kindness to her last night?

Lifting her skirts, she examined her leaf-covered feet, remembering his gentle touch as he'd applied the salve. So gentle for such a beast of a man. Equally confusing was the way his touch had made her feel. As if she were dancing in a field of flowers. But surely those sensations were merely a result of reaching the end of the most excruciating day of her life. Anyone's attentions would have caused the same reaction.

Having rid her hair of most of the snarls, she repinned it and returned her mirror and comb to her valise, then struggled to rise. An impossible feat when one wore a bird cage strapped to one's waist. Finally, she managed to lean forward on her knees, plant her hands in the mud—there was simply no way around that—and push herself to stand. Wincing at the pain burning across her feet, she made her way to Hayden.

"Wake up!" He didn't move. Searching the ground, she gathered a stick and poked him with it. "Wake up."

In one swift movement, he jerked upward, cocked a pistol, and swung its barrel at her chest. Magnolia screeched and leapt backward.

Hayden blinked several times, gaping at her, before he lowered his weapon and rubbed his eyes with a groan. "When are you going to learn it is dangerous to wake a man from his sleep?"

"I didn't realize you were such a grump in the morning."

"Well, now you do." He lay back down. "Leave me alone."

"Is there a creek nearby where I can wash and change my clothes?"

"You woke me to ask me that?" He growled.

"Yes I did. The sun is risen and we should not be dilly dallying."

Emitting a bestial sigh, Hayden sat up again, grabbed his canteen, and took a sip. "It's barely past dawn, Princess. I would have expected someone so accustomed to languid inactivity to sleep much longer."

"If you must know, I hardly slept at all. No thanks to you." She tossed the stick at him, missing him by an inch. He never flinched. Which only made her angrier. "I was assaulted all night long by feral insects and would have probably been eaten by a wolf if I hadn't stayed awake."

"I doubt your expert vigilance would have stopped a wolf." He handed her the canteen. "You get the last sip. We'll refill it when we find water."

Tipping it to her lips, she barely got enough of the precious liquid to wet her tongue. *No more water?* She stared in horror at her stained gown and the dirt smudges on her arms and hands. "But I simply must have my morning toilette." Besides, she was terribly sweaty, though it wouldn't be proper to mention that. "I've never slept in my clothing before and you have no idea how uncomfortable it is."

He didn't seem to be listening to her anymore as he stood, shoved the pistol into his belt, and retrieved his coat from the dirt. "Well, now that I'm awake, we shouldn't *dilly dally*, as you say."

"I'm a lady and I have certain needs." She hated the slight catch of desperation in her voice.

He turned to stare at her as if she'd dropped out of the sky.

"So, if you'll lead me to some water, *Hayden*"—she seethed out his name for effect—"I'd be most obliged." Better to establish who was in charge before things got out of hand.

"I am not God, Princess. I cannot produce water out of a rock no matter how much you demand it. However, if you need to relieve yourself, you may do so in the bushes. I will wait here."

Heat stormed up her face. "How dare you mention such a thing?"

He pinched the bridge of his nose as if he had a headache. "If we are going to be traveling together for four more days, I don't see how we can avoid such breeches of etiquette."

Magnolia flung her hands to her hips and tried to spit a retort, but only nonsensical stuttering emerged.

Hayden seemed to be trying to make sense of it but finally shook his head. "What about your feet?" He leaned over to examine her toes.

"I brought along a pair of satin dance slippers. Though this heinous wilderness will destroy them within hours, they will suffice for now."

He nodded his agreement then waved her off like a spoiled little child. "Run along. Take care of your business and be quick about it."

Magnolia's stomach growled, reminding her that she hadn't eaten anything since yesterday morning. "Aren't we going to eat breakfast?"

"We'll find some fruit along the way."

Magnolia had never met a more obnoxious brute of a man. As soon as she relieved herself, donned some new stockings, and slid her slippers over her bandaged feet, she returned to the clearing and handed him her valise.

His amused gaze shifted from the case back to her before one of his eyebrows lifted. "Why do I want this?"

"To carry, of course."

"You brought it. You carry it." He dropped it to the ground, then disappeared into the greenery.

Magnolia didn't have time to be angry. She didn't have time to pout or gather the tears that melted most men's resolve. No, it was all she could do to keep up with him or be lost in the jungle forever. She did have time, however, to pluck an orange from a passing tree and toss it at him. It would have struck him too, if he hadn't ducked. How he knew she'd thrown it, she had no idea, but his chuckle filtered in his wake like a slap to her face.

Several hours later, Magnolia wished she'd eaten the fruit instead. Not only was her stomach rasping out its final breaths, but she could no longer feel her feet. They'd gone from aching to burning to completely numb. She wished she could say the same about her arms. Pain stretched all the way from her fingers across her shoulders and down the other side as she shifted the valise—that had transformed into an anvil—to her other hand. It hadn't seemed so heavy the day before, but she hadn't been this tired, either. Her hair had loosened from its pins and hung in sweaty strands over her shoulders. The hem of her dress was so caked in mud, it felt like she'd sewn iron bars into it. Yet what worried her most was that her stomach had stopped complaining hours ago. She feared it had taken to eating her own flesh from the inside out, and if she ever had a chance to remove her clothing, she'd find her midsection completely gone.

Just when she thought about gulping down the rest of her pinga rum, Hayden stopped at a small creek to fill the canteen and eat some wild bananas he'd foraged along the way. But no sooner had she splashed water onto her face and arms and sat down to enjoy her fruit, than Hayden was ready to leave again. The man had the strength and stamina of a bull. And the personality to match. How could she have ever found him appealing enough to kiss?

A band of monkeys scampered on branches and swung on vines overhead, yapping and squealing—which was more than Hayden had said to her all day. More than once, she'd tried to engage the man in conversation, but all she'd gotten were grunts that sounded much like the monkeys above. Gazing up, she ducked to avoid any droppings that might further soil her gown and add to the putrid scent emanating from the stained fabric.

Trying not to think about her situation, Magnolia forced her thoughts to happier days back home in Roswell before the war, when her only concern had been what gown to wear and which social function to attend and with whom. Her parents had seemed happy then, hadn't they? That was before she'd made the fatal error that had cost them nearly everything. Then when the war took the rest, things had gone from bad to worse. Her parents had never treated her the same after that. Before Martin, she'd had freedom. Afterward, she was a prisoner. Before Martin, she'd been her father's princess. Now, he did nothing but scold her about everything from her attire, to her manners, to the way she wore her hair. Perhaps by regulating every detail of her life, he believed he could stop her from making another mistake, make her so perfect that she'd only attract the "right sort of gentleman." Of course, how he expected her to accomplish such a feat in the middle of the jungle, she had no idea.

"You owe your mother and me. You owe this family." She could still hear him say. "And by God, you're going to restore our family name and fortune or you'll be no daughter of mine. Do you hear me?"

Yes, she had heard him. And each time he'd said it since. Yet for all her trying, she still seemed to do nothing but disappoint him. Perhaps she would never be good enough. Batting aside a leaf the size of her body, Magnolia plodded ahead. Were her parents worried about her now or were they simply angry she'd left? Most likely the latter, for she had once again besmirched the Scott name.

Drawing a filthy handkerchief from her sleeve, she rubbed the perspiration from her neck and face, chuckling at what her father would say if he saw her now. Sunlight drew her gaze to her right where creeping plants, laden with clusters of pink flowers, circled a tree trunk in an arrangement too beautiful to describe. Stopping, she drew in a deep breath of mossy air, perfumed with orchids and a hint of the sea, and set down her valise. Just for a moment. She only needed a moment. Stretching her aching hand, she glanced at the luxuriance of tree ferns all around her, their massive leaves at least six feet long, in every shade from red to brown to green. A small bird with bright orange wings landed on a frond, studied her for a moment, and began to warble a tune. If she wasn't so miserable, she might say the jungle was stunning in all its dangerous beauty.

A shadow caught the edge of her eye. Turning she saw a man standing with his back to her, dressed in an elegant suit of fine poplin, complete with cane and silk top hat. A crackling sound filled the air. Magnolia froze. She rubbed her eyes. When she opened them again, the man glanced at her over his shoulder and winked. *Winked!* She'd know that wink anywhere, along with those green eyes, finely chiseled nose, and cultured whiskers. Martin? Martin Haley? Her blood ran cold. It couldn't be. He took off at a sprint.

"Martin!" Clutching her skirts, she tore after him, ignoring the pain shooting up her legs. She plunged through the foliage, shoving branches and vines aside, with one thought in mind. *Kill Martin Haley!* For what he'd done to her. What he'd done to her family. Her thoughts whirled. How could he be in Brazil? In the middle of the jungle? And dressed to the nines? No matter. She would kill him anyway. How, she didn't know and didn't care. She simply dashed ahead, blind with rage. Until he disappeared. Faded into the steam coming off the plants. Whirling around, she searched the trees, bamboo, vines, her breath heaving, her feet aching, her mind spinning. No sight of him.

Plopping to the ground in a puff of muddy skirts, she began to sob. Moments later, footsteps thudded, and she jerked her gaze up to see Hayden emerge from the leaves, fear rumbling across his face.

Was he afraid for her? Now, she *was* dreaming.

"What happened? Why did you run off?" He squatted and brushed a strand of hair from her face.

"It doesn't matter." She swiped her tears away and took the hand he offered. Once on her feet, she tugged from his grasp. "I can no longer feel my feet. I'm covered with bug bites and"—she hesitated—"sweat, if you must know. Yes, sweat."

The concern from his face vanished, replaced by his typical look of annoyance. "Forgive me if I don't have a carriage to convey your ladyship through the jungle. What did you think the journey would be like?"

"Must we walk so fast? And you don't listen to me. Or talk. And my arm hurts from carrying my valise." She glanced over the maze of green and brown. "And now I'm seeing things."

Hayden gave her a patronizing look. "Oh, do forgive me, Princess. I was under the impression you wished to get to Rio as soon as possible. Yet now I discover your real desire is to engage in idle chatter whilst we take a Sunday stroll through the jungle."

Magnolia would love to stroll over his face with her muddy feet at the moment. Instead she bent over, grabbed a handful of the black ooze, and swung her arm back to toss it at him.

He cocked his head, that devilish grin of his appearing on his lips. "Come now, are we reduced to such childish antics?"

"Apparently that's the only language you speak." She held the dripping mud up like a trebuchet about to release its fiery projectile. "I demand you give me the proper respect due a lady on this journey or you will not only be covered in mud, but you won't be paid."

He chuckled. "I will be paid, Princess. The deal was to get you to Rio. There was no mention of licking your boots along the way."

"In case you haven't noticed, I'm not wearing boots." She lifted her chin. "Why, you may ask? Because my feet are swollen to twice their normal size." Magnolia knew she was losing what was left of her sanity. She knew because she no longer cared *that* she knew. "I ache from head to toe. I can't feel my arm or my shoulders, and my stomach has shrunk to the size of a walnut. My body has become a buffet for a plethora of flesh-eating insects. And I'm in dire need of a bath."

At that moment, the sky split with a thunderous roar and a sudden deluge poured from the heavens. As if God tipped over an enormous pitcher, the liquid cascaded upon them, drenching everything in sight.

"Your wish is my command." Hayden grinned and swept an arm out in a royal bow. Then gazing up, he spread his arms wide, closed his eyes, and allowed the water to wash over him in sheets.

Water gushed over Magnolia, too, soaking her hair, streaming over her face, dripping from her chin, and flowing down her gown. Refreshing and cool. Puddles formed on the ground as water streamed off plants and leaves. She opened her palm, allowing the rain to wash away the mud. She felt like crying, like screaming. . .

Like dancing.

Thunder rumbled.

Their gazes met through the blur of rain. Water pooled on Hayden's dark lashes and glued his shirt to his muscled chest. He started to chuckle. Not a bombastic victor's chuckle, but the hearty, warm chuckle of friendship. He pointed at her as his chuckle transformed into laughter, deep rolling laughter, that caused him to bend over and hold his stomach.

An unavoidable giggle burst from Magnolia's lips. She glanced down at her saturated dress, then closed her eyes and lifted her face to the torrent, allowing her own laughter to ring free. When her glance took in Hayden again, looking like a drowned bear, her laughter grew louder, until she, too, spread out her arms and twirled around, basking in the refreshing rain.

CHAPTER 11

After several unsuccessful attempts, Hayden finally lit a fire with some sparse kindling and a few dry logs. The flames snapped and sparked. He blew on them, watching them rise to dance over the wood. Setting moist logs around the edge of the fire to dry, he stood, shook the water from his hair, and ran a hand through the saturated strands. The smell of spicy rain and musky forest filled his lungs.

Shivering, Magnolia inched to the fire, a dazed look in her eyes. Muddy water dripped from the hem of her gown. Sopping, flaxen curls hung down to her waist. Raindrops sparkled in her lashes like diamonds as she knelt by the warm flames and held out her hands. She looked like a forest sprite who'd tumbled over a waterfall. A delectable, delicious forest sprite. Hayden licked his lips.

A fine mist filtered through the canopy, coating everything in a silvery sheen as evening lowered its black shroud over the jungle. The scent of orchids and musky earth swirled about them. A hint of a breeze added the briny sting of the sea. Her lips trembled, and she hugged herself.

"You should change out of those clothes, Princess. Tending a sick woman is not part of the bargain."

She lifted her gaze to his. The numbness in her eyes transformed to ice. "What good will that do? It's still raining." She stared back at the fire. "I'm going to die out here in the middle of nowhere. I'm going to die in a puddle of mud and be eaten by worms and spiders and toads."

410

She slumped onto a carpet of wet leaves.

"Toads don't eat humans." Hayden could think of nothing else to say to such a ludicrous outburst. She lowered her head and let out an ear-piercing wail.

Splendid. He had no idea what to do with a blubbering female. He much preferred a shrew to this sobbing mass of dimity and lace. But she was right about one thing. The rain wasn't stopping, and although he would be quite comfortable curling up beneath a huge leaf somewhere, he could hardly expect her to do the same. Zooks! He'd known the woman would be more trouble than she was worth. Selecting one of the wet logs, he tossed it on the fire. The wood sizzled and hissed, sending smoke curling into the air.

With a grunt, Hayden shoved aside some hanging vines and headed into the jungle. Hopefully, he could find what he needed before the encroaching darkness stole everything from sight. After several minutes of stumbling around in the shadows, he followed the firelight back to the small clearing, bamboo, banana leaves, and palm fronds bundled in his arms. Magnolia looked up and wiped tears away as if she hadn't realized he'd been gone.

"What are you doing?" Her voice broke, reminding him of a little girl's, an innocent little girl who needed his help. Despite his best efforts, it touched a deep part of him that wanted to protect and provide.

"Making you a shelter." He set to task, hearing her sigh of relief even above the drone of the jungle. Choosing the largest tree trunk at the edge of the clearing, he began leaning the bamboo against it, tying the hollow stems together with twine and placing palm fronds and banana leaves on top. The rain turned from mist to drops that bounced off leaves and dirt, and he placed another log on the sputtering fire, hoping the flames wouldn't die out. Magnolia sat in the same spot, strands of hair glued to her cheeks, and eyes alight with disbelief.

"Where did you learn to do that?" she asked.

Hayden shrugged. "I slept in the woods outside Charleston when it became too dangerous in the city."

Her delicate brows dipped. "Outside? Why didn't you sleep in your bed?"

411

"I had none." Hayden returned to his task, stacking more leaves on top to form a watertight barrier, then tying more bamboo together to form a bed.

He heard her saturated skirts slosh as she struggled to rise, heard her unladylike curse and the slap of mud as she pushed herself up from her hands and knees. "Didn't have a bed? What of your parents?"

He clenched his jaw at her sympathetic tone, regretting his disclosure. He didn't want pity. Especially not from someone like her. Wealthy and pampered. The type of people who'd averted their eyes and held handkerchiefs to their noses when little Hayden had passed on the street, begging for food.

He slammed back into the jungle, returning within minutes with armfuls of dry leaves he'd found beneath an Inga tree. He laid them on the bamboo frame inside the shelter, ignoring those sapphire eyes of hers as they followed his every move. After a few more trips, he'd gathered enough to complete a bed for her to sleep on.

The rain lessened into a light drizzle as darkness took the final step onto the throne of night, issuing in the buzz and chirp of its evening subjects.

"Your shelter awaits, Princess." Hayden gave a mock bow with a sweep of his hand.

She eyed him with a mixture of gratitude and surprise. "I don't know what to say."

"Though I'm sure the words may feel foreign on your tongue, I believe thank you is in order."

Her lips drew into a tight line, and the harridan reappeared in her eyes. "Of course I know to say thank you, you untutored toad," she spat. But then her expression softened. "However I *do* thank you. Your kindness is most unexpected." She pressed down her sodden skirts with a ragged sigh as if saying the words had exhausted her.

Not sure whether he should be angry at being called a toad or appreciative of her first thank you, Hayden merely shrugged. "You should change into dry clothes and get into the shelter. I fear the rain may be with us for a while."

"And just where am I supposed to do that?" She gazed around

as suspicion tightened the lines on her face. Hayden smiled. Which caused her to lift a condescending brow—made all the more adorable because she looked like a drowned mermaid. If mermaids could even drown.

"Princess, I'm too tired and too wet to sneak a peek at your unclad body," he lied and gestured toward a clump of thick brush. "You may change behind that. I'll stay here and tend the fire." Which needed tending by the looks of the dying embers. Besides, the task would give him something to focus on. Anything but where his mind kept taking him—to the vision of her bare curves and silky skin, only enhanced by the tiny moans and whispery whines emanating from the bush as she struggled to disrobe. He shook the vision from his head, selected the least wet log, and placed it on the fire, suddenly feeling a bit aflame himself.

"Need any help?" He half-teased.

"You stay right where you are, Hayden Gale!"

Squatting by the flames, Hayden rubbed his stubbled jaw. The only women he'd known outside of those he'd swindled were the kind who had no compunction taking off their clothes in front of men. Some he'd befriended. Others he'd used. Most he'd forgotten. He had no idea how to treat a real lady, how to control urges he'd always satisfied on a whim. And despite her viper tongue, Magnolia was indeed a tempting morsel. Especially for a man who'd been hungry for a very long time.

A breeze blew against his wet clothes, etching a chill down his back. Perhaps if he stayed wet and cold all night, it would keep his thoughts in check. Either that or he'd catch his death. Which somehow seemed preferable over trying to resist the temptation that continued to grunt and groan from behind the thicket. Rising, Hayden searched for any remaining dry leaves to toss into the fire—

When Magnolia screamed.

Plucking a knife from his belt, he dashed toward the bushes, preparing to meet some wild beast or ferocious spider.

"Hayden!"

Diving through leaves, he grabbed Magnolia, shoved her behind him, and thrust out his blade to meet her attacker. Scattered firelight from the camp flickered over dark greenery that barely rustled beneath a weak breeze. Nothing was there.

"There it is! There it is!" Hoping over the dirt as if it were on fire, Magnolia let out another grating scream and pointed to the ground. The shadow of a snake—a rather large snake—slithered over the dirt, heading toward a curtain of vines. No doubt to escape the strident clamor.

Releasing Magnolia, Hayden dove and thrust his knife through its head. The thick body bounced and twitched for several seconds before finally stilling. After ensuring it was dead, Hayden reached for Magnolia, surprised when she folded against him, surprised even more by the soft press of her curves on his chest, the silky feel of her trembling body beneath her chemise. "Did it bite you?"

She shook her head.

Relieved, Hayden untangled himself from her arms and nudged her back. But the naïve temptress pressed against him again, sobbing hysterically. He groaned inwardly, keeping his hands at his side and clenching his jaw until it hurt, hoping the pain would help him focus. "Only a snake, Princess."

"But it's slimy and disgusting and it crawled on my leg." Her voice quavered.

Against his better judgment, Hayden folded his arms around her and rubbed her back. Her need for comfort oddly deflated his own needs at the moment. Besides, he might as well enjoy the feel of her while he could. Because he knew it wouldn't last.

"How dare you?" She stepped back and slapped him across the face.

Not long at all. He rubbed his cheek. "I was comforting you."

"You were taking liberties." Grabbing her wet skirts from the bush, she held them up to her chin. "In my frightened condition!"

Hayden huffed. "It was you who ran into *my* arms, Princess."

"You could have resisted me."

"You were hysterical. What was I supposed to do? Shove you aside and leave?"

"You should have noticed I wore nothing but my chemise and excused yourself."

"I had a snake to kill, if you remember."

She sniffed. "Well, after that, of course. Stop staring at me!"

Hayden was indeed staring at her, more from a stupefied confusion than any lewd intention. Besides, the darkness forbade him to make out the details he so desperately wished to see. And his desire to do so had vanished with her slap. Leaning over, he picked up his knife, still stuck in the snake's head and held up the beast.

Magnolia leapt back. "What are you going to do with that?"

Shoving aside the scraggly bush, Hayden headed back to camp. "Make dinner."

❦

Lowering herself onto a rock, Angeline nuzzled her face against her cat, Stowy's, soft fur and stared across the dark water of the creek. Wisps of night mist danced atop ripples as they tumbled over boulders to form a dozen tiny crystalline waterfalls. She loved this time of night. When everyone had retired to their huts and she could steal away for a few moments alone. A time when she could dip in the creek and allow the warm waters to wash away the filth of the day and caress her skin—a time to reflect on her life and her future; on her uncanny attraction to the preacher, James; on what she could do about Dodd's constant attention; on how she ended up being a seamstress in a town without a single bolt of fabric, though there were plenty of repairs needed on the colonists' already-worn clothing. But most of all, she needed time to reflect on whether she'd been mistaken in hoping she could escape her past by hiding in the middle of the Brazilian jungle.

Stowy glanced up at her with a *merow* to complain that she'd stopped petting him. Smiling, she scratched his head then ran her fingers down his back as he rumbled out a loud purr. "You're such a good companion, little one." She set him down beside her. "Now, stay here while I bathe." The cat promptly plopped on the dirt and folded his legs beneath his chest, reminding Angeline she needn't worry about him. Ever since they'd come ashore, Stowy rarely left her side.

It was as if he sensed dangers in the jungle and decided it was best to stay close. Everyone in New Hope had predicted he'd be devoured by some predator within a week, but here he was three months later, fit and fine. What a wise cat. Much wiser than her it seemed, for she had not fared as well in the wilds of city life.

Angeline began unbuttoning her blouse as she gazed across the misty creek. One of the farmers' wives had come across this isolated stream last month, and after telling the other women, they had all been sworn to secrecy about its location. The reason why stared at Angeline from just a few feet away. A round, stone basin, formed out of a rock outcropping, lay perfectly positioned beneath a gentle waterfall. Constantly filled to overflowing with calm, fresh water and surrounded by enough leaves to provide sufficient privacy, it provided a warm bath in the middle of the jungle—pure heaven to all of the colony's ladies. Well, if one didn't mind the mud, insects, and fish.

Drawing off her blouse, Angeline untied her ankle boots, removed her shoes, and took a quick glance around. There was no one around except a bright yellow parrot, who stared at her from a tree branch, and a rather frumpy looking frog perched on a rock in the middle of the creek. After removing her stockings, skirts, petticoats, corset cover, and corset, only her thin chemise remained. Thank goodness she'd given up on her crinoline weeks ago. The darn thing was far too cumbersome to work in.

After laying her clothes on top of a shrub, she fingered the ring hanging on a chain around her neck—a sparkling ruby mounted in a gypsy setting. On either side of the ruby, two white topazes shimmered in the moonlight. It was her father's ring. He'd always told Angeline that she was the red ruby in the center while the topazes were he and her mother, always guarding and watching out for her. Sorrow caused her throat to clamp shut at the thought, and she glanced up into the star-sprinkled sky, wondering if they were looking out for her now. Even though her mother died in childbirth, Angeline had always felt her love from beyond the grave, as she did her father's, dead some four years now. She had pulled the ring off his cold finger, placed it around her neck, and had never taken it off since. Not even when. . .

But she couldn't think of that now. Didn't want to think of that now. . .

Or what her parents would think if they knew what she'd become. "If only you hadn't died, Papa. If only you hadn't sent me to Uncle John's." Wiping away a tear, she kissed the ring and climbed to the rim of the basin. An unavoidable moan of pleasure escaped her lips as she slid into the warm water. The frog uttered a deep *ribbit*. She smiled at him, hoping he'd stay on his rock and wouldn't be tempted to join her. Floating her head back on the water, she stared through the canopy at the clusters of stars flung like pieces of glass across a velvet backdrop. She held her nose and dipped beneath the surface. The sounds of the jungle muted to gurgles and the heavy swish of liquid. So soothing—as if she were in another world. A world far away where there were no problems, no struggles, no heartache.

No past.

Her lungs ached and she broke the surface, back to reality, back to the hiss of wind and hum of the jungle and the crackle of a fire.

A fire? She scanned the clearing. A dark figure sat on the beach.

Covering herself, she shoved backward until stone struck her back. Water sloshed. A shriek stuck in her throat. A cloud shifted. Moonlight dappled the man in silver. He smiled, revealing a row of crooked, stained teeth. Brown hair as dull as paste hung limp to shoulders that sagged beneath a thick wool overcoat missing two buttons. Bushy, graying sideburns angled down his limpid jaw as he studied her and stretched out his booted legs. "How's about a little fun, missy?"

Blood raced from Angeline's heart, leaving her numb. *Joseph Gordon.* What was he doing in Brazil? "You can't be here." Surely she was going mad. The heat, the insects, the hard work, the fear of Dodd recognizing her from that one night in a tavern in Richmond. . . All of it had ruptured her reason, shredding it into nonsensical rubbish.

"Ah, but I *am* here." He chuckled and leaned forward on his knees, looking at her with that same wanton look he'd always worn during the six months she'd lived in Savannah. Before he and his inquisitive nature and constant beatings had forced her to move—yet again.

"How?. . . I don't. . . What do you want?" She finally said, eyeing her clothing on the bush. Out of reach.

"To tell you that you can't run from what you are, Clarissa. Not here in Brazil and not if you went to the farthest parts of the earth, nor to the bottom of the sea. No, no." He gave a feigned sigh of disappointment. "And you can't hide what you done neither."

Angeline swallowed, her heart sinking into the silt beneath her feet. It was all over. Old Joseph Gordan would have no compunction to sharing her dirty secret with everyone.

He grinned. "Yes indeedy, you and I are going to have barrels of fun getting reacquainted."

⚓

"What are you doing, Mr. Dodd?" Overcome at the shock of seeing the man in the jungle so late at night, Eliza's shout came out louder than she intended.

Dodd seemed equally startled as he leapt back from his position crouched behind a bush. Immediately, he regained his composure and smiled. "Why nothing at all, Mrs. Colonel. Nothing at all. Just searching for gold."

Eliza narrowed her eyes. The man only addressed her with her husband's military title when he was up to no good. Perhaps as a reminder to himself that she was married to the leader of the colony and he best behave. "Searching for gold in the dark?"

"I have eyes like a bat, madam. Eyes like a bat." He opened them wide as if trying to convince her.

Eliza moved her torch closer to study those eyes that now shifted away.

I bet you do, but not to see gold with. "And yet you have no shovel."

He frowned and stuffed his thumbs into his belt. "No sense in carrying around a shovel until I actually find treasure, now is there?"

Eliza groaned inwardly at the idiocy of his statement. But why argue with a fool?

"I assure you, your pirate gold is not at the women's bathing pool, Mr. Dodd." Angeline had told Eliza she was going for a dip, which was why Eliza was coming to join her. She could use a bath herself, and besides, it wasn't wise for any of the women to be out here alone.

"The women's bathin'. . . What are you talking about?" Mr. Dodd looked at her as if she'd told him he stood in the Sistine Chapel in Rome. "I had no idea Miss Angeline was at some bathing pool."

"I made no mention of Angeline, sir."

He rubbed his chin and gave a nervous laugh. "I just assumed since you two are friends and I hear she loves to bathe and she'd be the only woman to come out here alone without escort and disrobe in public. Not that I'm saying she did such a thing, but since you mentioned a bathing pool, I only assumed. . ." He shifted his stance and cleared his throat, still refusing to look at her.

The man was not only a greedy letch but a bad liar as well. "What exactly are you trying to say, Mr. Dodd?"

"Nothing. . .oh nothing. . ." He slapped his lips together and plucked a leaf from a nearby bush. "Never mind. It's late and my head is foggy. Good evening." And with that, he sauntered away, chuckling, as if she hadn't just caught him peering inappropriately at Angeline. Something she would definitely mention to her husband, Blake.

Shoving the foliage aside, Eliza's anger rose as she realized the ladies would have to find a new spot to bathe. But those thoughts were soon scattered when she saw Angeline standing on the shore, holding her loose petticoat up to her chest, her face as pale as the moon.

"Did you see. . ." She turned as Eliza approached and pointed a trembling finger to the sandy shore of the creek.

"See what?" Eliza scanned the clearing. No one was there except Stowy, who now circled his mistresses' ankles. "Come now, let's get you dried off. You're shivering."

She wrapped Angeline in a dry towel and led her to sit on a boulder. "Did Dodd bother you?"

"Dodd? No." Angeline's voice sounded hollow. "I saw someone. Someone I knew from Savannah." Stowy leapt into her lap.

Eliza's heart tightened as her thoughts drifted to the odd visions she and Blake—and now even James—had seen. "Who?"

Angeline's harried gaze skittered across the clearing. "When you emerged from the jungle, he simply vanished. Are you sure no one is here?"

"I don't see anyone." Eliza took Angeline's hand in hers, deciding it best not to tell her about Dodd. "Real people don't vanish. I'm sure it was just a bad dream. That's all." But she knew Angeline hadn't been asleep. None of them had been asleep when they'd seen their visions.

Dear Lord, what is going on?

CHAPTER 12

Holding her wet clothes over one arm and her valise in the other, Magnolia entered the clearing and made her way to the shelter. Setting her valise inside, she flung her wet garments over a nearby branch beneath the cover of a tree, doing her best to hide her personals. Just the thought of Hayden seeing them sent heat blossoming up her throat. Just like it had when he'd held her close with nothing between them but her chemise. The utter shame! Yes, she had screamed for his help. She'd been hysterical with fear. But any gentleman would have made a hasty retreat after killing the snake. Not taken her into his arms. Not rubbed her back and squeezed her tight. How could she possibly face him now?

More importantly, how could she deny the complete and utter pleasure she had felt in his embrace? Not just safe and secure, but on fire from the inside out. In a good way. A most pleasurable way. Mercy me, she'd kissed men before. She was well acquainted with the flutter in her belly upon such an action. But this, this sensation was beyond anything she had ever dreamed.

She needed a drink. She took in a deep breath, letting her nerves settle.

At least it had stopped raining. For now. Perhaps she should retire for the night and avoid looking at Hayden altogether. She heard him fiddling with the fire, could feel his eyes on her. Knew as soon as he looked at her, he'd see her embarrassment. No doubt he would utter some sarcastic quip, or worse, try to take further liberties. Reaching into her pocket, she pulled out her flask and took a sip, noting how dry it was in the shelter. She placed a hand on the bed of leaves. Thick and soft and raised off the ground to keep the ants and moisture away. An odd feeling warmed her belly—she wasn't used to being cared for. But no, she told herself, that must've been the pinga. She took another sip, wincing at the pungent taste when a most delectable scent caused her stomach to lurch.

Peering around the corner of her shelter, she saw Hayden holding a skinned snake over the fire. "Ready for supper?" he asked, his tone playful.

She crept toward him. Their eyes met. As she'd feared, heat swamped her, rising up her neck and face. The right side of his lips quirked. Magnolia stomped her foot. "Stop looking at me that way. You behaved the cad and now you remind me of it with your eyes." Jungle-green eyes that assessed her with impunity and something else that sent a tingle down to her wet toes. "You know I am at your complete mercy and yet you toy with me as an impudent boy would a poor little bird. Not that I'm as weak as a little bird, so don't get any thoughts in your bloated head—"

"Do you wish to eat or not?" He interrupted, one brow lifting.

She thrust out her chin. "I don't eat snake."

"Well, I have nothing else to offer, Princess." The snake flesh sizzled in the flames, sending up an aroma that caused Magnolia's mouth to water. She inched to the fire, saw that he'd dragged a log over for her to sit on and placed some dried leaves on top.

Hayden tore off a chunk of snake and popped it in his mouth, raising his brows at her as he moaned in delight. His wet shirt molded to his chest, carving lines around firm muscles. Damp almond-colored hair slicked back from a face that seemed more intense and angular in the shifting firelight.

Magnolia pulled out her flask and took another sip. What was wrong with her? She'd been courted by wealthy landowners, an English baron, even a governor's son, yet here she was ogling a man so far beneath her, the heel of her boot wouldn't touch his head.

An orphan. One of the many hapless street elves inhabiting Charleston, stealing and begging and causing mayhem.

"I'll have a sip of that," he held out his hand.

"*May I* have a sip, please?" she corrected him.

He cocked his head and studied her, his jaw tightening. "Thank you, Hayden, for saving my life from a snake," he taunted.

Magnolia fumed. "Did I not say thank you? Perhaps you were too busy fondling me to hear."

He laughed, a hearty laugh that echoed through the jungle. "How about an exchange then? I give you some food and you give me a drink." Rising, he approached and held out the stick of roasting snake flesh.

She gulped. "I couldn't possibly."

"Come now. It tastes like chicken. Besides, you must eat or you won't have strength to walk all day tomorrow."

Handing him the flask, Magnolia pulled off a chunk of meat. She closed her eyes, set it on her tongue, and forced herself to chew, trying not to gag at the thought of it. But Hayden was right. It did taste like chicken. Wonderfully delicious chicken. Her stomach welcomed it happily. She broke off another piece while Hayden sipped her pinga.

He lowered the flask and coughed, his face turning red. "What in the Sam Hill is this?"

"Brazilian rum. Thiago made it." She frowned and gestured for him to give it back. "And that's all I have for the journey." When he didn't return it, she tugged off another piece of meat and lowered herself with difficulty to the log. "But this snake is good. Very good. I'm going to think of it as chicken, however. How do you know it's not poisonous?" She stopped chewing and stared at him, fear trailing the last piece down her throat.

Hayden chuckled. Much to her dismay, he took another sip of rum before he handed the flask back to her. "Poisonous snakes are brightly colored. Besides, I cut off the head where the venom is stored."

Magnolia had no idea how he knew such a thing, nor did she want to know. She resumed chewing, finally feeling the effects of the pinga soften her frayed nerves. "So, you were an orphan in Charleston?"

Emboldened by the rum, she broached a subject that would be considered impolite to mention in society, but for some reason she was desperate to know more about this fierce, untamed man.

The fire cast a circle of light, skipping over the surrounding leaves and branches like a swarm of butterflies in a field of flowers. Pops and sizzles joined the drone of crickets and bullfrogs in a pleasant melody.

Sitting on a stump just a yard from hers, Hayden tore off another hunk of snake and stared at it for so long she thought he wouldn't answer her. "Eight years."

"What happened to your parents?"

"Father left when I was two. My mother was run over by a carriage when I was ten."

Magnolia's throat closed around a piece of meat. She coughed, struggling to breathe, and grabbed the flask for another sip. Her heart felt as thick and heavy as the air around her. What father would leave a wife and child? And his poor mother. . . "How horrible. Did you not have relatives, uncles, grandparents?"

He shook his head and tossed the snake into his mouth. His jaw rolled tight as he chewed. "No one."

Magnolia stared at the dirt. An ant scampered across the soil, forming a jagged path. First left then right, then left again as if it were lost and trying to find its way. Finally, it approached the fire then sped off in the other direction. All alone. Just like Hayden had been. While she'd slept in a feather bed, had a buffet of delicacies to choose from, and every luxury money could buy, he had been on the street, searching to find his way, scraping his sustenance from the dirt. "How did you survive?"

He grabbed a stick and poked the fire, sending sparks into the night. "I begged. Stole. Sometimes set traps and caught small animals, whatever I could."

His tone bore the nonchalance of a man who didn't want pity, yet pride and pain lingered in his expression. She wanted to touch him, to offer him comfort, but he seemed unsettled, like a powder keg about to explode. Besides, she didn't want to care for him. Caring meant risk. And risk meant pain. At least with men like him. Handsome, capable men with sultry smiles and mischievous eyes that made a woman's heart flutter, excitement and danger in their touch. She'd had her heart trampled by a man like that. But never again. They both sat silent for several minutes. Finally, he stood, strode to the edge of camp, and returned with two bananas. He handed her one.

"Yet you survived and obviously found a way to earn a living." She took the fruit, hoping to sweep away Hayden's somber mood with her compliment.

A breeze stirred the flames then spun around the camp, fluttering the surrounding leaves. Pinpricks of light flashed in the dark jungle. On and off. One there, and then another a few feet away. "Fireflies!" Shoving off the log, Magnolia jumped to her feet and twirled around, excited to see something so familiar. "Just like in Georgia! Do you see them? I've always loved fireflies ever since I was a little girl." Somehow it made her feel close to her homeland, as if it wasn't across an ocean, thousands of miles away.

Her eyes met his, and she found him smiling at her. Not a seductive sort of smile, but a smile of admiration. It did odd things to her insides, and she shifted her gaze away and sat back down. "What is it that you do, Hayden? To make a living, I mean."

This seemed to amuse him, though why she couldn't imagine. "You might say I'm a broker of sorts."

"A broker? And what does a broker do?"

He seemed to be pondering the answer as he tossed another log into the fire. "I arrange sales of properties and other investments." He smiled again, a smile of amusement, as if he'd just told her he was a clown with a traveling circus. At least that would be more interesting than being a broker from the sounds of it. In fact, it quite surprised her to learn that this uncultured man held such a professional job. Sailor, fisherman, blacksmith—those professions she could understand. But broker? "Sounds complicated," she said. "How did an orphan learn such a trade?"

He peeled his banana and took a bite. "One learns many things on the streets, Princess. You do what you must in order to survive."

Then why did his voice sting with guilt? Surely being a broker was an honorable pursuit. Perhaps not very lucrative, but honorable.

A monkey howled in the distance. Or was it something else? Something more menacing. Hayden didn't seem to notice as he stared at the fire, a pensive expression on his face.

Magnolia took another sip of pinga. My, but the man was acting strangely. Finally, after a quick glance her way, he rose and sat on a log on the other side of the fire, as if he couldn't stand to be near her.

She should be thrilled at his obvious disinterest. Relieved! Especially after their encounter in the bushes. Then why did the action disturb her so? She fingered a strand of moist hair lying in her lap and regretted not pinning it up appropriately. She must look a mess! Her father would be outraged. She could still hear him say:

"The Holy Scripture tells us that a woman's hair is her glory. Therefore, it must be properly combed and pinned up with modesty and decorum at all times. Otherwise you shame not only yourself, but your family and your God. Only women of tawdry morals wear their hair loose."

Corking the pinga, she slipped it in her pocket and retrieved her mirror from her valise. She barely recognized the woman staring back at her. Hair like coiled wet rope hugged the side of her face like a barnacle to a ship. Her lips were pale, her eyes dull, and red marks peppered her once porcelain skin. Retrieving her handkerchief, she quickly wiped the streak of dirt lining her forehead. How had she missed that before?

Perhaps her disheveled appearance was the reason for the look of disgust on Hayden's face, the reason he distanced himself from her. She ran fingers through the tangled strands of hair, shoved them away from her face, and held the mass of curls up behind her. She should pin it up. But she didn't feel like it tonight. Besides, who cared what Hayden thought? Letting her locks tumble down her back, she opened her flask and took another drink. Maybe she was worthless just like her father said. Especially without her beauty.

Firelight dappled leaves with golden light and flung sparks into the night. She glanced up to see stars winking at her through the canopy. She giggled at the sight and lowered her gaze. Things became blurry, distant. The pain throbbing in her heart numbed, and she tipped the flask to take another sip.

When Hayden plucked it from her grip.

❦

"I think you've had enough, Princess." Hayden shoved the cork in the nozzle and slid the flask into his pocket. Though he'd love to take another drink himself, he was already having trouble keeping his wits about him with this capricious woman. Capricious and whimsical and oddly delightful. And beautiful. No one had ever asked him about his childhood before. Or his occupation. Nor had anyone seemed genuinely sorrowful at his woeful story. In fact, the last person he expected sympathy from was the spoiled daughter of a rich plantation owner.

Yet the concern and pain burning in those blue eyes of hers had nearly done him in, broken his resolve to allow no one into his heart. No one close enough to really know him. No one who could hurt him—abandon him. He'd told her more than he'd intended. And she was more beautiful to him for having drawn his sad tale out from hiding. But now, he must shove his past back into the cobwebbed recesses of his mind and close the door on further conversation.

At least about him.

"Here, have some more snake." He handed her the stick.

"I don't want snake. I want my rum back." She held out her hand.

He put a piece of snake in it instead.

Those eyes that had been so beautiful when they were filled with concern for him now flashed like lightning. He gave his gaze permission to rove over her curves, heating his body in remembrance of the feel of her. Zooks, but she was a delicious morsel. And now a besotted one as well. In her condition, he would have no trouble seducing her. Like he'd done with so many women before.

Which was why he mustn't take a drink. And why he must sit as far away from her as possible.

She tossed the snake into her mouth. "My rum, if you please?"

"Let's save it for tomorrow, shall we?" He returned to his seat and threw another log on the fire.

A frown on her face, she began peeling her banana. "You're a monster, Hayden Gale." She mumbled. "And no fun at all." She bit into the fruit and fumbled with her hair, trying to set it in place without pins. "No, you are worse than a monster. You're one of those giant toads down by the river. You know the ones that are big and fat and ugly and have all those hideous spots on them? Yes, you're one of those. Except there's not a libertine's chance in a convent that you'll ever turn into a handsome prince."

Hayden couldn't help but smile.

Until she began to sing.

"Open the door, my hinny, my heart,
Open the door, my own darling;
Remember the word you spoke to me
In the meadow by the well-spring."

Hayden must find a way to stop the irksome sound. "Tell me of this fiancé of yours."

She stopped and stared at him. "I've told you. His name is Samuel Wimberly, and he's a renowned solicitor." She sat taller as if trying to convince him of the man's worth. "He was an adviser to Jefferson Davis, you know."

"If he was such a great match, why are you here in Brazil and not playing the doting wife back home?"

She released a heavy sigh and gazed into the fire. "My parents didn't think Samuel was good enough for me. They wanted someone with more money and a better name to help our family recover from my—" She froze, her eyes widening.

"From your…?"

"From the war."

"From *your* war?" he teased.

"Don't be silly." She waved a hand through the air. "It doesn't matter. Anyway, Samuel must have gone into hiding after the war because we couldn't find him. And my parents got some harebrained idea of pawning me off on a wealthy Brazilian of royal blood or a rich American who came here to escape the war. Apparently many of both can be found in Rio."

"Then why didn't they stay in Rio with you when we first arrived?"

"Because. . ." She glanced at him and flattened her lips. "Because they want to get settled first, establish a presence, a name. . .to attract the right sorts. . .you know, appearances and all that."

"Hmm." Either the woman was lying or she and her parents had beans for brains. "Surely being part of the landed gentry, your parents could have found a suitable match for you in the States. Why come to an unknown country?"

Knowing how much she hated Brazil, Hayden expected her to agree vehemently. Instead a shadow rolled across her face as she fingered a wet strand of her hair.

"My father says a woman's appearance is all that matters. And because I was born beautiful, it is my duty to marry well. That's what beautiful daughters do, you know, they are useful for making alliances that help the entire family move up social and economic ladders." She wobbled on her stump then perched her chin in her hand. "Trouble is I can't seem to *keep* myself presentable enough for him."

A lump formed in Hayden's throat.

The shadows beneath her eyes deepened. "I can never seem to please him. I can't keep my hair in a proper coiffeur nor my skirts without wrinkle and stain. And I've tried so hard. So very hard. Which is why he dragged me to Brazil." She stared down at the strand of hair in her hand. "I owe it to him to form a good alliance. To pay off my debt. And now I've gone and run away. Ruined everything for him once again." Her voice caught, and she released a long sigh. "I simply can't stand another minute in this place, surely you understand? The jungle, the dirt, the bugs…and I love Samuel. And he loves me. How am I to find a proper man out here in this desolate cesspool? I want to help my father, I do, but I fear he's given up on finding me a match anyway, and I'm fast becoming an ugly old spinster." She dropped her head into her hands and began to sob.

Hayden ground his teeth together. He had never cared for Mr. Scott, but now he liked him even less. How dare any father treat his daughter like a commodity? Treat her beauty as if it was something to barter with, something with which to increase his own station in life?

Look what he had created. A miserable woman not only obsessed with her appearance but desperate for a father's love. Perhaps life behind the gilded doors of the pampered elite wasn't as merry as they pretended. Sympathy rose for the woman before him, and Hayden found himself longing to bring her comfort.

The fire spat and sizzled. A lizard sped across the clearing and disappeared into the darkness. "What could you possibly owe your father?" he asked.

She looked up, eyes swollen and face moist. She swayed to the left, blinked, and finally balanced herself on the stump. "I made a mistake. A big mistake. It cost my family dearly. And tore my heart in two." A flicker of awareness strengthened her glossy gaze. "But I can't tell you about it."

"It was a man, wasn't it?" It had to be. A suitor, perhaps, who took advantage of her innocence. "Someone close to you?"

"How did you know?" She snapped her gaze to his then shifted to stare at the fire. "An evil man. A trickster. A liar."

Hayden's stomach twisted. Like him.

Rising, she began to pace, her skirts floating over the dirt. She wobbled, held out her arms, then turned to go the other way.

He'd better settle her before she fell. Slowly, Hayden made his way to her. The last thing he needed was her darting off into the brush on a whim. Over the years, he'd seen alcohol cause people—especially distraught people—to do dangerous things. And he didn't relish the idea of traipsing after her through the jungle. Especially in the dark. She stumbled over a root and barreled into him. He steadied her. She smelled of sweet rain. "Regardless of what you feel you owe your father, you shouldn't have to sacrifice your life for it."

Her eyes wavered over his. A tiny furrow formed between her brows. Finally, she reached up and ran her fingers over his jaw. "I always wondered what that felt like. So rough and prickly." She scrunched her face and studied him. "You are quite handsome, Hayden Gale." She slammed a finger over her lips and grinned. "But I'll deny I said that tomorrow."

"And since I am not a gentleman, I will, of course, remind you."

Raising her nose, she jerked from his embrace and took up a pace again, charging straight into the stump she'd been sitting on. "Ouch!" She started to topple. Hayden caught her, hoisted her into his arms, and carried her to the shelter. Kneeling, he placed her inside. It was best that she got some sleep before she said something she'd regret. And before he *did* something he would definitely regret.

Lying down on the soft leaves, she threw a hand to her head. "Everything's spinning. Why is everything spinning? It's a fine shelter, Hayden, it truly is, but what of all the spiders and lizards, ants, and snakes!" She sat up and reached for him. "Don't leave me, Hayden. It's so frightening here in the jungle."

Hayden could only stare at her. Was she kidding? *God, if You're up there, this is far too much temptation for one man.* Especially a man like him. It was the first prayer he'd uttered since his mother's death fifteen years ago. That time, God had not answered him, why did Hayden think He would answer now? "The critters will leave you alone." For the most part. "Besides, I'll be right by the fire. You're safe."

"There's room for two." She lay back down and patted the leaves beside her. "You made the shelter—you should sleep in it."

She had a point. A very delectable point. Groaning, he forced himself to stand. "Good night, Princess. Sleep well." At least *she* would get some rest, for it would be a long time before he settled down enough to fall asleep. A long time, indeed.

During those hours, Hayden made a pact with himself. This woman not only stirred him physically, but she had begun to stir his heart. And that was far too dangerous. Dangerous for him and dangerous for her. He'd made a practice of never mixing business and pleasure, of never getting too close to one of his "clients." Which was why he must keep his distance from the lovely Magnolia for the rest of the trip. He was only flesh and blood, after all.

CHAPTER 13

Finally some level ground! Magnolia trudged after Hayden, every inch of her legs and feet aflame. For the past two and a half days they'd ascended one hill after another as they wove their way through a range of verdant mountains—through steamy jungles, up windswept crests, and even down to an occasional beach, so close were they to the sea. Hayden told her they traveled near the coast to avoid the larger mountains inland—a range of majestic peaks she could now see rising in the west like angry gods spying on intruders to their land. She half expected them to grow weary of holding their heads above the clouds and suddenly collapse, swallowing her and Hayden whole. Part of her wouldn't care if they did. At least she'd be able to rest. But the muted sounds of a large city kept her plodding forward. That and the glimpses of civilization they'd passed—if one could call them that—in the form of several small farms and mud homes abuzz with naked children like bees around a hive. The adults greeted them with unabashed friendship and grand enthusiasm, beckoning them to come and share a meal. At least that was what Magnolia surmised from their exaggerated gestures, once they realized she and Hayden didn't speak Portuguese.

But Hayden declined each time, trying to make them understand that he and Magnolia were in a hurry to get to the city. Unfazed by the refusal, they continued to smile and wave at them until they were out of sight. Magnolia couldn't help but remark at how friendly Brazilians seemed to be.

"Beware of smiling faces and beguiling invitations, Princess. Everyone has a motive."

Those were the first words he'd spoken to her in days, other than grunts and nods and an occasional "Hurry up." Magnolia couldn't imagine what she'd done to prick his ire. Yes, she'd overindulged in drink that one night, but she had no memory of saying anything untoward or rude. Like she usually did when besotted. All she remembered were the personal details they shared of their lives. Which should make people feel closer, not push them apart, shouldn't it? Yet, all their intimate conversation had done was erect an impenetrable wall around this man.

"So, you *can* speak" The path widened and she quickened her pace to slip beside him.

"Only when I have something important to say."

"What are you implying?" Magnolia snapped, shifting her valise to her other hand while she shook out her aching fingers. "That I don't speak of important matters?" She huffed. "Besides, what is so important about your cynical distrust of people?"

He halted. Green eyes assessed her as if she were one of the pesky butterflies that continually landed on them in the jungle. Then turning, he moved on without saying a word.

"You can't trust most people, Princess," he said after a few minutes. "Once you realize that, you'll be better off."

Magnolia drew a sleeve over the perspiration on her brow, having long since given up proper etiquette. Trust. Something she'd sworn to never give another man. Yet, here she was trusting this one to put her safely on a ship heading back home. "Can I trust *you*?"

When he didn't answer, she stopped. "I *can* trust you, can't I?" she called after him, but her voice blended with the annoying whine of insects darting around her head, and she wasn't sure he heard her. In fact, she wasn't sure she could take another step. Every inch of her body throbbed, from the pounding in her head to the crick in her neck from sleeping on the ground, to the strain across her shoulders, the gnawing hunger in her belly, the spasms in her arms and fingers, her sore calves, and blistered feet. And to make matters worse, she'd been shaking ever since she'd sucked down her last drop of rum over a day ago.

In fact, she was quite sure she'd walked across the entire country, hiking up craggy cliffs with deadly drop-offs, sliding down muddy trails with no end, tripping on massive roots that crisscrossed the ground, all the while being strangled by the web of vines dropping from the canopy like ropes from a castle wall. Only climbing these ropes wouldn't bring one to the safety of a fortress but to an entirely different world ruled by monkeys and bats and birds. And then there were the bugs. She'd thought Georgia's insects were hideous. If she ever made it back home, she'd never complain about them again.

She stared at Hayden, marching on his merry way, with that cocksure swagger of his, oblivious to her at-death's-door condition. As usual. Yet he *had* taken care of her. Good care. Especially at night when he erected a shelter for her and provided something for dinner. One night he'd even caught a couple fish. Magnolia was sure she'd never tasted anything so delicious. Though he'd ignored her many shrieks during the night at the bugs invading her shelter, he'd stretched out and slept across the entrance like a sentinel. His presence had brought her more comfort than she cared to admit. And aside from that evening when he'd held her in her chemise, he'd been the perfect gentleman, stunning her with behavior so contrary to her initial assessment of the man. Mercy me, he'd even given her back her flask, though it had been nearly empty.

Now, it *was* empty and she craved a drink. Picking up her valise, she forced her feet to move before Hayden disappeared from sight. Infuriating man! But they were almost in Rio, and she could rid herself of him soon enough. The sooner the better before he realized she'd lied to him about the money. She shuddered to think what he would do to her when he found out. Most likely take every last cent she owned before she could purchase a ticket home. Then, what would happen to her?

No, as soon as Hayden led her to the harbor, she would steal away and buy a ticket on the first ship heading back to the States. Even now as the chatter of people and clank of the tramway convinced her civilization was near, her heart lifted a little. She needed a bath. That

the middle of the crowd. She leaned against him, weak and panting and looking like she was about to wilt. He must find shelter and food for her soon. She had endured far more than most ladies of her class ever would have been able to endure. More than *he* thought she would have. For a pampered sot, she had surprisingly kept up with his swift pace through the jungle. And aside from a few complaints here and there and some shrieking in the middle of the night due to bugs invading her bed, she'd stopped whining. One night, she'd even helped him gather firewood and palm fronds. He had wanted to thank her, wanted to tell her he was proud of her. But he thought better of it. No sense in teasing them both with a friendship that couldn't last. One that would be quickly severed when Hayden's deception came to light.

Pressed against the wall of a shop, Hayden slipped his hand into hers, lest he lose her in the mad crush. Much to his surprise, she gripped it willingly, desperately, and he hated the overwhelming need to protect her that welled inside of him. He'd never felt that way about a woman before, especially one he was about to swindle. Clamping down his jaw, he shoved through the crowd, focusing his mind on his plan, his goal, while squashing his emotions. Emotions made him weak, made him lose his edge. Any confidence man worth the money he swindled never allowed sentiment to interfere with a job.

Elaborate churches rose like guardians of light over the shadows of debauchery in the streets as the crowd drank and danced in celebration. The idol worship offended even Hayden's nonreligious sensibilities. Though he was sure they were shouting "Saint John! Saint John!" the entire festival seemed to have popped from the pages of some pagan ritual. Especially in light of the prostitutes lingering about. Large Negresses dressed in ruffles and lace, wearing high-heeled slippers, their necks and arms loaded with gold chains and ivory, and their heads adorned in colorful turbans, squatted before shops and dared to lounge even on church steps, baring bosoms to men who passed by.

Hoping to protect Magnolia from the sight, Hayden hurried her along, but her gasp and "Mercy me" told him he had failed. Rounding another corner, he led her away from the celebration, trying to recall the way to the immigration office. A donkey-led tramcar clanked along in front of them as dozens of mulattoes in every shade possible wove through the crowd, carrying sugarcane, bananas, oranges, prawns, and fish.

"Can you show me the way to the dock master? I need to see when the next ship leaves for the States." Magnolia finally released his hand and drew her parasol from her valise. "Perhaps there's one leaving tomorrow. I wouldn't want to miss it. Of course you don't have to accompany me. I could meet up with you later to say our good-byes."

Her voice sounded odd, hurried and clipped. When he glanced at her, she did not meet his gaze.

"They are closed in the afternoon," he said, not entirely sure of that fact, but it made for a good excuse to delay her plans. Besides, they'd passed several businesses and shops that had signs posted on their doors and no patrons within. Closed for the festival, no doubt. Which meant the immigration office might be locked up as well. Blast! He'd have to wait another day to find out about his father.

"Closed?" Her voice was so despondent, it nearly broke him.

"We'll go first thing in the morning." If—and only if—Hayden discovered his father had returned to America.

He turned down Rosario Street, where, if he remembered correctly, there was a hotel, Hotel d'Europe, which favored foreign guests. The least he could do before he swindled Magnolia out of most of her money—if it came to that—would be to provide her a decent room, a bath, and some food.

Shops lined the narrow street, their second stories housing for city dwellers. Carne secca and dried cod, along with bags of *feijjoes* and Minas cheeses sat in piles in front of the stores, emitting the most foul odor. Magnolia shifted her parasol and drew a hand to her nose, but her gaze soon found the bay and all discomfort vanished from her face.

"Look at the ships! Can you tell if any are American?" She halted, her eyes skittering over the water.

With the sun low in the sky behind them, the bay of Rio De Janeiro spread a panorama of glistening emerald across the horizon, dotted with boats, barges, and ships of all sizes: steamers, frigates, sloughs, brigs, and a Dutch trading ship, from what Hayden could tell. Large barks with high lateen sails, navigated by Negroes and laden with fruit, sped across the bay to the various pretty islets strewn like gems across the water.

"We'll check tomorrow. Come along." He offered his hand but she drew her valise to her chest and hugged it instead, giving him a look of suspicion. "Where are we going?"

"To get you a room for the night. You'd like a bath and a real bed, wouldn't you?"

Her face lit. Followed by a flash of her pretty white teeth. It was the first smile she had graced him with in several days. And he hated how good it made him feel. Like he was worthy. Like she trusted him. Like he'd do anything to keep that smile on her pink lips.

Even pay for the room at the Hotel d'Europe with his own money. Seven dollars. Good thing they accepted American money and didn't expect Reis, the local currency. Yet now Hayden had only five dollars left in his pockets. At least until tomorrow.

After unlocking the door to the room, Magnolia spun to face him, a look of horror on her face. "Where are *you* going to stay?"

Hayden rubbed the stubble on his chin and grinned. He'd love to tease her and insist they share the room, but she looked so pathetic and tired standing there in her stained, ripped gown and dirt-smudged skin, her hair all askew. "Is that an invitation?" All right, so he couldn't resist a little taunting.

"Of course not! How dare you insinuate—"

Hayden placed a finger on her lips. "Don't vex yourself, Princess, I can take care of myself."

At this, her eyes narrowed, and she swatted his hand away. "Very well." She set down her valise and started to close the door.

Hayden's boot halted its progress. "Why don't we settle accounts now?" He held out his hand. Something about the woman's demeanor pricked his suspicion. Surely she wasn't planning on running off before she paid him. She couldn't be that devious. Besides, she still needed him to escort her to the dock master tomorrow.

One brow lifted above eyes alight with enough mischief to confirm Hayden's suspicions.

"Do you take me for a complete fool?"

Hayden smiled. *Well...*

"Our bargain was that you'd bring me to the dock master. Besides, I won't know how much I have left over until I purchase my ticket." She pushed on the door then let out an exasperated sigh. "Now, if you'll please remove your mammoth boot, I'd like to rest."

Hayden studied her as she stared at the floor. Something wasn't right. But whether it was simply the woman's normal theatrics or something far more duplicitous he didn't know. He blew out a sigh. Magnolia was spoiled and pretentious and the most frustrating woman he'd ever met, but she wasn't shrewd. Especially not shrewd enough to trick the likes of him.

"If you try to run away with the money, Princess, I'll find you at the dock master's in the morning. There's only one in town."

Anger flared across her eyes, but only for a moment before she rubbed her forehead and leaned on the door as if she were going to faint. "I would never do such a thing. I'm just so tired, Hayden."

He shook his head, wondering whether to believe a word this woman said. "How about I return in a couple hours and escort you to dinner?"

She raised her eyes to his. Where moments before they'd spiked with annoyance, now they softened with what looked like sorrow. But that couldn't be.

"Thank you. That will be lovely," she said with a weak smile.

Hayden resisted the urge to run a finger over her cheek, to feel its softness, to see her response. Instead, he withdrew his boot. "Until then." He backed away from the door, expecting her to slam it on him. But she stared at him for another minute, her eyes becoming pools, before she closed it with a click that nipped his heart.

Reflecting on the woman's odd behavior, Hayden passed the time strolling the city streets, gazing at the oddities of this foreign place. Curiosity led him past the immigration office, just to see if it was open, and then inside when he found the door ajar. Though he'd wanted to have Magnolia—and her money—with him when he questioned Mr. Santos, he couldn't help himself from inquiring whether the man was there. A pudgy, grease-faced fellow wearing a suit that had gone out of fashion a decade ago informed Hayden, in rather broken English, that the immigration officer was away and wouldn't return until tomorrow. However, if the matter was urgent, Hayden might find him that evening at a party at the home of Adelino Manuel Guerra da Costa, one of the city's magistrates. The squirrely man even gave Hayden directions, but then quickly chastised himself with a chuckle saying that the party was by invitation only. His brandy-drenched belch a moment later confirmed Hayden's suspicions that the man would probably have given Hayden his mother as a gift if he had asked.

Regardless, Hayden emerged from the office into the heat of the languishing day with a huge smile on his face. He'd rather meet Santos with an advantage—a rather beautiful advantage carrying a pouch of gold. How could any man resist Magnolia? Within moments of lavishing him with her Southern charm, Mr. Santos would melt like warm butter in her hands. And Hayden would discover his father's whereabouts—if the swine had even returned to Rio. If not, perhaps he'd sent one of his colonists with information on a new location as Blake wanted Hayden to do. Hayden knew the immigration office kept updated records of each colony's precise acreage and position, and since his father was not where Mr. Santos had originally told Hayden he would be, he must have moved to a new area and reported the change. A huge gamble, but a reasonable one, and the only option Hayden had at the moment for finding the man. And finally ending his lifelong quest. Finally putting things right. For him. For his mother.

Alternatively, if his father had sailed back to America, Hayden would be able to escort Magnolia home and ensure her safety. He wouldn't have to swindle her, wouldn't have to betray her trust and return her to New Hope. For the first time in his life, the thought of not cheating someone pleased him immensely, along with the thought of spending more time with the lady.

He shook his head, wondering if he'd contracted some brain-eating jungle fever, for she'd done nothing but annoy him to distraction these past five days. No, that wasn't true. The lady had surprised him in more ways than one. The sad story of the debt she owed her father, how he used her for her beauty like some prize horse, how some swindler broke her heart, her concern over Hayden's unhappy past, her resilience these past few days—all had stirred something in his soul. Made him realize that, despite the wide gulf in their social standing, they weren't so different after all. Both of them wore masks to hide deep inner pain. And both were desperately searching for something to ease that pain.

Weaving around a Chinaman selling fish, Hayden shifted his thoughts to the immigration officer, Mr. Santos. A safer topic. If he waited until tomorrow to talk to the snake, he'd have to find a way to delay Magnolia from seeking passage on her ship. Besides, it had been awhile since he'd attended a party. He smiled. But how to sneak into the lavish affair without notice? And where to find some decent attire?

Preoccupied with his thoughts, he missed the turn and headed down a narrow avenue. Not until the clamor of voices, shouts of vendors, and bray of donkeys faded did he realize he was going in the wrong direction. Heat spiraled from the tiled roofs of houses lining the dirt road. He halted, spun around, and headed back, passing a group of abandoned buildings and a church that was no more than a mud hut with a raised tin roof and a brass crucifix affixed above the front door. The words "Igreja" were hand written on a sign tacked to the wall.

Wiping the sweat from the back of his neck, Hayden hurried past when the front door swung open and a thin man wearing a black priest's robe started toward Hayden. Ignoring him, Hayden continued walking. The last thing he needed was some castigating sermon. Yet, before he took two steps, the man touched his arm and spun him around.

"Portuguese?"

"Sorry." Hayden shook his head and continued onward.

"English then?" The priest followed him, a silly smile on his angular mouth.

"What can I do for you?" Hayden sighed and faced the man. An odd looking man for a priest. His slanted eyes, along with a long gray braid running down the back of his robe gave him a Far Eastern appearance. Yet his skin was brown, his body more reed-like than muscular.

The priest grew somber, his dark eyes studying Hayden as if searching for something. "You come from jungle, right? You part of colony from America, right?"

"Yes." Hayden's annoyance grew. All good guesses based on his appearance and accent. "I have no money, sir." He started walking again.

The man grabbed Hayden's arm. "Beware. Evil. Much evil there. Many men die. Many men disappear."

"What are you talking about?" Hayden wanted to call the man an old fool and walk away, but one didn't say that to a priest, even a crazy one. Sure, Hayden was probably going to hell—if there *was* such a place—but there was no sense in adding insulting a man of God to his list of crimes. But perhaps. . . "Do you know a man named Owen Godard?" Hayden spoke the alias his father had used on his journey to Brazil.

The priest shook his head and tightened his grip on Hayden's arm. "Many disappear."

"Did Mr. Godard disappear?"

"I do not know this man."

"Then who disappeared?"

"Other colonists like you. And men from Rio. Even priests who go to fight."

"Fight?" Hayden glanced down the street, anxious to leave.

"Fight the evil. From the *lagos incendito*." He folded his lips together and studied the ground as if expecting it to explode beneath his feet. Then he gripped Hayden's arm even tighter, his eyes flashing. "Fire lake beneath temple."

Hayden didn't know whether to laugh or feel sorry for the deranged man. Still, he hadn't time for this. He gently removed the man's boney fingers. "Fire lake, eh? Thank you for the warning. Now, if you'll excuse me." He turned and felt the claw-like grip on his arm once again.

"No. You listen. Much evil. Men not survive. Some tell of invisible beasts. See many visions. Some go mad."

Visions. Now the man had his attention. "How do you know about the visions? Where do they come from?"

"The beasts. They must be defeated."

"Beasts? Like wolves and jaguars?"

"No." He gripped Hayden's other arm, swerving him to face him. "Not natural. Not human. Only God can protect."

God again. How could a God who couldn't protect an orphan on the streets of Charleston possibly save them from these beasts?—if they even existed. No doubt the priest had seen some visions of his own.

Hayden placated him with a smile and a pat on his arm. "I promise to be careful." Tearing from his grip, Hayden stormed ahead. *I promise to not come down this street again!*

This time the man didn't follow him. But his authoritative voice did.

"Only one way to defeat. Only one way. You must go back. You are one of six. Consult the book. Only the six can defeat the evil."

Hayden wanted to ask him six what, but reason kept him moving. Evil, indeed. Outside of man's own selfishness, did evil even exist? Yet Hayden couldn't deny the heaviness that had weighed on him at the temple and the visions he'd seen—Katherine and the one of his father in the jungle.

Shaking the thoughts from his head, he reached the end of the street and started for the hotel. Just the ramblings of a crazy old priest. Or were they?

CHAPTER 14

In all her twenty-three years, Magnolia had never enjoyed a bath so much. Though the water was brown and had a coppery smell to it, and the tub itself was nothing but a sawed off ship's barrel, and the maids had dropped towels of questionable cleanliness on the dirty floor, Magnolia didn't care. She relished in the caress of warm water on her skin, washing away the grime and grit and filth of the past five days. If only she could wash away her fears for her future as well. Now, as she stood at the open window in her chemise, gazing at the ships teetering in the bay, and battling the hopeless tangles in her hair, those fears rose again like tenacious flood waters, threatening to drown her.

It was one thing to tromp through the jungle with Hayden protecting her, and quite another to face a journey on one of those ships with no one to stand up for her, no one to defend her should a sailor get the wrong idea about her traveling alone. And then, once in the States, she would have to find her way, unescorted, to her aunt and uncle's. Would they even take her in? Did they still live in the same home in Ohio? Since the war, they had not been on the best of terms with Magnolia's parents. Or perhaps it would be better to seek out Samuel in Atlanta. Surely he would provide for her until they could be married. Although the last time she'd seen him, he'd slammed out of their home in Roswell, leapt into his waiting carriage, and driven away in a rage.

"Humph!" Her father had joined her on their wide front porch. "It appears the man has a temper. I've done you a favor, Magnolia."

"Of course he was angry, Father. You broke off our engagement. Went back on your word as a gentleman. And for what?" She batted away her tears. "Because he doesn't make enough money? Isn't high enough on the social ladder? It isn't fair!" She'd rarely spoken to her father in that tone, but as she'd continued to gaze at Samuel's carriage rumbling away, she saw her future rumble away with him.

Her father swung to face her, his jaw tight. "If you hadn't played the fool and lost the family fortune, I wouldn't be forced to make such hard choices." Indignation puffed out his cheeks even as his eyes grew narrow and cold. "Thank God we still have a sliver of our good name. Something, along with your beauty, that should lure a better positioned and wealthier prospect."

Magnolia wilted beneath his fury and gazed down at her pink, tasseled shoes, lest he see her cry again.

"You have no right to speak to me of what is fair," he continued, his voice thundering. "You have ruined us and you will unruin us. Or by God you'll put me in an early grave!"

At that moment Magnolia finally realized she would forever be under her father's thumb. Like their few remaining house slaves, her life was his. He owned her, and he would never let her forget.

Of course she and Samuel had continued secretly corresponding. He still loved her and wished to marry her. And she, him. But no amount of convincing, cajoling, or crying had changed her father's mind. And after multiple attempts to wed her off to what remained of the landed gentry, wealthy politicians, and elite families in Georgia, he'd given up, sold what little they owned, and booked passage to Brazil. Apparently, the news of Magnolia's scandal had swept through Georgia like wildfire, and no decent gentleman with a reputation to uphold would consider joining himself with their family. But in Brazil "the slate would be wiped clean and no one would be the wiser," her father had said when he announced his decision. "And Brazil boasts of many wealthy land owners as well as those of royal descent with whom we can align ourselves."

Magnolia only had time to send a quick dispatch to Samuel, informing him of her father's plans. But word was he had gone into hiding after the war, and she had no idea if he'd received it or if he still loved her.

And, of course, now that she'd run away, she would never pay her debt to her father. She was a horrible, disrespectful daughter who only thought of herself. He'd told her that on so many occasions, she'd begun to believe it. Perhaps it was true, after all.

She combed through the last tangle and watched as a mulatto woman, four children in tow, walked past the hotel, each with baskets of fruit on their heads. The briny scent of the bay drifted in with the wind, floating atop the sickly sweet smell of decaying fruit. It was a peculiar city. A peculiar, beautiful city. A city filled with the most unusual, exotic people.

And yet she felt more alone in the world than she ever had. Would Hayden even come back? The way she'd treated him, she wouldn't blame him if he abandoned her to begin his search for whomever or whatever he was looking for. But then again, he would want his money, wouldn't he? Her chest tightened. If only the dock master was open, she'd be long gone. As it was, she'd have to find a way to run away in the morning, purchase a ticket, and board a ship without Hayden's knowledge.

Her hands shook and she clasped them together. Nearly two days without a drink had taken its toll on her body. Perhaps that was why her thoughts spun in such a whirlwind.

A knock on the door startled her and Hayden's voice on the other side caused an unavoidable smile to form on her lips. Coughing it away, she forced the traitorous glee from her voice and replaced it with petulance. "I'm not ready yet, Hayden. What do you want?"

"How would you like to go shopping, Princess?"

Shopping? She could almost see that pleased-with-himself grin of his through the door. "Shopping for what?"

"For a new gown."

Regardless of how nonsensical his answer was, how ludicrous the notion, she yelped her "Yes" and then dashed through dressing. Aside from a few moans, groans, and unladylike curses at the difficulty of putting her clothing on without her lady's maid, she managed to don her least filthy blouse and skirts and pin up her damp hair as best she could. By the time she opened the door, Hayden was leaning his head against the post, pretending to be asleep.

Pretending, she knew, because he usually didn't wear a playful smirk in his sleep.

"Oh, mercy me." She slapped him with her fan. "I didn't take that long."

He opened one eye, one devilishly green eye, and grinned, sending a thrill through her.

"You tease me, sir. But you have no idea of the complexity of a lady's attire. Without my maid, I must tighten my corset behind me and then tie on my crinolette. . ."—he was still grinning. Rather mischievously, in fact—"Well, never mind. Let's just say there are far too many things a lady must put on."

His brow cocked. "You need not wear them all on my account."

Heat sped up her back. "You are indeed a toad, Hayden. And why are you being so nice to me all of a sudden?"

He didn't answer. Instead he gestured toward her valise sitting on the floor. "We will need your money."

"*My* money?" Magnolia snapped. "But I don't know if I have enough. I mean. . ."—she fumbled with her fan—"For the ticket, of course, and then to pay you as well."

"Then we'll take it out of my share."

This confused her further. Surely a man who would only escort and protect a lady for a fee wouldn't so willingly purchase her a gown. Besides, unbeknownst to him, it would still come out of *her* money.

Magnolia bit her lip and looked down at her stained skirts and the tattered fringe drooping from the hem. She supposed she did have enough for traveling *and* a new gown. Besides, she couldn't very well allow Samuel to see her in these rags. He might mistake her for a street urchin and send her away!

"Very well." She plucked her purse from inside her valise and met him in the hall. "What is the gown for?"

"For tonight, Princess." He extended his arm. "We are going to a ball."

The oddest thing happened to Hayden. He actually enjoyed shopping with Magnolia. It was odd for a number of reasons. One, he had about as much interest in women's clothing and fripperies as—to use her analogy—a toad had for fine literature. Two, her spoiled coquettish ways normally caused his blood to boil. Yet today, strolling about Rio, seeing the way her eyes lit up at all the fanciful items being sold at market, watching her caress the silk scarves from India, bite into a fresh mango till juice slid down her chin, giggle at the colorful parrots and chattering monkeys hopping along the roofs, and successfully haggle with a woman for a beaded bracelet, Hayden found himself utterly enamored. She may be spoiled and a bit self-centered, but she was the epitome of femininity. All lace and fluff and softness.

She seemed to grow more beautiful with each passing moment. Her sun-kissed hair, dried by the gentle breeze, dangled from her chignon in golden ringlets. Roses blossomed on her cheeks. Even the sheen of perspiration on her face and neck made her glow like an angel. Hayden swallowed and tried to avoid staring at her as they turned down *Ruo do Ouvidor* and found a drapers as fine as any in Charleston. Bolts of taffeta, calicos, and gingham filled the room that smelled of French perfume and musty cloth. Neither the language nor monetary differences impeded Magnolia from bartering for a ready-made blue gown that hung in the back. Apparently a return from an unhappy customer who thought the needlework subpar.

So, with wrapped gown flung over her arm, Hayden escorted her back to the hotel with a promise to return after sunset. Of course he had nothing to wear himself besides the disheveled, torn suit he had on. But finding something suitable had never been a problem before.

So, it was with a jump in his step that he returned to fetch Magnolia promptly at 8:00 p.m. He attributed his exuberant mood to his upcoming chat with Mr. Eduardo Santos and the possibility of discovering the whereabouts of his father. Hayden was tired of chasing the man all over the world, putting his own hopes and dreams on hold. Once justice was served, Hayden could get on with his life, perhaps learn a trade, become a sailor, or help out in his friend's furniture shop in Savannah.

Entering the hotel, he tipped his hat at an attractive lady in the lobby and mounted the steps. He might even get married, have children. His conscience rose to chastise him for the ridiculous notion. No decent woman would marry a confidence man—a swindler who had ruined so many lives.

Magnolia opened the door to his knock and widened her eyes when she saw his gray cotton suit with black velvet trim and double-breasted cutaway coat. "Where on earth did you get that?"

No decent woman would marry a thief, either.

But that thought quickly dissipated at the sight of her. Her flaxen hair, adorned with sparkling beads, was swept back in a bun from which golden swirls fell across her neck. The shimmering blue of her gown only enhanced the color of her eyes. Ruffles bubbled like foam from her bell-shaped sleeves, while the lace embellishing her low neckline drew his unbridled gaze. He gulped and prayed for a breeze to drift down the hall and cool the heat swirling in his belly. The victorious sparkle of delight in her eyes told him she'd noticed his approval. But then she was accustomed to men fawning over her, wasn't she?

"So?" She tapped him with her fan as her eyes took him in. "How did you purchase such a fine suit?" Now it was his turn to be delighted for he could see the appreciation in her eyes as she scanned him from head to toe.

"I borrowed it." He winked and offered his elbow. Giving him a suspicious look, she gripped it and allowed him to lead her down the streets of Rio. With every step they took, every street corner they turned, they drew appreciative glances. Hayden's shoulders rose a bit higher, and for the first time he no longer felt like a thief and a rogue. For the first time in his life, with Magnolia on his arm, he felt like a gentleman. Not just pretending to be one. But a real gentleman. Strangely, it made him want to become one.

That illusion, however, slipped away once they reached the estate of Adelino Manuel Guerra da Costa. Though music and laughter spilled from the windows of the palatial two-story home onto the manicured lawn, sprinkled with flowering bushes and majestic palms, Hayden was forced to tug Magnolia to the side and head down the fenced outskirts of the property like the uninvited guests they were. She glanced back at the open front doors and the guests being greeted by their host and hostess and gave an adorable little chirp signifying her dismay.

"Where are you taking me?" Her voice turned shrewish.

Ignoring her, Hayden peered into the darkness, finally finding what he sought. "We can slip in through here." He gestured toward a broken spoke in the fence that created a two-foot gap.

"I thought you said we were invited."

"I said we were attending. I said nothing about being invited."

"Well, I shan't sneak in the back like common riffraff." Clutching her skirts, she flounced away.

Silently growling, Hayden caught up to her and spun her around. "There's no other way. Either we go in through here or we don't attend at all."

"Then we don't attend. Barging into parties uninvited is for uncultured plebeians, not someone of my station." She turned to leave.

He wouldn't release her arm. "Then I won't help you book passage tomorrow."

He couldn't quite make out her expression in the darkness but he was pretty sure she bared her teeth like a tigress. "Who says I need your help?"

Hayden ran a hand through his hair. "Listen, Princess. There's someone at that party I need to speak with. It's quite possible the information he has will lead me back to the States. In which case, I can give you a proper escort all the way home." He felt her relax. He released his grip on her arm. Zooks, but it felt good to speak the truth. For once.

"This man. . .he can help you find what you're looking for?"

"Yes."

"Then go speak to him. I'll wait here."

Hayden sighed, hating his next words. "I need you with me."

"How can I possibly assist?"

"This man is a scoundrel of the worst kind. He refuses to give away any information unless his pockets are lined. And believe me, even with the money you are paying me, I won't have enough. But he's soft on the ladies and—"

"So you're using me," she snapped. "It's why you bought me this gown, asked me to the ball. You planned this all along. In addition to taking my money." Her voice stung with pain.

Guilt sat heavy on his shoulders. She was right, of course. But he couldn't let his feelings for her or his own shame dissuade him from his mission. He forced desperation and remorse from his tone and replaced it with silky charm. "After all we've been through, would you please do me this one small favor?"

"All we've been through? You mean all you've put me through!"

Zooks, the woman aggravated him! Hayden clamped his jaw until it hurt. Music floated atop the scent of savory spices, giving him a grand idea. "There will be good food and plenty of spirits inside." Totally unfair of him to mention the alcohol, of course.

But it did the trick. He sensed her weakening.

She stepped away from him. "Very well." But her tone carried none of joy it had held just minutes before.

Hayden hated being the one who'd swept it away.

However, her blasted hoops wouldn't fit through the fence opening. His suggestion for her to remove them didn't fair too well. In fact, they unleashed a series of gasps and "I never" and "How dare you?" until finally she settled with a childish pout and a firm chin, demanding they leave at once.

Desperate, Hayden searched the area, found a stack of bricks, and formed a step for her to stand on. Then squeezing through the opening in the fence, he dragged over an old wooden bucket, leapt on top, and reached his arms above the railing. "Step on the bricks, and I'll grab your waist and hoist you over."

"You can't be serious."

"I am quite serious. Come now, it will be an adventure. Something to laugh about in years to come."

She said nothing.

"Nothing to fear—I'm right here." He moved his hands above the fence for her to see. "I'll catch you."

"You are a toad, you know."

"As you have informed me."

Her skirts swished. "I can't believe I'm doing this," she grumbled. "And as a favor to you!"

Their hands locked and Hayden hoisted himself onto the top of the fence. "Grab onto my neck." She did. It felt good. He found her waist. Straining, he lifted her to sit beside him. Thankfully the top of the fence was at least a foot wide. Still, she teetered. He jumped down to the bucket then turned to place his hands firmly on her hips. "Now, swing your legs over."

"Close your eyes."

"For the love of. . ." he ground out. "Very well." Lace and silk swished. The bucket beneath him wobbled. He grew dizzy. . .lost his bearings. He opened his eyes to a heeled boot slamming his chest. Groaning, he tightened his grip on her waist. The bucket teetered. Hayden lost his balance. The world spun and he toppled backward to the ground, dragging Magnolia on top of him. The air fled his lungs with a mighty squish. Neither said anything. The hem of her skirt circled her shoulders as her sweet breath puffed over his face. Her warm curves molded against him. Her lips were but inches from his.

And he did the only thing he thought to do.

He kissed her.

CHAPTER 15

The kiss sent a sultry ripple through Magnolia, ushering out her anger and embarrassment and inviting in an ecstasy she'd never known existed. She knew her gown had flown up around her face, could feel the braided hem of her skirts on her cheek. But lying atop Hayden's warm, steel-like body, she found she didn't care. Nothing mattered but the touch of his lips, the thrill spiraling through her. The way he cupped her head in his hands and drank her in as if he were a man deprived of drink for decades. Until a small flicker of reason invaded the pleasurable fog in her mind—a tiny shred of reason that forced her to remember who she was and what she was doing. And how another man, equally as charming as Hayden, had torn her heart in two.

She shoved from his chest. "Get off of me!"

"I believe it is *you* who are on me, Princess."

"Oooh!" Realizing in a flush of heat that she still straddled him, she flipped back her skirts then vaulted onto the grass. Crinoline flailing, she attempted to rise amid a flurry of unladylike grunts. Finally, rolling onto her hands and knees, she managed to stand. "How dare you take advantage of me—yet again!"

"If you hadn't forced me to close my eyes, I wouldn't have lost my balance." Hayden leapt to his feet, his voice raspy with desire. He turned his back to her as if trying to collect himself.

"It's a simple task to stand steady on a"—she glanced at the overturned pail—"bucket. I should have known not to trust you.

Now, look what you've done to my new gown." She swatted the twigs and grass from her skirts. "Could you not have allowed it to remain unstained for one evening?" An evening, that if she admitted, she'd been rather excited about. Hopeful, even, that beneath Hayden's rugged, raffish exterior, he was an honorable man, a man who might actually care for. . .oh what did it matter? He'd not invited her to a ball because he enjoyed her company or because he wanted to become better acquainted with her or treat her like a lady. No, he'd simply been using her. For her beauty. Like her father. Like everyone else.

Finally, he swung about and brushed grass from his coat. "Perhaps it was being so near to you that made me dizzy." Despite being unable to see his face in the shadows, she sensed a smile. He held out his hand. "Now, if you're quite done yammering, shall we go enjoy the party?"

Yam. . . Magnolia knew the daggers in her eyes were lost to him in the darkness, but it felt good to fire them at him anyway. "So much for the toad ever becoming a prince."

"Ah, but the evening is still young."

Though he tried to hide behind sarcasm, passion still dripped like dark molasses from his voice. And if Magnolia were honest, it tingled through her as well. But she no longer wanted to attend the ball. She didn't want to be used. She wanted to be loved. Wanted to be special. She wanted to have value beyond her appearance. Her vision grew hazy as tears filled her eyes.

Oh my, but she could use a drink!

Which was the only reason she now followed the rogue through the back entrance, past the kitchen, and into the warming room, where he waved off the servants' curious gazes with the excuse of getting lost.

The sound of an orchestra and the hum of chatter and laughter bubbled over Magnolia as Hayden led her upstairs to the main ballroom, where they joined the glittering throng. Dipping his head in greeting, he smiled at everyone as if he'd known them all his life. Most smiled in return, mainly the ladies, whose appreciative gazes drank him in as if they were parched and he were an oasis. Yet, not a single suspicious brow rose as they wove through the crowd. The ease with which this ruffian slipped into the role of an aristocrat astonished

Magnolia. From the stretch of his shoulders, the lift of his chin, and the swaggering confidence with which he strode through the room, people no doubt guessed he was a gentleman born and bred into luxury and privilege, not an orphan who grew up without benefit of home, food, and education. In fact, she'd met sons of earls who held themselves with less dignity. Strangely, the thought unsettled her.

He led her to a table laden with delicacies she could not name, an ivory-colored pudding, a bowl of creamy paste with a cocoa nut on top, and other assorted cakes. But it was the *vinho virgem*—French red wine—that drew her gaze. Hayden poured a glass and handed it to her. The sweet yet pungent taste lingered on her tongue and sped a heavenly trail down her throat. Ah sweet, sweet nectar! But when she raised her gaze to Hayden's devilish wink, she couldn't be sure if it was the wine or the way he looked at her that caused her blood to suddenly heat.

Clearing her throat, she glanced up at sputtering chandeliers that dappled light upon a fresco of orchids and ferns painted on the tall ceilings. Below, framing the room, high-backed chairs stood alongside gilded card tables while great oval mirrors with tawdry decorations hung on the wall. Young mulatto boys, dressed all in white, wove barefooted through the crowd, hoisting trays of drinks and cakes.

She took another sip while Hayden fetched his own drink and then led her through the maze of ladies and gentleman, their skin in every shade from dark as night to snowy white, all decked in silks and brocades as colorful as spring flowers in an open field. Magnolia could not keep from staring. She'd never seen a Negress wearing a gown that could be found in a ballroom in Paris, nor speaking with the confidence and education of any genteel woman back home. Men, bearing the blended features of both Europeans and Africans, sauntered through the crowd, women on each arm while their wives stood in corners, ignored. Even the priests partook of drink and engaged in playful dalliances.

In the center of the room, couples spun and bobbed as they floated across the floor like lilies on a pond. Portuguese thickened the air as the scent of orange blossoms and salt swept in through open windows, masking the miasma of perfume and alcohol.

Despite her sore legs and blistered feet, Magnolia found herself swaying to the music, wishing more than anything that Hayden would sweep her onto the dance floor and she could spend one night—just one night—forgetting that she was all alone in the world without a penny to her name and without anything to offer but her beauty.

But instead, the toad popped a sweet cake into his mouth and gestured with his drink to a man on the other side of the room.

"There he is. Mr. Eduardo Santos. The petulant squab speaking with the tall gentleman in the blue suit."

Magnolia stared at the man she was supposed to charm. Short in stature and as wide as he was tall, he reminded her of the toad she so often called Hayden. Thin, greasy hair crossed the top of his head in perfect rows as if he had plowed furrows in his scalp. His posh broadcloth coat with satin lining did nothing to enhance his boorish mien or the aura of base ignorance surrounding him.

She cringed and looked away. Right into Hayden's anxious green eyes.

"He's despicable," she said.

"You think so? Wait until you meet him." He chuckled and sipped his wine.

"Who is he, anyway?"

"The immigration officer."

The dance ended, and a flood of people cascaded to the refreshment table. Taking her arm, Hayden led her aside, whispering in her ear. "Take my lead, Princess, and use that seductive charm of yours."

"All of a sudden, I'm seductive and charming, is it? I seem to recall other names flung my way in the jungle. Shrew. Spoiled. Harridan." They twisted through the crowd as the scent of cheap perfume and cedar oil threatened to strangle her.

"I admit you are a woman of many talents."

Before she could come up with a witty retort, Magnolia stood before Mr. Santos. The taller man he spoke with excused himself and the immigration officer faced them, his dark eyes flitting over Hayden in brief recognition before landing on Magnolia like a bird of prey.

Delight, followed by desire, strolled across them as a feline smile lit his face.

"Mr. Santos." Hayden dipped his head. "What a pleasure to see you again."

The man seemed reluctant to draw his gaze from Magnolia. Though she did nothing to hide her disinterest. Finally he glanced at Hayden. "Yes, indeed. Mr. . . .Mr. . . ."

"Gale."

"Gale. Ah, yes." He cocked his head. "I thought you would have joined your American colony by now."

Despite his strong accent, Magnolia was impressed with the man's English.

"I did. But Owen Godard was not where you said he would be."

"Owen Godard." The man ran a finger over the thin hair on his forehead, his bulbous nose pinching. "Ah yes. I remember. Older gentleman. Small group of Americans. But I told you where he settled."

"He wasn't there," Hayden repeated.

The orchestra began playing a waltz.

Mr. Santos sipped his drink, staring at Magnolia over the rim of his glass. "But where are your manners, senhor? I must be introduced to this lovely creature."

Hayden's jaw tightened beneath a forced smile. "My apologies. This is Miss—my wife, Magnolia Gale." He placed a possessive arm across her back.

Under any other circumstances she would have enjoyed the protective action, but instead she stiffened and stifled a gasp. With great difficulty, she extended her gloved hand. "A pleasure, sir."

Mr. Santos ran his thumb over her fingers, fondling them as if he'd never touched a woman before. She tugged away before he could raise her hand to his lips and cause the wine to curdle in her stomach.

Hayden gave her a sideways glance, frowning as if displeased with the action. Which only made her angry. Just like her father, just like every man she'd ever met, Hayden used her like some pretty puppet to achieve his ends. Forcing down the agony burning in her throat, she looked toward the door. She should leave. She wanted to leave. But

Hayden said this man's information might make it possible for him to accompany her on the voyage home. And she was so very frightened of traveling alone. The thought of being safely escorted back to the States, even the slight possibility of it, kept her feet in place. Kept her willing to help Hayden.

Mr. Santos sipped his drink. "I had no idea you were married to such a beauty."

"My wife and I have returned to Rio in the hopes that Mr. Godard may have also returned recently," Hayden said. "Perhaps for supplies? Or to submit the appropriate paperwork to settle on a different plot of land?"

Impressed with Hayden's ability to lie without blinking, Magnolia wondered who this Godard man was and why he was so important to Hayden.

Wrinkles formed on Mr. Santos's forehead as if the attempt to recollect such a transaction taxed his tiny brain. "Hmm. Maybe he returned. Maybe not. I cannot remember, Mr. Gale. Perhaps"—the gleam in his eye turned greedy—"you have something to help me recall?"

Hayden released Magnolia, a tiny twitch in his jaw the only indication of his vexation. "I'm afraid I haven't any more money to give you, sir. I appeal to your generosity."

Mr. Santos frowned and slammed the rest of his drink to the back of his throat.

Magnolia rolled her eyes. *Yes, you supercilious buffoon, please do be generous.* Just the thought of getting any closer to this man made her insides squirm.

But she could tell from his rigid stance and the indulgent hunger in his eyes that he hadn't a generous bone in his body.

"What you can count on, senhor, is that I am not without honor. Mr. Godard's affairs are Mr. Godard's affairs, not yours. However with a bit of persuasion. . ." He assessed Magnolia as if she were a gift at Christmas.

Hayden shifted his stance and gazed across the room. Magnolia bit her lip. If he had a speck of decency, if he had a speck of chivalry within him, he wouldn't leave her alone with this wolf. Finally he faced

Mr. Santos and took his empty glass. "Allow me to get you another drink. And you as well, my dear." He winked at her. "While you two become better acquainted."

Magnolia growled inside. The man was a cad through and through.

⚜

Hayden had never hated himself more than he did at that moment. The look of spite in Magnolia's eyes as he left her with Mr. Santos shot a gaping hole in his heart. Gaping and vacant and empty—like his soul. Hayden used people for a living. He made money off of people's pain. Zooks, he'd certainly done far worse than leaving a lady with a lecherous fool. Then why did he feel like such a louse for asking her to do something that came natural to her? Innocent flirting. That was all. No harm done. Besides, what choice did he have? He must find out where his father had gone. He must put an end to this mad quest or he would surely go mad himself.

Yet everything within him wanted to whisk Magnolia away to safety—away from scum like Mr. Santos and anyone who could hurt her. He'd never felt protective toward anyone in his life, and he certainly didn't want to start now. It made him vulnerable. It made him lose focus on the task at hand. And he couldn't have that. Not that her kiss hadn't already distracted him beyond measure. The soft feel of her atop him, the passionate way she'd embraced him, caressed his lips. She'd stirred his passions into such a frenzy it had taken several minutes to regain his composure. So unlike him. He'd always been in control. In control of himself, his emotions. Of everyone around him. And if he was to succeed in serving justice to his father, he must stay in control.

Ignoring the coquettish glances from several women, he made his way to the refreshment table and grabbed a glass of punch. Tossing it to the back of his throat, he yearned for it to soothe his nerves. He would delay returning with fresh drinks—give Magnolia time to perform her magic. In the meantime, he could at least keep an eye on them should Mr. Santos cross the boundary of propriety. Hayden spun around to do just that.

But Magnolia and Mr. Santos were no longer there.

CHAPTER 16

When the pernicious fatwit suggested they take a stroll in the garden, Magnolia almost lost the wine she'd consumed. She'd wanted to say that she'd rather sit in a dung heap, but instead, she smiled and looped her arm through his as he escorted her from the room. She could do this. She knew she could do this. It would only take a few minutes of her bewitching charm to extract the information Hayden needed from this man. How many times had she done the very same thing back home in Roswell whenever she'd wanted a particular favor from a particular gentleman?

Except those particular gentlemen hadn't smelled like sour cheese, nor made her insides stir into a putrid brew. But no matter.

She tried to get Hayden's attention as they passed the refreshment table, but he seemed deep in thought. Mercy me, another drink would certainly make her task easier. Besides, she wanted him to see where they were going just in case Mr. Santos attempted liberties which weren't his to take. Certainly Hayden would come looking for her. Wouldn't he?

Glancing over her shoulder, she allowed Mr. Santos to lead her outside through a line of orange trees and cultured palms, framed by resplendent crotons and bamboo. Castor oil lamps hung from tree branches, flinging lacy ribbons of light on the grass below. He gestured toward a secluded spot at the far end of the garden where a stone bench edged a pond.

"We do not see—how do you say, much or often?—such lovely, cultured ladies in Rio," Mr. Santos said, gesturing toward the bench. Releasing his arm, Magnolia slid onto the hard stone as he took a seat beside her. Far too close.

"You are too kind, Mr. Santos." She inched away and tugged her fan from her sleeve—if only to use as a weapon.

"And your accent. I hear it from many new colonists but it makes music on your lips." He took her hand in his.

Something sour and thick rose in her throat.

"Mr. Santos, as you know, my husband is most desperate to find"— oh, what was that name again? How could Hayden leave her like this? Ah yes—"Mr. Godard. Any information you have would be greatly appreciated." She forced a smile that nearly caused her to choke as the man leaned even closer.

"*How* appreciated?" His breath smelled of wine and curdled milk.

"You would have our. . .*my* undying gratitude, sir. Wouldn't that be enough? Helping out a lady in distress. Why, you would be my true hero." She fluttered her fan about her face. "I just knew you were a gentleman when I first laid eyes on you. Why, I wager you are quite the ladies' man. Aren't you, Mr. Santos?" She tapped his chest with the tip of her fan and smiled.

He shrugged and pressed back the oily hair at his temples. "*Sim*, yes, I do have a reputation."

Magnolia could only imagine. She giggled playfully. Which apparently was all the enticement the man needed to lean in and nibble on her neck. "Why, sir, you forget yourself." She pushed him back, all the while giving him her most alluring smile. "I cannot possibly enjoy myself when my husband suffers so miserably from lack of information."

A breeze fluttered the palm fronds overhead and sent a ripple across the inky waters of the pond, stirring the cattails lingering at its edge. Distant orchestra music drifted atop the chirp of crickets in a pleasing melody that would have been peaceful except for the brute beside her.

That brute seemed to be pondering what to do. He finally flattened his surly lips. "Yes. I saw this Mr. Godard. He came back with a crazy tale about the land being bad. Cursed, sim, cursed is what he said. He moved his expedition west." He leaned in to kiss her.

Magnolia turned her cheek to him. "How far west?"

"Twenty of what you call miles, I believe." A groan of delight erupted in his throat as his lips seared her skin. "I have paperwork in my office with the exact location." He trailed slobbering kisses down her neck. "We can go there and I show you."

Magnolia would rather leap into a volcano. In fact, at the moment her skin felt as though a thousand lizards scampered over it. And her stomach wasn't doing much better. She pushed Mr. Santos away yet again, her heart plummeting like a stone in a pond. The information would take Hayden from her and send him back to New Hope. Leaving her to travel all alone. Yet, at the moment, she was preoccupied with preventing Mr. Santos from tossing her to the grass and having his way with her. Surely she'd learned enough about Mr. Godard to suit Hayden's purposes, for Magnolia could hardly stand another moment with this snobcock.

A snobcock who dove in for the kill. He nibbled on her earlobe, grunting like the swine he was. Shooting off the bench, Magnolia cast a quick glance around to see whether anyone was near to assist her. "Sir, you do yourself no credit with such beastly behavior." She kept her voice playful, not wanting to prick his ire in such isolated circumstances. Could she make a run for it? Surely a man as pudgy as Mr. Santos would not be able to catch her. "I bid you goodnight, sir."

She turned to leave.

He clutched her arm. "Where is my kiss?"

"A kiss was not part of our bargain, Mr. Santos. You have had your fun. Now, release me at once!" She struggled in his grip.

Leaves fluttered and a footstep sounded behind her, but Magnolia hadn't time to look before Mr. Santos said something about her paying him his due and shoved his mouth onto hers. She squirmed, causing his slobbering lips to slide over her cheeks and chin. More disgusted than afraid, she placed both palms on his chest and pushed him. Tripping on an uneven cobblestone, he stumbled backward toward the pond, arms flailing and curses flying, as he attempted to right himself. Before he did, Magnolia stormed toward him and gave him one final shove into the water. The immensity of his frame caused an enormous splash, which would have soaked her if she hadn't leapt out of the way.

Flopping like a fish in the shallows, he finally managed to sit in the silt near the shore. Water dripped from threads of hair hanging in his face. He sputtered and moaned and cursed her—*and her mother!*—to some hideous fate, which she dared not repeat.

Laughter rumbled behind her.

Spinning around, she barreled into a tree trunk that smelled like Hayden. Wait, it *was* Hayden. All six foot one of his sturdy frame. He held a glass of wine. Her nerves unwound at his presence. Or maybe it was at the sight of the wine. Either way, they quickly knotted again in anger. "You left me with that leech!" She punched his chest.

Which loosened a chuckle from his throat.

Mr. Santos attempted to rise from the pond, but slipped and splashed back in the water with a loud curse.

Grinning, Hayden led her back toward the house. "I was here the entire time. If things had gotten out of hand, I would have stepped in." He handed her the glass.

She gulped down the wine. "You waited long enough. The man was about to accost me. He *did* accost me, in fact."

"You seemed to have things in hand, Princess." Hayden winked and slid his hand into her free one. "In fact, I thought you handled yourself quite well."

He led her into the ballroom again. Magnolia blinked at the bright lights as music and the prattling of guests assailed her. She tugged from Hayden's grip and finished her drink. The comfort of his large hand around hers drained away her anger, bit by bit. And she wanted it to remain. At least for a while.

Returning the smile of a rather handsome Brazilian gentleman, Magnolia set down her empty glass and gathered a full one from the table. Hayden stole it from her hand. "Perhaps you've had enough."

"You are not my father. Besides, I deserve a reward for enduring that oaf slobbering all over me."

He held the glass out of reach. "And, pray tell, what did that slobbering oaf tell you about Mr. Godard?"

She studied him, wishing the wine in her belly would hurry and numb her conscience. All she had to do was utter one lie. One tiny lie and Hayden would escort her home. One tiny lie and all her fears of traveling alone would dissipate. One tiny lie and she could spend more time getting to know this mysterious man as she longed to do. One tiny lie. He certainly deserved it and worse after using her to get what he wanted. But the desperation in his eyes undid her. Whoever this Godard was, it meant everything to Hayden to find him. And she couldn't be the one to deny him that.

"Your precious Mr. Godard has moved twenty miles to the west. Isn't that what you wanted to know?" She speared him with a gaze.

"He is anything but precious." His tone was shattered glass. "But I do thank you for finding that out." The corner of his mouth twitched as he gazed absently into the room.

"So who is this Mr. Godard, and what did he do to invoke the wrath of Hayden Gale?"

The twitch intensified. "Let's just say he stole everything from me."

"Ah, now *that* I can relate to."

Hayden studied her. "You speak of this huge mistake you made. . . of your debt to your father?"

"I was taken in by a charlatan." But she had said too much already. "Perhaps he is the same man as your Mr. Godard?" She teased, trying to change the topic back to him.

Hayden laughed. "If you had crossed paths with my. . .Mr. Godard, I doubt you would be in Brazil. He rarely leaves his victims with enough to live on, let alone to travel."

"So it was money he stole?" Magnolia pressed, desperate to understand this man before her.

"No. Something far more precious." His vacant stare took in the room as sorrow stole over his features. Perhaps they had more in common than she first realized. She was about to inquire what exactly the man had taken from him when a commotion drew everyone's gaze to the veranda. Poor Mr. Santos hobbled into the room, scattering droplets on the tile floor and firing an angry glare over the assembly.

Ushering Magnolia aside, Hayden ducked behind a cluster of people as the man let out a frustrated growl and stormed out the other side of the room, demanding the servant retrieve his coat. A moment later the front door slammed, and Magnolia could only assume he'd left since the room suddenly burst with mocking laughter.

Hayden handed her the wine, his smile returning. "I suppose you *do* deserve this." The hint of adoration in those jungle green eyes made her want to do more for this man, anything he asked—just to keep him looking at her like that a little longer.

She sipped the wine, keeping her eyes trained on his. A grin lifted one side of his lips as he continued to stare at her, seemingly looking past the silk and lace, past the beads and fripperies, into her very soul, absorbing her with the delight of a man who'd found a priceless jewel. But that couldn't be right. She was no jewel. Her throat went dry and she looked away. She had to keep her focus. She couldn't allow this man to charm his way into her heart, for in the morning she had to leave him—buy a ticket and get on a ship and never see him again. An ache radiated through her at the thought. If only Mr. Godard had gone back to America. Then she wouldn't have to travel alone. And this wouldn't be her last night with Hayden.

But it *was* her last night with him. And despite the threat to her heart, she wanted to make it a night to remember.

He was still staring at her, an unreadable expression on his face. Was her hair out of place? Suddenly self-conscious, she began stuffing loose strands into her bun. But a gentle touch to her hand halted her, charmed her into saying, "I do have a favor to ask of you, Hayden."

"And what is that, Princess?"

"Would you dance with me?"

Was the princess flirting with him? By her coquettish grin and the way she lowered her lashes innocently, Hayden could come to no other conclusion. After he'd forced her to welcome that foppish squab's attentions, he wouldn't blame her if she poured her drink on his head and stomped off. Instead, she asked him to dance!

He cocked his head. She was up to something. But what? Perhaps she hoped to convince him to escort her to the States. Which—no matter how much he wanted to—he couldn't do. Perhaps she hoped to lessen the amount she owed him. Which now he needed more than ever if he was going to find his father. He glanced at the couples floating across the floor in a country dance. Whatever her reasons, the lady did have a point. Since they were here in the midst of this elaborate party, why not enjoy it?

He offered his arm. "I'd love to."

Delight brightened her smile as he led her onto the floor, took her hand, and joined the other couples bobbing and gliding to the music.

"Why did you tell Mr. Santos I was your wife?" Magnolia asked as they bowed to each other.

"I thought it might temper the man's passions." Hayden took her hand and together they strolled down the line of couples.

"Why temper them if their very existence brought you the information you sought?" Her voice was sharp, her chin lifted.

"If you're asking whether there was a limit to the price I would see you pay, there was." He took both her hands and spun her around. "And Mr. Santos had reached that limit when you shoved him into the pond."

At this she giggled, though an odd pain lingered behind her eyes. "Besides, I knew he could not resist your charms for long."

She gave him a disbelieving look, but for once, Hayden spoke the truth, for he was having trouble resisting her himself. The way little wisps of her flaxen hair bobbed about her neck as she danced, the delicate curve of her jaw, her high cheeks flushed with excitement, and her lips swollen and pink. The gossamer lace edging her low neckline rose and fell with each breath, drawing his gaze, though he tried not to look. Save for a few beads in her hair, she wore no jewels or baubles, no silver combs or satin sashes, yet she outshone every woman there. And those eyes—blue as sapphires—flashing like lightning. And just like lightning, they were electric and powerful. Especially when they looked at him as she was looking at him now.

They finished the dance, but at her request, they stayed on the floor and continued with a Scottish Reel. And then another dance and another, stopping only for refreshments and a stroll in the garden. Her laughter became his healing elixir, her smile his hope. Hours sped by like minutes, and for the first time in his life, Hayden found he was enjoying himself. Immensely. All because of Magnolia. Her coy glances, her witty repartee, the way she looked at him as though she saw a prince instead of a toad.

He knew she could have her choice of any gentleman present, most of whom bore the noble posture of gentility and wealth, not the stink of an impoverished orphan. Instead, she seemed to barely notice the men who looked her way, her attention fixed on him alone. She was his for tonight. The realization made his chest swell. He felt as though someone had placed a precious gem in his hand and charged him with its care. Instead of dodging the assignment, he cherished it.

Zooks, what was happening to him? No doubt it was the wine, the rich food, the music and opulence. It combined to spin a magical web, deluding him into believing that he was not a thief and an orphan and she was not a stunning patrician. And that perhaps they might have a chance together.

He brought her a glass of lemonade, ignoring her look of disappointment at the drink. But he'd had a hard time resisting her in the jungle when she'd been inebriated. He doubted he could summon enough self-control in this magical place.

"You dance marvelously," she commented.

"That surprises you?"

"Yes." She looked at him but there was no condescension in her eyes. "Where did you learn?"

Hayden grinned. "Here and there."

"Ah yes, I've seen your skill at sneaking into parties uninvited."

"It does come in handy. I will teach you some time."

She lowered her gaze as if a sudden sadness stole her joy.

He determined to gain it back. "You look lovely tonight."

She raised sparkling eyes to his. "Ah, a compliment. The first one you've paid me." She began fiddling with her hair.

He stayed her hand. "Your hair is perfect." He brought her hand to his lips and kissed it. The music, the laughter, the exotic sound of Portuguese, all faded around them as their eyes locked together. Time floated on a whisper—a whisper that held all his dreams in its breath. A whisper that danced around them, between them, caressing her face, stirring her curls, filling him with her scent, with a hope that dangled within reach. Her eyes shifted between his as if seeking an answer.

But what was the question? Was it the same one that burned on his heart?

Could a pampered rich plantation owner's daughter love a baseborn swindler?

But he already knew the answer.

Not in the real world.

Tonight was a fantasy, a dream. And it would soon come to an end. Especially when the sun rose in the morning and she found out the truth.

CHAPTER 17

Darkness cloaked the stairs leading up to Magnolia's hotel room. She tripped on one of the treads and Hayden's arm swung around her waist.

"I told you to stop drinking wine," he said.

"I didn't have too much," she shot back. "I simply can't see the steps." The only light came from a sputtering lantern on the landing above them. Not that she minded Hayden's arm around her. She'd felt his touch quite often during the night. With each possessive press on her back, each grip on her elbow, each squeeze of her hand, he'd been staking claim on her, making her feel cared for and protected for the first time in her life.

The steps creaked. Her skirts swished. The rhythmic tick of a clock joined the distant pattering of a mouse as they reached the top. The hallway spun and she leaned on Hayden. Perhaps she *had* overindulged just a bit.

What a wonderful evening! Dancing, the orchestra, the wine and delicacies. And Hayden looking so dashingly handsome. The way he'd swept her across the dance floor with the style and grace of any aristocrat while a multitude of envious eyes followed them. It was a dream, an incredible, magical dream. Yet now her feet felt as heavy as cannon balls.

Hayden was silent beside her. Was he distraught at their parting? Halting before her door, she spun to face him. Lantern light rippled over the firm lines of his jaw, his cheeks, and over the speck of sorrow in his green eyes. He stared at her lips and licked his own. For a brief, exhilarating moment, she thought he might kiss her again.

Instead he swallowed, shifted his stance, and leaned in to whisper, "I had a wonderful time tonight." His warm breath fondled her neck and spiraled a pleasurable shiver down her back. She gripped the door handle behind her. Anything to keep from throwing herself in his arms. From begging him to come with her to the States. From telling him that she'd never felt this way about any man before. Not even Samuel. Or it had been so long since she'd seen her fiancé that she'd simply forgotten? Regardless, she should say goodnight, slip inside her room, and close the door before she did something only an unchaste woman would do.

"I enjoyed myself as well," she replied, soaking in every detail of his face, his strong Roman nose, sculpted cheeks, thick brows and lashes that matched his dark hair, and the stubble that circled his mouth and trailed his jaw. She never wanted to forget him.

Hayden scratched that stubble now and met her gaze. The *tick-tock tick-tock* of a clock down in the lobby counted out their final moments together. Final moments only she knew about. For he no doubt assumed he'd be escorting her to the dock master come morning. Snoring rumbled down the hall. Hayden's breathing grew deep. He seemed as unwilling to leave her as she was him. Finally, he grinned. "So you didn't mind spending an evening with a toad?"

"I make concessions for toads who know how to dance."

"But you would prefer a prince?" He eased a lock of her hair behind her ear, suddenly serious.

The intimate gesture nearly caused her to blurt out *No! I much prefer the toad!* But instead she lifted her chin and said, "Of course. What princess wouldn't?"

He frowned. Good. She must stop this dangerous dalliance or she'd be done for. She forced her thoughts to what she must do in the morning—escape this man, leave him behind.

"Where will you stay tonight?" she asked.

"I'll find somewhere. I'm used to being on the streets, remember?"

Yes, she did. And it endeared him to her all the more. She'd never met a man like him. He'd suffered so much, grown up without a single advantage, yet he was more competent than any man she'd known. Even Samuel, who although he was a successful solicitor, could barely start a fire without a servant's help.

Hayden studied her, a sudden twinkle in his eyes. "Hmm. I do recall, however, that in your *Maiden and the Frog* story, the young lady made a bargain with the toad that allowed him to share her bed for two nights."

Magnolia would have slapped any other man for such an insinuation, or at least slammed the door in his face, but she knew Hayden, could hear the teasing in his voice. "You remember correctly, sir. But I believe he gave her something first, something invaluable to her survival."

"Alas, I have brought you to Rio, my princess."

"And you will be paid," she lied.

He sighed and loosened his string tie. "Very well. If you don't wish to see the toad transformed into a prince. . ."

Magnolia wouldn't tell him that he had already made the transformation. "But you forget the end of the story. After the toad spent two nights with the maiden, she had to chop off his head in order for him to turn into a prince."

Hayden rubbed his throat, his brow crinkling. "On second thought, I believe I'll remain a toad." He grinned, leaned over, and kissed her cheek. "Sweet dreams to you, fair maiden." Then with a wink, he turned and disappeared into the shadows.

❧

Chirp, tweet, chirp, tweet, the shrill clamor pierced Magnolia's ears and penetrated her blissful slumber. She groaned and tossed the quilt over her head. Mercy me, why did the jungle always have to wake up so early? *Wait.* She wasn't in the jungle. Moving her hands, she felt the scratchy fabric of the bed sheets. She wasn't in a hammock on a ship or on her feather bed in Roswell either. Or even on a bamboo cot in New Hope. Her mind snapped to attention. She was in some shamble of a hotel in Rio de Janeiro. But she wasn't complaining. It was the first night she'd slept on a mattress in nearly five months. *Chirp, chirp.* Drawing the cover from her head, Magnolia pried one eye open to find a small, plump, and very colorful bird sitting on her window ledge. Behind the winged annoyance, a pinkish-gray glow chased away the night.

"Shoo! Go away!" She swatted the air and closed her eye again. An unavoidable smile curved her lips as memories from last night came out from hiding. The ball, the music, dancing, Hayden. . .

She let out a satisfied moan and stretched across the lumpy mattress that was, no doubt, home to a myriad of tiny beasties. But what did it matter? She'd had such a marvelous evening—a fairy tale evening, an evening she wished had never come to an end. But it had. . .and today. . .

She shot up in bed, rubbed her eyes, and glanced once more at the window. Dawn. She must leave before Hayden arrived! The bird cocked his red-feathered head and stared at her curiously.

"I suppose I should thank you for waking me, little one."

Leaping from the bed, she made quick work of her morning toilette, all the while ignoring the pain lancing through her heart. Pain at leaving Hayden. Wasn't this what she wanted? To go back home, find Samuel, and get married? She shook her head as she made her way to the wardrobe, trying to break the spell Hayden had cast on her. Last night was a fantasy. Today, she was back to reality. Today she would begin her journey home.

After dressing, she packed everything in her valise and checked herself in the mirror, pleased she'd been able to pin up her hair in a fashionable coiffure all by herself. Removing a slip of paper and a pen and ink from her case, she scribbled out a note.

Hayden,
    I'm sorry. Hope you can forgive me someday. . .Yours affectionately,

                                                            Magnolia

Short and to the point. No sentimentality. He would appreciate that. No doubt he was still fast asleep somewhere and wouldn't see this for hours. And she'd be long gone. She hoped. For she didn't think she could handle saying good-bye to him again.

Releasing a heavy sigh, she cast one final glance at the bird who still stared at her from the window before she grabbed the door latch and swung it open.

To find Hayden sound asleep on the bench across the hallway.

Hayden peeled his eyes open and was rewarded with a vision of loveliness tiptoeing past him. Lovely until she saw him looking at her and her expression crumpled. She halted with a huff. "What on earth are you doing here, Hayden?" Her shrill voice bore no resemblance to the soft, enchanting cadence of last night. Had the princess turned into a pumpkin while she slept? All the better. For it would make his task today much easier.

Rubbing his aching eyes, he sat, leaned forward, and placed his elbows on his knees. "I was protecting you." *And keeping you from leaving without me.* He wouldn't tell her that he'd sensed something in her last night, something secretive, duplicitous.

"Protecting me?" The hard edge to her voice softened.

Hayden raked his hair back and gazed up at her. "Rio's not the safest town, nor are we in the safest location down here by the docks."

Her delicate eyebrows folded together, and she glanced toward the stairs as if she wished to escape. "How very chivalrous of you," she mumbled. Then why did she seem so troubled and distant?

She faced him, her smile tight as a stretched bow. "You must not have slept at all on that hard bench. Why don't you go lie on the bed? I believe we have the room until noon, do we not? In the meantime, I will go see about some food and perhaps stop by the dock master's." She batted the air around her face, her gaze skittering about. "After the news about this Godard fellow, I assume you aren't going back to the States with me. So, after I book passage, I'll return to say good-bye."

Uneasy at her nervous chattering, Hayden rose and cocked a brow. "And pay me."

"Of course." She gave an exaggerated giggle. "Well then, I shall see you in an hour or so. Do get some rest, Hayden. You look an absolute fright." Sorrow cracked her voice, and he thought he saw moisture cover her eyes before she turned to leave.

Hayden caught her arm. She didn't turn around.

"I've no need for further rest, Princess, though I'm thrilled by your concern." Why was she behaving so strangely? "Perhaps it's best you pay me now."

She tugged from his grip and took a step back, her gaze lowering to the stained and marred floorboards. A man emerged from the room next door, assessed them for a moment, then tipped his hat and headed downstairs.

Magnolia's jaw tightened. "I'm not sure how much my ticket will be."

"Then I will accompany you."

Speechless—for once—she stared at him. Or more like *through* him as alarm screamed in her eyes. Yes, indeed, there was definitely some tomfoolery afoot. Foolish girl! She obviously had no idea who she was dealing with.

After a vain attempt to press the wrinkles from his coat and trousers, Hayden escorted her from the hotel. Better to tell her the truth away from prying eyes and ears, away from people who might wish to intervene in the ensuing confrontation. And what a confrontation it would be when he told her he had no intention of allowing her to put her life at risk by traveling back to the States alone.

Except for a few people, wagons, and chickens milling about, the street was refreshingly empty. Bright fingers of sunlight curled over the edge of the water, spreading a coral ribbon across the horizon and splashing violet on the underbellies of clouds. Sugar Loaf, the peak guarding the bay, rose like a dark thumb imprinted onto the majestic painting. The smell of fish, salt, bananas, and mangoes swirled about Hayden as he battled a myriad of conflicting emotions.

Magnolia hurried along, head down, and valise pressed to her heaving chest. Perhaps she was simply nervous about her upcoming voyage. But soon enough, she would be relieved of such fears.

Of course, he had to get his money from her first. Before she got to the dock master and bought a useless ticket. Turning, he scanned the street, seeking a coffee shop or fruit stand where he could entice her to stop for a moment. Nothing but houses and hotels and a gaudy French theater lined the avenue. Dread clenching his stomach, he faced forward again.

Magnolia was gone.

His heart lurched. He scanned the sparse crowd for a flash of flaxen hair and blue skirts. There, darting down a narrow passage between a cigar shop and a stall selling fine silks. Cursing himself for his stupidity, he tore after her, down the alleyway, out onto a main street bustling with activity. Good thing he was taller than most for he had a clear view of her light hair threading the crowd like a needle through canvas.

So, she intended not to pay him, to go back on her word. Perhaps that had been her intention all along. His blood boiled. How dare she try to swindle him! The best confidence man in the Confederacy.

It didn't take long to catch her. In fact, he considered delaying the chase to grant her a few extra moments of hope. But sweat began to bead on his chest and neck, and his breath grew heavy, so he lengthened his stride, grabbed her elbow, and dragged her off the street into an alleyway.

Forcing her against the brick wall, he imprisoned her with his arms. "What in the Sam Hill are you doing, Princess?" His breath came out in heated bursts, filling the air between them.

Her chest heaved in time with his. Waves of freed hair tumbled down her shoulders. Perspiration shone on her face and neck. But her eyes were ice. "I hate good-byes."

"And I assume you hate parting with your money as well."

She ducked beneath his arm and darted to the left, but he snagged her and brought her back. "Ah, ah, ah, Princess. Not until you pay me my due." Not ever, actually. But he wouldn't tell her that until he got his money—money he desperately needed to purchase supplies and a scout to locate his father.

"It's always been about the money, hasn't it?" Spite hissed in her voice. "Not about helping a lady in distress. Even last night. You were playing a part, being kind just to get the money, weren't you?" The ice melted in her eyes, and he couldn't tell whether the tears were an act or real. *Baffling woman!*

He pushed off the wall and held out his open palm. "Nevertheless, we had a deal."

She swallowed hard, her gaze flitting from him to the street and back again. Finally, she sighed, retrieved the pouch from her valise, and slammed it into his hand.

The sheer weight of it delighted Hayden.

"You're welcome to what's left after you purchase my passage home. In fact"—she picked up her valise and started down the alleyway—"why don't we go buy a ticket now? Then I'll board the ship and you'll be free of me."

Hayden leapt in front of her. A breeze sifted through the passageway, cooling the sweat on his neck. He snapped hair from his face, studying her. She wouldn't meet his gaze. "I have a better idea. How about we count it first? Three hundred dollars worth of gold coins, if I recall?"

Her face blanched. She seemed to be having trouble breathing. She set down her valise and leaned against the brick wall with a huff of resignation. "Very well."

Tipping her valise on its side, Hayden poured the contents of the pouch onto the patterned fabric. A few gold coins sifted out from the top, but they were soon smothered beneath a massive pile of copper pennies.

CHAPTER 18

Magnolia gripped the wall behind her, snagging her last pair of good gloves, wishing she could melt into the bricks and disappear. The look of shock in Hayden's green eyes transformed into fury as hard as emerald. He clutched a handful of pennies and rose, thrusting them in her face. "You tricked me!" Nostrils flaring, his jaw reddened beneath dark stubble like embers beneath coal. "You lied to me!"

Magnolia's breath fled her lungs. A squeak emerged from her lips.

He flung the coins on the ground by her feet. Some struck her hem and landed on her shoes. Others crashed to the stone walkway, their *clanks* and *clinks* sounding hollow in her ears—hollow like her promise to Hayden. She couldn't blame him for his anger. She'd tried to avoid it. But now as he took up a pace before her like a raging bull about to charge, she grew concerned at what he might do.

He kicked the pennies down the street, growling. "I counted on that money. I trusted you."

Halting, he slammed his palms on the brick on either side of her and pinned her to the wall once again. The man could start a fire with that look in his eyes. As it was, Magnolia felt her heart sear beneath his stare. He tried to say something, bared his teeth, but only a groan emerged as he pushed off the wall and backed away.

Finally, she found her voice, shaky as it was. "I only had enough for my passage, Hayden. I didn't know what else to do. You wouldn't have taken me along without being paid."

"No, I wouldn't have." Clenching his fists, he crossed his arms over his chest.

"You left me no choice." Tears blurred her vision.

A flash of understanding lit his eyes before he narrowed them. "You prepared the trap before you even knew I would deny your request. You intended to trick me all along."

Unable to bear the pain in his eyes, she lowered her gaze. "I suspected money might influence you, yes. I'm sorry, Hayden. I hated lying to you." A bell rang from the harbor. She bit her lip and watched a woman pass by with a basket of fruit on her head. "Please let me use what little gold I have to buy my passage. As soon as I get home and marry Samuel, I'll send you ten times that amount."

He gave a cynical chuckle. "Fool me once, Princess." He shoved a finger at her and shook his head. Then kneeling, he gathered the gold coins and slid them into his pocket—seven coins that would amount to no more than forty dollars. Just enough to pay for her passage home and perhaps conveyance to her aunt and uncle's in Ohio. But now they were in the possession of this angry bull before her.

Angry and wounded and possessing a crazed look akin to a feral wolf. Oh, how she wished the ardor of the prior night would return, but she'd never see that again. She'd ruined that possibility with her lie. Ruined any affection that had grown between them. And now, there was truly nothing left for her in Brazil. Despite the heaviness in her heart, she put on her most charming smile and inched toward him. "I know I lied to you, Hayden, but I promise I will send you money. As much as you need." Self-loathing curdled in her belly at another possible deception. But how else was she to get home?

A breeze snaked an eerie whistle through the alleyway, flapping Hayden's dark hair across his collar. He shook his head and snorted. "Your pardon, Princess, if I no longer believe you. Besides, you're coming back to New Hope with me."

"What?" Magnolia screeched. "I will do no such thing!" She backed away. "I didn't come all this way, suffer all I have, to return to that barbaric place. Give me back my money this instant!" She gestured toward his pocket.

"Your money?" He snorted. "You mean my payment for escorting you to Rio." He grumbled out a curse. "Or at least my partial payment."

"The bargain was to buy my passage home and the rest would be yours."

"The rest of"—he glanced at the pennies strewn across the ground, his voice coming out strangled—"nothing is nothing!" Growling, he raked a hand through his hair, took up a pace, then stopped and collected himself. "Besides, it's not safe for you to travel alone. You'll be ravished or robbed. Or both."

Steam rose up Magnolia's back. Hot, furious steam. "I have nothing for anyone to steal."

"Then just ravished." He pointed toward the pennies. "If you want those, you best pick them up."

Grinding her teeth, Magnolia glanced toward the street, now bustling with people, wagons, and donkeys. A monkey skittered past the alley, stopped, cocked his head curiously at them, and then jabbered something that sounded like a rebuke before he darted away. She closed her eyes as a groan erupted in her throat. She must leave this savage country! She simply couldn't bear another five days traipsing through the jungle, dealing with insects as big as cats and snakes as long and thick as ship's ropes. Nor could she face her father again. If he didn't kill her for leaving, his continual berating would drive her to suicide.

She gazed at the coins scattered over the moist ground. Scattered and worthless just like her dreams, her hopes. Just like her. Yet something Hayden said haunted her dismal thoughts.

"You were never planning on putting me on a ship, were you? You merely told me that so I'd help you with that repulsive immigration officer."

He didn't need to answer. She saw the answer shouting from behind those green eyes of his.

He sighed and rubbed the back of his neck. "I fully intended to escort you home if Mr. Santos had informed me that Godard had gone back to the States."

"And if not?"

He shrugged. "Like I said, you wouldn't survive alone on a ship."

479

"What is that to you?" Blood surged through her veins, thick and scorching. "You lie to me, cheat me, use me. Why do you care if I survive the trip or not?"

He raised his brows. "I am not a complete monster, Princess."

"No, you are worse than a monster! You are a heartless beast, a cruel, heartless beast who preys on innocent women."

She must have struck a nerve for a hint of remorse shoved the pompous fury from his face.

"Listen, Princess," he began, hands raised in a truce.

But Magnolia couldn't hear him anymore. Rage seared through her, befuddling all rational thought. Lifting her foot, she kicked him as hard as she could.

She aimed for his thigh, hoping to knock him to the ground, but she must have struck a more sensitive area, for he toppled over with an agonizing groan.

A moment's consideration told her she didn't stand a chance of retrieving her money from his pocket so instead, she grabbed her valise and darted into the street. Tears mottled everything into a kaleidoscope of colors as she twined her way through the swarm of beasts and humanity. Creaking wagons, shouting vendors, and squawking birds blended in a perverted, dismal hum. She had no idea where she was going. She had no money, knew not a soul, and didn't speak the language. But what else could she do? She'd rather die alone in Rio than go back to New Hope. Besides, she was a capable woman. She would think of something, wouldn't she?

Her mind and heart a jumble of fear and panic, she clutched her valise to her chest and rushed forward, stumbling over the uneven cobblestones. She turned down a familiar-looking street and hurried past a huge church with white columns, lofty spires, and a scrolled bell tower. Halting to catch her breath, she studied the way the rising sun reflected off the stained-glass window, enhancing a portrait of Jesus on the cross. A young boy sat on a bench out front. A beggar? No. His clean, stylish attire and well-groomed hair spoke otherwise. He smiled at her, flashing a rank of snowy teeth before he went back to weaving a basket. Sniffing, Magnolia wiped her face and started up the pathway.

A church would be the perfect place to hide, to think, to decide what she should do next.

She pushed against one of the large, heavy doors. The aged wood creaked as it opened to darkness and a blast of cool, musty air. Stepping inside, scents of candle wax and incense wafted around her—pleasant smells that seemed to leech the worry from her pores. She would be safe here. A man like Hayden would never set foot in a church. Nor, she supposed, would he think she would either. Sliding into one of the pews, she set down her valise as her eyes grew accustomed to the dim lighting. Rows of empty wooden benches stretched to an altar laden with white linen, lit candles, and silver bowls. Beyond the altar and above the chancel hung a carved figure of Jesus on the cross. Golden angels with trumpets to their lips perched on either side of him. Of course Magnolia knew the story of the Son of God, who died to save mankind from their sins. She'd heard it preached repeatedly in her childhood. And while it made for an interesting tale, she'd never seen how it applied to her. Perhaps this Jesus *was* the Son of God. Perhaps He did die for her. But where was He now? Why didn't He show Himself? Talk to her? Help her figure out her disaster of a life? No, God had always seemed so far away, so unreachable.

Leaning back on the hard pew, she plucked her mirror from her valise and attempted to stuff her wayward hair back into her bun. How her father would scold her for entering a church in such disarray. Not only was her hair a mess, but perspiration covered her face and neck. Grabbing a handkerchief, she dabbed the offending moisture, all the while wondering, if God did exist, why He cared so much about appearances. Was He just like her father—always expecting perfection? If so, she wanted nothing to do with Him. Lowering her mirror, she dropped it back into her valise.

A gust of wind blasted over her, warm and scented with roses and vanilla, and so strong it loosened her hair once again from her pins. Magnolia turned to see where it came from when a voice sent her heart into her throat.

"Well, hello, dearest."

An old woman sat beside her. A very old woman. A stained, torn dress covered her from neck to ankles, divided by an old tattered rope tied around her waist. Furrowed skin hung from a skeletal face framed by shriveled sprigs of gray hair. Where had she come from?

"I didn't mean to startle you, dearest." Her voice cracked with age, but her eyes were bright and clear, and the light that shone from within them put Magnolia immediately at ease.

"My apologies. I didn't see you come in," Magnolia said. In fact, she hadn't heard a thing. Odd since every sound seemed to magnify through the hollow, high ceilings of the church.

The lady smiled, revealing a scattering of dull teeth over fleshy gums. Magnolia's annoyance rose. Of all the places to sit in the vacant church, why did the old woman sit beside her? Especially when Magnolia wished to be alone, to think, to figure how to get herself out of her predicament. The smell of sweat and age and foul breath curled her nose, and she turned to gaze up at the crucifix. "Forgive me, madam, but I would prefer to be alone to pray."

The woman chuckled. "Is that what you were doing?"

The sarcasm in her tone sent anger through Magnolia. "Yes, it was. Now if you please." She scooted away, wondering why the woman spoke fluent English with no accent.

She shifted even closer to Magnolia.

With a huff, Magnolia shoved her ever-rebellious hair into her bun and patted it in place. Then rising to her feet, she pressed the wrinkles from her skirts and grabbed her valise, intending to bid the woman good day. But a bony hand reached out and stayed her.

"You concern yourself far too much about your appearance, dearest Magnolia—far too much about your outside, when it is your inside that needs attention."

The words turned nonsensical in Magnolia's mind. She jerked from her touch. "How do you know my name?"

Again that smile, filled with such peace. "I know much about you, dearest."

Magnolia's legs wobbled, and she sank back into the pew, studying every line and crevice in the woman's face, trying to determine if she'd met her before. But no, she would remember someone this bent and wrinkled with age.

"You find me ugly, don't you?" the woman asked.

Magnolia lowered her gaze, unsure of what to say and yet somehow knowing this woman would see through vain flatteries. "No. . .yes. . . but you are old. It is to be expected."

"Old, indeed, dearest. If you only knew." She chuckled. "But this body is merely a covering, a used garment that one day will be shed. True and lasting beauty comes from within."

Sunlight shone through the stained glass, sending a rainbow of dusty spears through the church and haloing the figure of Jesus with brilliant light. The old woman gazed up at Him as if she knew Him, as if He were a dear loved one. "God cares not for the outside. His concern is the heart. He sees only the heart."

Pondering the woman's statement, Magnolia suddenly wondered at the condition of her own heart. Surely it was clean and good. She hadn't told too many lies, hadn't stolen from others. She'd been chaste and moral. She hadn't hurt anyone purposely, had she? Certainly not like many of her prudish friends back home.

The woman touched her again, and Magnolia felt a spark shoot through her. "Here and henceforth," the woman began, "your reflection will reveal the true beauty of your heart, the way you appear to those who inhabit eternity. Take care to adorn yourself with jewels that last forever."

Her words floated through Magnolia's mind, forming a tangled thread of nonsense. She was still staring at the woman when the old lady gripped the pew back in front of her and pulled herself to stand. With body curled and bent, she waved a bony hand above her head. A bright light flashed. Magnolia blinked. The woman's body unfurled like a new flower in spring. Her back straightened. Her shoulders stretched. Her withered gray hair plumped and lengthened into gold, silky strands. Creases on her skin faded and tightened, leaving a complexion that glowed. Her eyes sparkled, her lips grew rosy. Her rags transformed into white robes trimmed in silvery glitter.

Magnolia's heart stopped.

The woman smiled again. "This is how I look on the inside." Even her gruff voice had transformed into music.

The foyer door squealed. Magnolia turned to see a man enter. A gust of wind struck her with the scent of sweet roses. When she turned back around, the woman was gone.

CHAPTER 19

A church was the last place Hayden expected to find Magnolia. It was the last place he expected to find himself. Still throbbing from her assault, he approached her with caution, lest the wildcat reveal her claws again. But when he grew close, she made no move to run, made no move to fight. Instead she remained in the pew, her face a white sheet, her eyes stark and skittering. Finally she gazed up at him, her befuddled expression transforming into recognition, followed by fear, then resignation.

"I see you found me," she said.

"Perceptive as always, Princess."

She rose, teetered, and grabbed the pew back for support, the fight gone out of her. So easily, or did something happen? Hayden glanced through the church but no one was in sight. Just the crucified Jesus staring down at Hayden as if he weren't worthy to be in such a holy place.

A shiver etched between his shoulders.

Magnolia grabbed her valise. "I take it I am now your prisoner."

"Call it what you may, I will not allow you to put your life and your purity at risk."

She stepped into the aisle, raised a hand to her head and swayed. An act? No, not by the way she gasped as if all air had evacuated the church. Hayden grabbed her elbow, and she all but fell against him. Despite his anger, he wrapped an arm around her waist and felt her

485

tremble. "What happened? Are you all right?"

She sniffed and shook her head, but said nothing. Hayden found he quite enjoyed the pussy cat over the tigress. Besides, he could not deny his relief at finding her. At first, as he folded in agony from her kick, unable to move or even breathe, his anger told him to just let her go, just let her be. After all, he had what little money she possessed. If the shrew wanted to be on her own, what was that to him? But he couldn't do it. Couldn't even think clearly while she was wandering the streets alone. And in far more danger than her innocence realized.

Taking her valise, he ushered her to the door. No sooner did they step out into the blaring sun than the tigress reappeared. Tearing from his embrace, she shoved him aside, nearly knocking him down the steps. "You deceived me!"

He turned his body, shielding himself from another kick, and clutched her arm lest she try to run again. "*You* deceived me, Princess." He still couldn't believe that she'd swindled him so effectively, that she'd charmed her way into his heart with lies and promises. The notorious confidence man, Hayden Gale! It was not only unheard of, it was infuriating, and even worse, it was humiliating beyond all measure.

Halting at the bottom of the stairs, she snapped from his grip and faced him. "So, we lied to each other. Used each other. We are even." Squinting against the bright sunlight, she scanned the street. "How on earth did you find me?"

"The boy." Hayden gestured toward the bench, but it was empty now. He scratched his chin. "There was a boy. He called to me while I sped past. Told me an American lady was in the church."

Magnolia frowned and marched onto the muddy street, nearly bumping into a man who was being carried in a chair by four dark mulattoes. Thunder bellowed in the distance. She slowed and faced Hayden, her anger gone, her eyes soft wisps of sapphire. "Why don't we go home, Hayden? Back to the States. Just you and me." Her voice was honey. "I'm sure we have enough for two tickets. Let's leave this horrid place, return to the familiar comforts of home. Please?" Was it his imagination or did her bottom lip suddenly plump like the inviting cushion of a divan? One he normally would long to lounge upon. If he weren't so furious. Lashes lowering to her cheeks, she played with the lapel of his coat.

For a moment, he felt his anger receding beneath her feminine charms. Oh, but she was good. She was very good. He could see why most men melted at her feet. He'd never met a woman—or a man, for that matter—who possessed the same innate skill as he did to charm a piece of meat from a starving man. Together they could have amassed a fortune back home.

But he wouldn't fall for her schemes again. He shifted his gaze away.

She placed a hand on his arm. "If you escort me safely to my aunt and uncle's estate, I'll give you my entire dowry."

Hayden snorted. "Why do I find it hard to believe that such a dowry even exists?"

"Of course it does. Please, Hayden. This Mr. Godard is no doubt long gone by now. I know you say he stole everything from you, but you are here and alive and we both have a chance at getting out of this savage country. I can tell you don't wish to stay in New Hope, so why delay—"

But Hayden wasn't listening anymore. Just the mention of his father's alias sent renewed zeal through him. And as tempting as it was to run away with this beautiful, unpredictable, spitfire, he had a promise to keep to his mother. "I can't."

"Of course you can."

"No." Taking her arm, he started walking.

"Then leave me here. I can't bear to go back to New Hope." Her voice degraded to a sob.

"It isn't safe."

"What is that to you?"

Hayden wouldn't tell her that, much to his chagrin, and even after her deception, he cared very much what happened to her. "Perhaps your parents will offer me a reward for bringing you back."

He could hear the pain in her long, ragged sigh. Felt the ache in his own heart. She yanked her valise from his grip. "I assure you, sir, they will not. You are wasting your time."

Seconds passed in silence as she trudged beside him before blowing out a huff of surrender. "Well, if you insist on dragging me through the jungle again, can we at least stop and purchase some rum?"

Setting down his shovel, Wiley Dodd wiped sweat from his brow, plucked a map from his pocket, and spread the crinkled paper over the stump of a felled tree. A spindly insect dove at him. He swatted it away as sweat stung his eyes, blurring the lines on the map. He rubbed them and tried to focus despite the heat that spiraled down from the sun, making everything look like a mirage. But the hard, rocky ground was no mirage. His aching muscles attested to that. He'd been digging for days in the exact spot indicated on the map, but all he'd gotten for his trouble was a ten-foot-deep hole, a mound of dirt and pebbles, raw blisters on his hands, and a mood so foul it scared even the monkeys away.

He ran a finger over the points on the treasure map. He'd found the purple boulder shaped like a turtle fifty paces from the spot where the river split. He'd followed the edge of the shallow ravine in a semicircle to find the old cassia tree with the carved hole in the center. Inside, he'd gathered the twelve stones, along with several surly spiders, which he'd shaken off before they bit him. Upon each stone two numbers were etched. According to the map, the first, a number between one and four, indicated the direction—north, south, east, or west—and the other was the number of paces in that direction. Just finding the stones where the map said they would be, had caused him to yelp and leap like a man whose britches were on fire. It was proof that he wasn't mad after all. How he'd love to tell the other colonists, to show to them he'd been right, that there must be gold here in the Brazilian jungle, but they'd probably want in on the treasure.

And he couldn't have that. He'd worked too hard for too many years. First as a boy in a sailmaker's shop, sweeping the floors of scrap canvas and cordage, and stirring the kettle of tallow—doing whatever he could to support his mother and two sisters. Then as a sheriff, first in Norfolk and then in Richmond, sweeping the streets of equally useless scraps of humanity. Hard, dangerous work for so little pay. Now, it was fortune's turn to smile upon him—for once.

A drop of sweat landed on the map, and he brushed it away. He'd followed the directions on the stones to the waterfall. Or at least he hoped it was the same waterfall drawn on the map. Ten paces off, he'd found the group of larger rocks piled in the shape of a pyramid. And beyond them, a circle of mango trees, in the center of which stood the treasure. At least that was how it appeared on the map—a chest filled with gold. In reality, there was nothing but leaf-strewn, hard-packed dirt. And so he had dug. And dug. And dug and dug.

Scratching the back of his neck, he stretched his shoulders. Where had he gone wrong? He carefully folded the map and stuffed it into his pocket. After gulping down water from his canteen, he grabbed the shovel, leapt into the hole, and started digging again. His sweat soon returned, along with the mind-numbing thrum of insects and birds above. But when his shovel struck something hard, he no longer cared. The sweet chink of metal on metal brought a huge smile to his cracked lips.

⚜

Magnolia couldn't believe she was in the middle of the jungle again. After she had endured so much discomfort in order to get to Rio. After she could see the ships in the bay preparing to sail for home...

If not for the lying, thieving barbarian sitting across the crackling fire from her, she would have made it home, too. Somehow or another. She would have found a way. But instead, he had made her his prisoner—forced her to walk in front of him, never taking his eyes off her, so she "wouldn't get any fool notions about running back to Rio," he had said.

Many such notions had crossed her mind during the long day, but they now faded with the last vestiges of sunlight angling through the trees. She was too far enmeshed in the steamy web to ever find her way back. The brute obviously knew that too, for he sat on a log whittling a piece of wood, completely ignoring her. Beside him sat a knapsack filled with supplies he'd purchased with her money. *Her money!*

Leaning over, she unlaced the new shoes they'd also bought in Rio, a pair of black kids with shiny buckles. Plain, yet practical. Of course, after a day of traipsing through the jungle, they were already ruined. She rubbed her toes through her stockings, feeling the hardened skin of old blisters and hoping her feet wouldn't grow large and callused like some women's. She'd always prided herself on her petite, flawless feet.

"What are we going to eat?" she asked.

Without looking up, Hayden gestured to a pile of fruit he'd gathered earlier.

"But what about the dried pork you purchased in Rio?"

"That's for my search after we return."

"But it was *my* money. I should have some of it."

Finally he looked up, eyes darkening like the growing shadows of the jungle. "It was *my* payment."

"But the bargain was not completed. You did not see me safely on a ship to America."

He went back to whittling. Dark hair the color of almonds grazed his shoulders, stirred by a welcome breeze that whistled through the leaves. He shifted his boots over the dirt, clearly avoiding the discussion.

Magnolia felt like growling, but that wouldn't be very ladylike. Did the man have any idea what eating only fruit did to her delicate digestion? She dropped her chin into her palm, putting on her most adorable pout. Though why she bothered, she had no idea. It never worked on him.

He ignored her.

How rude! Especially when she had far more reason to be angry at him than he did her. What did it matter if he didn't have as much money as he'd hoped? He could still search for this Godard fellow. While she, on the other hand, had to face the wrath of her father for her betrayal, a lifetime of his criticisms, and a hopeless future in the primordial sludge of Brazil. Not to mention, her father would probably marry her off to some dowdy, feeble-minded Brazilian. A sour taste rose in her throat and she released a wilted sigh—a sigh that begged for Hayden's help.

Still, he ignored her.

And to think that only last night she'd thought she might be developing affections for him. There. She admitted it. Yes, she had felt something. Most likely just cheap wine. But he'd been so gallant at the ball. Such a gentleman. So handsome and charming and entertaining and clever. She'd had fun. For the first time in her recollection, she'd truly enjoyed herself at a party.

Now, that same man had transformed back into a toad—all angry and somber—dressed once again in his stained white shirt and black trousers tucked within muddy boots. And search as she might, she could find no resemblance between him and the man she'd been with last night. Perhaps it had all been an act. Hayden was just like all the other men in her life. He had used her for her beauty then used her for her money. And now, he was using her for a possible reward from her father. Pain lanced her heart, the blade turning and twisting until tears filled her eyes. Maybe that was all she was good for. Beauty and money.

She ripped a banana from a bunch and started to peel it as a chorus of katydids began their nightly orchestra. Fireflies flickered in the darkness, matched by stars beginning to twinkle through the canopy. She shoved away her sorrow. It did her no good. Besides, she was lonely and frightened and talking helped soothe her nerves. Even if the only person she could converse with was the man who had put her in this predicament.

"Who is this Godard anyway?"

He blew out a sigh. Was it her imagination or did his knife cut a little deeper into the wood? "I told you. Just someone I need to find." Setting down his carving, he tossed another log onto the fire, the flames reflecting red in his hard eyes. Magnolia swallowed at the fury she saw within them. Surely, that wasn't *all* directed at her.

"I have a right to know who he is," she said, "since it is on his account you are dragging me back to a father who will punish me to the end of my days for running away." Something flapped across the clearing, disappearing into the leaves. Magnolia hoped it wasn't a bat. She hated bats.

The tight lines on Hayden's face seemed to soften. He picked up his whittling again. "I am truly sorry about your father."

His tone carried remorse, but she wasn't buying it. "If you are truly sorry, you'd take me back to Rio and put me on a ship." She bit into her banana, the sweet taste flooding her mouth.

"Trust me. I'm doing what's best for you." His shirt sleeves were rolled up, drawing her gaze to the muscles flexing in his thick arms with each dig of the knife into wood.

"You are a toad, Hayden Gale."

He smiled.

Did the man truly care what happened to her on the ship? Or did he simply not wish to part with any of his—her—money? The thought that he might actually care brought a measure of comfort to her otherwise aggravated heart. Magnolia focused on a trail of ants edging the clearing. A monkey howled in the distance. "So this Mr. Godard, did he steal your lady, kill your dog? Ah, I know"—she nodded, studying him—"He lied to you. Deceived you like I did. But for something besides money. Hmm. . ."—she tapped her chin—"That would explain why you are so furious with me. You hate being tricked, outwitted. That's it. He made you out to be a fool, didn't he?" Like Martin had done to her. If so, she could well understand Hayden's need for revenge. She could even understand why he'd traveled all the way from Charleston to Brazil in search of the man, for she would do the same thing if she knew where Martin was. If she ever saw that fiend again, he would regret the day he laid eyes on her.

"Let it alone, Princess." Hayden's jaw tightened even further as his tone brooked no further discussion.

Tossing the empty banana peel, Magnolia plucked an orange from the pile, tore off the skin, and plopped a piece into her mouth. Sweet juice dribbled down her chin. Thankfully Hayden didn't see it before she wiped it away. Not that she cared what he thought of her. He was the worst sort of cad. The opposite of Samuel. Perhaps Samuel couldn't start a fire or build a shelter or catch fish. Maybe he couldn't find his way through the jungles of Brazil, but he knew how to treat a lady. He was cultured and well mannered and could converse on any number of topics—though most of them bored Magnolia. But that didn't matter.

He was courteous and kind and chivalrous, a true gentleman. And he would never lie to Magnolia. Or use her. Nor would he be churlish when she depended on him for survival.

"If you are intent on ignoring me, might I at least have some rum?" She'd seen Hayden purchase a flask in Rio, and the liquor would do much to relieve her tension.

He studied her, assessing her like a schoolmaster assessing a child. Finally he reached into his knapsack and handed her the flask. "Just a few sips."

"Am I to be rationed as well?"

"Until you learn to control your drinking, yes. I'll not have a besotted nymph running around the jungle."

"Nym. . .I do not overdrink!"

He snorted out a chuckle.

She frowned. "Then, why did you purchase it?"

"To control your shakes," he said. "And yes, I noticed."

Heat stormed up her neck as she uncorked the flask and tipped it to her mouth. Spice and fire slid down her throat and warmed her belly. Now, if it would only make the toad disappear. She took another sip.

"Easy now, Princess. Ladies don't gulp."

"How dare you!" Magnolia seethed. She attempted to rise but her insufferable crinoline pushed her back down. Carefully setting down the rum, she dropped to her knees, planted both hands in the dirt, and shoved herself up with a groan that she was sure would also be dubbed indelicate. "I am not a lush." She plucked the flask from the ground.

"When are you going to get rid of that cage you wear under your skirts?" He pointed his knife at her gown.

"Of all the. . .I. . ." She inhaled a breath. "What is under my skirts is none of your affair!" Mercy me, what had she just said? A tidal wave doused her in heat. She pressed a hand to her cheeks, certain that they were as red as pomegranates.

He grinned and continued whittling.

She sipped the rum, praying it would loosen the tight noose around her nerves. "What do you know about ladylike behavior, anyway? I imagine the only ladies you associate with are those who make taverns their home."

He chuckled. "In which case, I should not consider your behavior out of the ordinary with all the spirits you consume and the way you kiss a man without provocation."

"Without prov…kiss!" Rage strangled her. Followed by humiliation as the truth of his words struck home. Was she nothing but a common hussy? Had it been her lack of moral character that had caused her to fall for Martin's lies? Was that the reason her father constantly reprimanded her about her appearance? To hide her wench's heart? The old woman's words blared like a trumpet in her mind. *Here and henceforth your reflection will reveal the true beauty of your heart, the way you appear to those who inhabit eternity.*

Dropping to her knees, she set down the flask, opened her valise, and yanked out her gilded mirror. Eyes blurry with tears, she slowly raised it to view her reflection. Gray hair, frizzled and scorched, circled a face furrowed with lines and marred with dark spots. Her thin, leaden lips were drawn and cracked. Dark wells tugged at the skin beneath her eyes as hooded lids slanted over her once luminous eyes.

Magnolia screamed.

Chapter 20

Magnolia's scream sent Hayden leaping over the fire, knife drawn, ready to defend her against some reptilian, multilegged invader. But when he landed beside her, no such creature was to be found either on the mirror she continued to hold up to her face, or on her arm, her skirts, or anywhere around her. Her screaming reduced to sobs as she continued to stare at her reflection, gingerly touching her cheeks.

"What is it?" He nudged her hand and the mirror away, grabbed her shoulders, and forced her to look at him. Tears streamed from blue eyes as liquid as the sea. "She was right. She was right. The old lady was right," she kept repeating.

"Who was right? About what?"

"How can you look at me?" Jerking from his grasp, she turned her back to him. "I'm grotesque."

Hayden could make no sense of her ramblings. It couldn't be the rum. She'd only had a few sips. "You're anything but grotesque, Magnolia. You know that." He touched her shoulder but she moved out of reach. "Why all the theatrics?"

"You used my common name." She sniffed. "Not Princess." Her shoulders rose and fell upon a sob that seemed to calm her until she glanced in the mirror and started wailing again.

"By all that is holy, what is wrong?" Hayden's patience was fast coming to an end.

"Can't you see? Look." With her back still to him, she held the

495

mirror up and gazed at him through the reflection. Nothing but her beautiful tear-streaked face stared back at him. Her eyes assessed him, the terror within them fading into confusion.

"Don't you see me?" she finally asked.

"Of course I see you. Lovely, alluring you."

"I look the same to you in the mirror?"

He studied her reflection again. "Except for your red, swollen eyes."

Leaning over, he picked up the flask, suddenly needing a drink himself. The pungent liquor warmed his throat. And heated his suspicions. "You did all this, behaved like a rattlebrain, just to lure a compliment from me?" He shook his head. "Of all the conceited, egotistical, selfish—"

"I did no such thing!" Stomping to her valise, she tossed her mirror in and slowly turned to face him, studying him as if gauging his reaction. Finally she planted her fists at her waist. "How could you think something like that? Do you find me so shallow?" Her eyes flashed like lightning, but then the anger faded, and she lowered herself onto a log, skirts puffing about her. Caked mud covered the hem from their long trek through the jungle, her new gown already ruined. But she didn't seem to care.

Instead, she stared at the fire as if in a daze, her tears drying on her cheeks. Hayden had no idea what to do. The great confidence man who could see past any facade, who could read people and match his own behavior to theirs in order to achieve his goals, now found himself at a complete loss.

Yes, he'd been furious at her for tricking him, for being the only one who had ever managed to swindle the infamous swindler. But perhaps that was just his pride. Besides, how could he blame her for doing something he did for a living? They both had good reasons for their deceptions. She to escape her father's tyranny, and he, of course, to finally end his quest for the man who had killed his mother and ruined his life.

The croak of a frog joined an owl's hoot in the distance as a breeze stirred the leaves into a crescendo of laughter. Laughing at him, no doubt. At his weakness for this Southern sprite. Slipping the flask inside his pocket, he squatted and poked the fire, sending sparks into the dark sky. Still, Magnolia didn't move. Hayden had been outwitted by a conceited debutante. But what bothered him more than her lie was the pain he'd felt when he discovered it—the agonizing pain of betrayal by someone he trusted. Sure, he had his suspicions. In his profession, he'd learned to be leery of most people. But deep down he supposed he had truly believed Magnolia. Otherwise, why would he feel such a palatable ache deep in his heart?

Something bit his neck and he slapped away the offending varmint. Had any of his victims felt this gut-wrenching pain? Memories of his vision of Katherine pricked his conscience. She'd seemed so upset, so tormented. But that hadn't been real, had it? In truth, he had no idea what her reaction had been. He'd never stuck around to witness the trail of destruction he'd left behind. By the time his targets discovered they'd been swindled, he was long gone. He'd always imagined their fury, their rage, but he'd never thought about their heartache.

Not until now.

Magnolia began mumbling something about being ugly inside and some old woman in a church, but Hayden couldn't make sense of it. Zooks, was the woman going mad now on top of everything else? He pictured himself hoisting a foaming-at-the-mouth lunatic over his shoulder and attempting to carry her through the jungle. The idea held no appeal. Finally, he suggested she retire, and much to his surprise she nodded and crawled into her shelter.

Two hours later, her deep breathing assured him she was asleep. Squatting by the opening of the shelter, he stared within, cursing himself for making the frond roof so snug that not a sliver of moonlight gave him a view of her face. What was it about this woman that had him so bewitched? She was spoiled, pompous, self-centered, and whiny. Besides, she hailed from a class of landed gentry that was as far from his own heritage as Queen Victoria was from a chimney sweep. To make matters worse, she had a viper's tongue in that sweet little mouth of hers. Sweet indeed! He rubbed his lips, remembering her taste. Honey and spice and passion. His body reacted, and he shifted his stance.

But she was also witty and smart and charming and feminine and passionate, and deep down she cared for others. And much like him, she'd also been given a rough start in life. Maybe she hadn't grown up a destitute orphan, but she'd grown up equally unloved by a critical, demanding father who valued her only for her beauty and held her captive to a mysterious debt she couldn't pay. It was no wonder she behaved the way she did.

Hayden sighed and rubbed his chin, studying the edge of her lacy petticoat peeking from beneath her skirts and the way her stockinged feet curled at her side. When he found his father and completed his mission, he would take Magnolia back to the States with him. He would hand her over to her fiancé, this solicitor Samuel Wimper. . . Wimperly or whoever he was. Just the sound of his name created an image of a spare, lanky man with greased hair, spectacles perched on his nose, and wearing a fancy frock coat.

But she obviously loved him or she wouldn't have gone to such trouble to find her way back to him. Hayden rose and circled the fire, hating the sudden pain that made his heart feel like an anchor. Hating it because he didn't understand it. Because he'd never felt it before. And because the woman who had caused it was forever outside his reach.

James emerged onto the sandy bank to find Miss Angeline, her skirts hiked up to her knees, standing in the river, slapping clothes against a rock. On the shore, Stowy, her inseparable cat, pounced on leaves and frogs and anything that dared move. Sunlight set Angeline's hair aglow in spirals of glittering amber trickling over her elegant neck. James had never seen a more beautiful sight.

Despite the rushing river and the warble of birds, she must have heard his boot's tread, for a pistol appeared in her hands so fast, he hadn't seen her draw it or from whence it had come.

He raised his hands, taken aback at the familiar way she held the weapon. Not with the hands of a seamstress, but with the hands of one accustomed to handling a gun. "I surrender."

Her eyes sparkled, and her shoulders lowered…along with the

gun. "Do forgive me, Doctor. I've been a bit skittish lately."

"No need. I'm glad for it. It isn't safe for you to be out here alone." Which was why he had come in the first place. He'd seen the other women leaving with basketfuls of wet laundry, but not Angeline. Though James hadn't spoken to her since he'd made a fool of himself and run off during his sermon at church, he'd kept his eye on her. Especially after Eliza had told him about Dodd's propensity for peeping at the women.

James approached, sweeping a cautious glance over the clearing, then to the bank on the other side of the river. Afternoon sunlight rippled in silver ribbons across water that stretched at least forty yards before thick jungle kept it at bay. No sign of intruders or Peeping Toms. "You should always have at least one other person with you."

Stuffing the gun into her belt, she waded to shore, but then glanced down at her raised skirts and lowered them immediately, face reddening. James smiled. How refreshing to find such a modest woman. In fact, all of the women in the colony seemed in possession of the highest morals. And if James had his way, he intended to keep it that way. He'd had his fill of unscrupulous women.

"To deliver thee from the strange woman, even from the stranger which flattereth with her words. . . For her house inclineth unto death, and her paths unto the dead. None that go unto her return again, neither take they hold of the paths of life."

The words of Proverbs, words he had memorized and recited each day, stood to attention in his mind.

"I'm nearly done here." Angeline's voice snapped him from his musings. "And though I appreciate your concern, Doctor, I can take care of myself." She scooped up Stowy and stroked his fur, eyeing James with those exquisite violet eyes of hers. "Is there something I can do for you?"

He shifted his boots in the sand, wondering why the lady always turned his insides to porridge. "I'm checking with all the women to make sure they feel safe in the colony and aren't being bothered by any of the men." He invented a half-truth, ignoring the twinge of guilt that came with it. He'd fully intended to talk to Angeline after Eliza told him about Dodd, but he hadn't gotten around to it yet.

Her brow furrowed. A breeze stirred a pile of leaves, and Stowy leapt from her arms onto the pesky foliage. "Are you applying to be our town's constable as well, Doctor?" She smiled.

He suddenly felt rather silly, like an awkward schoolboy with his first infatuation. "No, I believe being preacher keeps me busy enough." He slanted his lips, wondering how to explain his concern without seeming like a lovesick fool. "The colonel and I want to keep an eye on all the single ladies in New Hope." Truss it, that didn't sound right either. "I mean we. . .well, in the absence of a lawman, we feel responsible for the ladies who live alone."

A tiny line formed between her brows. She studied him as if he were an oddity. James swallowed. Splendid. If running from the pulpit at church hadn't convinced her he was utterly mad, surely his present ramblings were proof enough.

A fish leapt from the lake, drawing Stowy to the edge. Was it overly hot today? Sweat moistened James's neck and arms, and he had a sudden desire to jump into the water. Even better, jump in with Angeline. The thought did nothing to cool him off.

She approached, the hem of her skirts scraping over hot sand. "I assume Eliza told you about Mr. Dodd." She raised a hand, shielding her face from the sun and darkening her eyes to deep lavender. Soothing, entrancing lavender.

"He hasn't done anything except stare at me and make me uncomfortable," she continued. "Let's hope his hunt for gold keeps him otherwise occupied."

"Indeed."

"But I thank you for your concern, Doctor."

She was so close he could smell the lye soap from washing clothes and her own sweet scent that reminded him of coconut. He cleared his throat, trying to clear his head as well.

"I do see that perhaps my concern for your safety has been exaggerated." He pointed toward the pistol stuffed in her belt. "I've never seen a lady draw a weapon so quickly. Where did the daughter of a shipwright learn such a skill?"

Angeline couldn't tell James that she'd learned how to load and shoot a pistol the hard way. That she'd had to defend herself against the worst possible monster. After that, it had been a matter of survival. "Oh, here and there." She offered him a coy smile, hoping he'd let the topic drop. Stowy jumped onto a rock at the edge of the lake and began swatting at fish swimming beneath the water.

"I also understand you had a disturbing vision," the doctor said, drawing her gaze back to him.

Those eyes, such a magnificent shade of bronze, exuded a strength equal to the metal itself. Somehow that made her feel safe in his presence. That and the way thick muscles in his chest flexed beneath his gray shirt. Power and strength that could subdue any villain. Power and strength she could have used three years ago. Power and strength coupled with the concern pouring from his expression that could have saved her a lifetime of misery.

Her pulse raced. She forced it to slow. James was not who he seemed. She must remember that.

"The vision, Miss Angeline?" He lowered his gaze to hers and stared at her quizzically.

"Yes. Forgive me. I did see something. But it was dark and late and I was very tired."

"Would it surprise you to know that I, too, saw a vision? That morning a week ago when I ran out on my sermon."

So that would explain his odd behavior. At the time she'd thought he'd become ill. "I couldn't imagine what had gone wrong."

"You haven't been back to church since. I feared I frightened you away." A burst of wind tossed a strand of his wheat-colored hair into his face. She longed to reach up and ease it aside.

"I told you I'm not much for religion." She lowered her gaze and saw the pink scar on her arm. Horrified, she unrolled her sleeves to cover it before James noticed. She didn't need any more questions she couldn't answer without lying.

But he must have seen it for he rubbed his own scar—the one on his cheek that angled down the side of his mouth like an oversized dimple. "Do say you'll come back to church. I promise not to become a babbling fool again."

How could she resist such a boyish smile? "I will make an attempt." She straightened the cuffs of her sleeves, wanting to know more about this man. Wanting to know why he was so different from the man she'd met a year ago. "May I ask what you saw in *your* vision?"

James turned and stepped toward the river. The mad rush of water surrounded them, drowning out the ever present buzz of the jungle. Sorrow darkened his eyes and formed tiny lines at the edges. Finally he answered, "It was a young corporal who died on my operating table during the war."

Angeline's stomach tightened. She had seen someone from her past as well. And so had Eliza. "From the ship before we even arrived, Eliza saw her dead husband standing on shore."

James faced her. "And Blake has seen someone too."

"Perhaps it is just the strain of moving to a different country, eating unfamiliar food, starting a new colony." Angeline would not allow for any other possibility. She couldn't. New Hope was her last chance at a normal life.

A cloud swallowed up the sun. "Being the preacher, I feel responsible for the emotional wellbeing of the townspeople. And these odd visions reek of something amiss in the spiritual realm."

Angeline stifled her laughter. Not at the man himself. No, James was nothing to laugh at. He was all man and strength and wisdom. It was his insistence on being a spiritual leader that gave her pause. She stared into those bronze eyes, so clear now. Yet only a year ago, those same eyes had stared at her, glazed and murky, as she'd led him upstairs to her room.

Taking a step back from him, she fingered the ring dangling on a chain around her neck—her father's ring. The only man she had ever trusted.

If James had truly changed and become a godly man, he wouldn't want to associate with the likes of her.

And if he hadn't, Angeline had had enough of lying, hypocritical men to last a lifetime.

CHAPTER 21

A rather obtuse insect of epic proportions and sporting a pair of orange wings had decided he loved Magnolia more than any creature in the jungle. He'd been following her for hours, buzzing about her face, trying to get her attention, looking for a place to land where he could shower her with his affections which, no doubt, would be in the form of some vile bug ooze. Which, of course, she couldn't possibly allow. So, she'd been swatting at him all day, and trying to stab him with the tip of her parasol, until her arms ached and her frustration was about to burst.

Hayden had reverted into being a toad again. For two days he'd barely said the same number of words to her. He'd been polite. He had provided for her. Mercy me, he'd even carried her valise, but whenever she tried to engage him in conversation, he replied with nonsensical grunts and groans. Did all men revert to barbarians when living in the wild?

She swung her closed parasol at the fawning bug again just as Hayden, marching in front of her, shoved aside a large leaf and released it. The green monster descended on her as if the sky had changed from blue to jade and was crashing to earth. It slapped her face and swaddled her in suffocating foliage.

Sputtering, she coughed and thrust it away, her insides seething. "How kind of you."

He grunted.

The only reason she could find for his rude behavior was that he'd seen her horrifying reflection in the mirror and was completely repulsed. Yet he'd claimed she looked the same. Perhaps he was lying, though she couldn't think of a single reason for that. Fine, if he wanted to be so shallow as to not even talk to her because of her appearance, then she didn't want to talk to him either. Oh, mercy me, was she truly old and ugly? She hadn't looked in the mirror since that night. Didn't want to see. Didn't want to know. She hoped it was just a bad dream—a delusion her mind had conjured from what that demented, shriveled-up woman had said. Surely that was it. But if so, what was wrong with Hayden? Magnolia knew she wasn't useful around camp. She couldn't even light a fire or catch a fish or build a shelter. She was worthless. As usual. And now, without her beauty, what good was she? That had to be the reason for his disdain. He couldn't still be angry about the money. After all, he'd lied to her as well! If not for him, she'd be on a ship right now enjoying the fresh ocean breezes, not being smothered by air as thick as syrup.

Wiping perspiration from her neck, she gazed up at the canopy, a lattice of vines and branches and leaves over which skittered hundreds of birds, monkeys, and crawly things that she preferred would stay above. A swarm of white butterflies flitted among the foliage like a band of tiny angels sent to keep watch on God's creation. She wished that were so, for at least then someone would know how miserable she was.

Hayden tromped in front of her, his hair tied behind him. The sound of his boots crunching on dry leaves rose in a steady, soothing cadence. His damp shirt clung to muscles that rippled across his shoulder and down his back with each graceful move. Unfortunately, being right behind him, Magnolia could hardly avoid such an alluring sight—alluring and hypnotizing and warming down to her toes. She realized she felt safe with this man—a man who was nothing at all like her Samuel. Samuel, who always dressed in the latest fashion from the heels of his leather Congress shoes to the top of his silk hat. His short-cropped hair was never out of place, his face always stubble-free, his movements so refined they could be considered dandyish.

Completely opposite from the wolfish gait of the man before her.

She drew in a breath of sweet jungle air, remembering Samuel's impeccable manners and how he always smelled of cedar oil and cigars.

The pesky bug swooped down upon her again. She shrieked.

In a move so quick she had no time to react, Hayden spun around, gun in hand, cocked it, and fired.

Magnolia squeezed her eyes shut, her one thought being that perhaps she'd been premature in her feelings that she was safe with this man.

Shock buzzed through her as the smell of gunpowder stung her nose. No pain seared her body. Her head felt intact. Her heart still beat. Slowly, she opened her eyes to see Hayden shoving the gun into his belt. He gave a wink before he continued onward.

"You"—she struggled to find a voice but it felt as if it had been shot clean through—"could have killed me."

"I didn't."

"Why did you do that?" She stumbled after him, glancing around for the bug that, no doubt, had been blown to pieces.

"I was tired of hearing you moan and groan every few minutes."

"Well, mercy me, I'm sorry to have disturbed you, but since you make me keep up with your impossible pace and won't give me a moment's rest to catch my breath or take a drink, you are bound to hear a little moaning from time to time." She swept a large vine aside with her parasol, shrinking back at the colorful lizard scampering up it. "I'm doing the best any lady could do under the circumstances."

He continued onward. "Perhaps if you remove that cage you wear under your skirts, your gown won't scrape against the branches as much."

Ugh. She wanted to swat him with her parasol. Instead, she burst into tears. "And you won't even speak to—" She barreled into him, realizing he'd stopped.

His hand was raised; his dark brows dipped. Only then did she notice the normal hum of the jungle had quieted, replaced by a crackling sound. It sizzled all around them yet seemed to come from nowhere. "What—?" Hayden laid a finger on her lips, silencing her. His body stiffened. He scanned the tangle of green. His gaze froze while his chest rose and fell like a ship in stormy seas. "Did you see that?" he whispered.

"No. What?"

"Not what, who," he mumbled before rubbing his eyes and starting forward again, his steps cautious. After a few minutes the crackling ceased and the thrum of the jungle returned. Tension spilled from Magnolia's shoulders. The last time she'd heard that sound, Martin—the fiend who'd destroyed her life—had appeared out of nowhere. And she was in no mood to deal with him.

Within an hour, the sound of rushing water drew them to a stream cutting through a narrow gorge. Steep, moss-covered cliffs rose on two sides where cascades of water plunged some sixty feet over bare rocks, splashing into deep pools at the base. With no more than a "stay here," Hayden went off in search of fruit, leaving Magnolia to stare at the refreshing pond. She longed to disrobe and plunge beneath its swirling waters, but Hayden could return at any moment. Instead, she settled for removing her stockings and shoes and dipping her feet in the cool liquid. The reflection of her legs bounced off the water in squiggly lines and a frightening idea occurred to her. If she hung her head over the water, what would her face look like now? Had she simply been delirious with exhaustion two nights ago? After one quick glance over her shoulder, she leaned over the calm pool.

Hayden plucked a ripe mango and scanned the tree looking for another one, wondering if he'd lost his mind. Perhaps the assault of insects, the stifling heat, and the overwhelming temptation of Magnolia had finally sizzled away all his reason. Or at least his eyesight. For he was sure he had seen old Mr. Carson sauntering through the jungle as if he were walking down East Plume Street in Norfolk. But of course, that couldn't be. Unless the man had immigrated to Brazil, which would be totally out of character for the timid, weak-minded goosewit. Besides, what would he be doing alone in the middle of the jungle?

Shoving the impossibility aside, Hayden spotted a banana tree and headed in that direction, thankful for a moment's reprieve from

Magnolia. Not because she annoyed him. Quite the opposite, in fact. Though he'd maintained a rapid stride the past two days, she'd kept pace with him, offering nary a complaint. An occasional moan and hapless sigh, yes, but no complaint. At night, she'd helped gather firewood and ate what he provided without a single grumble. Not one—even though he knew her feet ached and she was hot and weary and covered in bug bites. Even though he was returning her to an abusive father and keeping her from a fiancé she loved. He found her resilience admirable, her forgiveness commendable, her company, dare he admit, pleasurable.

In fact, he felt a strange urge to provide for her, to protect her, if only to draw an adoring look from those sapphire eyes. But that would make him like all the other men who fawned at her feet, begging for one favorable glance, one cherished kiss. And he hated himself for it. He wouldn't allow himself the indignity. Not the great confidence man, Hayden Gale. So, what else could he do but try to ignore her as best he could? A task made all the more difficult when, even covered in filth and bug bites, she glowed like a lantern on a dark night. No wonder insects surrounded her. If Hayden could fly, he'd hover around her too, just for the chance to land on those luscious lips.

Slapping a mosquito on his arm, he reached for a bunch of bananas when sizzling filled the air. A chill iced down his spine. He scanned the jungle. Nothing out of the ordinary. Snapping off the bananas, he headed back to the waterfall, determined to ignore the puzzling sound. Just his imagination. Or perhaps merely a swarm of insects in the canopy. Though the sound didn't come from above. He batted aside a leaf and froze.

Mr. Carson sat on a tree stump.

Hayden closed his eyes and drew a deep breath. When he opened them Mr. Carson was staring at him inquisitively.

"You aren't real," Hayden said.

The man flinched then glanced over his body. "I assure you, sir, I am as real as you."

"What are you doing here, Mr. Carson? Did you move to Brazil?"

"Brazil?" He glanced over the jungle as if seeing it for the first time. "What does it matter where I am, Mr. Grenville, or whatever your name is?" Steel eyes speared Hayden.

He swallowed and began to circle the man, remembering the vision of Katherine that had seemed so real in the temple. But she hadn't been there. And neither was this man here now.

"You sold me a shipyard that wasn't yours to sell." Mr. Carson released a heavy sigh, following Hayden with his eyes. "Turns out it belonged to a shipwright named Paine. But you knew that, didn't you?"

Hayden stopped a few yards from the man, resisting the temptation to pounce on him to see if he was flesh and bone. "What do you want? If it's your money back, I don't have it."

The man's gaze grew distant, his face folding in sorrow as if he remembered something dreadful. "I trusted you."

For being only a vision, Mr. Carson sure was causing a rush of guilt to burn in Hayden's throat.

"I lost everything. My wife left me. Took the children and went back to her father's farm."

Hayden had no words to say. What could he say? Mr. Carson was a gentle man with a limited mind—the perfect target. He'd wanted to be a shipwright. And Hayden had found an empty shipyard that had recently been sold to another man. It had been easy to forge the necessary papers.

"I killed a man," Mr. Carson said. "Mr. Paine, in fact. When he came to claim his property." He swallowed and looked down. "I thought he was trying to steal from me. We fought. I pushed him." He thumbed a tear from beneath his eye. "I didn't mean to shove him so hard. He fell out a window to his death."

Hayden's heart crumpled like old vellum—old and stained with guilt. The vision of Katherine rose fresh in his mind as well as the other dozen or so people he'd cheated. And for the first time in his life, he felt like sinking into the mud beneath his feet—deserved to sink into the mud and be buried like the scoundrel he was.

"I'm sorry." The words echoed hollow and heavy in the humid air. "I'm truly sorry."

Mr. Carson only stared at him, his eyes now blank and lifeless.

A woman's shriek drew Hayden's gaze over his shoulder. *Magnolia!* When he looked back, Mr. Carson was gone. Shaking the vision from his mind, Hayden wheeled about and dashed through the jungle, plowing a trail of scattered leaves and branches. He found her sitting near the creek, face in her hands, sobbing and muttering something about being grotesque and repugnant. His anger sparked. But her wails continued, long and painful. This was no act. Dropping beside her, Hayden took her hands. They trembled just like his. Something horrible was happening to them both, and the sooner they got out of this jungle, the better.

◦◦◦✧◦◦◦

Magnolia studied Hayden as he scoured the jungle for wood. She rubbed the aches from her stockinged feet, proof that they'd walked much longer today than usual. No doubt Hayden wished to get back to New Hope as soon as possible and rid himself of her. Though she'd really been trying to be less whiny and annoying and not cry all the time. But when she'd seen her aged face in the pond earlier that day, she'd been unable to stop the tears.

Of course Hayden had pretended not to be annoyed, had tried to console her, but she could see the frustration on his face. Or had it been fear? Regardless, since then he'd seemed preoccupied and had hardly spoken a word to her. As usual.

And she was still old and ugly. Was this to be her curse? Never to see her reflection as it truly was? Only to see how she would look in sixty years or longer? Never to see if she had a hair out of place or a smudge on her cheek. Never to see when she truly aged.

What had the old woman said? That Magnolia's reflection was a picture of her insides. But how could her insides be *that* ugly? She was a nice person, wasn't she? Even after Hayden had dragged her back into the jungle, she'd tried hard not to complain. She'd even thanked him for taking care of her. Why, she hadn't even mentioned the blisters on her feet! Perhaps if she tried even harder to be kind, to think of others, then that gruesome reflection would disappear. Oh, how she wanted it to disappear.

509

Hayden tossed another log into the fire, took a seat, and picked up the chunk of wood he'd been whittling. Strands of dark hair hung over his jaw and jerked with each strike of his knife. Magnolia reached for another piece of turtle meat and plopped it into her mouth. "Um." She hoped to draw those magnificent jungle-green eyes to hers, but he remained focused on his wood. She swallowed the turtle. It was actually quite delicious. At first she'd been hesitant to try it, but after all the effort Hayden put forth—not to mention skill—to catch the thing and then break the shell and roast the meat, it would have been rude to refuse. Besides, she was so weary of fruit.

As darkness fell, shadows crept out from the jungle like unholy specters. Frogs began to croak. Crickets chirped. Somewhere in the distance an animal howled. She hugged herself, longing for conversation, companionship, anything to get her mind off the dangers surrounding them. As well as the ones she'd face when they returned to camp.

"You must think me mad," she said, "crying like a fool by the pond."

"No. I think you have an unnatural obsession with your appearance that is making you see things."

The sentence contained more words than he'd spoken to her in three days. She was so thankful to hear his voice, she didn't even mind the insult. Well, not entirely. It *was* quite loutish of him to say. Nevertheless, she'd just promised herself to be kinder to others and kinder she would be. As a start, she would forgive his affront. There. That was easy. Yet as she watched him stare at the flames and sensed a deep sorrow cloaking him, her chest suddenly felt heavy. She tried to force herself to not care, to still be angry at his deception, but found the task fruitless. Something bad had happened to Hayden, aside from his being an orphan and having to struggle to survive. And it had to do with this Mr. Godard. She wanted to know. And baffling as it was, she wanted to take his pain away.

"Is there something bothering you, Hayden? Do you wish to talk about it? Perhaps it will make you feel better. My mother always said that keeping problems to yourself makes you old before your time."

The flicker of surprise in his green eyes quickly faded. At least he looked up at her. "It's nothing," he said, returning to his work.

Oh, mercy me, this wasn't going well. "It's me, isn't it? My whining?" Though she'd been so well behaved, she doubted that was the case.

"Not everything is about you, Princess."

Magnolia blew out a sigh. She took another bite of turtle, desperate to draw out Hayden's sad tale, but not wanting to anger him or, worse, push him away. Perhaps a change of topic. Her thoughts drifted to the old woman in the church, the way she had gazed at the figure of Jesus with such love, such complete devotion, as if that immovable sculpture actually loved her in return. Was it possible to love and be loved by a God she couldn't see or hear?

"Do you believe in God?" she asked.

"Not sure." He stomped his boot on a spider crawling in front of him as a low growl rumbled through the trees. Drawing his pistol, he laid it beside him on a rock.

"Do you suppose God cares what we do? I mean, do you think He watches us?"

Hayden shrugged. "If He exists, I'm sure He has better things to do than look after us."

Though Magnolia hadn't thought much about God, Hayden's statement saddened her. "Our reverend back home said that God loves all of us, that He is always with us to help us."

Hayden chuckled. "If your reverend is anything like Parson Bailey, I wouldn't put too much credence on his words."

"Well of course he isn't! He doesn't steal from people." Magnolia bit her lip as her stomach churned with frustration. She reached for the flask sitting on the ground between them and tipped it to her lips. Hayden only allowed her a few sips each night and she hated to use them up so early, but the man was beyond infuriating. He eyed her, one brow raised. She corked it and set it down.

"When will we arrive in New Hope?"

He returned to his whittling. "If we get an early start, we should be there tomorrow evening."

Magnolia's insides shriveled. Then she would have to face her father's wrath. And her time alone with Hayden would come to an end.

511

"When will you leave to search for Mr. Godard?"

"Soon."

"You never told me exactly what he did to you."

"You ask too many questions."

"Perhaps it's because I care, you big oaf." She huffed. "You're always telling me I'm self-centered and now that I'm asking questions, I'm too meddlesome."

She received the first smile from him in days.

Prompting her to ask one more question. "How long will you be gone?"

His smile faded. "If I had been able to purchase a guide, I wouldn't be gone long at all, but as it is, it could be weeks." He scraped his knife over wood, flinging shavings into the air.

"I suppose you blame *me* for that."

"Do you see someone else here who robbed me of money that was my due?" He glanced around.

She jumped to her feet, instantly regretting the movement for the pain in her tired legs. "Of all the nerve. Your lie was far larger than mine. Besides, at least you got something out of the deal. All I'm getting are blisters and bug bites."

He grinned. "And a trip to Rio de Janeiro like I promised."

"Oooh." She fisted her hands, regretting that she'd ever felt sorry for the rogue or wanted to ease his pain. "I cannot wait to be rid of you. Bedeviled, odious toad!"

"Ah, but according to the story, us toads are only princes in disguise." His tone taunted her.

"Even if I could chop off your head in the morning, you'd never turn into a prince."

"Just a headless toad." He dug his knife into the wood. "And then you'd be lost and all alone in the jungle."

"Quit patronizing me."

"Quit behaving like a minx." His eyes glinted with amusement.

Something moved behind Hayden. The fire crackled. Leaves fluttered. A man materialized from the jungle, tipped his hat at Magnolia, then dashed away. "Martin!" Clutching her skirts she darted after him, ignoring Hayden's call to stop. Smacking leaves and vines aside, she caught sight of his suit up ahead, a gray mist floating through the darkness. "Come back here this minute!" The charlatan was obviously following her around Brazil. To taunt her, no doubt—to flaunt the fact that he'd ruined her and her family. Ruined Magnolia's prospects and chained her to a debt she could never repay.

He stopped and glanced over his shoulder. A shimmer of moonlight caught his smile. She knew that devious grin anywhere. He took off in a sprint. She tore after him. What she would do with him when she caught him, she had no idea. Kick him, for one thing, give him a tongue lashing for another. Tie him to a tree and leave him to rot would be her preference.

She raced ahead, leaves and branches assaulting her as she went. Dashing into a clearing, she scanned the shadows, her chest heaving. Martin was nowhere in sight.

A low growl stiffened the hairs on her arms. She slowly turned around.

A pair of golden eyes gleamed hungrily from within the shadows. The creature stepped toward her, fangs bared.

CHAPTER 22

James eased aside the rotted doors of the ancient temple, trying to shrug off the morbid foreboding that had smothered him before they'd even spotted the dilapidated structure. What made the feeling worse was that Eliza had insisted on joining the expedition. Her smile as she passed him now and entered the courtyard did nothing to assuage his unease. He hadn't wanted any of the women to witness the horror of this place. He hadn't wanted them to feel the terror and grief of the hundreds, perhaps thousands, who had been tortured to death within its walls; but once Eliza got something in her mind, it took a battalion to defeat that will of hers. Not even her husband, Blake, seemed able to control her. And he was the leader of the entire colony!

"Besides," she had said, "perhaps Mr. Graves is injured and is in need of medical attention." Though she hadn't meant it, the statement stabbed James like a knife. She was right. His fear of blood made his doctoring skills useless.

Blake went in behind her, then Dodd, running a hand through his mop of light hair, and finally Mr. Lewis, the old carpenter, whose wary eyes shifted back and forth over the scene. Begging off with an excuse of illness, Thiago had remained at New Hope. But James knew it was fear that kept the Brazilian guide away. Even Eliza seemed out of breath as she gazed at the courtyard: the ancient roasting pit, the obelisks carved with the silent screams of victims. "This place." She lifted a hand to her mouth. "I can *feel* the evil."

"Don't say I didn't warn you." Blake circled an arm around her waist as James shifted his own shoulders against an uncontrollable shudder.

He'd seen something on the way there, a vision perhaps, a memory maybe, or more likely an invention of his overheated mind: his father pacing through the jungle, head bent over a Bible clutched in his hands, muttering to himself as he'd always done every Sunday before giving his sermons. The sight tore open a wound in James's heart he'd thought long since healed. Then his father was gone, like a puff of smoke dissipated by the wind. Just like he had vanished from James's life that fateful night over a year ago.

The ground shook, jerking him to the present and shifting pebbles over the hard earth. Rocks tumbled off the temple's roof and peppered the cracked stairs like hail. An eerie *caw caw* lifted their gazes to a massive black bird soaring overhead.

Mr. Lewis plucked a flask from within his vest and took a sip, his ruddy face paling. James had wanted to bring Moses—sturdy, dependable, godly Moses—just in case they ran into trouble, but the poor man's eyes had grown so wide at the mention of the temple James hadn't the heart to insist. So, they were stuck with Lewis and of course Mr. Dodd, who had jumped at the chance, greed sparkling in his blue eyes. Which meant he hadn't found his pirate's gold yet. If he had, he'd be long gone to Rio and back to the States.

James hoisted the knapsack over his shoulder. "Let's find Graves, give him these supplies, and get out of here."

The group headed for the building and mounted the chipped, moss-laden steps.

Stopping at the top, Blake faced Eliza. "There's no need for you to go any farther, dear. If Graves is hurt, I'll bring him to you."

"Quit fussing over me, I'll be all right." Carrying her medical bag in one hand, she squeezed her husband's arm with the other and gave him one of her knowing smiles. "If he's too badly hurt, you won't be able to move him."

With a sigh of frustration, Blake took her hand in his and led the group into the inner sanctuary. Mr. Lewis nursed his flask of liquor, jumping at every shadow while Dodd dashed about excitedly, examining the ancient writing on the walls, peering beneath bits of broken furniture and pottery, even inspecting the steaming spring. James, however, made a beeline toward the back where a flaming fire kept guard over the entrance to the tunnels. The tended fire, along with the flickering light from deep within the tunnel, gave him hope that Mr. Graves was still alive.

"Mr. Graves!" James's shout echoed over the walls, hollow and metallic as if it weren't human.

Plucking one of the unlit torches from a pile on the floor, Blake dipped it in the fire and swept the flame over the dark opening. "Graves!"

A stench reminiscent of spoiled eggs wafted from the hole. Eliza covered her nose.

"Gold!" Dodd exclaimed as he climbed the stone altar and pointed to a large moon and stars embedded in the wall. "They are made of gold! Why didn't you tell me there was gold here?" Flames flickered excitement in his eyes.

"They aren't yours," James said. "Leave them be."

"Whose are they, then? No one owns this place." Plucking out a knife, Dodd dug around one of the stars, scattering dirt onto the altar. "I'm staking my claim first. You are my witnesses."

A low rumble sounded, much like a distant train. The ground shook. Dust showered them from above. Screeches preceded flapping as a group of bats took flight.

Eliza gasped and gripped her husband's arm.

Dodd stopped digging and leapt from the altar.

"Perhaps someone or something has already staked a claim, Dodd," Blake teased.

"I'm going down." James gathered a torch and lit it in the flames.

"I'll stay here and guard." Mr. Lewis clung to his flask as if it and it alone could save him from whatever lurked in the tunnels.

Blake nodded, took his wife's hand, and followed James into the tunnel, Dodd on their heels.

Jagged rock formed the walls of the oval passageway, twisting the torch's glow into angular patches of light and dark. Foreign letters scribbled atop ancient paintings passed in James's vision: pictures of people in various poses of work and play, some so faded he could barely make them out. Figures hunting, fishing, playing, and dancing leapt out at him as his flame brushed over the moist walls. Most likely etched there by the cannibals who built the temple long ago. Eliza ran her hands over the scribblings as they went along. "They're beautiful."

As if in defiance of her words, the pictures suddenly became gruesome: men with knives raised over animals, blood dripping from their blades, others stabbing victims laid out on slabs, fires blazing, faces twisted in agony. But what drew James's attention were the paintings of enormous winged beings carrying staffs with lightning bolts firing from their tips. He tripped over something and stumbled forward, his torch revealing piles of rock and dirt that, no doubt, marked Grave's progress.

Hot waves as thick as boiling molasses rolled up from below, dousing them in sweltering heat. Eliza visibly struggled to breathe, but still refused her husband's suggestion to go back.

Around a corner, a lit torch hanging on the wall revealed a set of stairs leading downward—downward into the pit of hell, it seemed. Rocks and dirt littered each step, and James braced against the walls to keep from slipping. Behind them, Dodd moaned his displeasure, mumbling something about wishing he'd stayed with the gold.

At the bottom of the stairs, they found another turn, another torch, and ground that angled ever more sharply down into the bowels of the earth. An odor akin to rancid meat curled around them.

The ground trembled again. A low rumble that was more like an agonized groan rolled through the small tunnel. James's spine stiffened. Pebbles flew at them from all around. Ducking, Blake covered Eliza with his body. A small rock struck James's neck and tumbled down his back. He shrugged off the pain and pressed onward.

"That's enough. I'm taking you back." Blake tugged on his wife, ignoring her complaints, pushing past Dodd, and starting upward when James's torch revealed a jagged opening in the tunnel wall. "Here! Over here!" he called.

Shoving the flame first, James stepped through the hole, hearing Blake retrace his steps behind him. At least ten torches flamed from hooks on the walls of a large cave, their flickering light transforming the stalactites hanging from the ceiling into shadowy fangs. Two circular alcoves were hewn out of solid rock on the wall to their left. Within each one, a giant pole, made from some type of metal, ran from ceiling to floor where massive iron shackles lay broken. Above the alcoves, something was written in what appeared to be Latin over a single Hebrew word.

Blake squeezed in behind him, followed by Eliza and Dodd.

"By all that is holy. . ." James finally said. "What is this place? And why is it so hot?" Sweat sucked his shirt to his skin.

"I don't think holy has anything to do with it," Eliza remarked, her voice unusually timid.

Scuffling sounds drew their gazes to a small opening on their left. Blake and James pulled their pistols and leveled them at the spot just as Mr. Graves emerged. Or at least James thought it was the crazy politician.

He gave them a cursory glance before carrying the large rock he was holding across the room and dropping it onto a pile with a loud *thunk*! Spinning to face them, he withdrew a soiled handkerchief and wiped his face, managing to smear the black smudges into streaks. Stripped down to a once-white shirt that was now blotched in mud and a pair of torn trousers, and with his black hair matted to his head and his cultured goatee growing like wild brush, he resembled nothing of the polished, sophisticated senator's son from Maryland.

James almost felt sorry for him. Would have felt sorry for him if he wasn't burning alive and enduring the worst stench of his life. He shoved his pistol into his belt and coughed, trying to expel the fumes from his lungs.

"I knew it was you," Graves said, his tone hurried and annoyed. "Knew you were here. They are agitated because you are here."

Lowering his weapon, Blake swiped a sleeve over his forehead. "Blast it, what are you talking about, Graves?"

But Graves didn't seem to hear the colonel. Instead, his dark, bloodshot eyes skittered over them as if trying to solve a puzzle. "But there are only three. There cannot be six. Six would ruin it."

Grabbing the knapsack, Eliza started toward the madman. "When was the last time you ate, Mr. Graves? Or got any sleep?"

Blake leapt in front of his wife and snagged the satchel from her hands.

She peered around him. "Are you injured, Mr. Graves? Give him some water, Blake, please."

"Would ruin what?" Dodd fingered his pointed chin, fixated on what Graves had said earlier. "You aren't talking about gold, are you?"

"Everything. Why the six would ruin everything, my friend! That's what they told me."

Friend? When had Graves ever called anyone *friend?* Or been this excited about anything? James handed his canteen to Graves. "And just who are *they?*" he asked.

"The rulers of course. The glorious ones. I'm helping them." Graves scratched the top of his head, making his filthy hair stand on end. Grabbing the canteen, he glanced to where he'd entered the room as if someone were waiting for him below.

"Helping them do what?" James fingered the handle of his pistol.

"They call to me, you know. They need me." He tipped the canteen to his mouth. Water dribbled trails of gray mud across his beard before splattering on his shirt. "There is power here. Power for the taking."

Dodd's brows shot up. "Do they have any more gold like I saw above in the temple?"

"Better than gold, my friend. Better than gold."

Dodd frowned as if there was no such thing.

Moving to the first alcove, James knelt to examine the broken irons lying at the bottom of the pole. "Who was locked up here?"

"They were, of course." Graves huffed his impatience.

"We brought you some food." Eliza elbowed Blake.

Reaching in the knapsack he pulled out an orange and handed it to Graves.

"You really should come back to New Hope," Eliza said. "It isn't safe here, and your hands. . ." She pointed at the cuts and scrapes all over his once soft, uncallused hands. "I need to look at those."

"No time. No time." Refusing the orange, Graves dropped the canteen to the ground and darted back the way he'd come, disappearing inside the hole.

Dabbing the sweat from her neck, Eliza gazed after him. "We can't leave him. He'll die here alone."

"What do you suggest we do with him?" Blake shook his head. "I have nowhere to restrain him."

"He's right." James dropped the irons, stood, and gazed curiously up the long pole. "We aren't equipped to care for the insane. We can't even lock up criminals."

"I agree." Dodd opened his watch and looked at the time as if he had an appointment. "Leave him here. He's harmless."

Blake gave Eliza a reassuring smile. "I promise we will bring him food and water every week. At least until we can provide a safe place to keep him while his mind recovers."

Graves returned with another rock and tossed it onto the pile, slapping his hands together.

"These writings." James pointed above the alcoves. "Rather curious. A Latin phrase above Hebrew. This one says "Deception and"—he gestured toward the other. "That one Delusion."

"You know what they say?" Graves's voice quivered with excitement. Grabbing a torch, he scrambled across the cave, leaping over rocks and stalagmites with the expertise of a bobcat through a field of thorns. Deep into the shadows, his light revealed a shelf carved out of the rock. He took something from it and darted back, hefting a thick leather-bound book at James. Odd thing for cannibals to have, James thought. Hebrew lettering lined the left side of the cover while a crescent moon and cluster of stars were engraved on the right.

"What does it say?" Mr. Graves pointed to the words as he leapt up and down with the giddiness of a child getting a gift. "What does it say?"

James ran his hand over the ancient Hebrew. "It says, *The Judgment of the Four*."

CHAPTER 23

Magnolia's blood turned to ice. She couldn't breathe. She couldn't move. She couldn't think. The wolf's golden eyes locked on her, no doubt assessing her ability to resist her tastiness as a meal. The beast growled again, malevolence dripping from rows of sharp fangs. And Magnolia knew it was all over. She would die here, her flesh ripped apart and devoured by this monster. Foolish, foolish girl. Why hadn't she stayed with Hayden by the fire?

She flashed to her parents. Would they mourn her? Would Hayden?

Ever so slowly, she retreated a step. The wolf drew back on his haunches. Magnolia's heart stopped. She closed her eyes and prayed, *God if You're there, help!*

Footsteps thundered. Leaves crackled. The wolf roared. Magnolia dropped to the ground and covered her head with her arms. She sensed the wolf leaping, felt his hot breath on her skin, his ravenous spittle on her hair. Then another growl shook the ground. This one human. Someone shoved her back. She landed in a tangle of shrubs and vines and opened her eyes. A shadow, a man—no, Hayden—had the wolf in a stranglehold, the fiend's barbed teeth just inches from his neck.

Untangling herself from the vines, Magnolia leapt to her feet. Hayden and the wolf tumbled over dry leaves. Moonlight glinted off the knife in Hayden's hand as he strained to keep the wolf's fangs at bay.

"Oh, God, no. God, please no." Dropping to her knees, Magnolia groped for a sharp stick, a rock, anything to use against the ferocious animal.

Man and beast fought, growling, tumbling, rolling over the ground like storm clouds on the horizon. Her fingers clamped around a rock. The wolf was on top of Hayden again. Magnolia could smell its foul breath, his animal smell, raw and primitive. She also smelled blood. But whose? Hayden's heavy breath filled the air. Along with his agonizing moans and grunts as muscles strained to exhaustion. She hoisted the rock, aimed for the wolf, but he twisted and dug his fangs into Hayden's arm.

Hayden roared in agony. Magnolia lunged for the beast and slammed the rock at his head. Yelping, the wolf released his hold. Golden malevolent eyes swung her way. Magnolia's blood turned to ice. She tried to scoot back over the ground. He leapt for her. His razor-sharp teeth filled her vision. But then he let out a tormented shriek and fell to the ground at her feet. Hayden's knife stuck in his side. With a howl of his own that was almost beastlike, Hayden pulled it out. The wolf gave a painful wail and limped away. Within moments, the jungle swallowed him up as if he'd never been there.

Dropping to his knees, Hayden gripped his arm. His breath exploded into the humid night, his knife pointed at the place the wolf disappeared. Magnolia crawled toward him, every inch of her trembling. He turned and gathered her close, pressed her tightly against him, his muscles still twitching from battle. No words were said, just their heaving breath mingling in the air between them, their hearts pounding against each other's through flesh and bone, their minds reeling in shock. Finally Hayden rubbed Magnolia's back and kissed her forehead. The metallic smell of blood jarred her senses.

"He bit you!" She backed away, trying to see his arm in the darkness. But she didn't need to see. She could hear the blood dripping onto the dry leaves. *Plop, plop, plop.*

"Just a scratch." Hayden's chuckle sounded weak.

"Let's get back to camp." She stood, forced strength into her wobbling legs, and tugged on his good arm. Sheathing his knife, Hayden rose, wrapped an arm around her, and started through the greenery. "You're still trembling," he said.

"I don't think I'll ever stop."

Back by the fire, she grabbed the canteen and an old petticoat and sat beside Hayden, preparing herself for the sight that would meet her eyes, trying to settle her nerves. Blood seeped between his fingers and trickled onto the ground below. But his eyes were on her, an intensity in their green depths she'd not seen before. Despite her fear, his gaze sent a flutter through her heart. Without asking permission, she grabbed the knife from his belt, ignoring the wolf's blood splattered over the blade, and ripped her petticoat into thick strips. Then turning toward him, she tore his sleeve from shoulder to wrist and pried back the torn fabric.

Blood dribbled down biceps bulging and bunching from exertion.

Bracing herself, she peeled his hand from the wound. Punctures littered his skin like bubbling wells. His flesh hung open, revealing muscle and bone. Magnolia gasped, groaned, looked away. Her head swam.

"That bad, huh?"

"No. . .yes. . ." She pressed a cloth over the wounds, wondering how he could even talk, let alone joke, with the pain he must be enduring. "But you'll need stitches." Stitches she had no idea how to apply. Though she'd seen Eliza stitch wounds a dozen times, she'd never done them herself. She drew a deep breath and faced him again. She had no choice. They were at least a day or more from New Hope and she couldn't very well leave Hayden's flesh hanging open to the insects and filth of the jungle.

Gathering her strength, she poured water on a cloth and wiped blood from the gashes. He winced. "Sorry, but I need to clean the injured area."

He took one glance at his arm then swerved his gaze to the jungle. "I'm suddenly glad you learned nursing from Eliza."

"Some." Her heart scrambled into her throat. "Enough." She hoped. "Here, hold this."

Hayden pressed his hand on the cloth while Magnolia retrieved the flask of rum.

"This is hardly time for a drink, Princess." His grin turned into a grimace.

"Alcohol prevents infection."

"You would waste your precious rum on me?"

She uncorked it. "Hard to believe, isn't it? Now, this will hurt."

His jaw knotted but he gave her a nod.

She poured the pinga on his wound. He didn't move. Didn't scream. But pain seared in his eyes. What had this man endured to make him so tough? "You don't have to play the valiant hero for me," she said.

"You're not impressed?"

Of course she was. More and more each day. "Does it matter what I think?" She rose and sifted through her valise, not wanting to see, by his expression, what his answer was. There. She found the tiny leather purse and pulled out the thread and needle she'd brought just in case she needed to mend her skirts. Not that she'd ever mended anything herself before, but in lieu of a lady's maid, she was sure she could figure it out.

When she returned to his side, his eyes were squeezed shut. So he wasn't as tough as he pretended. After pouring rum on both needle and thread, she sat beside him and drew a deep breath. "This will hurt." Her hand trembled. Doubts flooded her. Who did she think she was? She couldn't do this. Other than her mother's failed attempts to teach her to embroider beads onto her skirts, she'd never sewn a stitch. Let alone human flesh! Her father's words pierced her confidence: *"Magnolia, God gave you one gift and one gift alone, and that is your comely appearance. So, focus on that, my dear, and forget the rest. Then you'll attract a wealthy man worthy of such beauty."*

She gulped. Firelight flickered over the needle, taunting her to continue. Somewhere in the distance, an owl hooted.

As if sensing her hesitation, Hayden opened his eyes, their intensity diving deep into hers. "Go ahead, Princess. You can do this. I trust you."

Trust me? Yet there it was in his eyes. Faith. Belief—belief in her abilities, that she was more than a face and figure. Warmth swirled through her, bolstering her courage.

He reached up and tucked a strand of her hair behind her ear. The gentle gesture nearly melted her on the spot. She dropped her gaze to the wound. *Focus, Magnolia. Focus!* "No distractions." Her nerves ignited like flint on steel.

"Then I *do* distract you."

"Be still."

"Aye, ay—"

She pierced skin and slid the thread through. His Adam's apple plummeted. A tiny moan reverberated in his chest. She hated hurting him. Making another pass, she looped flesh together. He faced her. His rapid breath spread hot waves over her cheeks.

He grabbed a lock of her hair and twirled it between his fingers. He smelled of sweat and blood and. . .Hayden. "I told you to be still."

"Touching you helps keep my mind off it."

She shifted her eyes between his. She still could not believe he'd risked his life to save her. Could not believe he'd leapt between her and a ravenous wolf.

She tugged on the thread.

Wincing, he ran the back of his fingers over her cheek. She allowed the familiarity if it helped him cope with the pain. What it did to her insides was anything but painful. She slid the needle through again. "Almost done."

The fire cracked and spit.

He fingered the lace at her collar and brushed fingers over her neck.

Magnolia's skin buzzed beneath his touch. She finished the stitch, snapped the thread, and tied it off. "I don't know how long that will hold, being common thread and all." Taking clean shreds of petticoat, she wrapped them around his arm, his muscles still rock hard even with the wounds. "But that's the best I know to do." She just prayed it wouldn't get infected. Prayed she'd done it right. Done something right when it mattered most of all.

Hayden couldn't take his eyes off Magnolia. Instead of curling up into a ball and whimpering as he would expect someone of her station to do after they'd nearly been eaten by a wolf, she'd taken charge, hadn't faltered in her task, and had stitched up a wound that would make most women swoon.

"You are a brave girl."

Shock blinked on her face. "Hardly." She washed her hands with canteen water and gathered the bloody cloths.

Placing a finger beneath her chin, he lifted her gaze to his. Those blue eyes, normally flashing like lightning, were soft, even timid. "You didn't run when you had the chance. You stayed. Risked your own life to knock the wolf off me." He eased a thumb over her chin, not wanting her to move and rob him of the look of ardor in her eyes.

"How could I do any less after you saved me?"

"Any other woman would have run. And most men I know, as well." He snorted.

She jerked her chin from his touch, one brow arching. "You always said I was crazy. Now you have your proof." She bundled the bloody cloths in her arms, inching away from him.

Yes, crazy and brave and charming and wonderful. And apparently uncomfortable beneath his complements. He flexed his arm, not showing the pain in his face. Though the wounds still throbbed, the bleeding had stopped. With his good hand, he tore off the remainder of his shirt and tossed it aside. "Guess that leaves me without a shirt." Since he'd returned the one he'd "borrowed" in Rio. When he looked back at her, she was staring at his chest.

A flood of pink crawled up her neck, and she fumbled with her skirts in an attempt to stand.

He gripped her arm, gently, yet firmly, keeping her beside him. "Thank you. For stitching me up. You did a good job."

She gave a little smile and stared into the jungle. A breeze stirred her loose curls, tossing one onto her cheek. "Why did you come after me, Hayden? You haven't spoken to me for days. I thought you hated me. Couldn't wait to be rid of me." She moved her gaze to his chest then quickly dropped it to the ground between them.

He took her hand and raised it to his lips. So soft. "I could never hate you." Before he'd even entered the clearing, he had heard the wolf's growls, knew she was in mortal danger. Yet, oddly, not a single thought of self-preservation had entered his mind. The great Hayden Gale who always put himself above others had rushed headlong into certain death to save another.

She searched his eyes, as if trying to assess his sincerity. There, the affection he'd seen moments ago returned. Was it possible that a woman like Magnolia could care for him?

"But you—but I thought—" she stuttered. "Didn't you just say, not moments before, that you blame me for not having enough money to. . .?"

But Hayden wasn't listening anymore. Her rambling faded into the background as he absorbed her with his gaze, longing to take her in his arms. Zooks, the woman could argue about anything, even their affection for each other.

". . .and when I asked you to look in the mirror, why the very sight of me caused you to run off into the jungle. And every time I've tried to stir up conversation you. . ."

He grinned, delighting in her feminine gestures and expressions while she prattled on.

"So as you can clearly see—"

His lips met hers.

CHAPTER 24

Hefting the heavy book they'd found at the temple, James trudged through the jungle back to New Hope. Behind him, Blake and Eliza discussed what to do with Mr. Graves, while behind them, Dodd and Lewis argued about the best way to extract the gold moon and stars from the temple wall. But James didn't care about the treasure. Or Graves, if he were honest. He was still trying to shake off the foreboding presence he'd felt in the tunnels. In fact, he hadn't been able to get away from that place fast enough.

A flock of blue-and-green parakeets chattered above him as a swarm of gray butterflies flitted between thick hanging vines. The melancholy *caw caw* of a toucan sounded in the distance. A lizard skittered up a tree trunk beside him then stopped to bounce up and down on all fours. James smiled, took a deep breath of the musky air, and allowed the rhythm of life to settle his nerves.

That was when the crackling started. At first soft and slick like the sifting of grain through a sieve. Despite the humidity, the hair on James's arms prickled. One glance over his shoulder told him Blake and Eliza didn't hear it or perhaps, so engrossed in conversation, didn't notice. He faced forward again and swatted a leaf aside, scanning the jungle. A flash of periwinkle blue caught his eye, a glimpse of raven hair, graying at the temples. His heart cinched. Continuing forward, he kept his gaze on the vision, for that was what he knew it was. Just a vision, a dream from his past. His mother stopped and glanced over her

528

shoulder at him, at first smiling with that I'll-always-love-you-smile a mother gave her only son, but then sorrow squeezed the life from her expression. She looked so real, James's eyes filled with tears. He shifted them away and continued onward. He wasn't going to make a fool out of himself again.

"You left me," she said as he passed her. "You went off to war." Her voice floated on the edge of sorrow.

James plodded forward, but she kept pace with him, walking through ferns and trees and vines as if she were made of nothing. Of course she was made of nothing. She was a vision. A mist. Then why did she look and sound so real?

"Don't leave me, Jimmy, not again. I died of a broken heart, you know. Died because you left me." Tears trickled from her eyes.

You're not here. You're not here. You're not here, James repeated in his head, keeping his gaze forward. *What is happening, Lord?*

"Jimmy, oh, Jimmy." She began to sob, and James could stand it no more. He stopped and stared into her swimming brown eyes. Oh, how he'd missed those loving chestnut-colored eyes. God in heaven, help him.

Then she disappeared. But not before he saw a tiny smirk lift one side of her lips. Gripping the book to his chest, James bent over, nausea welling in his stomach.

"What is it?" Eliza caught up to him.

"Have some water, Doc." The colonel handed him the canteen. "This heat can get the best of a man."

James pushed it away. "No." He straightened himself. "Let's just get back to town."

Eliza's look of concern transferred into one of understanding. "You saw something, didn't you? A vision?"

James nodded and stormed forward, ignoring further questions.

A few minutes later, they emerged from the jungle onto the path leading back to New Hope. Taking advantage of the widened trail, Blake and Eliza slipped beside James as they made their way past fields speckled with sugar cane sprouts. Finally the thatched roofs of their huts came into view. The sight brought a smile to James's lips. After the macabre gloom of the temple, their quaint settlement was like a ray of sunshine.

"Seems you have some studying to do." Blake gestured toward the book.

James ran his hand over the aged leather, faded and cracked. "Indeed. If I remember the Hebrew my father taught me."

"I was surprised when you told me it was Hebrew. I would have never recognized it," Blake said. "What baffles me is how a book written in Hebrew, an archaic language not used in centuries, ended up in Brazil. And buried beneath a pagan temple, of all places."

James sighed. "I quite agree. It doesn't make sense."

Eliza leaned forward, peering at James from Blake's other side. "How did your father know Hebrew?"

"He studied it. Wanted to understand the Old Testament better. My mother thought he was a bit overzealous." James chuckled but suddenly sobered. Was that why he'd seen a vision of her? Because the Hebrew had brought her to mind?

Blake rubbed his sore leg. "And now Graves wants you to translate it for him."

"I'll do it," James said. "But only to satisfy my own curiosity. Whoever wrote this was well educated." He'd already determined that from the few pages he'd perused.

Blake swatted a bug. "Perhaps it will give some clue about the purpose of the tunnels."

"And who or what was chained up below."

"I just wish we could help Mr. Graves," Eliza remarked as she stepped over a massive root. "And I'm still worried for Magnolia. It's been two weeks, and we've not heard from the scout we sent after her."

"Yes, I'm concerned as well." Blake raked a hand through his hair. "Yet if she ran after Hayden, he'll take good care of her."

James chuckled. "And no doubt bring her back as soon as he can. There's no love lost between those two," he said as they entered the town.

Blake halted, lifting a hand to keep Eliza back. Dodd and Lewis caught up with them and stopped.

"What is it?" James followed their gazes to the meeting shelter.

The rest of the colonists were huddled together on the dirt floor, surrounded by a band of armed men, muskets and pistols at the ready. James blinked as shock sped through him. Upon seeing them, a tall man with curly black hair sauntered their way. Jeweled pins decorating his silver-embroidered waistcoat sparkled in the sunlight as he continued toward them, sizing them up with his gaze.

Halting, he placed one hand on the hilt of a short sword hanging at his side. "I am Captain Armando Manuel Ricu of the pirate ship *Espoliar*. Now, tell me where is the gold?"

At the very least, Hayden expected a slight protest from Magnolia, a feigned indignation, perhaps even a slap when his lips descended on hers, but instead, she moaned in ecstasy and pressed her curves against him. He wrapped his good arm around her and deepened the kiss. She moaned again, ran her fingers through his hair, gripping it in bunches as her passion grew. She tasted fresh and sweet, and he grew thirsty for more of her. Not just more of her physically, but more of her in every way. She'd become a part of him and he needed to feed that part with knowledge of her, with her laughter, her fears, her hopes and dreams.

He gripped her face and rubbed his thumbs across her jaw, directing her mouth to move with his, leading her in their passionate dance. She withdrew, her eyes brimming with desire as they shifted between his. Releasing her face, he brushed hair from her cheek. "Magnolia," was all he could think to say. "Sweet, sweet, Magnolia."

The air between them thickened, charged with a power that made his heart swell, his blood pulse, his head spin. Time slowed as their eyes searched each other's. A breeze stirred leaves into a dance. Branches swayed. Fireflies sparked in the darkness. Something connected between them. Something deep and abiding.

She leaned her forehead against his, her breath puffing over him like warm fog. "I can't believe this is happening." She gave a little laugh and reached up to touch his good arm, hesitating at first then running a finger over his rounded bicep.

"That you enjoyed my kiss?" Hayden took her other hand and planted his lips upon it. "Or that you are kissing a man who's wearing no shirt?" He grinned.

"Both." She smiled, caressing his stubbled jaw.

"Sorry. I haven't shaved since we left Rio."

"No, I like it." She smiled. "It feels like sand on my cheek."

Everything inside Hayden that was real—his heart, soul, and spirit—ached. With an exhilarating, pleasurable ache. What was happening to him? Was this what it felt like to fall in love? Both thrilling and terrifying at the same time? Now as she gazed at him with such admiration, with such longing, he wanted nothing more than to wrap his arms around her and protect her, keep her safe, and give her all his love forever.

He kissed her cheek, then trailed kisses down her jaw and back to her lips, finding them as sweet as ever.

"Thank you for saving me, Hayden," she breathed out.

"My pleasure."

She backed away. A tear slipped down her cheek. "No one has ever risked their life for me."

He eased a curl from her forehead. "Because no one has taken the time to realize what a treasure you are."

At this, she melted in his arms and began to sob. Unsure if he had said something wrong, he embraced her, burying his head in her hair that smelled of moss and orchids.

When she'd spent her tears, she kissed him, deep and powerful, and he realized he'd said the right thing. But her passion soon stirred his own to near boiling, and against everything within him, he nudged her back.

"We should stop."

"Yes, of course." She seemed embarrassed, leaned forward on her knees and started to rise. Hayden stood and helped her to her feet, bringing her hand to his lips for another kiss. He'd love nothing more than to continue kissing her all night, but she was unlike the other women he'd known. She was special, precious, and he didn't want to ruin things with unbridled passion and regrets.

He stretched his wounded arm. "Thank you for tending my wound."

"It was my first." She gathered her salve, clean strips of petticoats, and thread and needle, and returned them to her valise. "Good night, Hayden."

"Good night, Princess." And for the first time, as he watched her walk to her shelter and cast a loving glance at him over her shoulder, he meant the title in the purest sense of the word.

Halting just a few yards from New Hope, Magnolia glanced down at her attire. She still wore her cleanest gown, the one she'd purchased in Rio, though it was anything but clean anymore. She'd pinned her hair up as best she could—without using her mirror—and scrubbed most of the dirt from her skin. It was going to be hard enough facing her father without looking like a filthy street waif. As it was, her nerves were in so many knots, they resembled the tangled vines crisscrossing the canopy. She knew he'd be mad, furious even. What she didn't know was what her punishment would entail, nor how much debt would be added to her already massive bill.

Hayden stood beside her, allowing her a moment. No doubt he knew how nervous she was, had listened to her fearful chatter all day, had apologized more than once for bringing her back home. But all she could think of now was how exquisite he looked without his shirt. He shook his hair, raked a hand through it, and winked at her as sweat glistened on the rounded muscles in his arms and chest. Heat flooded her belly and she looked away. The jungle was good for Hayden. He seemed to thrive in the wildness of it. Oh, mercy me, the shame! She'd been raised with more manners than to stare at a man's chest or the muscles rippling in his back as he moved through the jungle like a cougar. Just as she'd done all day from her position behind him.

"Are you ready?" He reached for her hand. She took it and allowed him to lead her forward as she remembered their kisses from the prior night. She'd never experienced such sensations—had never known they existed. Neither had she felt such deep affection for a man. The emotions had consumed her, filling every crack and crevice of her need to be loved, cherished, adored. He had said she was a treasure worth having. No one had ever said that to her before. And it made her want to never leave his side.

Thank God Hayden had the strength to stop kissing her. He truly was a gentleman. More than she ever realized. More than most of the sophisticated men who'd courted her. Yet now she feared for her heart even more than she feared her father's wrath, for she had no idea whether Hayden harbored any true feelings for her. No doubt he'd kissed dozens of women before. He was a charmer. And she'd already had her heart broken once by a charmer. And once was more than enough.

On their right, Hayden pointed out the green sprouts of sugarcane and coffee plants rising from rows of rich dirt. They'd barely been gone two weeks and the fields looked completely different. Magnolia wondered where the men were, but realized it was nearing supper and everyone would be back in New Hope.

They skirted a large puddle and memories assailed her of the time she'd been so enamored at the sight of Hayden working in the field, she'd tripped and fallen into the mud. Of course, he'd come to her rescue. At the time she thought he was nothing but a plebian oaf.

But now she realized he'd rescued her from far more than a little mud.

Brushing aside the final leaves of a large fern, he escorted her into town. At first glance, things seemed normal. Quiet, but normal.

"Everyone must be eating super," Magnolia said as they made their way down the main street, though no smell of cooking food reached her nose.

Her chest tight, she slowed her pace, dreading seeing her father, dreading the looks of censure she would receive from both him and the other colonists, the sordid rumors that would fly when they saw her with a bare-chested Hayden. Hayden was taking his time as well. She hoped it was because he didn't want to release her to her father's care, because he loved her and wanted to stay with her. Oh, why didn't they just turn around and disappear back into the jungle where they could be together? Where they could frolic and play in the waterfalls and sleep under the star-lit canopy. One word from him and she would do it, she would give up being clean and sleeping on a bed and having her belly full. Just to be with him. But he'd not said much to her all day.

They approached the meeting shelter. The sight that met Magnolia's eyes halted her on the spot. Sent her heart vaulting into her throat. A band of colorfully-dressed men armed with pistols and swords circled the colonists. Magnolia shook her head. She must be seeing things. Hayden gripped her arm and tugged her back. He'd seen them too. But it was too late.

They'd been spotted.

Before Hayden could draw his pistol, a group of men swamped him, forcing his arms behind his back and ignoring his cry of pain. Another foul-smelling man dragged Magnolia to the others and tossed her to the ground. Her stomach twisted in a knot. She gulped for air. Terror sped across the faces of the colonists, all held at gunpoint.

Magnolia's mother shrieked and started for her, but one of the assailants barred her with the barrel of a musket. She collapsed, quivering, into her husband's arms. Magnolia couldn't tell if her father was happy, angry, or ambivalent to see her, his stare was so benumbed.

It took four men to drag Hayden to sit on a stump. Their eyes met. His brimming with fury, hers pleading for help. He gave her a nod as if to assure her all would be well. But she knew that wasn't true. Gathering her skirts, she struggled to stand, grimacing when the assailants laughed at her attempt. Finally she rose, brushed off her skirts and swallowed down her fear.

An ostentatious brute with the swagger of a dandy approached. His lips slanted at an odd angle as he placed a jeweled finger on his chin and took her in with his vulgar gaze. "What have we here?" he said in a heavy Portuguese accent.

"Just another one of our colonists," she heard Blake say.

Magnolia peered around the man to see Eliza clinging to Blake, terror shadowing her face. The colonel's jaw bunched as his eyes sped across the group, no doubt planning some means of defense or escape. Angeline trembled beside James, who moved to shield her from the monster's view. The rest of the colonists gathered their children close and cowered beneath the weapons pointed their way. A few women sobbed. But at least everyone seemed in one piece.

"Since no one tells me where is the gold. . ." The brute spun around and waved an arm through the air, his lacy cuffs fluttering in the breeze. "And I know you found it. I will take a woman for myself. One every night until you tell me the truth." He turned and slid a finger down Magnolia's cheek. The man reeked of sweat and filth.

Disgusted, she turned away.

"Starting with this delicate flower."

Blood abandoned her heart. Her knees began to quake. Before Magnolia could move, he hoisted her onto his shoulder and stomped away, his men following after him. The last thing she heard was her mother's scream and Hayden's growl before someone silenced him with a thud.

CHAPTER 25

$\mathbf{M}$agnolia struggled against the ropes binding her hands to the captain's bed. Yet for all her toil, she gained only bloody wrists and searing pain. Stretching out her legs, she adjusted her bottom on the hard deck. What sort of man kept a lady tied to a bed frame and sitting on nothing but wood that felt like stone for hours?

A pirate.

She shivered as the sounds of drunken revelry filtered through the deck head: a vulgar ditty accompanied by an off-key fiddle, shouts, curses that bruised her ears, random pistol shots, and the distant clang of a sword. The same raucous din she'd been hearing all night. Ever since Captain Armando Manuel Ricu had kidnapped her from the colony and dragged her on board his ship and into his cabin. When he'd tied her to his bed, sunlight angled over his oak desk and mahogany paneling. But hours ago, a curtain of black dropped over the stern windows, encasing the room in darkness. How long could these pirates carry on with their revelry?

She hoped a lot longer.

Terror gripped her at the thought of what the captain had planned for her when he retired for the evening. How could the colonists have allowed these horrid men to steal her away? How could Hayden? They'd all just stood there, staring wide-eyed at the barrels of the pirates' pistols... doing absolutely nothing. Even her own parents! Even when the vile pig-of-a-captain flung her over his shoulder and carried her away.

And for what? *Gold.* Magnolia grimaced. Dodd and his infernal gold! He must have found it. He must have buried it where no one would ever think to look. She could tell by the malicious twinkle in his eyes when the pirates had demanded it be returned or they'd start kidnapping the women one by one.

The ship rolled over an incoming wave. Magnolia braced herself against the deck, but her weight pulled against the ropes. Pain shot through her wrists. The wood creaked and groaned, voicing her inward protest. Why, when anchored mere yards off shore, did the ship insist on pitching and lurching as if it was out at sea? The same familiar smells that had haunted her on the long voyage from Charleston to Brazil now saturated her lungs: moist wood, mold, salt, tar, waste. . . and something else, something new that made her nose twitch. She couldn't place the foul odor, but surely it emanated from the beasts who inhabited this putrid bucket they called a ship.

Hanging her head, she stared at her soiled gown. Her eyes burned, but no tears came. She'd already spent every last one of them—could feel their salty tracks drying on her cheeks and neck. Mercy me, she must look a fright. But what did it matter?

She was about to become a pirate captain's mistress. Lose her innocence to that vulgar Philistine. And maybe her life. Ah. . .there the tears were. *Crack!* A pistol shot snapped her gaze to the deck head. Her ears perked, desperate to hear the sounds of a battle as her friends stormed aboard to save her. But instead, the cackle of sordid laughter accompanied the return of the discordant fiddle.

And Magnolia began to sob again.

Why wasn't anyone rescuing her? Tears spilled down her cheeks. One dropped onto her wrist, seeping beneath the ropes, stinging her raw skin. Why wasn't Hayden coming to save her? Had their kiss meant so little?

Perhaps she had not been the kindest person in the world. Yes, she had often complained about her situation. She had sabotaged the ship that brought them here, had told a few lies, grumbled at the lack of food and comforts. Yes, she'd tried to swindle Hayden into taking her home. She often drank too much, though most of the colonists weren't privy to that particular vice. Her eyes locked upon a half-empty bottle of port sitting atop a chest at the end of the bed, and she licked her lips. Drat. . .just out of her reach.

Regardless, she was a nice person, wasn't she? She had assisted Eliza in the infirmary many times. She had hauled water from the river. She had gathered wood and picked mangos a few times for breakfast. She'd even saved Hayden from a wolf! Surely those things—huge efforts for someone of her station—made up for her occasional bad humor.

The ship rolled. Boot steps thundered outside the door. Magnolia's heart charged through her chest as if it were looking for a place to hide. She wished she could do the same.

The door burst open, slamming against the bulkhead, and in walked Captain Armando Ricu—all sinewy six-foot plus of him. Tawdry music and laughter swirled in behind him like a hellish minion. The deck tilted, and he gripped the door jamb, a perplexed look in his glassy eyes as he lifted his lantern and surveyed the cabin. Curly black hair that would be the envy of any woman flowed halfway down his back over a waistcoat embroidered with silver and pinned with so many jewels and diamond-encrusted brooches, it made him look like a floating candelabra.

Trophies from his conquests, no doubt. Magnolia gulped.

He staggered into the room and set down the lantern. Then planting his fists on the wide belt at his waist, he focused on Magnolia as she attempted to curl into a ball small enough to avoid detection.

It didn't work.

"Ah, there you be, *amor*." His broken English was only further befuddled by the slur of alcohol. "Time to join the *festa*."

If by festa, he meant festivities, Magnolia would have to decline—wanted so desperately to decline, to blink her eyes and wake up in the middle of the jungle, sitting around the fire with Hayden, eating fruit and bantering back and forth as they so often had done.

Instead, the toe of the man's boot—made of some kind of repulsive reptile—appeared in her vision then landed on a fold of her skirt, marking her taffeta gown.

If only that was all that would be stained this night.

Tiny specks of light spun at the edge of her vision. Her breath huddled in her throat. *Oh, God. Help me. Please help me.* That was twice she'd appealed to the Almighty in the last few days. More than in her entire life. In truth, she rarely had much need to ask for anything. Except when her parents had dragged her to Brazil. And by then she had just been plain angry at God for allowing such an atrocious thing to happen.

Captain Ricu plucked a knife from his belt. Lantern light gleamed on the blade as it plummeted toward her. Magnolia tried to scream but only managed a pathetic whimper. The sound of splitting hemp reached her ears. Her wrists flew apart. Fingers as thick as bamboo grappled her arms and yanked her to her feet. Pain etched across her shoulders. The pirate thrust his face into hers, measuring her with eyes that seemed afloat in barrels of rum. Rum. The spicy scent of it filled the air between them and caused Magnolia to lick her lips, despite her predicament. What she wouldn't give for a drink or two, or eight, right now. Anything to send her into the bliss of unconsciousness, that secret place wherein existed no pain, no pressure, no insect-infested jungle, no pirates!

"Yes, *muito bonito*. We have fun, you and I, *é?*"

The cabin spun in her vision. *This can't be happening.*

Laughing, the captain shoved her onto the bed, slammed the door, and returned to her in one stride.

Magnolia scrambled backward across the ratty mattress. Hard wood knuckled her back, preventing her retreat. There was nowhere to hide. Nowhere to escape.

Captain Ricu slipped out of his jeweled waistcoat and tossed it onto a chair. Reflections from the gems twinkled on the deck head like stars. And for a moment, Magnolia dreamed she was far away in a small boat drifting at sea, staring at the night sky. Far, far away where no one could touch her. . .

But the pirate's belch broke her trance. He removed his sword and pistols, tore off his stained shirt, and leaned on the bed frame, eyeing her like a tiger eyeing a hunk of meat.

Magnolia squeezed her eyes shut. Seconds passed, yet no meaty claws seized her. Instead, a latch creaked and a blast of briny wind sent a chill down her back. Boot steps and a grunt of surprise from the captain opened her eyes. He had risen to his full height and spun around toward the now open door.

A stream of angry Portuguese shot from his mouth.

Whatever he said, it did not deter the intruder. Mercy me, was she now to be fought over like prey? All hope drained from her. Her eyes landed on the bottle of port and she started for it. Not for a drink, but to use it as a weapon. Battling against layers of petticoats, she was almost there when a voice, a wonderfully delicious voice, brought breath back into her lungs. She almost dared not look for fear she'd slipped into madness.

"Step aside, *Capitão*, I'm taking the lady back."

Magnolia peered around Captain Ricu's massive frame to see Hayden dressed in black trousers, a white open-collared shirt, a red neckerchief at his throat, and pointing a cutlass at the captain.

Her heart surged.

Captain Ricu chuckled, hesitated, and stared at Hayden as if he'd just told a joke. But when Hayden's blade poked the captain's chest, his stance immediately stiffened. In a speed that defied his inebriation, the captain ducked and charged Hayden, knocking the blade from his grip. It clanked to the deck.

Shrieking, Magnolia scrambled to the edge of the bed and reached for the fallen cutlass, but the captain kicked it beneath his desk and dove for his sword. Hayden charged forward. He shoved the captain. The man toppled backward over a chair. Kicking the broken seat aside, Hayden jerked the man up and slammed him against the bulkhead. Before the pirate could react, Hayden shoved his muscled forearm against his throat until the man's face transformed into a bloated beet.

"I said I'm taking the lady back," Hayden seethed. Lines of red appeared on his shirt from where the wolf had bitten him.

Heart slamming against her ribs, Magnolia jumped off the bed and grabbed the bottle of port. Captain Ricu sputtered and blubbered, his eyes wide. Hayden released him and slugged him in the stomach.

Bending over, the pirate coughed and gasped for air. For the briefest of seconds, Hayden's eyes flashed to Magnolia. The concern and affection within them nearly brought her to tears.

Would have brought her to tears if she hadn't seen Captain Ricu straighten and raise his arm to strike Hayden, a malicious smirk on his lips.

Hayden groaned and dropped to the deck. Magnolia screamed. The pirate captain rubbed his neck, spit on Hayden, and headed for her. Clutching the bottle to her chest, she backed away, but a thick wardrobe blocked her retreat.

A slow predatory grin lifted the captain's lips. "Sorry for *interrupção*, amor."

The grin vanished. Shock sparked in his eyes before he toppled like a felled tree. He struck the deck, and the ship seemed to tremble with the impact. Releasing his grip on the pirate's ankles, Hayden pounced on top of him and landed a punch to his face. The captain growled like a bear, clutched Hayden's throat, and tossed him aside. Both men leapt to their feet.

Captain Ricu slammed a fist across Hayden's jaw. The impact spun him around, squirting a circle of blood through the air. Magnolia shrieked and started toward him. Wiping blood from his mouth, Hayden glared at the pirate.

"Is the woman worth your death, Capitão?" Hayden's voice held the sarcasm of victory.

Captain Ricu's chuckle defied the fear racing across his eyes. "Is she worth yours, *idiota*?"

Hayden charged the pirate, landing blow after blow against his jaw and into his belly. Groaning, Captain Ricu raised his hands to block the assault. By his size and ruthlessness alone, he should have had the advantage over Hayden, yet it was Hayden who now had the pirate's back pinned on his desk, a stranglehold once again on his throat.

The pirate coughed and sputtered as his hands groped over the surface, knocking over quill pens and trinkets. He found his pistol. Magnolia tried to scream, but her throat slammed shut.

The pirate leveled the barrel at Hayden's head as the sound of the weapon cocking echoed in the room. Hayden froze. Releasing the beast, he stood and backed away.

Captain Ricu, one hand on his throat, one hand on his pistol, got up from the desk as a victorious grin played on his lips. "Any last words, *imbecil*?"

CHAPTER 26

Magnolia's heart beat so hard, her chest hurt. Without so much as a thought, she charged toward the pirate and slammed the bottle of port atop his head. Shards of glass and maroon liquid sprayed over her, and for a moment, she thought her assault had no effect, for the man simply stood there, unmoving. But finally, his shoulders drooped, his breath escaped in an eerie moan, and he slumped to the deck, striking Magnolia with his arm in the process.

She fell backward and landed on the mattress, the severed bottle neck in her hand. Tossing it aside, she tried to settle her breathing.

Boots crunched over broken glass and a strong, bloodied hand appeared in her vision. She gazed up to see Hayden, looking more like a pirate than a gentleman, grinning at her. He winked. "I've come to rescue you, fair maiden."

She gripped his hand. Warm, strong fingers curled around hers and lifted her from her seat, pulling her into an embrace that sent ripples through her belly.

"Your stitches!" She shrieked, pulling back and staring at the red blotches on his shirt.

"They're fine. Eliza saw to them." He glanced at his arm and shrugged. "Just bleeding a little."

She fell into him. "I didn't think you were coming." All the tension, the fear, released in a shuddering sob.

He kissed her forehead, took her face in his hands, and locked his eyes upon her. "I will always come for you, Princess."

Emotion clogged in her throat as she searched those eyes for any hint of insincerity, any hint that he was playing her for some selfish purpose. What she saw there instead caused more tears to fall. This time, tears of joy.

She ran a hand over his jaw, still red from the pirate's strike. "Have a care, Hayden, or a lady might think you seek something more serious than passionate kisses."

"And what if I did?" His lips quirked into a smile as he wiped moisture from her face. "Would the lady be agreeable to such a notion?"

The words shot straight from her heart, past her good reason, past her care for Samuel Wimberly, past her parents' approval, and spilled from her lips. "The lady would."

Hayden's wide smile sent her head spinning, and he drew her into his arms again, barricading her with his strength.

Reminding her of their precarious situation.

She tugged from his grip, her gaze snapping to the open door. "The pirates! How will we get past them?" Oddly, however, the ship had grown silent.

He smiled. "Don't worry about them." He took her hand and assisted her over Captain Ricu's prostrate form. "I expect they'll be unconscious for several hours. Thank you, by the way, for knocking this particular one out."

"Well, I couldn't very well let him shoot you, now, could I?" She gave a coy smile. "Even though you do look like a pirate, yourself."

He led her up onto the main deck. "As it turns out, the other pirates were of the same opinion. There were so many of them aboard the ship, they didn't even realize I was not one of them."

Even in the dim moonlight, Magnolia could make out bodies strewn about the deck in various poses as if they'd dropped in the middle of their revelry. If not for the loud snoring, she would have thought them dead. "Did you drug them?"

"Only with pinga." Hayden took her hand and assisted her over the fallen fiends. "Turns out Thiago had made a particularly potent batch. And lots of it. After bringing it on board, it was only a matter of persuading the pirates to overindulge." They reached the railing. He chuckled. "As easy as convincing babies to drink their mother's milk." A salty breeze and the sounds of waves lapping against the hull greeted them. Hayden stuck two fingers in his mouth and let out a shrill whistle. "Of course, once I saw the captain go below, I knew I didn't have much time."

All of her worries, all of her fears had been for naught. She fell against him, never wanting to leave his side. "Why aren't you as besotted as they?"

"I only pretended to drink. The more inebriated they became, the easier it was to fool them." He stroked her hair.

A moist thud sounded from below. Hayden leaned over the railing. "Ahoy there."

"Ahoy," a muffled yet familiar voice drifted up from the water. "Ready here."

Grabbing the rope ladder, Hayden leapt over the railing and assisted her onto the bulwarks. Then side by side, he helped her clamber down the shifting cord to the waiting boat. She really was going to have to get rid of this crinoline! Wobbling, she crawled to take a seat beside Colonel Blake, who smiled her way. James sat at the bow, lantern in hand.

"A rescue party. I am very grateful, gentlemen."

"We had fun," James said.

Hayden grabbed an oar and shoved off from the hull then hooked it in the oarlock.

Magnolia's gaze swept up the massive ship that seemed like an impenetrable mountain rising from the sea. "But won't the pirates simply come back ashore when they wake up?" Even now, dawn's glow curled over the horizon.

"We cut the anchor chain." Hayden grunted as he plunged the oar through water. "Good thing the ship is old and it was made of hemp."

"Then we tied it around the rudder," James added with a chuckle.

Magnolia gazed back at the *Espoliar* already drifting out to sea with the morning tide.

Leaning forward, Blake heaved his oar, propelling them through water that purled against the tiny craft with gurgles and splashes. "By the time they wake up, they'll be far away and have no way to steer."

An incoming wave struck the boat and Magnolia held onto the thwarts. "But they'll fix it, of course."

"Eventually, but by then, hopefully they'll have moved on to other conquests."

"I suppose Dodd may be right about his gold," James said, "if these pirates are so intent on finding it."

Blake sighed. "Perhaps. Many a foolish man has wasted his life searching for buried treasure that is never found."

"What happens if they do return?" Magnolia asked, dreading another encounter with Captain Armando Manuel Ricu.

The boat struck sand and Blake hopped into the shallow waves. "Then we'll be ready for them."

⚓

Propriety tossed to the wind, along with the fear of Mr. Scott's inevitable protests, Hayden flung an arm around Magnolia's shoulders and drew her close as they walked back to New Hope. She leaned her head on his chest and snuggled beside him, causing his heart to leap. Was it possible she returned his feelings? Was it possible she loved him and not that ninny of a solicitor back home? From the look in her eyes, he could see no other possibility.

Yet, now as the sun peeked over the horizon and unrolled its golden fingers over the landscape, Hayden knew he'd have to release her to her parents. He hoped they had missed her enough to forgive her for running away. He hoped they'd be kind, but when he saw them standing before their hut, his hopes vanished.

"Unhand her this minute, you officious reprobate!" Mr. Scott stormed toward Hayden, his jowls quivering.

"Papa!" Magnolia clung tighter to Hayden, but he pried her fingers loose and nudged her forward. Though Hayden would love nothing more than to get into a tussle with the man, it wouldn't be proper. And he was just too tired.

547

"This officious reprobate just rescued me from being ravished by a band of pirates!"

Her mother gasped in horror and drew Magnolia into her arms.

"Yes, yes, I knew he would." Mr. Scott waved the comment away. "Especially with the colonel's help."

"I assure you, sir," Blake said as he approached. "It was Hayden who risked his life."

"Oh, dearest," Mrs. Scott blubbered. "I'm so happy to see you. The pirates didn't harm you, did they?" She ran her hands over Magnolia's face and arms.

"I'm all right, Mother. Thanks to Hayden."

"But why did you leave us in the first place?" her mother continued, her lip quivering. "We were so worried. We sent a scout after you, but he hasn't returned."

Magnolia exchanged a glance with Hayden. "We saw no sign of anyone. I hope he didn't fall into trouble."

"Indeed." Blake's tone bore concern. "I'll send a few men to search for him."

Mr. Scott snorted. "I wouldn't bother. He's, no doubt, as much of a liar as this man."

"Papa, Hayden rescued me. Saved my life more than once. And he took good care of me these past two weeks."

But Hayden doubted the man heard her. Instead, he held up a lantern and stared in disgust at the stains on her dress and the dirty hair dangling about her shoulders. "He also stole you away."

"I ran away, Papa. He had nothing to do with that."

He shifted malevolent eyes to Hayden. "But I'm sure he took advantage of the situation."

Hayden's jaw began to twitch. "I return her to you, sir, pure and unscathed. Otherwise she would be on a ship bound for the States."

"Humph." Mr. Scott grabbed Magnolia's elbow, turned, and headed toward the door of their hut. "Her reputation is ruined. Completely ruined. Now, no one will have her."

Mrs. Scott blithely followed them inside.

Hayden hung his head and whispered into the wind. "*I* will have her."

Chapter 27

Two nights later, something startled James out of his sleep. Tossing a shirt over his head, he grabbed his pistol and darted out of the hut. He was sure he'd heard a woman's scream. It sounded like Sarah, the teacher, whose hut was next door to his. Stumbling in the dark, he spotted a man holding a woman in a tight embrace.

"What is the meaning of this?" He shoved the man aside. Patches of moonlight shifted over his face.

"Thiago, what on earth are you doing? Explain yourself at once."

Blake and Eliza appeared out of the shadows, their hair askew and concern lining their expressions. Several colonists followed in their wake, carrying torches and rubbing eyes filled with alarm.

"I do nothing." Thiago's expression was defiant.

"Then why was she—?"

"James, no." Sarah stepped between the men. "Thiago was helping me. I had a terrifying dream. . .a vision. . ." She pressed a hand to her forehead, stumbled, and seemed to melt before their eyes. Thiago captured her in his arms then gently set her down on a stool and knelt beside her.

The tender display caused emotion to rise in James's throat. He hadn't realized that a bond had formed between the teacher and the Brazilian guide.

"I hear her scream," Thiago said. "I come running. She is frightened, trembling. All I do is hold her."

Some of the colonists moaned and shuffled back to their beds.

James retreated. "Forgive me, Thiago. I thought. . .it looked like. Well, never mind."

Colonel Blake shifted his weight. "It seems to be a night for dreams."

"You too?" James said. Out of the corner of his eye, he spotted Angeline heading toward the group, eyes puffy with sleep and russet hair spilling down her back.

"Yes." Blake swung an arm around his wife and drew her close. "A nightmare about the war. I haven't had one of those in quite some time."

"I've been having dreams as well." James sighed. "Events from my past. Odd."

Lydia began crying, and before Sarah could get up, Eliza slipped inside the hut to retrieve the baby and handed her to her mother.

"I don't think it was a nightmare." Sarah rocked her daughter. "I was awake, couldn't sleep all night. I stepped out of the hut for some air and that was when I saw him."

"Who?"

"My husband. My dead husband. Only he wasn't dead." She glanced over the crowd. "I'm sorry to wake everyone."

Eliza shared a knowing look with her husband.

"I've seen visions too," Blake said, lifting his voice for all to hear. "My dead brother for one."

"Me, as well," one of the colonists added.

"And me," Angeline spoke up.

Several of the remaining colonists offered their own stories, and soon the air was filled with tales of various sightings. Despite the frightening accounts, an odd relief swept through the crowd as each person realized they weren't alone.

Yet James couldn't shake the dread settling like a stone in his stomach. If they weren't crazy then. . .he fingered his chin and stared at the ground.

Blake eased beside him. "What is it?"

"Just something I read in that book from the temple."

Blake hushed everyone. "What?"

"Something about visions. No, it was delusions. I didn't think about it until now. My Hebrew is a bit rusty. I can't make out all the words, but it said something about four generals, Deception, Delusion, Destruction, and Depravity."

"Generals? From what army?"

James shook his head. "I don't know, but there was an entire section on Delusion that used words like vision, memory, manipulation, torture. . . . Not pleasant stuff at all."

"Perhaps it's just some account of a war the Portuguese and Indians fought long ago," Dodd offered.

Eliza hugged herself. "Do continue to read and let us know, won't you, Doctor?"

"Of course."

"Superstitious rubbish," one colonist grumbled and ambled away.

"I see things too." Thiago crossed himself. "It comes from temple. There is evil there. We should leave. Find another place. My charms not strong enough."

"God can protect us, Thiago," Eliza said.

"Exactly," James added. "We have nothing to fear." Then why did he suddenly feel so terrified?

⚜

The orchestra wasn't at all like the one Magnolia had enjoyed at the soiree in Rio, but the fiddle, guitar, and harmonica, accompanied by a young lad slapping a beat on a wooden stump, delighted her ears nonetheless, drowning out the normal thrum of the jungle. As well as her father's constant castigation. She wished the music would delight her spirit, but that, along with her body, had been kept locked behind a prison of her father's wrath and her own guilt for three days. Three long, miserable days during which he had not let her out of his sight. Not even at night. Though she'd tried twice to escape.

The first day she'd been home, her father had worked himself into such a frenzy yelling at her about what a spoiled hoyden she was, he'd nearly collapsed from exertion. In fact, Mable, their slave, had been

551

forced to run into the jungle and pick fresh fruit just to revive him. Once back to sorts, however, he continued his castigation, stating how Magnolia had not only broken his heart but her mother's as well—though the woman didn't seem heartbroken at all, simply upset that her husband was shouting so much. Then he growled on about how she'd worried them sick, though for the life of her, she found no evidence in his tone. But finally he got to the crux of the matter—the real reason for his anger. Magnolia had run out on her debt to them. Her debt to make up for her courtship with Martin. For bringing him into their lives, for falling for his schemes. For allowing him to ruin her family.

"Your beauty is our only hope to reinstate our wealth and name in this new land," he had said, stomping back and forth on the dirt floor of their home-in-progress, barely a frame of wood and stones. But of course he hadn't wanted to shout at her in town where everyone could hear. "And then you run out on your mother and me, leaving us destitute and without hope. You ungrateful girl!"

She should have shown him her reflection. That would certainly crush his hopes to toss her as bait into the pond of rank and fortune. How his face would wrinkle in disgust and his eyes pop out in horror if he saw the image she saw in her mirror. For some reason the thought brought a smile to her lips, though it quickly faded at the remembrance of that reflection earlier when she'd been dressing for the party. So upset at the sight, Magnolia had decided not to look at it ever again. Besides, now that she was home, she had Mable to fix her hair and ensure her face was clean.

Torches were lit and couples began dancing across the cleared area beside the meeting shelter, drawing Magnolia's gaze. She envied their happiness, their freedom. Their peace. At least her father had given her a slice of that peace today. He hadn't said a word to her. No doubt he'd exhausted not only himself but his store of insults. For the time being, anyway. However, his silence had finally given Magnolia a chance to steal away and tell her mother what had happened. Though obviously hurt that Magnolia ran off, her mother seemed to understand and even sympathize with the harsh treatment Magnolia received from her father. Regardless, the woman refused to say anything negative about her husband, always kowtowing to his needs, his wants, while ignoring her own. Magnolia wondered how she could be related to such a weakling. But the truth was, even if her mother wanted to leave, she had nowhere to go and no money to get there.

Just like Magnolia.

So now, she sat, squished between her father's stiff presence on her right and her mother on her left—like two sentinels guarding their most precious asset.

Worst of all, she'd been forbidden to speak to Hayden. Ever. At least they had allowed her to attend tonight's celebration—in honor of her return and the pirates' defeat—though she was sure it was only to save face.

One of the ex-soldiers came up to ask her for a dance, but her father waved him off before the man uttered a word.

The scent of roasted wild boar still lingered in the air from dinner. Although delicious, the food hadn't settled well in her agitated stomach. She scanned the couples, seeking the one face she so desperately longed to see. Had he meant what he'd said on the ship? That he'd always come for her? That he wanted something more than a frivolous dalliance? Or was he simply playing the part of the charming gallant in order to woo the lovely lady? She had to know. Must speak to him.

Before he left tomorrow.

Which frightened her all the more. He was leaving her. Magnolia's mother had heard from Mrs. Matthews who had heard from Sarah that Hayden was going on an excursion to seek this Mr. Godard, and he didn't know when he'd return. Or if.

"It's for the best," her mother had said, patting Magnolia's hand. "You know how your father detests him."

Perhaps he wouldn't if he knew that Hayden had saved her life more than once, cared for her and protected her. But that probably wouldn't make a difference. Hayden lacked the two things her father sought the most—wealth and rank.

Blake swung Eliza past in a polka, and she smiled at Magnolia from her husband's arms. The colonel's hobbled gait was barely noticeable when he danced with his wife. The sight warmed Magnolia.

As did the sight of Thiago, one hand on a tree trunk, leaning over to smile at baby Lydia in Sarah's arms. Across the way, James extended his elbow for Angeline and led her onto the makeshift dance floor. Mr. Dodd leaned over a table beneath the meeting shelter staring at a map in confusion. Perhaps he hadn't found his gold, after all. Lewis, ever the cheerful besotted soul, sat on a wobbly chair drinking from his flask and bobbing his head to the tune. Of course he was happy, he had spirits to numb his soul.

She raised her hand and noticed the slight tremble. Another thing she'd been denied these past days. Finally Mable returned with a tray of drinks. Not the kind Magnolia needed, but warm lemonade would have to do. She took a sip, her lips puckering. They were running short on sugar.

Moses headed toward them, across the clearing, hat in hand. Magnolia's attempt to warn him with her eyes failed as his were locked on Mable. He stopped before them. "Missah Scott, would it be all right if I ask Mable to dance? If she wants to, dat is."

Mable's eyes lit up as she gazed up at the tall black man.

But Magnolia's father had a way of crushing any happiness that crossed his path.

He waved him away. "Slaves don't dance."

"Oh, let her dance with him, Papa," Magnolia said, resisting the urge to pour her lemonade on his head.

"I said no! Why the colonel allows these freed Negroes to attend our party is beyond me. Now, go fetch the frond fan, Mable. I'm getting hot. And you"—he flicked his fingers at Moses—"run along."

Dejected, Moses trudged away. Magnolia opened her mouth to say something she'd probably regret when the sight of Hayden stopped her.

He strode into the clearing as if he owned the place. No longer looking like a pirate, he wore gray trousers tucked into high boots, a white shirt, a black waistcoat, and a string tie. Unlike in the jungle when he wore his hair loose and wild, he had combed it and tied it behind him, so unconventional for the fashion of the age, but one of the things she adored about him.

Their eyes locked and he winked at her as if he knew a grand secret. And her heart nearly beat through her chest.

Still he made no move toward her. No doubt he knew the effort would be fruitless.

The dance ended and people scattered for refreshments. Blake approached. "Mr. Scott, if I may intrude on your time, something has come to my attention regarding your home. A few of the farmers passed by the other day and told me there may be a flaw in the frame that will compromise the integrity of the entire structure."

Her father jumped to his feet. "Absurd! I know what I'm doing and have inspected every inch.'"

"Would you like me to show you, sir?"

"In the dark?"

"We have torches," Blake said, his expression grave. "I fear we should not wait."

Her father tugged on his waistcoat. "Very well." He turned toward his wife. "Look out after her." He nodded at Magnolia. "She is not to dance."

Mrs. Scott agreed, her shoulders slumping. Yet as Blake led the man away, Magnolia saw a slight grin lift the colonel's lips.

Moments later, Eliza asked Magnolia's mother to taste an orange pie she'd made with mandioca root, begging the accomplished woman's advice on the taste of the flour substitute. After Magnolia insisted she'd behave, her mother left, seemingly oblivious to the sparkle of mischief in Eliza's eyes.

For the first time in three days, Magnolia was alone.

No, not alone. Hayden appeared before her and offered his hand. "Would you care for a stroll?"

CHAPTER 28

Hayden led Magnolia away from the party, relishing the feel of her delicate hand in his once again. It had been pure torture not being able to speak to her the past three days. Especially after he'd made up his mind. But she was with him now. His plan had worked, thanks to his friends. Unusual nervousness buzzed through him as he shoved through a fence of leaves and led her into a small, private clearing. Two torches, planted in the soft bank of a bubbling creek, cast flickering light over the water.

Magnolia smiled. "Did you prepare this for me?"

"Of course."

She stared almost shyly at the reflection of golden flames bouncing across the dark water as if she were afraid to face him.

"I've missed you," he said, caressing her fingers.

She swung her blue eyes to his, the shield over them dissolving. "I have missed you too." Her voice was filled with longing. "Thank you for getting rid of my parents. Very clever." She grinned.

He shrugged. "How else was I to speak to you?"

She lowered her gaze. "Papa has been horrible."

Hayden squeezed her hand, tugging her closer. "I'm sorry. You don't deserve that."

"Maybe I do." Rare contrition shrouded her features.

"None of us are perfect," Hayden said. "But no one deserves to be treated like a commodity. Especially not from a father." It would almost be better to grow up without a father like Hayden had than to be reprimanded daily by an unloving one. His heart strung tight.

A breeze whistled through the canopy, joining the gurgle and splash of the brook and the buzz of katydids. She gazed into the jungle, sorrow shadowing her face, and he longed to bring the life back into her eyes that he'd witnessed on their journey. But it seemed every drop of hope had been squeezed from her these past three days. Magnolia attempted a smile. "Regardless, you have stolen me away from him for a brief time, and I thank you for that."

"I hope to steal you away for much longer," he said. Flames glinted in her eyes. He searched their depths for her response. Desperate to know. Feeling as if he teetered in the balance between life and death.

Then delight sped through him at what he saw in those sapphire pools.

"Whatever are you implying, Hayden Gale?" She thickened her Southern drawl.

He raised her hand to his lips. "I would like to court you properly, Magnolia, if you'll accept my suit."

The lace at her neckline rose and fell like the beat of angel wings, breathless, eternal, full of promise. Finally, she flung her arms around his neck and kissed him. A passionate, hungry kiss that revived his heart and sent flames down to his toes. Enveloping her in his arms, he drank in her sweet savor, never wanting the moment to end. When they parted, he leaned his forehead against hers. "I have something for you."

Reaching into his pocket, he pulled out the carving he'd just finished that morning.

Magnolia held it to the light. "It's a toad." Surprise heightened her voice. She looked at him. "This is what you were carving on our way back to New Hope?"

"Your nickname for me."

"I never meant it."

He tapped her chin with his finger. "Come now. You meant every word of it."

"Well, perhaps." She smiled and fingered the carving as if it were made of gold. Then lifting it to her lips, she kissed it. "We shall be good friends, shan't we, little one?"

"Now you're making me jealous. It wasn't meant as a substitute for me. Just a reminder."

"I need no reminders. Ever." Lifting her hand, she traced his jaw, her touch so gentle, so full of affection, his head grew light. But then the sparkle in her eyes dulled, and she glanced down. "My father will never permit a courtship between us. He has other plans for me."

The night song of a whippoorwill trilled its agreement. Hayden hefted a sigh. "Plans that don't include an impoverished con—broker, I'm thinking."

"He's forbidden me to ever speak to you again." Thankfully, she missed his near blunder, which reminded him that he should disclose his true profession—or his former profession—to her if they were to be courting. But later. Not now. The sound of music and laughter drew her gaze back to town. "Father will be returning soon. I shouldn't stay." She kicked the leaves by her feet. "It's hopeless Hayden, don't you see? I have nowhere else to go." Her voice broke as tears filled her eyes.

Placing a finger beneath her chin, he raised her gaze to his. "Ah, but you do. I have already spoken to Sarah. She would be happy for you to move in with her in exchange for help with baby Lydia. And Eliza is offering you a position at the clinic. Your work there will more than pay for any food and other necessities you need."

She stared at him as if he'd asked her to swim back to Georgia. "*Work* for a living?"

Hayden clenched his jaw. How could he want to kiss her one moment and strangle her the next? "Yes, work. Like most people must do to survive. Do you want to be free, Princess?"

"Of course." A tear slipped from her eye. "Yes, of course. But you don't understand—I owe my family."

"Whatever it is, we will pay them back. Together."

Another tear joined the first. "You would do that for me?"

He cupped her face in both hands. "I would do anything for you."

"Magnolia!" Her father's voice echoed off branches and leaves, clamoring like a gothic gong and drowning out the pleasant music.

Hayden took her hand in his. "Shall we go announce our good news?"

⁂

Magnolia's joy was soon swallowed up by apprehension as they made their way back to town. She feared not only what her father would say but what he would do. If her courtship with Hayden ended in marriage—ah, dare she hope?—she might never be able to pay back the money she owed her parents, and she'd certainly never gain them the prestige of title or position.

She fingered the toad carving in her pocket. But to become the wife of such a man! Was it possible? When she was with Hayden, everything seemed possible.

Breaking free from her father and living independently as a single woman, for one. It simply wasn't done. At least not for a genteel lady. But could she do it? Could she rise from her bed every morning and spend her days working like an impoverished washerwoman? She *had* enjoyed helping Eliza in the clinic, but it had been her choice to be there and her choice when she would leave. Yet. . .she had felt useful for the first time in her life. And Eliza said she had a gift for nursing. Wouldn't it be wonderful to have value beyond her appearance? Perhaps that would cause her reflection to transform back into one of beauty.

The thought elated her. Along with being loved by such a strong, courageous, kind man. And of having a lifetime to love him in return. It was too good to be true. Too much to hope for! Yet there he was, walking beside her, his warm, rough hand enveloping hers, the taste of his kiss lingering on her lips, his manly smell wafting in the air between them. And she knew she could face anything, even her father's wrath, with Hayden by her side.

He squeezed her hand and gave her that wink that melted her heart before they burst into the center of the square.

Her father, his face bloated like a jellyfish—with a sting just as potent—charged toward her. Her mother followed, ringing her hands. "Where have you been? I told you to stay away from that man!"

Before her father could yank her away, Hayden released her hand

and stepped in front of her. Equal in height, the men stared each other down, one snorting like a bull, the other calm and determined.

The music faded into contrary chords before ceasing altogether, giving way to protests and grunts as all eyes swerved to the brewing altercation. Still, Magnolia's father kept his eyes locked on Hayden's, like cannons about to fire. Magnolia knew that look. It was a look that had caused strong men to wither and staunch women to cry. But Hayden did not falter.

"You will step aside at once, sir, and hand me my daughter."

"Only if she wishes to come to you." Hayden's voice bore neither rancor nor intimidation.

"Of course she wishes to come to me, you hawkish popinjay!" With narrow, seething eyes, her father peered at her around Hayden. "Magnolia, come here this instant!" Her mother stepped beside her husband, a strength in her expression Magnolia had never seen before.

Gathering her own strength, Magnolia stepped forward, slipped her hand once again into Hayden's, and lifted her chin. "I cannot, Papa. Hayden and I are officially courting."

He let out a guttural laugh and glanced at the gathering townspeople. "Rubbish! There's nothing official about such nonsense."

"And I am moving to town," Magnolia continued. "Taking a position at the clinic." She feared he would read the tremble in her voice as doubt.

But he seemed not to notice as maroon exploded on his face. "A position? Moving!" He loosened his necktie, his chest pitching like a ship on high waves.

A gust swirled through the square, sending the lanterns sputtering and casting patches of light over the crowd. Magnolia thought she saw her mother smile.

Colonel Blake and James pushed through the mob to stand beside them.

Magnolia's father gave a bitter chuckle, casting another incredulous glance over the bystanders. Then leaning close to her—so close she felt his spittle on her neck—he said, "You will stop this foolishness at once! You are embarrassing your mother and me. We will discuss this at home." He clutched her arm.

Magnolia winced, and Hayden grabbed her father's wrist. So tightly, her father's jaw twitched with the silent struggle until finally he released Magnolia. Rubbing his hand, he gave Hayden a look that would have killed him if he had been armed.

Magnolia drew a shaky breath. "I have made up my mind, Father."

For once, her mother wasn't sobbing. Instead, she stared at Magnolia with pride.

"You ungrateful girl," he hissed. "This is the second time you have walked out on your bargain, and it will be the last."

Hayden took a step forward. "We will pay you what she owes."

Her father measured him with a scornful gaze then glared at his daughter. "You are a bigger fool than I thought, Magnolia, but do not take me for one." He tugged on his waistcoat, stepped back, and waved them away. "You are no longer my daughter."

Gasps sped through the crowd.

Eliza eased toward them. "You can't mean that, Mr. Scott."

A tangible pain speared Magnolia's heart. Her mother began to sob. Hayden squeezed her hand and drew her close as her father strode away, head held high, ordering her mother to come along. But Magnolia didn't have time to consider the implications of his words before the sound of crunching leaves—a multitude of crunching leaves—rose from the jungle. Blake, James, and most of the men, including Hayden, headed for their rifles and pistols, leveling them toward the noise while ushering the women behind them. Magnolia joined Eliza and Angeline as everyone watched to see what new dangers emerged from the trees.

Seconds passed like minutes. The leaves parted and a group of men marched into town. No, not just men, women and children too, their clothes torn and stained, their faces weary and frightened. Eyes widening, they froze at the sight of the guns pointed their way. Some of the men in the group plucked out pistols and returned the favor.

But Magnolia's gaze fastened upon a single man leading the pack, his arms raised and an impudent grin on his lips. Her heart seized. It couldn't be. It simply couldn't be. Surely, it was just another vision.

"Hold up there, gentlemen," the vision spoke, his slick voice confirming her fears. "We come in peace. We are settlers from the Confederate States, just like you."

"Martin!" Magnolia managed to growl the name. She started toward him, but her father stormed past her. "Mr. Haley? Mr. Martin Haley!"

The man lowered his arms. His eyebrows shot up over eyes filled with shock. Magnolia's mother shrieked.

"No, sir. You are mistaken. That is not my name." He spoke with his usual aplomb.

But the closer Magnolia got to him, the more she recognized the cultured goatee and thin mustache, the gray streaking the temples of his black hair. Those firm cheek bones and stark green eyes. Handsome, charming Martin.

Her father stopped before him. "I don't care what you call yourself. You stole all my money, sir! And I demand it back."

Wondering where Hayden was, Magnolia glanced over her shoulder to find him staring at Martin as if he were a ghost. No, worse. A monster, from the look of fury blazing in his eyes.

Blake approached the group. "What is the meaning of this? Who are you and who are these people?"

"Ah, you must be the man in charge." Martin faced the colonel with the same smile he used on everyone he wished to deceive. "As I said, we are but settlers like yourself. In fact"—he waved an arm over the town— "we are the ones who inhabited these huts before you."

"This man stole from me and I demand reparation!" Magnolia's father bellowed.

But Magnolia was tired of talking. Barreling forward, she planted her hands on Martin's chest and shoved him backward. He stumbled but quickly righted himself. Brushing off his coat, he smiled—a sweet, sickly smile that made her stomach turn. "Ah, dear Magnolia, how good to see you. Of all the places to find each other. . .Brazil." He chuckled.

A few of the newcomers took up positions at their leader's side, weapons raised, and defiance written on their faces.

"I am not your dear," Magnolia spat. "You are a liar, a cheat, and a thief!"

Seeming to forget he had an audience, her father shoved a finger in Martin's face. "You charmed my daughter into an engagement, wormed your way into our family's graces, and took me for everything I had with some spurious investment! You owe me, sir! You owe me, and you will pay. By God, you will pay!" Lunging for Martin, he locked fingers around the man's neck and squeezed.

Martin's eyes bulged. He clawed at her father's hands, gasping and croaking. Several women in his group screamed and the two men at his side cocked and pointed their pistols at her father's head.

"That's enough, Mr. Scott!" Colonel Blake shoved his way between them and pried them apart. Martin gasped for air. "Settle down! Everyone, lower your guns!" Blake shouted to the colonists.

But Magnolia didn't want to settle down. She wanted to gouge Martin's eyes out for what he'd done to her and her family. She was just about to attempt that very thing when Hayden nudged both her and her father aside, cocked his pistol, and leveled it at Martin's forehead.

Martin retreated, real fear skittering across his eyes for the first time.

"Hayden, no!"

"What are you doing, Hayden?" Blake grabbed Hayden's arm but he shrugged him off.

"Put the gun down." James came up from behind.

But Hayden didn't move. Didn't breathe, as his eyes remained locked on his target. A drop of sweat slid down his cheek onto a jaw strung as tight as a sail under full wind. Magnolia had never seen him this enraged, this focused. It frightened her.

"Please, sir, whatever you have against me, let us settle it like gentlemen." Still Martin's voice was as slick as oil.

With an ominous growl, Hayden flipped the weapon, raised it, and slammed it atop Martin's head. The odious man toppled to the dirt with a groan.

Shock filtered through the crowd as Blake knelt beside Martin and gazed up at Hayden. "Why did you do that? Who is this man?"

Hayden stuffed the gun into his belt. "He's my father."

CHAPTER 29

Shoving aside the bamboo door, Hayden headed into the night. Unfortunately the air was just as heavy and oppressive outside as it was inside his hut. Or maybe it was seeing his father that strangled the breath out of him. After he'd flattened the heinous man, Hayden had stomped into the jungle, trying to gather his thoughts and smother his anger. But after hours of batting aside leaves and slapping insects, his thoughts were even more convoluted and his fury hotter. So he'd had a drink of that pinga Magnolia loved so much and had gone to bed. Yet sleep taunted him with heavy lids that would not shut and a wounded heart that kept him awake.

Taking in a deep breath of air, thick with musk and earth, Hayden stretched the kinks from his back and gazed down the dark street. Not a single light shone from any hut. Nor were any watchman in sight. This would be the perfect time to visit his so-called father at the clinic, where he was spending the night after Eliza dressed his head wound.

Yet as Hayden plodded down the street, it was Magnolia who consumed his thoughts. Though he'd been frozen with rage at the sight of the man he'd been so desperate to find for fifteen years, Hayden had heard everything that transpired.

Magnolia had been engaged to his father!

He still couldn't believe it. His stomach lurched even as the thought twisted a cyclone of impossibility in his mind. How could she have fallen for such a scoundrel? A born liar, a charlatan of the worst kind. A shark who preyed on people's hopes and desires only to gobble them up at the last minute. How could she be that foolish? And more importantly, how could he court a woman who had once been in his father's arms, perhaps even kissed him and who knew what else? Disgust sent acid into his throat as he passed Blake and Eliza's hut. The sound of night creatures joined the rush of the river in a cadence that was usually soothing, but tonight the noise only clanked and gonged against Hayden's shock and fury.

His father had swindled the Scotts from all their wealth. That was the debt Magnolia spoke of so often. Now things began to make sense. Still, what kind of parents blamed their innocent daughter for being tricked by a master manipulator? And then used her mistake to enslave her with guilt into obeying their every command. He squeezed the back of his neck, his muscles coiled tight.

He was too confused to deal with his feelings toward Magnolia at the moment. Right now, he had to focus on the only thing that mattered—honoring his promise to his mother.

Pushing aside the canvas flap, he entered the clinic. It smelled of blood and lye and herbs. He groped for a match and a lantern and brought light to bear on the sleeping form of his father. A pile of cloths sat on the table, tempting Hayden to place them over his father's mouth and nose and finish the task quickly. But that wouldn't be a fitting punishment. His father must know who was killing him and why. Hayden wanted to see the fear, the realization in his eyes, and perhaps even a spark of regret.

"Wake up." He poked him, noting the bandage wrapped around his head. "Wake up."

With a growl, Patrick—for that was his real name—peered through tiny slits. But upon seeing Hayden, he jerked to sit up. Rubbing his forehead, he blinked as if trying to focus. "Come to finish me off?"

"Something like that." Hayden crossed arms over his chest.

Patrick glanced over the room as if looking for a weapon and, upon finding none, released a sigh. "Well get on with it then or get out." He swung his legs over the bunk.

If anything, at least the man was no coward.

"You don't recognize me?" Hayden heard the fury strangling his own voice.

"Should I?"

"Perhaps the name Hayden Gale will spark your memory, *Patrick*." He spit the name like the dirt it was.

Every muscle in the man's face stiffened. All except his eyes. They shifted over the dirt floor as if wishing a tunnel would open up beneath him. Seconds passed before he let out a ragged breath, attempted a grin, and lifted his gaze to Hayden, allowing it to wander over him. "You grew up well, lad."

Hayden huffed. "Is that all you have to say?"

With a diminutive slant of his lips, Patrick shrugged. "What else is there?"

A muscle twitched in Hayden's jaw. "You. . .left"—he squeezed out the words, barely able to contain his rage—"when I was only two. Mother. . ."

Patrick rose, stretched his back nonchalantly, all the while keeping a wary eye on Hayden. "Ah, yes. Elizabeth. Lovely lady. How is she?"

"Dead."

His brow folded, and he plopped into a chair beside the examining table. "How?"

"Run over by a carriage on her way home from slaving all day as a seamstress." Veins throbbed in Hayden's forehead. "Too exhausted to even look where she was going."

Genuine sorrow shadowed Patrick's face. Or was it a ruse? "A shame," he said.

"A shame?" Hayden started toward the man, intending to slug him, then stopped. "A shame!" Spit flew from his mouth. "You left her without means to survive. Forced her to toil her life away from dawn till dusk just to feed us."

"She was a resourceful woman. I knew she'd make it."

"But she didn't!"

Patrick flinched. "Listen, lad, I was a different man back then." He ran a finger across his finely coiffed beard, a shadow rolling across his expression. "I made a mistake marrying her. I loved your mother,

I truly did, but a man like me couldn't possibly be tied down."

"You mean a liar, a cheat, and a scoundrel like you."

"Perhaps." He jerked his head to the side and sighed. "In the end, I knew she deserved better."

"In the end you thought of no one but yourself."

Hayden's words seemed of no effect on the man as he pressed fingers on the bandage around his head and winced. "She had family. A father and a brother, I believe."

"Grandpa died of smallpox, and Frederick took to sea to find his fortune."

He seemed to ponder the information for a moment. "How was I to know that?" His indignant tone further infuriated Hayden.

"You would have known if you had bothered to check on our welfare. Even once. Did you check even once?"

Patrick shifted his gaze away. Lantern light glinted in green eyes that held a hint of remorse before he straightened his shoulders and faced Hayden again. "Well, boy, it appears you turned out just fine." He slowly rose and slapped Hayden on the back as if they were old friends—the confidence man at his finest. "How odd that our paths crossed all the way here in Brazil."

"Not so odd." Hayden jerked away from him. Was Patrick so dimwitted that he didn't understand what Hayden intended to do? What he'd sailed across an ocean to do? "I came looking for you."

"Me?" Patrick's brows pinched together, but then a hint of fear slowly claimed his features. "How did you know what I looked like?"

Reaching into his pocket, Hayden pulled out the tintype, snapped open the leather case, and showed it to the man.

Patrick took it, eased fingers over the portrait, and smiled. "Your mother had this made of me."

"And she gave it to me on her deathbed."

He touched the gray at his temples. "I'm older now."

"Yet you haven't changed one bit."

"Everyone changes, lad." He handed it back to him.

Hayden held up a hand. "Keep it. I don't need it anymore."

With a shrug, Patrick set it on the table.

"Do you have any idea what I suffered?" Hayden stretched his fingers, itching to strike the man. "I was only ten when she died. I lived on the street, hungry and cold, sleeping in refuse."

"You can hardly blame me for my ignorance." One brow arched over an expression of annoyance.

"You wouldn't have helped me even if you *had* known, would you?"

Patrick's silent stare was all the answer Hayden needed. He fisted his hand, intending to strike him, strangle him, whatever it took to wipe that smirk off his face. Patrick cringed, bracing for the attack. Fury pooled in Hayden's fist, throbbing through each muscle and bone, until it felt like it would explode. But no. Not yet. He lowered it, stretching out his fingers, gathering his control. Hayden must first find out about Magnolia. Taking a deep breath, he stared out the window.

"No doubt those hard times made you the strong man you are today." Patrick's tone had lost its edge, bordering on conciliatory. Good. He was starting to understand the danger he faced. "Perhaps I did you a favor," he continued. "I wouldn't have been much of a father anyway."

"Why are you here in Brazil, Patrick?"

"For gold, lad!" His eyes glittered greed. "I have a map given me by a reliable gentleman who told me there's a fortune buried near here. Why else would I subject myself to this bestial jungle?"

Wealth, of course. Hayden should have known. "You'll have to fight Dodd for it first."

"Dodd, who's Dodd?"

"Never mind." Hayden shook his head. "So you dragged these poor settlers here on the guise of starting a colony when in truth you plan on finding the gold and abandoning them?"

"I needed funding for the trip, didn't I? Besides, they'll be quite all right. They truly believe they can recreate the South here." He chuckled.

"You're still a monster who uses people," Hayden growled, disgust curdling in his belly. "And what about Magnolia?"

"Miss Scott?" Patrick grinned. "A rare treat, that one. I would have loved to have stayed and sampled more of her wares, but alas there was money to be had."

This time Hayden *did* slug him. Right across the jaw, sending him tumbling backward, arms flailing, and finally dropping to the ground with a thud. He moaned, rubbed his jaw, but managed to swing out his legs and trip Hayden. He fell beside his father, but quickly leapt up and struck Patrick again. Blood spilled from Patrick's nose as he scrambled to rise. Hayden clutched his collar, lifted him, and slammed him against the wall. The bamboo cracked. Palm fronds quivered above them.

"When I find the gold, I'll split it with you," Patrick screeched, his eyes sparking in terror. "Anything you want."

"I don't want your money."

"What do you want? To kill me for something I did over twenty years ago?"

"No, I'm going to kill you for the man you are today. And for the promise I made Mother on her death bed to avenge her untimely death."

Tossing Patrick to the ground, Hayden wrapped his hands around the man's neck and squeezed with all his might. His eyes bulged. His face grew purple as he tried to seize Hayden's fingers, desperate for release, desperate for life. As Hayden's mother had been when she'd gasped her last breath. *This is for you, Mother. Finally, you will have justice.*

A plea for mercy seeped from Patrick's eyes. Hayden searched for the joy, the thrill he expected to feel as he squashed the final breath from the man who had ruined his life. But instead, remorse pinched him. Guilt. And a sense of evil he'd never felt before. Still he squeezed, unable to release his hold. He would have continued, too, if strong hands hadn't pried his fingers away and shoved him off the man. Blake gave Hayden a look of horror as he pushed him back. Patrick coughed and sputtered and gasped for air, rubbing his throat.

Eliza darted in, glanced at the scene, and went to check on Patrick.

"Blast it! What is wrong with you?" Blake shoved Hayden outside.

Hayden paced back and forth before the clinic, clenching and unclenching his fists, struggling to restrain his fury before he did what every fiber in him longed to do—barge back into the hut and finish the job. Before he could do just that, Blake dragged him down the street, stoked the embers in the main fire pit, and ordered Hayden to sit on a stool.

"What's this all about, Hayden?" Blake glanced toward the clinic where Eliza was still tending the monster's wounds.

Hayden stared at the flames.

Selecting a log from a nearby pile, Blake tossed it onto the fire. "I tried to find you, to talk about what happened, but you disappeared."

"I needed to think."

"Think about how you were going to kill him? Blast it, man!" Blake limped around the fire and rubbed his leg. "Is he the reason you went to Rio?" He halted and stared at Hayden. "Is he the reason you stowed away on our ship?"

Hayden nodded. "Back in Charleston, I heard he was in town, heard he'd signed up for your colony."

"Hmm. But, apparently, he started another colony and arrived sooner than we did," Blake said.

"He must have taken a steam ship." Hayden ran a hand through his hair. "What does it matter? You don't know what he's done to me."

"Then tell me. Tell me so I understand." Blake pulled up a stump and sat down. The look in his eyes was one of true concern—a look that said *I care. You can trust me.* Hayden had never seen that look before, except recently in Magnolia's eyes. And perhaps glimpses of it in some of his friends here, but never like this. Sincere concern. Holding the power to lure all his secrets out from hiding.

A breeze whipped through the clearing, stirring dried leaves into a spin and dancing through the flames. A monkey howled in the distance. Hayden hung his head, released a heavy sigh, and slowly began to spill the story of how his father had abandoned them, how his mother had been crushed beneath carriage wheels, how he lived on the street, hungry and cold. And with the telling of each devastating event, Blake's shoulders sank lower and lower.

Leaning forward, Hayden planted his elbows on his knees and stared at the leaping flames. "I promised Mother on her death bed I would get revenge, that I would find my father and make him pay."

Blake squeezed the bridge of his nose. "Was that what *she* wanted?"

The question shocked Hayden. He shot Blake a venomous look. "She was unconscious by then and slipped away an hour later. But I know she would have wanted retribution for dying so young. Who wouldn't?"

"Really? From what you've told me of her, I doubt she would have wanted this kind of life for you."

"You know nothing of her," Hayden snapped.

"No. But I know much about revenge."

Hayden nodded. Indeed. He'd heard Blake's sad tale. How his entire family had died in the Atlanta burning, how his little brother had been killed on the battlefield. He had seen the fury in the colonel's eyes when he'd discovered Eliza's dirty little secret. Yet Blake had changed. Changed so much he ended up marrying a woman with the blood of his family on her hands.

"I don't know how you overcame your anger, your need for revenge, Blake. I could never forgive what my father did to me. . .to my mother. Her memory depends on it."

"If your mother was a godly woman, she's happier now than she's ever been." Blake's smile in contrast to the morbid topic confused Hayden.

"For over a year," Blake continued, "I wanted to kill any Yankee who crossed my path. I almost did kill a few." He chuckled then locked eyes with Hayden, the lines on his forehead deepening. "The only way I overcame my bitterness was by handing my need for revenge over to God. By understanding that if He could forgive me for so much, I had no right not to forgive others. Besides, when you receive God's love and forgiveness, it changes you. Makes you a better man."

Hayden flattened his lips. He'd be a better man when his father was dead. "God's never been there for me. Perhaps for someone like you—a West Point graduate, a colonel who served your country courageously, a man of honor." He shook his head and stared at the ground. "You don't know what I've done."

"I don't have to know. And God doesn't care about your past. He only cares that you turn to Him, ask His forgiveness and His help to forgive others."

Hayden studied the ex-colonel. When he'd first met him on board the ship, Hayden thought he'd found a kindred spirit and immediately became friends with the man whose bitterness and rage Hayden understood. But now that rage was gone, and a joy and peace surrounded Blake that Hayden envied. What would it feel like to be at peace? He had no idea—no remembrance of a time when he'd been at ease with himself and with life. But he would know soon enough. When justice was served.

Rising, Hayden grabbed a stick and tossed it into the fire. Perhaps forgiveness would bring him peace. But he'd have plenty of time for that after he got his revenge. "My father must pay for what he's done. If your God is so forgiving, He'll no doubt pardon my father's offenses as well. But, for my mother's sake, I cannot let that happen. Don't you see? It is up to me to see that her murder is avenged."

The fire hissed and crackled, sending sparks into the night.

"Hayden, you're not judge and jury of the world. That's God's job. Let Him handle it."

Hayden grew tired of all the God talk. "What are you going to do about Patrick?"

"Patrick. Is that his name? Hmm. Well, I can hardly turn him and his colonists away. You saw how hungry and worn they looked." Blake rubbed his eyes. "Besides, we could use the help, and they *did* inhabit this town before us."

"But they didn't build the huts," Hayden argued, his mind refusing to believe Blake could be so fooled.

"No, Patrick said they found them like this."

"Then let the colonists stay and banish my father."

"I can't do that and you know it. The man has done us no wrong."

Blood drained from Hayden's heart and fired through his veins. "He's a confidence man. A swindler! He's only here for the gold. He'll charm his way into this colony and infect it like a plague. And like a plague, he must be isolated, cut out with a knife, before we all fall ill."

Blake's gray eyes assessed him. "Perhaps. If so, he'll show his true colors soon enough. Either way, killing him is not the answer." Blake rose. "Rest assured, I will keep an eye on him. And so will James. We won't allow him to harm New Hope or anyone in it."

Hayden repressed a laugh. Though Blake was a competent leader, he had no idea who he was up against. But Hayden did. And he had no intention of allowing that man to stay. Perhaps Blake was right about not murdering him, but Hayden had other ways to exact his revenge.

CHAPTER 30

Babies made the sweetest sounds when they slept. Or at least Lydia did. Little gurgles and tongue clicks and grunts of innocence bubbled through Sarah's hut. Though the sound was far more soothing than Magnolia's father's snores, she still could not sleep, envying every second of the babe's worry-free existence—the sweet repose of innocence. If only Magnolia were a child again on her parents' plantation, when her mother and father were happy and her father doted on her as if she were a princess. Before she'd grown up and disappointed him. But those days were gone. They'd been gone for a long time. And now her father had disowned her.

Rubbing her aching head, Magnolia sat up in bed. Thoughts flitted through her mind, scattered and jumbled, some too painful to light on. Others too thrilling to ignore. Such as the one she embraced now, the one where she had accepted Hayden's suit! She could barely remember the joy she felt at that moment, so brief had it been before Martin had barged into camp, strutting like a bloated goose as if he owned Brazil. Just like he always did everywhere he set his imperious boot. *Hayden's father!* How could it be? Swinging her legs over the cot, she dropped her head into her hands. The Godard man he'd been searching for. The man he'd given his life to find was her ex-fiancé. A putrid taste flooded her mouth.

Shouts drifted through the bamboo and mud walls, and she wondered who else was having trouble sleeping. Flinging on her robe, Magnolia glanced at Sarah and Lydia sleeping side by side on the cot and smiled. Moonlight fluttered silver ribbons on both their faces, as if God Himself gently caressed them while they slept. Was that what it took to get God's affection? To be as good and sweet as Sarah? If so, Magnolia would forever be in His disfavor. Just like she was in her father's. Shoving her feet into slippers, she headed outside. To walk. To think. To clear her head. Anything to soften the ache in her heart.

After Hayden had struck his father, he'd stomped off, not once looking her way. Not once! Magnolia knew he was angry. Knew he was as shocked as she at their twisted, vile association. What she didn't know was what he thought of it all. What he thought of her. Mercy me, she didn't even know her own thoughts anymore. Martin had ripped her heart in two and stolen everything from her family. So desperate to be loved, to be cherished, to be of some value to someone, she'd ignored the warning signs along the way: the twinkle of greed in his eye, the twist of doubt in her gut, his sudden interest in investing in new racetracks in Kentucky.

Yet now those doubts rose once again. Was his son any different? Wasn't Hayden just as much a swindler as his father? Hadn't he tricked her with the same sugar-laced words and rakish grins and idle flattery? Perhaps even his offer of courtship was just a part of some nefarious plan to discredit her family again. Although how he could cast any further reproach on them, Magnolia could not imagine. Ah, she was just being silly. Hayden was nothing like his father, and until he gave her a reason to believe otherwise, she would trust him.

Night insects and birds hummed atop a cool breeze swirling off the river. Wrapping her robe tighter, she started down the street when the flicker of a fire caught her gaze. A few more steps and she saw Blake sitting on a stump, Hayden pacing before him deep in conversation. She knew that pace, knew that stubborn cut of his jaw. Her traitorous heart leapt at the sight of him, and she longed to run to him, to know his thoughts, to comfort him in his pain, but instead she just stood there watching.

Soon, Blake rose, said something to Hayden then walked away.

Hayden rubbed the back of his neck and stared at the fire with such anguish, it brought tears to her eyes.

Slipping from the shadows, she entered the clearing, halting when her footsteps brought his gaze to hers. Eyes the color of the jungle assessed her as if she were some unearthly being. Pain clouded them before they hardened like jade.

"Hayden, I. . ." Magnolia took a step toward him, but he held up a hand.

He faced the fire again, his Adam's apple diving in his throat.

"We should talk," Magnolia said.

"I can't."

"I had no idea he was—"

"I know." His cold, distant tone carved a hole in her heart.

"I'm so sorry, Hayden. I'm sorry he hurt you. He hurt me too. Lied to me. Ruined my family."

The strident rasp of crickets filled the air. Above her, a cloud cloaked the moon, stealing away its milky light. "Are you angry with me?"

"You were engaged to my father." He breathed out the words as if still in shock.

Magnolia swallowed, forcing back tears. Only a few hours ago Hayden had gazed at her with such love. Now his eyes were cold and hard. "What does it matter?"

"You and he, you—" Again repugnance braided his expression. "Every time I see you. . .every time I look at you, I will see him. I will see him and you. . .together."

"Well, we are *not* together now!" Magnolia fumed. "And we haven't been for years. Are you going to be equally repulsed by every man I've ever courted?"

He kicked a rock and fisted hands at his waist. "No. Just my father."

A terrible fear began to wind its way through her soul. "How can you be angry at me for something I did in complete innocence? Surely if either of us has a right to be mad, it is I, since it was one of your relatives, your very father, who ruined my family."

Snorting, he raked his hand through his hair and moved to the other side of the fire as if he couldn't stand being close to her.

"Do you think this is easy for me?" Though she'd wanted to sound angry, her voice came out a whimper. "You already swindled me once. Perhaps you *are* your father's son, after all."

He crossed arms over his chest, steely and defiant. Why was he behaving this way? She hadn't done anything wrong. Desperate, she reached out to him, clinging to the hope of his love. "But I want to trust you, Hayden. All you need do is tell me I can. Tell me one more time that I can."

Nothing but the crackle of fire and buzz of katydids met her ears. "Please, talk to me." A tear slid down her cheek.

Still no response.

Dread sank in her gut. "What does this mean for us, Hayden?"

His eyes rose to hers over the fire, the flames reflecting his pain. "I don't know if there is an us."

Knife in hand, Hayden whittled a fresh piece of wood, his anger chipping away at the branch with no design in mind. Much like his life. Lots of cuts and chips and broken parts that formed nothing but a nonsensical shape without beauty or reason. Dawn had broken an hour ago and still he sat in the same spot, ignoring everyone around him and even refusing a plate of fruit Eliza had offered. One thought consumed his mind, and one thought alone—revenge. Even as one feeling consumed his heart. Pain. Pain at the loss of Magnolia. Yet the two were so inextricably connected, he could not separate them. Both cut through his soul, leaving him bitter and empty. The former with a ravenous desire to fill, the latter with a hopelessness he'd never experienced. He hated hurting Magnolia, hated the anguish in her eyes when he'd proclaimed an end to their brief courtship. But what choice did he have? He couldn't look at her without envisioning her in his father's arms.

Speaking of the monster, Patrick finally strolled into the clearing, nodding his greeting at everyone and thanking them when they expressed concern for his injuries. As he passed to grab a plate of fruit, his eyes brushed over Hayden. A new confidence—a smugness—made its home deep within them as if he knew Hayden could not touch him.

Unfortunately for Patrick, he was wrong.

"You aren't getting any ideas." Blake's voice speared conviction through Hayden's thoughts as the colonel took a seat beside him.

"No." He continued whittling. None that he'd tell Blake. Unless Blake agreed to toss Patrick from the colony so Hayden could hunt him down like the animal he was. But he knew the honorable colonel would never do that. No, Hayden would have to wait to find his father alone. Then he'd knock him out, tie him up, and deposit him in the middle of Brazil far away from New Hope. The cultured coxcomb wouldn't survive two days in the wild. A fitting punishment for someone who stripped his victims of all their comforts and security and left them to die.

Patrick's laughter drew Hayden's gaze. His father sat with two women from his colony, both staring at him adoringly and giggling at his every word. The seductive curve of his mouth, the gleam of interest in his eye, his engaging chuckle, the way he looked at each woman as if she were a rare treasure, Hayden knew those tactics well. He'd used them on countless women himself.

"What are you going to do about Mr. Scott?" Hayden asked, noting that the colonel's gaze was also locked on Patrick. "I'm not the only one who wants Patrick Gale dead."

Before Blake could answer, the man in question barreled into the clearing like a steaming locomotive, Mr. Dodd at his side. The two men halted before Patrick. "Arrest this man at once!" Mr. Scott pointed at Hayden's father.

With a groan, Blake excused himself and headed toward the altercation. Hayden followed, the irony of his agreeing with Mr. Scott, for once, not lost on him.

Blake halted beside Dodd. "What's all the fuss?"

Several colonists stopped eating and glanced at the group, while others gathered around.

"The fuss, if you must know"—Mr. Scott gave him a superior look—"is that I'm having this thief arrested. Mr. Dodd was a sheriff back home. Ergo, he is best suited to be the law here. At least until we can set up a proper election or however they work it in Brazil." He scanned the mob and, upon realizing he had an audience, raised his voice. "We have three witnesses who can testify that this man robbed me and my family of all we owned."

"Absurd!" one of the women at Patrick's side exclaimed.

Patrick plopped a slice of orange in his mouth and smiled.

Dodd scratched his head. "Well, I suppose I could oblige you if we had a proper jail."

"We can lock him in the tunnels you told me about, Mr. Dodd. You mentioned there were chains down there."

"No one is arresting anyone," Blake said.

Patrick nodded. "At last, a word of reason." The ladies breathed a sigh of relief.

Mr. Scott bunched his fists. The lines framing his mouth seemed to have deepened overnight. "Colonel, this man is a criminal and must be punished."

Hayden stepped forward. "I couldn't agree more."

Mumbles of both protest and agreement thundered through the colonists.

"Hold up, everyone." Blake raised a hand. "Is anyone here a witness to the theft of Mr. Scott's wealth?" When all grew silent, Blake continued, "I thought not. Then, Mr. Scott, I'm afraid it is your family's word against Patrick's."

"Are you calling me a liar, Colonel?"

"No. I'm simply saying we don't have enough proof." Blake shifted weight off his bad leg. "Besides, as Mr. Dodd said, we have no jail, no judge, and no jury. If you want to see justice done, I suggest you escort Mr. Gale back to the States."

"Why would the man come with me, when all that waits him is the noose?!" Mr. Scott shouted, his baleful eyes narrowing upon Patrick.

The man merely shrugged and rubbed his goatee. "Why would I leave Brazil to waste time and money on a trial that would surely declare me innocent?"

Mr. Scott lunged for Patrick, but James leapt between them and forced the old plantation owner back.

"You can't just let him run free!" Mr. Scott blazed.

Blake rubbed his forehead. "What would you have me do with him?"

"String him up on a tree."

"Here, here," Hayden agreed, drawing his father's reptilian eyes.

"You know I cannot do that." Annoyance edged Blake's tone.

"I appreciate that, Colonel." Patrick smiled. Handing his plate to one of the women, he rose, brushed off his waistcoat, and gazed over the crowd. "Your colony has chosen a wise and just leader."

Ah, now the flattery began. Hayden's stomach curdled. But, thankfully, Blake didn't seem to fall for it.

"However, Mr. Gale." The colonel stared the man down with that I'm-in-command-and-you-will-obey look he must have given his troops on the battlefield. "That something unlawful occurred between you and the Scotts, I have no doubt. Simply because I don't have the means to discover what that is, doesn't mean I won't be keeping a firm eye upon you and your activities in our town. Should I find even the slightest hint of anything nefarious in your dealings with anyone, you will be banished from this colony. Do I make myself clear, sir?"

A flicker of anger, a promise of defiance, crossed Patrick's eyes before they clouded over with seeming compliance. "Of course, Colonel. I wouldn't have it any other way."

The lady to Patrick's right stood and brushed aside her chocolate brown curls. "Colonel Blake, is it? You are quite mistaken about Owen. . .this man you call Patrick. He is a noble man of the highest character." She sent a spiteful glance toward Mr. Scott. "He couldn't possibly have done what this man claims."

Other members of Patrick's colony shouted their agreement.

Mr. Scott seemed about to lose his breakfast. Patrick, on the other hand, nodded his thanks to his admirers before he turned to address Dodd. "Mr. Dodd, I heard you were searching for gold, sir."

Suspicion clouded the ex-lawman's face as he clipped his thumbs into his belt. "What's it to you?"

"Well," he began, drawing the man in. "I happen to have a map. . . an old pirate's map." Patrick raised dark brows.

"So do I." Dodd twitched his crooked nose, studying the man.

"Great news, great news. Precisely what I'd hoped." Patrick rubbed his hands together. "You see, my map is one of three. Perhaps yours is another?" Reaching into his waistcoat pocket, Patrick pulled out a crinkled piece of vellum, carefully unfolded it, and showed it to Dodd, whose eyes widened at the sight.

"It does look similar to mine," Dodd said. "But I found nothing at the spot it led me to. Just another piece. . .of. . ."—Dodd's words slowed as realization rolled over his face—"a . . .map."

"Indeed?" Patrick grinned. "Mr. Dodd, I do believe we need to talk." He glanced over the crowd. "In private."

Mr. Scott jerked from James's grasp. "What does this have to do with this man's arrest?"

Patrick thrust out his chin. "It has everything to do with your complaint, Mr. Scott. For here is what I propose. You say I stole money from you. I say I did not. However, I am a fair and generous man, and I do feel badly for you and your wife and, of course, your lovely daughter."

At the mention of Magnolia, his gaze brushed over Hayden, and the look of victory in his eyes nearly caused Hayden to draw his pistol and shoot the man on the spot. But that would be too nice a death.

"And besides," Patrick continued. "Whatever sort of man you thought I was before, by the very testimonies of the people who have spent months living with me, you can see that I am different—transformed, as it were." One arm drawn over his chest, he bowed toward Mr. Scott. "I wish to make amends for whatever harm you perceive I've done to you."

Hayden glanced over the crowd, expecting to hear rumbles of laughter, or at the very least, see eyes rolling in disbelief, but they all stood mesmerized by the man.

"Mr. Dodd and I will find this gold, I assure you." Patrick raised his voice for all to hear. "And when we do, I shall pay you and your lovely wife every penny you say I stole. How does that sound?"

"Why would you do that if you aren't guilty?" James eyed the man with suspicion.

"Because I am generous. And because if the information regarding this treasure is true, there'll be more than enough gold to pay this man and make us all rich!"

Nausea clambered up Hayden's throat. How could anyone believe such nonsense? But Mr. Scott made no protest. Instead, a hint of greed flashed in his eyes.

"Those pirates certainly thought there was a fortune here," one of the colonists said.

"But the gold is mine." Dodd frowned.

"Not if you need my third of the map to find it." Patrick grinned. "So, Mr. Scott, you can either have the colonel banish me from the colony and remain poor forever, or you can allow me to find the gold and make you a rich man once again."

Hayden chuckled, drawing everyone's gaze. "The man is lying. Can't you see that?"

Mr. Scott glared at Patrick, a vein throbbing at his temple. "I am not a man to be trifled with a second time, Mr. Haley or Gale, or whoever you are. But at the moment, I don't see that I have a choice."

Hayden shook his head in disbelief.

"Find your gold, sir," Mr. Scott continued. "If it even exists. You have six months to do so before I take matters into my own hands" —he swung a determined gaze at Blake—"regardless of what you say, Colonel."

"I would expect nothing less." Patrick gave a placating grin. "You shall have your money, Mr. Scott"—he lifted his chin and scanned the assembled group—"and then I will invest the rest of my share in this town and make it the Southern Utopia we all came here to embrace."

Ah, such seductive words frothing from devious lips with such aplomb that everyone cheered and smiled at him like the puppets they were. And he, the puppet master, skillfully pulling their strings. Hayden frowned. Yet, how many times had he, himself, lied to people, persuaded them with the same laud and puffery, put on a facade of honor and integrity while placating them with the same reassuring smile? All the while robbing them behind their backs of everything they had. Sometimes in front of their eyes.

A horrible realization struck him. One he should have seen long ago. In his quest to find his father by entering the man's world, Hayden had become just like the man he hated.

Chapter 31

Squeezing through the rotted gate, Hayden entered the temple square. How Blake and James had talked him into coming here again, he couldn't say. It seemed like a good idea at the time—a chance to get away from bumping into Magnolia everywhere he went, as well as from stewing in fury while he plotted revenge against his father. But now, as he glanced over the gruesome faces carved into obelisks and the huge fire pit whereupon those faces, along with their bodies, had been roasted, he much preferred his own internal angst than this temple of horrors.

But sweet Eliza had insisted that she check on Graves and bring him some food, and Blake would not have her come alone. In fact, he organized a regular posse consisting of Thiago, Moses, and of course James, who was anxious to return due to his reading of some ancient book Graves had given him. However, now as James entered the courtyard, he moved with the determined, wary look of a warrior rather than the interest of a scholar. The preacher-doctor was a constant surprise to Hayden for he knew the man harbored secrets from his past. Yet he played the part of a respectable man of God so well, Hayden couldn't help but admire him.

Thiago and Moses entered in after Hayden, looking less than pleased to be there, with Blake and Eliza bringing up the rear.

"Let's get this over with." Hayden started toward the temple stairs. "Though I don't see why you care so much for Mr. Graves, Eliza. If it were up to me, I'd leave him to his own devices."

Releasing her husband, Eliza slipped her arm through Hayden's. "We all have moments of insanity in our lives, do we not?" Her coy smile made him wonder if she referred to Hayden's recent attempt to murder his father. If she only knew the other horrid things he'd done, she wouldn't dare to touch him now. "Perhaps if someone had cared for us during those times," she continued, "we would have come to our senses sooner."

"You can't argue with my wife's compassionate heart." Blake leapt on the stairs, kicked aside a piece of crumbling stone, and helped Eliza up. The adoring way he looked at her clouded Hayden with sorrow. His chances at loving and being loved like that had died with the revelation of Magnolia's relationship with his father.

James faced the young interpreter. "Thiago, will you join us inside this time? There are some carvings I need you to look at."

The Brazilian's chest bellowed like the wind, but his jaw remained firm as he followed James up the stairs.

"I'll wait here," Moses said.

Blake nodded at the man, flung a sack of food and water over his shoulder, and led his wife inside the temple. Hayden followed, wondering if he shouldn't wait outside with Moses. But his curiosity got the best of him. The last time he'd been here, they'd gone no farther than the altar in the back. Since then, he'd heard Graves had managed to excavate tunnels beneath the building.

Minutes later, the oppressive heat in those tunnels threatened to melt Hayden on the spot. The deeper they went, the hotter it became. Eliza wilted in her husband's arms as he led her along, while James and Thiago discussed the odd carvings on the wall. Put there by the cannibals who built the temple, Thiago guessed, and telling a tale about a huge battle between the gods.

"And these." Thiago held up the torch and pointed toward drawings of figures that looked like giants with wings. "These are powerful beings who fought." He ran his finger over the rough stone. "Here see, they are put in chains. Defeated."

Sweat stung Hayden's eyes. He wiped it away, moving past them.

What difference did some ancient fable make when one was roasting alive? With each step he took, more air seeped from his lungs, while his damp clothes clung to him like tarpaper. And what in tarnation was that smell? A smell that got worse when, at the bottom of two sets of stairs, they entered a torch-lit cave. All the chamber needed to complete Hayden's vision of hell were volcanoes of fire belching from the ground.

Leading her to sit on a boulder, Blake handed Eliza his canteen. The woman shouldn't be here at all, but Hayden knew Blake oft had difficulty bridling his stubborn wife. Which reminded Hayden of Magnolia. Despite how things ended between them, a smile tugged his lips. A smile that soon faded when James lifted a torch to reveal strange symbols scrawled above two alcoves.

"Yes, yes. Deception and Delusion," he mumbled to himself as he knelt to examine the broken chains at the bottom of a long pole. "They are in the book. *The Judgment of the Four*. They are two of the four mentioned."

"I don't understand," Eliza said.

Hayden ran a sleeve over his forehead. "What nonsense is this, Doc?"

James shook his head. "I haven't translated it all yet. But they were some kind of powerful beings."

"Like the carvings on wall." Thiago's gaze skittered about the eerie cave. "The defeated ones."

Hayden snorted. "Where is Graves?"

As if on cue, sounds echoed from an opening to their left and out crawled Mr. Graves. Though he'd been sinister-looking before landing in Brazil, the dust-laden, long-haired, rag-attired man who emerged into the room now harbored such a macabre aura about him, Hayden's sweat turned cold.

"Ah, Mr. Graves." Eliza approached him. "We've brought you some food and water."

"I have no need of it." He waved her away, but by the way his clothes hung on him, Hayden thought he should reconsider.

"Still, we will leave it for you," Eliza said as the man brushed past her, his suspicious eyes flitting over her. "What are you doing here? Come to spy?"

Blake drew his wife back. "We were worried about you."

"No need." Graves swatted dirt from his stained and torn shirt. Cuts marred the skin on his arms and neck. "Unless you hear them and wish to help, it would be best if you didn't come at all." His dark glance roved over them. "Good. Just four of you." He wiped sweat from his forehead, leaving a streak. "There can never be six," he muttered, his expression suddenly tightening.

James and Hayden exchanged a glance that said they agreed the man was mad. Or at the very least, he couldn't count, though their fifth member, Thiago, now remained at the entrance as if ready to bolt at the first provocation.

The anxious twist of Graves's lips soon raised into a sinister grin. "I tried to stop you, you know."

"Stop us from what?" Eliza asked.

"From coming to Brazil. But I was wrong."

Hayden stepped toward the crazy man, his curiosity roused. "How did you try to stop us?"

A maniacal gleam crossed his eyes. "Don't you remember? The storm, the mists, the illness, the first mate's injury, the fire"—he paused, thinking—"oh, and the birds."

Of course Hayden remembered. That voyage from Charleston to Rio had been fraught with one odd disaster after another. Even Captain Barclay had commented that in all his years of sailing, he'd never seen such bad luck. Which was all it was. Just bad luck. "You cannot expect us to believe you caused any of that," Hayden said.

One brow arched in imperious delight. "You'd be surprised what kind of power is available for those willing to call upon it."

James rubbed the scar on his cheek. "There are only two types of power on this earth. The power of God and the power of the devil."

Graves chuckled. "Indeed, dear doctor, indeed."

"But why?" Blake asked. "Why would you want to stop us?"

"For revenge, of course!" Graves erupted in fury, fisting his hands. "I was to be a senator, then president someday. If not for the South seceding, I would have been!"

Whether it was the scorching heat, the stench, or the lack of food for days on end that had done it, Graves had gone undeniably insane.

"Someone had to pay, you see." Graves's hurried tone spiked with anger. "So I tried to destroy your hopes, your dreams, as you destroyed mine. But I was wrong. We were meant to come here." He waved a bruised, filthy hand over them. "Besides, you will soon suffer enough, and I will be more powerful than any president could be."

Blake gathered Eliza close. "Then, we will leave you be, sir."

Breaking free from her husband, she stepped toward Graves, extending a hand. "Mr. Graves, please come back with us. You aren't safe here."

"You are dabbling in things you don't understand," James said. "Dangerous things."

"Evil things." Thiago added from the entrance.

Eliza took another step. "Please, we care about you. Come back with us."

For a mere second, the evil glint in Graves's eyes softened, replaced by a look of pleading, as if a part of him, buried deep within, cried for help. But then it was gone, hardened into granite as black and infinite as a bottomless pit.

"Ah, but that's where you are wrong," he said. "You'll see. When I gain my power, I will crush your little colony to dust."

❦

The next evening, Hayden sat whittling in the center of town, longing for some peace after a long day's work. But that was not to be. He could hear his father returning from his treasure hunt. The fiend's spurious laughter grated over Hayden—that gloating I-don't-find-you-amusing-but-I'll-laugh-anyway-to-win-your-favor chuckle that Hayden knew too well. Why? Because he had perfected it himself. Trying to ignore the grating sound, he chipped away at the piece of wood in his hand. He still didn't know what he was making. Other than a mess. But whittling kept his hands from doing what they longed to do—wringing his father's neck. Why hadn't the man fallen off a cliff or been bitten by a poisonous snake, or better yet, devoured by a wolf? Surely that would be a just end. But apparently God wasn't just, or surely He would have punished Patrick long ago.

Which meant it was still up to Hayden.

All around him, the townsfolk clustered in groups after supper, talking about the day's events and their plans for tomorrow. Both Blake and James had tried to engage Hayden in conversation, but his mood was too dour for company. He'd spent hours with them, chopping down trees for a barn and a dock, hoping the hard work would get his mind off of his situation. But all it had done was delay the inevitable confusion and despair that haunted his evening hours. The more Hayden sought to catch his father alone, the more people surrounded him like a fortress of worshipping toadies. It was as if God protected Patrick, while leaving his victims defenseless.

The odious man now sauntered into the clearing, a lady on each arm, conversing in his cavalier tone and looking none the worse for wear after a day of hunting gold. Dodd, on the other hand, followed behind him, carrying shovels and pick axes and appearing as if he'd wallowed for hours in the mud with pigs. Amazing. His father had even charmed Dodd into doing his work for him. Hayden scored another slice of wood and flicked it aside as colonists gathered to hear news of the treasure hunt.

A captive audience was the golden goose to a man like Patrick. Swinging about, his eyes twinkling, he began an embellished account of their adventures, drawing gasps from the ladies and admiring grunts from the men. Mr. Dodd, however, shook his head and circled the group to get his supper.

Hayden's own meal rebelled in his stomach. Rising, he slipped the knife into his belt and wood in his pocket and made his way to the edge of camp. Plunging into the jungle, he kept going until he could no longer hear his father's voice, until the familiar buzz and hum of night creatures suffused all other sounds. He sat on a log and breathed in the thick air, scented with orchids and lemons and musk. Dim light from a half-moon spread a dusting of silver on branches and leaves. Brazil truly was a beautiful place, teeming with life. But Hayden couldn't stay.

Once he got his revenge—in whatever form that took—he would go back home. In fact, depending on the type of revenge he exacted, he might be *forced* to go back home. The thought unnerved him, and he shifted on his seat. He would miss his new friends, his honest work. And most of all, he would miss Magnolia. But what choice did he have? Every time he looked at her, his mind conjured up a myriad of sordid images of her in his father's arms. Even worse, she seemed to be enjoying herself. Hayden shook the pictures from his head. No, he must start anew. Perhaps help his friend in his furniture shop in Savannah, learn how to survive on honesty and integrity rather than lies and deceit.

Like his father.

Visions of the man pranced tauntingly through Hayden's mind— his mischievous grin, swaggering gait—along with the wake of hapless victims fawning over his every witticism. Especially the females. Yet how was Hayden any different? He dropped his head into his hands, not wanting to consider the question, yet not able to avoid the suffocating truth of its answer. Crackling sounds echoed, louder and louder, finally fading into female moans and sobs. Hayden looked up. A mass of pearly moon-dust materialized in front of him, glittering in the starlight. It floated through the air like a cloud that had lost its way, uttering the woeful cries of a woman. Hayden could only stare at it, transfixed in confusion as it began to twirl and spin in a mad rush that soon took the shape and form of Miss Grayson.

Hayden swallowed. His heart raced.

"Hello, Joseph," she said, a vacant look in her once lustrous brown eyes.

Joseph Murphy, the name he'd used all those years ago.

"What? Nothing to say? The charming Joseph, with ever a witty retort on his lips, has suddenly gone silent?" She raised her chin, that pert little chin he had so adored—at least for a time.

"I'm sorry, Julianne."

"Oh, *now* you're sorry." Clutching her skirts, she sauntered about the clearing as if she were strolling through a ballroom. Yet not a twig snapped, not a leaf stirred beneath her silk slippers. "But you weren't sorry when you ran off with my dowry." She swirled to face him, her hooped-skirt bobbing. "Left me with a ruined reputation and no prospects."

Just as his father had done to Magnolia.

The words spun a tempest in Hayden's mind. Shame fisted in his throat, threatening to strangle him. He gripped his neck and forced himself to breathe. Julianne wasn't real. She was only a figment of his guilt-laden mind. Yet, as he stared at the agony folding her beautiful features, he suddenly wished she *were* real. Then he could tell her how sorry he was. Then he could somehow make up for what he'd done.

"What I did was wrong." He slowly rose.

"Wrong?" Her voice spiked, her eyes flashed. "It was more than wrong. It was cruel, heartless, and wicked. You don't know what happened to me, do you, Joseph? After you left?" Gathering her pink satin skirts, she floated across the clearing like a lily on a pond. "I never married, of course. Watched all my friends find love and have babies. But worse than that, I became the laughingstock of Williamsburg. A cursed woman whom the Yankees found easy prey when they stormed in to occupy our town."

Nausea bubbled in Hayden's gut. "No."

"Yes."

"I'm sorry." He stepped toward her, but she withdrew. "I didn't mean to. . . I didn't want to hurt you."

"Then why *did* you, Joseph? Why?" A tear spilled from the corner of her eye.

Visions didn't cry, did they? Hayden sank back onto the log. "I was trying to find my father."

"And you have finally found him, haven't you? A man after your own heart."

Hayden stared at the dirt. "No, I was only pretending to be like him, penetrating his social circles. It was the only way to find him."

He kicked a rock with his boot. How his mother would have hated that. "No!" He hung his head. "I'm nothing like him."

The swish of skirts sounded, and Julianne knelt before him, studying him. Her eyes, now devoid of tears, turned hard as quartz.

"Then you must kill him. It is the only way."

Up close, she looked so real. The shimmer of her skin in the moonlight, the wisps of hair dangling over her forehead, even the locket around her neck. "How will killing him help you?"

"He started this. He's the reason you swindled me, ruined my life. He should pay."

Which was exactly what Hayden had planned to do. Yet there was something familiar in Julianne's face. An expression. . .a madness. . . that brought a memory of Graves to mind.

Revenge. Was Graves's insanity the destiny for all those who sought revenge?

And what of Blake? The man had every reason to seek retribution from the Yankees, but he'd forgiven. The comparison between the two men shook Hayden to his core.

As if she could read his thoughts, Julianne's face contorted. Flames flickered in her hard eyes. "Kill him," she hissed. "It's what you've wanted your entire life. Now's your chance."

"I don't know what I want anymore."

"You fool! You weak, pathetic fool." She rose and brushed off her skirts, her face angular and harsh. But then it softened back into its familiar graceful curves. A glaze covered her eyes. "You must do it for me. The price for my forgiveness."

A breeze swept through the trees, swaying leaves and bringing shadows out from hiding. Dark mist slithered over the ground, swirled around her feet, and rose to circle her skirts like a cobra beneath its master's flute. And for the first time in his life, Hayden sensed pure evil. Dark, heavy, powerful, all-consuming. And with it came a heady lust, an irresistible yank on his heart to obey her words. To murder his father.

"Do it!" she shouted, her eyes fiery coals.

"Oh, God." Hayden dropped to his knees. "Help me!"

All went silent. All save the frogs and crickets and night herons. He lifted his gaze. Julianne was gone. So were the shadows. Instead, a spire of moonlight lit the spot where she had stood. "God?" Hayden's breath tangled in his throat. "Jesus, are you there?"

A breeze played upon his face, spinning through his hair and cooling the sweat on his neck. "You exist. All this time I thought you were a fable, a myth." Burning traveled from his throat to his eyes. He would not cry. He hadn't cried since his mother died.

"I'm so sorry, Lord. I've hurt so many people. Ruined so many lives." A tear escaped. He batted it away. "I don't deserve Your attention. I deserve nothing but judgment and pain."

Palm fronds fluttered, like angels laughing. No, not laughing, singing! Soft words sifted through his soul, "I LOVE YOU, SON. YOU ARE FORGIVEN."

Son? No one had ever called Hayden that before.

A father of the fatherless, and a judge of the widows, is God in his holy habitation.

The verse blared in his mind from a time long ago when he'd sat in the back of a cold, dark church in Tennessee and listened to the first sermon he'd heard since his mother died. Yet now as an overwhelming feeling of love and belonging fell on him, he could not deny that God was present, wrapping His arms around the little orphan boy shivering and starving on the streets of Charleston.

God had been there all along. He'd always had a Father. One that would never abandon him.

Rising, he closed his eyes to the moonlight and allowed the wind to dry his tears.

He was a new man.

CHAPTER 32

Is that everything?" Magnolia corked the bottle of plantain tincture and placed it on the shelf, straightening the others beside it.

"Yes," Eliza said. "It's more than enough. However did I run this place without you those two weeks you were gone?" She stuffed a loose strand into her bun then wiped down the examining table. "You are such a huge help."

Magnolia smiled, feeling a lift in her heart for the first time in four days—four days since Patrick Gale had arrived in town and ruined her life. Again. Yet, in the meantime, she had more than proven her service to the colony—that she could earn her keep, take care of herself, and have no need for her parents' support. The realization was exhilarating. Or it would be if she weren't so melancholy. "Truly? Or are you just being kind?"

Eliza gave her a look of reprimand. "I wouldn't lie to you, Magnolia. You have a real knack for nursing. And you're a hard worker. At least you've become one since your trip to Rio."

Had she? Had she been that lazy before? "Don't tell my father that. He considers *work* akin to profanity." She chuckled.

"Good to hear you laugh again." Eliza threw the dirty cloth into a bucket.

Magnolia gazed out the window where the setting sun angled through palms and lined the floor with wavering strips of light. "As long as I don't think about things, I'm all right. Which is why I truly appreciate you allowing me to help in the clinic. It keeps my mind off my problems." Untying her apron, she drew it from her waist.

"Which one? Patrick or Hayden?" Eliza gave her a teasing smile.

"Both, I suppose. Though I'm relieved Patrick has been spending his days with Dodd hunting gold, sparing me the discomfort of his presence." Yet as relieved as she was of their absence, she'd been equally dismayed that Hayden had been absent as well.

"I don't know whether to pray that Patrick and Dodd find the gold soon, or that they never find it." Eliza began picking up dirty scissors, knives, needles, tweezers, and other medical instruments. "Hayden doesn't believe his father will stay long after they do."

Of course he wouldn't. Magnolia would bet her life the charlatan would break his promise and run off with any treasure he found, leaving her still indebted to her parents. But the worst of it was Hayden would leave as well, ever in pursuit of his blasted revenge.

Eliza touched Magnolia's arm. "Your parents shouldn't have blamed you for what happened. You were all fooled by the man."

"Perhaps." Magnolia tossed her dirty apron into a basket and looked down. "I don't know. But that's kind of you to say." She bit her lip. "But, then, you've always been kind to me, Eliza. Even when I blackmailed you for liquor on board the *New Hope*."

Eliza's golden eyes twinkled. "It all ended well. And your issue with drink? Has that ended well?" She picked up the tray of instruments and gave Magnolia a questioning look.

"Truth be told, I still struggle with it now and then."

The door flap swept open and Angeline entered, thankfully cutting the conversation short. Smiling at them both, she handed Eliza a bundle of dried herbs, while Stowy, her cat, circled the hem of her skirts. "Suma root. Complements of Mrs. Matthews. For your medicine chest."

"Wonderful." Setting down the tray, Eliza skirted the examination table and set the plants on a shelf. "Perhaps if we don't have too many patients tomorrow, Magnolia, I can show you how to crush these and create a tincture."

"I'd love to learn." Though Magnolia tried to interject excitement in her voice, her doleful tone drew Angeline's gaze.

"Why, Magnolia, I just came from the meeting area and I'd swear Hayden wears the same sour face you do," she said. "Perhaps you both suffer from the same malady?" She smiled.

Magnolia picked up the tray of instruments and carried it to the side table where a bucket of clean water waited. She hated that the entire town knew Hayden had broken off their courtship. She hated the whispers that ceased when she came near, the smirks, the looks of pity. She did not want to be pitied. *A Scott is never pitied*," her father always said. And besides, what's done was done.

"His father's appearance has upset him greatly," she answered Angeline.

"No doubt." Angeline twirled a lock of her russet hair. "As I'm sure it has upset you. I just don't see the point of you both denying your affections for each other."

"He doesn't want me anymore. Not after discovering I was engaged to his father. In fact, you can have him, Angeline. He's never hidden his interest in you." Magnolia flinched when her voice came out more clipped than she intended, but Angeline didn't seem to notice.

"His gaze follows *you* everywhere in camp. He doesn't even know I exist."

Forcing Angeline's words from her heart where they would only cause more pain, Magnolia raised her gaze to find both her friends staring at her curiously. A loose strand of hair tickled her shoulder, and she tucked it in place. "I must look a fright. And look at the dirt in my fingernails." She held them up before her.

"You always glow, Magnolia," Eliza said. "Surely you know that. Besides, a woman's beauty doesn't come from hairstyles or jewelry or clothing. It comes from within."

Magnolia studied Eliza, half expecting to see the old woman from the church materialize in place of her friend. But it was only Eliza, with the usual approval beaming from her eyes. So accepting, so loving of everyone. So unlike Magnolia. *Beauty comes from within.* Could it be true? Could everything she'd ever thought or ever learned be so completely wrong?

Scooping up Stowy, Angeline bundled the cat in her arms. "I quite agree, Eliza. True beauty is more than fripperies and finery. Thank goodness, because it's far too difficult to keep up appearances in this jungle."

"Isn't that the truth?" Eliza chuckled, placing the instruments in water. "I do miss a few of the finer things back home, hot baths, for one."

"And perfume," Angeline added.

"And being fitted for a new gown..." Eliza said.

"And wearing satin slippers with no fear of getting them muddy."

"And—"

"But how does one adorn one's inside?" Magnolia interrupted, drawing both their gazes.

Eliza approached and squeezed her hand. "Only God can do that. All you have to do is ask Him. He loves you, Magnolia. He formed you in your mother's womb to be unique and talented and beautiful and... well, just to be you."

Eliza's statement followed Magnolia as she made her way down the main street later that day. Was that what the old woman in the church was trying to tell her? That she had to turn to God? It was all too confusing. Though the scent of roasted fish permeated the air, her stomach knotted. She had no desire to eat. All she wanted was to find someplace alone where she could nurse her broken heart.

A child's laughter drew her gaze to Mr. Jenkins, one of the famers, coming home from working in the fields. His little girl, Henrietta, ran into his arms without a care about the layers of sweat and grim covering the man. He spun her around, showering her with kisses as her giggles rose to join the birdsong above them. Frozen in place, Magnolia watched as he lowered her to a bench and sat beside her, listening with rapt attention as she told him about her day. He didn't rush to clean off the filth from the fields or dash to get his supper. No, he sat and listened as if she were the most important thing in the world to him—his special princess. Mercy me, he didn't even notice that her dress was stained and her hair was a rat's nest! Nothing but love poured from his gaze onto his little girl. Tears flooded Magnolia's eyes. Was that how a father was supposed to treat his daughter? Not with harsh words and impossible expectations? But simple adoration?

The vision blurred before her, and she started on her way again, lowering her gaze lest others see her crying. She dipped into Sarah's hut, lit a lantern, then took it, along with her flask of pinga, and dove into the jungle. She needed time alone. Time to think, to sort things out, to plan. And to cry.

Shoving aside leaves, she entered her favorite spot by a small creek and sat on a boulder beside the rippling water, finally allowing her tears to flow. One by one they slid down her cheeks and leapt from her jaw into her lap. She swiped them away. What good did it do to cry? She stared at the brook, her eyes drawn to a small pool of calm water by her feet. Dare she take a peek? Or would it just distress her further? Either way she'd better decide before the setting sun stole the remaining light.

Leaning over, she cringed at the reflection and jerked back. Still old and ugly. And she'd been trying so hard to be kind and think of others! Helping out Eliza in the clinic, assisting Sarah with baby Lydia, working in the garden the other women had planted. Even carrying buckets of water from the river. But she was still ugly inside.

Uncorking the flask, she gulped the pinga. Burning spice sped down her throat and warmed her belly. She tipped the flask to her lips once again. Perhaps if she drank enough, the grotesque image would disappear from her mind.

Perhaps she should take her ugly self back to Georgia. Without Hayden, there was no point in staying in this uncivilized jungle. Yes, she had made friends—true friends—for the first time in her life. And she had employment—a trade. She was not useless as her father had always declared. But after tasting Hayden's love, how could she live in the same town with him day in and day out? Even if he did end up leaving, there were too many memories of him here.

And then there was Patrick. What if he didn't find his gold for months? How could she live in such close proximity with the monster who had ruined her life? It was too much to ask. If she could find a way home, she might be able to locate Samuel and at least have a chance at contentment and peace. And comfort. Not happiness anymore. She could never be happy with anyone but Hayden. She ground her fists on her forehead. "Oh." If only Patrick hadn't shown up and ruined everything!

Leaning back on the boulder, she plucked a leaf and fanned herself. "I'd kill him myself if I had the chance."

"Who's that, my dear?" Shoving leaves aside, Patrick Gale materialized out of the foliage and headed toward her.

"What are you doing here?" Setting down her flask, Magnolia jumped to her feet, feeling the rum crawl back up her throat. "Don't come any closer."

Yet Patrick continued onward, the ever-present grin on his lips. "Don't fret, my dear. I come as a friend not an enemy."

"You will always be my enemy."

"Always? I had hoped for a truce." Lantern light shifted over his face and sparked desire in his eyes. Eyes the same color as Hayden's yet devoid of the gleam that was uniquely his.

"You hope in vain, Martin, or Patrick, or whoever you are. Not another step. I'm warning you."

"Such threats. Tsk tsk. I well remember the days you longed to be near me. In my arms. With my lips on yours." He stopped before her—too close—eyeing her lips as if they were made of cake and he wanted a taste.

He smelled of the same lavender-spice cologne he'd always worn, and she wondered how he could still have some left after months in the jungle. But Martin had always been a resourceful man. She stepped back, fear clamping her gut. She shoved it aside, choosing anger instead. "Do you honestly expect me to run into your arms after you lied to me, cheated me, ruined my family, and broke my heart?"

"No." He fingered his graying goatee. "But you can't deny there is still a certain attraction between us." He reached up to touch her cheek.

She backed away. "I will deny it with my dying breath. Now, leave."

An animal growled in the distance, reminding her of the wolf that had attacked her. She shivered and stared at the beast hunting her now. His face was drawn in sorrow. But she knew it was a ruse. Everything the man did was a ruse to get what he wanted.

"I have come to apologize and to tell you I've changed. Can't a person change?"

Instead of charming, he looked sinister in the shadows of light and dark. Sinister and miserable. And old. What had she ever seen in him? "Some people do change, I suppose. Others never will."

He pressed the hair above his ears into place. "I want to make things up to you, dearest."

"Don't call me that!" Crossing her arms over her waist, she gazed over the swirling brook, envying its soothing dance. "I am in the middle of a savage jungle with no money, no prospects, and no future. All because of you. I doubt you can ever repay me."

"Ah, but I can. When I find the gold, I fully intend to repay your parents every dollar I stole."

She snapped her gaze back to his. "I hope that you do, sir, but I shan't count on it. As I shan't count on anything you say ever again."

He folded his lips in a smile—a patronizing smile—as if he had come to her rescue just in the nick of time. "We could run away together. Back to the States. You could have beautiful gowns and jewels and ladies' maids to service your every whim." He scanned her, frowning. "It would seem my offer could not have come a moment too soon. I've never seen you so out of sorts, dearest." He brushed something from his coat sleeve. "The jungle is no place for a lady like you."

Memories of their time together invaded like a cold mist. Magnolia's stomach shrank. She'd been so young, so impressionable, so eager to please this sophisticated man, that she'd allowed him to critique her every move, her every word, as well as her appearance.

Just like her father.

He leaned forward and sniffed. A victorious grin lifted his perfectly coiffed mustache. "I see you've done away with your prudish ways and have finally taken to drink."

"You thought me a prude?" She gave a bitter laugh. "Is that why you constantly pushed me to savor your spirits? Or was it to lower my defenses so you could have your way with me?"

He sighed. "But it never worked, did it?" Drawing a flask from inside his waistcoat, he tipped it toward her. "Scotch?"

Magnolia licked her lips and looked away.

Unscrewing the cap, he took a sip. "If you can find it in your heart to forgive me, dearest, perhaps we can start over?" He slipped the flask back into his pocket. "Begin a courtship anew. You always were my favorite."

"Your favorite what? Victim?" Magnolia snorted, suddenly wondering what *his* reflection would look like in the pond. "You sicken me, sir. I'd rather die a thousand deaths than tolerate one touch from you!"

"*Tant dramatique!*" The salacious glimmer in his eyes brightened. "I always loved your passion." He leaned toward her. "Perhaps a kiss for old time's sake?"

Magnolia raised her hand to slap him. He caught it and tugged it behind him, pinning her against his chest. Scotch and lavender combined in a repulsive odor that stung her nose. Her head spun. Her legs wobbled. She struggled to free herself and cried out. He grabbed her other arm and held it down. Lips descended on hers.

Then he was gone. Disappeared in a mad swoosh. Magnolia stumbled to catch her balance and peered into the shadows to see Hayden shoving Patrick to the ground.

"Haven't you done enough?" Hayden growled, then picked the man up by his lapels and shoved a fist into his gut.

Coughing, Patrick bent like a snapped twig and held up a hand to stay his son. When he recovered his breath, he stood upright and chuckled. *Chuckled!* Though Magnolia could see the hesitancy in his eyes. "Well played, son. Well played. But I had no intention of hurting her."

"Do not call me that." Hayden seethed, snapping hair from his face. "Now leave before I finish what I started the other night."

Patrick held up his palms. "You would murder an unarmed man?"

"You would ravish an innocent woman?"

Magnolia didn't know whether to be elated that Hayden had come to her rescue or frightened at the ensuing battle. She scanned the clearing for something with which to strike Patrick.

Hayden took a step toward his father, hands fisted at his sides. "Go!"

One corner of Patrick's lips twitched. "Very well. Calm yourself, boy. I'm leaving." Straightening his coat, he tipped his head toward Magnolia and started away. Hayden unclenched his fists and glanced at Magnolia. Just one tiny glance that took his eyes from Patrick for but a second. And the beast took advantage and slugged Hayden across the jaw.

His head jerked to the side. He stumbled backward. Yet even before Hayden recovered, he pummeled his father in the chest, knocking the man off balance. Grabbing his coat to keep him upright, Hayden slugged him in the stomach. A left and then a right before landing a final blow to his head. The vile man once again fell to the dirt.

Patrick rolled across the leaves, reaching inside his coat. Scrambling, turning, grunting, he finally leapt to his knees. Blood seeped from lips that formed a slow grin—a devilish grin that seemed to have a life of its own in the flickering light. Plucking a pistol from within his coat, he leveled it at Hayden. Hayden froze. The gun cocked. Magnolia's breath halted. Patrick pulled the trigger.

CHAPTER 33

The sharp crack of Patrick's pistol reverberated in Hayden's ears.
Magnolia screamed. Gun smoke pinched his nose. Sweat dribbled
down his neck as a numbness crept up his legs, his thighs, and onto
his torso. He patted his chest, searching for the wound that surely
must be there, all the while wondering why he felt no pain. Perhaps
the absence was God's way of sparing those who were dying from last-
minute agony. Yet, when he raised his hands, no blood appeared on
them anywhere.

His father had missed.

Dashing to Hayden, Magnolia seemed equally shocked, her teary
eyes scanning him from head to toe before falling into his arms. He
absorbed her like a root absorbed water, her feminine scent wiping away
the anger and smoke from his nose. It was good to hold her again.

Tossing down his gun, Patrick cursed and drew a knife.

Nudging Magnolia behind him, Hayden faced his father. "Killing
your own son? I thought at least *that* was beneath you, Patrick."

"You've become a nuisance, Hayden. Besides, you already tried to
kill your own father, so what does that make you?" Moonlight glinted
on the blade as he flipped the knife expertly in his hand. "And it
appears you've stolen my lady's affections. An insult that cannot go
unchallenged."

Fingers twitching at the chance to put an end to this, Hayden
slowly drew the knife from his belt. He could kill his father right here

and now. And what better excuse? The man had assaulted Magnolia and shot at Hayden. No one would blame Hayden at all.

Patrick circled him, his eyes obsidian in the darkness—empty, hard obsidian that reminded Hayden of the vision of Julianne, the way her eyes had changed, the presence of evil surrounding her.

"Stop this at once! Both of you!" Magnolia shouted, her voice broken and desperate.

Patrick charged, his blade gleaming. Hayden sidestepped then barreled into the man's side, sending them both to the ground. Round and round in the mud and leaves they went. Patrick groaned and grunted, his spittle spraying. Pain sliced Hayden's arm. Releasing his father, he leapt back and jumped to his feet, holding back the blood beneath his sleeve.

"Hayden, no!" Magnolia cried.

Patrick bounced up with more agility than his age should have allowed. Brushing leaves from his coat, he stretched his neck. A malicious grin alighted on his lips. "How does it feel to have your father's cast offs?" He gestured toward Magnolia.

"How dare you?" Magnolia stomped her foot, bent to pick up a rock, and tossed it at Patrick. He ducked, chuckling. Groaning, she went off in search of another while Hayden assessed his enemy.

"If you're fool enough to release such a treasure what is that to me?" Hayden dove for the man, seeing nothing but the path from his knife to Patrick's heart.

But Patrick blocked that path with a quick thrust of his arm and then twisted to ram his blade toward Hayden's stomach. He would have succeeded in planting a fatal wound if Hayden hadn't lunged backward. As it was, Patrick's attack loosened the knife from Hayden's hand. It fell with an ominous thud to the dirt. Heart in his throat, Hayden searched the ground to retrieve it, but darkness kept it hidden.

"Aha!" Patrick sauntered toward him, his expression one of ravenous glee.

A flash of blue calico blocked him from view. "Stop this nonsense, Patrick!" Magnolia pounded on his father's chest. "He is your son. You beast! You horrible beast!"

Hayden charged toward her. Foolish woman. The man would take no thought to kill her if she became a nuisance. He reached out to shove her aside when Patrick grabbed her wrists and locked them together. "Ah, my dearest, how utterly quaint." She tried to kick him, but he sprang out of her way. "The woman fights better than you do, Hayden!"

The sight of Patrick's knife gleaming in the moonlight so close to Magnolia's throat kept Hayden in place. "Leave her be. Your fight is with me."

"As you wish." Patrick released Magnolia with a violent shove, sending her crashing to the ground in a puff of skirts.

Fury took charge. Hayden fisted Patrick in the stomach. His groan was but momentary. Leaning over, he grabbed something from the ground and then rushed Hayden. Hayden could barely react before something struck him over the head. His vision clouded. His legs liquefied. And he dropped to the ground, fighting to keep conscious.

Tossing a rock aside, Patrick pounced on him, jamming Hayden's shoulders into the dirt. Overhead, branches and leaves spun around a sprinkling of stars. He heard Magnolia's faint sobs. A glimmer flashed in his eyes and pain seared his neck. His father's face filled his vision, crinkled in rage. "Why did you have to find me? Why didn't you leave me alone? Now, you force my hand."

Hayden knew it was all over. His father would kill him. *God help me!*

His head began to clear. His strength returned. His father still hovered over him, knife to Hayden's throat, hesitating. Was there some goodness in the man after all?

"Sorry," was all Patrick said before he inhaled as if to gather strength for the task. In a burst of energy, Hayden kneed him in the groin and shoved him aside. Moonlight flashed on the knife as Hayden plucked it from his father's hand and held it to his throat.

"One move. One breath. And it will be your last."

Lantern light circled them as if they were performers in some gruesome play.

Terror etched across Patrick's eyes.

This was the moment Hayden had waited for his entire life. The moment he had planned, sought after, dreamed of during long, sleepless nights. This was the moment he would honor his mother's memory. This was the moment he would have his revenge.

The blade quivered over his father's coarse skin.

Magnolia groaned. Her skirts swished. If the man had hurt her!

A stream of blood trickled from the tip of the blade. Just another inch and Hayden would cut the artery that fed this vile man's brain.

FORGIVE.

Forgive? Had Hayden heard correctly? Forgive the death of his mother? Forgive the years he'd spent on the street, eating scraps not fit for rats. Forgive the frostbite and lice and sores and a belly that had clawed up his throat at the mere scent of food. Yet. . .hadn't God forgiven Hayden of all his wicked acts? Until now, Hayden had no idea how difficult that task must have been for God—forgiving those who hurt Him, who reject Him and renounce Him. Sending His own Son to die in their stead—Hayden's stead.

Hayden swallowed, gripping the knife tighter. Could Hayden send someone he loved to their death for this man? No.

But what of justice, God?

I AM JUSTICE.

Patrick swallowed, deepening the cut. His breath heightened.

Hayden's fingers trembled. Sweat dripped onto his father's chest. Hayden was not God. Not even close. He couldn't forgive him.

I LIVE IN YOU.

He ground his jaw together so hard he thought it would burst. But still he waited, seeking the strength of his new Father. If God *was* inside him somewhere, that strength would come.

And it did. Pity replaced anger. Sorrow replaced the need for revenge. And he shoved off his father and stood.

"Go." He waved the blade toward the jungle. "Go!"

Patrick struggled to rise and, without a word, dashed into the leaves.

After ensuring he was gone, Hayden searched for Magnolia but found only a lump of shadowy skirts. Terrified, he knelt beside her, reaching for her, praying she wasn't injured. Arms emerged from the darkness and looped around his neck. "Oh, Hayden, I thought he would kill you."

"So did I." He chuckled, feeling the blood trickle down his neck beneath his shirt. "Are you hurt?"

"I must have hit my head. I couldn't move. By the time I was finally able to sit, you held a knife to Patrick's throat."

"Can you walk?"

"I think so."

Hayden wrapped an arm around her waist and lifted her to her feet. She stumbled and leaned on him as he led her back to the creek and lowered her to a boulder. Grabbing the lantern, he examined her head. No blood. Just a slight bump. The sight caused his anger to rise again. He forced it down.

"I'm all right, Hayden, but you. . ." She touched the bloody gash on his arm and gasped when she saw his neck. Pulling a handkerchief from her pocket, she dipped it in the creek and dabbed the wound, her face puckering in angst.

He stayed her hand and engulfed it in his, searching her eyes, longing for things to be the way they used to be. She cupped his cheek, running her fingers over his jaw. "You didn't kill him. It's what you've always wanted. Why?"

Releasing her hand, Hayden stood. He drew a deep breath and stared at the moonlit water whirling and bubbling down the creek bed. "I've come to realize revenge only causes more heartache. Forgiveness is better." He shifted his shoulders and smiled. "Quite freeing, actually."

"Forgiveness? I never would have expected you to say such a thing."

"God has changed me."

"God? Now I know I'm dreaming." She stood and pressed the cloth to his arm. "We should have Eliza look at this."

He placed his hand over hers. "You took care of me when I had far worse injuries."

Her eyes lifted to his, liquid sapphires brewing with turmoil. "Would that we had never left the jungle, Hayden."

He'd give anything if that were true. If they could both go back to a time before Patrick appeared. Before everything changed. But they couldn't. And despite her care for him now, despite the look of love burning in her eyes, they never could. "I'm leaving Brazil."

Jaw dropping, she jerked from his touch. "Leaving? Why?" But then her hand was on his again, sudden joy lighting her face. "Take me. We'll go together. Like we planned."

Hayden shook his head and looked away, not wanting to see the pain in her eyes—not wanting to see his own pain reflected there. "I can't."

"I don't understand." Her voice etched with desperation.

Hayden made his way to the creek and stared over the water flowing past in peaks and valleys, much like his life. "Every time I look at you, I see you in my father's arms."

"Well stop seeing that, you stubborn fool! And see me only in *your* arms."

"Would that it were that easy." He faced her and was sorry he did. She'd never looked so lost, so completely and utterly lost. Not because of the dirt blotching her face. Not because of her hair tumbling over her shoulders. But because of the look of desperation, of hopelessness in her eyes. "You are a constant reminder of him. I've wasted fifteen years thinking of that man. I need to forget him for the next fifteen."

"He and I were engaged less than a year. Nothing untoward happened between us."

"I know that." Against his better judgment, he caressed her cheek. So soft. He never wanted to forget it. "You are a lady through and through."

She leaned into his hand and closed her eyes. A soft sigh spilled from her lips. Before they drew tight and she tore away from him. "So, God helps you forgive him, but you cannot forgive me!"

"There's nothing to forgive, Princess."

"You have no right to call me that. Not anymore." She took up a pace, bunching her skirts with her fists.

Hayden sighed. "I'm truly sorry." More sorry than she knew. For if he didn't leave soon, he was sure he'd toss aside his resolve and take her in his arms. But now he'd sparked her temper. Good. Her ire would aid him greatly.

"Sorry?" She shot him a feral look. "You are no better than my father—punishing me for succumbing to Patrick's charms!" A tiny vein pulsed in her neck. "And just like Patrick, you ask to court me one minute and the next you trample my affections beneath your traitorous hooves. You think you are different from your father. You are not!" She halted, spearing him with her contempt. "You are a man who lures women to fall in love with you only to break their hearts." The anger faded and the tears began. Grabbing her skirts, she took the lantern and darted from the clearing. Leaves swallowed her up like darkness swallowing light.

CHAPTER 34

James plopped the open book down on Blake's desk and pointed to the lines of Hebrew he'd finally managed to translate. "You need to know this."

"What? More ancient prophecies? More riddles we can't solve?" Blake laid down his pen and rose, stretching the kinks out of his back. "It's far too beautiful a morning for such dismal tidings." He glanced out the window where the rising sun flung spires of emerald through the jungle, stirring its creatures to life. "Besides, we need to weed the fields before it gets too hot. Then we can work on more irrigation troughs and start on the cane mill." Blake studied him. "You haven't slept, have you?"

"No." James rubbed his eyes and stared at the elegant Hebrew letters. Letters that couldn't have been penned by anyone other than a Hebrew scholar or a learned man. Certainly not the cannibals who had built the temple. "I had to figure this out."

Circling his desk, Blake shoved the book aside and leaned back on its surface. His eyes filled with concern. "You've become far too obsessed with these ancient fables."

James cocked a brow. "That's what they say about the Bible too."

Blake frowned. "Indeed." He glanced at the page and released a heavy sigh. "But this is not God's Word."

"No. But it means something. I know it. I feel it in my Spirit. Something important."

609

"Very well." Blake rose and walked to the window where a breeze brought the scent of mandioca cakes and boiled banana. James's stomach stirred. He'd been so caught up in the translation, he had skipped supper last night.

"What have you discovered?" Blake turned and gripped the back of his chair with both hands.

"From what I can gather, the judgment of the Four refers to four beings of enormous power. The first half of the book describes a battle that took place. The Four lost the battle, were judged, and then locked beneath the earth in chains." He glanced up at Blake. "The same story told by the pictures painted along the tunnel walls."

"But you don't know that for sure. Thiago could have guessed or even fabricated the story to match the book."

"He didn't know what was in the book."

"Hmm." Blake stared at the ancient manuscript. "So, I assume these beings were locked in the alcoves we found in the bottom chamber?"

"Yes. But, as you saw, their chains are broken. Do you remember their names?"

"Deception and Delusion."

James nodded.

"So, you're saying these beings were freed somehow?" Blake asked.

"That's what I'm thinking." James ran a hand through his hair, trying to curb his excitement. "Haven't we all been seeing visions lately? Delusions? Deceptions?"

Blake huffed. "Oh, come now, you don't think. . ."

"I do." James took up a pace, something he'd been doing all night long. "Something or someone has been reading our minds, conjuring up visions from our past, visions that are meant to torment."

"I don't know." Blake released the chair and rubbed his sore leg. "It sounds a bit farfetched. So, why can't we see these beings?"

"They live in the spirit realm. . .like angels and demons."

Blake snorted. "And the other two?"

"Hopefully still locked up." James halted as a breeze stirred the papers on Blake's desk. "You *do* remember that Graves was digging farther below."

"Humph." Blake eyed him with understanding. "All right, let's say I believe this nonsense. How were these powerful beings freed in the first place?"

"I'm not sure. But I believe this next section"—James planted a finger on the open page—"will tell me. I just can't quite decipher it." He scratched his head.

"And you think Graves is trying to release the other two?"

"I wouldn't put it past the man."

Blake rubbed his chin, lines furrowing on his forehead. "Continue your translation and keep me informed if you discover anything else. A year ago I would have laughed at all this, but now after what I've seen, after my encounter with God, I do believe there is another realm we cannot see."

"Indeed, the Bible speaks of it often."

"As I have discovered in my readings." Blake's smile soon faded beneath a sigh weighted with responsibility. "Speak about this to no one but me."

James nodded, happy his friend didn't think him a fool. He was about to thank him when one of the night watchmen stormed into the hut, his face aglow with excitement. "There are three men heading toward our town, Colonel. And one of them looks like Captain Barclay!"

James and Blake exchanged a puzzled look. The man who had captained the ship that brought them from Charleston to Rio? But as soon as they saw the old sea dog's ruddy, bearded face emerge from the greenery, hearty greetings were exchanged. In fact, everyone in town soon gathered around to welcome the captain and his mates, anxious for news from home.

"I didn't expect you back so soon, Captain," Blake said as everyone clustered near the meeting shelter to partake of breakfast and drill the seaman with questions.

"Nor did I!" Barclay laughed and drew off his neckerchief to dab his forehead. "I feel like a pig roasting on a spit! Is it always so hot here?"

James laughed as did many of the colonists. "You get used to it."

"I won't be here long enough, I hope," he said. "Ah, but yes, I picked up my cargo in New Orleans, delivered it to Norfolk and then passed by Charleston for another group of colonists headed toward Brazil. I just dropped them off in Rio and thought I'd gather your mail from the immigration office and bring it to you." He plopped a piece of mango into his mouth and groaned his pleasure as juice dribbled into his beard. "So here I am!" He reached into his pouch, withdrew a packet of letters, and began reading off names.

James hung back, sipping his coffee. There'd be nothing for him, of course. He had no one back home who would be writing to him.

His gaze landed on Angeline. She sat beneath the bamboo roof of the meeting house, her apron still on from helping prepare breakfast, a forlorn look on her comely face. He longed to know her story, for it appeared she had no one at home either. Nor did Blake or Eliza, though they seemed to be enjoying the colonists' excitement. Hayden was leaning on a tree at the edge of the clearing. James had heard the man intended to leave again, and he was sad for it. But he could understand in light of his father's presence. Would that Patrick Gale would leave instead, but they couldn't force the issue. They'd left the South to find freedom and it wouldn't be right to dictate who could stay and who couldn't.

"Miss Magnolia Scott. Magnolia Scott!" Captain Barclay shouted, and the lady emerged from the crowd to retrieve her letter, a look of confusion on her face.

Magnolia gripped the letter, still not believing the return address: Samuel Wimberly, 235 Washington Street, Atlanta, Georgia, United States. Her fingers began to shake as she left the others to find a quiet place to read.

> *My dearest Magnolia,*
> *When I heard you had immigrated to Brazil, I could hardly believe it. What possessed your parents to drag you to such an uncivilized post? I sincerely hope it was not because of the way*

things ended between us, for I have been wallowing in misery ever since. The despicable war stole away the years we should have been together. But now that hostilities are at an end, at least the formal kind, I have found myself in a position of great influence in aiding the North as they rebuild our precious South. Great influence and great wealth, my dear. Enough to provide for you and your family in the manner in which you were accustomed before the unfortunate incident with that incorrigible confidence man. Do write back to tell me you'll return and marry me. Better yet, send no post but hop on the ship that delivered this letter and come back to me post haste. I wait with great anticipation to see your lovely face again.

You are ever in my fondest dreams,
Samuel Wimberly III Esquire.

"Oh my." Magnolia's mother flung a hand to her mouth as she perused the letter Magnolia had reluctantly handed her. Curiosity had driven her to Magnolia's side within minutes of receiving the post, had opened her mouth to finally speak to her. Something she hadn't done in days under the watchful eye of her husband.

"This is wonderful news! Just wonderful!" Her mother squealed. "I knew he wouldn't forget you."

"Why are you speaking to her?" Magnolia's father burst around the corner of the hut. "I told you—"

Giddy with delight, her mother shoved the letter toward him, stopping him in his tracks. "What's this?" he puffed out, his chin doubling as he perused it.

Magnolia waited while he read, her mind still whirling in shock and confusion. She'd never thought she'd hear from Samuel again. Mercy me, she hadn't even been sure he'd take her back if she *had* managed to return home. But this. That he missed her and still wanted her! It was wonderful news.

Wasn't it? It wouldn't be wonderful if Hayden loved her and still wanted her. The news would bear no effect on her whatsoever, except the pain at writing Samuel a letter of rejection. But that was only a dream.

"That settles it." Magnolia's father slapped the paper. His smile appeared at odds with his normally flat lips "We head home immediately!"

"This is my decision." Magnolia straightened her shoulders. "And besides, you disowned me."

"For accepting the courtship of that nincompoop!" He waved the letter toward the center of town. "This changes everything."

"If I accept, it does, yes." For once Magnolia returned her father's pointed stare. Yet no fear crawled up her spine at the fury blazing in his eyes.

"Surely you aren't still considering receiving the attentions of that ghastly man! Why, he's the son of the beast who ruined us."

"I'm well aware of that, Father." Despite that sordid fact, Magnolia would have Hayden if he wanted her. She hugged herself as the sound of laughter and gaiety drifted from the meeting area of town.

Her mother laid a hand on her arm. Was it Magnolia's imagination or were there more streaks of gray in her mother's brown hair since last she saw her? "We hear he's leaving town anyway, dear. Abandoning you just like his father did."

She tugged from her mother and backed away. "He's not abandoning me. He's hurt and confused." Then why did it feel like a boulder just dropped in her stomach?

"This is what you want!" Her father clenched his jaw to keep from shouting. "You've been complaining about coming to Brazil from the moment we set foot on the ship. You tried to sabotage the voyage, for Pete's sake. And all your poor mother and I have heard since we arrived here is how miserable you are."

"Then, why did you take me away from Samuel in the first place?"

"You know very well we couldn't locate him after the war."

"And he didn't have enough money or power to suit you. Odd how you've changed your mind now that he does." Magnolia cocked her head. She'd never spoken to her father with such an imperious tone. She'd always been so afraid of him. So fearful of his disapproval. But something had changed within her. And she found it exhilarating!

His dark eyes narrowed but not before she caught a hint of pain within them. "You've acquired a sharp tongue these past few days."

"I've acquired far more than that, Father. Confidence, for one. Freedom, for another. And along with both the realization that I can take care of myself."

"Bah!" He folded the letter and handed it back to her.

Magnolia took it as her mother's pleading eyes shifted between them. "Please don't quarrel. Not when we've received such good news."

"Your mother is right." Her father expelled his fury on a long sigh. "Let us put things behind us, dumpling. Finally, we can leave this jungle and live the life we were destined to live."

Magnolia didn't miss the use of her pet name, the one he used to call her when she was young and still in his favor. Nor did she miss the slight catch in his throat. For a moment, a brief, happy moment, he had looked at her like he used to before Patrick came into their lives. She swallowed down a burst of emotion. Perhaps things could be mended between her and her father. Perhaps he loved her just a little. She'd already made up her mind to return home anyway. Even if Hayden left, Patrick would still be here, and she couldn't stand to be in the same town with that man.

She glanced at the letter in her hand. She had loved Samuel once, hadn't she?

"What if Patrick finds gold?" she asked her father.

"Then he can send it to us. I'm sure Blake will see to it." She'd never seen her father's expression so soft, so placating. How quickly the power had shifted between them.

With or without the gold, if she married Samuel, her debt to her parents would be paid. And the idea of sleeping in a proper feather bed, of having steaming sudsy baths, a wardrobe full of the latest fashions, and a bevy of servants to wait on her every need was not without some appeal. No bugs. No thirst. No excruciating heat. She looked at her hands, once soft and white, now bruised and scraped. No mud. No hard work.

No purpose. No fulfillment. No love.

"Darling." Her mother tucked a strand of hair into her bun. "We must get you married before the bloom of youth is gone. Or it will be too late."

❦

The bloom of youth, the bloom of youth, the words chanted over and over in Magnolia's mind as she strolled through a field of spring flowers, brushing her fingers over their colorful petals. Aquamarine, purple, gold, vermillion, amber, crimson—a thousand shades like dots of paint swaying on a canvas of green. A gentle breeze refreshed her skin and fluttered the delicate curls at her neck. She closed her eyes and breathed in the perfume-scented air. Sunlight blanketed her in warmth. Was there ever a more beautiful sight? Clutching her skirts, she ran across the field, dancing and laughing as the soft blooms tickled her stockings. Near breathless with glee, she stopped to pick one particularly beautiful blossom and drew it to her nose. A mixture of lilac and vanilla delighted her senses as she examined the crimson and orange petals, admiring their beauty and their silky feel.

The bloom of youth.

The flower began to shrivel in her hand. The petals browned and curled inward, then wilted into parched folds, drooping from the stem. Tossing down the blossom, Magnolia mourned the loss of such beauty when suddenly all the flowers around her began to brown and wilt and shrivel into dry, wrinkled twigs. Within minutes, the field became a crackling desert.

A chilled wind whipped the hem of her gown and blew the dried flowers away as if they'd never existed. Leaving nothing but gray, cracked ground. Leaving Magnolia all alone. In a dry and barren place. An ugly place. A tear slipped down her cheek.

A white speck appeared in the distance, gliding toward her. A person. A lady. The lady Magnolia had met in the church in Rio. The beautiful version with her glittering white robe, shimmering golden hair, and a face that would put Helen of Troy to shame. Halting before Magnolia, she smiled.

"Favour is deceitful and beauty is vain, but a woman that feareth the Lord, she shall be praised." Each word was as crisp and resonant as the plucking of a harp string.

"What does that mean?" Magnolia asked. "What happened to the flowers?"

"For what is your life? It is even a vapour, that appeareth for a little time, and then vanisheth away."

The woman smiled again and Magnolia smiled back, sensing only kindness, not judgment in her peaceful expression.

"Why are you telling me this?"

She raised a small mirror to Magnolia's face.

Magnolia turned her head. "I don't want to see."

"You must, child. You must." Grabbing Magnolia's chin she forced her to look at the hideous, wrinkled reflection. "This is—"

"I know. I know. This is my true appearance. What's inside of me." Magnolia squeezed her eyes shut against the sight and began to sob.

"Look again, child."

Magnolia shook her head. "No. Take it away."

"Look again."

Slowly prying her eyes open, Magnolia noticed the woman had flipped the mirror around to the other side. Beauty, pure beauty like she'd never seen before, stared back at her. The woman in the mirror glowed. She sparkled like a diamond, her skin luminescent, her hair spun silk, her eyes pools of glittering sapphires.

She couldn't pull her gaze away. "Who is she?"

"This is how God sees you when you turn to Him. When you accept the sacrifice of His Son, Jesus, you are cleansed, purified. You become His beautiful princess. Man looks on the outward appearance, but God looks at the heart."

Magnolia woke with a start, the lady's words echoing in her mind. *God looks on the heart. God looks on the heart.* A dream. A bizarre dream. Glancing to make sure she hadn't woken Sarah and Lydia, she swung her legs over the cot and rubbed her eyes.

Hadn't she discovered recently that she was more than a beautiful face? That she had value beyond her appearance? Besides, she was no fool. She knew her outward appearance would fade one day, that the bloom of youth would shrivel as her mother had said. And if Magnolia focused only on that, spent her time perfecting only that, what would be left when it was gone? Wasn't her soul, her character, more important? More lasting? Something that would never wrinkle or fade or die? But would only become more beautiful?

She'd once thought Patrick handsome but now that his true heart was revealed, she found him repulsive. And what of Sarah? She was no beauty and yet, she was the sweetest woman Magnolia had ever known, and more beautiful for it. Magnolia's heart shrank as she wondered how people truly saw her.

All these years her father, and oft times her many suitors as well, had spoken only of her appearance: complimenting, commending only her outside. Seeing her beauty as her only value. Making her believe she had no other redeeming qualities.

Rising, she grabbed her flask and tiptoed out of the hut, plopping on the bench.

"Oh, Jesus. I've been so wrong. About You. About myself."

She sipped the pinga and gazed up at the few stars peeking at her through the leaves above. "Do you truly see me as beautiful as I was in that second reflection?"

Wind stirred leaves by her feet into an exotic dance that tickled her legs. She giggled. "Is that You, God?"

"Precious one. Beautiful one."

Falling to her knees, Magnolia couldn't help the tears that streamed down her face. She tipped the flask to her lips again when the words "You don't need that anymore" flowed like warm water over her soul. Corking the flask, she set it on the ground and bowed her head.

"All this time I never spoke to You unless I wanted something. I never thought You cared. What a waste." She wiped her moist cheeks. "I'm sorry for being such a spoiled, vain, selfish girl. I don't want to be that way anymore. I want to be beautiful on the inside, not just the outside."

A whippoorwill sang in the distance as a sensation filtered through her. She had always been loved, regardless of what she looked like or what she'd done or what she would ever do. God's love was a gift that carried no conditions, no prerequisites, no debt. And even before she'd been born, He knew her. He'd fashioned her in her mother's womb as Eliza had said: special, unique, beautiful, and valuable.

And for the first time in her life, she felt all of those things as God's presence enveloped her.

CHAPTER 35

So you're going to let her get on that ship and sail out of your life?" Blake asked.

Hayden rubbed his aching eyes and stared at his two friends who had barged into his hut before the sun even had a chance to rise.

"You tell us you gave your life to God, forgave your father, released your need for revenge, which I'm very happy to hear, by the way"— James crossed beefy arms over his chest—"and now you're going to lose the woman God gave you to love. Just because of your foolish pride."

Hayden suddenly regretted telling Blake and James about his encounter with the Almighty. He wouldn't have even mentioned it if they hadn't insisted on knowing why he'd changed his mind about seeking revenge on his father and had decided to leave.

"Besides, if you're planning on going back to the States anyway, why not sail with Captain Barclay instead of walking to Rio?" Candlelight flickered mischief in James's eyes. "Not that I want you to leave. Not that I want either of you to leave. But if you're on the same ship with Magnolia, at least there's more of a chance you'll come to your senses."

"Or do something I'll regret the rest of my life."

"Like marry the lady? Why would that be so bad?"

"You don't understand." Hayden flung his shirt over his head and tucked it into his trousers. He'd hoped to sneak away that morning without anyone seeing. He'd said his good-byes to those that mattered the night before, painful enough as *that* was. More painful than he'd ever thought leaving people could be. Afterward, he'd had a fitful night of staring at the bamboo and palm fronds over his head, listening to the hoot of a nearby owl and the distant growls of jungle predators. A night of waiting for the first glow of dawn to give him permission to rise and slip away. But his friends had cornered him before he'd had a chance.

"I understand more than you think." The lines in Blake's forehead deepened as they always did when he was concerned.

Hayden studied him. Perhaps the colonel did know about revenge and forgiveness and the love of a decent woman. But his life had turned out well. His hopes had been realized. Hayden's hopes never would be. A breeze whipped through the window, ripe with the scent of orange blossoms and rain.

"She's leaving because she doesn't think you want her," James said.

Sitting on his cot, Hayden pulled on his boots. "She's leaving because she will finally get to marry her rich solicitor like she's always wanted." The news had carved a hole in his heart while at the same time giving him the peace of knowing she'd finally be happy.

Blake marched to the window, fists at his waist. "What other choice have you given her?"

"She could stay with the colony. Work in the clinic." Even as he said it, Hayden remembered how determined she was to repay her debt to her parents. Another reason to marry this Wimby fellow. He ran his hands through his hair and grabbed his only possession, his knapsack containing his knife, pistol, canteen, and the few supplies he'd purchased in Rio.

James released a heavy sigh and rubbed the scar on his cheek. "You could stay with the colony too. Why run away if she is gone?"

"You seem to forget my father is still here."

"If what you say about him is true, he won't be here for long."

Indeed. The man would either find his gold and leave or give up and move on to the next conquest. Regardless, even if his father left, New Hope was too full of memories. Hayden would see Magnolia's face everywhere he turned, catch glimpses of her flaxen hair among the leaves, picture those sapphire eyes staring at him from across the fire. No. He couldn't do it. Better to have a clean break, get far away from any reminders. Of her and his father.

"Look, I appreciate what you both are doing." No one had ever cared enough for him to look out for his best interests. The thought brought a burning sensation to his throat. He swallowed it down and glanced out the window. He would truly miss his friends. "But I must go."

Blake spun around to face him. "Do you love her?"

He wanted to say no. That she was just a passing fancy like so many other women in his life. But Magnolia was so much more than that. She was all spark and spunk and wit and courage, tenacity, kindness, and goodness. Besides, his newfound faith forbade him to lie. "More than anything."

"Then go to her, man," Blake said.

Hayden hung his head and stared at the packed dirt that made up the floor of his hut. "She was with my father. I cannot shake it from my mind. I don't think I ever can."

James gripped his shoulder. "Then you must ask God for help."

Blake nodded his agreement. "I understand what you are suffering. I thought I could never look at Eliza without remembering what her husband did to my brother. But God can heal all those memories, all those wounds. Like James said, you have but to ask."

"At least say good-bye to her." James raised a brow. "She inquired about you this morning, before she and her parents followed Barclay to the coast, wondering if you were awake."

"I've never seen a woman so distraught," Blake added. "Her parents had to drag her away sobbing. Doesn't seem like a lady happy about her upcoming nuptials, if you ask me."

"Sobbing?" Hayden shifted his boots over the dirt. Why was she sobbing? All she'd talked about during the entire trip to Rio was Samuel this and Samuel that. Could she really be that upset about leaving New Hope? About leaving Hayden?

"Truss it." James glanced out the window and groaned. "They've probably already set sail. Captain Barclay wanted an early start."

Hayden's gaze shifted between his friends, the urgency in their eyes igniting a fire in his heart. And then in his legs. Without a word, he dashed from the hut, tore down the street, and barreled into the jungle, all the while praying that Magnolia was still there.

A wave crashed upon the shore, reaching its foamy fingers toward Magnolia. For a fleeting moment, she thought to step into it—hoping the waves would grab her feet and drag her out to sea, down into the cool waters where all was silent and calm. Where her life would slowly leak from her body and abandon her to peace.

Her parents stood a ways off, chattering excitedly about finally leaving Brazil and returning to civilization and the lifestyle they deserved. But Magnolia drowned them out, instead focusing on the warble of birds, the buzz of insects, the flutter of leaves—all playing a melodious orchestra behind her. The delicate hum of life. A lump formed in her throat. She would miss it. How odd that she would miss it so! Those sounds would always remind her of her time with Hayden in the jungle. The best time of her life. She nearly chuckled at the thought. The entire trip she'd been nothing but hungry and tired and hot and sweaty and covered with bug bites. She'd slept on a hard bed of bamboo, had been attacked by bats and a snake and nearly eaten by a wolf.

And she'd been deliriously happy.

Pulling the toad Hayden had carved for her from her pocket, she fingered each curve and line. It truly looked like a toad. From the large eyeballs protruding from its head, to the thin dish-shaped mouth, to the rounded body, and the tiny webbed toes. Amazing talent. Memories of all the times she'd called him a toad surfaced to make her giggle even as tears slipped from her eyes. At least she would always have this part of him.

Shouts rang from the ship. Squinting, she ran her gaze over the silhouette of the brig, its masts stark against the rising sun. A beautiful ship, indeed. Then why, whenever she saw it, did her stomach sink to her shoes?

One of Captain Barclay's sailors began rowing the skiff to retrieve them after bringing his captain and the other men on board. It was only a matter of minutes now before her feet would leave the shores of Brazil forever. She should be happy, elated! She would marry Samuel, be well positioned in society, and live in ease and luxury. A month ago, this would have been the happiest day of her life. But a month ago, she had been a different person. Now, those things no longer mattered to her. She knew her value came from God, from the changes He wrought within her, not from adornments she placed without. She'd even looked in her mirror that morning, expecting to see herself old and wrinkled, but found some of the lines on her face had softened, some of the bald patches on her head had filled in with hair. It was a good start. But it came too late to save her relationship with Hayden.

She really couldn't blame him. Nor could she blame God. She, alone, was responsible for entangling herself with Patrick Gale. She would accept the consequences, no matter how bitter. And God's will would be done in the end. A breeze swirled around her, and she raised her face to the sun, basking in the warm fingers of heaven's love. Though her heart was breaking, she belonged to God now. All would be well.

The boat struck shore and the sailor leapt out, splashing through the water as he dragged it onto the sand.

"Come now, darling!" her mother shouted as the man hefted their portmanteau into the craft.

The sooner she left, the better. With a heavy sigh, Magnolia slipped the toad into her pocket and started toward them.

"Magnolia!"

She was surely hearing things, conjuring Hayden's voice from her memories, perhaps to instill it in her heart. But there was no need for that. She would never forget the deep, raspy timbre. When she reached her parents, their eyes sped behind her, widening in alarm.

"Magnolia!"

She turned to see Hayden marching toward her through the sand, his dark hair blowing behind him, his shirt flapping in the breeze, a look of longing and determination on his face.

Her heart stopped beating. The breath leached from her lungs. And elusive hope sprouted fresh within her again.

Hayden's overwhelming relief at seeing Magnolia was shoved aside by a much more powerful emotion—fear. Fear that he'd face her and see only his father, despite the petitions he'd lifted up to God on his sprint through the jungle. Fear that she'd come to her senses during the night and realized Wimby was a much better prospect. Fear he'd have to accept, once and for all, living without her. But as he drew close, the look in her eyes spoke of none of those things. In fact, he saw nothing but love and hope and pleading expectation.

Mr. and Mrs. Scott clutched both her arms and dragged her to the boat. "Time to go!" her father shouted. "We mustn't keep the captain waiting."

The sailor clasped Magnolia's hand to assist her into the wobbly craft while her father grabbed the other. And for a moment Hayden thought he'd lost her.

But suddenly, she tore away from them both, and clutching her skirts, headed toward him. How lovely she looked with the sea breeze dancing through her hair and the sunlight painting gold on loose strands about her neck, her pink lips slightly parted in expectation and a flush blossoming on her cheeks. Hayden's breath escaped him.

"Get back here at once, Magnolia!" Mr. Scott shouted, while Mrs. Scott held a hand to her mouth.

"In a moment, Father. I will speak to the man," she replied without turning around. Mr. Scott, his face red and blustery, started to follow her, but she swung to face him. "In private." The shock of her stern voice halted the man and put a smile on Hayden's lips. Turning, she closed the distance between them and stopped, all Chantilly lace and sweet Georgia peach. He could think of nothing else except that he wanted to kiss her. No vision of his father came to mind, no stench of him surrounded her at all. *Thank You, God.*

"I thought I'd never see you again." Her blue eyes searched his as if seeking an answer to a question deep within. "You didn't say good-bye."

"I couldn't."

He wanted to touch her, to brush aside the curl that had blown across her cheek, but he dared not. She had every right to be angry with him. To not want him after he rejected her love.

"I don't think I can ever say good-bye," he said, gauging her reaction.

Her lips parted. Her eyes moistened. "What are you saying?"

He took her hand in his and placed a kiss upon it. Then dropping to one knee in the sand, he gazed up at her. Maybe he was making a complete idiot out of himself, but he didn't care. For the chance to love Magnolia, he'd play the fool a thousand times.

Her eyes widened. Her chest heaved. Her parents groaned. And Hayden said, "Will you marry me, Magnolia? Will you stay here and start a new life with me?"

A tear slid down her cheek, touching the tip of her upturned lips. Was that a smile of joy or of mockery? She gaped at him as if he'd asked her to wed a wolf. Rising to his feet, he released her hand.

"I know I have nothing to offer you. No house or fortune. And especially not a good name." He gazed out to sea, his heart ready to implode. "You must think me rather presumptuous."

"Presumptuous? Always, sir. But at the moment I find you completely. . .completely wonderful and incredible and"—her nose wrinkled—"and wonderfully incredible." She giggled. "I can't seem to find the words."

"A first." He grinned, his heart daring to hope.

She frowned. Blasting that hope. "What about Patrick?"

"Patrick? Who's Patrick?" He feigned confusion then raised a brow. "And what of Samuel?"

She laid a finger on her chin. "I don't believe I know anyone by that name."

"But I fear your parents do." Hayden nodded their way, noting the horror on their faces.

"Then they can marry him." She laughed.

Happiness burst within him. Like none he'd ever known. "So, what is your answer, Princess?"

She fell so hard into his arms, it nearly knocked him over. "Yes! Yes! Yes! Forever, yes!"

CHAPTER 36

Hayden had never been this nervous. Not during his biggest scam when five thousand dollars, along with his very life, was at risk. Not even when he'd crossed blades with the notorious swordsman Monsieur de Chambolier after Hayden had entertained flirtatious dalliances of his wife. He shifted his polished boots over the dirt, eyed his clean, pressed gray trousers, straightened the black silk embroidered waistcoat he'd borrowed from Blake, and tugged on the cuffs of his pristine shirt—the sleeves a bit too short for his long arms. But nothing eased the knot in his stomach. He glanced at Eliza, standing off to the side, smiling at him with that pleased, knowing smile of hers. Hayden tugged at his black necktie. Why had he tied the thing so tight?

Women to his left giggled, joining the cacophony of birds and insects and the off-key thrum of Mr. Lewis's fiddle. Hayden glanced across the courtyard, seeking his bride, but all he saw were the cheerful faces of the colonists lined up to witness the nuptials. Angeline, cat bundled in her arms, smiled his way, as did Sarah, bouncing Lydia against her chest, Thiago by her side. Mr. Dodd nodded his approval with a sly grin. The Jenkins, their daughter Henrietta between them, stood at the end of a crowd of other colonists, several farmers, ex-soldiers, the blacksmith, the baker—all grinning like clowns. More colonists crowded together on the other side, even some from his father's group. Magnolia's mother stood on Hayden's left, flowers in hand and a pleasant smile on her face. Conspicuously absent were

Magnolia's father and Patrick.

Which was fine by Hayden.

He gazed at the strings of orchids festooning the thatched roof of the open-air meeting shelter, complements of New Hope's women, who had seemed more than excited to be planning another wedding. Vines covered with feathery flowers of white and scarlet circled support poles and tables, while violet petals littered the ground. A breeze flickered two rows of lit candles that formed a pathway from the main street to where Hayden stood. He gave a sigh of impatience as the scent of sweet lemonade and molasses cakes swirled beneath his nose.

Rays of a setting sun speared the jungle, dappling the area with glittering saffron.

James cleared his throat, drawing Hayden's gaze. The man stood in front of him, prayer book in hand, but his eyes were on something behind Hayden. He turned to see. . .

Magnolia.

Dressed in a shimmering white gown, trimmed in golden lace and embroidered with beads—complements of Angeline—and with her pearly hair swept up in a mass of curls, she looked more angelic than human. Her gloved hand rested in the crux of Blake's elbow as he led her through the rows of flickering candles. Their eyes locked, and he couldn't believe God had given him such a princess.

Releasing Blake with a nod of thanks, she stopped beside Hayden. The flowers in her hands quivered. Her eyes sparkled with love. A breeze tugged loose a single strand of her hair, sweeping it across her neck. She reached up to put it in place, but he took her hand in his and smiled. And he vowed right there before God and man to take care of her, protect her, and love her all of her days.

⚜

Thump-ump, thump-ump, thump-ump, the pulsating sound echoed in Magnolia's ear. As it had all night. Lulling her to sleep with its soothing cadence, while at the same time keeping her awake with the knowledge that it came from the heart of the man she loved. The man that lay beside her, his strong arm around her waist, his chest beneath her head where she had laid it after they'd become one flesh, just like the scriptures said. He'd adored her with his body and then adored her with his words of love and promises of care and affection and joy for a lifetime, until he'd finally drifted off to sleep.

The night had passed in a brushstroke of paradise as she lay ensconced in his warmth and strength, listening to his deep breathing, feeling the rise and fall of his chest, inhaling the male scent of him, and praying for God to bless and strengthen and protect this man forever. Closing her eyes against the glow of dawn creeping in through the window, she wished it would retreat, go back to the rising sun, and push it down beneath the horizon for just a little while longer. Just a little while longer in Hayden's arms, a little while longer absorbed in his love.

A parrot screeched outside the window. Hayden stirred. He reached up to rub his nose. Propping her chin on his chest, she watched him. His mouth twitched. He groaned and released a heavy breath. Then his arm tightened around her and he snapped his eyes open, shifting them to her as if surprised to find her in his bed. A slow grin appeared on his lips. "I thought I only dreamed last night."

"Do you often have dreams of such a"—she raised an eyebrow at him—"sensual nature?"

"Only about you, wife." Easing a lock of hair from her forehead, he propped himself up on his elbow, his eyes drinking her in. "Last night was magical."

Magnolia smiled, felt a blush rising, and lay back on the pillow, gazing up at him. "Let's never leave this cot. Stay here forever."

"Wouldn't that give the townspeople something to talk about?"

"Let them." She laughed, running her fingers over the dark stubble on his chin.

His gaze landed on the toad carving on the table. "So, now that I've spent the night with you, I suppose you must chop off my head so I can become a prince."

"It's two nights you must spend with me, Mr. Gale. After tomorrow, I shall have to see." She grinned. "But I do believe you are well on your way to becoming a prince, even with your head attached."

He rubbed his throat. "Good thing, Mrs. Gale. I've grown quite fond of my head."

"I rather like it myself." Propping herself up, she trailed kisses up his neck. "Especially this neck"—she continued on to his chin—"and this scratchy jaw"—she planted one on his nose—"and this nose and these ears"—she nibbled on his ear.

Groaning, he nudged her back onto the pillow and trapped her with his arms. "If you continue such provocative amusements, you will get your wish and never leave this bed."

"I don't believe you for one minute. Are you swindling me again, Hayden Gale?"

He grew serious. "Never again, for you have swindled the great swindler, Princess, and stolen his heart forever."

"I shall take good care of it, Hayden. You need fear nothing from me. I will cherish it forever and never betray your confidence, and I will—"

His lips met hers, and the rest of her thoughts flew out the window.

EPILOGUE

What in the Sam Hill are you talking about, Doc?" Hayden shook his head. "You're not making any sense." Besides, the man had dragged Hayden away from Magnolia on only their second night together as man and wife. He glanced down the dark street, lit in intervals by flickering lanterns, toward their hut where he'd left her sleeping.

"I know you're anxious to return to your wife," Blake said, drawing Hayden's gaze back to see him smile. "I am as well. To mine, that is." He chuckled at his faux pas. "But let's hear James out. He's been translating this book Graves gave him from the tunnels, and I'm sure he wouldn't have woken us unless it was important."

"Yes." James stared at the open book lying on the table in the meeting shelter. Light from a lantern perched beside it spilled onto the page littered with odd characters. The doc seemed unusually tense as he pushed from the table, took up a short pace, then stopped again. "I finally figured out what this section says." He nodded to the book. "The Latin phrase written above the alcoves is a key to release the powerful beings."

The impact of his ominous declaration was lost on Hayden. Just the preacher being a preacher, he supposed. But the news seemed to distress Blake. He planted a boot on a stool and leaned forward, his jaw stiff, his eyes intent.

"What powerful beings?" Hayden asked.

James gave Hayden a look as if he'd asked if the sun rose in the east. An event Hayden hoped he'd miss before he returned to his bed. "Ah, yes. Sorry," James said. "Remember those alcoves in the tunnels beneath the temples, the ones with the poles and broken chains?"

"Go on."

"This book tells how they got there. There was a battle. Probably on that scorched field we saw behind the temple." His eyes lit up as if he suddenly realized the connection. "Anyway, those powerful evil beings were subdued and locked below. Four of them."

Hayden had heard some rattlebrained tales before—had told a few himself—but this one could get a man locked in an asylum. "But there was nothing there."

"Two were gone. Yes." James scratched his thick hair. "I know how they escaped." He exchanged a look with Blake. "Remember the writing on top of each alcove?"

"Yes. Latin and something else written in another language." Hayden pointed toward the book. "Words that looked like this."

James nodded and shifted his gaze between them. "All someone needs to do to free the beings is say the Latin phrase out loud. Here, let me read this section. When the man of darkness in whom there is no light"—he slid his finger across the characters from right to left—"speaks the key to the four winds, the chains are broken."

Blake nodded as if James had just read facts from a scientific treatise. "But who released the first two?"

"Indians, pirates, cannibals. I don't know. The person merely has to say the phrase, not understand it. And he or she must be evil. A bad person in whom there is no light."

Hayden rubbed the back of his neck. "So who locked them up there in the first place?"

"I don't know. God...good angels."

Hayden snorted. "And you think these beings might be bad angels?"

James huffed his displeasure at Hayden's skepticism. "I know it sounds farfetched, but yes, I believe these beings could be angels who followed Satan in the fall."

Farfetched? Hayden shook his head. More like pure madness. "So, why would whoever conquered them make a way for them to be released?"

James flipped back a few pages. "It's hard to explain, but it says here that because the earth was given to mankind, fallen as he is, there had to be a way for man to release these beings. It had to be man's choice of good over evil. . .free will"—he looked up at Blake—"like we talked about before. God does not want puppets. If we choose evil, He allows us."

The excited way he spoke, the fear lacing his tone, brought Hayden's own fears to the surface. Were his two friends becoming as mad as Graves? Perhaps if Hayden simply excused himself and returned to bed, he'd wake up tomorrow to find their senses recovered. "Fascinating, gentlemen, but I have a new bride waiting for me." He turned to go.

"Graves is close to releasing the next being." James's forceful tone spun Hayden around and caused Blake to squeeze the bridge of his nose with a groan. "That's what he's been digging for," James continued. "Two of them were locked in the chamber we saw. Another two were locked below them. The worst two. More evil than you could possibly imagine." He gripped the edge of the table. "If what Graves said about sabotaging our journey was true, we know he was evil to start out with. But now, you've seen him. He's not only evil, but he's gone mad as well. If he knows any Latin at all, all he has to do is say the phrase above the open sepulcher out loud and the third being will be free."

Graves raised the lantern over the alcove he'd just uncovered. Finally. After weeks of digging, he'd finally removed enough rocks and dirt to clearly see the curved trench that ran from the muddy floor to the craggy roof of the cave. Water dripped and hissed all around him as steam rose from cracks. Sweat streamed down every aching muscle in his body and burned over cuts and abrasions. But he didn't care. Excitement set his hair on end. The chains were intact, suspended in midair as if still restraining something. . .or someone, yet now as he flooded the area with light, he could see no one there.

"I did what you said." He wiped sweat from his face, leaving a streak of mud on his sleeve. "I did what you said." He took a step closer.

Ah. . .there they were, the voices again. His friends, his companions for the last two months. Happy voices, praising him for his faithfulness, his hard work, his dedication, promising him rewards beyond his wildest dreams. Graves smiled. Finally all his work would pay off. Finally he would have immeasurable power.

Say the words. Open the chains.

Water dripped on his face from above—steaming water that smelled of sulfur and stung his skin. He leapt on a boulder and raised the lantern higher, illuminating the Latin above the sepulcher. Squinting, he tried to make out the letters, tried to remember their pronunciation from his lessons as a child.

The words sounded foreign on his cracked lips, but he shouted them aloud with glee. Their echo magnified and bounced off the walls with a power he would soon possess. A low rumble resounded from below. Louder and louder it grew until it thundered in the chamber. The walls shook. Dirt showered over him. Stalactites speared down from above. One struck Graves's shoulder, piercing his flesh. Crying out, he tumbled from the rock and landed in the mud. Another pierced his leg. He screamed in agony and raised a pleading hand to the sepulcher. Chains rattled. Iron split apart, and the dark outline of an immense being took form. Eyes as hot as coals stared down at Graves.

"Help me," Graves cried, reaching toward the creature.

The being pulled a sword with a blade as long as a man from his scabbard, stepped from his prison, and raised it over Graves's head.

Before he completely vanished.

Graves released a heavy breath. He never felt the blade on his throat until it was too late.

◦◦◦◦◦◦◦

A loud boom like the roar of a cannon drew all men's gazes to the jungle. The ground trembled. The lantern wobbled on the table and slivers of thatch filtered down from above.

The three men exchanged wary glances. The shaking stopped. Night birds and crickets returned to their song, and a mighty gust of wind sent the lantern flame sputtering patches of light and dark over the prophetic Hebrew book.

"So what is the name of this third being?" Hayden asked, suddenly rethinking his position.

James pointed to a word in the book then eyed them both. "Destruction."

Author's Historical Note

For purposes of the story, I chose the location for the colony of New Hope to be roughly one hundred miles south of Rio de Janeiro, near a wide river that flows from the mountains down to the sea. The river and the colony are fictitious and are not actual landmarks in Brazil. There was, however, a colony named El Dorado, led by Frank McMullan, that settled south of Rio de Janeiro in the São Paulo province, near the São Lourenço River. Shortly after the colonists' arrival, Frank McMullan took sick and died, leaving his partner, William Bowen, a gruff, greedy man more interested in finding gold than planting crops, in charge. (Many legends abounded of a lake of gold near the area!) The resultant power struggle caused great dissention among the group. That division, along with sickness, lack of food supplies, money, and no way to get their crops to market caused the demise of the colony in 1870, three years after it began.

The fairy tale Magnolia recites to Hayden during their trek in the jungle comes from James Orchard Halliwell-Phillipps: *Popular Rhymes and Nursery Tales*. London 1849. I copied it here for your enjoyment.

The Maiden and the Frog

Many years ago there lived on the brow of a mountain, in the north of England, an old woman and her daughter. They were very poor and obliged to work very hard for their living, and the old woman's temper was not very good, so that the maiden, who was very beautiful, led but an ill life with her.

The girl, indeed, was compelled to do the hardest work, for her mother got their principal means of subsistence by traveling to places in the neighborhood with small articles for sale, and when she came home in the afternoon she was not able to do much more work. Nearly the whole domestic labor of the cottage devolved therefore on the daughter, the most wearisome part of which consisted in the necessity of fetching all the water they required from a well on the other side of the hill, there being no river or spring near their own cottage.

It happened one morning that the daughter had the misfortune, in going to the well, to break the only pitcher they possessed, and having no other utensil she could use for the purpose, she was obliged to go home without bringing any water. When her mother returned, she was unfortunately troubled with excessive thirst, and the girl, though trembling for the consequences of her misfortune, told her exactly the circumstance that had occurred.

The old woman was furiously angry, and so far from making any allowances for her daughter, pointed to a sieve which happened to be on the table, and told her to go at once to the well and bring her some water in that, or never venture to appear again in her sight.

The young maiden, frightened almost out of her wits by her mother's fury, speedily took the sieve, and though she considered the task a hopeless one to accomplish, almost unconsciously hastened to the well. When she arrived there, beginning to reflect on the painful situation in which she was placed and the utter impossibility of her obtaining a living by herself, she threw herself down on the brink of the well in an agony of despair.

Whilst she was in this condition, a large frog came up to the top of the water and asked her for what she was crying so bitterly. She was somewhat surprised at this, but not being the least frightened, told him the whole story, and that she was crying because she could not carry away water in the sieve.

"Is that all?" said the frog. "Cheer up, my hinny! For if you will only let me sleep with you for two nights, and then chop off my head, I will tell you how to do it."

The maiden thought the frog could not be in earnest, but she was too impatient to consider much about it and at once made the required promise. The frog then instructed her in the following words:

> Stop with fog,
> And daub with clay;
> And that will carry
> The water away.

Having said this, he dived immediately under the water, and the girl, having followed his advice, got the sieve full of water, and returned home with it, not thinking much of her promise to the frog. By the time she reached home the old woman's wrath was appeased, but as they were eating their frugal supper very quietly, what should they hear but the splashing and croaking of a frog near the door, and shortly afterwards the daughter recognized the voice of the frog of the well saying:

> Open the door, my hinny, my heart,
> Open the door, my own darling;
> Remember the word you spoke to me
> In the meadow by the well-spring.

She was now dreadfully frightened and hurriedly explained the matter to her mother, who was also so much alarmed at the circumstance that she dared not refuse admittance to the frog, who, when the door was opened, leapt into the room, exclaiming:

> Go wi' me to bed, my hinny, my heart,
> Go wi' me to bed, my own darling;
> Remember the words you spoke to me,
> In the meadow by the well-spring.

This command was also obeyed, although as may be readily supposed, she did not much relish such a bedfellow. The next day, the frog was very quiet and evidently enjoyed the fare they placed before him, the purest milk and the finest bread they could procure. In fact, neither the old woman nor her daughter spared any pains to render the frog comfortable. That night, immediately supper was finished, the frog again exclaimed:

> Go wi' me to bed, my hinny, my heart,
> Go wi' me to bed, my own darling;
> Remember the words you spoke to me,
> In the meadow by the well-spring.

She again allowed the frog to share her couch, and in the morning, as soon as she was dressed, he jumped towards her, saying:

Chop off my head, my hinny, my heart,
Chop off my head, my own darling;
Remember the words you spoke to me,
In the meadow by the well-spring.

The maiden had no sooner accomplished this last request, than in the stead of the frog there stood by her side the handsomest prince in the world, who had long been transformed by a magician, and who could never have recovered his natural shape until a beautiful virgin had consented, of her own accord, to make him her bedfellow for two nights. The joy of all parties was complete; the girl and the prince were shortly afterward married and lived for many years in the enjoyment of every happiness.

Abandoned

Memories

Behold, I give unto you power to tread on serpents
and scorpions, and over all the power of the enemy:
and nothing shall by any means hurt you.
LUKE 10:19

Dedicated to everyone who feels weak,
for when you are weak, He is strong.

Cast of Characters

James Callaway—Confederate Army surgeon turned Baptist preacher, James signed on as the colony's only doctor but suffers from a fear of blood. Feeling as much a failure at preaching as he does at doctoring, James endeavors to rid the colony of all immor-ality, but instead ends up in a fierce battle between good and evil.

Angeline Moore—Signed on as the colony's seamstress, Angeline is a broken woman with a sordid past, which she prefers to remain hidden. Tough and courageous on the outside, inside she longs to be loved. She mistrusts all men and claims she can take care of herself, but the colony's doctor keeps hindering her plans. To make matters worse, she is constantly haunted by visions from her past.

Magnolia Scott—A spoiled plantation owner's daughter, who at first hated Brazil and hoped to return to Georgia, Magnolia, instead, fell in love with Hayden Gale. Now she is learning to value character over beauty as she receives God's love and distances herself from the constant belittling she received as a child. If only the reflection of her soul would become more radiant.

Hayden Gale—Con man who joined the colony in search of his father, whom he believed was responsible for the death of his mother. At first bent on revenge, Hayden, by the grace of God, has now forgiven the man and wants to make a good life for himself and his new wife. Instead, he finds himself thrust into the middle of a spiritual battle.

Colonel Blake Wallace—Leader and organizer of the expedition to Brazil, Blake is a decorated war hero who suffers from post-traumatic stress disorder. By God's power, he has learned to forgive his enemies and now hopes to start anew with his wife, Eliza. But when strange disasters strike the fledgling colony, Blake feels the weight of responsibility grow even heavier.

Eliza Crawford Wallace—Blake's wife and Confederate Army nurse who runs the colony's clinic. Once married to a Yankee general, she was disowned by her Southern family and nearly ostracized by the colonists when the truth came out. Eliza is impulsive, stubborn, courageous, and kind—qualities she will need in the upcoming battle.

Patrick Gale—Swindler, con man, and all-around crook, Patrick came to Brazil in search of gold. He is Hayden's father and ex-fiancé to Magnolia—and the man who swindled her family out of everything they had.

Mr. and Mrs. Scott—Once wealthy plantation owners who claim to have lost everything in the war, they had hoped to regain their position and wealth in Brazil by marrying off their comely daughter to a Brazilian with money and title. Unfortunately, their plans came to naught.

Wiley Dodd—Ex-lawman from Richmond, Dodd is fond of the ladies and in possession of a treasure map that points to Brazil as the location of a vast amount of gold.

Sarah Jorden—War widow who gave birth to her daughter, Lydia, on the ship that took them to Brazil, Sarah signed on to teach the colony's children.

Thiago—Personal interpreter and Brazilian liaison assigned to New Hope to assist the colonists settle in their new land.

Moses and Delia—A freed slave and his sister, along with her two children, who want to start over in a new land away from the memory of slavery.

Mable—Slave to the Scotts.

CHAPTER 1

October 18, 1866
The jungles of Brazil

The ground shook like a ship in a sea squall. Dirt and rocks pelted Angeline. . .striking. . .stinging. Her heart seized. Covering her head, she spun and staggered back the way she'd come—up toward the tunnel entrance and into the temple, where at least she wouldn't be buried alive. Unless the roof of the ancient shrine caved in. A violent jolt struck, launching her against the rock wall as if she were made of paper. Pain radiated up her arm. Her legs quivered like the ground beneath them, and she fell onto the shifting dirt.

The hand that engulfed hers was rough like old rope, powerful, yet warm. An equally powerful arm swung around her waist as tremors wracked the tunnels. "Hang on. You're safe," James spoke in her ear, covering her head with his own. Pebbles rained down on them. Coughing, Angeline flung a hand to her mouth when the quaking finally stopped.

She drew a deep breath, her lungs filling with dust scented with spice and man and James. And standing there, ensconced in his embrace, fears that had risen so quickly when the ground had begun to shake suddenly vanished. She hated herself for it. She pushed from him. The stench of sulfur and mold instantly swept away his masculine aroma and resurrected her terror.

James stared at her oddly while he said to the men, "I told you we should not have brought the women."

Brushing dirt from her skirts, Eliza, who stood in front of them with her husband, Blake, turned to face him. "You had no say in it,

Doctor. We insisted. Did we not?" She smiled at Angeline. "There's nothing to fear from a little shaking."

Angeline wasn't so sure. But then again, she didn't possess Eliza's courage and strength. Few women did. Those qualities, along with a multitude of others, were the reason Angeline admired her friend so much—the reason she'd cast aside her fears and agreed to venture into the eerie temple they'd found in the middle of the Brazilian jungle.

And then down into the tunnels beneath.

Yet at the moment, Eliza looked as if someone had dumped a bucket of chalk powder on her head. If Angeline weren't so frightened, she'd giggle at the sight. But her alarm at being so far below ground during an earthquake stifled any laughter. She never should have come along. The men had insisted on investigating a loud explosion they'd heard last night that had shaken the ground all the way to their settlement of New Hope. When they feared it came from the temple, Eliza's concern for Mr. Graves mounted, but now that Angeline had seen the ancient ruin and experienced the stink and heat of the narrow tunnels that spanned beneath it, she wondered why anyone would want to return. Or live here, as Mr. Graves had done since they'd arrived in Brazil.

Mr. Graves was one of the reasons Angeline had joined them today—to witness for herself the madman "digging his way to hell," according to some of the colonists' reports. Exaggerated reports, she was sure, but after Eliza had regaled her with further tales of gruesome obelisks, prison alcoves hewn in rock, strange Latin and Hebrew inscriptions, and Graves's obsession with releasing powerful, invisible creatures, Angeline's curiosity had gotten the best of her—regardless of James's insistence that she remain in town. Or maybe because of it. Angeline grew tired of men dictating to her. Telling her how to live and what to do and how to behave.

And using her like a dried-up commodity.

So, she'd come. And now, despite the heat and the terror and the pain, the look of approval in Eliza's eyes made it all worth it. Almost.

"We ladies don't fear a little earthquake, gentlemen. Do carry on." Eliza's courage caused Angeline's shoulders to lift just a little. The woman was nearly two months along with child, yet here she was burrowing into the depths of the earth right beside her husband.

Oh, how Angeline longed to be brave and independent like Eliza. Not weak and submissive as she'd been her entire life. Angeline had not only come to Brazil to start a new life but to become a new person. To put both her past life and her past self behind her. If only she could. . .

The ground trembled again and she pressed a hand against the wall. Sharp crags pricked her fingers as they slid over rock that seemed to sweat in the infernal heat. "If there was an explosion here last night, I'm surprised these tunnels didn't collapse."

"Indeed," James said, shifting his torch to his other hand, "though these walls appear to be solid enough." He ran a sleeve over his forehead, leaving a streak of mud. "Still, being below ground makes me nervous."

"I couldn't agree more." Blake, an ex-colonel in the Confederate Army and the leader of their colony, raised his torch and wiped dust from his wife's nose. He planted a kiss on it and shook his head. "I told you it wasn't safe."

"Which is precisely why I didn't want you coming here alone." Eliza brushed dirt from his shirt. "Besides, we have to discover if Mr. Graves is injured."

The colonel huffed his frustration and glanced at James with a shrug. But James was still examining the tunnel walls. "Odd. I wonder how primitive cannibals managed to score these tunnels out of rock."

"This place is filled with nothing but questions." Hayden's voice preceded his appearance from the shadows behind them. "The main one gnawing at me now is why we are bothering to check on Graves when he's made it plain he wants nothing to do with us." He ran a hand through dark hair moist with sweat.

"Where are Patrick and Dodd?" the colonel asked.

"They spotted the gold moon and stars above the altar." Hayden's lips slanted. "Need I say more?"

James snorted and leaned toward Angeline to whisper, "Are you sure you want to continue?"

"Yes, I've come this far. I might as well go on." Though her bodice was glued to her skin and sweat trickled down her neck and the fetor that rose from deep within the tunnels was enough to wilt a sturdy oak tree, she would prove herself brave. At least this once. Anything to keep James gazing at her with such admiration.

"Let's get on with it, then," Hayden said, urging them forward. "I've got a new wife to return to."

Eliza smiled and looped her arm through her husband's. "She was so sweet to take over the clinic in my absence."

"I'm glad she did," Hayden replied. "I wouldn't want her coming to this vile place."

Vile indeed. Angeline had forced her eyes shut at the sight of the images of torture carved into stone obelisks that littered the temple yard above. As well as the huge fire pit where no doubt the cannibals had roasted their victims so many years ago. Thankfully, James had ushered her past it all and into the temple before she'd had time to visualize the scenes in her mind. Something she was prone to do, especially with bad memories.

Trying to not lean on James for support, she followed Eliza and Blake as they descended an uneven set of stairs into a dark hole that grew hotter and hotter with each step. The walls narrowed. Air abandoned the space as if too frightened to go farther. She couldn't blame it. Coughing, she gasped for a breath, but only the foul odor of death and decay invaded her lungs. James patted her arm. Torchlight cast ghostly shadows over walls and ceiling. Angeline shivered and nearly tripped.

"Almost there." Blake's voice reverberated through the narrow passage.

They descended another set of stairs cluttered with dirt and rocks then crawled one by one through an opening that led into a large cave. Stalactites and stalagmites thrust from floor and ceiling like giant fangs of some otherworld creature—its mouth gaping wide to receive them. Blake lit torches hooked on walls about the chamber. Their flames cast talon-like shadows leaping over rock and dirt. Angeline's gaze flew to two empty alcoves carved upright into one of the walls. Her breath caught in her throat. Eliza's description did them no credit, for they were much larger, much taller, and so perfectly hewn from stone that Angeline could only stare in wonder.

"Mr. Graves!" James shouted, his voice echoing like a gong. "Mr. Graves!"

Nothing but the *drip*, *drop* of water and howl of wind replied.

Angeline took a tentative step toward one of the alcoves, her eyes fixed upon the iron shackles lying loose at the bottom of a long vertical pole. Her mind tripped on the impossibility of such a place existing beneath an ancient temple, of smooth alcoves carved in a perfect semicircle out of solid rock, of a metal pole and chains that formed some ungodly prison.

A blast of heat swamped her, coming from nowhere, yet all around. Air as hot as a furnace seared her lungs. Sweat moistened her face. The tunnel began to spin. James clutched her arm and handed her a canteen. She took several gulps, allowing the hot but refreshing water to slide down her throat.

"How could Graves stand to be down here so long?" Hayden said from behind them.

"Graves!" Blake shouted. Lifting his torch, he slid through another opening to their left, Eliza on his heels. With a heavy sigh, James followed, escorting Angeline through the narrow crevice into yet another cave. Most of this chamber was filled with large rocks stacked to the ceiling as if the roof had collapsed. The smell of sulfur and feces stung Angeline's nose, and she covered her mouth as her gaze latched upon a single empty alcove carved out of the wall—the same as the two in the cave above.

Leaping atop a boulder centering the room, James raised a torch and tried to peer above the mound of rocks. "There's another alcove back here. I can see the top." He jumped to the ground and approached the empty one then kneeled to examine the broken chains at the bottom. The clank and jangle of iron thundered an eerie cadence through the cavern. Angeline tensed. Dropping the chains, James stood and lifted the torch to reveal writing etched above the alcove. In a foreign language. No, two different languages from what Angeline could tell. James's Adam's apple plummeted, and he snapped his eyes to Blake's.

"Same as the other?" Blake asked.

James nodded.

Hayden approached, glancing up at the writing. "Destruction?"

But James didn't answer. Instead, his wide eyes focused on something on the ground hidden from the rest of them by the boulder.

"What is it?" Blake circled the large rock, glanced down, then turned to stop Eliza from following him.

But it was too late. She shrieked and buried her face in her husband's shirt.

"What's wrong?" Angeline started forward, but James darted to her and held her back.

"It's Graves."

Blake groaned. "Without his head."

CHAPTER 2

Angeline hated funerals. They reeked of finality and no more second chances. They spoke of an eternity hounded by memories one could never escape, mistakes one could never rectify. The last funeral she'd attended had been her father's. She could still see Reverend Grayson in his long black robes, Holy Book in hand, his words dribbling on the fresh mound of dirt, empty and meaningless as the drizzle of rain that had battered her face. She could still see the crush of people—black specters hovering beneath billowing umbrellas—come to pay their respects to a beloved member of their community, a pillar of Norfolk society, businessman, scholar, man of God. Pushed through a window to an early death by a misguided man inflamed in anger. She could still see Uncle John and Aunt Louise standing on either side of her. Her aunt wearing an impatient scowl, her uncle a look of interest. Though that interest was not on the funeral or the reverend or the crowd. But on her—a devastated seventeen-year-old girl. She hadn't known at that time just how far his interest would take him.

Or how far it would take her.

"Mr. Graves made few friends among us." James's voice drew her gaze to where he stood before a fresh heap of dirt, much like Reverend Grayson had done that dreary day three years ago. Only this time, the sun was shining and they weren't in a graveyard in Virginia but in the middle of a lush jungle in Brazil.

Tall, thin trees surrounded the clearing, their vine-laden branches bowed as if paying respect to the dead. Colorful orchids and ferns twirled up their mighty trunks. Luxuriant lichens swayed in the breeze. Birds of every color flitted through the canopy, providing music for the ceremony—albeit a bit too cheerful for a funeral. But not many of the colonists mourned the loss of Mr. Graves. Stowy shifted in her arms, and Angeline caressed the cat who'd been her dear companion since the ship voyage to their new land.

"He spent his time in Brazil deep beneath the earth on a quest for power that made little sense to most of us," James continued. The preacher-doctor looked nothing like Reverend Grayson either. Where the reverend had dark short-cropped hair, James's light hair hung in waves to his collar. Where the reverend was a thin, gaunt man, James was tall and built like a ship—like one of her father's ships. Where the reverend had an angular face, James had a round, sturdy face with a jaw like flint and eyes of bronze that reached to her now across the fresh grave.

She lowered her gaze. That was another way the two men were different. With just one glance, one brush of his skin against hers, James could evoke a warmth that sizzled from her head to her toes. She'd never felt such a thing from a man's touch. And a preacher, at that. Sweet saints, the shame!

"Perhaps we failed Mr. Graves somehow by not trying harder to befriend him. If so, may God forgive us."

Angeline knew the remorse in James's tone was genuine. He truly cared for each and every colonist. Yet she still could not reconcile this man before her with the one she'd met a year ago in Knoxville, Tennessee.

"May God forgive Mr. Graves for sins that would keep him from entering heaven's gates."

Forgiveness. Bah! Angeline well knew there was a limit to God's forgiveness. And from what she knew of Graves, he, like her, had far exceeded that boundary. A breeze, ripe with the scent of orange blossoms and vanilla, wafted through the clearing, fluttering ferns and spinning dry leaves across the ground. A butterfly, its wings resplendent with purple and pink, landed atop Eliza's bonnet as if she were the only worthy subject in the crowd. Beside her, her husband, Colonel Blake, hat in hand, stared at the ground with his usual austere, determined expression.

The butterfly took flight and settled on Sarah's shoulder. Ah yes, another worthy soul, Sarah Jorden, Angeline's hut mate, and one of the sweetest, most godly women she knew. Her baby Lydia, now five months old, was strapped to her chest and thankfully asleep at the moment. Being the resident teacher, children flocked to Sarah as they were doing now, tugging on her skirts, vying for her attention. Delia grabbed her two wayward lambs and ushered them away, casting apologetic looks at Sarah. Angeline wondered if the freed slave woman was happy here in New Hope, where she endured much of the same racial aversion she would have experienced back in the States. Delia took her spot beside her brother, Moses, at the back of the crowd.

"Oh death, where is thy sting? Oh grave, where is thy victory?" James spoke with enthusiasm as if he actually believed the poetic hogwash.

The shifting canopy scattered golden snowflake patterns over the crowd. A sunbeam set the butterfly's wings aglitter as it danced through the air, skipping over Mr. and Mrs. Scott. The wealthy plantation owners were under the impression they still lived on their Georgia plantation and the colonists were their slaves. Yet no one paid them much mind. Angeline smiled. Especially their daughter, Magnolia, the object of Mr. Scott's glower at the moment.

But Magnolia didn't seem to notice as she stood hand in hand with her new husband, Hayden, at the foot of the grave. The butterfly landed on their intertwined hands, bringing another smile to Angeline's lips. Despite the somber occasion, the couple couldn't hide their happiness, nor the loving glances they shared—glances that held such promise. A promise of intimacy and love Angeline would never know.

"For God so loved the world, that he gave his only begotten Son, that whosoever believeth in him should not perish, but have everlasting life. . . ."

Wiley Dodd's eyes locked upon hers as the butterfly passed him by. She tore her gaze from the hungry look on his face. The ex-lawman remembered her. She was sure of it. She could see the mischievous twinkle in his eyes, the knowing glances when he passed her in town. Why didn't he simply tell everyone her secret? What was he waiting for? Despite the heat of the day, her fingers and toes turned to ice.

The butterfly landed on her arm, instantly warming her. She hadn't time to ponder the implications when the crackle of flames sounded in her ears. Glancing up, she expected to see a lit torch, but none was in sight. Neither did anyone else seem to hear the sizzle that grew louder and louder. Wind wisped through the clearing, fluttering black feathers atop a hat that drifted at the outskirts of the crowd. No, not just any hat.

Heart slamming against her ribs, Angeline peered across the grave and through the assembled colonists, trying to make out the woman's face, but the lady wove through the back of the mob, her hat bobbing in and out of view. A hat of ruby velvet, trimmed in a black ribbon with a tuft of black feathers blowing in the wind. Angeline knew that hat.

"I am the resurrection, and the life: he that believeth in me, though he were dead, yet shall he live," James droned on.

The lady stopped. The crowd parted slightly, and the woman tilted her head toward Angeline.

Aunt Louise!

The butterfly took flight. And so did Aunt Louise. But not before Angeline saw a devious smile curl her lips. Setting down Stowy, Angeline clutched her skirts, barreled through the colonists, and plunged into the jungle after her.

"Aunt Louise!" Greenery swallowed a flash of ruby red in the distance. Thrusting leaves aside, Angeline headed in that direction, ignoring the scratch and pull of vines and branches on her gown. "Come back!" Why was the woman even here in Brazil?

Batting aside a tangle of yellow ferns, Angeline burst into a clearing and stopped, gasping for air. She scanned the mélange of leaves in every shade of green for a glimpse of ruby or flutter of black feathers. The *caw, caw* of a toucan echoed from the canopy, drawing her gaze to a golden-haired monkey scolding her for interrupting his mango lunch.

"Aunt Louise!"

There. A flash of red. Lifting her skirts, Angeline plowed through the greenery, her eyes locked on one target: the insolent smirk on her aunt's face. The red grew larger in her vision. The smirk wider. Until finally Angeline stopped before the lady. She caught her breath while studying every inch of her father's sister, wondering how two siblings could be so different, wondering why the woman had despised Angeline more than any relative should. Despised her from the feathers atop her promenade hat to the tiny lines strung tight at the corners of her mouth, to the pearls on her high-necked bodice, the black velvet bows on her pannier skirts, and down to the tassels on her patent leather boots. Boots that tapped impatiently on the dirt as they used to do on the wooden floor back in her Norfolk home.

"What are you doing here?" Angeline asked when her breath returned.

Louise cocked her head. "I could ask you the same. Aren't you supposed to be polishing the silverware like I ordered?"

Angeline stared at her. That was the last chore her aunt had assigned her to do before. . .well, before her life disintegrated. "What are you talking about? I no longer live in your house."

Finely trimmed brows rose. "And why is that, *Clarissa*?"

Angeline cringed at a name she hadn't heard in years.

"Ah, yes. Now I remember." Her aunt strolled about the clearing, the swish of her skirts an odd accompaniment to the drone of insects. She spun to face Angeline, spite pouring from eyes as dark as the feathers atop her hat. "Because you're a vulgar strumpet who stole my husband's affections!"

Blood surged to Angeline's heart, filling it with shock and fury. "I did nothing of the kind." She couldn't tell the lady what had truly happened. It would be far too cruel. Even for a woman who had done nothing but mistreat her.

"I curse the day you entered our home," her aunt hissed. "I knew you were wanton refuse just like your mother."

The woman might as well have forced a bag of rocks down Angeline's throat for the way it made her stomach plummet. Her mother had died giving birth to her, leaving a hole within Angeline, deep and vacant. Yet as the years passed, she couldn't help but hear the whispers floating through town behind raised fans and smug looks. When she questioned her father, he told her that her mother was the most kind, loving, compassionate person who ever lived and to ignore any rumors to the contrary. So she had. Until she moved in with Uncle John and Aunt Louise and their constant degradation of her mother's character eroded the memory implanted by her father.

"I was only seventeen," Angeline said. "I wanted you to care for me.

I *needed* you to care for me—like a mother cares for her own daughter." She hung her head. "But instead you worked me to death."

"I wanted no children. Nothing to steal John's attention from me." She fingered the emerald weighing down her finger then stretched out her hand to examine it in the sunlight. With a snort, she snapped her hand to her waist. "But there you came, young and beautiful, a bouquet of lace and curls no man could resist."

"I had no choice. I had nowhere to go."

"Humph." Aunt Louise gazed out over the jungle as if she stood on Granby Street in Norfolk.

Angeline took a step toward her, the longing for a mother's love shoving aside her misgivings, her memories, giving her a spark of hope that it might still be possible. "Did you ever love me, even just a little?"

Aunt Louise swept eyes as cold and dark as an empty cave toward Angeline. "No one will ever love you." Then, spinning on her fancy heels, she shoved through the foliage and disappeared.

Batting away tears, Angeline darted after her. She had to tell the woman what had really happened. No matter the pain. No matter the cost. She had to make her understand. She had to beg her forgiveness.

After Angeline had sped off in a frenzy, James could barely concentrate on the rest of the funeral. What would cause the woman to dash away in the middle of a ceremony? Certainly not her grief over Graves's death. As it was, her departure caused quite a stir in the otherwise solemn occasion, so he hurried through the remainder of his eulogy before closing his Bible, handing it to Blake, and dismissing the gathering. Now, as he shoved through the leafy jungle, he could think of only one thing that would cause her to run. And that one thing sent an icicle down his spine. That and the fact that whoever *or whatever* had beheaded Graves might still be on the loose.

Destruction. The name etched above the empty alcove. The name of the third being described in the ancient Hebrew book Graves had found in the caves and given James to translate. A being that, it appeared, Graves had somehow freed from its prison. Having seen firsthand what the first two beings, *Deception* and *Delusion*, could do, James feared more than anything the power of this third beast. That was, if he hadn't gone completely mad and all this nonsense about a fierce battle, the judgment of the four, a molten lake, and invisible angelic beings was just that. Pure nonsense.

But for now, he was more concerned with Angeline's safety. Shoving aside a tangle of hanging vines, he caught a glimpse of her standing in the middle of a clearing talking to the air. His chest tightened. Suspicions confirmed, he sprinted toward her, but she took off again. He lengthened his stride, ignoring the scrape and jab of branches on his arms as he kept his eyes on her blue skirts flickering in and out of view through the maze of leaves. She stopped again. James rushed toward her, calling her name, but she didn't seem to hear him. Instead, she stood near the brink of a tall precipice. What he saw next made his blood freeze. Gathering her skirts, Angeline started for the edge.

CHAPTER 3

Aunt Louise halted between an acacia tree and a massive fern. She turned and gave Angeline a grin of victory. Gathering her breath, Angeline hoisted her skirts and darted toward her. Still her aunt remained. . . smiling. . .gloating. Making no attempt to run. Perhaps she'd decided to speak to her after all. Good, Angeline had more than a few things to say to the woman who had caused her so much pain. She wasn't a young girl anymore. She wasn't timid, in mourning, or desperate for love. Nor was she at her aunt's mercy for survival. This time, the conversation would be different. Just a few more steps. . . "So, are you ready to—"

Strong arms grabbed her from behind, cinched her waist. "Let me go!" Angeline tried to pry off fingers that tightened like vises. She lunged to break free, staring at her aunt's smirk that now faded to disappointment.

"Angeline, stop!" The male voice blared in her ears. Her behind hit the ground. Her back flattened on leaves. And James's face absorbed her vision. "Holy thunder, woman, what are you doing?" Lines of terror spiked from the corners of his eyes.

Angeline pummeled his chest with her fists, but she might as well have been pounding on steel. He pinned her arms to the dirt.

Panic tied her stomach in a knot. Too many men had forced her to her back, held her down against her will. Memories pierced the fear. Bestial grunts and groans, hands groping where none should touch. The struggle against muscles too strong to move. Like now. She kneed the man above her, grinding her fists in the mud. "Get off of me! Get off of me!"

Releasing her, he leapt back, hands in the air. "I wasn't. . .I wasn't. . . doing anything untoward, Miss Angeline. Forgive me."

Breath clogged her throat. She rose and inched backward on wobbly arms, staring at the man she least expected to make advances on her. The preacher-doctor, James.

But they weren't advances. Not from the look of concern in his eyes. Nor the remorse that followed. Not a speck of desire could be found in either. She knew desire. Could spot it in a man a mile away.

"You were about to run off a cliff." He gestured with his head toward the right as he collected his breath.

Making no sense of his words, she glanced toward the spot where she'd last seen Aunt Louise. But there was nothing there but the jagged edge of a precipice and the empty space beyond carpeted with spindly treetops.

Air fled her lungs. The jungle reeled in her vision, and her arms gave out. Before she hit the ground, James caught her and cradled her against his chest. She couldn't be sure whether it was the feel of that rock-hard chest or the sight of the cliff where none had been before that made her head spin. But spin it did.

"There was no cliff. . .just jungle. . ." she muttered. "And my aunt was there. . .no cliff."

James brushed hair from her face. "Your aunt? Did you see her?"

"Yes. . .Aunt Louise!" Alarm forced its way through the fog in her mind. She pushed from James. "Did she fall? We have to help her!" Struggling to rise, she refused his help and started toward the overhang.

"No." He pulled her to a stop, caressed her hand with his thumb. "It was a vision. It must have been a vision." Concern poured from his eyes.

Angeline tugged from his grasp and swallowed. Like Mr. Gordan, whom she'd seen last month. "But she looked so real. She spoke to me."

"They all do." He led her to sit on a boulder then knelt and eased a strand of hair behind her ear. The intimate gesture sent heat firing to her toes. She wiggled them, wondering if it was simply nerves. But it was far too delightful to be anything other than what she feared—the thrill of a man's touch. Not just any man. Looking away, she shook it off. She wanted nothing to do with men ever again. Especially this one: preacher, doctor, drunk? She had no idea which. Nor could she forget their brief encounter over a year ago.

Thankfully he seemed to.

Yet, if he was nothing but a womanizer and carouser, why did he affect her so? Both in the past, when she'd met him on the streets of Knoxville, and now, when he seemed so different. People change. Isn't that what they said? She wanted so badly to believe that. She *had* to believe that or the rest of her life would surely be doomed.

❦

Nerves strung tight, James rose to his feet. If only to put some distance between him and Angeline. The woman drove him mad. In a good way. In a dangerous way. Truss it, he'd almost lost her! He breathed a silent prayer of thanks to God for helping him reach her in time. One second later and she would have been gone. He couldn't imagine New Hope without her. He couldn't imagine life without her. Although they had no formal understanding—and if the lady had a lick of reason, she'd never agree to one—they *had* formed a friendship these past months. Possibly a bit more, if he sensed things right.

Sunlight filtered through the canopy, weaving gold threads through her hair, the color of burgundy wine. A sudden thirst overcame him, and he licked his lips and shifted his thoughts to the funeral then to the spider skittering up the tree at the edge of the clearing, anything but on her. But then she raised moist eyes to his, the same shade as the lilacs circling the vine behind her. And just as striking. She bit her bottom lip, full and soft as a rose petal, and looked at him with such need, such innocence.

He took another step back. He must focus. He was the town preacher, not the town rogue. For once in his life, he must resist this tempting morsel. For once in his life, he could not fail. He ran a sleeve over his forehead and studied the cliff.

"You didn't see the drop-off?"

"No."

"That means they are turning deadly." He frowned.

"The visions?"

"And whatever or *whoever* is causing them."

"I still can't believe Aunt Louise wasn't real." Her voice trailed off as she wrung her hands in her lap. "She tried to kill me. But why?"

James shook his head, wishing he had answers.

"You think they have something to do with the temple?" she asked. "The empty alcoves and broken irons and Graves's death?"

He nodded and smiled at the way she wiggled her nose, shifting her sprinkling of freckles. Adorable as always. A flock of green parakeets with black heads landed on the branches of a nearby tree and began chattering, while uneasiness crossed her violet eyes. She fingered a button of her bodice. Another thing he admired about her—her modest attire. High-necked blouses, long sleeves, and her hair always put up in a bun, though now some strands broke free and dangled in the breeze. Angeline was a lady in the truest sense. In fact, all the women in New Hope seemed to possess the highest of morals. Something James was extremely thankful for. He'd had his fill of unscrupulous women back in Tennessee and would not allow them to taint the new Southern utopia they were building here in Brazil.

"And this Hebrew book you're translating. . ." She broke into his musings. "The one Graves gave you before he died. Will it tell us more?"

"That is my hope."

"Who do you think killed the poor man?" She rubbed her throat, no doubt thinking of the manner of his death.

"Whoever it is, you have nothing to worry about, Miss Angeline. Blake and I will protect the colony." He had hoped to set her at ease, to erase the fear lining her face. Instead, she slanted her lips and huffed.

"Don't placate me, Doctor." Her sharp tone surprised him. "I may be a woman, but I don't wilt like a flower. In fact, I shed my petals years ago."

But not all her thorns. James smiled, remembering the gun she'd pulled on him last month when he'd surprised her at the river. He scratched the stubble on his chin. "Truth is, I don't know who killed Graves. But I do believe there is something peculiar going on. Something supernatural, even." He shrugged. "Demons, angels, curses, who knows? Something only God can help us with."

Her snicker brought his gaze back to her. "You don't believe in evil, Miss Angeline?"

Her eyes sharpened. "Evil? Absolutely." She stood and brushed dirt from her skirts as if she could brush away memories of that evil.

"It's God I have trouble believing in." She raised her chin.

That would certainly explain why the lady never attended church. "I'm sorry to hear that." What had happened to this beautiful woman? Whatever it was, James longed to know more about her, to ease her suffering if he could. Memories of their ship voyage from Charleston to Brazil rose to prick his suspicions. Perhaps she had not seen a vision at all just now, but had intended to fling herself off the precipice. It wouldn't be the first time she'd attempted to leap to her death. Yet she had seemed much better since they landed in Brazil—happier, more settled.

A breeze rose from the ravine and swirled through the loose strands of her hair. Her gaze shifted to the cliff. "How did you know? Where I was?" Her brows—the same lush russet as her hair—scrunched together. "How did you know I was in danger?"

"You ran so quickly from the funeral, I assumed something had either frightened or upset you. So I followed."

"Your duty as town preacher, no doubt? Comfort the afflicted? Save the tortured soul from hell?" The cynicism in her voice stung him. But he refused to let it show.

"Something like that." He chuckled. "Though, I must say, you do make my job sound rather nefarious."

A tiny grin flitted across her lips. "My apologies, Doctor."

"Please call me James."

She glanced down as if he'd asked her to reveal her deepest secret. He would ask her to do just that if he thought she'd tell him. The warble of birds and buzz of insects filled the awkward silence. James shifted his boots over the ground, littered with dried leaves. "When I saw you heading for that cliff. . ."—he'd felt his heart tumbling over with her—"and you weren't slowing down. . .I. . .I'm just glad I made it in time."

His heart cramped even now. . .even though she was safe. And he realized for the first time how much he truly cared for her. In all his twenty-eight years, he'd never truly cared for a woman. He'd never had time. From an early age, he'd spent his days studying Greek, Hebrew, and theology under his father's tutelage, and his nights resisting the delights other young men his age embraced: courting young girls, attending parties and plays, playing All Fours or Faro at the local tavern. All innocent enough activities, but out of reach for a preacher's son studying to follow in his father's footsteps.

Angeline moved toward the cliff, stared into the canyon, and hugged herself.

Trouble was, James hadn't wanted to be a preacher. He'd wanted to be a doctor. So, after proving himself an abject failure at pastoring, he ran away to apprentice under a physician in Charleston while attending the Medical College of South Carolina. The news broke his father's heart. And his mother's. Especially when the war began and he volunteered to serve.

Blood. There had always been so much blood. Day after endless day. Night after endless night. It was as if the world and everything in it had been painted red. And no matter how he tried, he could never scrub the stain from his hands. He stared at those hands now. They shook at the memory, and he fisted them at his sides.

A dark cloud rolled overhead, stealing the sunlight and settling a smoky dust on the scene. And now here he was in the fledgling colony of New Hope—a haven for Southerners after the war—preaching again. Not doctoring. He chuckled at the irony, drawing Angeline's gaze over her shoulder. "Something amusing?"

"Just pondering life's twists and turns." The most recent twist had him bearing the spiritual well-being of an entire town when he couldn't even bear his own.

Thunder bellowed, and a gust of wind brought the spicy scent of rain upon a gentle mist. He found himself remembering what she had looked like drenched from seawater...how her blouse had clung to her underthings, mapping out her bountiful curves.

She whirled about, caught him staring at her, then narrowed her eyes as if she perceived his thoughts. "We should go."

No, he wasn't fit to be a preacher at all.

"Yes, of course." Though he hated to leave. Though he knew these rare tête-à-tête's were beyond appropriate. Yet he so enjoyed them.

They set off side by side, crunching the leaves beneath their shoes and brushing aside foliage as they went.

"If you should see another vision, Miss Angeline, please oblige me and do not follow it."

"I will try," she responded with a slight smile, "but I so desperately needed to talk to this particular one."

James understood that all too well. He had tried to refrain from talking to the vision of his dead mother a few weeks ago, and he'd been no more successful than Angeline. "I suppose that's why they appear. They know we can't resist them."

"Perhaps they are just cruel tricks of our imaginations. Memories rising to taunt us."

"I doubt it. If so, all the colonists' imaginations are ravaged with the same plague."

She swatted a leaf, not even flinching at the large beetle that grazed upon it. "We all have our demons, do we not, Doctor?"

James touched her arm, stopping her, always amazed at how petite she was—at least a foot shorter than his six feet. "Whatever your particular demon is, Miss Angeline, whatever is bothering you, I hope you know you can talk to me." He cleared his throat. "As your pastor of course."

She tugged from his grip and forged ahead. "If I talk to you of my demons at all, Doctor, it will not be as my pastor."

The rest of the hike back to camp was made in silence as James pondered the unusual woman beside him. Part angel, part dragon. Both terribly wounded. By the time they burst onto Main Street, black clouds broiled low over town like a witch's cauldron. Though most of the colonists had no doubt taken refuge in their huts, Blake, Hayden, and Magnolia stood beneath the cover of the meeting shelter, peering up at the frightening sky.

James started toward them when a bright flash turned everything white as if someone had struck a giant match over the scene.

Thunder roared. The ground shook. He blinked, waiting for his vision to clear when Blake's shout pounded in his ears. "Fire! Fire! The sugar mill!"

CHAPTER 4

Setting down the bucket, Angeline leaned back against a tree and tried to settle her rapid breath. She plucked a handkerchief from her pocket and wiped the perspiration cooling her face and neck as she examined what was left of their sugar mill. What once had been the building's frame lay in piles of smoking, charred remains. Several of the town's men, including James, stood staring at the ruins, water pails locked in their grip as if there were still some chance to save it. The colonists, who had only moments before formed a human chain of water from the river to the mill, began to drop like wounded birds to the ground, their chests heaving, their haggard faces aghast at the futile result of their hard efforts.

Magnolia appeared beside Angeline, her normally flawless skin streaked in soot and sweat. Wincing, she stretched her fingers on both hands, no doubt from the same ache that afflicted Angeline's after an hour of hoisting buckets full of water.

"I can't believe this happened. Of all the places for lightning to strike." Magnolia fingered her hair, attempting to stuff strands back into their pins.

"I agree. Any other building would have been better."

"My parents' house, for one." Despite the dire situation, Magnolia gave a sly smile as her gaze traveled to her mother and father standing in the distance, eyeing the disaster with shock and dismay—as they had done through the entire ordeal.

A month ago, Magnolia would have been by their side, thinking herself too superior for such menial work. Especially too superior to bring herself to such a state of perspiration and filth to save a mere mill. What had changed her? Marriage? Angeline glanced at Hayden, the roguish stowaway who'd stolen Magnolia's heart. Word was he'd been a confidence man before coming to Brazil. The swindler and the Southern belle. An odd match, indeed.

Cursing under his breath, Hayden tossed down his bucket, splattering water over the dirt.

Magnolia cocked a brow. "I better go calm him down." After giving Angeline's hand a squeeze, she joined the men standing just feet from the smoking remains.

Angeline did the same. For the first time since she'd been a young girl, she had friends—friends who cared, friends on whom she could rely. Though if they knew her secrets, she doubted they'd have much to do with her at all. Smoke burned her nose and throat. James's bronze eyes swept her way, at first hard and pointed but then softening around the edges. He tapped her on the nose then held up a finger covered in soot and smiled. Heat surged up her neck.

"You brat!" She laughed and wiped her nose.

Blake cursed and took up a pace before what was left of the mill, instantly stifling their playfulness. "It took us a month to cut down trees, shape the logs, and erect this frame."

Angeline felt sorry for the leader of their new colony. It was a hard enough task to organize such a diverse group of people while struggling to create a new town and eke out a living in the jungle. He certainly didn't need any further setbacks.

"Perhaps we can salvage the rollers." Eliza, his wife, gestured to the round iron objects used to press sugarcane that now lay in a glowing heap inside the building. "And the gears. It appears the fire didn't destroy them."

Blake nodded and rubbed the back of his neck. "Yes. Thank God for that."

"And we still have the donkeys." Magnolia pointed to the two animals tethered off to the side. One of them brayed in response.

"Indeed." Blake heaved a sigh and turned to face the colonists, raising his voice for all to hear. "Thank you all for working so hard! You pulled together when we needed you the most."

"A lot of good it did us," one man shouted.

Moses, the burly ex-slave, lowered himself to a stump and wiped sweat from his forehead. With no thought to his own safety, he'd been up front with Blake, James, and Hayden, enduring the full heat of the flames. His sister, Delia, and her two children approached him, and he swept both little ones on his knees in a tight embrace.

"Where'd the lightning come from?" Mr. Lewis, the old carpenter, pulled a flask from his coat and leaned against a tree.

Thiago, the Brazilian guide the emperor had assigned to their colony, glanced upward and scratched his head. "Look at sky now."

All eyes snapped above, where sunlight speared the canopy.

"It was black as night a minute ago," Hayden said.

"It is curse," Thiago added with a shiver.

As if he were searching for something, James's gaze spanned the sky then lowered to the wide river from where they'd drawn the water, before taking in the rows of huts that made up their town.

Eliza slipped her hand into her husband's. "The good news is we have plenty of time to rebuild the mill before the sugar is ready for harvest."

"And at least no one was hurt," Angeline offered, trying to lighten the dour mood.

Eliza nodded and placed a hand tenderly over her belly as if she could caress her child before it was born.

Magnolia leaned against Hayden, and he swept an arm around her, drawing her close.

Angeline's closest friends had found love on this journey. Love and marriage and happiness. She should be happy for them. She *was* happy for them. She hadn't come to Brazil to find a husband. A husband was the last thing she needed. Or wanted. Then why did the sight of her friends arm in arm make her feel so alone?

James shifted his stance and glanced her way. Was he as lonely as she? No matter. Lonely or not, she must avoid the doctor—for a number of reasons. The one foremost in her mind was the way she'd felt all hot and tingling when his body had been atop hers, when his warm breath had wafted over her cheek, when his arms had kept her from tumbling to her death.

To her death? Sweet saints, she'd almost darted off a cliff! Her legs wobbled at the memory.

James finally lowered his bucket to the ground and stretched his back. No matter how hard she tried, she couldn't keep her gaze from traveling his way. Damp, sooty hair stuck out in all directions and hung to his collar where it curled at the tips. A muscle twitched in his tight jaw, and dirt blackened the tiny scar on the right side of his mouth. She remembered the night he'd received that scar. She had tended to the wound in a room above a tavern in Knoxville, Tennessee. But she wouldn't ask him about it, lest he ask her where she'd gotten the scar she kept hidden on her arm.

Nevertheless, he'd been so kind to her today in the jungle. So caring. He'd made her feel safe. But she didn't want to feel safe with him. She never wanted to feel safe with any man again. Out of the two men she'd ever trusted—the two men she should have felt the safest with—one had died and the other had betrayed her. She took a step away from James.

No. She would not be fooled again.

The colonists struggled to rise and began ambling toward the river to clean and refresh themselves. Angeline was about to join them when James grabbed Blake's arm. "Have you considered this may not have been a natural act?"

The colonel's dark brows dipped together.

Hayden snickered. "I suppose you think some invisible beast did this, eh, Doc?"

Magnolia glanced at her husband. "Come now, Hayden, how can you deny what we've all seen?"

"I didn't want to say this in front of the others"—James scanned the five of them who remained—"but we all saw it firsthand. The empty alcove. The next beast gone. Have you ever seen a sky turn that black and oppressive in so short a time? And the lightning. Did it strike anywhere else? And now the sun returns within minutes?" He shook his head.

"It *is* rather strange." Eliza hugged herself.

"Perhaps what we should be more concerned with," Blake said, his face drawn tight, "is who killed Graves and why. And whether the murderer is still close by."

"What if it isn't a *who* at all?" James lifted a brow toward Blake.

Blake seemed to be pondering the possibility while Hayden

offered a cynical chuckle.

"Regardless," James continued, "we should post extra guards at night."

"Indeed," Blake agreed.

Angeline felt her admiration rising for the doctor as it did every time he spoke with such authority. Though Blake was the leader of the colony, James had assumed a position of power right beside him. As had Hayden. Wise and strong, the three of them had engendered the confidence of the people. And Angeline's confidence as well. Even though she didn't always agree with James's position on spiritual matters, she trusted his judgment.

"What does your Hebrew book say?" she asked.

His eyes met hers. "Not enough at the moment. I need to translate more of it."

Blake rubbed his leg where an old war wound still pained him. "Well, until you do, let's assume this was nothing more than a natural disaster. I don't want to scare the entire town with fables and myths."

"Speaking of myths and fables," Eliza said. "Where are Dodd and Patrick? We could have used a few more men to help."

Hayden huffed. "Where else would my father be but out searching for gold?"

Taking a small brush from his pocket, Patrick Gale swept dirt from a boulder and took a seat. A drop of sweat trickled down his back, making him squirm while loosening a curse from his lips. "Blast this infernal heat!" He gazed up at the maze of vines and branches webbing the canopy, where birds of every color and size skipped and chirped and whined and essentially made nuisances of themselves. So many! Studying the shoulders of his Marseilles cotton shirt, he was relieved to not find spatters of bird droppings. "Over there. I said to dig there." He pointed his jeweled finger to a portion of the creek a few feet from where the imbecile, Dodd, had planted his shovel.

Dodd leaned on the handle and gave him his usual exasperated glare. "Apologies, your *lordship*, but perhaps if you got off your bottom and helped now and then, I wouldn't make so many mistakes."

"We only have one shovel." Patrick spread the three maps on his lap.

Squatting, Dodd cupped water onto his head, allowing the liquid to saturate his golden hair and trickle from the ends onto a chest bare except for tufts of hair scattered across it like brambles on a plain. "I'm the one doing all the digging, Patrick, while you sit in the shade and study those maps."

That the man had ever been a sheriff astounded Patrick. Though one might consider him brawny enough, the deficit of a single intelligent thought must have made the job difficult at best. Dodd shook the water from his hair, spraying droplets over the dirt. Ah, yes, that's what he reminded Patrick of—his grandfather's dog, a Greyhound to be exact. Thin, powerful, with the same sharp, crooked nose, and just as clumsy and witless.

Patrick waved away a swarm of gnats. "How many times must I inform you, Mr. Dodd, that if we are ever to find this gold, I must spend my time examining every detail of these maps? Since you have been in possession of two of them for months and have made no progress, might I suggest that it may take a superior mind to decipher them? In which case, the best use of my time is in their study, and the best use of yours is digging where I tell you to dig."

Dodd spit off to the side, no doubt an indication of his thoughts on the matter. "If you're so smart, then why have you led me to dig in three different spots in the last two weeks and we've come up empty each time?"

A *caw, caw* rang above them as if even the birds laughed at the idiocy of such a question.

"This is not science, my friend. This is a puzzle, a code which one can interpret different ways depending on the position of each map in relation to the others." Patrick stared at the maps. "Whoever designed these was a genius. Quite impressive."

"So you have said." Dodd gripped the handle and thrust the shovel into the gravel lining the creek bed then tossed the silt atop a growing pile on land. "All I have to say is we better find the treasure soon or I'll be taking over the map deciphering." He forced the shovel in again.

Patrick shook his head. It was like dealing with a child—an unruly child. And if he'd wanted to do that, he would have raised Hayden instead of left him and his mother when the lad was but two. But Dodd must be tolerated, for he provided the brawn for their venture.

At the mature age of forty-three and with his experience and skill, Patrick had certainly risen above such menial work. He'd certainly risen above living in a hut and eating bananas like a monkey as well. Ah, the struggles he endured to line his pockets with gold!

To make matters worse, not only must he suffer in this bestial jungle, but he was forced to watch his ex-fiancée, the lovely Magnolia, stroll about town on his son's arm, the two smiling and cooing at each other in a nauseating display of marital bliss. Why she chose him over Patrick, he'd never understand. Though Hayden had inherited Patrick's good looks, he'd definitely received his plebian mannerisms and limited wit from his sweet mother. And to think Hayden had become a swindler like Patrick. A very bad one at that, to look at him now. Impoverished, living in a thatched hut in the most pathetic attempt at a colony Patrick had ever seen. No, Hayden was going nowhere.

Not like Patrick. He had plans. Big plans. Wind stirred the crinkled edges of the map, and he pressed them down, gliding a finger to the drawing of the well in the center. He folded the map across the figure then folded the other two maps at the precise points he'd determined and slid all three together. Yes. Yes. It was definitely this creek. He was sure of it. The treasure had to be here.

"Hurry up, Dodd. Hurry up, our gold awaits!" he shouted with exuberance.

Sweat streaming down his face, Dodd's blue eyes speared him with disdain, but Patrick waved him away with a snort.

"*More gold than ye can carry,*" the old pirate had told him over a sputtering candle in the back room of a tavern in St. Augustine. "*More gold than ten men can carry. Why, ye'll be the richest man in America.*" The man had looked to be near one hundred years old. He had a glass eye in one socket, no teeth in his mouth, and three missing fingers on his right hand. But Patrick believed him. The old pirate knew things no one else could.

That's when Patrick had decided to come to Brazil. As luck would have it, the end of the war drove many Southerners in the same direction. All he had to do was organize a colony, collect everyone's money, and he had a free ride to the land of promise.

Only the land of promise had turned out to be filled with insects the size of a fist, snakes that could strangle a man while he slept, and

CHAPTER 5

Magnolia sidestepped a massive root and continued down the path to the river's edge. "Mable, I'm so happy my mother released you for the day."

"I's glad too, Miss Magnolia. I thank you for your kindness." The slave girl's voice teetered on the edge of nervousness as she hurried along beside Magnolia. "If she knew what you were doin' she'd be stormin' mad."

"Don't you worry about her, Mable. She will never know." Magnolia winked. A habit she'd acquired from Hayden. "Wells, I thank you just the same, Miss." The Negro beauty graced Magnolia with a rare smile that flashed a row of alabaster teeth. No wonder Moses found the woman comely and charming and sweet. She was all those things and more. Why hadn't Magnolia noticed how special Mable was when she'd been her personal slave?

"I'm so sorry, Mable, for all the times I mistreated you." Magnolia swatted an oversized fern aside.

"You diden mistreat me, Miss."

Halting, Magnolia gave the slave a look of reprimand. "Yes I did, and you know it. I was rude and condescending and behaved like a spoiled chit. While you were always kind to me."

Mable looked down at worn shoes peeking out from beneath her equally worn skirts. "You've changed, Miss."

"Yes I have." They continued walking as the drone of insects heightened with each hop of the sun across the sky. It was not even noon, and perspiration already spread a sheen over Magnolia's arms.

673

She looped one of those arms through Mable's. The slave tugged away. "People will see us, Miss."

"I don't care a whit. God has changed me, Mable. He exists and He loves me and He loves you too! And He doesn't like slavery. All are equal in His eyes." It was a revelation the Almighty had shown Magnolia recently, and she wished more than anything she could force her parents to free Mable, but they were having none of it. Their excuse was they couldn't afford to pay her, and the girl had nowhere else to go. For the time being, Mable seemed content with her station in life, but Magnolia had other plans.

Plans that included the large black man standing at the edge of the river, staring across the wide expanse of sparkling blue and green. The man who caused Mable to stop and gasp in delight as she and Magnolia burst from the leaves onto the tiny beach. The young slave girl stepped on a twig, and the snap brought him around and split his face in a wide smile.

"Go." Magnolia released her. The girl hesitated. "You have only a short time."

"Thank you, Miss." Her eyes glassy, Mable sped toward the stocky freedman and disappeared in his bearlike embrace. Magnolia knew she should turn away and continue on with her business, but she couldn't help but stand and soak in the glow that beamed from both their faces as Moses led Mable to sit on a boulder and took her hands in his. A glow Magnolia knew all too well with Hayden.

When one is fortunate enough to find real love, it should not be denied. Especially not because of the color of one's skin. My, but she *had* changed. She patted the mirror weighing down her right pocket and wondered if that change would at all be seen in her reflection.

A bee buzzed around her head, interrupting her musings. Batting it aside, she made her way to the river's edge, set down her bucket, and lowered herself to a rock. A much easier feat without the crinoline she'd finally discarded for good. The gush and roar of the river bathed her in peace while sunlight rippled silvery jewels over water as blue as the sky. She pulled the mirror from her pocket and laid it facedown on her lap. Colorful flowers painted on porcelain stared up at her. A chip cut into the gilding that circled the painting, no doubt broken during her long trek to Rio de Janeiro through the jungle with Hayden. Ah, such fond memories! Yet, despite the flaw, the mirror her father had given her all those years ago was still beautiful.

But would she see beauty on the other side? Or was the prophecy spoken over her by the old woman—or perhaps angel—in the church still in effect? She hadn't looked at her reflection in weeks—too fearful to see no change at all. Mable's laughter drew her gaze to the couple holding hands and beaming at each other like lovesick children. She faced the river again. Taking a deep breath, she flipped the mirror over and held it to her face. She'd become so accustomed to her aged reflection, she no longer gasped in horror. Brittle gray hair sprang out above creviced, loose skin; thin cracked lips; and eyes that hid behind drooping lids. But wait. She touched her cheek. Wait. Not as many lines wrinkled her skin. She brushed fingers over her lips that now held a tinge of pink. And her hair. . .a few strands of blond sprang from among the gray. She *had* improved! Her heart was growing less dark, more filled with light. Thanks be to God!

Hearing footsteps, she quickly stuffed the mirror back into her pocket and turned to see Sarah approaching with baby Lydia strapped to her chest and two buckets in her hands.

"Ah, marriage agrees with you, Magnolia. I've never seen you smile so much!" Sarah set down her pails and gazed over the river. Across the rushing water that spanned at least twenty yards, an armadillo emerged from the thick jungle, stared at them for a moment, then dipped his snout in the swirling current.

"I never thought I *could* be this happy," Magnolia said, hearing the lively bounce in her own voice. "Hayden is everything I could ever want in a husband and more. He's absolutely—" She halted when she saw the dazed look of sorrow in Sarah's eyes. "Oh, do forgive me. I'm going on and on when you. . .when. . .I wasn't thinking."

Sarah smiled. "That's quite all right."

"I can't imagine enduring the pain of losing a husband." Magnolia would simply shrivel up and die should something bad happen to Hayden.

Gurgling, Lydia reached up to touch her mother's face, and Sarah kissed the child's chubby fingers, gazing at her daughter with love. At least she still had something left of her husband. "The war stole many men from their wives," Sarah said. "But Franklin is in a better place now."

Magnolia nodded as she watched the armadillo disappear into the jungle again. "A month ago, I would have laughed at such a declaration. But now I understand."

Sarah brushed a strand of brown hair from her eyes. "It is wonderful, isn't it, knowing how much God loves you? Knowing Him?" She spoke with the excitement of a young woman in love, putting Magnolia's own zeal for God to shame.

"I'm only just beginning to know Him, but yes, it's better than I could have ever hoped."

"I've seen a great change in you in such a short time."

"If only I could change faster." Magnolia ran fingers over the mirror hidden in her skirts.

"Be patient." Sarah knelt and dipped a bucket in the water. "Allow God to work in His own time."

Magnolia took the other bucket and lowered it to the swirling water. "I miss sharing a hut with you."

"But I imagine you enjoy your new companion far better?" A devilish twinkle appeared in the teacher's eyes.

The insinuation behind those eyes set Magnolia's face aflame. A flicker brought her gaze down to the ever-present gold cross hanging around Sarah's neck, a symbol of her genuine heart and saintly ways. Sarah Jorden, the epitome of piety and grace. Then why had God taken her husband from her at so young an age? "Do you ever get lonely?"

Sarah set her bucket down. Water sloshed over the brim, and she dipped a hand in and brought it to her neck. "Sometimes I miss the feel of a man's arms around me."

"I am sure Thiago would be happy to oblige you in that regard." Angeline's spirited voice startled them, and they looked up to see the russet-haired beauty approaching, pail in hand, and ever-present black cat following on her heels.

A tiny smile peeked from the edge of Sarah's lips. "You shouldn't say such things, Angeline. I hardly know him. Besides, he has some strange beliefs about God."

"Sweet saints." Angeline set her bucket down and scooped up Stowy. "Why is that so important?"

The smile on Sarah's lips faded. "Because our paths would eventually go in very different directions. No, I have no interest in the

Brazilian guide, nor does he have any in me, I assure you."

Angeline bit her lip and stared at the river, caressing Stowy. Magnolia wondered if she thought of James. The poor lady always seemed so conflicted, so sad. Magnolia should pray for her. What a grand idea! She'd never done that before—prayed for someone else.

"James is a godly man." Angeline confirmed Magnolia's suspicions as the woman kissed Stowy and set him down. But her next statement shocked Magnolia. "Perhaps you should pursue him, Sarah."

"Me?" Sarah chuckled. "I've never been much for competition. Whenever you're around, the man is drawn toward you like a bee to nectar."

⤙⚓⤚

Both women grinned at Angeline, mischief twinkling in their eyes. Grabbing her pail, she brushed past them to the river's edge, not wanting them to see her expression, whatever that may be. For she didn't know which of the emotions spinning inside her—joy, terror, excitement, or sorrow—revealed itself on her face.

"Don't be silly. He's simply being kind like any preacher would."

"He *does* know his scripture well," Magnolia commented. "He's been teaching me and Hayden in his spare time."

Angeline didn't want to hear about God and scripture. She heard enough of such pious talk from Eliza and Sarah and James, and now Magnolia. The Southern belle had been one of the few women Angeline could count on to not mention God in every conversation. What had happened to her? A leaf floated by on the current, and Stowy batted it then pounced down the bank in pursuit. Squatting, Angeline dipped her pail in the water. "Seems we are all in need of water at the same time."

"I need some for my garden before the children arrive for their lessons," Sarah said.

Magnolia gestured to her left and smiled. "I came for them."

Shielding her eyes, Angeline glanced at Moses and Mable down shore, hands locked and heads dipped together. "It is a good thing you are doing, Magnolia."

"It's the least I can do. They deserve a chance at happiness too."

Angeline frowned. Why did happiness always have to involve a

677

man? Couldn't a woman be happy alone? She hefted her full bucket. "I'm bringing this water to the men in the fields. They should be taking their noon break soon."

"Men? Or perhaps one man in particular?" Magnolia gave her a sly look.

"You are incorrigible!" Angeline shook her head as the three ladies started back. Though Mable reluctantly parted from Moses, neither the girl's smile nor the skip in her step faltered all the way to town. When they emerged onto Main Street, she thanked Magnolia, said her good-byes to Sarah and Angeline, and started back to the Scotts. Thiago, the handsome Brazilian, appeared out of nowhere to help Sarah carry her buckets.

"No interest in him at all, hmm?" Magnolia leaned toward Angeline after they'd left, and they both giggled. "I'll accompany you to the fields. I wouldn't mind seeing Hayden." She smiled at Stowy trotting along beside Angeline. "That cat follows you everywhere."

"Not everywhere."

"I remember the day you found him on board the *New Hope*."

Chasing rats in the hold of the ship, if Angeline recalled. Even so, the cat had been riddled with fleas and near starving. "He's been a good friend." Loyal, trustworthy, caring. More than she could say about most people.

They crossed the street that ran through the center of their tiny settlement, separating two rows of bamboo huts, about twenty in all, housing forty-two colonists. Actually more than that, now that Patrick Gale had shown up a couple weeks ago with his own group of settlers. Blake had assigned a few men to build more huts, but it was slow going since he needed all able hands to work the fields. Would they ever turn this crude outpost into a civilized town? Angeline hoped so as she and Magnolia took a well-worn path to the edge of the fields.

Surrounded by jungle on three sides, sun baked the plowed land, luring green stalks of sugarcane from the ground where they'd planted the splices they'd brought with them on the journey. Barely a foot tall, they spiked across the fields on one side while tiny coffee sprouts dotted the other. The coffee beans would take at least three years to ripen, but the sugar would be ready within a year. Plenty of time to rebuild the mill and process the cane for market. Spotting the ladies, the men tossed picks and shovels down and headed toward the shade.

Angeline had come to Brazil to start a new life. To erase the memories of her past and start over. To be a lady. Or at least *try* to be one. So far she'd been accepted and had gained the respect and care of others. Now, as she watched men come in from the fields, men she'd grown to care for as brothers, an odd feeling welled inside her. A sense of being normal. Of being part of a family. Maybe her risky move to Brazil had been a good decision after all.

If only the ex-lawman, Dodd, would keep his mind busy with gold and not with trying to remember her from the time they'd met back home.

If only the half-clad man heading her way would stop sending her head into a spin.

And her heart.

Against her will, Angeline's gaze locked on James. She'd seen him at a distance without his shirt. But never this close. Thick-chested with his shirt on, the lack of it revealed mounds of corded muscle rolling under taut skin—gleaming like a golden statue of some Greek god. And this man was a preacher? Not like any preacher she'd met. Sweet saints, she'd seen men without their shirts before—far too many of them. Why did the sight of this one send a buzz over her skin? Stowy meowed and leapt onto a stump, gazing at him too. "Indeed, Stowy. Indeed," she said out loud without thinking.

Magnolia raised taunting brows in her direction.

Angeline smiled. "Just admiring from afar."

Except now he was close. Thankfully, he grabbed a shirt hanging on a branch and tossed it over his head. She must avoid him. She tried her best, but he followed her. Offered to carry the bucket while she ladled water for the men. He didn't speak, just smiled at her with that knowing smile of his that made her feel safe and cared for. Skin flushed with sun and health, he smelled of sweat and loamy earth. Since arriving in Brazil, the sun had painted gold threads in his wheat-colored hair that now blew in all directions in the swift breeze. Drat! She was looking at him again.

Blake accepted the ladle and gulped down water, thanking her. "This time next year, God willing," he spoke to the men lounging around him, "we should produce enough sugar to pay off our debt for this land."

"And buy better farming tools." Hayden sat on a log beside Magnolia.

"And new fabric for a gown," Magnolia said, making everyone laugh.

"Anything for you, Princess." Hayden slid hair behind her ear and kissed her cheek.

Mr. Lewis, the old carpenter, stood off to the side chopping logs for fires. Angeline headed toward him, offering him water. New fabric would be nice, indeed. They hadn't had any new cloth in ages, leaving Angeline, as the town's seamstress, with not much to do but mend tears and holes.

Lewis slogged down the water with a "thanks" before returning to work. Did the man ever take a break? Shaking her head, Angeline finished serving everyone, ending with James, who took a hearty drink himself before plucking Stowy from the ground and curling the black cat against his chest.

Angeline gaped at the sight. "He won't allow anyone to touch him but me."

"And me, it would seem." James grinned.

Of course. She sighed. God was no doubt playing some cruel trick on her. Wasn't it bad enough the man affected her to distraction? Did Stowy have to like him too?

"Lewis, take a break, man," Hayden shouted.

"Naw, I want to get this wood chopped before it gets dark." The old carpenter wiped sweat from his forehead and continued hefting his ax in the air. Though he tipped the sauce a bit too much and not many people took him seriously, Mr. Lewis never shied away from hard work.

Angeline felt rather than heard something zip past her. She *did* hear the *thwack* of blade in flesh. Followed by a blood-chilling holler. Jerking around, she saw one of the farmers, Mr. Jenkins, drop to the ground, his shoulder a burgeoning mass of red and a bloody ax lying on the ground beside him.

CHAPTER 6

"I can't." James backed away from the examining table where Mr. Jenkins lay moaning in pain. His wife stood on one side of him, gripping his arm and dabbing sweat from his brow, her face mottled in terror. Eliza stood on the other, pressing a fresh cloth to the man's shoulder. Like an army of red marching across a white plain, blood saturated the rag within minutes. James's stomach vaulted. His hands shook. He snapped his gaze away. Unfortunately it landed on the faces of his friends staring at him in confusion—and judgment—Blake, Hayden, and finally Angeline, whose look of disappointment lured his eyes to the dirt floor of the clinic.

"Hold this." Eliza ordered before the swish of her skirts sounded and she dipped into his vision, demanding he look at her by her strong presence alone. "I've never stitched a wound so deep before. Please, James. I need you."

He swallowed hard and glanced at Magnolia holding the dripping cloth in place then over to Mrs. Jenkins, who cast a pleading look over her shoulder.

"Maybe you can talk Eliza through it," Hayden offered.

Approaching, Blake gripped his shoulders. "You can do this. I know you can."

James wasn't so sure. In fact, the tremble now moving from his hands down to his legs said otherwise. Nodding, he gathered what was left of his strength and took a shaky step toward Mr. Jenkins, focusing on the tortured expression on the man's face instead of the blood bubbling from his shoulder. But the red menace crept into his vision like a rising flood—one that would surely drown him.

Eliza began preparing the needle and sutures. Magnolia's frightened glance measured James as he slowly made his way to her. She slipped a clean cloth over the wound and tossed the bloody one into a bucket. *Splat!* Blood dripped from the table—*drip. . .drop. . .drip. . .drop*—like a doomsday clock ticking away the last minutes of Mr. Jenkins's life. Ticking away the last minute of James's consciousness, for he was sure he would faint any second. He inched beside the table, legs like pudding, heart slicing through his chest like the blade had sliced through Mr. Jenkins.

Afternoon sun angled through the window, lighting the macabre scene in eerie gold. Mrs. Jenkins sobbed and leaned to kiss her husband. One of her tears dropped onto his face, and James watched as sunlight transformed it into a diamond rolling down his cheek.

Such beauty in the midst of pain. James drew in a deep breath, trying to settle his nerves, but the metallic scent of blood filled his nose and sent the contents of his stomach into his throat. He rubbed his eyes. The room grew hazy. . .

The examining table became an operating slab in the middle of a medical tent. Mr. Jenkins transformed into a soldier, his chest ripped open, his kidney cradled in James's hands. The *thu-ump, thu-ump, thu-ump* of the man's heart grew dim. . .distant. . . .

"What are your orders, Doctor?" A nurse, apron sprayed with blood, stared at him with eyes filled with panic. The same panic that had kept him frozen in place.

"Doctor? He's dying. . .he's dying. . .do something!"

"James." Eliza touched his arm. She handed him the needle. . . slowly as if she had no energy. "Are. . .you. . .ready?" Her words were garbled and distant. Like she was there, but not there. He faced Mr. Jenkins. The soldier remained. An officer. The single gold star on his collar stood in stark contrast to the blood oozing from his midsection. The nurse continued shouting, "We're losing him. . .he's dying! Doctor. . .Doctor. . ."

James dropped the kidney. It disappeared. Along with the nurse and the wounded officer. He drew a breath. Just a vision. Not real.

But once, years ago, it had been *very* real.

"Pour rum into the wound," he ordered, taking a step back. His head grew light. "Stitch the blood vessel." Another step back. The room spun. "When the bleeding stops, suture the wound." He turned, pressed a hand over his heaving stomach. "I can't. I'm sorry. I can't." Ignoring their protests, he barreled out the bamboo door to a burst of fresh air and stumbled forward, praying for strength to return to his legs before he made a complete fool of himself and toppled to the ground.

People stared at him, whispering. No doubt mocking him as he charged down the street and dashed into the jungle, foisting the brunt of his anger out on leaves and vines that stood in his way. And all the while wondering why the cruel visions continued to assail him. Especially since it had been over two years since he'd left the battlefield. Did they come from these invisible beasts the Hebrew book described, or were they just figments of his tormented guilt? He remembered that injured major well. It was the first time he'd held a man's kidney in his hand—a kidney shredded from a cannon blast. He'd tried to remove it to save the man's life. He had failed. The poor soldier died in a pool of his own blood.

Halting, James pressed hands to his knees and heaved onto the ground. When there was nothing left in his belly, he wiped his mouth and gazed up in the canopy, where life went on in a myriad of chirps and chatters as if he weren't completely losing his mind below. Only a madman saw visions of men who died long ago. Men who died under his knife. Under his hands. Hands that still trembled. He held those hands up before him now. Not a doctor's hands anymore. He'd failed at that profession. He'd also failed at preaching, but God had given him a second chance at that. This time he was determined to be a good preacher, to avoid temptation, and to be a spiritual guide to the colony.

If only he could stay away from blood.

⊱⊰

Angeline woke with a start. Her heart raced. Heat stormed through her. Tossing the coverlet aside, she swung her legs over the edge of the cot. Another nightmare. Just like all the others. A kaleidoscope of haunting images from her past: rain splattering on her father's muddy grave; the vacant, lifeless look in Uncle John's eyes as he stared at the ceiling; Aunt Louise's maniacal laugh of victory; dim taverns, male hands reaching for her, groping. Lowering her chin, she rubbed her eyes. The odor of stale beer and sweat clung to her nose. Would she never be rid of it?

A gray hue lit the window. Almost dawn. One glance told her that Sarah and Lydia were still fast asleep on the other side of the hut. At least she hadn't woken them as she'd done so often these past months. A ghostly tune rode upon the wind stirring the calico curtains. Angeline cocked her ear. Was she hearing things now as well? An off-key piano banged "God Save the South," a tune she'd heard many a time at the Night Owl tavern in downtown Richmond.

Rising, she tore off her night rail and quickly donned her blouse and skirt. Did visions play piano? Tired of being bullied by whatever or whoever was causing these nightmares, she intended to find out. As she passed the foot of her cot, she brushed fingers over Stowy curled up in a ball. The cat opened one eye then nestled farther into the coverlet, obviously too lazy to join her. After slipping on her shoes and stuffing her pistol in her belt, she burst onto Main Street to a blast of dewy air and the smell of musk and orange blossoms.

Still the music continued. More angry than frightened, she charged toward the meeting shelter when a shadow leapt in front of her. Shrieking, she barreled backward, heart bursting. The music stopped. A nebulous form drifted in her path. "Who is it?" Struggling to breathe, she plucked out the pistol and leveled it at the shape.

"Just an old friend." The voice rang familiar. Eerily familiar.

Moonlight speared the clearing, and the figure of Dirk materialized—Dirk Clemens, if she remembered correctly. "You're not real." The gun shook in her hands, defying her statement.

"That's not what you said back in Richmond, dear heart." His voice was sickly sweet.

"Get out of my way." She attempted to shove him aside with the barrel, but the pistol swooshed through air, sending her off balance. She tripped, quickly regained her footing, then spun to face him. He grinned and cocked his head. Her heart crawled into her throat. *He's not here. He's not here.* "Leave me alone!" Turning from him, she dashed down the street.

"You can't fool these people for long. They'll soon know *what* you are."

His sordid chuckle faded as she rushed onward, vision blurring, drawn by a lantern in the meeting shelter. Surely the women weren't up already preparing breakfast? No, it was James. Sitting at the table, leaning over a book.

Like a beacon of hope and light, he drew her to him, longing for the safety and comfort of his presence. Head bent, eyes narrowed, brows bunched together, he didn't seem to hear her approach. Wiping tears from her cheeks, she hesitated, hating to disturb him. A breeze sent the lantern light rippling over him like waves upon the sea. She was within a few yards of him now, so close she could hear his deep breaths, see the dark stubble on his chin, the way the wind swayed the tips of his hair over his collar. Dawn's prelude cast a heavenly glow around him that left her speechless. Somewhere a whippoorwill sang. She dared not move, dared not breathe. She could stare at this man forever. Just watching him seemed to unravel her tight nerves, slow her heart, and steady her breathing.

He looked up then. Right at her as if he'd sensed her presence, known she was there. Surprise melded into delight before the burn of shame torched his bronze eyes. No doubt at his performance in the clinic yesterday.

Laying down his pen, he stretched his back. "Forgive me, Angeline, I didn't hear you."

"It is I who am sorry, Doctor. For disturbing you."

He released a heavy sigh. "Don't call me that. As you saw today, or yesterday, rather, I am anything but."

"I imagine you are a great doctor."

"Imagining it is all you'll be able to do, I'm afraid." He snorted.

Angeline wanted to tell him that perhaps he could overcome his fear someday, but she'd heard too many useless platitudes in her life to foist one on this wise man.

"I'm sorry you had to witness my atrocious behavior." A muscle twitched in his jaw as he stared at his book.

"We all have our fears."

"And what are *your* fears, Miss Angeline? Nothing seems to rattle you, save visions flying off cliffs." He gestured toward the pistol stuffed in her belt and grinned. "God help those visions should they ever turn into flesh and blood."

Angeline smiled and took a step closer. "I wish they would." For she would have blown each one back to hell where they belonged. She ran her fingers over the gun's brass-plated handle, finding comfort in the hard metal, in the power resident within. She'd sworn to never allow a man to touch her against her will again. But how could she fight things that weren't even there?

James stood, concern bending his brow. "Did you see something?"

She stared at him, hesitating to add fuel to his supernatural fancies. "Outside my hut. . ." She glanced that way. "Someone I knew from long ago."

He took her hand and led her to a stool. "Sit down. You're trembling."

"I'm all right." She took the seat anyway. Mainly because his touch sent a spire of heat through her that she didn't want him to notice.

"The visions are getting more intense." He took a seat opposite her, leaning elbows on knees, and studied her with such unabashed concern, she squirmed.

"Is that the Hebrew book?" She gestured toward the volume on the table. Bound in cracked, aged leather, the yellowed pages crinkled at the edges and contained strange letters that looked more like drawings than words.

He nodded with a deep sigh, gazing at the book as if it held the secret to life. A breeze ruffled the ancient paper as the croak of frogs and buzz of night insects serenaded them.

"Any clues as to what's happening?"

"Many, yes. None I think you would believe." He gave a cynical snort.

"Those pesky invisible beasts again?" She grinned, desperate to wipe the frown from his face.

Eyes aflame with conviction met hers. "Yes. Chained in a catacomb below the temple for many years—maybe thousands."

She wanted to believe him, she truly did. But all this God and angels and devil stuff? It was beyond ludicrous. If there was a God, why had He ignored her all these years? "I don't understand. If these beings are so evil that they had to be chained up, why would anyone release them?"

"I don't think the cannibals knew what they were doing or what lay beneath the temple they were building."

"And Graves?"

James rubbed the scar angling down the right side of his mouth. "Graves sought power above all else. Somehow they convinced him that would be his reward. Poor fellow." His forehead tightened as he stared at the strange letters.

"You *do* realize how silly all this sounds?"

"Yes." He smiled. "And I tell you at great risk to your good opinion of me." His tone bore humor, but his eyes begged acceptance.

"You are right about my good opinion, Doctor. And I assure you, it is intact." Oh my, she shouldn't have said that. Lowering her gaze, she stared at the hands in her lap then across the dark jungle surrounding the meeting area. "So what happens next?"

"I don't know. I fear my command of Hebrew has faded over the years." He rubbed his eyes and seemed to slump in his seat. "It's been quite awhile since I studied under my father."

"You've been up all night, haven't you?"

"Couldn't sleep."

Something she could well understand. "So what will this newly released beast do? *Destruction*, was it?"

"Yes, and I have no idea. But if his name is any indication. . ." He chuckled.

Rising, Angeline pressed down her skirts, only now noticing she'd forgotten to pin her hair up. Drat. She so wanted to appear a proper lady to this man. She expelled a ragged sigh. "Why can't everything just be normal? I simply want our colony to succeed and everyone to be happy."

James stood. "We all do."

"Why, if it ain't the two lovebirds up to watch the sunrise?" Dodd's taunting voice scraped over Angeline. Turning, she faced the man as he strolled into the clearing, a malicious grin twisting his lips.

"We were only talking," Angeline said.

"*Sure* you were."

James slipped in front of her as if he could barricade her from the fiend. If only he could. "What do you want, Dodd?"

"Nothing." He scratched his mop of blond hair that had become even more unkempt with each passing month. "Heading out early with Patrick to search for gold and wanted to find a banana or mango or something to fill my belly." He made his way to the end of the table and plucked an orange from the basket of fruit.

"Apologies for the interruption." He tossed the orange in the air, caught it, and grinned at Angeline before he sauntered away, immensely pleased with himself, though Angeline could not imagine why.

"Odd man," James commented.

Unnerving was more like it. Dodd had the power to bring Angeline's entire life to ruin—if he truly remembered her.

The hum of crickets soon gave way to morning birdsong as Eliza and a few other women approached with yawns and sleepy eyes. Sarah, holding baby Lydia, swept a knowing glance between James and Angeline, muttering something about how she should have known where Angeline had run off to so early. Which, of course, caused James to squirm and Angeline to drag the woman away before she said anything else to embarrass her. Besides, Angeline should help prepare breakfast.

Before they'd even managed to boil water for coffee, Blake strode into the meeting area making a beeline for his wife. Despite his limp from a war wound, he moved as though he were still a colonel in the Confederate Army marching before troops. That authoritative demeanor abandoned him, however, when he halted behind Eliza, wrapped his arms around her and leaned to whisper in her ear. Whatever he said brought a blush to her cheeks and a smile to her lips as he locked hands with hers and laid them upon her belly.

Angeline turned away from the touching scene, joy and sorrow vying for dominance within her as she continued to slice bananas to be fried for breakfast.

A clap brought her gaze to Thiago, who rubbed his hands together and sought out Sarah, shouting, "Good morning, all. Where is coffee?"

Grabbing his book, James smiled at Angeline and started to walk away when a high-pitched whining filled the air. Soft at first, like the trill of a flock of birds, it grew louder with each passing second. Others heard it too. James spun around.

"What is that?" Angeline asked.

"Stay here," he ordered as he and Blake shoved through the leaves on the north side of the clearing.

Ignoring his command, she followed the men through thick brush that led to the edge of the sugar fields. In the east, trees scattered light from the rising sun into threads of gold over the terrain. Something moved in the distance. No, not something. The field moved. Darkness shifted and rippled over the ground as if someone had tipped over a giant bottle of ink.

Thiago burst through the leaves and leapt into a tree, climbing to the top with an agility only a native Brazilian could muster.

"What is it, Thiago? What do you see?" Blake shouted.

"Ants. Army ants! Thousands of them!"

CHAPTER 7

"I can't find Stowy." Angeline's frenzied gaze shifted first east then west down Main Street, while the increasing high-pitched drone of army ants sent a cold rod through James's spine.

Grabbing her hand, he pulled her in the other direction. "The cat will be all right."

"I will not leave him." She tugged from his grip and tore down the street. Growling, James sped after her. He had no idea how much time they had left before ants overwhelmed the town. Nor did he wish to find out until he and Angeline were safe in the river with everyone else. He glanced between two passing huts toward the sugar fields. Alarm charged his legs into a sprint at what he saw—a black horde swallowing up everything in its path like some biblical plague. And it was nearly upon them. Daring another glimpse, he rushed headlong into—*thump*!

Blake grabbed James's arms, his face sweaty and red. "What are you doing? Get to the river!"

"It's Angeline." James tensed as his gaze caught her green skirts up ahead. "She's looking for her cat."

"There's no time for this tomfoolery!" Blake shouted over the eerie whine. "Get her to the river if you have to carry her there."

James nodded and sped away. Gladly. He wouldn't mind at all hoisting the stubborn redhead over his shoulder. If only to teach her a lesson. She should listen to those in charge who knew what was best for her, not run around half-cocked looking for a mangy cat!

There. He caught a flash of her russet hair disappearing in the trees on the other side of the meeting shelter. Heart pounding against his

690

ribs, he darted after her. Since they didn't know how wide the trail of ants stretched, Thiago told them the river would be their best chance to avoid being overwhelmed. Or eaten! Though army ants weren't known to attack humans, they did eat insects, snakes, toads, and the occasional small mammal. *A mammal like a cat.* Even so, their powerful bite made you wish for death, particularly when there were hundreds swarming your body. Hundreds that, if they got inside your nose and mouth, could smother you. Just thinking about it made the hairs on James's arms stand on end. What a horrible way to die.

Punching through leaves and branches, he skirted the edge of the fields, horrified at the sight. As if the sea had breached its boundary, a tidal wave of black and brown swept over the terrain, moving rapidly toward him, drowning everything in its path.

Everything.

That meant the crops too—the sugar and coffee. A hollow cave formed in his stomach. He'd been so frightened for the safety of the colonists, it hadn't occurred to him that they were losing everything they'd worked so hard to accomplish in the past two months. Squawking drew his gaze upward where a crowd of birds screeched and trilled, flapping and diving for insects driven out from hiding by the advancing army—an army that was advancing far too fast! And with scouts, apparently, as a few moved ahead of the pack, crawling over leaves and twigs in a haphazard path. One scrambled atop his boot. He shook it off, terror pricking his heart.

A flash of green snapped his gaze to the left. At the edge of the field, Stowy pounced on the intruding ants as if they were but a few common insects to be toyed with while Angeline dashed toward him, skirts and hair flailing and voice crying, "Stowy! Stowy!"

James took off in a sprint, calculating the distance between them and the ants, realizing as he did so, that by the time he arrived, they'd be smothered alive.

⚜

Hayden tugged Magnolia toward the river.

"Must we go in the water?" Clutching her skirts, she wrinkled her nose.

"Yes."

691

Resisting her husband's pull, she halted at the bank and gazed over the colonists. Eliza and Sarah beckoned her onward, their skirts billowing atop the rushing river. Thiago handed Lydia back to Sarah then treaded knee deep before the frightened group of people. "Move back. More. Move back." He gestured with palms up. Soon everyone waded farther into the current until the water reached their waists. Even Magnolia's parents! Her mother clung to her father, her face as white as the eddies that swirled and lapped at their clothes.

"Magnolia, you must come in!" It was the first words her father had spoken to her since she married Hayden. She returned a tentative smile.

She hated rivers. "There's dirt and bugs and snakes."

Hayden gestured behind her. "Or ants. Whichever you prefer, Princess." She gave him a sassy grin and glanced over her shoulder. A pulsating black sheet flowed toward her. The closer it came, the more she could make out the individual ants with their spindly legs and spiked antennae.

She leapt into Hayden's arms.

Chuckling, he carried her into the water and set her down. Despite the heat of the day, a chill etched up her back as the current knotted her skirts between her legs. Yet no sooner had her slippers sunk into the silt than the ravenous horde struck the water's edge. For a moment she thought the ants would form ships with their hideous bodies and sail out to get them, but, although a few did get caught in the tide, the rest split down the middle like the parting of the red—or in this case, black—sea and scurried down the bank of the river and off into the jungle.

Still they came. Endless waves of ants as big as a man's thumb, scurrying, scrambling, eating everything that stood in their way. Magnolia's legs grew numb. No doubt sensing her exhaustion, Hayden moved behind her and pulled her against him, wrapping his arms around her waist.

A somber mood descended on the colonists as they fought to keep their balance in the strong current while watching the endless swarm strike the shore. Other than the whine of the ants and the rush of water, the jungle was quiet—terror silencing its creatures. Sweat formed on Magnolia's brow.

A few of the women began to sob. One man cursed.

Magnolia glanced over at Blake and Eliza. The colonel stared straight ahead, his eyes as cold and hard as a river pebble. She imagined he'd worn much the same look after losing a battle in the war. For they all knew the truth. They'd lost this particular battle. The ants had devoured their crops and left them with nothing.

Looking for the rest of her friends, Magnolia scanned the group of colonists. Panic soon overcame sorrow. "Where are Angeline and James?"

Angeline leaned over to scoop up Stowy, ready to scold him for his disobedience when from the corner of her eye, she saw the ground advancing toward her. No, not the ground—a wall of ants. And they were only a foot away! No time to ponder how they got there so quickly, no time to chastise herself for her foolishness, she clutched Stowy to her chest, intending to run, but her legs felt like tree stumps—heavy and rooted in place. Her heart crumbled into dust as ants swarmed her, first swallowing up her slippers then swelling up her stockings. Pain like a hundred matches torched her skin.

Arms of steel clamped her waist and hoisted her up, smashing her against a thick chest. Stowy let out an angry wail, but Angeline managed to keep a tight grip on the cat as they bounced up and down in the arms of her rescuer. Her legs stung, her arms stung. Ants crawled over her and onto James's arms and neck. His hot breath gusted her cheek. His jaw bunched. His eyes focused. His pace slowed. He let out a growl that seemed to boost his strength to run faster.

Angeline closed her eyes. How could she have been so stupid? She'd put them both in danger, for a cat. But not just any cat—Stowy.

James let out another bestial groan.

"Put me down. I can run," she shouted then shrieked as an ant crawled on her face. She slapped it away. The land sloped upward. James ascended, huffing and panting like a steam engine. His face grew red. Sweat dripped from his jaw. He ground his teeth and continued. Finally at the crest of the hill, he set her down and leaned forward on his knees, gulping in air as if he'd surfaced from a deep lake.

Setting Stowy down, Angeline slapped ants off her skirts and blouse, trying ever so hard not to shriek like a typical goose-livered female. But when she felt something crawling on her thigh. . . Screaming, she turned her back to James, lifted her skirts and punched the vermin away. Two vermin, in fact. The hugest ants she'd ever seen! When she faced James, he smiled at her, his hands still on his knees, his breath still bursting from his lungs.

And an ant on his face. She dashed toward him and struck his cheek.

He shot back, eyes blinking. "Not exactly the response I expected after saving your life."

"There was an ant. . ."

"Thanks." He rubbed his jaw. "I think." Then, as if concerned more of the pesky critters were on him, he raked furious hands through his hair, shaking it over the ground. Nothing fell loose, but when he righted himself, he looked like a soft-quilled porcupine.

She would laugh if she weren't so frightened. "Are we safe here?" She peered down the hill.

"For now. They seem more interested in our fields and town."

"So many of them." Angeline gathered Stowy to her chest and slid beside James. Through the tangle of trees and vines, a dark wave flooded the land below. "Where are they all coming from?"

"Where are they going?" James added. "And more importantly, why, of all places, did they choose to devour *our* fields?" Hopelessness drained the life from his normally cheerful voice as the continual drone of destruction rang through the jungle. A gust of wind stirred leaves overhead, dappling him in sunlight and setting the perspiration on his forehead aglow.

Sweet saints, he'd risked his life for her!

"Thank you for saving me." Angeline swallowed as visions of her and Stowy smothered in ants filled her mind and resurrected pain from a dozen bites still burning her skin. Heart racing, she glanced down, expecting to see her skirts covered with the evil vermin. "I still feel them on me." She thrust Stowy at James and frantically brushed her arms and skirts, slapping and striking and punching. Panic sent her heart spinning along with her body as she ran hands through each strand of hair.

James gripped her arm, stopping her. "There's nothing on you,

Angeline." He leaned over until their eyes locked—his calm and as strong as their bronze color, hers flitting between his until their peace flowed onto her. She nodded and took a deep breath.

"Did they bite you?" James asked.

"My legs. They still sting."

"I should examine them."

"No need." She looked away. If this man's touch on her arm made odd things swirl in her belly, what would his fingers do on her bare legs? Best not to find out.

Stowy meowed and reached for Angeline. James held him up. "And you, you pesky varmint. We were nearly eaten alive because of you."

Angeline smiled at his playful tone. Most men would be furious at Stowy and even more furious at Angeline for going after him. But James was no ordinary man.

No ordinary man would have risked his own life to save hers either. Twice now. No, three times. Once aboard the ship and twice in Brazil. Which made her indebted to him. And she hated being indebted to anyone. Neither did she like being rescued. Being rescued was for weak women looking for a hero. And Angeline knew there was no such thing as heroes. Or happy endings. Never before had anyone swooped in to rescue her when she'd been in danger. Men had swooped in, that much was true, but much like these ants, they had stung and stung and then left her covered with bites and scars.

No, she didn't need a man to help her. She didn't need or want *anyone*.

"Why are you always rescuing me?" Her curt tone snapped James around to face her. Shock transformed into confusion and finally into anger.

"Because you are always doing foolish things."

Angeline wanted to tell him to leave her alone the next time he thought her foolish, but the whine of the ants suddenly grew louder and a line of the vile pests appeared over the ridge of the hill. Grabbing her hand, James plunged deeper into the jungle. With one arm tucked to shield Stowy, he shoved aside leaves and branches with his shoulder, forming a safe cocoon for Angeline following in his wake.

She tried to focus on her legs moving and her lungs breathing and not the feel of James's hand forming a fortress around hers, guiding her to safety. She wanted to let go of him and find her own way. She wanted to never trust anyone again. But, for the life of her, she couldn't seem to release her grip.

Finally, he halted, shoved her behind him, and turned to stare down the path.

Ants continued to advance, their scouts weaving down the trail ahead of the pack. Not just down the trail, but now coming at them from every side. Where had they come from? There was nowhere else to run. Angeline squeezed her eyes shut.

They were going to be eaten alive.

A grunt, followed by the sound of tree bark scraping and James's voice, drifted from above. "Grab ahold!" She pried her eyes open to see his hand reaching down from a low-hanging branch. A sheet of ants marched toward her, inches from her feet. Slapping her hand into his, she heard him groan, felt her feet leave the ground, her legs failing. Ants swarmed the dirt beneath her and stormed up the trunk. Sweat slicked her hand. It started to slip from James's grasp.

CHAPTER 8

Dangling in midair over a horde of army ants, Angeline gazed up at James. His tight grip on her wrist slid. Just a fraction. But it slid. Sweat dripped off his chin. His determined gaze pierced hers like a rod of iron forming an impenetrable bond between them. "I won't let go. Do you hear me? I won't let you go."

With a torturous groan, he hoisted her up, grabbed her waist, and set her on the branch beside him. The ants continued their insatiable crunch and snap over the jungle floor below, but she dared not look. "Won't they climb up the tree?" she breathed out, trying to settle her heart. Stowy leapt into her lap and meowed in complaint.

"I don't think so. Thiago said this species stays on the ground or beneath it."

Yet even as he said it, the little pests continued to skitter up the trunk.

"Come." He stood, pulled himself up to a thicker branch above, and reached down for her and Stowy. He did the same again and again until they were high above the ground.

"Where did you learn to climb so well? You're nearly as good as Thiago." Angeline took his hand one last time as he hoisted her onto the final branch.

"Summers in Tennessee."

He found a spot where several branches grew together, forming a flat area as big as a cot. Plopping down, he helped Angeline to sit beside him, his breath bursting in his chest. Hers was too, especially thinking the ants had followed. But when she dared a glance down, none were in sight, at least not on the tree. The ground, however, rolled and swayed like storm clouds at night. Leaning her head back on the trunk, she lowered her shoulders and ran fingers through Stowy's fur. The cat seemed to understand their tenuous predicament and curled up in her lap.

"You're trembling." James swung an arm around her and drew her close.

"Who wouldn't be?" She wiggled from beneath his touch. "With a horde of army ants beneath our feet." She hated that she'd put a frown on his face, but she rarely allowed anyone to touch her—especially a man.

Taking the hint, he moved away. "If I act inappropriately, you still have your pistol." He gestured toward the weapon stuffed in her belt as a rakish grin appeared on his lips.

She laughed and plucked out the pistol, laying it beside her. "I'd forgotten all about it." Though as uncomfortable as it was pressed against her belly, she didn't know how. She raised a coy brow. "Don't think I won't use it, Doctor."

"Oh, I have no doubt, Miss." He lifted his hands in surrender. "You can count on me to be a gentleman."

Yes, she did believe she could. But that only made things harder. She looked away. "I suppose I should thank you, yet again."

"Not if you don't mean it."

A breeze swirled through the leaves of the tree, dousing her with the scent that was uniquely James—all musk and man. "Of course I mean it. . . . I *do* thank you. It's just that. . ." She sighed. "Never mind." Bundling Stowy close to her chest, she suddenly wished she weren't alone with James. He had a way about him that made her want to share things she wouldn't share with anyone. She supposed it was the preacher in him. His duty to care for people and listen to their problems.

He stretched his legs out, dangling one over the side of their wooden platform. "But you'd rather not accept anyone's help, is that it?"

She searched his eyes for any mockery but found only concern. "Do you find that so odd?"

"For a lady, yes."

"So you assume all women are weak and in need of help?"

His brows shot up, and a grin touched his lips. "Whoa, I didn't say that. I meant no disrespect, Angeline."

She looked away. "Forgive me. I suppose it's just the stress of being chased by killer ants." She forced a smile, trying to lighten the conversation. It wasn't James's fault she trusted no one.

Placing a finger beneath her chin, he turned her to face him. "There's no shame in needing help." His eyes seemed to look right through her, and she found the sensation unsettling to say the least.

She jerked from his touch. "It depends on the price."

Price? The woman baffled James. They'd barely escaped a rather unpleasant death—one he'd pulled her from twice—and all she could talk about was not wanting his help. Or anyone's. "There is no price."

"Maybe not this time," she mumbled, petting her infernal cat.

James rubbed the back of his neck. What had happened to this poor woman? He so desperately wanted to know more about her. Why did she oftentimes carry a pistol in her belt? What made her turn from lady to dragon in a matter of seconds? Why did she seem so frightened of Dodd? Why, when she thought no one was looking, did a deep sorrow linger in her eyes?

The drone of ants lessened below, though the ground still moved. She followed his gaze, and her breath seemed to heighten.

"We are safe here," he reassured her. "If they were coming up, they would have done so by now."

"I fear for our friends. I hope they are all right."

"I'm sure they made it to the river." He drew his knees up and placed his elbows atop them. "Where we should have gone."

Angeline frowned, the freckles on her nose clumping together. "You should have gone without me."

"Despite your aversion to rescuing, I couldn't do that."

"And *I* couldn't leave Stowy either." She lifted the cat and planted a kiss on its head.

James suddenly wished he were in Stowy's shoes—or paws. He shook the thought away. It was such wayward thinking that had caused his many falls from grace. Angeline was a lady of the highest morals who didn't deserve to be ogled or thought of with impurity. Despite the fact that she looked so incredibly beautiful and vulnerable at the moment. A sheen of perspiration made her skin glow and transformed curls framing her face into dangling rubies. The rest of her russet hair tumbled in waves over her shoulders, down her back and into her lap, where Stowy played with a strand clutched between his paws. James swallowed.

Thankfully, the screech of a macaw sounded, followed by the chorus of birds returning to their song, jarring his thoughts. What was wrong with him? They'd almost been smothered by ants, their crops were ruined, and all he could think about was how being close to Angeline made him feel so alive.

She peered through the canopy, her gaze scanning the ground below, where the swarm of ants had thinned considerably. "How long before it's safe to return to New Hope?"

Eyes the color of the violets his mother used to grow in their garden in Knoxville searched his. Only, the violet in Angeline's eyes was more like a bottomless pool of swirling emotions. Emotions he longed to explore, along with those lips of hers she so often bit when she was nervous. He looked away. "We should wait until there's not an ant in sight. I don't want to risk getting trapped."

Nodding, she leaned back against the trunk and folded up the sleeves of her blouse against the sultry heat. A flicker of sunlight brushed over a pink scar on her forearm. He'd seen scars like that before. Many of them. All caused by knives embedded in flesh. But why would such a lovely lady like Angeline have been the victim of such violence? His gaze shifted to the ring she wore on a chain around her neck. Normally she kept it tucked within her bodice, but perhaps it had loosened during their mad dash through the jungle. Since it appeared to be a man's ring, he'd always wondered about it but had been afraid to pry.

Now seemed like the perfect time.

"That ring you always wear around your neck, it must be important to you."

Her lips flattened. "I realize, Doctor, that we find ourselves inappropriately alone, but that does not grant you entrance into my personal life." Her strident tone surprised him. Though he didn't know why. The woman could switch moods faster than a chameleon could colors. Flinching at the sting in his heart, he held up his palms. "Douse those flames, your dragonship; I was just asking."

"Dragonship?" A sparkle lit her eyes, softening the hard sheen of only a moment before. "Sweet saints, where did that come from?" She laughed.

"Sorry. Old habit." James shrugged, thrilled to see her anger flee. "I used to read stories about dragons when I was a little boy. They fascinated me." He shrugged. "Were dragons good? Evil? How did they make the fire that came out of their snouts?" He winked.

"So am I to be compared to a dragon now?" She laughed as the tension dissipated between them. "You are a strange man, indeed. A doctor, or rather preacher, who is fascinated by creatures that don't exist."

Her gaze snapped to his, and he knew she also referred to the invisible beasts he claimed were tormenting the colonists.

A bird landed on a branch and eyed them curiously before beginning a serenade in a variety of tones and notes and pitches that would shame a symphony orchestra.

Despite the joyful tune, she grew quiet. After several minutes, she lifted the ring and fingered it like it was the answer to all her prayers. "It was my father's. He gave it to me on his deathbed."

Sunlight cut a swath through the canopy and swayed over the ruby in the center, setting it aflame.

"It's beautiful," James said.

"Yes." She stared at it as if lost in another time.

"When did he die?"

"I was only seventeen."

"And your mother?"

"At my birth." She swiped away a tear, and James felt like a cad for bringing up such morbid memories.

She held the ring up to him. "My father told me I was the ruby in the center and he and my mother were the topazes on either side, watching out for me." She smiled but her voice caught.

"They must have loved you very much," James said. And with their death, this poor lady was left an orphan at only seventeen. Had family taken her in?

She withdrew the ring, kissed it, and slipped it beneath her bodice. "So now you know." She sounded disappointed.

"I can keep a secret."

"It's not a secret. It's just mine to know and no one else's."

"Then I am indeed honored you shared it with me."

She gave him a sly smile. "You coerced it out of me, sir. Took advantage of my weakness."

"Weakness? You? Never."

An expression akin to disbelief shadowed her face before she glanced away. He longed to bring those violet eyes back to his.

"Friends share things about their lives." He shifted on the hard bark. "It helps them know each other." Did she consider him a friend? He hoped so, though he wanted so much more.

She scooted away and peered down through the branches. "The more a person knows about someone, the more power they have over them."

Shock kept James silent. For several minutes, he watched her pet Stowy and gaze at the ground, no doubt searching for ants. Strands of hair blew in the breeze across her waist. "I want no power over you, Angeline."

"No?" Turning, she raised a disbelieving brow before glancing down again. "Everyone wants something."

James scratched his jaw. What had happened to make this lady so cynical?

"The ants are gone," she announced.

He inched beside her and peered through the lattice of leaves toward the distant fields. Small patches of dark still moved across ground that looked gray and empty in the blaring sun. "We should wait awhile longer. Just to make sure."

Regardless of whether the lady or the dragon appeared, James was rather enjoying his time with Angeline. When they climbed down from this tree, only God knew what they'd have to face: the loss of their crops, all their food, perhaps even their town. And he could only hope and pray there'd been no injuries. Or deaths. But for now, he would relish being close to a woman he'd spent five months with and yet felt he hardly knew. Every moment in her company only endeared her more to him. And made him want to dig deeper and deeper to understand everything about her. He'd never felt that way about a woman. Never thought he'd find a woman interesting enough and pure and good enough to marry. Yet, here was a woman he could care for. Here was a woman he could love. Perhaps his philandering wasn't his own fault at all. How could any man resist a woman who flaunted herself before him like a French praline?

"I lost my father as well," he said hoping to resurrect the conversation. "Just a few years ago."

She stopped petting Stowy. "Then you understand."

"Yes. Though I was much older than you, it was hard nonetheless."

She nodded but said nothing. He wanted to continue talking. . . wanted to find that connection they seemed to have earlier. But he couldn't tell her that he'd been responsible for his father's death—that he might as well have shot the man himself. Instead he said, "I was not the same person back then."

This piqued her interest as she swept an attentive gaze his way.

Prompting him to continue. "I've done some horrible things that I'm not proud of. Shameful things."

She didn't seem surprised, nor did she inquire what things. Instead, she simply stared at him with an odd approval as if he'd just informed her that he bore the bloodline of the prince of Wales.

Angeline could hardly believe James would divulge such information. Yet once he said it, she could hardly stop herself from pressing him to reveal more. Most of her mistrust of the doctor—aside from him being a man, of course—stemmed from their brief encounter over a year ago in a Tennessee tavern. Though she doubted he remembered her, was he now confessing the sins of that night?

"We've all made mistakes, Doctor," she said, releasing Stowy to wander around the branches. "The important thing is that we move past them and become better for them."

He scrubbed the dark stubble peppering his jaw. "Indeed. And also that we repent and allow God to change our hearts."

She scoffed inwardly. It was she and she alone who had changed her life. Not God. But she wouldn't tell James that and start another theological debate.

"So what *were* these sins, exactly?" She raised a brow, half teasing, half desperate to know.

"Ah, who is being overbold now?"

She smiled.

"Drinking." He hesitated, searching her eyes, then lowered his gaze. "Women." Was that red crawling up his neck? "Too many of both."

Memories of him lying on a ratty, stained bed above a tavern that blared and thumped with music and laughter drifted through her mind. He'd been so drunk, he could hardly stand. And covered in blood. Too much to have come from the gash at the side of his mouth. But he'd been kind. And sad. Terribly sad about something. Which is why she remembered him from all the others.

Now, she laid a hand on his and said the words that screamed true within her—words she wanted so desperately to be true. "You are right. You're not that man anymore."

This brought his eyes up to search hers, the hope within them conflicting with the pain and despair that had filled them that night long ago. He pressed a thumb on the scar on the right side of his mouth. "Thank you for saying that."

If only she believed it of herself. Shoving aside her morbid thoughts, she offered him a smile. "And now we both know a secret about the other."

"Mine is much more incriminating."

"But safe with me."

He nodded, and his trust in her caused her heart to swell.

Stowy pounced on James's leg and began gnawing at his trousers. "Hey, you little rascal!" Clutching the cat, he flipped him on his back and knuckled his tummy. Stowy pawed James's hand in a mock battle for dominance he was sure to lose.

Watching how gentle and playful James was with Stowy, Angeline's heart felt lighter than a feather. Perhaps she *could* trust this man. He *had* changed, hadn't he? He'd made mistakes, but he freely admitted them. And when he could have lied about his past, he'd been honest with her. Besides, hadn't Angeline changed? Hadn't this new life in Brazil offered her a second chance? How could she deny the same to James?

Setting Stowy between them, James raised his gaze to hers. A breeze ripe with oranges and mossy earth swirled around them, toying with the hair at his collar as they stared into each other's eyes, searching, wondering, hoping. . .daring to trust.

Raising his hand, he cupped her jaw and swept a thumb over her cheek. Angeline's heart quickened. A tingle ran across her skin. He glanced at her lips and licked his own. And she knew he wanted to kiss her. More than that, she desperately wanted to kiss him back.

CHAPTER 9

J ames! Angeline!" Blake's baritone shout jarred them apart, drew them embarrassed to the edge of their tree terrace to see their friends combing the jungle below. With an odd reluctance, James had assisted Angeline and Stowy to the ground, ending their precious time together—moments that had given him hope for a promising future.

A hope, however, that was dashed as he now stood beside Hayden and Blake and some of the other colonists before their desolate fields. Where once stalks of sugarcane had poked through fertile ground, where once coffee seedlings budded fresh leaves, now there was naught but barren dirt dotted with bare twigs. Stunned silence shrouded the group, save for the occasional sob from the women and curse from the men.

A few leftover ants skittered about, separated from their army, their fate in the hands of angry colonists who stomped the life from them. One man even pulled a pistol and shot one, causing everyone to jump. Finally, however, when it became obvious no amount of staring would bring back their crops, the group assembled, one by one, in the meeting area, somber and dejected, and—all but James and Angeline—soaked to the bone. Blake stood in front of the crowd, Eliza by his side, while James took a spot beside him, should the leader of the colony need reinforcement.

Yet from the expression on the colonel's face, he needed much more than reinforcement. He needed encouragement. And hope. Something they all lacked at the moment.

"What are we gonna do, Colonel?" one of the farmers asked before

Blake could even begin.

"We are going to plant again," he responded without hesitation.

The colonists' groans were silenced by a lift of his hand. "We still have most of the sugar splints. Though the ants stripped them, they didn't eat them entirely. With some care, they should sprout again. The coffee might too, though we still have some seed if need be."

"Preposterous!" Mr. Scott, Magnolia's father, bellowed. "Start over again?"

"But we have no food," a woman whined.

Eliza stepped forward. "We still have rice and beans. They didn't eat through the burlap sacks."

"And we have fish from the river," Angeline offered.

"And fruit and wild boar from jungle," Thiago said. "I can teach men to hunt better."

Mr. Lewis took a swig from his flask and wiped his mouth on his sleeve. "All that work wasted."

"It will be wasted if we give up." Hayden ran a hand through his moist hair.

"I say we quit and go home," one of the ex-soldiers shouted, glancing over the mob. "Enough is enough."

"Besides, how can we pay the emperor what we owe him for the land now?"

"We will pay him when we can pay him," James said. "Come now, surely you aren't ready to give up after one setback? Not after all we've endured to make it this far."

Shadows crept out from hiding as the sun lowered in the sky, bringing a breeze that caused many of the colonists to shiver in their wet clothes.

"We've had more than our share of trouble," one man yelled.

Another farmer slapped his hat on his knee. "At least back in Georgia, I wasn't in debt."

"But we are still alive!" Angeline said, sharing a smile with James that caused his heart to leap. "No one was hurt. And our huts, tools, and dried food are intact."

Standing beside his sister, Moses, the freedman, scooped one of her children in his arms. "I says we stay." His gaze met Mable's, who stood beside her owner, Mr. Scott.

707

The elderly man let out a bloated grunt. "And, pray tell, who cares what a slave thinks? I, for one, plan to leave."

"Freedman, Papa. He's not a slave anymore." Magnolia nodded at Moses before turning to her mother, who wrung her hands together in her usual worried fit.

Breaking through the crowd, Patrick Gale sauntered into the clearing like a king surveying his subjects. "True, we expected hardships in this new land, but we certainly didn't expect complete destruction. I say none of us should feel guilty for leaving now."

Grunts of assent rang through the air.

James frowned. Of course the man wanted people to leave. Fewer people to stake a claim on his gold. If he ever found any, *and* if he intended to share it with the colony like he promised. Dodd, his partner in the mad treasure quest, sat off to the side, nodding his agreement.

"Go back to what?" Blake shifted weight off his sore leg. "Back to destruction, devastation, and tyranny? Why, I'd rather deal with nature's blows than man's, wouldn't you?"

A few nodded. Wind whipped leaves by feet that were bare and muddy due to wading in the river.

"What if the ants come again?"

Crossing his arms over his chest, James shrugged. "What if they do? What if our crops fail or our cane press breaks or the river dries up? Life is full of struggles. But also blessings. Remember, God is on our side."

Several colonists shook their heads in dismay, but Eliza smiled his way. "Indeed, Doctor. And He will see us through."

As if disagreeing, the last rays of sunlight withdrew through the trees and left them in darkness.

Lanterns were lit, but most of the colonists retired to their huts, too tired and wet to argue anymore. James was surprised when Angeline didn't join them. Especially after the harrowing day she'd endured. Instead, Stowy still in her arms, she stoked the coals in the brick stove and put on some water for tea then joined him and the remaining colonists around the fire Blake lit in the center of the clearing.

Flames reflected over her loose hair, casting it in a fiery red that reminded him of the dragon he'd called her earlier. Holy thunder, he'd nearly kissed her! Her gaze briefly met his, but she bit her lip and quickly looked away, as if embarrassed.

Blake's somber tone brought James from his musings. "So, are you thinking what I'm thinking, Doc?" The colonel led his wife to sit on a log and lowered himself beside her.

"If you're thinking this could be the work of *Destruction*, then yes." He scanned his friends' reactions, not wanting to seem foolish but not wanting to hide his suspicions either. Especially should they be true. "First Graves's death, the earthquake at the tunnels, the lightning strike, and now this. Either we have encountered a string of terrible luck or something else is going on here."

"What on earth are you talking about?" Dodd scratched his thick sideburns and spat in the dirt.

"We are talking about the ancient Hebrew book I'm translating, the one Graves found in the tunnels. We're talking about the cannibal temple, the empty prison alcoves beneath it, and these odd visions and disasters that keep happening. They are linked somehow."

"Nonsense!" Patrick's tone was spiked with haughty disbelief as he adjusted his necktie. "I, for one, have encountered no visions. And these disasters are nothing but misfortunes common to any new settlers. Tell them, Diego!" He motioned toward Thiago.

"I am called Thiago." The Brazilian guide didn't hide his disdain for the man. "But *sim*, they are all natural events." He moved beside Sarah, who sat on a chair, baby Lydia in her lap.

Magnolia slid her hand into Hayden's. "But so many disasters so close together?"

Patrick's slick gaze took her in like a crocodile would a rabbit, before he shifted eyes toward his son, Hayden. Though there was a physical resemblance, the similarities between them stopped there.

Hayden drew his wife closer. "Though I hate to agree with Patrick, I'm not ready to believe that some evil supernatural beast has caused our visions and all these misfortunes."

"I hope you are right." Blake rubbed his eyes and tossed another log in the fire. It crackled and spit, sending sparks into the night.

"I do as well." James lowered to sit on a stump. But he doubted it. He must interpret more of the book. It was up to him, and him alone, to figure out what was happening. Not only because he was the only one who knew Hebrew but also because he was the only one who was fully convinced that something spiritual was afoot. A sudden weight pressed on his shoulders. Of all the people to bear such responsibility. . . *God, what are You doing? I've done nothing but fail my entire life.*

Even the rising croak of frogs and crickets seemed to mock him.

"What will happen if some of the colonists leave as they've threatened?" Hayden shifted his stance. "We will lose good men. Good workers."

"Regardless," Eliza said. "None of *us* are leaving. We all believe God brought us here. We must fight and not give up."

"God. Bah!" Patrick snorted before shaking his head and turning to leave. "I shall leave you with your foolish notions."

Good riddance, as far as James was concerned. Magnolia seemed to agree as she released a sigh and leaned against Hayden.

James faced Angeline. "What about you, Angeline? Do you wish to leave?"

She caressed Stowy's fur a moment before lifting her eyes to his, causing his heart to nearly break at the pain he saw within them. "I have nowhere else to go."

Neither did James. There was too much pain back in the States. For him. For all of them. They had no choice. They must make a life here in Brazil, or they would have no life at all.

❦

A month passed. New sugar stalks sprouted and coffee was replanted, and soon the fertile Brazilian soil pushed up infant sprouts in a promise of coming abundance. Though ten colonists had packed their things and started on foot for Rio de Janeiro, the spirits of those who remained lifted with each passing day—each passing day in which no further disasters struck. The river provided an abundance of fish and the jungle a bounty of fruit. And Angeline's nightmarish visions had decreased. Even Dodd seemed more preoccupied with finding his gold than gawking at her. Perhaps the worst was over. Perhaps God was indeed on their side.

Angeline couldn't help but hum a cheerful tune as she flitted about her hut in preparation for the day. She had several shirts and trousers that needed mending as well as a torn quilt. And in the afternoon, she would assist Sarah in teaching the children. Yet, if she was honest, it was the thought of James that had her in such good humor. His attentions toward her had become more frequent and intense, made all the sweeter by her growing knowledge of his character and honor. Yes, he *had* changed. He wasn't the same man she'd met in Tennessee over a year ago. Why, he'd even encouraged her to attend Sunday services, and she had found him to be a good preacher, fervent and heartfelt. This was a man she might well be able to trust. A man who could make her forget her past—sweep away the horrid memories like so much dust—and give her hope. Hope that she could live a normal life and find happiness like a normal woman.

A voice sounded from outside the canvas flap that served as a door to the hut she shared with Sarah. Her heart jolted in her chest. She knew that voice, a deep throaty voice that held a zest for life and a hint of hope. Checking herself in the small mirror on the wall, she pinched her cheeks and swept the flap aside. A bouquet of violet hibiscus and pink orchids filled her vision, flooding her with beauty and fragrance. Behind them, James's smile sent a streak of warmth down to her toes.

"Good day," he said. "I came across these in the jungle this morning and they reminded me of you."

If she didn't know how sincere he was, she'd laugh at his mawkish attempt at wooing her. Yet, despite his age of eight and twenty, he bore a charming boyishness that made her blush.

And she hadn't blushed in years.

"Why, thank you, Doctor. . .I mean James," she corrected herself and plucked the flowers from his hand. "They are lovely."

"Indeed." His bronze eyes poured life and love into hers, momentarily mesmerizing her. She could stare at them all day—at the depth of promise they held. But people were beginning to stir from their huts, curious gazes drifting their way.

The soothing rush of the river and flutter of leaves in the breeze whisked over her ears, accompanied by the happy warble of birds. A sleepy-eyed Hayden walked past, smiling at her and giving a knowing wink to James. James shifted his boots on the dirt and ran a finger down the scar angling the right side of his mouth as his gaze flitted about the town.

"Did you want something, James?"

"Yes. I. . .I hoped you would accompany me on a stroll after supper.

Down to the beach. It's so lovely there in the evening."

"A stroll?" She teased with a grin. "Alone with you?"

The right side of his lips curved upward as he leaned toward her. "I hope you know by now that you can trust me, Angeline."

His breath warmed her cheek. "I do."

"I have something to ask you."

Her legs turned to noodles, and she leaned on the door frame. *He was going to ask if he could court her!* He'd hinted about it often enough the past few weeks, though she had refused to believe it was possible. Her being courted by so fine a gentleman! Her being treated like a true lady.

Wiley Dodd emerged from his hut across the way, smothering her hopes with his frown. "How quaint." He chuckled. "Another early morning rendezvous. And flowers too?"

Releasing a sigh of frustration, James slowly turned to face him. "Shouldn't you be looking for gold, Dodd?"

"There's more than one type of treasure, Doc." He flashed his brows and winked at Angeline.

"But only *one* that can satisfy your insatiable greed, so be on your way, Dodd. And learn to mind your own business in the future." James's brass tone held an undeniable warning that sent emotion burning in Angeline's throat. Never had a gentleman stood up for her before.

"Threats, threats." Dodd clicked his tongue. "And from our preacher too. What is the world coming to?" He peered around James, his eyes locking on Angeline. "Have a pleasant day, Miss Angeline."

Acid welled in her belly. She tore her gaze from his. Why wouldn't the man leave her be? His petulant whistle as he strolled away grated on her worst fears.

James turned and took her hand in his. "Don't let him bother you. He's harmless."

Angeline wasn't so sure.

"Till supper then?" He placed a kiss on her hand and started down the street, glancing one last time at her over his shoulder. Diving her nose in the bouquet, she watched him walk away in that confident, boyish gait of his, light hair rippling in the breeze, white shirt, tan trousers tucked within his black work boots that stomped toward the fields for his day's work. A feeling welled up inside of her she'd never known before, an ache so palpable she pressed a hand over her heart.

She loved James. At least she thought it was love. He stirred her body, soul, and spirit like no man ever had. Like she never knew a man could. But more than that, she cared for him, wanted the best for him. But therein lay the problem—one that was becoming more real the more her feelings grew. For if she truly loved him, she'd run as far away from him as she could.

⤜⧉⤛

Dodd slapped aside an oversized leaf with his shovel and trudged after Patrick. The man claimed to have discovered some new secret twist on the treasure maps during the night and was once again leading the way to the "gold that would make Dodd a king." After three such grand declarations and nothing to show for it but sore muscles, blisters, and empty holes, Dodd's frustration level was rising—along with his doubts.

"If this new information of yours don't produce gold, we are switching roles. I'll be the brains and you can be the brawn."

"Don't be absurd, man." Patrick's ever-annoying imperious tone continued to eat away at what was left of Dodd's patience. "We must remain in the stations nature has given us. It will work out for the best in the end. You'll see."

"Nature ain't given me the station of digging, I can swear to that." Or trekking through a jungle so sultry it felt like wading through a hot bath. What Dodd wouldn't give for a real hot bath. And a shave and a drink. And a woman. Which brought his thoughts back to Angeline and the memory of her and the doc acting all intimate that morning.

Patrick halted and Dodd barreled into him, releasing a string of curses. "For crying's sake, tell me when you're going to stop."

"What has got you in such a foul mood today, Dodd?" Patrick fingered his goatee and scanned the jungle.

Dodd did the same but saw nothing but a web of green and brown strung between thin trees that reached for the sky. "How can you tell where we are going? Everything looks the same."

"That's why I'm the brains, my friend." Patrick continued marching forward as a band of yellow monkeys raced through the canopy, chattering like gossiping women at tea.

713

"I'm guessing it's a woman," Patrick said.

"What's a woman?"

"The reason for your foul temper."

Dodd cursed the man's blasted intuition.

"It's the seamstress, isn't it?" Withdrawing a handkerchief, Patrick dabbed his neck. "That voluptuous redhead."

"None of your business," Dodd growled, crushing a lizard beneath his boot.

"Ah, but it is my business, especially if I am to endure your company day after day. Why not make a play for her?"

"She doesn't want me. We have a past."

"Ah, interesting. Tell me more."

"I'll tell you nothing."

Patrick chuckled. "She and the good doctor seem to be forming an attachment."

Which was exactly what grated on Dodd. "What's that to me?"

"Only that if you want her, you must be a man and take her."

"Like you did Magnolia?" Dodd snickered.

Patrick turned on him, eyes like slits and jaw distended. "I allowed my son to have the wench." He poked Dodd's chest with his jeweled finger. "And you'll not forget it. I will have any woman I want after I find this gold."

Dodd smiled as the man resumed his march. The only pleasure he'd had on these torturous excursions were the few times he'd gotten under the pompous horker's skin. Yet, he could not deny the wisdom in the man's words. Dodd was in need of female companionship. And there was a perfectly lovely female for the taking, one that he could force to do whatever he wanted. Then what was he waiting for?

⁂

Dipping a cloth in the brook, Angeline wrung it out and brought it to her neck and face. She wanted to look her best for her stroll with James, but her day had been so busy, she hadn't had time to bathe properly. Besides, after Dodd discovered the women's bathing pool a few months back, they really hadn't found a new spot where the ladies felt safe from prying eyes.

A flock of parakeets darted from branch to branch in a nearby tree chirping and playfully pecking each other's beaks, drawing a smile from Angeline. Water trickled over a mound of boulders as it made its way down the creek bed while Stowy sprawled on a flat rock, soaking in what was left of the sun before it dipped behind the trees. Angeline moistened her cloth again. Sitting on a fallen log, she allowed the cool water to soothe her skin, all the while wondering at the peculiar feeling of happiness that invaded her soul. A happiness that brought back fleeting memories of her childhood before her father had died. Had it only been four years ago? It felt like a lifetime, so foreign were these sensations of contentment and joy.

Visions of the past few years attempted to barge into her thoughts, but she shoved them back. Today she would accept James's suit. Today she would put her memories behind her and become a real lady. She had already changed her name, why not change her past along with it? James need never know anything different. How could keeping her secret be wrong when she knew she could make him happy? Yes, she would make him very happy. She loved him, and love could never be wrong.

Unbuttoning the top buttons of her collar, she dipped the rag in the creek again and dabbed her chest. *Thu-ump, thu-ump, thu-ump,* she could feel the pounding of her heart against her fingers, proving her excitement for the coming evening. The crunch of leaves snapped her to attention. Plucking her pistol from her belt, she slowly stood and swerved to aim at a shadow emerging from the jungle. Retreating sunlight slicked over blond hair, slid down a pointy nose, to finally ride on the smug shoulders of Wiley Dodd.

CHAPTER 10

"What do you want, Dodd?" Though the barrel of the gun quivered in Angeline's hand, she kept it leveled at the vile ex-lawman.

He strutted toward her, his grin reminding her of Stowy after he caught a mouse—pleased with himself and very, very hungry. A hungry gaze that now lowered to her unbuttoned shirt. Taking a step back, she determined to shoot the man if he came any closer.

"You have a bad habit of spying on women at their bath, sir," she spat.

He clipped thumbs in his belt and eyed her. "I meant no offense, I merely came to talk."

"I have nothing to say to you." She gestured toward the jungle with her gun. "Now, leave."

"Ah, but you had plenty to say to me that night at the Night Owl."

Angeline's heart plummeted. She wanted to say she knew of no place by that name. She wanted to call him mad. But they both knew she'd be lying.

He grinned. "I see you understand me quite well, my dear."

"I am not your dear, and I don't understand at all. Who cares if you remember me from some tavern?" She lifted one shoulder. "What is that to me?"

"Nothing to you, I'm sure. But everything to your doctor beau. You *have* noticed how he abhors immoral women? Why, he talks about it all the time—how he wants to keep our new town free of such vices as harlotry and the like."

Nausea bubbled in her stomach. Of course she'd noticed. It was all she'd thought about the last month as she and James had grown closer. "Well, it's a good thing there aren't any harlots here."

He raised a taunting brow. "Aren't there?"

She lowered the gun, all hope lowering with it. "I knew you recognized me. You knew the minute we boarded the ship that brought us here, am I right?"

He circled her, assessing her as a panther would a rabbit. "Who could forget such a face?" He halted in front of her. "Or such a figure."

A lizard skittered up a tree behind him, the perfect example of the man before her. Slimy, slick, and sneaky. "Then why wait until now to say something?"

He cocked his head. "Because, my dear, I knew you would never come to me of your own will, so we could. . .how shall I say?"—he tapped his chin—"Become reacquainted?"

A hiss followed by a growl drew her gaze to Stowy, who glared at Dodd from his perch on a rock. Even her cat could spot a bad seed. "I wish no reacquaintance with you."

"Was our one night so terrible?" He ran a finger down her cheek. "Your moans of pleasure still ring in my ears."

"Moans of disgust, you mean." She jerked from his touch and snapped angry eyes his way. "Yet men like you always think them from delight."

A slight tic appeared at the corner of his lips. His eyes narrowed, and for a moment, she thought he might strike her. But then he thrust a finger in the air as if testing the wind. "But since you brought up the topic of pleasure, that is the reason I'm here."

The sun dipped below the trees, hiding its warmth and light from the hideous scene.

Stowy circled the hem of her skirts.

"I am a lonely man."

"That does not surprise me." Scooping up her cat, she stormed past him, but he clamped her arm. Tight. She winced.

He spun her around. "Then we will be lonely together, for once the good preacher hears about your prior profession, I do believe he'll have nothing more to do with you."

Though Angeline had known the threat was coming, hearing it out loud sent such a wave of agony through her, she nearly crumbled to the ground. Would have crumbled to the ground if the beast weren't still gripping her arm. She tore away from him, her breath coming hard and fast.

"Why? Why are you doing this now?" When she'd fallen in love. When she finally had a chance at happiness.

Blue eyes sparked with mischief. "Because now you have a reason to do as I say, my dear. Before James showered you with attention, you may have been willing to have your reputation besmirched. But not now. Not when you have everything to lose."

Everything to lose. Yet, hadn't she lost it all the second Dodd had set foot on the ship? Or was it the second her uncle forced himself on her all those years ago? Perhaps she never really had any chance of happiness at all. Tears flooded her eyes, and she lowered her chin.

"Come now." Dodd approached and leaned to peer up at her. "It won't be so bad. You will come to me in the night. Once or twice a week will suffice. I'm not greedy. And during the day you may carry on your callow dalliance with the doctor or preacher or whatever he is. You see, unlike your pretentious preacher, I am willing to share. What you see in the man is beyond me."

Anger dried her tears, and she lifted her head. "He's everything you are not."

"Yet I will have *you* in my bed while he carries on like a sheep-headed minion." He smiled. "What do you say to that?"

She stared at him, knowing she had no cards to play. No choice but to obey. Just like she'd had no choice in what she'd become. Dodd absorbed her with his gaze again, and the thought of him touching her sent a foul taste creeping into her mouth.

"Cat got your tongue?" He chuckled, reaching to pet Stowy, but the cat hissed at him again. Frowning, he withdrew his hand. "Well, you best get your voice back, my dear, because I'll expect your answer in two weeks. Yes, yes, I'm not completely without compassion. I will grant you some time to consider your options. Enough time to realize you have none."

And with that, he kissed her on the cheek before she could stop him then turned and strutted away, whistling a discordant tune.

Clutching her skirts, Angeline made her way to the water's edge and dropped to the ground. Groping for the rag through blurry vision, she found it and scrubbed and scrubbed and scrubbed her cheek until her skin was raw and stinging and her tears fell in a puddle on the sand. She'd been wrong. So completely wrong. It was impossible to escape her past, to put her memories behind her. She would always be what she had become. Her dream was shattered—her new life abandoned.

❧

Angeline was not at supper. After James had frantically searched for her, Sarah informed him that she wasn't feeling well and had retired early. Though desperate to see her and concerned for her health, he forced himself to stay away from her hut and instead barely touched his meal of papayas, beans, and fish, while the rest of the colonists chatted idly around him. And why, in the name of all that was holy, was Dodd staring at him with that impish grin on his face? Continually staring and smiling like the blunderhead he was.

Rising, James handed his plate to Mr. Lewis, whose appetite for food matched his lust for liquor. He took it with an appreciative nod as James grabbed the torch he'd prepared to take on his journey to the shore—he and Angeline's journey—and dipped it in the fire. He'd even left the fields early to assemble logs on the beach so they would have a fire to sit around while he asked if he could court her. Perhaps he was just a foolish romantic, but he wanted everything to be perfect. Perfect for the perfect lady.

Shoving aside leaves, he plunged into the jungle, seeking some time alone to nurse his disappointment. Which was silly. The woman couldn't help feeling ill. He only hoped—no, prayed—it wasn't anything serious. *Lord, please take care of her. I intend to make her my wife with Your permission.* No sooner had he lifted the silent prayer than he realized he hadn't been very diligent in praying recently. Nor had he asked God's blessing to court Angeline. There'd been so much to do after the ants destroyed everything. Parts of the fields had to be re-plowed and replanted, the sugar splints tended to, huts repaired, the mill rebuilt from the fire, as well as their normal tasks of digging irrigation ditches and foraging for food. Plus James had been spending so much time with Angeline. An unavoidable smile lifted his lips as he thought of those precious moments. Still, that was no excuse to ignore God. He was the preacher, for heaven's sake! Was he destined to fail at it all over again? Just like he'd done with his father. Like he'd done with that woman who had destroyed him. He marched ahead, plowing through a curtain of vines, hoping he hadn't been showered with spiders or beetles or other insects. Insects that now buzzed in their nighttime chorus.

A growl echoed through the trees. Distant but ominous, it caused the hair on James's arms to prickle. Yet it was the sound that followed that made his stomach twist in a knot. Crackling like a fire but not coming from his torch. He knew that sound all too well. He swerved the flame through the darkness, the blaze flaring like the tail of a comet. The crackling increased. A figure—all smoke and mist—emerged from the leaves. James stood his ground, heart beating through his chest.

"Who are you?" he demanded.

The figure took form and shape and stepped into the light. Skirts of violet poplin floated over the ground, festooned with pink velvet bows. Satin embroidery drew his gaze to the creamy skin bursting from her low neckline, where her hair, the color of pearls, dangled in lustrous spirals. Eyes as green as the jungle around them looked at him with longing. *Tabitha.* Blood rushed through his veins and began to curdle in his mind. She smiled. He took a step back and blinked, trying to erase her from view. Still she remained, cocked her head.

"Don't you remember me?" she said in that honey-sweet drawl that had once sounded like music to his ears.

Of course he remembered her. She was the woman who had ruined his life. "You're not here."

An adorable pout appeared on her lips. "Why, what a horrid thing to say, dear James. After all we've meant to one another."

James knew she was a vision—from one of the fallen angelic beasts. She had to be. But she looked so real. Her skin was as sparkling and luminescent as he remembered. Her lips plump and moist. Her curves in all the right places. It was the sight of those curves and the peek she'd given him when she leaned forward in the front pew of his church that had become his demise. Week after week. Sunday after Sunday. The way she stared at him as he preached from the pulpit, the way she eased her tongue over her lips, the desire in her eyes, every movement a dance of seduction that had driven him mad.

"We meant naught to each other," he said, though he wondered why he spoke to a vision. "You seduced me."

"Did I now? Or was it *you* who drew me into your lair?" She stepped toward him, the rustle of her skirts joining the buzz of insects. "And what a lion you were." Her tone dripped with desire as she looked him up and down.

Shame seared his belly and rose up his neck at the memories: the clandestine rendezvous, the long nights of passion. The way he felt nauseous with guilt the next day. The lies. The deception. Her irresistible pull on him again and again. Even now, even as an illusion, she stirred his body to life.

He rubbed the scar beside his mouth—the one her husband had put there. "You're a wicked woman. Nothing but a pig with a gold ring in her snout who lures men to destruction!" he quoted from the Bible. Proverbs, in fact, had much to say about loose women.

Feigning a look of pain, she sighed and twirled a lock of her hair. "You came of your own free will, if I recall."

Tearing his gaze from her, James stormed through a tangle of leaves and headed back toward town.

"You have another woman now, don't you?" Her voice trailed him. "You think she is better than me? You are a bigger fool than ever, James Callaway!" The sound of her laughter bounced off trunks and leaves and rang in his ears all the way back to camp. All the way to his hut, to his cot, where he plopped to sit and dropped his head in his hands. Reaching beneath his bed, he pulled out a small chest, opened it, and brought a Bible to his lap. His father's Bible. He breathed in the smell of it—leather and fire smoke and aged vellum—and pictured his dad sitting in his favorite high-back chair by the fireplace in their home, reading the words on each page over and over as if they were precious.

"This is yours now, son." The hands, strong yet veined with age, handed the book to James. "Read it every day. Memorize its words and they will bring you life. Abundant life!"

James could have died happy right there for the look of pride in his father's eyes, instead of the usual disappointment ever since James had forsaken the church and run off to become a doctor. To make matters worse, during his long absence at war, his mother had died of heartbreak. And fear. Fear that she'd never see her son again. But James *had* returned, like the prodigal coming to his senses, and now he would take over the pastorate of his father's church—the Second Baptist Church in Knoxville, Tennessee.

Rain tapped on the thatched roof, jarring him back to the present. Clutching the Bible to his chest, he blinked back the tears burning his eyes. Tabitha had tricked him and led him astray. And now his father was dead. "I'm so sorry, Father. I failed you. I failed you in the worst possible way."

CHAPTER 11

W hy won't you look at me?" James asked Angeline as she hovered over the brick oven beneath the thatched roof of the meeting shelter.

Swerving around, her skirts flinging about her legs, she gave him a tight smile. "I *am* looking at you. I'm just busy at the moment, Doctor." Her voice sounded stilted. She turned and continued to slice the wild onions, mushrooms, and herbs Thiago had found to add flavor to the rice. Rain tapped a baritone cadence on the thatched roof and formed puddles in the dirt across the town square. The deluge had not lessened since it began last night.

"I've been searching for you all day." James shook his arms, sending droplets through the air. "Are you feeling well?"

"Well enough, thank you." She continued her work. Wisps of hair, stirred by a breeze, danced over her neck while the musky scent of moist jungle filled his nose.

"I was sorry to hear you were ill last night. I so longed for our stroll on the beach." He took a step toward her and swiped a hand through his wet hair. The rain had kept the colonists in their huts most of the day, save a few hardy souls who scavenged the jungle for food. And James, who had scavenged the town for Angeline. He had searched every hut, looked in the frame that would become the barn, hunted through the burnt mill, ventured over to the beginnings of the Scotts' house, but Angeline was nowhere to be found. Until a few moments ago when a flash of blue skirts and red hair sent his heart racing and his legs darting to the meeting shelter.

Still, she said nothing. Thunder grumbled, shaking the roof and loosening a few raindrops onto the table.

He dared another step closer. The fire swamped him in smoke. Coughing, he blinked the sting from his eyes and touched her arm, staying the knife in her hand. "What is wrong, Angeline?"

A tremble passed through her. She drew in a shaky breath and stiffened her jaw, still avoiding his gaze. "I'm helping prepare supper."

"I didn't ask what you were doing." Voices sounded in the distance. He leaned toward her. "Why are you treating me like I have the plague? Did I do something to offend you?" Though he couldn't imagine what. Tabitha came to mind, and sudden terror flooded him. Had she appeared to Angeline? Had she told her what he'd done?

Violet eyes, brewing with turmoil, lifted to his. But there, he saw it—a speck of affection hid beneath the angst. Or was he only hoping? She opened her mouth to say something. . .

"There you both are." Eliza darted beneath the frond roof, removed the cloak from her head and shook out the water. "Thank you for starting the rice, Angeline. That's just what I was coming to do."

Other feminine voices rode on the wind accompanied by the splash of boots in mud.

Releasing Angeline, James stepped away. *Confound it all!*

Lifting her skirts, Magnolia ducked beneath the roof. "Now look at my gown." She slapped at the mud clinging to her hem while Mrs. Jenkins, Sarah, and a few other women joined them. "When is this rain going to stop? I feel like a waterlogged goose."

Eliza chuckled. "Surely it can't last much longer." Shoving a wet strand of hair behind her ear, she leaned to inspect Angeline's work. "Would you believe Blake is still sleeping? One day of rain and he's as lazy as a sloth." She smiled and glanced up, but instantly frowned, no doubt at the tension strung tight between James and Angeline. Tension that threatened to eat away at his gut if it wasn't resolved soon.

Slapping her hands together, Eliza skirted the table, mumbling something about helping skin the fish.

Taking Angeline's elbow, James turned her to face him. "A word, please?"

"I have work to do." She glanced over her shoulder at the ladies chattering and donning aprons. "Besides, people will hear."

"Then whisper." He leaned toward her ear. "Why are you angry?"

She smelled of rain and coconut and sweet onions, and he longed to see her smile at him again. Lightning flashed and the droplets pounded even harder, splattering mud onto the raised bamboo floor.

"I'm not. We'll talk later." She tugged from him and started to go but not before he saw tears mist her eyes.

He pulled her back. "I'm not letting you go until you tell me what has you so upset. If someone has hurt you. . ." If so, he'd forget he was a preacher and pummel them into dust.

She jerked from his grasp. "You can't always rescue me, James." Anger burned in her eyes. . .anger and something else. Despair? "Sometimes you just have to let go."

"What does that mean?" A sudden chill bit through his wet shirt.

She swallowed and stared off into the jungle, where rain streamed off the tip of a giant banana leaf like a spigot. A drop squeezed through the roof and landed on her forehead. James reached to wipe it, but she swatted him away. Thunder bellowed. "It means let me go, James. Let *us* go."

⚜

The words felt like barbed spikes as they passed over her tongue. Sharp spikes that stung her lips, her ears. And her heart. James stepped backward into the rain. Water cascaded down his face, blurring his expression of shock and agony and beading in his lashes that hung limp over pain-filled eyes. She wanted to take it all back, retract every word, and lose herself in his arms forever.

But she couldn't.

Rain slicked his hair and dripped from the curled tips to his collar. His wet shirt clung to every line and muscle in his chest. Still he stared at her. "I don't understand. I thought. . .I thought we cared for each other."

Blood pooled in her head. Behind her, the women's voices grew muted and distant. "We do care." She forced a smile. She would give him that much. A friendship to cherish.

Lightning flashed a deathly gray over him, enhancing the benumbed look on his face. Flattening his lips, he nodded then turned and walked away.

Taking her heart with him.

Impulsively, she sped after him, tears joining the rain on her cheeks.

He must have heard her for he stopped and faced her, confusion bending his brow.

She must be strong. If she stayed away from him, if she pretended not to care, Dodd would have no leverage over her. Then perhaps she wouldn't have to give herself to the lecherous swine. She wouldn't have to go back to her old way of life. And James would be spared the pain of discovering the truth. Even if Dodd eventually told him, it was better to break James's heart now than crush it later after they entered a doomed courtship. Either way, things must end between them.

But she could tell him none of this.

Instead they stood, rain sheeting between them, water dripping off their chins and lashes.

"I'm sorry," she finally said. Then fisting her hands, she forced herself to turn and walk away. Tears came as hard as the rain.

Dreams were not meant for her—not for little girls who had become harlots.

※

Distant groans wove their way through the slumberous maze in Hayden's mind. *Tap, tap, tap,* just like the thrum of incessant rain on the roof of his hut—the thrum he'd become so accustomed to these past three days, it actually helped him fall asleep. That and the feel of his wife cradled in his arms. The last thought brought a smile to his lips while another whimper finally burst through his mind, jerking him awake.

Magnolia thrashed beside him. "No. Don't leave me! Don't leave me!"

Leaning on his elbow, he drew her trembling body close. "Princess, wake up. You're dreaming." He shook her gently then kissed her forehead. With a moan, her eyes popped open, her chest heaving against his. Releasing a breath, she flung her arms around him.

"Hayden, it was such a terrible nightmare." Her voice quivering, she clung to him as if he were a lifeline in a storm.

"I was all alone in a tiny boat at sea."

Nudging her onto the pillow, he brushed hair from her face and planted a kiss on her nose. "Shhh, it's all right now. Only a dream."

"It was so real, Hayden. I was old. All wrinkled and gray-haired and feeble. And I had no oars." Tears dampened his fingers as he caressed her cheeks. "You and all our friends were leaving me...sailing away on a big ship, and I had no way to get to you."

He cupped her face in his hands. "It's the enemy feeding on your fears of being old and useless, you know that."

She nodded as another tear spilled from her eye. Hayden kissed it away before it slid into her hair then drew her close again. If only he could kiss away all her fears, all her pain as easily. "Do you know how beautiful you are? Both inside and out?" Did she really know? Had Hayden been able to convey to her just how much she meant to him? How precious she was?

He felt her relax as she squirmed closer.

"Magnolia, you are useful to everyone in this town. You are kind and cheerful, and you make us all laugh. Besides that, Eliza finds your help in the clinic invaluable."

"You are right." Joy returned to her voice. "God *has* given me purpose. And He has shown me what true beauty is." Turning on her side, she curled her back against him, erasing all slumber from his body and stirring it to life.

He ran fingers through her hair. "I love you, Magnolia. More than life itself," he whispered in her ear, his passion rising.

"And I you," she mumbled, her voice trailing off.

Hayden caressed her arm, brushing fingers over her soft skin, and thanked God yet again for giving him such a wonderful wife. Yet when he lowered his lips to hers, only the deep breaths of sleep responded to his kiss.

Smiling, he laid back on the pillow with a sigh, willing his body to relax. Another time. She needed her rest. She'd had so many nightmares lately. Hayden's own visions had increased as well. In fact, each day a parade of people he'd swindled in the past accompanied him wherever he went, showering him with either looks of hatred or tears of agony. He ignored them most of the time. Citing scripture often sent them scurrying—something he'd learned from the doc. Another thing he'd learned from the doc, as well as from the hours Hayden had spent with God, was that Hayden was forgiven. God had adopted him into His family. He had a new Father and a new life. No silly vision of the past would ever change that.

An hour passed, and unable to relax, he rose, tucked the quilt beneath Magnolia's chin then donned his trousers and shirt. Maybe a walk in the cool night rain would settle him.

All the rain did was soak through his clothes into his skin and finally send a chill through his bones. He slogged down Main Street, once terra firma but now nothing but a puddle—a rising puddle that squished beneath his boots, cloaking them in mud. When would this rain end? He was about to turn around and head back to the warmth of his wife and his bed when a flickering light coming from James's hut tugged his curiosity. At least he wasn't the only one not sleeping. Besides, he'd been meaning to speak to the doc about something.

Hayden found James leaning over a makeshift desk, a Bible on one end and a candle and large open book on the other.

Hayden cleared his throat.

James spun on his seat. "Hayden, I didn't hear you." He rubbed his eyes and set down his pen.

"It's the rain. It drowns out everything." Hayden shook the water from his hair then noticed his trousers dripping on the floor. "Sorry."

"No matter. After three days of rain, everything is wet anyway."

"Where are your bunkmates?" Hayden gestured toward the empty cots.

James sighed. "Off making rum is my guess. You know Lewis." He tilted a pocket watch on his desk to see the time. "But at one in the morning, they should be back. What brings you here so late? Have a seat." He gestured toward the only other chair in the room.

Hayden remained standing. No sense in soaking the furniture as well. "Magnolia had a nightmare again."

James nodded as if the information didn't surprise him. "Many are suffering from nightmares." He leaned forward on his knees, his shoulders slumping. "I wish I knew what to do. I can't seem to stop these demonic visions and dreams."

"I doubt any preacher could." Hayden gestured toward the old book on James's desk. "Perhaps you'll find the answers in there."

James nodded as lightning burst outside the window. "Let's hope so. But you didn't come to talk about that."

"No."

James leaned back in his chair, the candle casting shadows over his face. "Well?"

"It's Angeline."

He frowned, but then alarm shot across his face. "Is she all right?"

"Yes, yes, she's fine." Hayden held up a hand. "Surely you would know better than I."

"No." James lowered his chin. "I haven't spoken to her in a few days."

Hayden finally took the seat. "I thought you two... Word was that you were going to ask to court her?"

James frowned. "It didn't work out that way."

"I'm sorry." Hayden couldn't imagine the pain he would have felt if Magnolia had turned him down.

Yet it was probably for the best. Hayden had noticed the doctor's interest in Angeline when they'd first set sail for Brazil. Then when he'd observed the playful dalliance between them here in town, he'd ignored it as innocent flirting. However when they began to spend more and more time together and he saw the loving glances between them, he'd become worried. Angeline had an obligation to tell James the truth. She should have told him the truth already, before they'd grown so close. And despite Hayden's hatred of meddling in other people's affairs, he could not risk the safety of his good friend. How could he ever forgive himself if something horrible happened? No, if Angeline accepted James's suit, Hayden was obligated to tell him he was courting a murderer.

CHAPTER 12

"What about Angeline? Did she say something about me?" James could tell from the look on Hayden's face that whatever he had to say wasn't good news.

"It's nothing." Hayden shrugged and moved to the window where James had attempted to cover the opening with palm fronds—two of which had already blown off and the rest now bent in the wind. "It doesn't matter anymore."

Rising, James stretched the ache that spanned his shoulders and had now begun to migrate to his heart. He had tried to avoid thinking of Angeline the past few days, had buried himself in his translation. But fleeting glimpses of her around town without so much as a word or a smile had left him feeling as dry as a desert, despite the deluge outside. Now, Hayden had gone and brought her to the forefront of his thoughts again, resurging his loss. "If she's in danger, please tell me."

The flap opened and a blast of rain-saturated wind shoved Blake inside. He shook water from his coat and ran a hand through his wet hair. "I thought I heard voices." His glance took in his friends before he slapped Hayden on the back, sending a spray into the air.

James smiled. These two men had become like brothers to him. Brothers he'd never had, being an only child. "If I'd known I was going to have company, I'd have asked Lewis for some of his rum."

"Blaa!" Blake stuck out his tongue and shivered. "That stuff tastes like seaweed."

"Ah, it's not so bad when you really need a drink." Hayden chuckled.

Thunder rode through the town, shaking the tiny hut. A few droplets squeezed through the extra fronds James had fastened on the roof. Soon there'd be no dry place in the whole colony. "The storm worsens."

"Which is why I came." Blake gestured for Hayden to take the only empty chair, but when the man shook his head, the colonel slid onto the seat, stretching his leg out before him with a wince. "Can't sleep lately."

"A common problem it would seem," Hayden said as he attempted to steady the canvas door that flapped and flailed like an injured goose.

Blake pinched the bridge of his nose. "Eliza's been suffering from terrifying visions of the war, and my nightmares have gotten worse. And this storm"—he glanced up as the pounding of rain intensified, reminding James of the war drums that haunted his dreams as well— "there's something strange about it. I feel it."

So had James. Which is why he'd been up studying more of the ancient book from the temple. He glanced at that book now with its Hebrew letters scrawled from right to left. Next to it, his own scribbles in English darkened a separate parchment in an attempt to translate a language he'd barely learned as a child.

Lightning flashed white through tiny slits and holes in the fronds that made up the wall. Wind snaked around corners in an eerie tune, sputtering James's candle.

The flap opened again, and Eliza pushed past Hayden, fear sparking in her eyes until they landed upon her husband. "I woke and you were gone." She moved and fell against Blake.

He embraced her. "I'm sorry, love. I didn't want to wake you."

"You know I hate it when you're not beside me."

James had never seen the woman quite so needy before, but he supposed the incessant storm had everyone on edge.

"I was just telling the men about your visions and my nightmares," Blake said.

"My visions have increased recently as well," Hayden added.

"Yes." Picking up his pen, James tapped it on the edge of the book. "Things are definitely getting worse."

"Have you discovered anything new in your translation?" Blake rubbed his leg as a barrage of rain struck the east wall, quivering the fronds.

"I'm finding out bits and pieces about the power of these beings and why they were put in chains. The first one, *Deception*"—he glanced at his friends—"has the power to deceive people by feeding them lies buried within half-truths. The lie could be anything from something about another person, or your own self-worth, the existence of God, to a lie that *Deception*, himself, isn't even real."

Hayden's lips slanted in skepticism.

Ignoring him, James continued. "The next one, *Delusion*, has the power to create visions, mirages, various illusions."

Blake rubbed the back of his neck while Eliza took his other hand in hers. "We've all experienced that, haven't we?"

A clap of thunder slammed the skies. James jerked, blood pumping, wondering if someone or *something* didn't wish him to continue.

Hayden held the flap down against another burst of wind. "And the one Graves released?"

"*Destruction*," James said. "He has the power to alter nature. He cannot kill anyone directly, but he can change their surroundings in order to destroy them."

"The lightning strike, the ants." Blake ground out, rubbing his jaw.

"Possibly."

"But where did these beings come from?" Hayden asked.

"From the pit of hell is my guess," James said. "Apparently, these particular fallen angels had become extremely powerful or perhaps they broke the boundaries God had set for them—some cardinal rule they were not permitted to break. In any case, God decided to lock them up until the end of the age. He sent Gabriel and other angels to do battle. The four evil beings lost and were chained beneath the earth near"—James shook his head, hesitating to tell them what he wasn't sure he'd translated correctly—"near a branch of the lake of fire that burns at the center of earth." He gazed at them, assessing their belief but found only stunned confusion. He sighed. "Although I don't think the temple was there at the time."

Groaning, Hayden swallowed hard, his face growing pale.

"What is it?" James asked.

He took up a pace, eyes darting over the hut, mumbling something they couldn't hear over the storm. Finally he halted and faced them. "There was a priest in Rio. He told me there was a fire lake beneath the temple."

"A priest?"

"Yes, some odd man I bumped into on the street. It was nothing, really. He was muttering crazy things. But I do remember him mentioning the fire lake. I thought him mad at the time, but now. . ." Shock leapt in Hayden's green eyes as he gaped at them.

"Did this priest say anything else?" James moved to the edge of his chair.

"Something about six. I don't remember." Hayden rubbed his eyes.

"Surely it's a coincidence." Eliza hugged herself. "If all this is true, why would God allow these angels to be so easily released?"

"Not easily," James said. "If the cannibals hadn't built their temple in that exact location and then dug tunnels beneath it, these beings would still be locked below and we'd be knee-deep in sugarcane, coffee, and the utopia we sought."

Eliza frowned. "Then it would seem Satan told the cannibals exactly where to build their temple."

James nodded. "A reasonable assumption." Though he could tell from her clipped tone that she was being facetious.

Blake snorted. "But why didn't God bury them so deep they'd never be found?"

Tossing down his pen, James leaned back in his chair. "I don't know. Something to do with man's free will, I'd wager."

"I'm starting to hate this free will thing." Blake huffed.

"It does have its downfalls."

Hayden shifted his stance. "Do you know how crazy this sounds? Invisible evil angels buried beneath the earth?"

"You saw their prisons yourself. How else do you explain your visions? And what this priest said?"

"I don't know." Hayden scrubbed his face. "Perhaps something in the food?" Though his tone bore humor, his expression was one of desperation—desperation for the normal life they all longed for. "The mandioca root we've been eating can be poisonous if not cooked right. And Thiago has been instructing the women to grind it into flour since we got here."

Eliza smiled. "Your skepticism is good, Hayden. We should all question things. But ultimately, we must put the matter to God and see what He says."

733

Blake lifted the flap and glanced out onto the street. "Perhaps we ought to pray for the rain to stop before we all drown. Wha—?" He disappeared outside. Hayden ran after him. Rain pelted James's face as he followed and peered down the street—more like a brook for all the water streaming down it. A muffled shout came from the darkness. Blake charged ahead, his figure dissolving in the downpour. A man emerged from the shadows, another man hanging limp in his arms.

Eliza appeared beside James, lantern held high.

"It's Mr. Lewis. Help! He's hurt."

Hayden grabbed Mr. Lewis from the man's tired arms. Blood expanded on his saturated shirt and stormed down his trousers, coming so fast the rain couldn't wash it away.

James's throat closed. He stepped back.

"What happened?" Blake asked over the roar of the storm.

"Wolf! He was attacked by a wolf!"

James was a fish. A fish swimming through a lake plump with swaying ferns and dancing vines. He breathed in water. He coughed up spray. His boots sank in puddles up to his ankles. He yanked one from the clawing mud. If only he *were* a fish. It would be much easier to swim through this sodden jungle with fins and gills than plod through it with feet and lungs.

Dawn had crested the horizon over an hour ago, but you wouldn't know it for the cloak that settled over the thick brush. If only that cloak would protect them from the rain that continued to spew from angry black clouds broiling across the sky. Rain that speared the leaves overhead like a thousand arrows before pummeling the group of five men below in a hail of violent grapeshot—saturating, stinging, biting.

The musket slipped in James's hand. Readjusting his grip, he wondered if it would even fire if they found the wolf. Blake moved ahead of him, his soaked shirt plastered to his skin, water dripping from his black hair. To James's left, Hayden slogged through puddles, looking more like a sea otter than a man. Another colonist angled away on James's right while Thiago led the way up front.

James ground his teeth. He should be back at the clinic helping Eliza and Magnolia tend to Lewis's wound, but instead he was traipsing through the jungle, soaked to the bone, looking for a wolf that was no doubt long gone.

If only there hadn't been so much blood. . .

At least he had caught a glimpse of Angeline when she'd stormed from her hut, hooded cloak askew, at the sound of Lewis's shrill screams. Their eyes reached for each other through the gloom of night, and he thought he saw sorrow in hers before she snapped them away.

Thiago halted, knelt, and examined the muddy ground, water trickling from strands of dark hair hanging at his jaw. Blake and James caught up to him as the Brazilian stood and shook his head. "We lost him. He not come this way. The rain hide tracks."

As James had tried to tell the man before they left town. But Thiago had insisted they must hunt and kill this *Lobisón*, the man-wolf he claimed had attacked Mr. Lewis. If they did not, Lewis would become a wolf himself. Or so the legend said.

Rubbish. Just a ludicrous Brazilian superstition. One James supposed he should be thankful for since it had allowed him to escape a situation where his ineptitude would be on full display. He had a feeling Blake would rather be in the jungle than witnessing the bloody mess as well.

A guttural howl pierced the rain—distant and hollow. Thiago's dark eyes narrowed as he scanned the maze of dripping green. "He watches us." Rain beaded on his long lashes and slid down his jaw.

"What happens to Lewis now?" Hayden shouted over the din of the storm, the tremor in his normally staunch voice more than evident.

"We wait. If his blood is poisoned, he become wolf in three days."

Above them, a colorful bird squawked at the ridiculous statement. James couldn't agree more.

Hayden's brow darkened as he absently rubbed his arm where Magnolia had stitched up a wolf bite two months ago.

Blake leaned toward him. "What's that?" He pointed beneath his chin. "Is that fur growing on your neck?"

Hayden flung a hand to his throat, eyes flashing. Frantic, he brushed fingers over his neck, chin, and jaw before he released a long sigh. Blake, James, and even Thiago chuckled as Hayden gave them a look of annoyance. "Amusing. Very amusing."

On the way back to town, James caught up with Thiago. "You

realize that this myth of Lobisón is just that, a myth. Surely you don't believe that men become wolves."

The Brazilian interpreter shrugged. "Many of my people see Lobisón." Shoving aside a large fern, he gave James a curious look. "You are man of God. There is much we not know about world and spirits. Like evil angels you speak of."

James flattened his lips. The man did have a point, but his answer made James wonder at his spiritual condition. "Do you believe in God, Thiago?"

"Sim, Mr. James." He nodded.

"And His Son, Jesus?" A frog croaked, and James barely missed stepping on it as it splashed across the path.

"Jesus opened way to heaven." Thiago shook water from his hair. "We pay money to priests for family to go. That's why we must make many friends in life, so many will pay our way."

Shocked at the man's words, James felt an urgency stir his spirit. He was the town's spiritual guide, and he couldn't very well let this kind man continue in darkness. But how to reach him? "That isn't really how it works. There is no price to pay. Jesus paid it on the cross. Then He gives us power to live good lives. He delivers, heals, and protects us."

Thunder rumbled in the distance. One glance over his shoulder told James the other men followed close behind, heads bent against the rain.

"There are women in Rio who heal people too." Thiago sloshed through a rather large puddle. "Wise women use herbs and oils and many other things. One time they crush roasted worms and sing a chant to cure my toothache. They also make love potions. All you need is lock of hair from your beloved." He frowned. "Wish I had some of Miss Sarah's hair."

James grew sad at the man's beliefs that seemed to be a strange mixture of Catholicism and sorcery. "You don't need a potion to make a woman love you. Nor do you need incantations for healing. And you especially don't need anyone to buy your way into heaven." He longed to set the young Brazilian free from beliefs that entrapped him in fear. Worse than that, beliefs that would eventually send him to hell.

Lightning flashed, and James kept pace with Thiago as they shoved through a wall of slippery vines. "In fact, you can't buy your way into heaven at all," James shouted above the storm. "God grants everyone entrance as a free gift to those who receive His Son. There is nothing else you need to do except get to know Him and follow Him."

Another growl of thunder shook the sky, and for a minute, James thought he'd overstepped the Brazilian's bounds. But finally Thiago said, "I will think on this, Mr. James."

James smiled.

They stopped at the river before heading back into town. What once had been a smooth-flowing finger of blue and green gently caressing the land, now had transformed into the bulging muscle of a raging bully shoving his way through the jungle. The sandy beach that had once spanned several yards up to an embankment had disappeared beneath a torrent of rushing gray water. At its edge, foam clawed the sheer rock where they stood, licking and groping like a hungry child bent on having his way.

Spears of rain stabbed the water, bouncing and skipping over the surface, sounding like the clash of a thousand swords. James swallowed.

"You don't think it will overflow its banks, do you?" He glanced at Blake, whose stern expression formed his usual unreadable mask. Hayden stood frozen at the sight. "We *are* in the middle of a valley."

"True, but the river flows to the sea," Blake answered, yet James didn't miss the slight hesitation in his voice.

Hayden released a sigh of relief and kicked a stone into the frothing mass. "Right. There's always an outlet for the water, then."

Then why did James suddenly feel like he was sinking into the mud? And fast.

CHAPTER 13

Angeline sank into the murky water, deeper and deeper. Shapes of life beyond the surface above grew blurry and hypnotic. Dark and cold, silence invaded her soul. Her lungs screamed for air—clawed her throat for life's last breath. In a moment, death would grant her the peace that had eluded her in life. But the water continued to slosh and gurgle, refusing to be silenced.

Drip. Drip. Water splattered on her eyes. She popped them open. Darkness slithered over a thatched roof where the *rat–tat–tat* of rain had drummed a steady cadence for five days. *Drip.* Another drop struck her neck. Light burst. A baby cried. *Lydia?* Water splashed.

"Angeline!" Sarah screamed.

Lantern light blinded Angeline before Sarah's anxious face filled her vision. "Angeline! The river, it's rising! We must get up!" Holding a lantern in one hand, she gripped Angeline's arm in a pinch with the other, the pain finally forcing her to surface from her morbid dream.

"Get dressed!" Sarah shouted as she sloshed toward the other side of the hut. "I need to get Lydia."

Knot in her throat, Angeline swung her legs over the cot. They landed in a foot of water—cold water that smothered her skin and sent a shiver up her back. Water that was rising. Fast!

"What's happening?" She stood, grabbed a petticoat, skirt, and blouse off a hook and began putting them on as best she could. No time for a proper corset. Thunder boomed. Thatches quivered, sprinkling drops onto their liquid floor.

"It's the river!" Sarah shouted over the roar of water as she bundled

Lydia in a blanket and headed for the door. "Hurry!"

Before she could open the flap, Blake stuck his head in. "To higher ground! We haven't much time!"

Tying her skirts on, Angeline grabbed Stowy and followed Sarah out the door. Darkness haunted a scene ravenous with the gush of water. In the distance, she made out Blake ushering the townspeople toward a hill that rose to the north. Madness, chaos all around! Shouts and screams zipped past her ears. People sloshed in all directions through the surging torrent. Lanterns speared light onto angry water. Rain pelted the surface like rabid pebbles.

She felt her neck. Her father's ring! Swerving, she dove back into the hut, the river at her thighs now. Groping in the dark, she waded through water that felt as thick as molasses and found the table by her bed. She searched the chipped wood. There. The chain. The ring. She grabbed it and flung it over her head. Lifting her hair, she tucked it safely within her bodice. Stowy clawed her shoulder and meowed in protest.

The river reached her waist.

Stomach twisting, she plunged out of the hut, trying to settle the cat. Dark water swirled around her, tangling her skirts and shoving her legs backward. She lost her footing. Throwing out an arm for balance, she forced her shoes back into the mud. In the distance, dots of light ascended into darkness like angels flying back to heaven. The colonists had left her behind.

Her friends had left her behind!

She headed toward the lights, fighting both the rising current and her rising terror. The water surged, spinning its greedy claws round about her. Pulling, tugging, twisting. Ravaging her like an unwelcome lover. Rain lashed her head and arms. Her hair hung in ropes of lead. Lightning etched across the sky—a gray flash of death that left a vision imprinted on her mind: a liquid grave rising to swallow her alive, trees bowing in defeat, huts collapsing. Then all went dark again.

Nothing but the roar of the river and growl of thunder remained to keep her company. And Stowy's fearful whines. The water reached her chest. Terror sucked the breath from her lungs. Her skirts felt like chain mail. Her legs tangled in the heavy fabric. Clenching her jaw, she thrust through the river, trying to shove the raging water aside with her arm. Her muscles ached. Her head grew light. The lights in the distance faded. She wasn't going to make it. She was going to drown in the middle of the Brazilian jungle, her body swept away to be devoured by some beast when the waters receded.

A fitting punishment for her crimes.

Her eyes burned, but no tears came. Wasn't it enough she'd been forced to give up James? Give up any chance at true happiness? What else did God want from her? Would He never be satisfied until she had paid for her sins with her life? *God, if You're listening, I won't pray for myself, but please save the rest of the colonists. My friends. James. And please give him the happiness he deserves.*

Her breath rasped over a dry throat. Her chest hurt. Water gripped her shoulders. Stowy's nails clawed her skin as he clung to her neck. *God, please save Stowy!* The current grew swift. A shadow moved toward her. A thicket of branches and twigs. Sharp wood jabbed her. Knocked her over. Her feet swept out from under her. Water absorbed her face. Thrashing, she fought to keep her mouth and Stowy above the surface, gulping and choking as the river spilled into her lungs.

⚓

Handing Mrs. Matthews—who'd been separated during the confusion—back to her worried husband, James raised his lantern and turned, scanning the remaining colonists hiking up the hill. Sporadic lanterns dotted the jungle, spiraling and bobbing haphazard trails through leaves and vines. He squinted to make out faces in the brief glimpse afforded him. Anxious, pale faces, some casting fearful looks over their shoulders at the liquid death rising behind them. A fountain of bubbling pitch that snapped twigs and broke branches, devouring all in its path.

Thunder blasted, accompanied by the screech of birds and howl of creatures abandoning the forest floor for the canopy. James's blood mimicked the mad rush of the river—hot and violent. And mind-numbing. Shock buzzed across his skin. Everything was ruined. Everything they'd worked so hard to build, destroyed. But he couldn't think of that now. The river had breached its banks so quickly, they all would have surely drowned if he hadn't been up translating more of the book—the book he'd handed Thiago for safekeeping only moments ago, along with his father's Bible. Perhaps James should thank God for his obsession with the ancient manuscript.

After alerting Blake and making sure the eldest colonists were up and moving, James had gone in search of Angeline and Sarah, the only two single women in the colony, but poor Mrs. Matthews had latched onto him in hysterics, refusing to release him until he found her husband. Now, as James searched the colonists bringing up the rear, he thought he saw Sarah in the distance. Surely Angeline was with her.

Making his way down the slippery hill, he wiped rain from his eyes and batted aside sopping leaves, all the while encouraging colonists he passed—their arms full of clothing, tools, and weapons—to keep moving.

Thunder bellowed, shaking the ground. Shoving aside a cascade of vines, James nearly ran over Blake. Two muskets were strung over his left shoulder beneath which he hefted a sack of rice. Eliza, arms loaded with blankets and a satchel—no doubt full of medicines— clung to her husband's other side, her expression stiff with alarm.

"Keep moving, my friend. We don't know how far the river will rise." Blake's normally controlled tone was laced with fear.

Sarah stopped beside them, nestling Lydia to her chest against the rain.

"Where's Angeline?" James scanned the three of them. Their eyes grew wide. Dread swept over him as they all glanced at the rising river. Lightning scored the sky, flickering a deathly pallor over the scene and a shroud of terror over his heart.

"She was right behind me!" Sarah shouted over the roar of water and rain.

Blake's jaw bunched. He turned to Eliza. "Go ahead. I'll catch up."

James clutched his friend's arm. "No, I'll go back for her. You get your wife and Sarah to safety." Turning, he marched down the hill, not waiting for an answer. Below him, the jungle floor sped past in a mad dash, snapping branches from trees as if they were matchsticks. Somewhere out there, Angeline was fighting for her life. He would find her. He must. He could not fail. *God, please, not this time. I cannot fail at this.*

Helpless to move, helpless to fight, Angeline allowed the swift current to carry her away. Terror had long since abandoned her, leaving a numb submission behind. Her only fear now was for Stowy. Somehow he had managed to hang on to her neck, his sharp claws digging into her skin. *Hang on, precious one. Hang on.* Maybe he could find a tree to leap onto and save himself.

Tumbling, twisting, turning, the angry river flung her onto rocks, bashed her against tree trunks, scraped her against branches until every inch of her screamed in pain. She prayed for mercy. She prayed she would drown. But every time her head went under the water and she almost lost consciousness, the river shoved her back into the air, forcing her to gasp for a breath. And Stowy to screech in terror. How long could this go on? If each bruise and cut were punishment for her sins, it was going to be a long night. Rain lashed the top of her head. Shadows rushed toward her like ghouls. She closed her eyes.

And heard her name. "Angeline!"

God? No, probably the other guy. She wouldn't answer him. She'd meet him soon enough.

"Angeline!"

She opened her eyes. The dark outline of a patch of trees rushed toward her like soldiers in a demonic army. A branch swung low from one in the middle. A man's arm extended. Water filled her mouth. Gasping, she choked it out and tried to focus. She struck the first tree. Pain seared across her side. Dipping beneath the surface, she bobbed up again and shook water from her eyes. The hand was definitely there. Unless she was dreaming. If not, she'd have one chance to grab it.

And once chance only.

"Angeline! Grab ahold!" Desperation screeched in the voice—a voice she knew.

Oh, God. Please help. I really don't want to die. I am not ready to be judged.

Lightning flashed, flickering over the lowered hand. Large and strong. She slammed into the tree's buttress. Water gushed over the top, shoving her over with it, legs and arms flailing. The hand flashed in her vision. She reached for it. The current pushed her under again.

No! Gathering what little strength remained, she shoved her feet against the buttress and lunged back up. She hacked up water. Stowy uttered a deathly wail. Angeline reached once more.

Fingers met fingers. Palms met palms. And a grip tighter than a corset fastened around her hand.

Water sped past her, bubbling in defiance of losing its prey. She glanced up. James looked down upon her. "Hang on! I've got you!"

CHAPTER 14

It was a miracle. That was the only explanation for Angeline's appearance beneath the very tree James had climbed in the hope of spotting her in the frothing waters. Now that he had a grip on her, he would never let go. Ever. He growled as he gathered every ounce of strength to pull her up toward him. Desperately, she clutched his arm. He reached down with his other hand, grabbed the belt around her waist, and hoisted her the rest of the way onto the wide branch where he sat. She fell against his chest, their heavy breaths mingling in the misty air as the river raged beneath them. A shiver wracked her body, and he thought he heard her whimper. Wrapping his arms around her, he leaned back against the trunk, encasing her in what little warmth he had left through his soaked garments.

A sandpaper tongue licked his cheek. Jerking back, he squinted in the darkness, smiling when he realized it was Stowy. How the cat had survived, James had no idea, but he was sure Angeline would have sacrificed her own life for her feline companion.

Lightning flashed, giving him a brief glimpse of the tree. A kapok tree, if he remembered Thiago's lessons on Brazilian flora. Thick branches reached up toward the angry sky like hairy dragon claws, their tips swaying in the wind. A sturdy tree, James hoped. The tree God had led James to after he'd done the only thing he knew in order to find Angeline—plunge into the mad, chaotic water, grab onto a piece of wood, and pray with everything in him.

Angeline shivered again and he gripped her tighter, squeezing her between his thighs to let her know he wasn't letting go. Wind fluted an eerie tune through branches, stirring leaves into applause. Rain squeezed through the canopy above and drip-dropped on their heads.

Another blast of thunder shook the sky—farther away this time. Good. Perhaps the storm was passing. Perhaps the rain would finally stop and the river would recede. But what would be left of their homes? Their town? Their crops? He couldn't think of that now. Couldn't think of the watery beast just yards beneath their dangling feet, gobbling everything in its path. For now, he and Angeline were safe. And Stowy too. Whispering a prayer for the rest of the colonists, he leaned his head back on the rough bark and closed his eyes. A few minutes later, Angeline relaxed in his arms and snuggled against his chest. Stowy began purring.

James fell into a semiconscious slumber and dreamed he was on a ship full of cats pouncing over a sunny deck in pursuit of mice. Above him, bloated white sails sped them to some unknown destination. The gurgle and rush of the sea against the hull tickled his ears while voices clambered up hatches from passengers below. Yet no one but James was on deck. No captain, no first mate, no helmsman. Wind whipped his hair. The ship bucked over a swell, and he steadied his feet on the deck when he caught a glimpse of darkness in the distance. Not the type of darkness when a huge cloud covered the sun or when night approached, but a vast wall of black spanning the horizon. Flames burst through the ebony slate in a savage, frightening pattern. Like lightning. . .yet more ominous, more threatening. . .as if the jagged flares had a mind of their own.

James froze. A thousand needles punctured his heart. He leapt up the ladder onto the foredeck for a better look. The ship sped on a course straight for the dark menace. And somehow he knew that if he didn't stop it, everyone on board would die. His glance took in the sails, the wheel spinning out of control. He had no idea what to do! Even if he did, how could he lower sails and turn the ship all by himself?

The smell of coconut tickled his nose. The sweet scent filled his lungs and tantalized his memories. A bird squawked.

James snapped his eyes open with a start.

Angeline was staring at him. Sitting as far away from him as possible on the branch, she petted Stowy in her lap. Morning sun cut through branches and leaves and set her damp hair aglitter like liquid fire. A drop from above splattered on her shoulder, soaking into the fabric of her blouse. For a moment they simply stared into each other's eyes as if they were both lost in dreams they didn't want to end.

Finally she lowered her gaze. "You saved my life. Again."

A bird chirped above them and Stowy leapt from Angeline's arms in hot pursuit. She reached after the cat and lost her balance. James lunged to grab her waist and settle her. Their gazes met again, just inches apart this time. An emotion he couldn't name brewed within her violet eyes, but whatever it was, it made him never want to look away. His heart ached all over again from the loss of her.

She shoved his hands away as if he had leprosy.

"If you want me to apologize for coming to your rescue, I fear I cannot." James glanced down to see what his ears already told him. The waters had receded. Well, most of them. A shallow stream trickled over the land, shoving tangled nests of branches, twigs, and leaves through the mud, some bunching in knots to form beaver dams. The *tap*, *tap* of water from the canopy provided a cheerful accompaniment to the warble of birds. A pleasant tune so different from the mighty roar of the storm the night before.

But how could James possibly keep his focus on muddy water, birds, or storms when Angeline's lips were so close to his face he could feel her breath on his cheek?

"No, I. . ." she began and James leaned back against the trunk, lest he do what every impulse within him drove him to do—kiss her.

"I. . ." She lowered her chin. "How did you know where I would be?"

James shrugged, trying not to notice the way her damp blouse clung to her curves. "I didn't. When I saw you weren't with the others, I jumped in the river and prayed I would find you."

"You did?" Tiny brows collided above her freckled nose as her eyes searched his.

"Of course. I knew you must be out there somewhere. Either in the water or clinging to a tree."

"But the chances. . ." Moisture covered her eyes and she looked away.

"Are good with God." He smiled. When she didn't respond, he swung his leg over the branch and gripped the bark on either side.

Angeline sat inches from him, one hand pressed on the branch beneath her, one nervously fiddling with her tangled hair. Yet she seemed so distant and cold she might as well have been miles away.

A flock of orioles, plumed in brilliant yellow and black, landed in branches above them and began their morning serenade as if all was right with the world. Totally oblivious, it would seem, to Stowy who flattened himself, his ears back, his tail jerking as he slunk toward them. Yet were they oblivious? Were they too busy praising God to notice the danger lurking all around? Or did they simply trust Him to care for them? As God had cared for James and Angeline through the storm.

"You shouldn't have come after me, James. You could have died." Angeline's tone turned petulant as if he had dipped her hair in ink or put a frog in her stew.

Which completely baffled him. He knew he should be angry at her for her ungrateful attitude, but he couldn't find it within him. "I'm sorry for saving your life, your dragonship."

A smile peeked from her lips. "You said you weren't going to apologize."

"Force of habit, I suppose." His chuckle fell limp when he noticed her torn sleeves and the cuts and bruises marring her arms. "You're hurt." He reached for her, but she grabbed her arm and drew it close, wincing.

"I guess I hit a few trees."

James studied her, not able to imagine the horror she must have endured being helplessly carried away by the current. For him, he'd been more concerned about finding her. But she must have believed she would die. His gaze landed on the scar on her arm.

"But this"—he gestured toward it—"is old. What is it from?"

Her body stiffened. She attempted to cover it with shreds of her sleeve.

"Forgive me. I shouldn't have asked."

She raised a brow. "Another apology, Doctor? It does, indeed, appear to be a habit with you."

"Only when I'm with you, for I seem to constantly cross some invisible boundary that awakes the sleeping dragon."

She looked away but not before he saw her smile.

"Nevertheless, when we get back, have Eliza look at your wounds." Since it was obvious she wouldn't allow James to touch her.

She nodded, and James stretched the aches from his back and ran hands down his still-damp trousers, longing for her to understand the depth of his feelings, but she wouldn't look at him. Instead she peered through the lattice of shifting leaves and drew in a deep breath of air scented with sodden earth and salt.

"We are near the sea," she finally said before looking down and wobbling slightly, her face blanching.

"The river pushed us toward it. Here, grab this branch and don't look down." James guided her hand to a bough angling beside her shoulder then reached over to pull a scrap from her hair.

She snapped her eyes to his.

"Just a twig." He held it up before her horrified gaze. "I assure you, I wasn't taking liberties." Though he wouldn't mind coiling his finger around the lustrous curl he'd just briefly grazed.

Moments passed in silence. Surely she wasn't angry at him for saving her life! He'd never met such a puzzling woman. He longed for the camaraderie, the friendship they had formed the last time they'd been in a tree together, but that had drifted out to sea with the raging river.

"I cannot believe what happened," she finally said. "The river came up so quickly."

A breeze gusted through the leaves and chilled his wet shirt. He adjusted his position on the branch. "Too quickly. It doesn't make sense. It was as if someone broke a dam upstream." Yet he had his suspicions—suspicions that had nothing to do with natural causes.

"You don't suppose there's anything left of our town?" She bit her lip, her voice vacant of hope. "And the others. They are safe?"

"Yes. They all made it up the hill in time." He wanted to tell her all would be well. He wanted to kiss the worry from the freckles tightening on her pert nose, but he truly wasn't sure anymore. Not after all the disasters they'd suffered. "I don't know about our huts. Or our crops."

She faced him again, staring at him with sad eyes. Wind eased a curl across her cheek, and reaching up, he brushed it behind her ear. She took in a quick breath.

So he *did* have some effect on her.

Fear sped across her eyes before she attempted to scoot farther away from him. "We should go find out."

"We should wait until the water is gone. If the town is destroyed, there's nothing we can do about it now."

When another branch blocked her progress, she let out a huff of displeasure. What in the surefire blazes had James done to deserve such aversion? Whatever the reason, it wouldn't dull the pain lancing through his heart at the moment. She'd made it plain she didn't want a courtship. What he hadn't realized was that she also found him repulsive.

Moments passed in silence. Stowy sent another flock of birds scattering before he began pouncing on leaves instead. Finally Angeline attempted a smile. "How odd that we are stuck in a tree again. I wonder if this will become a regular occurrence?"

"I hope so. Apparently it's the only time you'll talk to me."

"I *talk* to you."

"Not since you told me our relationship was over."

"Not over. Just different." She stared down at the muddy ground. "I've been busy. And it's been raining."

He wished those were the only reasons. But he knew better. Regardless, he would cherish the time they had now. Even if she wished she were anywhere else but with him.

Gathering her mass of damp curls, she tugged them over her other shoulder. They tumbled to her lap where she attempted to untangle them with her fingers.

Red streaks drew his gaze to blood on her neck. "What are these?" He brushed more of her hair aside and examined what looked like scratches. Deep ones.

She fingered them absently. "Yes, I'd forgotten. Stowy. He hates the water."

As if on cue, the cat swatted at her from the branch above causing Angeline to giggle. A wonderful, delightful sound that helped loosen the tightness in James's gut at both her cold demeanor and the sight of fresh blood.

He swallowed, plucked a nearby leaf and pressed it on the wounds. "You may need stitches."

James's voice sounded hollow and trembling, as though it came from within a cave—a very cold cave. Though she'd been trying not to look at him, she swerved her gaze to his, noting that his eyes were on anything but her neck and his face bore resemblance to white parchment.

Moving his fingers aside, she held the leaf in place, remembering all the times he had been paralyzed in the presence of blood. At first she'd thought it ludicrous and weak. Especially for a doctor, but now that she knew him—had witnessed his strength and bravery—she knew this was no simple phobia. "It must have been horrible for you on the battlefield," she mumbled the thoughts filling her mind.

"You would never know it now, but I used to be quite a good surgeon," James said with a sordid chuckle, still not looking at her neck. "They would send the worst cases my way. . .the ones with limbs blown off and entrails bubbling from bellies."

The visual sent a sour taste into her mouth.

"Forgive me, Angeline." He laid a hand on her arm, but she moved aside. The man had no idea how his every touch played havoc with her insides. And her emotions. When she awoke, cocooned in his arms, she'd felt safe and warm and loved. And she found herself wishing time would stand still and she'd never have to leave his embrace. But that could never be. So, she'd moved as far away from him as she could and watched him sleep—a restless, fitful slumber that tore at her heart to discover what caused him such angst and to put an end to it with her love.

"You were quite accustomed to seeing blood, I imagine," she said.

A drop of rainwater landed on his forehead from above and he shoved it into his hair—damp, chaotic hair threaded in strings of gold and tawny brown that curled when they reached his collar.

"Is it possible for one person to see too much blood in a lifetime?" His jaw flexed as he gazed into the jungle. "Perhaps there is some limit set by God that man cannot go beyond. Similar to the threshold of pain that thrusts men into the bliss of unconsciousness. I reached my limit is all." His bronze eyes searched hers, brimming with sorrow and shame, yet sturdy as the metal whose color they favored.

"I cannot imagine what you went through."

"I wouldn't want you to. I wouldn't want anyone to. Yet, it was nothing compared to what our soldiers saw on the battlefield."

"Yet you saved many lives."

"A few."

"How could there be shame in that? Or what happened to you afterward? In fact, you should be proud of your service." Unlike her. While he was saving lives, Angeline was ruining them. Her own included.

Stowy leapt onto James's leg, pouncing on a shifting spot of sunlight. They both chuckled, lightening the dour mood. Perhaps lightening it a little too much, for when the laughter died, their eyes met again, and his hand swallowed hers. This time, she allowed it. The rough feel of his skin, the warmth, the way his fingers folded over hers, protecting, caressing. Eternity was made of moments like these, moments when time halted, dangling on the line strung between their gazes. Moments when there were only two and the strength of their love seemed to power the universe. She soaked it in, storing the memory deep in her heart.

For it could never happen again.

She couldn't have this man. Or Dodd would ruin his chance at happiness, his chance at marriage and children with a true lady. Angeline must be strong. Breaking the trance, she turned and gazed below. "The waters are low enough now. Perhaps we should go. It isn't proper for us to be here alone."

"People will understand. Besides, you're safe with me." With a touch to her chin, he brought her to face him again. "You know my feelings for you."

She did. And it threatened to undo her carefully erected shield. But Dodd's ultimatum rose like a sword beside that shield—one she must use to keep James at bay. For his sake.

Sunlight angled over his jaw, over his dark stubble so at odds with his light hair.

She tugged her hand from his. "You must accept the way things are, James. I'm sorry."

"And how exactly *are* things?"

That I'd give anything to be loved by you. "We can be no more than friends." Moisture blurred her vision.

"I don't understand. You feel something for me. I see it in your eyes."

"You are mistaken." She waved a hand through the air. "I have a terrible fault, you see, of making everyone feel cared for. I've been that way since I was a little girl." She laughed to cover up the sob caught in her throat and turned from him.

"Does this character flaw include crying when rejecting someone you have no feelings for?" Again he moved her chin to face him. She lowered her lashes as two traitorous tears sped down her cheeks. He thumbed one away.

Oh, God if You're there. Please give me strength. She closed her eyes beneath his touch. His kissed the other tear away. Before she could jerk back, his lips descended onto hers. His breath filled her mouth.

And she lost herself in his taste, his male scent, the tender touch of his lips, so unlike other men who'd kissed her.

Her skin tingled. Her body grew weightless and drifted toward the sky. If only she could fly away with James, away from everyone, away from her past, away from Dodd.

What am I doing?

Shoving him back, she punched his chest, grabbed Stowy, and inched away with one thought in mind. Get as far from James as she could. The branch bounced, she shrieked, lost her grip, and toppled to the bough beneath her. Landing hard. Squashed between her chest and the bark, Stowy let out a painful howl.

"Don't move, Angeline. Stay there." She could hear the creak of wood as James made his way down to her.

No! He would touch her, hold her, rescue her again. She couldn't allow it. Her heart couldn't take it. "Stay away!" She struggled to rise. Cradling Stowy, she slid to the branch below. It was too thin, too slick from rain. She slipped. Her feet met air. One arm flailing, she reached for another bough, but her hand scraped over bark. Her leg caught on something. The rip of fabric filled her ears. Along with Stowy's mournful screech.

Splat! Angeline landed on her derrière in the mud. Stowy flew from her arms and alighted on a pile of broken branches beside her.

"Angeline! Are you hurt?" James shouted.

Water soaked through her skirts into her petticoat and nightdress. A croak brought her gaze to a toad sitting atop a rock to her left. A giggle burst into her throat, but she forced it back. "You! You made me fall!" She lifted her hands and shook off the mud as James skillfully navigated the tree, swung down on the final branch, and landed on the ground with a splash.

He started toward her. "If you hadn't been in such a hurry to get away from me—"

"Because you made improper advances!"

Stopping, James cocked a brow. "If I had made improper advances, you would not have fallen, I assure you."

"What is that supposed to mean?" She reached for the gun at her waist, but her hand met the empty belt around her skirt. "Are you saying you would restrain a woman against her will?"

"Missing your pistols, your dragonship?" He quirked a grin that made her want to giggle, to toss mud at him, to drag him down with her until they both burst forth with laughter. But instead she forced anger into her tone. "If you wish me to be a dragon, I shall oblige you!" She had no idea what that meant, but it was the only retort she found on her lips.

He chuckled. "Dragon or not, I would never restrain a woman."

"Why? Because you are so captivating, so virile, so exciting that women swoon in your arms?" Though honestly she couldn't blame them.

This, however, seemed to hit the mark as the grin faded from his lips and he lowered his chin with a sigh.

Angeline felt like sinking into the mud.

Instead, James extended a hand to assist her up. Refusing it, she struggled to rise, got caught on her skirt, fell down again, growled, then shoved herself up to stand. She wanted to thank him for saving her life, for risking his own for the likes of her, for being so wonderful and charming and honorable. . .

Reaching up, he wiped mud from her cheek. She stepped back. "We should get going. Come Stowy." She turned to gather the cat in her arms, but he leapt into James's instead.

Clutching her skirts, she started sloshing back toward town. *Traitor.*

CHAPTER 15

The crash and fizzle of ocean waves—normally soothing to Angeline—grated over her like a washboard on skin. Still, she was thankful to see the storm's retreat on the horizon, waving farewell in robes resplendent in amber, coral, and ruby—a promise for a sunny day on the morrow. Yet no amount of sun could brighten the colonists' dour mood. Especially after a day of scouring the jungle for castoffs left by the river, hidden booty shoved behind bushes and stuffed up trees in some kind of demonic treasure hunt. And always the trinket disappointed. A shirt here, a hat there, an iron pot over there, but not enough left of the things they really needed.

"Thank God we found some of our clothes scattered about." Ever the optimist, Eliza plucked a sopping pair of trousers from a bucket and flung them over the line the men had strung between palms.

Angeline finished hanging a petticoat and stretched the aches from her back. She'd given up on the ones in her legs long ago.

"Mercy me, Eliza." Magnolia stuffed a wayward hair into her bun. "Our entire town is destroyed. We have no homes, no food, no cots, and now we are forced to sleep on the sand like burrowing crabs. I hardly think a few clothes will aid our situation."

Angeline quite agreed, but she wouldn't say so. There was already far too much complaining firing about the camp.

"Without proper attire we'd be *naked* crabs burrowing in the sand." Eliza smiled, an infectious smile that caused all of them to grin, Sarah included, who assisted with the laundry on Angeline's left.

However, Magnolia's smile soon faded. "Honestly, what is to

become of us? The entire town is washed away. Not a single hut remains."

Angeline stooped to retrieve a dripping coverlet, her gaze drawn to James chopping wood down the beach. After the colonists had hauled everything they could find of use down to the shore, Blake had organized the men for different tasks. Some chopping wood, others building shelters, a few fishing. He'd asked some of the women to search for fruit, though most of it had been stripped from the trees by the mighty claws of the river. The rest of the colonists scoured the jungle for scattered goods. All except Dodd and Patrick, who insisted their time would be better spent looking for the gold that would—how had Patrick put it?—*rebuild the town into a thriving metropolis*. Angeline had met too many men like Patrick Gale in her life to give credence to a single word he spoke.

As if in defiance of her thoughts, Sarah added, "Towns can be rebuilt, Magnolia."

"And they can be destroyed again, as well," came the lady's retort.

Destroyed was a fitting description of New Hope. Demolished might be better. Every hut, bamboo pole, palm frond, and even the fire pit had been washed away. All that remained as evidence that civilized people had lived there was the stone oven beneath where the meeting shelter had once stood. In fact the ground was still so soggy and littered, there was no place to sleep. And it would take weeks to pick up all the debris in order to build again. Which is why they decided to settle on the beach for now. Though much of the sand near the mouth of the river had been washed away, this northern section of coast remained unscathed, save for mounds of wet sand and downed palm fronds.

So much loss. So much sorrow. As Angeline glanced at the colonists scattered across the beach set to various tasks, she wondered what would become of their attempt at a Southern utopia. Already she'd heard rumblings from some who wanted to quit and go home.

Two of those mumblers headed toward them now. Magnolia's parents. Mr. Scott, gray hair askew, face red, arms stiff by his sides, marched in front of his wife who scurried along behind him, wringing her hands while the torn fringe of her hem dragged over the sand. Mable, their slave, followed on her heels.

Magnolia released a heavy sigh as they halted before the clothesline.

"Magnolia," Mr. Scott began, lifting his chin as if addressing an assembly. "We have decided to return to Georgia on the next ship. Brazil is obviously no place for civilized people."

"And dearest"—Mrs. Scott placed a hand on her daughter's arm, her tone desperate—"we want you to accompany us."

"In fact, we insist," Mr. Scott added.

Magnolia released an annoyed sigh. "In case you have forgotten, I am married now, Father."

"Do you think I could forget such a travesty?" Glancing around, he restrained his rising voice, or rather attempted to. "Since you ran off with that ruffian, I haven't had a full night's sleep!"

His belligerent tone drew a few gazes from others down the beach, including Moses, who halted from chopping wood to wipe sweat from his face. His eyes latched upon Mable.

"I didn't run—" Magnolia began then gave a tight smile and faced her friends. "Why, excuse me, ladies." Her Southern drawl reappeared as she lifted her skirts, looped an arm through her father's, then escorted him and her mother out of earshot.

Angeline's pity rose for the lady. Though Angeline had lost her father at a young age, he'd been nothing like Mr. Scott. Perhaps Magnolia would be better off without him. Perhaps the entire town would. All except Moses, whose longing gaze toward Mable spoke of a growing affection that would be severed should the Scotts leave and take their slave with them.

While Magnolia argued with her parents, Eliza eased beside Angeline, flung an arm around her shoulder, and squeezed her close, causing her bruises to throb. But the affection of such a good friend was well worth the pain. "You are very quiet, Angeline. Such an ordeal you endured being swept off by the river. We were so worried for you."

Angeline smiled. "I thought for sure I would drown."

"It's amazing James found you at all."

"A miracle," Sarah said as a breeze nearly tore the garment from her grasp. "And you and James spending the night in a tree?" The mischievous twinkle seemed so out of place in the pious woman's eyes. Under normal circumstances, Angeline would have feigned a giggle or a blush or something else appropriate for maidens. Instead she only felt shame and sorrow.

Her traitorous eyes swept to the man in question, standing over a log, ax hefted above his head, muscles strained. And she remembered the feel of those muscles encasing her in a fortress of protection. Not since she'd been a little girl snuggled in her father's lap had she felt so safe. And loved. The loss of him joined the ache in her heart for her father. "He's a good man."

"And quite fond of *you*." Eliza shook water from a man's torn vest and held it up to the fading light.

A child's belly laugh drew Angeline's gaze to Thiago playing with Lydia in the sand. Anxious to change the topic, she gestured toward the Brazilian. "He's so good with her, Sarah. You must be pleased."

"Yes." Seemingly lost in her thoughts, Sarah smiled as she glanced at the handsome Brazilian swinging six-month-old Lydia around in a circle. Perhaps a woman like Angeline would never marry and have children, but a saint like Sarah certainly deserved happiness.

Leaves parted, and Dodd emerged from the jungle just feet from where they hung clothes. His wink sent a chill scraping down Angeline before another chill followed when Patrick Gale sauntered onto the beach after him. Had they found their gold? No. Not from the scowl on Patrick's face. Another man, one of the farmers, burst from the trees, his chest heaving, his eyes searching the beach and then dashing toward Blake, shouting, "Mr. Lewis is missing. We can't find him anywhere!"

꧁◆꧂

James tried to keep his focus on the flames instead of on Angeline, who sat on a stump across from the huge fire. But his gaze kept wandering her way. Her hair, tied in a braid, tumbled over the front of one shoulder down to her waist, where Stowy batted the curled tips. Firelight reflected such sorrow in her violet eyes, it made him long to sit beside her and make her smile again as he had in the tree. Before she'd become a dragon and spurned his kindness. Ah, the woman's fickle moods! He would never understand her. Perhaps that was part of her allure. Yet, despite that allure and her insistence otherwise, he *knew* she felt something for him.

Resisting the urge to approach her, he lowered to sit upon one of the logs framing the massive fire, where colonists assembled for a town meeting. Or a beach meeting, since there was no longer a town. A salty breeze whipped the flames into a frenzy before blasting over James, filling his lungs with the smell of fish and brine and wood smoke. Crashing waves serenaded them, drowning out the drone of the jungle just yards away. One by one, the colonists took positions around the fire, some sitting, some standing, all looking hopeless and worn. It had been a long day of hard work—a long day of disappointment.

Stretching the aches from his back, James glanced toward the row of shelters he and some of the other men had managed to erect. Not nearly enough for everyone, but at least the ladies would have some protection from the elements.

"What are we gonna do, Colonel?" one of the ex-soldiers finally said when all were assembled. "What's the plan?"

"Plan? How can there be a plan?" Mr. Scott bellowed, thumbs stuck in his torn lapels. "The only reasonable course is to count our losses and head home."

Grumbles of assent followed.

Blake rubbed the back of his neck and stared into the flames. Was it James's imagination or did the colonel's shoulders sit much lower after this last disaster?

"That is one possible course, Mr. Scott," Blake said, glancing at his wife, Eliza, who stood by his side. "We could give up and leave, go back home like the failures the North claims we are."

"Better failures than dead," one man spat.

"But *have* we done our best?" Hayden spoke up, gazing over the group. "At what point do we give up on our dream?"

"When your dream is out to kill you, that's when," the blacksmith's wife muttered, followed by bitter chuckles.

"What do you make of all these disasters, Colonel?" another man asked.

Blake exchanged a glance with James, an approving glance followed by a nod James took as permission to share what he knew. He rose to his feet, shrugging off his hesitation. They were all in this together; they might as well know everything. Even if it sounded completely and utterly mad. "We think this may be the work of a supernatural force."

"Poppycock," Dodd scoffed, fingering his gold watch.

Ignoring him, James continued. "There's a book I've been translating written in ancient Hebrew. We found it at the temple."

"You talking about a curse, Doc?"

"Yes and no." James assessed the group, knowing full well most would think him unhinged. "We believe Mr. Graves released a supernatural being called *Destruction* and it is he, or *it*, who is wreaking havoc on our colony."

"Balderdash!" the baker shouted then scanned the group with a chortle. "I do believe the preacher's still got water on the brain from the flood."

Chuckles joined the crackle of the fire. Yet some of the colonists remained somber, staring intently at James, waiting for him to continue.

"Released from what?" one asked.

"A prison of some sort. . .where Graves was digging." James fisted hands at his waist while a gust of wind sent hair into his face. He snapped it away.

One of the women hugged herself. "What sort of being are you talking about, Doctor?"

Halfway above the dark horizon, the moon peeked from behind a heavy cloud, casting them in murky light. "An evil one, Mrs. Wilson. An invisible one."

More chuckles erupted.

"He speaks the truth." Blake's commanding tone silenced them. "I've seen this temple myself. It's a strange, evil place with broken chains that once imprisoned something, or someone."

"I have seen it as well," Hayden offered, much to James's surprise since the confidence man had been nothing but skeptical.

"And me." Angeline added, her gaze brushing over him—too quick for him to thank her.

Wind sprayed them with sand and Magnolia stood, brushing off her skirts. "Haven't we all had frightening visions? People long since dead appearing out of nowhere and talking to us?"

Nods bobbed around the group.

"Then why is it so hard to believe that some supernatural being is causing them?" She gave James a satisfied smile and sat back down beside Angeline.

"You mean there's more than one of them?" One of the farmers scratched his head.

As if she could stand no more talk of evil beings, Mrs. Scott released a blubbering whimper and leaned on her husband's arm. For once the man responded with kindness, drawing her close.

"Yes, we believe so," James said.

"All the more reason to leave." Mrs. Jenkins stood, drawing her young daughter into her skirts. "I don't want Henrietta exposed to some unearthly evil."

Though she said nothing, Delia, Moses's sister, nodded her agreement while gathering both her children close as well.

"Let's say this thing exists." Mr. Jenkins swung an arm around his wife. "How can we fight it?"

A crab skittered over James's boot. He flipped it aside. "I don't know yet. I need to translate more of the book."

"What if we can't fight it? What if it keeps trying to destroy us?"

Patrick, who'd been standing to the side keeping unusually quiet, now cleared his throat and pushed through the throng, fingering his graying goatee. "Come now, you can't seriously be swallowing this gibberish? Invisible creatures? Bah! There are no such things. We are intelligent, civilized people, not unschooled savages." He scanned the crowd with imperious green eyes. "I have not had a vision."

"Nor have I," Dodd added.

A cotton farmer from Louisiana stood. "Begging your pardon, Mr. Gale, madness or not, if this is something evil, all the more reason to leave. At least back home, I didn't have the devil to contend with."

"Indeed," one man yelled.

"I couldn't agree more," another added.

"Ah, I didn't say that you shouldn't leave. In fact, I think you should," Patrick added. "There is nothing for genteel people here."

James's anger boiled. "Have you considered that perhaps God brought us here to defeat this evil?" Shame burned in his gut that he hadn't thought of that until now. If that was true, God would make a way, wouldn't He?

Moses stepped out of the shadows from beside his sister. "I say we's got to try. God will be wid us."

"I ain't listening to no Negro," the cooper hissed, causing James to cringe and the crowd to start muttering.

"Sorry, Colonel, Mr. Gale," one of the ex-soldiers said, crossing his arms over his chest, "but I've made up my mind to leave. The next time Captain Barclay sails to our shores, me and my family will be on his ship headed home."

"Us too," a farmer said.

"And us."

While others stood and announced their intentions to do the same, James swept his gaze to Angeline, still staring at the fire. He wouldn't blame her if she wanted to return as well, yet she said nothing.

Mr. Scott moved to stand behind Magnolia. "You will return with us, Magnolia." His normally strict tone held a hint of pleading that drew his daughter's gaze and caused her to rise.

Hayden took her hand in his. "Perhaps you should go, Princess. There's nothing but hardship for you here right now. We will rebuild the colony, create better homes, bring a crop to harvest. And then I'll send for you when it's safe."

"Finally some sense from the man," Mr. Scott announced.

Ignoring her father, Magnolia gave her husband a look of reprimand. "Are you daft, Hayden Gale? I have no intention of ever leaving you. Not now. Not ever. We will get through this together."

Considering the way the woman had complained all day, James was taken aback. Yet even from where he stood, he felt the love stretching between husband and wife.

Blake turned to Eliza, glanced over her swollen belly, and started to say something, but she silenced him with a lift of her finger. "Don't you dare even say it. I'm staying with you."

"But the baby—"

"Will be perfectly all right. I will have this baby here in Brazil. And he or she will be the firstfruits of this new land. Proof that we can survive anything." Eliza glanced over the crowd. "And we *can* survive if we stay together."

James swallowed and lowered his gaze. Would a woman ever love him, be as devoted to him as Magnolia and Eliza were to their husbands? He glanced at Angeline. Her expression had changed from one of exhausted sorrow to tangible fear. James followed her gaze to find Dodd looking at her. . .no, more like leering at her. If he continued,

James's fist would pummel those eyes until they were too swollen to look at anyone for a very long time.

But that wasn't a very nice thing for a preacher to think.

"Sorry," one of the ex-soldiers announced, "but I still intend to leave."

"Us too."

"And us."

"Very well." Blake released a heavy sigh and circled an arm around his wife, ushering her close. "I understand. I won't try to stop you."

"We've lost everything, Colonel. Not only our homes and our meager belongings, but now our crops. Twice. And worst of all, our hope."

"We still have our lives." Hayden raked a hand through his hair. "And each other."

"What of Graves? What of Lewis?"

"Graves died from his own foolishness," Blake said. "And we will search for Mr. Lewis tomorrow."

The fire sputtered and snapped as a wave thundered ashore.

"He probably drowned when the river rose," one woman offered.

Thiago tossed a log into the fire, shooting sparks into the black sky. "Or he become Lobisón —Wolfman."

Groans and wide eyes filtered over the group. A woman gasped.

James chuckled. "Hogwash. Come now, everyone. Let's keep our wits about us."

"Wits? You go on about curses and temples and supernatural beings, and you're telling *us* to keep our wits about us?"

James rubbed his chin. The man did have a point. Yet he didn't have time to respond before a distant sound echoing through the trees made the hair on his arms prick to attention.

The eerie howl of a lone wolf.

CHAPTER 16

Angeline hefted the basket of fruit in her arms. With only one orange and a half-spoiled mango, it wasn't terribly heavy, but she had an ache in her shoulder that wouldn't go away. Perhaps it was sleeping on the sand these past two weeks. Or perhaps it was an ache to match the one in her heart every time she saw James and had to force herself to avoid him. Avoid talking to him, seeing him, being anywhere near him. Which was difficult to do when they lived on the same beach. On the occasions when their eyes met, she saw the hurt in his, the yearning. And she wanted to scream, to cry. . .to run into his arms. But that was not possible. Not with Dodd watching her every move, slinking around the beach and jungle, eyeing her like the wolf that serenaded them each night with its baleful howl.

Was it possible that Mr. Lewis had, indeed, transformed into the beast? For they had not been able to find hide nor hair of him since the flood.

She glanced into the canopy, searching for fruit, but instead saw dozens of colorful birds hopping from branch to branch, trilling their happy tunes. Always happy. Always carefree. Oh, how she envied them. They had naught to fear from flood or ants or invisible beasts. A verse from scripture rose in her mind. . .something about how birds neither sow nor reap, but God cares for them. She pushed it aside. Comforting words meant for others. Not her.

Lowering her gaze, she scanned the delicate green lace of life that surrounded her. Where had the other ladies gone? Magnolia, Sarah, and the two other women who'd been sent in search of fruit. Nothing but ferns and vines and leaves large enough to be gowns met her gaze. Not to mention the occasional spider or lizard or frog. But they didn't bother her. She had bigger reptiles to deal with. Still, Blake had instructed the women to stay together.

In truth, she relished the time alone. Sharing a shelter with four other women had not allowed her any time to think, to decide what to do about Dodd. Even though, deep down, she already knew her answer. And that answer saddened her more than anything.

Batting aside a leaf, she moved forward, her boots sinking into the still-sodden ground. Perspiration dampened her neck and brow and made her long for the ocean breezes she left behind only moments before. Prying her shoe from the mud, a memory forced its way into her thoughts. Of a dark night and another muddy puddle. Of another pair of shabby boots—with holes in the toes—stepping into the muck as she made her way down the streets of Richmond. The icy mire had seeped into her stockings and crept up her ankles until her legs shivered. Not wanting to risk being recognized, she'd hid her face in the folds of her cloak as she kept to the shadows—hungry, cold, wet, and wishing for death. Angeline tried to shake away the memories. The depths to which she'd been reduced—begging on the streets like an urchin.

Little did she know, she would sink lower still.

She drew in a deep breath of the humid air so full of life, hoping some of that life would infiltrate her soul. But instead she heard crackling rising from all around. Fearing what it foretold, she stopped and squeezed her eyes shut. But the voice slithered over her ears nonetheless. It was the same voice of kindness, of charity, she'd heard that night over two years ago. The voice that had saved her.

And brought her to her doom.

She opened her eyes.

"Oh, you poor dear," Miss Lucia said, clipping Angeline's chin and turning her face side to side, just as she had done that dark night. "Such a fright. And so thin. Why, I declare, you are in dire need of a hot meal and an even hotter bath. I have just the thing for you, darling. Now, don't you worry."

Angeline could do nothing but stand and stare at the woman with her ample bosom and rounded hips, bedecked in glitter and feathers just as she had been that night. She'd been stunned by the woman's interest in her. Wary, of course, but too hungry and tired to care. Now, with Miss Lucia standing before Angeline looking as real as any of the trees that circled them, all the emotions of that night returned—raw and festering like open sores. She had allowed Miss Lucia to take her to an upstairs room at the Night Owl. She'd eaten her food, taken a bath, and slept in one of her feather beds. The woman had been so kind, Angeline wondered if this was what it felt like to have a mother, an older woman to care for her and love her and teach her the things women must know. On Angeline's fourth day at the Night Owl, she discovered Miss Lucia would skip over the first two and only provide the third.

Now, placing a jeweled hand on her rounded hip and tapping her fan to her chin, Miss Lucia sashayed around Angeline. "Yes. . .yes. . . you will do nicely." She had dressed her up in a lovely gown of creamy taffeta with a red silk ruche. And a bodice far too low for Angeline's tastes. "Now, you go out there, honey, and be friendly. That's all I ask in return for my hospitality." And then she'd smiled, that pearly smile of hers, made all the whiter by her brightly painted red lips.

The trees shrunk into tables, branches into men with tankards. The leaf-strewn ground into a floor strewn with other far nastier things: spit and ale and tobacco. And Miss Lucia nudged her into the crowd. All eyes shot to her like darts to a bull's-eye, leering, salivating. Hands reaching, swatting her behind, pulling her onto laps.

"Leave me alone!" She shoved them away. "Don't touch me."

A meaty hand gripped her arm. She struggled to free herself. "Let me go!"

"Angeline!"

She looked up and saw Dodd smiling at her with a grin of merciless victory. The tables and men faded. One glance over her shoulder told Angeline Miss Lucia was gone as well. Yet Dodd remained. She tore from his grasp and backed away, rubbing her arm. "You're real."

"In the flesh, my dear. But I believe you were having a dream. Or perhaps a vision?"

"A nightmare since you were in it." She reached for her pistol but remembered she'd lost it in the flood. Then, stooping, she picked up her basket and fruit. At least she'd have something to swat him with should he come nearer. "What do you want?"

"It's been two weeks, my dear. I must hear your answer."

"Surely you've seen that I'm no longer associating with James. In fact, I've told him to leave me alone."

A breeze lifted strands of his blond hair as his narrowed eyes assessed her. "What does that matter to me?"

"Your threat was due to our courtship, was it not?"

"*Threat* is such a nasty word. I prefer to call it an arrangement." He fingered a leaf by his side. "And yes, your pending affair with the good doctor prodded me to action, though I had hoped you would come to me on your own."

"And why would I do that?"

"Because of *what* you are." Incredulous, he looked at her as if the fact were inescapable.

Shame and fear burned in her throat. "I am not that woman anymore."

"Ah ah ah." He wagged a finger. "You can never erase such a blemish from your soul. What does the scripture say about fallen women. . . something about pigs with rings in their snouts?"

Perspiration slid down her back. "What would you know of the Bible?" What would *she*, in fact? Just snippets from her childhood when her father would read to her. Thankfully, she remembered no such reference to jeweled pigs.

"Regardless. The *arrangement* stands. You come to me twice a week and I keep your shameful little secret." Blue eyes scanned her from head to toe. He licked his lips.

She had no doubt the carnal letch would keep to his word if she complied. Even if he also knew the other truth about her, she doubted he'd give up her services to tell anyone. Nevertheless, she had but two cards to play with this huckster. She forced a complacent expression. "And why should I care if you tell everyone?"

He smiled. "Because I've been watching you, my dear, and I see how much you value your newfound friends. All that would disappear if they knew who you really were. In fact, the pious doctor may even ostracize you from the colony. He does seem to have an aversion toward trollops."

The word burned her ears and sped to the canopy, where birds gobbled it up and spit it back down. *Trollop, trollop, trollop.*

Dropping the basket, she covered her ears.

"Come now, it's not so bad. Why, you could even start up your own business in New Hope. Lord knows the town needs a little entertainment."

"Never! I came here to get away from that."

He cocked his head. "Yet we can't change who we really are, can we?"

Tears burned behind her eyes, but she forced them back. She had thought she could change. She had thought she could become a real lady.

"Perhaps you are right." She glared at him. "You are still the vulgar swine you always were."

He flinched as if wounded. But that couldn't be. The man had no heart to wound. "My point is proven, then."

Angeline stared at the ground, expecting to see her heart, her very soul bleed from her boots into the mud. She had but one card left, but it broke her heart to play it.

"I will leave."

Finally she got a reaction out of him. "What?"

"I'm going back to the States." She lifted her chin, enjoying her moment of power. "Thiago is taking a group to Rio tomorrow. I intend to accompany them." Back to a land where her past was known and she was wanted by the law. Back to horrid memories and a hopeless future.

But what choice did she have?

A slice of sunlight angled over his crooked nose as his eyes filled with malice. "I will still tell them."

"I'm sure you will." She knelt to pick up her basket and fruit and then pivoted on her heels. "Good day, Mr. Dodd."

Fingers as tight as bands clenched her arm and yanked her back. "No wench walks away from Dodd!"

Pain burned into her shoulders. She struggled against his grip and was about to kick him in the shin when James, hair askew, face red, stormed into the clearing. "What did you call her?"

⋘⊶✦⊷⋙

James couldn't believe his ears. Or his eyes. He knew Dodd had a fetish for Miss Angeline. He'd seen the way he gaped at her, licking his lips as if she were his next meal. Which was why he'd followed the man when he plunged into the jungle. But this! Grabbing her. Calling her foul names! Charging forward, he shoved Dodd, sending him toppling backward. Eyes firing like cannons, Dodd righted himself and brushed his vest where James had touched.

Despite the heat, Angeline's face was white as frost. Her moist eyes, filled with terror, shifted between him and Dodd.

He'd kill the man for frightening her. "How dare you touch her!" He barreled toward him. Dodd's eyes widened, but he had no time to react before James clutched his collar and thrashed him against a tree trunk. "What kind of lawman are you?" He ground Dodd's back into the rough bark, but fear had fled the man's face, replaced by superior smugness that ignited James's rage.

"I did the woman no harm. Ask her yourself."

James glanced over his shoulder, expecting to find Angeline relieved, perhaps even grateful to have been rescued from such a monster. Instead she trembled like the leaves all around them. "Let him alone, James," she said almost sullenly.

"He should be taught how to treat a lady," James growled.

Dodd snickered, and James tightened his grip on his throat.

"I said leave him be." Angeline's voice turned commanding. "He did me no harm."

Something was wrong. Why would such a strong, independent woman like Angeline—one who became a dragon at the slightest provocation—allow a worm like Dodd to defame her good character? James released the fiend.

Stretching his shoulders, Dodd circled him with a wary eye.

"Nevertheless, you will apologize for insulting her character," James said.

Dodd and Angeline glanced at each other as if they shared a secret. "There is no need," she said. Pleading filled her misty eyes.

"There is *every* need." He grabbed Dodd's arm and squeezed until the man winced. "Apologize to the lady."

For some reason, Dodd found this amusing. "My apologies, *milady*." The title rode like a taunt from a jester's lips.

Releasing him yet again, James stepped back, resisting the urge to punch the smirk from his lips. Dodd winked at Angeline, cast a scathing look at James, then turned and sauntered away, whistling a happy tune.

Shoving a hand through his hair, James faced Angeline. "Why grant mercy to such a beast?"

She wouldn't look at him. "Everyone deserves mercy, James. Being a preacher, surely you know that."

"Mercy is one thing. Justice another. And if Dodd isn't taught a lesson, he'll try to harm you again."

Her gaze skittered across the jungle. "If you don't mind, I should be getting back." And without another word, another explanation, or even a thank you, she turned and headed down the trail.

James caught up to her. "I know I've gone and done the unthinkable and rescued you again. How will you ever forgive me?" He intended to bring some levity to the confusing situation, but her scowl only deepened.

"You didn't, and I do." Her tone was placid, her eyes straight ahead.

James forced down a groan of frustration. "What is it between you and Dodd?"

"I don't know what you mean. I hardly know the man." She brushed aside a patch of ferns, her shoes making *splat, splat* sounds in the mud.

"He's dangerous. I see the way he looks at you."

"As he does all the women. He's harmless, I assure you."

But the quaver in her tone spoke otherwise. They proceeded in silence for several minutes, James leading the way so he could move the thick foliage aside for her.

"Please do not wander off alone again." He held back the final leaves before they emerged onto the beach. "Will you promise me that?"

"There is no need. For I won't be here to wander." She stepped onto the sand and hurried forward, no doubt desperate to relieve herself of his company.

Stunned as much by her words as by the slap of bright sunlight, James followed and touched her shoulder, halting her.

"What are you saying?" He didn't want to believe her words—prayed he'd heard her wrong.

She glanced toward the waves washing ashore, a forlorn look on her face. "I'm leaving for Rio tomorrow with the others."

Her words scattered into nonsensical phrases in his mind. He'd accepted that she didn't want a courtship. That she found him repugnant. But he could not accept never seeing her again.

"If it's because of me, I have received your message loud and clear. I understand your sentiments, and I won't be pursuing you."

Wind tussled her fiery hair. "It's not you." A glint of affection sped across her eyes. . .ever so slight. Then it was gone. She started walking. "I'm tired of sleeping on the sand and eating fruit and fish. It was a mistake coming here. Our utopia has failed. I have the good sense to know when to accept that." She didn't sound convincing.

"But you have no one back home."

"That's none of your concern, Doctor." Shielding her eyes from the sun, she gave him one final glance before she swirled about and walked away.

Leaving James feeling like one of the empty seashells lying at his feet.

❧

Angeline couldn't take another minute of this agony. It was bad enough she hadn't slept all night. Bad enough she had to witness the torment carved on James's face yesterday. Now she must endure the tears of her closest friends as they stood around her bidding her farewell. Magnolia, Sarah, and Eliza embraced her over and over, wiping tears from their eyes, begging her to stay. Another moment of such genuine affection and she might give in. Throw her past to the wind and remain with the only friends she'd ever had.

Yet how long would they be her friends once the truth was known?

The sun finally burst above the horizon, spreading its honeyed feathers over sea and land, and causing Angeline to blink. Good thing, for she didn't know how much longer she could hold her tears at bay. Releasing Eliza's hand, she hefted her satchel over her shoulder and glanced at Thiago, who was preparing his own sack for the journey. Only seven of the colonists dared to make the five-day trek to Rio, preferring to take their chances in the jungle rather than remain in the ill-fated colony waiting for a ship to arrive. She shouldn't be one of them. She didn't believe the colony was doomed. She believed they all had a chance at life and hope and new beginnings.

Her gaze landed on James in the distance. With trousers hiked to his knees, he stared at the sunrise, arms folded over his chest, waves swirling about his legs. Even now, she felt drawn to him like a plant to the sunlight. He glanced over his shoulder and their eyes met, though she couldn't make out his expression. Had he sensed her looking at him? No matter. Turning, he hung his head and started walking in the opposite direction.

She would never see him again. Now the tears finally came.

"See, you're crying." Magnolia looped her arm through Angeline's and handed her a handkerchief. "You don't wish to leave us after all."

"Of course I don't wish to leave such good friends." Angeline dabbed her cheeks and glanced over the three ladies. "But I *must* go."

"I still don't understand." Eliza tossed hair over her shoulder. "After all we've been through, surely it can't get any worse." She gave a sad smile.

"And you have been so strong." Sarah positioned Lydia higher on her hip. "Why leave now?"

"I wish I could explain, but I can't."

Lydia reached chubby fingers toward Angeline, gurgling happy sounds upon a stream of drool. Despite her tears, Angeline giggled and took the baby's hand in hers, planting a kiss upon it. "I will miss you, little one. Be good for your mother." Turning toward her friends, she opened her arms. "I will miss you *all* terribly." The women fell into her embrace. Over their shoulders, she spotted Blake, Hayden, and some of the colonists making their way toward them, no doubt to say good-bye. All except Dodd, who leaned against a rock cliff by the water's edge, scowling at her, and Patrick, who was engaged in a heated discussion with Magnolia's parents. What they argued about, Angeline could only surmise. Though the couple was anxious to leave the colony, they had opted to wait for the comfort of a ship rather than traipse through "the primordial sludge of Brazil," as Mr. Scott had put it.

Boom! Thunder split the sky. Releasing her friends, Angeline glanced upward. Nothing but white clouds against a cerulean background. Sarah scanned the horizon and shrieked. Eliza's wide eyes met Angeline's. Swinging her arms around her friends, she shoved them to the side and forced them to the ground. An eerie whine scraped Angeline's ears. The beach erupted in a fiery volcano.

The dirt beneath them trembled. Sand showered over them like hail, pelting their backs as they huddled together. No one dared speak. In the distance, a woman screamed. Men shouted. Baby Lydia sobbed. The rain of sand ceased. Angeline glanced up to see a smoking crater just a few feet from where they'd been standing.

Struggling to her feet, she helped her friends rise, her mind numb with confusion and fear. Gunpowder and smoke bit her nose. Dazed, the women stood staring at the crater. A shout sounded. All eyes fixed on the sea where the outline of a tall ship drifted like a giant sea serpent before the rising sun. Smoke curled from her charred hull.

A man on the deck held something to his mouth.

"This is pirate ship *Espoliar*. Surrender or die!"

CHAPTER 17

Sweat streamed down James's back that no amount of sea breeze could cool. Not even the continual gust swirling about the colonists as they were forced to line up at sword point before the pirate crew and their captain. Some of the men, James included, had made a valiant dash to retrieve pistols and what few supplies they had left amid a spray of grapeshot. They'd succeeded too—had even managed to gather the hysterical colonists and dive into the jungle. What they hadn't counted on was the preplanning of the pirate captain in the form of a dozen muskets that greeted them through the leaves. Now, back on the beach, those same muskets, along with a mishmash of swords and pistols, in the hands of over thirty pirates dressed like colorful parrots, tore any remaining hope of escape to shreds.

The sun, high in the sky, set the sand aflame and sea aglitter as waves crashed on the beach with an ominous thunder that matched the pounding of James's heart. Several yards offshore, the *Espoliar*, complete with a dozen bronze lantaka rail guns and a jolly roger sporting an hourglass and cutlass, bobbed and dipped with each incoming wave.

Captain Armando Manuel Ricu brazenly strolled before them, pantaloons and loose shirt flapping in the wind. A mane of curly black hair framed a long face with a tuft of dark whiskers crowning the chin. Every time he moved, sunlight glinted off dozens of jeweled pins scattered across his embroidered waistcoat like stars across the night sky, blinding James.

The twisted scene could match any of those pulled from a storybook espousing an age of piracy long since dead. Yet it was a scene James had witnessed not three months before in similar grueling detail when this same Captain Ricu had stolen Magnolia and brought her aboard his ship. If not for Hayden's ingenuity and courage, they would not have rescued her in time. Even now, after nudging Magnolia behind him, Hayden stood, arms crossed, face like flint, an impenetrable fortress protecting his wife.

James hoped it would be enough to deter the flamboyant captain. Though Eliza eased beside Blake and met the pirate's gaze with valor, the remaining women stood behind the line of men, hugging the children close. Mr. Keen, the poor farmer on James's right, couldn't stop his hands from shaking. Down the line, another man kept muttering to himself. Dodd stared straight ahead as if he'd gone numb. Yet, Patrick Gale fingered his goatee and kept glancing toward the jungle as if devising a plan of escape. Only for him, no doubt.

Mrs. Scott's whimper brought James's gaze around to see the lady swooning in her husband's arms. Moses stood beside Mable, while his sister and her children cowered behind his massive frame. James's eyes met Angeline's. He'd assumed she was with the other women, but instead she'd moved behind him. Though the corners of her mouth tightened and her chest rose and fell like a billowing sea, she gave no other indication of fear. He smiled and nodded, hoping to offer her a reassurance he didn't feel before he faced forward again.

Captain Ricu stopped before Hayden, studied him intently, then drew a knife longer than his arm and pointed it at his chest. Hayden didn't blink.

"I remember you. You striked me in my cabin. And you. . ." He dipped his head, first to one side of Hayden—and when Hayden moved to block his view—to the other side, before he reached to pull Magnolia forward. "You be the pretty thing I took to bed."

One of the women gasped.

Despite the terror screaming from her blue eyes, Magnolia lifted her chin. "*I* was the one who struck you, not this man." In a valiant effort to protect Hayden, she placed a finger on the pirate's blade and moved it aside.

But Hayden was having none of it. Eyes like slits and jaw bunching, he shoved between them, tugging Magnolia from the pirate's grip.

"Almost," he ground out. "You *almost* took her to bed. But she's my wife now, and you'll not be taking her anywhere."

Captain Ricu chuckled, turned, and said something in Portuguese to his men, which caused an outburst of laughter among the slovenly band. He faced Hayden again. "One thing to learn"—raising his voice, he shifted his gaze over all the colonists—"all must learn. I am Captain Ricu and I take what I want when I want."

Hayden clenched fists at his sides. Not a good sign. James must do something before he slugged the pirate captain and mayhem ensued, no doubt ending in an early death for them all. Stepping forward, James opened his mouth to speak when Blake beat him to it.

"What is it you want, Captain?" The colonel's annoyance rang louder than his fear. "As you can see, we have lost everything in a recent flood. We have nothing of value. So, take what you want and be gone with you."

Captain Ricu sauntered toward him. "You are leader, yes?" He sized Blake up with eyes as dark as coal, waiting for Blake's nod of affirmation. "You remember me?"

"Of course." Blake frowned.

"Then you know why I come." He flung hair over his shoulder in a feminine gesture that defied his fearsome appearance.

Dodd, standing on James's left, took a step back, trying to hide himself in James's shadow.

"We have no gold," Hayden shouted over the wind. "We didn't have any the last time you came and we don't have any now."

The captain's eyes snapped his way but halted upon Eliza. He curled a finger around a loose strand of her hair. "What say you, *bela*?"

Stiffening, Blake flung an arm in front of her. She pushed it down. "I know of no gold, Captain."

"Search our things and see for yourself," James said.

"I no need your permit, *idiota*!" Captain Ricu barked at James then suddenly swung around and snapped his jeweled fingers. One of his men came running with a surprisingly white handkerchief, which the pirate took and swiped over his face and neck before he flung it back at the man. With a sigh, he faced the colonists again and took up a pace before them, eyeing them up and down as if they were slices of meat hung to cure. In defiance of his ominous presence, the jeweled pins on his waistcoat made a delicate jingling sound. Or was it the bells he wore on his boots? He halted before Mr. Keen who stood beside James. "What be this?" His lip curled as he raised his knife toward the poor man.

Drops of sweat quivered on Mr. Keen's trembling jaw. James reached toward the farmer to tug him away, but sunlight blinked off the gold earring in Ricu's ear, temporarily blinding him. Mr. Keen's legs gave out, and he fell to his knees. The pirate leveled his blade beneath the man's chin and raised him to his feet, sniffing the air as if he smelled something foul. A drop of blood trickled down the farmer's neck.

Another string of Portuguese spilled from the captain's lips, ending with the emphasized word *covarde*, which brought the expected chuckles from his men.

"Leave him alone." Taking Mr. Keen's arm, James shoved him out of the pirate's reach. "Can't you see he's scared out of his wits?"

Captain Ricu turned to James with a chuckle. "And *você*? Are you scared out of these wits?"

"No."

Ricu swerved the knife toward James's chest. He felt the prick through his shirt but didn't flinch. Instead, he returned Ricu's staunch gaze with one of his own and was surprised by the intelligence he saw in the pirate's dark eyes. He also saw bloodlust. And something else that made him squirm—a crazed gleam. Uttering a silent prayer, James braced himself to be run through, to feel his lifeblood poured out upon the sand and end his days on this Brazilian shore. But the pirate suddenly whirled on his shiny heels and pranced down the line of colonists. Yes, pranced. Like a giddy schoolboy. " 'Tis a map I seek. Three maps in truth." He waved his hand through the air, the lace at his cuff fluttering in the breeze.

Patrick slid his boot across the sand and exchanged a frightful glance with Dodd. Captain Ricu, who seemed to miss nothing, headed toward them.

"What maps are these, Captain?" Blake asked. "I know of no maps."

Ricu spun about. "Three old maps. Three maps that need a fourth. Fourth one I have." He patted his pocket, dark brows flashing. "Maps that lead to vast gold to make a man rich for many lives."

James glared at Dodd. This blasted gold would be the ruin of them all!

A cloud gobbled up the sun, giving them a moment's reprieve from the heat. James rubbed the sweat from the back of his neck and scanned the pirates again. If only they could catch them off guard, storm them, and grab their weapons before they knew what was happening. But not these men. Though filthy and bearded and wearing clothes in every color imaginable, they stood soberly, some leaning on the tips of weapons thrust in the sand, others holding them at the ready, awaiting their captain's command—alert and loaded like a line of cannons on a warship.

Ricu snapped his fingers again, bringing another man with a handkerchief to his side.

A stream of angry Portuguese shot from his mouth as he flung the cloth back at the pirate, who plucked it from the sand and scurried away while another man approached with yet another cloth. This one seemed acceptable as Ricu again wiped his face and neck and tossed the cloth to the ground.

James's stomach knotted. Bad enough they'd been captured by a pirate, but a mad one?

A seagull squawked overhead as if laughing at the scene. One of the women behind James began to sob.

"They have the maps, Captain. I'm sure of it," one of the pirates spoke in perfect English before he spat a black glob onto the sand.

"I know, you *imbecil*!" Ricu snarled at him then faced the colonists with a grin. A silver tooth winked at them in the sun.

A tic twitched in Blake's jaw.

James fisted his hands at his waist. He'd about reached his limit of this lunacy. "Map or no map, no one here has found any gold. Feel free, Captain, to search our things." Join Dodd and Patrick in their treasure hunt for all James cared. It would serve the two greedy curs right.

Charging toward James, Ricu pricked James's throat with his knife. Angeline gasped.

"I am free with or without your permit, *senhor*! You keep that in head, eh?"

James eyed the man. Yes, he would keep that in his head. Along with how the pirate's own head was a bit unhinged.

Blake stepped forward. "He meant no insult, Captain, merely that we will make no trouble for you."

A moan sounded from Dodd's direction.

Ricu snorted, withdrew his blade, and ran his disinterested gaze over the colonists. "No trouble! Ha!" He tossed his knife in the air. It flipped several times, sun glinting off the metal, before he caught the handle with expert precision. "Search them and their things." At this, half his crew scattered like cockroaches in sunlight. He stopped before Blake. "You have till sunrise tomorrow, senhor, to give maps to me."

Blake swallowed as Ricu paced once more before the colonists. His eyes locked on something behind James. Shoving James aside, he grabbed Angeline by the wrist. She squirmed as he dragged her across the sand. James charged him.

A dozen pirates leapt in his path. The smell of sweat and alcohol stung his nose.

Ricu wheeled about and glanced from James to Angeline. "Ah. . . she be your *amante*, eh?" He grinned, his gaze landing on Hayden. "Take him." He snapped his fingers, and two of his men hauled Hayden at sword point from his spot. "I hang him in morning."

"No!" Magnolia shrieked, reaching for her husband.

"For what?" Blake demanded, his face a knot of fury and fear.

"He stole woman from me, cut my anchor chain. For this he die."

Tears spilled down Magnolia's cheeks as she started for Hayden, but Eliza and Blake held her back.

"Can we have the other women?" one of his men asked.

"No!" Ricu snapped, glaring their way, before turning and fingering a strand of Angeline's hair. She turned away in disgust. "Not before I try all first. Captain's. . .how do you say. . .privilege." His gaze took in Magnolia then skittered to Eliza, Sarah, and some of the other women as if he were deciding in what order to ravish them.

Every nerve in James's body ignited. "If you hurt her. . ." he seethed, nodding toward Angeline. "And if you kill this man, you will never get your precious maps."

"So, you have maps?" One dark sinister brow rose. "Good. Bring them to me when sun rises and I may not hang this one."

"And the lady?" Blake said. "You will not touch her."

Instead of answering, Ricu grinned, a wide grin that reached his eyes in a salacious twinkle before he dragged Angeline away.

Chapter 18

Give us the maps!" James gripped Patrick by the throat. The posh man stumbled backward, clawing at James's fingers, terror bloating his face.

Strong hands tore James from the villain and pushed him back. "This isn't the way." Blake's look was stern, but his eyes held understanding.

"What *is* the way with the likes of him?" James caught his breath. Fury pounded blood through his veins as Patrick coughed and gasped and finally rose to his full height, the fear on his face replaced by indignation that only further infuriated James.

"Give them the maps, Martin. . .Patrick. . .whoever you are!" Magnolia spat out through sobs. "If there is any decency in you, give them the maps. Hayden is your son!" She hung her head as more tears streamed down her cheeks. Eliza wrapped an arm around her and drew her close, trying to offer comfort that James knew was pointless.

Blake stood his ground between James and the two men who possessed the only things that might save Angeline and Hayden. Running a hand through his hair, James took a step back, uttering a silent prayer for strength not to kill both of them on the spot.

Night had flung a dark curtain over the beach, a heavy curtain that suffocated any remaining hope from the colonists. Hope that had leeched out during a day of watching the pirates scatter their few remaining belongings across the beach and then storm away, angry and spewing threats when they didn't find anything of value. A palpable terror buzzed through the camp. No one could eat. Few even spoke. And most had retired early for the evening. All except those who, unable to sleep, now sat around a fire.

His gaze sped down the beach where the pirates assembled around another fire, chortling and singing as they passed a bottle of some vile liquor. Two bobbing lanterns marked the location of the ship offshore where all was silent. No drunken ballads, no shouts, no woman's scream pierced the crash of waves on the sand. He prayed that was a good sign. He prayed the mad pirate was leaving Angeline alone. Perhaps he'd gotten drunk and passed out before he could touch her. The alternative was too horrible to consider. And he'd had nothing but time to consider it during the long afternoon. Only Blake's level head had kept James from plunging into the waves and swimming to the ship, where he would no doubt be hung alongside Hayden or shot dead as soon as his feet landed on deck. That would do Angeline no good. Though sitting here doing nothing at all was doing her no good either.

"Don't worry." Eliza followed his gaze. "We'll get her back." She hugged Magnolia. "We'll get them both back."

"You don't know that." James's hope, dare he say even his faith, had abandoned him the minute Ricu had dragged Angeline away. The look of terror in her eyes nearly did him in—would have caused his demise if several pirates hadn't blocked his path. Even then, he'd attempted to storm through them. If Blake hadn't restrained him, he'd probably be six feet under at the moment.

He could not lose her. Not like this.

"We *do* know that," Blake said. "Because we are going to give them what they want." Turning, he faced Patrick and Dodd with that commanding look of his that must have sent soldiers scrambling to do his bidding. "Even if I have to tear off every inch of your clothing, piece by piece, I will find those maps."

"Please!" Magnolia's misty eyes raised to both men. "How can you be so cruel?" She ran fingers down Stowy's fur, trying to calm the jittery cat in her lap. "Mercy me, what is a map compared to a human life? Compared to any of our lives?"

Patrick fingered his goatee. "Fools! Do you think if we give them our maps, they will be satisfied? Why, they'll probably kill us all anyway."

A gust of wind sent flames leaping into the sky as if in agreement.

James snapped hair from his face and glanced at the armed pirates commanded to patrol the beach lest the colonists try to slip away in the night. "I can't believe even *you* would allow your own son to die."

Patrick stared at the fire. "He was as good as dead the second they dragged him away."

"Don't you need their map to find this gold?" Eliza grabbed Stowy from Magnolia, trying to calm the agitated cat. "Ricu seems to believe you need all four."

Patrick eyed Dodd, and a look of understanding passed between them. "Indeed, it could be the reason for our lack of success."

A howl sounded from the jungle—a wolf's howl. An icy chill skittered across James's neck, joining the one in his heart.

"Then you have nothing to lose by giving them your maps," Blake said. "For all we know there might be no gold at all."

"There *is* gold, I assure you." Dodd nodded with a grin.

James clenched his jaw, trying to restrain his fury. "Have you any idea what Angeline might be suffering right now? Because of your greed!"

Dodd's expression was oddly remorseful. "The pirate would have taken her anyway. Just as he'll take the other women eventually."

A shudder passed over Eliza as she shared a glance with Blake. He slipped his hand in hers.

Patrick clipped thumbs in the lapels of his coat. "We could still plan an escape. Why not wait until they are well into their cups and the guards asleep and then slip into the jungle?"

"And leave your son to die, you gruesome beast!" Magnolia started to rise, but Eliza forced her down.

"There is nothing I can do about that, map or no." Patrick brushed sand from his shoulder. "In battle there are sacrifices to be made."

Shoving past Blake, James slugged the man across the jaw.

Patrick's head swerved, blood squirting from his nose. Firelight reflected flames of hell in his eyes as he righted himself and charged James. But it was Dodd, this time, who blocked the assault. "We will give you the maps. I could not bear it should the lady die." Thrusting his hand down one leg of his trousers, he plucked a wrinkled but carefully folded paper from inside what must be a secret pocket, and handed it to James. He jerked his head toward Patrick. "His are sewn into the back of his waistcoat."

Blake and James tore off the man's embroidered vest before he could protest.

"Of all the—! You have no right!" Patrick wailed. "This is thievery!"

Ripping the silk fabric, Blake pulled out two pieces of paper. Patrick, face erupting in rage, started for the colonel. James shoved him aside. He caught his balance and yanked his ruined vest from Blake's hands. "Thieves! The lot of you!"

Ignoring him, Blake nodded at James. "Let's go rescue Hayden and Angeline."

Captain Ricu shoved Angeline onto the bed and then plopped in a chair to remove his boots. It was the fourth time he'd entered the cabin since he'd locked her inside. His cabin, the captain's cabin, she deduced from the size and lavish furnishings. Each time he'd returned, the stink of alcohol was stronger, his eyes more glazed, his threats more insidious. Yet each time she thought he would ravish her, each time he pinned her to the bed and started to rip her bodice, he'd shoved away and stormed out in a groan of frustration.

She didn't know how much more terror she could stand. Hours of pacing, fearing the worst, followed by minutes of horror when it seemed he would attack her, only to have the cycle start all over again. He was either completely mad, incapable of performing, or perhaps he actually had a heart beneath all that glittery bravado. She opted for the first one. Part of her wished he'd get it over with and then toss her to the sharks. What was one whore worth, after all?

Not much, according to Miss Lucia, who, when Angeline had begged for a few nights off a week, had responded with, "Honey, you're comely of face and figure to be sure, but I can find a dozen girls just as pretty to replace you if you'd rather go back on the street again and starve."

The woman's voice had been so casual and amiable as she sauntered about the upstairs parlor, long cheroot in hand, that Angeline hadn't felt the true impact of her words for several seconds. When she did, her heart crumbled in her chest. The woman Angeline had come to care for as a mother had just told her she was replaceable.

Replaceable and expendable.

Ricu tugged off one boot and tossed it aside. Darkness coated the stern windows and squeezed the last of Angeline's hope from her heart. This time, the pirate would follow through with his threats. He removed his other boot and stood. Chest heaving, she braced herself against the ratty mattress. Lantern light oscillated over the fiend and shimmered off the jeweled pins scattered across the vest he now removed and pitched onto his desk.

She swallowed and wondered how Hayden fared. Once they had stepped on board, he'd been quickly dragged below. He'd cast one last glance at her over his shoulder, an attempt, no doubt, to reassure her, but all she saw was fear in his eyes. Though the thought of hanging terrified her, she envied Hayden his quick release from this earth. Her fate at the hands of this lecherous swine would be far worse.

That swine now wobbled before her, a lustful gleam in his eyes. Hair as black as night curled around his face and hung past his shoulders. Mighty shoulders. Thick shoulders that could subdue her without effort—that had no doubt subdued many women before her.

"Ah, you and me, we have good time, eh?" he muttered.

The ship rolled over a wave. He stumbled to the left. Took his eyes off her for a moment. Angeline flew from the bed to the other side of the cabin, avoiding the urge to open the door and run. Better to deal with one pirate than dozens. *Dear God, if You're there. . .* she began but then realized God would not be concerned with a prostitute getting ravished.

Ricu whirled about and grinned. "You wish to play chase?" He rubbed his hands together and took a step toward her.

"I wish for you to leave me alone."

"But I am Captain Ricu!" he bellowed, brows dipped as if he could not fathom such a thing. "I take what I want when I want." He staggered toward her.

Angeline darted behind the oak desk. Her eyes grazed over the silk handkerchief she'd seen there earlier, so delicate and out of place among the stained maps and rusty nautical instruments, and so different from the stack of common white handkerchiefs sitting beside it. An idea formed. Picking up the cloth, she waved it in the air.

Ricu halted and stared at it as if an angel appeared before him. Sorrow melted the glee from his features.

Angeline forced calm into her voice. "Who gave this to you, Captain? A lady friend, perhaps?" She drew it to her nose, inhaling the sweet fragrance of gardenias and lilac, then ran her fingers over the silk embroidered initials, AMV. There could be only two reasons a pirate would have such a thing. One, he'd stolen it from a woman he'd assaulted, or two, a woman he loved gave it to him as a remembrance. Angeline prayed it was the latter. And from the look on his face, she was right.

He snagged it from her grip, his angry scowl softening with its touch.

"Who is she?" Angeline dared to ask.

He ran his thick jeweled thumb over the initials. "Abelena Martinez y Vicario," he replied, still staring at the cloth as if he could materialize the woman from its fabric. "From Santa Domingo."

Angeline allowed a tiny smile. Inconceivable as it was, this beast, this pirate *was in love*! Completely mad but definitely in love. She thought of James. Perhaps insanity and love went hand in hand.

"She must love you very much to have given you such a personal gift."

Growling, Ricu marched to shelves built into the bulkhead. He grabbed a bottle, uncorked it, and tipped it to his lips. Angeline inched to the other side of the desk, as far away from this volatile man as she could get.

"Where is she now?" she asked, trying to settle her thrashing heart, desperate to say the right words to keep this man at bay.

He took another swig. "Home. Her father say I not have enough wealth to marry her."

"So that is why you need the gold?"

Without warning, he tossed the bottle across the room. It struck the door and shattered on the deck in a dozen glassy shards. Brandy dripped down the wood as the pungent smell filled the room. Angeline's heart crashed into her ribs. She swallowed and dared to glance his way, fearing he intended to toss her next. But his face had softened again.

"I get gold. Be very rich." He flung hair over his shoulder and swaggered toward her, his glazed eyes scanning her like a lion would its prey.

Angeline must think fast. "Would she want you to ravish women?" she blurted out.

He halted. "She will not know."

"She *will* know—deep down." Angeline placed a hand on her heart. "If she's a proper lady, she'll perceive the goodness of your heart. You cannot hide that from her. If she's a good, decent lady, the gold won't matter. It's your character, your heart that will please her most."

He cocked his head and gave her a quizzical look as if the thought had never occurred to him.

"She won't want to marry a murderer. She won't want to marry a man who hurts women."

He let out a loud belch and fisted his hands at his waist, studying her as if she were some freakish animal he'd never seen before.

Angeline lifted her chin, trying her best not to behave as frightened as she felt. "That is why you couldn't touch me all night. You love her, and you know she would be displeased."

"You not know her."

"But *you* do. Would she want your gold if she knew how you came by it?"

He fingered the dark whiskers crowning his chin. "But I am a pirate. It is what I do."

"Perhaps it's time to find another profession."

Turning, he gripped the edges of his desk and stared out the stern windows. Water purled against the hull. The deck tilted. Wood creaked and the lantern squeaked on its hinge as seconds counted down to her fate.

"Then I let my men have you." He pushed from his desk and started for the door.

Angeline's breath fled her lungs. "That would be the same thing as ravishing me yourself!"

He spun around, his brow wrinkled. "Not same. I get no pleasure from it!"

"But you would be allowing it, don't you see?" She took a step toward him. "It's the heart that must change first, proven by your actions."

He shook his head and kicked a broken piece of glass aside. "My crew will not understand."

"But you are their captain. They listen to you. They obey you. Unless of course"—she shrugged—"they do not respect your authority."

"Of course they respect!" He stretched his neck as if trying to make himself larger. Angeline allowed herself a tiny smile. This man may be a murderous, raping, deranged pirate, but he had an Achilles' heel. A woman named Abelena Martinez y Vicario. A woman who, even from a distance, could quite possibly save them all.

"And the man you have on board. You can't hang him either," Angeline said pointedly.

He suddenly looked like a young lad who'd just been told he wouldn't be receiving gifts at Christmas.

"Hayden was only protecting his lady when he came on your ship and fought you. Wouldn't you do the same for your Senorita Vicario?"

His gaze lowered to the handkerchief still clenched in his hand.

"If I not kill him, I look weak."

"If you *do* kill him, you will look weak to your lady. If you really want to change, Captain Ricu, you must start now." *Please start now!* her thoughts screamed above the blood pounding in her head. "Find your gold. Keep your men focused on that, and leave us be. That will show your lady your true heart."

"Humph." He fingered the handkerchief for several seconds, his thoughts taking him elsewhere. No doubt to his memories of this Spanish lady who dared to love a pirate.

A knock on the door startled him from his daze. He approached her and before she could stop him, clutched the fringe of her neckline and ripped her bodice down the front. Buttons shot to the ground like scattered seeds. Angeline leapt back, heart in her throat, wondering how she could have misread the man.

He shoved her onto the bed. She closed her eyes. Boot steps thumped. The door squeaked open. And a blast of salty air swept over her.

A man addressed the captain and said something in Portuguese. Angeline opened her eyes to see a sailor leering at her from the entrance. The captain replied then slammed the door in his face.

He turned and grinned. "Your people give me maps."

CHAPTER 19

J ames's worst fears became reality when, escorted by two rather
rank-smelling pirates, he, Blake, Patrick, and Dodd stepped into
Captain Ricu's cabin. Angeline sat trembling on the man's bed,
gripping pieces of her shredded bodice to her throat. Her violet eyes
lifted to his, and a hint of a smile graced her lips—which didn't make
any sense at all. He dashed her way and pulled her into his arms. She
fell against him with a ragged sigh as unavoidable visions of what
the pirate had done to her screamed through his thoughts. Nudging
her back, he marched toward Captain Ricu who stood behind his desk,
arms crossed over his bejeweled vest and a smirk of satisfaction on his
lips. James could get one punch in, maybe two, before the pirates could
stop him. After that, he didn't care.

"You will pay for—"

Angeline pulled him back and shook her head, her eyes filled
with warning, her expression telling him all was well. But how could
that be?

"Pay for what, little puppy?" Ricu chuckled.

Blake stepped between James and the pirate. "The woman returns
with us."

Ricu snorted and waved his hand at her in dismissal. "Take her.
I am done."

Growling, James tried to shove Blake aside, but once again
Angeline's gentle touch drew him back.

Still clutching torn fabric to her throat, she leaned toward him and
whispered, "He did not touch me, James."

787

He scanned her once more for any cuts or bruises. What remained of her pins could not contain the tumble of russet hair falling past her shoulders. Her skin was flushed, shadows clung to her eyes, but otherwise she appeared unscathed. He removed his shirt and flung it around her shoulders. She thanked him and buttoned it up then sat back down on the bed, refusing to look at him.

Was she lying? Trying to keep him from getting killed in an altercation with Ricu? He wouldn't put it past the sweet lady. But at least she was alive. That's what mattered now. And getting her back to camp.

Taking a protective stance beside her, James turned his attention to Captain Ricu, who was demanding to see the maps and eyeing Blake, Dodd, and Patrick as if they were cockroaches who dared to crawl into his cabin. At his nod, the chime of metal on metal echoed off the bulkheads as three crusty pirates drew swords and aimed them at the intruders. Ricu opened his palm and gave a grin of victory.

Withdrawing the papers from his vest pocket, Blake tossed them on the desk. "No need for that, Captain. We will comply." Minutes passed as Captain Ricu carefully unfolded each map and laid them side by side on the desk. Out the stern windows, a murky ribbon of gray burst on the horizon as the sun attempted to rise on the macabre scene. Shadows of light and dark from the lantern above swayed over the four aged maps as everyone—even the pirates—inched closer for a better look.

Finally Ricu pointed a long black fingernail at the maps and declared, "These maps are forestries! They make no sense." He spat something in Portuguese, which was no doubt a curse.

"Forgeries," Dodd corrected.

Slapping both palms on his desk, the pirate leaned toward Dodd, his black hair dangling in twisted curls over the maps. "You try trick Captain Ricu!" One of his crew pressed the tip of his sword in Dodd's back.

Dodd's face blanched. "No, I was just correcting. . .repeating—"

"Captain, if I may," Patrick intervened. "These maps are genuine, I assure you. In fact"—he straightened his string tie and put on a superior look—"I know the secret to translating them, and if you are willing to bargain—"

The captain laughed, a disbelieving laugh that ricocheted off the deckhead. "Who are you to know such secrets?"

Patrick lifted his chin. "Why I—"

"Our deal was only the maps," Blake interrupted. "We have delivered them. And now we demand you leave us and our colony be."

"Demand!" Ricu gave a hearty chuckle, his pirates joining in. But then with a snap of his finger, his men silenced, and fury overtook his features. "No one demand Captain Ricu."

"But there's gold. I know there's gold," Dodd began to whine. "I got my map from a very reliable source. Paid good money for it. And he"—he thumbed toward Patrick—"has figured out how to read them." He picked up one map and placed it atop the other. "You see, you have to bend—*ouch!*" Dodd glared at Patrick who settled his foot back onto the rolling deck.

Ricu slapped Dodd's hand away. "No touch maps." Then, opening a drawer, he pulled out a bottle of amber-colored liquid, took a long draught, capped it, and slammed it on the desk before he glared at Patrick. "You tell me secret now."

Patrick fingered his goatee, his lips slabs of stone.

At the snap of Ricu's jeweled fingers, one of his men leveled a blade at Patrick's back. The normally composed man's eyes began to twitch.

The ship teetered over an incoming wave, creaking and groaning. While the rest of them stumbled to keep their balance, the captain stood, arms crossed over the trinkets shining on his waistcoat, like a statue of some Greek god demanding worship.

"I am Captain Ricu, and I take what I want when I want." Eyes as dark and hot as coals measured each one of them like a judge deciding a prisoner's fate. He rubbed the handle of a pistol stuffed in his belt, and James wondered if the captain was trying to decide who to shoot first. He knew they had nothing to bargain with. Pirates were notorious torturers, and James was sure Patrick or Dodd would sing like birds at the mere threat of such measures. He was also sure the captain knew that as well.

"Captain, we will gladly share our knowledge of these maps as long as you promise not to harm any of us and release Angeline and Hayden," James put forth.

For once Patrick didn't protest. Though it may have had something to do with the blade jabbing his back.

The creak and moan of timbers marked the unbearable passage of time as the mad pirate considered James's proposal. Or perhaps he was merely deciding the most painful way to kill them all. Golden sunlight cast an amber halo around Ricu's dark curls. Plucking a handkerchief from his desk, he wiped his face and neck, his gaze assessing each one of them in turn. Finally, he grinned and waved the cloth through the air. "I agree. You"—he pointed toward Patrick—"tell us how to read maps." He gestured for his man to lower his blade.

Patrick released a breath. "And what do I get in return?"

Ricu gave an incredulous huff. "Your lives."

"We accept," Blake and James said in unison.

Standing knee deep in water, James extended both arms toward Angeline. "May I?"

She knew he intended to carry her from the small boat, but just the thought of being held in those powerful arms, nestled beside that powerful chest, sent warning bells off in her heart. It was bad enough James had rescued her once again—along with the others—but then the man had gone and stripped to his bare chest in an effort to preserve her modesty. No man had ever wanted to preserve her modesty. Quite the opposite, in fact.

She nodded her assent. But as she feared, the way he lifted her as if she weighed no more than a cat, the feel of his muscles encasing her in steel, his masculine scent, and the look of protection and care in his bronze eyes threatened to break down all the barriers she'd so carefully erected between them. Thankfully, once he put her down on the sand, Eliza and Magnolia dashed toward her, flinging their arms around her and asking how she fared. After ensuring them she was well, both ladies flew into their husbands' arms. As the pirates rowed back out to the ship, Dodd and Patrick slogged off, grumbling under their breath.

"I'm all right, Princess." Hayden pushed his overzealous wife back. "Not a mark on me, see?"

"We are all safe, for now." Blake smiled at his wife, who quickly slipped from his arms and eased beside Angeline. "Are you sure you aren't hurt?" Eliza brushed hair from Angeline's face, her gaze suddenly dropping to James's shirt. Fear laced her eyes. "Oh, you poor dear. Come with me." She swung an arm around her and started off when Angeline stopped her.

"He never touched me." She faced her friends.

"But your. . .your bodice. . ." James said.

"He ripped it, yes, but only to make his men believe he had ravished me."

"I don't understand." Blake's dark brows bent.

"I can't say that I completely do either." Angeline leaned onto Eliza, suddenly feeling weak. "He fully intended. . ."—her voice muddled as if the fear of her predicament suddenly struck her—"intended to. . ."

Eliza squeezed her close.

Angeline drew a breath. "But the man has a weakness."

"Aye, he has barnacles for brains." Hayden snorted.

"Better than that. A lady." Angeline smiled. "Crazy as it sounds, Captain Ricu loves a real lady. And he wants to change his ways so she'll love him back."

Looks of shock assailed her, followed by declarations of disbelief.

"It's true. It's why he didn't touch me. It's why I believe he won't allow his men to harm the rest of the women either. They fear him. With good reason." She trembled as memories of his many attempts to ravish her saturated her thoughts. "I convinced him his lady would be abhorred at such a thing."

"You placated him for one night," Hayden said. "I don't trust him. Men like him rarely change."

"You changed." Magnolia smiled at her husband.

Without warning, Stowy leapt into Angeline's arms and began burrowing beneath her chin, bringing levity to the somber topic and a speck of joy to Angeline's heart. She kissed the cat on the forehead and stroked his fur as purring filled the air.

"Seems you were missed," Eliza said.

"By more than the cat." The tone of James's voice chipped away at her heart. But she couldn't allow it.

"I agree with Hayden," she said. "I was spared, we were all spared this time. But I have no faith this man's love or desire or whatever it is he harbors toward this woman will placate his passions forever."

"Indeed. He's as volatile as a rusty cannon." Blake shifted weight off his bad leg. "We must find a way to escape, to sneak back to Rio. Perhaps the emperor would allow us to move to another location."

"But we haven't paid a single *réis* for this one." James shook his head and squinted toward the rising sun.

Blake flattened his lips. "I'm not admitting defeat. Not yet. We can still start a colony elsewhere." Nods of affirmation spread among Angeline's friends. But she didn't join them. How could she? Though her heart seemed ready to crack in a million pieces, she still intended to part ways with these beloved people. She had no choice. Extricating herself from Eliza's calming embrace, she gave an excuse of exhaustion and walked away, ignoring their offers of help, ignoring the look of love in James's eyes, and ignoring the tears that now spilled down her cheeks.

CHAPTER 20

Angeline finished the final chorus of "Hark the Herald Angels Sing," and sat down in between Eliza and Blake on one side and Sarah and Lydia on the other. She could hardly believe it was Christmas Day. Dates seemed of little consequence here in Brazil, especially with all the tragedies of late. And with the sun blaring overhead, it certainly didn't feel like Christmas, neither in temperature nor in temperament, for no one was very cheerful. Yet when James insisted they hold a service, they'd all banded together to haul logs and stumps and a few chairs salvaged from the flood to form pews in their thatched-roof church.

With the crash of waves thundering behind him, James rose to stand before the crowd, open Bible in hand. His gaze landed on something behind Angeline, and his slight flinch caused her to glance over her shoulder at the two pirates sitting in the back. She'd seen them come up during the singing but assumed they'd leave when the sermon began. Yet, there they sat, arms crossed over their colorful waistcoats, scarves blowing in the wind, pistols and blades sticking out everywhere like bloodthirsty porcupines, and looking like attending church was a normal occurrence. In fact, the past two weeks of living among pirates had proven much easier than everyone had anticipated. Though they drank too much and their leering gazes caused some of the ladies to squirm, they kept mostly to themselves. Angeline was sure it was because the fear of their captain was stronger than their passing passions.

James's voice brought her gaze around as he began to recite a passage from scripture. Wind tossed strands of his wheat-colored hair in a chaotic dance that made him look like a little boy at play. No, not a boy at all. He was all man. Every six-foot brawny inch of him. Not to mention all the manly qualities stuffed within that handsome frame: courage, selflessness, determination, honesty, integrity. . .and the way he looked at her like she was worthy. Just like he was doing now.

She loved him.

If a woman like her could love a man. If the burning in her belly whenever he was near was love. If her desire for his happiness above all else was love.

James glanced over the assembly as he began his sermon. Something about Jesus and a woman at a well. An odd take on the Christmas story, but regardless, Angeline found herself mesmerized by the deep tenor of his voice, the way the sun angled over his shoulder and kissed the tips of his hair blowing in the breeze, how his bronze eyes flamed with passion while he spoke. Why hadn't she attended church more often? If only for the opportunity to gaze at him without anyone thinking her forward. Even Thiago had made an appearance today and seemed enthralled with the message as he sat on the other side of Sarah.

Angeline smiled at little Lydia asleep in her mother's arms then glanced at Eliza's rounded belly on her other side. What would it be like to carry the child of the man she loved? The thought shamelessly brought her gaze back to James. Despair threatened to send her running from the crowd, but instead she lowered her eyes to her hands clasped in her lap. She could entertain no hope of such joy as long as Dodd threatened her. Thankfully, the annoying rodent had been too busy searching for gold with the pirates to bother with her. It had been a nice reprieve, but she knew it wouldn't last. Whether they found gold or not. Whether the pirates stayed or left, Dodd was not the type of man to give up what he considered a worthy prize.

Which is why she must leave as soon as possible. Before her feelings for James grew to the point of shattering her heart. Before Dodd blurted out the truth and exposed her shame to everyone. She couldn't bear the rejection, the shock, the looks of disdain from people she'd grown to love. As if sensing Angeline's angst, Eliza gave her a tender smile and placed a hand over hers, bringing tears to Angeline's eyes. She gazed out to sea.

"She was a prostitute, a woman who'd had five husbands and was living with a man out of wedlock." James's voice sharpened in her ears. "Yet Jesus traveled a day's journey out of His way just to speak to her, just to tell her God loved her." He took up a pace before them, eyeing them each in turn. "To tell her to stop drawing from a broken well that did not satisfy, but to receive the living water He offered. " His eyes latched upon Angeline's. "Then she would never thirst again."

The light in those eyes seemed different somehow. Brighter, dazzling even. And they seemed to pierce her very soul. Forcing back the mist in her own eyes, she lowered her gaze to the sand by her shoes. Yet, his words kept repeating in her mind. Jesus traveled a day's journey out of His way for a prostitute. To tell her God loved her. Could the same be true for Angeline? She began to tremble. But if God loved her, why had He allowed so much heartache? Why had He allowed her to become what she'd become?

A fire crackled. A voice, distant and sounding much like the thunder of the waves called her name. Her eyes flew up and scanned the shore. A man stood with his back to her, staring at the sea. He turned around, his braided frock coat flapping in the wind and a suggestive grin on his rounded face. "Come here, Angeline. The water's warm."

Her heart dropped like a stone.

"Angeline," another man called, drawing her gaze to the other side of James, where the old trapper, Swain, stood beckoning her toward him with a curled finger. "Come for a swim, my precious peach." Perspiration dampened her skin. Her breath clogged in her throat. No. Not two of them here at the same time! And why now?

To remind her she wasn't worthy enough to sit in a church service. That she had no right to be here among proper folk. She glanced around the crowd to see if anyone saw the men when a third one appeared just feet away. Charlie Wilkins, one of her regulars. Smoke curled from the cigar hanging from his lips while he counted out dollars in his hands, just as he used to do when he paid for her services. He glanced down at her, eyes cold and void. "Go in the water, Angeline. You aren't clean. You must be clean to sit there."

Angeline couldn't breathe. She couldn't live with the memories anymore. She wanted to shut her eyes and never open them again. She *did* shut her eyes, but the voices continued. She covered her ears, but they rang in her head. "Whore. Hussy. You'll never change. The water, the water, it's the only way," all three men brayed in unison. Eliza squeezed her hand. James's voice grew distant. Sweat slid down her back. Every breath became a struggle. "Filthy whore. The water will cleanse you. The water, the water, the water—" Punching to her feet, she barreled straight through ole Charlie and dashed toward the sea with one thought in mind. To silence the memories. To end the pain.

James plowed into the sea. Waves assaulted him, stinging his eyes and shoving him back. In the distance, green fabric floated atop water where Angeline's russet hair had disappeared. He fought off the next wave and dove into the foaming churn. Memories of another rescue at sea flooded his mind. Of another attempt by Angeline to end her life. God be praised, this time they weren't in the middle of the ocean, this time he'd had enough warning. He'd seen her fidgeting in her seat, watched her frightened gaze skitter back and forth across the beach, saw her chest bellow like the wind, her lips tremble, her hands cover her ears. He had some idea as to the cause and intended to conclude his sermon posthaste in order to come to her aid. But no sooner had he glanced down at his Bible than she had already reached the water's edge.

No vision, no matter how terrifying, was worth her life. Something else affected this poor lady, and James had allowed his affection for her to get in the way of being her spiritual advisor. Curse him for being a selfish fool! He thrust upward for air, gulped it down, then dove again. His hand touched her gown. Grabbing the fabric, he pulled her toward him and circled an arm about her waist. He kicked and they sped upward, breaking through the surface with a mighty splash. She spit and coughed until air took the place of water in her lungs. A wave thundered over them. James fought to stay afloat. She slumped against his chest, weighing them down. Breath heaving, he swam to shore, inhaling more water than air. Strength slipped from him with each thrust of his arm through the water. They went under. They weren't going to make it. His feet struck sand. Gathering his remaining strength, he shoved against the seabed, burst through the surface, and hoisted her in his arms. Bracing against the crashing surf, he carried her to the women's shelter and laid her on a bamboo pallet. Eliza ushered him out, promising to care for her as the other women gathered around.

Lungs still wheezing for air, James took up a spot beside Blake just outside the hut. He wasn't going anywhere until he heard how Angeline was doing. He knew she was alive. He'd heard her breathing. But he was more worried about her emotional state. An hour later, Eliza and Magnolia emerged from the ladies' hut, concern darkening their faces. A crowd formed to hear the news.

"She's well, James," Eliza started. "No harm done. At least not physical." She frowned. "She spoke of seeing visions. More than one. And voices that told her to throw herself in the sea."

Blake's jaw tightened as he stared out over the waves. Magnolia brushed the back of her hand against a wayward tear. Hayden drew her close, and she gazed up at her husband then over the crowd that seemed equally stunned by the event. "Whatever she saw, it terrified her to the point of not wanting to live."

"I can't imagine." Sarah hugged Lydia to her chest. "The poor dear."

"I say the lady has gone quite mad," Mr. Scott's bellow fell limp in the wind.

"How can you say that?" Though her voice quavered, Mrs. Scott's unusual defiance of her husband had all eyes shifting her way. "We have all seen these visions. Why, you told me just this morning that—"

"Enough, Mrs. Scott!" He moved to stand behind his wife, his shout dwindling into nervous laughter as he pressed a hand on her shoulder.

"Indeed, Mother." Magnolia snapped angry eyes toward her father. "There isn't a one of us who hasn't seen something."

"I swear there's spirits haunting this place!" one of the famers said. "If it weren't for these blasted pirates, we could all leave, go home, and be done with these visions."

Thiago crossed himself and eased beside Sarah. Lydia lifted her chubby hands toward him, and Sarah gave him a coy smile as she handed him the child. "Even I see dead grandmother yesterday," he said. "Last week, I see brother who died of sickness."

Most of the colonists nodded, understanding glances exchanged between them. A few groaned and stared at the sand. Others gaped vacantly at the sea as if unwilling to even think about what they'd seen.

Confirming James's fears.

"The visions are getting worse." He ran a hand through his damp hair and released a sigh, heavy with dread. "I need to get back to the book. Interpret more." He lifted his gaze to the storm brewing behind Blake's gray eyes. The same one that brewed in James's stomach. "This has got to stop before we *all* drown ourselves in the sea."

CHAPTER 21

Magnolia eased her face over the surface of the water, searching past the ripples for any sign of youth in her reflection. Was it her imagination or was there a clarity to her eyes that hadn't been there before? A plumper look to her skin? A few blond hairs among the gray. She sat back with a sigh. Mercy me, becoming beautiful on the inside was sure taking a long time! *Lord, can You work a little faster?* She bit her tongue, wondering if she was wise to ask for such a thing. Didn't that mean more struggles and trials? *Oh, bother, Lord. You will be gentle, won't You?* Of course He would. He was her Father, and He had proven Himself loving and trustworthy. She smiled and ran fingers through the cool water as a flock of thrushes warbled a happy tune above her. Eliza had sent her to find some fresh water for Angeline, and along the way, she'd happened upon this lovely creek surrounded by clusters of multicolored ferns. Which made for a bit of privacy off the beaten track. Privacy that had become a rare commodity since they'd moved to the beach, and Magnolia couldn't help but stay just a moment and breathe in the peace.

If only peace would settle on the entire colony, but with everything that had happened and with pirates guarding their every move, how could it? Her thoughts sped to Angeline, and she lifted up a prayer for her friend. What could she have possibly seen that had stolen her hope and driven her into the sea? Perhaps it was a combination of the disasters that had struck the colony, the uncertainty of their future, the threat of pirates, and these hellish visions. If Magnolia hadn't found her strength in God, her peace in His watchful eye, she'd most likely go mad as well.

"Thank You for that, Father," she whispered. In fact, she had much to be thankful for. Her husband, for one. "And thank You, Father, for Hayden—"

"Someone call me?" The leaves rustled, parted, and her husband strolled into the clearing with the fluid assurance of a panther stalking its prey.

What a luscious sight he was. But she wouldn't let him know her delight, lest it go to his head. She feigned a frown. "You shouldn't sneak up on people. How did you find me?"

"You are not supposed to venture out alone, remember?"

"I know." She pouted. "But I wasn't going far. And Eliza needed water."

He knelt beside her, grinned, and ran a gentle thumb over her cheek. Their eyes met, and she saw a familiar gleam within his that sent an eddy of warmth down to her toes. Suddenly conscious of her appearance, she patted her windblown bun and stuffed wayward strands behind her ear.

"Where is your brush and mirror?" Hayden twirled one of her curls around his finger. "The ones your father gave you. I haven't seen them since the flood."

"Because I lost them in the flood." She stilled his finger and brought it to her lips for a kiss.

He gazed at her curiously, moving his hand to caress her jaw. "But during the mayhem, you insisted on going back into our hut for something. I thought it was to gather them. They were so important to you."

She reached inside the pocket of her skirt and withdrew the wooden toad.

Hayden's look of shock brought a smile to her lips. "You went back for that silly thing?" He chuckled.

"How could I not? You made it for me." She ran fingers over the smooth wood. "It reminds me of our time in the jungle. When we first fell in love."

Hayden swallowed up her hand with both of his and gazed at her with such adoration, she nearly melted into the sand. "I still cannot believe you are my wife." He sat beside her and kissed her cheek then leaned his forehead against hers.

Magnolia drew in a deep breath of him as her body itched for his touch. "It hardly seems like we are wed anymore." Not since all the colonists had moved onto the beach and she'd been forced into the ladies' shelter. Oh, how she ached for her husband each long night. But she wouldn't dare say such a thing. Women weren't supposed to have such longings, were they? She pressed a hand over her flat belly. "How am I to give you sons and daughters when we are never alone?"

He cocked a brow, a twinkle in his jungle green eyes. "We are alone now, Princess."

She gave him an inviting smile that lured him to trail kisses up her neck, across her chin, until finally his mouth claimed hers. Every cell within her tingled as he laid her back on a bed of soft leaves and consumed her with his love.

∽◦✧◦∾

Dodd didn't like this one bit. Not one bit. Though he'd told the pirates there was nothing but evil and death here, warned them that a man had been decapitated by some unearthly being, still they insisted on descending into the tunnels beneath the temple. Now, as Dodd felt his way along the stone walls and attempted to find footing on the uneven ground with only a single torch to light their way, a heaviness settled on him like none he'd ever felt. It squeezed the breath from his lungs and made his soul feel clogged with soot. Patrick stumbled before him with pirates fore and aft, while Moses and a few other colonists brought up the rear. All excitement faded into silence as they descended into the oppressive heat.

These tunnels were their last hope. For two weeks, they'd folded the maps together in every possible combination. Four combinations, in fact, all leading to different locations. Three of which they'd dug up until they struck water or rock. Well, in truth, it was Dodd, three colonists, and Moses who'd done the digging, while Patrick and Captain Ricu attempted to best each other with exaggerated tales of conquest and valor. Patrick Gale could charm a snake into giving up its nest of eggs. Dodd only hoped his charm continued to work on the wily pirate.

As if in defiance of the thought, Dodd tripped and nearly barreled into the pompous shyster. A sharp crag on the wall sliced his hand. He cursed as they rounded a corner and began traipsing down a set of stairs hewn from the hard dirt. Why, oh why, did the final location for the gold have to be at this gruesome temple? Once Dodd had spotted the crumbling walls surrounding the shrine, his blood had turned to needles. He'd only been here twice before, but it had been enough to convince him he never wanted to return. At least not below ground. Something evil lurked down there. If there was such a thing. Good and evil. He'd never considered himself a religious man, but the sense of depravity that permeated these ancient walls was enough to make him reconsider his standing with God.

Perhaps Moses was doing enough praying for them both. Dodd could still hear the man mumbling petition after petition to the Almighty as he hobbled behind him. Forced below at sword point, the poor freedman's face had nearly turned white—if that were even possible for a Negro.

Sweat pasted Dodd's shirt to his skin. Colorful curses spewed from the pirates' lips, most in Portuguese. The ones in English made even ole tavern-inhabiting Dodd's ears curl. At least he wasn't the only one suffering.

Up ahead, Ricu's torch sputtered and grew dim. A darkness as thick as tar seeped into Dodd's lungs. He wheezed in air. Something skittered over his hand. Stifling a scream, he drew his arm close. A stench that seemed to emanate from an open grave rose with the heat and stung his eyes.

They trekked down another flight of stairs and in through a hole that led to the first chamber. Ricu snapped his fingers, sending men to light torches and search behind every rock, every stalactite and stalagmite of the cave. While the pirates examined the alcoves and chains and weird writing on the wall, Dodd, Moses, and the other colonists hovered near the opening, saying nothing. Patrick, however, strolled through the cavern seemingly oblivious to the fiery heat, putrid odor, and the foreboding heaviness in the air. Odd. Everyone who had ever gone this deep beneath the temple had complained of all those discomforts and more. Everyone except Graves, and look where he was now. Six feet under.

The eerie *tap, tap, tap* of dripping water grated over Dodd's nerves as Patrick returned to stand beside him.

"There's another chamber below," Dodd whispered as he gestured to a barely discernible cleft in the shadows of the rock wall. "If they don't find the gold here, it could be there."

Grinning, Patrick fingered his goatee. "Then we can come back later ourselves."

Precisely what Dodd was thinking. Though the idea of returning to this horrid place sent a hornet's nest buzzing in his chest. Yet, what was a little fear and heat when it came to finding enough treasure to make him a king? He was almost ready to believe that the torture of this place might be worth it after all when one of the pirates shouted something in Portuguese and pointed toward the other opening.

Confound it all! Dodd ground his teeth together as they descended into the lower chamber. Though similar in shape and size to the one above, it seemed smaller. But perhaps that was due to the wall of rocks—some small, others as large as a man—stretching nearly to the ceiling and cutting the room in half. Instead of two alcoves, only one was hewn from the cavern wall. The same broken chains lay at the bottom of a tall metal pole that poked through the top of the circular recess. James claimed invisible beasts had once been chained in these alcoves—the same beasts that now taunted the colonists with visions. Dodd thought the idea as ludicrous as the preacher himself. A preacher who hardly preached and a doctor afraid of blood. And they were supposed to listen to him?

Shoving the torch into one of the pirate's hands, Captain Ricu spread the maps atop a flat rock and beckoned to Patrick. After folding the scraps of parchment into place, he pointed at them, his long black fingernail forming a divot on the paper. "This is right place." His voice, normally commanding and belittling, held a hint of vulnerable excitement. "It must be!" He swirled around, studying the cave as a child would a toy store before he gestured back toward the maps. "Here, see drawing of—how do you say—*sepulture, caixão.*" His sweaty forehead wrinkled as he flung a clump of long curls over his shoulder and snapped his fingers.

A pirate appeared with a white handkerchief in hand. Without looking up, the captain took it, wiped his face and neck, and tossed it back to the man.

"Coffin," Patrick offered, eyeing the strange empty alcove. "I believe you mean coffin, Captain. Yes, it does appear to be a coffin of some sort, or perhaps a prison."

Curious, Dodd inched forward to peek at the map and saw a drawing of what definitely looked like a coffin standing on its edge. Why had he not seen that before?

Ricu folded up the maps, stuffed them in his pocket, then grabbed the torch from his crewman. "The gold be here! The gold be here!" he announced, the bells on his boots and trinkets on his vest jingling with excitement. Shouts and cheers rang from his men while a sharp snap of his jeweled fingers sent them searching every inch of the cave. Dodd made a pretense of joining them, trying to hide his own excitement at being so close to his dream. Indeed the gold must be here. But now to get rid of these pesky pirates! That's when he saw the blood—a large rust-colored circle staining the dirt. Graves's blood. Where Dodd had heard the man's head had been sliced clean off.

Phantom pain seared across his throat. Clutching it, he backed away and bumped straight into Moses. The Negro's eyes were as white and wide as eggs as he continued to mutter prayers.

"Frightened by mark in dirt?" Captain Ricu kicked the stained sand in some sacrilegious tribute to poor Graves before leveling a scowl at Dodd that would make a general whimper. "Get to work!"

Dodd darted away, nearly tripping over Patrick, who knelt to examine the chains at the bottom of the alcove. An hour passed—the longest hour of Dodd's life. His lungs were scorched, and his back had nearly split in two from hauling large stones back and forth across the chamber. But not one sparkle, not one glimmer, not one speck of gold was found. One of the pirates climbed the wall of rocks and shouted something in Portuguese to his captain. A conversation ensued, and finally Captain Ricu spewed a string of curses. "We come back tomorrow," he growled. "Bring tools to dig through rocks. Bring more men. It take many weeks to break wall down, but I know gold is here!"

And from the look of zeal in Patrick's green eyes, Dodd knew he agreed. That zeal was still evident as Dodd marched through the jungle beside Patrick on their way back to the beach. Thankful to be out of the hellish tunnels, Dodd drew in a deep breath of air saturated with life and earth and moss, so opposite the stagnant smell of sulfur and rot beneath the temple. The sun withdrew her light from the trees as she dipped behind the mountains, turning the pirates stomping before Dodd into shifting ghouls.

Ghouls or not, pirates or not, Dodd longed to find hope in the situation. Still both glee and gloom battled for dominance within him. Glee at finally finding the location of the gold. Gloom at knowing he'd probably never possess any of it. But why, then, did Patrick now whistle a happy tune beside him?

"If you're withholding some liquor from me," Dodd chortled, "I'll ask you to kindly share. I could use a drink about now."

"No drink, my friend, could produce such joy as fills my heart at the moment. Liven up, there, lad. We have found the gold and it is ours for the taking." A band of squirrel monkeys cackled overhead, mimicking Dodd's sentiments at Patrick's silly declaration.

"And how do you figure that, when you know as well as I these pirates will take it all for themselves."

"Because we shall steal it from them, of course."

Ducking beneath a spiderweb, Dodd shook his head, frustration bubbling in his gut. "For the genius you claim to be, you sure aren't so smart. How are—"

"Shhhh, keep your voice down, man."

Dodd drew closer and whispered, "How do you propose to steal gold from over forty well-armed pirates when we have less than thirty men and no weapons?"

"Simple. We swindle them." Patrick flashed his brows up and down in that sinister yet charming way of his. Then at Dodd's obvious look of confusion, he continued in a whisper, "We cause a mutiny, my friend. We offer some of the crew a higher share than their captain and then take over the ship."

Dodd restrained a laugh. "That's your brilliant plan? Become a pirate." He batted aside a rather large beetle. "But we know nothing about sailing, and we still have to share."

"Only with a few. The fewer the better, to my way of thinking. Besides, we have something else they want."

"And what is that?"

"Women. Their captain forbids his men to touch them, but we will offer them freely. Why, they'll be so immersed in their carnal pleasures, they won't even notice when we run off with the gold."

Women like Angeline. Dodd smiled. No, he hadn't forgotten about their little arrangement. He'd simply been too busy and too tired to take what was his. Now that the pirates were keeping the colonists hostage, she couldn't leave and therefore had no choice but to comply with his demands. Surely his request was not a terrible inconvenience for a woman of her immoral standing. Dodd would honor his bargain. He wouldn't tell anyone about her past as long as she complied. After all, he was not without compassion. Yet, just the mere thought of getting his hands on her luscious body made him giddy all over— almost as giddy as the thought of getting his hands on all that gold.

Patrick's elbow to Dodd's ribs brought him out of his musings. "What do you say, friend? Are you with me?"

Though he detested the man and hated being called his friend, Dodd had to admit, if anyone could pull off a mutiny, it would be Patrick. With the perfect timing, a lot of charm, and the right incentives, they just might convince enough pirates to side with them. And some of the gold was certainly better than the no gold they'd get from the pirates.

As if sensing his thoughts, Captain Ricu flung his ebony locks over his shoulder and glanced at Dodd, a menacing grin on his lips. Blood churning, Dodd tripped on a root, caught his balance, and looked away. Ricu laughed and faced forward again, slashing leaves aside with his blade as if he'd been born in a jungle.

A wolf howled in the distance. Dodd shivered and peered into the shadows. They'd never found Mr. Lewis. But the idea he had turned into a man-wolf, this Lobisón, was beyond absurd! Nearly as absurd as the belief that invisible beings caused army ants and floods and visions. Visions Dodd had yet to experience. No, he would not fall prey to such lunacy. He must keep his wits about him. Especially if they were going to swindle these pirates. For Dodd knew that if Captain Ricu even suspected their duplicity, he'd slit both their throats and hang them from a tree to rot.

CHAPTER 22

"I'm sorry, James." Angeline stared at the sand. Embarrassment had kept her in the tent all day, along with a desire to avoid the man standing before her. But desperate for some fresh air, she'd finally emerged onto the beach after everyone had dispersed from supper.

And ran straight into the handsome doctor.

"No need to apologize." He shoved hands in his pockets, reminding her of an awkward schoolboy. Which only endeared him to her even more. "You are definitely keeping my swimming skills honed."

Though a slight upturn of his lips indicated he toyed with her, she couldn't help but feel ashamed. "You mock me."

"No." He withdrew his hands and touched her arms. "Forgive me. I shouldn't have made light of it. I'm just happy you're safe."

"Thanks to you." She moved from his touch. A gust of wind struck and she hugged herself. A few colonists wandered by, staring at her as if she were possessed with an evil spirit.

James took her elbow and led her aside. "What did you see, Angeline? Or perhaps I should ask who? Whoever it was and whatever they said, nothing could be so hopeless. Not when you have friends who care deeply about you."

Like you? Are you one of those friends? She searched his eyes. Flecks of gold sparkled against deep bronze in the setting sun. But she knew he was. And that made everything so much worse. She glanced at the jungle—a seemingly impenetrable fortress of green that moved and swayed and squawked and howled like a living, breathing entity. Perhaps if she dove into it, it would swallow her whole. Save her from

Dodd and her past and from making more of a fool of herself than she already had.

James reached out for her but then pulled back. "I fear I'm not very good at comforting people."

Angeline looked at him again, at the way the wind tossed his hair in every direction, at the dark stubble on his jaw. She smiled. "Yes, you are."

He shrugged. "What I meant to say before was, I'm a good listener if you'd like to tell me what's bothering you."

What was bothering her? Men from her past kept appearing out of nowhere, taunting her with words and crude gestures. Dodd was blackmailing her into sharing his bed. And she loved this man who stood before her with all her heart but could never tell him. She could never be his. "Nothing is bothering me. I thought I saw something in the water. I was tired, delirious. . . I wasn't thinking."

He blew out a sigh that spoke of disbelief.

She must lighten the mood before he delved deeper into her secrets, before that look of affection and love in his eyes made her want to tell him everything. She gave him a scolding look. "Now, what did I tell you about rescuing me, Doctor?"

He smiled, studying her. "Guilty, as charged. Do say you'll forgive me once again."

She would forgive him. She *did* forgive him. And though she was happy to be alive, she wanted no more rescues—from him or anyone else. Rescues meant trust and dependence on others. And she wasn't ready to allow herself those luxuries, to become vulnerable, open to betrayal.

Blake started a fire and the colonists began to congregate. Though the night was warm, Angeline continued to shiver.

"You're trembling," James said.

"I can't seem to stop."

"Come by the fire. We can talk later." He led her to sit on a log beside Eliza then sped off as if he couldn't get away fast enough. She didn't blame him. She not only spurned his every advance, but now she'd gone and proven herself completely deranged. A person could dismiss one leap into the sea. But two?

Stowy jumped into her lap and nudged her with his head. At least the cat didn't mind if she'd gone mad. She petted him as Eliza smiled and asked how she was feeling. Magnolia and Sarah did the same as they joined the group. Though some of the colonists stared at her as if she had a disease, Angeline found no hint of wariness or judgment on any of her three friends' expressions. Or even on Blake's or Hayden's. These people truly were her friends. She would miss them terribly. She'd heard the pirates return just after supper more excited than usual, declaring they'd finally found the location of the gold. Of course, they'd announced similar success on many an occasion, so Angeline wasn't allowing her hope to rise that they'd soon gather the treasure and leave. But if they did, that meant she could finally get away as well. Away from the voices and visions, away from the threats, and away from the torture of seeing the man she loved day in and day out, longing to be with him but knowing he would always be out of her reach.

⚓

Grabbing a blanket from among his things, James sped back to the fire and flung it around Angeline's shoulders. She looked up at him with the strangest mix of shock and sorrow. He wanted to tell her that he longed to hold her until she felt safe again. He wanted to tell her that if she'd allow him, he could love all her problems away, but Captain Ricu joined them at the fire, drawing all eyes and a few whimpers from the ladies. He'd not addressed them as a group since the first day he and his pirates had landed, and his presence now sent a tangible fear through the colonists.

"So you think you've found your gold, I hear." Blake kept his tone nonchalant.

"Aye, we have. We be sure of it." The twinkle in Ricu's dark eyes confirmed his statement as he planted hands at his waist and surveyed the crowd.

"Where?" Hayden asked as he took a spot in front of Magnolia.

"In the temple." Dodd clipped thumbs in his belt. "Can you believe it? Under our noses the whole time."

Silence, save for the crackle of the fire and sizzle of waves, permeated the group as nervous eyes skittered about. James shared a worried glance with Blake and Hayden.

"You mean the moon and stars above the altar?" Eliza asked, voicing the hope they all felt.

Pressing hair back at his temples, Patrick pushed his way through the crowd. "No. You may have those if you wish." He flicked his hand through the air. "It is the gold *beneath* the temple that is the fortune we've been searching for."

James couldn't believe his ears. Of all the places for this infernal gold to be located, why that heinous place?

"Did you actually see this gold?" Blake crossed his arms over his chest.

"Nay." Captain Ricu stepped over a log and stood before the fire. "But maps led us straight to it." He patted his colorful vest—where said maps were, no doubt, safely tucked—sending his pins sparkling in the firelight. "I should realize it before. The cannibals, the temple. It makes sense."

"I don't understand." James took a spot standing behind Angeline.

"I ne'er told you tale of how I came by map?" A blast of wind tossed Ricu's black curls behind him. "Aye, quite a tale it be." His eyes, the color of the hot coals in the fire, sped to Hayden. "Thanks be to this *estúpido* who cut my anchor chain."

Ricu, now having gained an audience, lowered himself onto a stump, leaned forward on his knees, and swept his gaze over the assembled colonists. "We drift for week, hoist and lower sails, try stay close to shore so we fix anchor and not run into ground. We find berth in inlet near the port of Itaqui. And while we fix anchor chain, we go to town's tavern.

"There we met Bartolomeu Henrigues or Blastin' Bart as he call himself, a Portuguese pirate, at least hundred years old. We had merry time drinking and playing cards into long night. But when I told him of gold I sought, he pull map from waistcoat. And this be the tale he told." The captain's eyes were alight with adventure while everyone leaned toward him to hear over the pounding waves.

"His grandfather be a fierce pirate who sail under Portugal flag and raid along coast of Brazil and Caribbean. Legends of vast amount of gold—enough to buy entire world—lure him to land on Brazil shores. A search of jungle brought he and crew to strange temple with stone obelisks and steaming water pool."

"Just like the one we found." Magnolia's voice came out numb with shock.

"Aye." Ricu nodded, fingering the tuft of dark hair on his chin. "Only few cannibals remain and pirates torture them to find where gold be, but they ne'er say a word, kept make gestures about fierce beast who come up from ground and made tribe go *louco* and kill each other."

A few of the ladies gasped, including Mrs. Scott, who leaned against her husband.

James swallowed a lump of dread.

"Then pirates see things. Dead people talk to them. Terrible nightmares. Yet they keep search for gold, dig where cannibals say it buried. But *visão* get worse and worse, and nightmares grow until pirates get crazy and shoot and stab each other." Red and gold flames danced over Ricu's face as he stared at the fire, mesmerized by his own tale. Or perhaps as frightened by it as most of the colonists seemed to be.

James gazed at Angeline, longing to see her expression, but her back was to him. Would that be their fate if they remained? If they allowed the visions and nightmares to continue? Would they all go mad and either kill each other or themselves?

"What happened to them?" Dodd asked, the joy of only moments ago slipping from his expression.

Ricu grunted. "Only four remained and fear to kill the others. They not care about gold, but they not want such fortune lost, so they draw four maps that when put together lead to gold. Then they each take map and leave Brazil. Go in different directions, get far from each other and temple. They say if God want, others bring maps together and get gold." Ricu patted his vest yet again and proclaimed, "Blastin' Bart gave me one map. These men"—he pointed at Dodd and Patrick—"had others. That is story."

Moonlight dripped pearly wax on Captain Ricu's ebony locks as the fire snapped and spit sparks into the night sky. Some of the colonists continued to gape at him as if they thought him as crazy as the pirates he spoke of. Blake gazed numbly into the fire. Eliza looped an arm through Angeline's, while Hayden drew Magnolia close, a fear rolling across his features that James felt in his gut.

"You can't dig there, beneath the temple," James spoke up, forcing authority into his voice. "You'll release the fourth beast."

811

Captain Ricu stared at him as if he were a two-headed fish that had just emerged from the sea. A similar expression twisted Patrick's features. Dodd, however, dropped his gaze to the sand.

Patrick released a long sigh. "Of course we can. And we will."

"Dodd, you know this to be true." James turned to the ex-lawman. "You've seen what we've seen. You know what happened to Graves when he released the third beast."

Though hesitation sparked in his gaze, Dodd shrugged. "I'm not sure what I've seen."

"Beasts! *Ridiculo!*" Ricu spit onto the sand, his outburst causing a few colonists to flinch.

James shook his head. "But, you just told us there *were* beasts, Captain, the ones who drove the cannibals and pirates mad."

A rumbling broke forth from the captain's throat. "You believe?" He tried to contain his amusement. "This be louco pirates' tale."

"But you believe the part about the gold." Eliza raised a brow.

Snorting, Ricu rose. "We dig up gold. You see. I am Captain Ricu, and I take what I want when I want."

And with that, he marched away.

Later that night, after everyone had retired, James sat alone by the fire with the ancient book in hand and his father's Bible lying on a log beside him. He alternated between praying, reading the Bible, and interpreting more of the Hebrew script. But his eyelids kept sinking, and he wasn't sure he was learning anything useful. He chastised himself for not studying Hebrew with more diligence when he'd been a young man learning to be a preacher like his father. But back then, he hadn't taken life very seriously, except the feel of a beautiful woman in his arms. What a wastrel he'd been and a disappointment to his parents. Especially when he'd run off to become a doctor and joined the war.

The wind had lessened, the waves now stroked instead of pounded the shore, their caress so soft, he could hear the pirates snoring down the beach. Sand crunching brought his gaze up to see Blake and Eliza heading his way, their drooping eyes telling him they'd lost their battle with sleep as well.

Blake acknowledged him with a nod before tossing a log into the fire and taking a seat beside his wife. Moments later Hayden and

Magnolia joined them.

"I *thought* you were still awake when I left the tent." Eliza patted the spot beside her for Magnolia, who sat, adjusted her skirts, and drew her long braid of flaxen hair over her shoulder. "I heard you leave and decided it was better to have company than lie in the dark alone with my thoughts." She gazed up at her husband standing by her side. "No sooner did I step outside than Hayden dashed up to me."

He winked at her. "At your service, Princess." He turned to James. "So, Doc, can the pirates release this fourth monster?"

"You finally believe?" James gave a grin of victory he didn't truly feel before he closed the book and set it down. "Only a man with pure darkness in his heart who speaks the phrase above the alcove can release the beast."

"Whose heart is darker than a pirate's?" Magnolia dug her toes into the sand.

"But what pirate knows Latin?" Eliza added with a hint of hope.

"What cannibals do?" James shrugged. "They don't have to know the language. They only need to speak the words out loud. We can't risk it. We must stop them from digging for that gold. If the fourth beast exists, we cannot allow him to be set free. From what I'm reading, his release would affect the entire world."

"The entire world? How can that be?" Hayden asked.

"Oh my." Eliza shook her head.

Magnolia grabbed her husband's hand and gazed at the jungle. "Look what *Destruction* has done to us already."

"Nearly destroyed us," Blake said.

Wind blasted over them, whirling sand through the air. Hayden coughed. "And I don't think he's finished."

"Then even if the pirates get their gold and let us go, leaving Brazil wouldn't help." Blake's forehead wrinkled.

"No." James glanced up to see Angeline emerge from the shadows, the same blanket he'd given her wrapped around her shoulders.

"I heard voices."

"We didn't mean to wake you." Eliza stood and gestured for her to sit beside her.

"I wasn't sleeping." She lowered to the log. "What are we discussing?"

When no one answered, she lifted her violet eyes to James, moist and glimmering in the firelight. Moonlight circled her head like a halo. James swallowed. Was there ever a more beautiful woman? "Pirates and beasts," he said. "Not exactly topics to aid restful sleep."

"But important ones we need to discuss," Blake added.

Stowy peeked out from Angeline's blanket and began pouncing on the firelight flickering over the cloth. "What I don't understand is how a fortune in gold came to be hidden beneath the temple," she said. "Whose gold is it?"

"I don't know," James said. "Perhaps it was put there as bait to lure men to dig up the beasts."

Blake nodded. "Good thinking, Doc. That makes sense. Why else would it be placed in the tomb of the last beast?"

"Mercy me, who would do such a thing?" Magnolia asked.

James rubbed the back of his neck. "It's almost like God Himself planted a test for mankind. Much like the tree of the knowledge of good and evil. Will man choose evil for riches? Or will he deny himself and choose good?"

"But the pirates drew the maps that led to the gold, not God," Eliza shot back.

James smiled at her defense of the Almighty. "No, but God knew they would. He also knew what the first two beasts would lead man to do. Beasts whom I believe the cannibals released accidentally."

"Is that to be our fate?" Angeline's voice caught. "Are we to end up killing each other?" She lowered her chin, and James knew she thought of her plunge into the sea.

"We won't allow it to get that far," Blake stated with authority.

An ominous growl sounded from the jungle, drawing all their gazes. Several minutes passed as the crackling of the fire joined the sound of waves lapping ashore.

"Wait, I just remembered something." Hayden rubbed the stubble on his jaw, his eyes wide. "Remember that priest I told you about? The one I met in Rio?"

James nodded. "You said he mentioned a fire lake."

"Yes, and something about a temple and pure evil. A force that could not be defeated." Hayden stared at the fire. "He also said something really odd. At the time I thought he was crazy. He told me I was one of the six. That I had to go back. That only the six could defeat the evil."

"Six." James thumbed the scar on his cheek. "Didn't Graves say something about six?"

"That's right," Eliza said. "I remember him saying that there weren't six yet. That there can never be six."

"Six what? People? Us?" Angeline asked.

"I don't know, but I'm hoping this book holds the answer." James gripped the large leather tome and drew it back into his lap.

"The answer to stopping pirates?" Hayden snorted. "I doubt it. We have no weapons and they outnumber us."

"No. Not pirates." James swallowed. "The beasts."

Hayden chuckled and ran a hand through his hair. "Yes, that's so much easier than defeating pirates!"

"Not by might, nor by power, but by my spirit, saith the Lord," James said, wondering where the phrase came from. Had he read it in scripture? Either way it poured from his mouth before he gave it a thought. The effect was astounding. Instead of snorting in disbelief or taunting him for uttering a religious platitude, his friends nodded and stared at the sudden explosion of sparks from the fire ascending into heaven.

James had no idea how they would get out of this mess. But he knew one thing: This was not just a battle against pirates. This was a battle against pure evil.

CHAPTER 23

Angeline's face hit the sand. Hard. Grains imbedded in her cheek. They filled her nose and mouth. Wind howled in her ear, holding her down. Muffled screams surrounded her. What was happening? She'd been dreaming of trains—large trains with their *chug-a-chug* clank of wheels turning on iron tracks, their huge snorts of steam filling the air, and their mighty roar when they reached full speed. It was that roar that woke her, sent her barreling from the women's shelter with Stowy in her arms.

Straight into a wall of wind that knocked her to the ground on her stomach, shoved the air from her lungs, and sent pain across her shoulders.

Through the blur of sand, she saw the pink hue of dawn lining the horizon, lifting the shroud of night. She tried to move, but it felt like a hundred bricks lined her back. Sarah dropped to her knees beside her, Lydia bundled in her arms. She tugged on Angeline's arm. Her mouth moved but the wind stole her words. Hayden clutched Angeline's other arm, and they hefted her to stand, only to be shoved backward. All three of them rammed into the women's shelter. The wood snapped with a loud crack, and the palm fronds that made up the roof flapped and flailed until the wind broke them free and they billowed toward the sky like wings of a giant bird. The other shelter beside it suffered the same fate, disappearing into the clouds as the tempest scooped up clothing and supplies and tossed them like an angry, spoiled child.

Thiago darted toward them gesturing toward a cliff down shore. Shielding her eyes from the wind and sand, Angeline scanned the beach. Blurs that must be people darted back and forth, falling to the ground and then struggling to rise again. Beyond them, the sea was calm, clear, and smooth. . .

Like glass. *What?*

The sting of sand and salt in her eyes was, no doubt, making her see things. She rubbed them, but it only made them hurt more. Still, the placid sea remained. Thiago wrapped an arm around Sarah and started toward the massive rocks at the north end of their beach where several people took shelter. James came alongside Angeline, while a call for help sent Hayden down shore. Protecting her with his body, James drew her close, shoving his back to the wind. But it kept changing direction. Stowy let out a chilling howl, and Angeline hunched to shield him between her and James as they turned and twisted their way over the sand. Or, more like, *through* the sand as there seemed to be more of it in the air than on the ground. Grains pricked her skin and clothes like a thousand needles.

Pieces of wood, clothing, even small tools flew through the air. A chunk of firewood struck James. He moaned and forged ahead. His scent of sweat, smoke, and James filled Angeline's nose, bringing her a modicum of comfort.

Once at the cliffs, he pressed her against the rock wall, kissed her cheek, and sped away to help others. The wind's violence reduced to but a slap as the cliff absorbed the force of its punch. Angeline hunkered down, along with other colonists, and shielded her face as best she could. Something struck her head. Loosening her grip on Stowy, she reached up to rub the wound. The frightened cat leapt from her arms and sprinted away. Within seconds, his black fur was swallowed up in a cloud of sand.

"Stowy!" Shoving from the cliff, Angeline dashed after him, fear cinching her throat shut. Someone called her name, but it didn't matter. This wind would toss Stowy around like a rag doll, and she couldn't stand to lose him. Dodging flying branches and half blinded by sand, she plunged into the jungle. "Stowy!" A flash of black fur up ahead kept her stumbling forward.

Leaves slapped her. Branches stabbed her. Dirt and sand assailed her. Her skirts billowed, then slammed against her legs, then flapped right, then left. Her hair flailed about her head as if someone tugged on it from all directions. She struggled for each breath, barely able to hear her own thoughts—even the ones that shouted the invisible beast's name, *Destruction*. Was he the cause of this mayhem?

"Stowy!"

The cat crouched near a boulder, his fur standing on end, his eyes skittery with fright.

Someone darted past her, dove onto Stowy, rolled onto his side, and came up with the cat in his arms. Wind tossed light hair in a frantic dance above sky-blue eyes.

Dodd.

He smiled, rose to his feet, and fought his way through flying debris toward her. Dodging a large frond, she reached for Stowy, but he held the cat back. Instead he leaned toward her ear and shouted, "I know a cave nearby. It'll be safe. I'll take you there." His spit splattered on her neck.

"I'm not going anywhere with you!" She tugged on Stowy until finally Dodd released him. He took a step back, disappointment burning in his eyes. Then grabbing her hand, he tugged her forward. "I'll keep you safe," he shouted, ducking a flying branch.

Jerking from his grip, she hugged Stowy and backed away. The wind drove her against a tree trunk, whipped hair in her face. Squinting against a blast of dirt, Dodd went for her again, but she turned and sped away. A crack as loud as thunder pummeled her ears. She spun around. Something above Dodd moved. A massive branch loosened from the canopy and came crashing down. Dodd's eyes met hers. She started toward him, gesturing for him to move. He looked up. Terror rang in his eyes just as the branch struck him.

James closed his eyes and drew a breath, hoping to steady the thrashing of his heart. But when he opened them again, the wooden spike still protruded from Thiago's chest. Blood gurgled from the wound around the chipped wood. James's stomach cycloned, feeling much like the windstorm that had obliterated their camp earlier that day. Sarah knelt beside the unconscious Brazilian, her eyes red rimmed. She grabbed his hand while Magnolia and Eliza stared at James expectantly. Rising to his feet, he glanced over the wounded—at least a dozen. All lying on the sand beneath a slapdash bamboo roof some of the men had hastily erected. All attended to by Magnolia, Eliza, Angeline, and a few other colonists, who now stared at him as if he held the patients' survival in his hands. But they were wrong. Avoiding Angeline's gaze, he ducked beneath the bamboo and darted down the beach.

She followed him. He knew, because her coconut scent drifted on the ocean breeze and swirled beneath his nose. He continued walking, lengthening his stride, too embarrassed to face her. She caught his arm and turned him around. But there was no pity in her violet eyes. Concern, determination perhaps, but no pity.

"Eliza and Magnolia need you, James. You can't just walk away."

He glanced across the beach where colonists scavenged for anything left by the wind. "I'm not a doctor anymore."

"They don't know whether to pull out the wood or not. They need you to tell them what to do." She squeezed his arm. "Dodd needs you too. And the others. You don't have to look at the blood."

In the distance, Blake marched across the sand, stopping to speak to one man, then slapping another on the back, before shouting orders to a group who combed the beach for goods. His commanding voice was an encouragement to a colony that no doubt wondered if maybe next the ground would open up and swallow them whole.

Sobbing drew his gaze to Mrs. Scott, sitting on a stump, her slave, Mable, trying to comfort her. The windstorm had stripped the colony of what little the flood had left them. James felt like crying himself, except that would make him appear even weaker than he already was. Useless as a preacher—evidenced by the woman standing before him who had tried to kill herself two days ago—and useless as a doctor.

"Will you at least try?" Angeline's windswept hair fell in tangled waves over her shoulders. A curl blew across her face and tickled the freckles on her nose. She slid it behind her ear and stared at him, her pleading eyes shifting between his. And he knew he'd do anything to please her. Even if it meant his own death.

Which is exactly what it felt like he faced as he headed back to the makeshift clinic. Rolling up his sleeves, he approached Thiago, saw the relief on Eliza's face, then shifted his gaze to the blood bubbling from his friend's chest. And froze. His own blood turned to ice. He glanced away, his gaze landing on Dodd, lying in the corner, a lump on his head the size of a lemon. Angeline said a branch had fallen on him. The man hadn't woken up or even stirred in the two hours since they'd carried him from the jungle. Beside him lay Mr. Jenkins, a gash on his arm. Mrs. Swanson had a broken leg. Next to her, two farmers suffered mild abrasions, and the rest had minor aches and scrapes.

But it was Thiago who caused James the most concern. And the most terror.

"Please, James." Eliza pressed a cloth on the blood and looked up at him. "Tell us what to do."

"We have to pull it out," he said without looking at the wound. Angeline knelt beside Thiago to help. Sarah dipped a cloth in a bucket and dabbed the Brazilian's head, her hand trembling.

"But what if it struck an organ?" Eliza asked.

James risked a glance. Blood pooled around the wooden spike. His breath beat against his chest. His head grew light. Cursing himself, he looked away. At least the location of the wood indicated no organs or major arteries had been punctured. "If it pierced his heart, he'd be dead. If his lungs, he wouldn't be breathing like he is." If it was another organ. . .well, James doubted he could operate. "Have lots of rags available, some alcohol if we have it."

"We don't," Eliza said.

"I have some." The shame in Magnolia's voice drew James's gaze as she pulled a flask from a pocket of her gown. "I don't drink it anymore," she offered as an excuse when all the ladies gaped at her.

James drew a deep breath. The coppery smell of blood sent his heart hammering. Sweat beaded on his neck and arms. "Get a needle and suture ready. Pull the wood out, dab the blood, pour the alcohol on the wound, and sew him up as best you can."

Silence answered his instructions, prompting him to glance their way. All four ladies stared at him in horror.

Sarah grabbed Thiago's hand, tears streaming down her cheeks.

Eliza tossed her hair over her shoulder, her expression tightening. "You make it sound so easy."

James stared at the palm trees blowing in the wind just outside the clinic, at the gauzy foam bubbling on shore, anywhere but at the blood. "It *is* easy." For anyone but him. "You can do this, Eliza. I know you can. I promise I won't leave."

Angeline lifted Lydia to sit on her lap, caressing the soft skin of her cheek. So soft, so innocent. Had Angeline ever been this innocent? She couldn't remember. The baby uttered sweet gurgling sounds and grabbed Angeline's chin, staring up at her with a drooling smile and eyes as green as moss filled with trust and wonder. *Trust.* How trusting Lydia had to be. She was completely dependent on others for everything: food, water, protection, even for moving from place to place since she couldn't yet walk. Yet she had complete trust with no fear of harm or betrayal. How wonderful. How different from the way Angeline felt—from the way most people felt. What happened to people to make them so jaded and skeptical when they reached adulthood? Betrayal, rejection by someone they trusted. What a shame. Angeline hoped Lydia would not suffer such a fate. She hoped—dare she even pray?—that this little angel would never suffer abuse or a broken promise or heartache.

Or become what Angeline had become.

"You're good with children." James's voice jarred her from her musings and made her blood warm at the same time. Plopping to the sand beside her, he drew up his knees and laid his arms atop them. "Want some of your own someday?" His lips curved in a half smile that sent her mind reeling with possibility.

Angeline kissed Lydia's head and stared out to sea, where morning sunlight cast golden jewels atop waves. Of course she did. But she never would. The thought burned her throat with emotion, keeping her silent. It was just as well. Lydia pointed to Stowy perched on a rock beside them and said, "Day da."

"That's Stowy. He's a cat," Angeline said. "C...a...t."

James laughed. "I fear she's a bit too young to understand you."

"It's never too soon to start learning." Angeline smiled. She'd been taking turns with Eliza and Magnolia looking after Lydia for Sarah, who insisted on keeping vigil beside Thiago ever since they'd removed the spike two days ago. Angeline didn't mind. She cherished her time with the child. It gave her a chance to pretend, just for a moment, that she was a decent lady with a family of her own.

"How is Thiago?" she asked.

821

James tried to hide his concern, but she knew him too well. "He's over the worst of it. We shall see."

"And Dodd?" Dodd had not woken up in two days and she hated herself for being overjoyed.

James plucked a large shell from the sand and handed it to Lydia, who promptly stuck the edge into her mouth and began sucking on it. He released a heavy breath and squinted at the sun traversing across a cerulean sky. "I fear it's a coma. If he hasn't woken up by tomorrow, there's no guarantee he ever will."

"Poor man," she said, though her heart leapt at the prospect. Dodd's eternal sleep would solve all her problems. Well, the biggest one, anyway. She could stay with the colony—what was left of it. More importantly, she could stay with James. Start a new life like she always wanted. Abandon her memories to the past where they belonged.

"In the meantime, we must keep water and soft foods down him as much we can," James said.

James and Dodd had never been friends. In fact, quite the opposite. Yet the concern in his voice for the man put Angeline to shame. Because of his fear of blood, James thought himself weak. But he was the strongest, most courageous man she knew. Though sweat had beaded his brow, though his hands had trembled and his chest heaved, he had stood by Eliza and Magnolia, instructing them minute by minute while they tended to Thiago. He hadn't even left his post when his legs had begun to tremble. He'd just sat down and continued.

His eyes met hers. And in their depths she saw a life played out with the two of them—a life of love and passion and children and joy. A mist covered her own eyes, but she couldn't turn them away.

"What are you thinking?" He cocked his head as a breeze stirred the tips of his hair.

"I'm thinking about you."

Hope shone in his smile. Confusion formed a line on his brow. He brushed a curl from her face. "I thought you said. . ."

That she didn't want his courtship? "I can think, can't I?"

"As often as you want." He chuckled. "As much as you want."

Lydia pulled the tip of the shell from her mouth and tossed it at him.

He caught it, drool splattering on his hand. Laughing, he lifted his gaze to Angeline's. "As long as they are good thoughts."

"Always." She knew she shouldn't have said that. She knew she should keep her feelings to herself. But something broke free within her. Maybe it was all the near-death disasters the colony had suffered, maybe it was Dodd's coma, maybe it was the hope she saw in James's eyes. A hope she felt mirrored in her own.

Lydia grabbed Angeline's hair and tugged. She winced as James peeled back the chubby fingers to free the strands. Then relieving her of the child, he hoisted the baby in his arms and stood, twirling her around and around until she giggled so hard it made them both laugh. Angeline stared, mesmerized, at the child cradled in James's arms, her tiny hand splayed over his rounded biceps. He tickled her gently, and she laughed and drooled on his shirt.

He glanced at Angeline and smiled, and she wondered what it would be like to have children with such a man.

Oh God, if You're up there and You listen to women like me, please, please, don't let Dodd wake up.

CHAPTER 24

It's the beast, *Destruction*." James glanced over the colonists and the few pirates who had assembled the following evening around the fire. "He caused the windstorm. I'm sure of it."

Snorts and chuckles ensued.

"Pshaw!" one colonist said.

Ricu planted his hands on his waist. "Ridículo! I should not told you my tale."

James had not expected—nor wanted—Ricu to join their meeting, but he was not in a position to stop the man from doing much of anything. Still, his presence would only make what James had to say more difficult.

Hayden looked up from whittling a piece of wood. "We knew about the beasts before you got here, Captain."

From Magnolia's lap beside him, Lydia flailed her chubby hands in the air and yelped in agreement.

"Humph!" Ricu uttered a curse, lifted his hand, and snapped his fingers. One of the pirates placed a white handkerchief in his grip. The captain studied it intently before dabbing it over his neck and forehead. Firelight glinted off his jewel-pinned waistcoat.

James gestured toward the pirate's ship anchored several yards offshore. "How do you explain your ship? Not a sail torn, not a timber rent. No damage at all from the wind."

"And the water was as smooth as glass during the storm," Angeline said, petting Stowy. "I saw it."

Ricu scratched his whiskers and studied his ship, fading with the setting sun, before offering only a grunt in response.

"*Destruction* or not, we lost what little we had left," one of the ex-soldiers said.

"All that remains are some clothes, a couple of pails and baskets, a wagon and some tools," the blacksmith grumbled.

"And our lives," Eliza offered.

Moses added his "Amen," drawing the scowls of some. He stood beside Mable and slipped his hand in hers, making sure the Scotts couldn't see them from where they stood at the edge of the crowd, arm in arm, looking much older than their fifty-some years.

James smiled at the freedman. In fact he was smiling a lot these past few days. And all because of the alluring russet-haired beauty sitting on a stump beside him. Since the windstorm, something had changed for the better between them. He had no idea why, but he wasn't complaining. She gazed at him now, her eyes sparkling in the firelight and a smile curving her lips. And he found he didn't care whether they had no shelter or food or whether invisible beasts attacked them or pirates kept them prisoner. If Angeline continued to look at him like that, he could survive whatever came his way.

"Indeed." A cool breeze struck them as Blake stepped before the group. "We are all alive and have plenty of food. We should thank God for that."

"Some Southern utopia," a lady muttered under her breath.

Mr. Jenkins, a bandage wrapped around his arm, stood and cast a wary glance toward Ricu before turning to Blake. "There ain't nothing for us here, and you said the emperor might be obliged to relocate us."

"I don't want to start over on another plot of land in this dreadful jungle," another man said. "I just want to go home. Back to the States."

"Here, here," two people shouted at the same time.

"Ah, and with a quick stop at Rio de Janeiro," one woman added with a dreamy sigh. "What I wouldn't give to sleep on a bed again."

"And have a new gown made," Magnolia agreed but was instantly silenced by a look from Hayden.

James exchanged a glance with Blake. That was their plan. If the pirates ever released them, they would travel to Rio, take out a loan from the emperor, and purchase new supplies and a new plot of land. But that couldn't happen until the pirates left. And the pirates wouldn't leave without their gold. And James couldn't allow them to find it and release the final beast. If that fourth monster were freed—from what James had interpreted in the Hebrew book—it wouldn't matter where they went. Life would never be the same anywhere on the planet. But how to explain that to people who, though they'd witnessed the same things James and his friends had, thought the notion of invisible beasts utterly ridiculous?

Captain Ricu emitted a growl that would stir the hairs on a bear. "I say who leaves and who not leaves! If you go Rio, you will tell about gold."

"Ah, let them go, Captain," Patrick pushed his way through the crowd and gave Ricu a smile as if they were the best of friends. "They won't tell anyone. Who would believe them anyway? Look at them." He waved a hand over the group, his nose wrinkling. "They look like beggars and wastrels. And if they do say anything, by the time anyone gets here, you'll have dug up your treasure and been long gone."

Hayden shook his head at his father's performance and continued his whittling. What did Patrick hope to accomplish by siding with pirates? Did he actually believe they would hand over any of their gold to him? No, Patrick was many things, but he was not stupid. The charlatan was up to something. But what?

"I need men to help dig," Ricu returned, fingering the butt of a pistol stuffed in his belt as he scanned the colonists, no doubt seeking strong men he hadn't yet worn to a frazzle. For the past four days, he'd selected five of their men and dragged them to the tunnels. And each day they'd returned hungry and parched and covered in cuts and bruises. James wondered why he hadn't yet been chosen. Perhaps because Ricu knew he was a doctor and thought it best to keep him uninjured. Hayden had already gone twice, poor man.

The pirate captain drew his blade. "Tomorrow I take you, you, you, you"—he pointed the tip toward each man in turn, the baker, two ex-soldiers, Blake—"and you." Jenkins the farmer.

The chosen men's expressions dropped.

"*Capitão*, why not bring all the men?" One of the pirates rubbed his shoulder and winced.

"No room in tunnels. Too many to guard." Sheathing his sword, Ricu gazed out at his ship, the silhouette barely discernible in the shadows. "We will get gold soon." He sneered at the colonists. "Then I think about if I let you go." He waved his hand in the air, the lace at his cuffs fluttering in the breeze. And without another word, he turned and marched away, joining his fellow marauders already well into their cups down shore.

An eerie howl, more heartrending than frightening emanated from the jungle, drawing all eyes to the green fortress just yards away.

Hayden tossed another log on the fire. Sparks shot into the darkening skies.

"Wish they'd at least share their spirits," one man grumbled.

A cry for help, followed by "Doctor, Doctor!" shrieked from down the beach as Sarah flew at the group in a flurry of fear and hysteria.

She yanked on James's arm. "Thiago is much worse!"

And worse he was. His skin flamed. His breathing was ragged, and the wound in his chest had turned green and smelled putrid. Infection had set in. And James had no medicine. Nothing to give him at all.

The man fluttered his eyes open as he drifted in and out of consciousness. Sweat glued his black hair to his head and neck. His chest rose and fell like erratic waves at sea as he tossed over the sand in discomfort. Finally, he settled and his hazy gaze landed on James.

"Am I to die, Doc?" Thiago's voice came out weak and raspy.

James swallowed. One thing he swore he'd never do was lie to his patients. He had never done so in the war, and he wasn't about to now. "Unless a miracle happens. . .I'm sorry."

Sarah broke into sobs, and Thiago turned his head toward her. "No tears for me, sweet Sarah." She took his hand and raised it to her lips. James knew the couple had grown close. He just hadn't realized *how* close. His heart hung like a huge boulder in his chest as Eliza continued to dab a cool cloth on Thiago's forehead while Magnolia sat nearby, looking stunned. James rose just as Blake and Hayden arrived. He shook his head at their questioning looks. Then ignoring their anguished expressions, he stormed out of the clinic and kicked sand with his boot. "Truss it!"

"Don't blame yourself." Blake followed him. "It's not your fault."

James held up his hands and looked at his friends with disgust. "Maybe if I had been the one to operate on him, he'd have a chance."

A night breeze tossed Hayden's hair in his face and he jerked it aside. "And maybe not." He gripped James's arm. "Magnolia tells me you instructed them as well as if it were your hands doing the fixing."

Jerking from him, James took up a pace, rubbing the back of his neck. "If only I had some vinegar or mercury. Anything to treat him."

"Have you tried praying?" Blake asked as James passed him.

"Did you *see* him?" James halted. "He's beyond prayer."

"No one is beyond prayer," Hayden said.

James shook his head. He had never considered praying. Not once. And he was the colony's preacher! Shame doused him as he charged back into the clinic, Hayden and Blake on his heels. He gave a cursory glance at poor Dodd lying alone on the other side of the bamboo structure before dropping beside the Brazilian once again. He would pray for Dodd later. Right now, he laid a hand on Thiago's shoulder. "God, please heal this man. Like You did in the days of old. I command this infection to depart from him so he will live and know You. In Christ Jesus' name, we ask. Amen."

The others mumbled, "Amen."

Though she offered him a smile, even pious Sarah seemed skeptical. Minutes later, instead of a miraculous recovery, Thiago began to cough up blood.

CHAPTER 25

T hiago didn't die that night. Nor the next. In fact, after three days, he still barely hung to life with the thinnest of threads. Angry at God, angry at himself, James did the only thing he knew to do. He grabbed the Hebrew book and his father's Bible and headed into the jungle away from the incriminating glances that labeled him a failure at both doctoring and pastoring. Lowering himself to sit on a boulder by his favorite creek, he gazed up at the canopy where colorful birds engaged in a dance equal in style and grace to any waltz back home. A blue lizard skittered up a tree while a frog croaked from somewhere near the water. The gentle ripple of the creek soothed his ears, a welcome change from the boom and sizzle of waves. A glint caught his gaze, and he looked up to see a spiderweb that spanned between two trees, its silky threads sparkling in a ray of sunshine. A tiny black spider sat in the corner awaiting his prey. No doubt it had taken him days, even weeks, to spin such a magnificent web. Such patience, such ingenuity. All to trap some unsuspecting victim.

Is that what the fallen angelic beasts were doing to the colonists? Luring them into their web with the glint of gold? James released a heavy sigh, set his father's Bible aside, and opened the Hebrew book to the place he'd marked. Why, oh why, had God entrusted the fate of the colony, maybe even the world—if he were reading things correctly—to a failure like James? He had to do better. He had to work faster. The answer to stopping the beasts was in this book, and he had to find it.

After two hours of interpreting, James had achieved little more than an achy back, tired eyes, and sweaty skin. He slapped a mosquito that landed on his arm, wondering if he was wasting his time. But he *had* learned one thing: the name of the fourth beast—*Depravity*. He'd also learned that once *Depravity* was released, all four beasts would not be restricted to this small section of Brazil. Instead, they'd be free to travel the world, wreaking havoc and destroying lives wherever they went. He'd suspected as much from prior hints in the text, but now he knew for sure.

He knew another thing for sure. They had to stop *Depravity* from being freed.

Pondering why God would allow such awful beasts—or fallen angels or whatever they were—to be free in the first place, James set the book aside and knelt by the creek, splashing water on his face and neck. Sitting back, he opened his father's Bible and ran fingers over the pages. Oh, how his father had loved this Book. Not a day had passed when James had not seen him sitting by the hearth absorbing its words as if his very breath depended on them. James had read the Bible too. When he'd had time. And of course his father had forced him to study it, training his son to become a preacher. But James had never been quite in awe of the Holy Scripture as his father had been. Perhaps that had been his problem all along. Yet now, could the answer to his current dilemma with the beasts be found within?

Flipping to the Gospel of Matthew, he started reading when crackling sounds tightened his nerves. A woman's voice, cooing his name, made his blood run cold. He brought his gaze up to see Abigail Miller, standing in the middle of the creek, water up to her neck, golden locks floating like silk atop the liquid. She smiled, that sultry smile that used to melt his insides but now made them turn into slime.

"You're not here." Setting the Bible down, he stood and rubbed his eyes.

"Of course I am." She started for him, water slipping off her like the layers of clothing she had shed for him on many a night. When she reached the shore, her wet chemise molded every curve of her glistening skin. He turned away, cursing his body for reacting even as disgust soured his mouth.

"Reading your Bible, I see. Like a good little preacher's son." Her tone was teasing, playful, like she'd always been with him. "But it never really did you any good, did it? You're too passionate a man to be restrained by some distant God." .

"What do you want?"

She sidled up to him. "I want you. I've always wanted you."

Pulse racing, he stepped back. "You only wanted to ruin me."

"Of course not, James." She pouted, water sliding down her face like glistening diamonds. "I only wanted to make you happy. Weren't you happy with me?"

He had been. At least he thought he'd been. But what he'd mistaken for love had been only lust. And what he'd mistaken for a lady had been nothing but a trollop. A devouring trollop. Much like the spider he'd seen earlier, Abigail had cast her web for the young preacher and snared him without resistance. Widowed and older than James, she had opened up a new world to him—a world that was exciting and passionate, filled with carnal pleasures he'd never imagined. But it was all an illusion. A deadly one, for when his father, along with their parishioners, discovered his immorality, he'd been removed from the pulpit. "*For a time of correction*," his brokenhearted father had said. But shame drove James away. To become a doctor and join the war.

He stared at the leaves, the vines, the rays of sun spearing the canopy, desperate not to glance her way, desperate to give her no opportunity to entice him again. Women like her had ruined him. Twice. Abigail, who had driven him to war, and Tabitha who had ruined his life afterward.

"Thinking of me?" The new voice startled James into daring a peek. He wished he hadn't, for now both of them stood staring at him with innocent eyes that belied their scantily clad bodies.

Growling, he covered his own eyes, pleading with God to get rid of them, when a new voice, a male voice, added to his misery. He should just turn and leave, run as fast as he could back to the beach, but this particular voice owned a piece of his heart. And that piece forbade him.

"Father." He opened his eyes to see the man who had sired him, the man he had respected most in the world, standing by the creek, face pale, agony burning in his eyes and blood oozing from a pistol shot to his heart.

"Why did you let this happen?" Blood dribbled from his father's lips. "Where were you?"

James's chest caved in. The scar on his cheek began to throb. He rubbed it and fell to his knees, drowning in his agony and shame. He could not bear the sight, the memory of what he'd done. Would it never escape him?

It had been the most horrible night of his life.

And the most incredible. He'd faced a crossroads that fateful evening. One path led to death. The other to life. An angel had come alongside him—a woman who had ministered to him during the night, who had sang hymns and quoted scripture and helped him choose the right way.

"James, are you all right? James." Someone touched his arm. Small hands, gentle fingers. Abigail, Tabitha? Could visions touch? He jerked away and scrambled backward only to see Angeline staring at him, her face creased with worry.

He blinked the moisture from his eyes and looked away. "Yes. Forgive me."

"You saw a vision."

He nodded and slid a thumb over the scar on his cheek. The one he well deserved for what he'd done.

"Who was it?" Her eyes flitted between his, searching, caring. . .as her hand reached up to caress his jaw.

He took her in his arms. He couldn't help himself, and for once she allowed his embrace. She felt so small, so fragile. Here was a real lady. Pure and honorable and innocent. Not the kind of woman who lured men into traps and destroyed their lives. This was exactly the kind of woman who could redeem him.

❦

The fear Angeline expected to feel locked in a man's embrace never came. Even though James was much bigger than she was, much stronger, able to do whatever he wanted with her, she felt no apprehension. Instead, she felt cherished, protected. And loved. This preacher-doctor stirred her heart and soul like no man ever had. And now, dare she hope for a chance to stay in these arms forever? She drew in a deep breath of him and gazed into his bronze eyes still filled with angst from whatever horrifying vision he'd seen. If only she could erase the memory and bring him the comfort he always brought her.

But then he smiled and the agony left his eyes, replaced by such affection, it brought moisture to her own. He slid a strand of her hair behind her ear, and even that slight gesture sent her senses whirling. She'd never known a man's touch could evoke such feelings. She'd always thought women merely endured lovemaking, that it was nothing but an unpleasant burden for the sake of bearing children. Or in her case, surviving.

But James had woken things within her that bordered on a bliss not of this world. It was *that* bliss that forced her to step back from him now. It would be too easy to give in to his charms, but she was not that woman anymore. She was the lady she saw reflected in his eyes, the proper lady, the virtuous lady. She wanted *so badly* to be that lady.

Approval beamed in his expression as he took her hand in his. "Forgive me for being forward." He gazed down uncomfortably. "You have captivated me, Angeline. I know I shouldn't ask again, but I can't help it. These past few days, you've given me reason to hope that perhaps you've changed your mind about our courtship?"

He looked so hopeful, so vulnerable, as if his heart teetered on the cliff of her answer. And, oh, how she wanted to say yes to keep it from falling. And hers from falling with it. If only. . . She hated herself for even thinking it, but if only Dodd would never wake. . . How cruel of God to dangle the gift of happiness before her on the thread of another's death.

Her breath came rapid as he lifted her hand to his lips for a kiss. Hadn't James said that the longer Dodd remained asleep, the less the chance he would ever wake? Maybe God wasn't cruel at all. Maybe He was giving her a chance at love. But what of Dodd's chance? He was a vile man who deserved what he got, wasn't he? If that were the case, then she deserved an equal fate. A person could go crazy with such thoughts!

James smiled and lowered her hand. "It wasn't that difficult a question to answer."

"My answer is. . .yes." She breathed the word before her good senses smothered it.

James shook his head as if he hadn't heard her correctly. "What did you say?"

She raised a sly brow. "I said yes, I accept your courtship."

833

His smile was blinding. His eyes alight with glee. Taking her other hand, he brought them both to his lips and kissed them over and over.

Warmth sped down to her toes as a giggle rose in her throat.

"I don't know what changed your mind, and I don't want to know as long as you don't change it again," he said, lowering her hands but not releasing them. "I do not have a perfect past, but I will make every attempt to make myself worthy of you."

She already knew a part of that imperfect past and wondered at the rest. Yet all of it would seem like a monastic interlude compared to her former life. She was the one who must prove herself worthy of him. Or at least forever hide from what she had once been.

"May I kiss you?" he asked.

No one had ever asked her that before. They'd simply taken what they wanted. She could feel his pulse throb in his hand, could hear his deep breathing, could smell his scent of wood smoke and salt and James. And she could stand it no longer. She pressed her lips against his. Unlike the few stolen kisses they'd shared before, this one had meaning. It carried a devotion and a passion free to express itself within commitment. Each stroke, each caress of his lips on hers held the promise of unending love. Her toes wiggled. Her head spun. She pressed against him. Those beefy arms of his she loved so much surrounded her, hands running down her back, fingering her errant curls. All the while his mouth drank her in with such affection, she thought she would explode in pleasure. Was this what real love was like?

Then suddenly he was gone. He backed away and turned to the side, gathering his breath. "Forgive me. I lost myself."

Forgive him? For what? Angeline blinked to clear her head, waiting for her body to settle.

He looked at her. "I should not have taken such liberties with so fine a lady as you." Shame haunted his eyes as he took her hands once again in his. "It won't happen again. You deserve more respect than that. You deserve my utmost respect."

Respect? Her?

He ran a thumb down her jaw, and she leaned into his hand. He trusted her. He believed her to be pure and innocent. And, oh, how she loved pretending that she was. Even for a moment. But how could she base their courtship on such a horrific lie?

Yet there would be no courtship without the lie.

Her brain hurt from the conundrum. Besides, how was she to think clearly with him so close, with the taste of him on her lips?

Footsteps and the swish of leaves broke into her dream as Hayden crashed into the clearing. His glance took in their locked hands before he turned to James.

"It's Thiago. Come quickly!"

Grabbing the ancient book and his Bible, James darted after Hayden, pulling Angeline behind him, but after a few minutes of her skirts getting stuck on every passing branch, she insisted he go ahead without her. They were almost at the beach anyway, and she needed time to think. But no sooner had James and Hayden disappeared into the greenery than the crackling sound of a fire burned her ears. She shut her eyes, knowing what was coming, but then decided it would be best to hurry along and join the others rather than face whatever heinous vision was about to appear. Unfortunately, it wasn't just one vision, but a half dozen of her former clients who took up a stroll on either side of her. Clutching her skirts, she tried to ignore them.

"Your beau there thinks you're a lady," the oldest one remarked, whose name she couldn't recall. Though she did recall his stench.

"You sure got him fooled!" Mr. Keiter slapped his hat on his knee.

One of her more refined clients brushed dust from his suit of fine broadcloth. "If I were him, I'd want to know what sort of woman I was marrying. It's only right, you know."

Grief and fear stole her newfound joy. She covered her ears.

Milton Daniels, one of her regulars, leapt in front of her, halting her in her tracks. He swept strands of greasy hair to the side and frowned. "You never kissed me like you kissed him. You was holding out on me!"

You're not here! You're not here! She screamed inside her head. But his words stung, nonetheless. All of their words pierced a place in her soul where light had risen, where hope had begun to shove the darkness aside. It crowded back. Closing her eyes, she barged right through old Milton, feeling not a whisper of his body on her skin. They weren't real. But what did it matter? They had done their damage.

Tears spilling down her cheeks, she shoved through leaves and

835

burst onto the beach, hoping they wouldn't follow her.

"Ah, why don't you try and drown yourself again? That's the only way out." A shout and morbid laughter trailed her onto the sand, but when she spun around, no one was there.

CHAPTER 26

"Healed?" James blinked at the sight of Thiago leaning on Sarah's arm as they strolled down the beach. He would shrug it off as yet another vision if not for the fact that everyone saw the same thing. Blake and Eliza stood arm in arm, beaming smiles on their faces. Hayden, Magnolia, the Scotts, and Moses also stared at the wondrous sight.

"Is it so surprising?" Blake slapped James on the back.

Magnolia cocked a brow. "You *did* pray for God to heal him, did you not?"

James swept his gaze to Thiago. The Brazilian glanced up, and upon seeing James, a huge smile broke his tight expression as he and Sarah started back toward the group.

Waves crashed onshore, tumbling and foaming, much like the thoughts in James's head.

"You heal me, Doc!" Thiago exclaimed on heavy breath as he and Sarah stopped before him.

Shaking his head, James scanned him from head to toe. Though his face was pale, he'd lost weight, and he seemed weaker than an overcooked noodle, he was indeed very much alive. "May I?" James gestured toward the bandage on his chest, and at Thiago's nod, he peered behind it and sniffed. No bad smell, no discoloration. He stepped back, his mind trying to make sense of what his eyes told him.

"You heal me," Thiago repeated.

"God healed you," Sarah said with a smile.

"Yes." James shook his head to shake off the trance that had overcome him. "It was God who healed you, not me. I didn't do anything." Nothing at all, in fact, except direct Eliza and Magnolia to make a mess of his wound. And then say a simple prayer. "This is truly a miracle," he mumbled in disbelief. Slowly, the realization sank into his thick head and then trickled down to his heart, where a spark ignited. He glanced over the crowd. "This is a miracle! This man was dying." He gripped Thiago's shoulders and shook him. "You were dying!"

"I know." Glistening white teeth shone against his tawny complexion. "And now I am not. It is your God."

Moisture clouded Sarah's eyes as she clung to the Brazilian's arm.

From across the beach, Angeline approached and eased beside James. "What's happen—" Her eyes latched upon Thiago. "You're well again!"

"Sim, Miss. Mr. James pray and God heal me."

An adorable line formed between her eyebrows. "Indeed? Healed?" She blinked and exchanged a shocked look with James. A gust of wind blasted over them, cooling the sweat on his brow.

"God healed many people in the Bible." Hayden shrugged and snapped hair from his face. "Why can't He heal now?"

James stared at the sand by his feet. "I'm ashamed I didn't have faith that He would. I just prayed and went away without hope."

"None of us truly believed." Eliza gazed up at the sun, now high in the sky, as if she could spot the Almighty Himself, smiling down at them. Perhaps He was.

"God is bigger than our weaknesses." Magnolia's smile spoke of an intimate knowledge of that fact.

"Aaaa-men!" Moses proclaimed.

"There must be another explanation," Mr. Scott grumbled. "God no longer heals or does miracles. Those were only stories in the Bible."

"The evidence is to the contrary, sir." Blake jerked his head toward Thiago.

"Come along, Mrs. Scott." The elder man dragged his wife away, but her eyes were on Thiago, and her smile said she believed.

"This God," Thiago began, his voice weak but the light in his eyes strong, "He loves me. Just like you say, Doc. In your sermons. He loves everyone?"

"Yes, He does." James smiled.

"Indeed." Eliza gave Thiago a hug.

Magnolia wiped a tear from her eye.

"You need your rest." James placed a hand on the man's back. "Have Sarah take you to lie down, and Eliza and I will be there in a minute to examine your wound."

"And someone get the man something to eat!" Hayden shouted, causing them all to chuckle.

❦

Angeline couldn't sleep. Whether it was the thrill of accepting James's courtship, the haunting visions of her clients, or the excitement of Thiago's healing that kept her awake, she couldn't say. But finally, growing bored listening to the blissful slumber of the other ladies, she crawled off the leaf-strewn bamboo that served as their bed and stepped out from under the palm frond roof. The shelter the men erected didn't afford much privacy, but at least it would keep them dry should it rain. Speaking of. . . She drew in a deep breath and was sure she smelled the sweet scent of rain on the wind. Her legs began to quake. She used to love the rain, but after the flood, even the slightest hint of it made her nervous. Yet there were no clouds on the horizon. Just a full moon that hovered like a pearl atop black glass, sending ribbons of milk onto water and sand. So peaceful. Peaceful except for the snoring from the men sleeping on the beach and one pirate belting out a ditty from the ship.

She wondered which of the shadowy mounds was James but thought it best not to seek him out. A flicker caught her eye from a lantern at the clinic and she headed that way, hoping for some company. Anything was better than being alone with her thoughts. Or worse, being alone should any of her former patrons return to haunt her.

Sarah smiled up at her as Angeline ducked beneath the roof.

"How is he?" She gestured toward Thiago, who lay fast asleep on one of the homemade pallets while Sarah kept vigil beside him.

"He finally fell asleep." She gazed at him adoringly before snapping her eyes back to Angeline. "Lydia is all right?"

"Yes, yes." Angeline cast a quick glance at Dodd's shadowy form at the other end of the clinic before she sat beside Sarah and adjusted her skirts. "She's sleeping peacefully beside Eliza. I think Eliza is practicing for when her own baby comes."

Sarah smiled and pressed a hand atop Angeline's. "And you? Why are you not able to sleep?"

"Too much on my mind, I suppose."

A breeze swept in and flickered the lantern sitting on a stump beside them.

"Like pirates and evil beasts?" Sarah raised one brow at Angeline. "Or is it the good doctor who invades your thoughts?"

Heat creeping onto her cheeks, Angeline lowered her chin. "Am I that obvious?"

"That you both care deeply for each other is quite obvious." Sarah squeezed her hand.

"He is such a wonderful man. I fear I don't deserve him."

"Don't be silly." Sarah's face scrunched. "Of course you do."

"No." Angeline pulled her hand from Sarah's and began toying with her hair. "You don't know me. Not really."

"I know you are kind and thoughtful and intelligent and strong. Any man would be fortunate to gain your affections."

Angeline gave a tiny smile. "Perhaps I am some of those things now. But. . ." How much should she disclose to her friend? Lantern light glimmered on the cross Sarah always wore around her neck, reminding Angeline that this pious woman had probably never done a single vile thing in all her life, nor even thought a single vile thought. "My past—"

"Oh, pish posh, who cares about your past?" Sarah dipped a rag in a bucket of water and rang it out.

"I've done terrible things, Sarah. Things that if James knew about them, he'd never speak to me again."

Sarah's gaze snapped to hers. "I doubt that very much. He's a man of God, and God is in the business of forgiveness."

Angeline couldn't help the snort that emerged from her lips. "There are some things I'm sure even God does not forgive."

Wind whipped through the makeshift clinic, sputtering the lantern and stirring the sand.

Setting the rag atop a pile, Sarah slipped a strand of hair behind her ear. "There is nothing God doesn't forgive except rejecting the sacrifice of His Son." Brown eyes as warm and soft as a doe's assessed her.

Angeline studied those eyes now, searching for some hint of doubt, some hint of insincerity, but all she found was concern. Swallowing a burst of emotion, she concentrated on the rhythmic lap of waves onshore.

Sarah leaned toward her. "Do you want to know a secret? A deep, dark secret that I've never told anyone?"

Angeline could not imagine this woman having any secrets, especially nefarious ones.

"Lydia is not my husband's child," Sarah said.

Angeline lifted her gaze to Sarah's, sure she hadn't heard the woman correctly. "What do you mean?"

Frowning, Sarah glanced down at Thiago. "You see, I didn't love my husband. Not the way a wife should. I know that now." She fingered the ripped fringe at the edge of her sleeve. "After he went off to war, I got terribly lonely. There was a man who helped out on our farm. He was strong and protective and kind. I don't know how it happened, but. . ."

Angeline squeezed her hand. "No need to go on. I understand." And she truly did understand. She understood too well how one moment—one weak moment—and one foolish decision could have dire consequences for the rest of your life.

Distant thunder rumbled as the *tap*, *tap* of raindrops danced over the roof.

Sarah folded her hands in her lap, refusing to meet Angeline's gaze. "Do you think differently of me now?"

"No." Angeline touched her arm. "I think of you as human." Her eyes moistened. "I always thought you were so perfect, Sarah."

Sarah chuckled and wiped a tear from her cheek. "Oh my, how we do make assumptions of others." She smiled. "Thank you, Angeline. You are a true friend." She squeezed Angeline's hand. "Now, I've told you my secret. Yours cannot be half as bad."

Withdrawing her hand, Angeline grew somber. "Far worse, I'm afraid." Minutes passed. Lantern light flashed over Thiago's sleeping form as the pattering of rain tapped all around. "I don't think I can speak it out loud."

"Then you don't have to," Sarah said. "But you must know that God forgave me, Angeline. I knew what I'd done was wrong. I dismissed the man and repented. Truly repented. And I've never felt such love and peace." She touched Angeline's chin, bringing her gaze up to meet her own. "Whatever you've done, it doesn't matter. If you repent and change your ways, God promises to forgive and remember your sins no more."

If only that were true. Angeline desperately wanted it to be true. She glanced at the man sleeping so peacefully beside them. "If you marry Thiago, will you tell him about Lydia?"

"Marry?" Sarah's brows lifted, but a sparkle took residence in her eyes. "Where did you get that fool idea?"

Angeline squared her shoulders and raised her chin. "That you both care deeply for each other is quite obvious," she repeated in a voice much like Sarah's, which caused them both to laugh.

When they ceased, Sarah took Thiago's hand in hers. "I do care for him. And now that he's truly following God...well, who knows what will happen? But to answer your question, yes, I must tell him. You cannot base a marriage on a lie."

CHAPTER 27

The smell of fire-roasted fish made James's mouth water as he led Blake toward the edge of the jungle to speak to him in private. But no sooner had they stopped when just a few feet away, leaves parted and Patrick made an entrance onto the beach with his usual aplomb, feigning an exhaustion James was sure was not caused by hard work. Separating from Patrick, Captain Ricu and his band of pirates sped toward their end of the beach, no doubt anxious to drown themselves in rum, while five colonists glared at Patrick as they passed and nodded toward Blake and James. Patrick waved at two single women from his original colony who'd been awaiting his arrival like giggling toadies. They came running with a bucket of fresh water and towels in hand.

"Why, of course the excavation is going well!" Patrick answered Blake's question as he drew cupped hands of water to his face and neck. "It's this fiendish dust that disturbs me. Not to mention being forced to live in such squalor like an ignorant native, sleeping in the sand and eating food only fit for a monkey." He took the towel a young lady handed him and dried his face. "The things I do for gold, Colonel."

Blake rubbed his sore leg, annoyance written on his features.

"How close did they get today to unearthing the fourth alcove?" James crossed his arms over his chest.

Patrick dried his face and handed the towel back to the woman, whose look of silly adoration threatened to ruin James's appetite. How the man managed to garner such devotion, he could not fathom.

"Thank you, my dear." Patrick's sickly sweet smile caused the lady's face to redden. "Now if you ladies wouldn't mind getting me a drink while I talk to these men, I'd be so appreciative."

After casting him flirtatious smiles, they both flounced away. His eyes followed them. "Such lovely creatures, don't you agree, gentlemen?"

"I have a wife, sir"—Blake gave a sigh of frustration—"and she is all the lovely I need."

"Oh, quite. I forgot how prudish you religious sorts could be." Patrick planted hands at his waist and stared over the sea that was transforming from turquoise to gray in the setting sun. "The alcove. Ah, yes. Surely you don't still believe it is the tomb of this fourth invisible beast? Come now, gentlemen. I'm surprised men of your intelligence have succumbed to such balderdash." Winking, he elbowed James. "I've got some prime farmland in the swamps of Louisiana for sale, if you're interested." He laughed at his own joke but then sobered when neither of them joined in.

How could this buffoon be Hayden's father? The physical resemblance was uncanny, but inside they were as different as the Rebs were from the Yanks.

In the distance, James spotted Hayden heading their way.

"All right. All right. Lost your sense of humor in the war, I see. Now, let me think." Patrick tapped his chin. "The alcove. Indeed, we are almost upon it. Another few yards of rock to be cleared. I'd say a week or two at the most and then"—he rubbed his hands together— "we'll find the gold. Enough gold to rule the world."

Hayden halted before his father, his jaw tight. "But you won't see any of it, Patrick. So why the excitement? Why do you volunteer to help every day?"

"To benefit us all, of course! Do you think I do this for myself?" Patrick placed a hand over his heart as if wounded. "The sooner these vile pirates find the gold, the sooner they are gone. And the sooner we are all free."

"Wonderful performance. Bravo, bravo." Hayden clapped. "But you forget who your audience is."

Patrick frowned and brushed sand from his shirt.

"You're up to something," Hayden added. "I just can't figure out what it is yet."

James agreed. He hadn't known the man very long, but he'd discovered two undeniable traits. One, Patrick only thought of himself, and two, he was only in Brazil for the gold.

Patrick gave a feigned look of guilt like a little boy caught with his finger in a pie. "I suppose I do have a plan to get some of the gold for myself." He shrugged. "But what does it matter whether I take it or the pirates take it, either way you and your pathetic little colony will be left alone." He grinned as one of the women returned with a mug of water. "Why you're sweeter than a peach pie, Miss Belinda."

James groaned inwardly. How could he get across to this greedy blaggard the danger he faced—the danger they all faced—should the fourth beast be freed? "All I'm asking, sir, is that you consider what you are doing. There are forces at work which we cannot see in the natural."

"Of all the lunacy!" Patrick laughed, Belinda joining him. "Invisible monsters and visions and the destruction of the world. Pshaw!" A devious look twisted his features as he leaned toward James. "I fear the sun has addled your brain, preacher or doctor—or whatever you are."

Belinda's giggles grew louder. James's heart turned to lead.

"Now, if you'll excuse me, gentlemen." And off he strolled, the young lady on his arm.

Hayden glared after his father. "Good thing I've forgiven him, or I'd probably kill him on the spot."

James flattened his lips. "It must be difficult to live so close to him after all the damage he caused you and Magnolia."

"He'll be gone soon enough. But I do wonder what he's about. He has a plan to get that gold, a good one. You can bet on that."

Blake shook his head. "He'll probably get himself killed."

A breeze spun around them, cooling the sweat on James's neck as crickets buzzed from the darkening jungle. In the distance, colonists began to gather around the fire for supper.

"I interpreted more of the book last night," James said. He'd wanted to discuss his findings with his friends all day, but they'd been busy building huts and foraging for food. Besides, he needed time to ponder the new revelation, to ensure he was right, to ask God what to do.

Wind stirred sand at their feet as Blake and Hayden stared at him in expectation.

"I've discovered who these four beasts are." James hesitated. He knew this would make him sound like the addlebrain Patrick had just called him, yet it was no crazier than the idea of invisible beings in the first place. "They are four of Satan's fallen angels. In fact, they were—or are—generals in Satan's army." He glanced at his friends, but their expressions were unreadable. "Apparently, I was correct in my assumption that they stepped outside the boundaries God had placed on them, did something they had no permission to do, so God sent Gabriel with a contingent of warring angels to battle and subdue them."

Only the crash of waves and snap of a distant fire responded. James tightened his jaw, bracing for the laughter he expected from Hayden.

Instead, Blake moaned and gave an agreeing nod. "Perhaps that charred area behind the temple was the battlefield."

"My thoughts exactly." James turned to Hayden. Skepticism screamed from his eyes, yet he remained, waiting to hear more.

"Like I told you before, the angels' punishment was to be imprisoned underground near a hot spot until the end of this age."

"The fire lake the priest I met spoke of," Hayden said.

"Yes." James rubbed the back of his neck. "The book speaks of a river of fire that runs through hell in the center of Earth then flows up to the Earth's crust in only three places."

"Then the cannibals came along," Blake said. "Erected their temple right on top of it, dug tunnels, and happened upon these beasts."

"As I said before, I don't think they understood what they'd found or what they'd released."

"Not until it was too late," Blake added, gazing at the surf.

Hayden cursed, his mood growing sullen. "You told us that the person who recites the Latin phrase must have a black heart, an evil heart." He glanced at his father sitting on a rock, entertaining a group of people with some embellished tale. "If anyone has an evil heart. . ."

Blake groaned. "Tell us again what happens if this fourth beast is released?"

"He is called *Depravity*. Need I say more?" James heard the fear in his own voice as darkness settled on the beach. "And from what I've read, his release multiplies the power of the others and enables all four of them to leave this place and wreak evil over the entire planet."

"There's no telling how much damage they will do. How many lives will be lost." Hayden's gaze remained on his father.

Blake's body stiffened. "We've got to stop the pirates. We've got to stop Patrick from releasing that fourth beast."

James glanced at Captain Ricu climbing the rope ladder to his ship. "Pirates have gunpowder. . .do they not?" He lifted his brows and scanned his friends.

A slow grin spread over Hayden's lips while Blake nodded his understanding.

"We blow up the tunnels," they all said in unison.

"It's the only way," James added. "God is on our side. I believe He sent us here to stop these beasts." He'd been sensing that for days. But now he hoped his friends would agree.

Blake squeezed the bridge of his nose. "Perhaps. But even if we can destroy the tunnels, the pirates won't give up on the gold. Not when they know it's still down there."

"But it will buy us time." James stared at the ship, a shadowy leviathan floating offshore. "But how do we get on board and steal enough gunpowder to blow up those tunnels?"

Chapter 28

James glanced over his shoulder at the pirates guarding the beach. Though a few of them had left at sunrise for the tunnels—along with several of the colony's men—the rest stayed behind in order to keep the remaining colonists from escaping. "They are sneaking aboard tonight," he answered Angeline, who had asked about their plans to steal the pirate's gunpowder.

"Who?"

"Hayden and Blake," James said as he slammed the ax through a thick piece of bamboo. He'd been attempting to reinforce the women's shelter when Angeline approached. Storm clouds on the horizon portended rain, and he wanted a dry place for the ladies to congregate.

"Why aren't you going?"

Wind tore a curl from her pins and sent it bouncing over her neck as her concerned gaze snapped to the pirate ship. James set down the ax and wiped sweat from his brow. Since she'd agreed to their courtship, she'd been seeking him out, starting conversations, sitting with him at meals, strolling with him on the beach, looking at him with those exquisite violet eyes so full of admiration. He felt like he was living in a dream, a dream ripe with hope and love and every possible joy. Yet at the same time he felt guilty for feeling such happiness in the midst of so much struggle and danger.

He took her hand in his and caressed her fingers, thrilled when she no longer pulled away. "They need me here to protect the colony should. . ." He stopped, not wanting to alarm her.

"They get caught." She finished, her lips tightening. "I'm thankful you aren't going. Is that selfish of me?"

"Is it selfish of me to wish I *was* going?" He chuckled. "To want to do something—anything to stop this madness."

Swaddling his hand in both of hers, she brought it to her chest. "I fear for them. I fear for us all."

He ran a thumb over her cheek. She was so small, but he knew inside her petite frame, a dragon lurked—a dragon filled with strength and determination. And he loved her all the more for it. "They will be all right. God will go with them."

She smiled. "I wish I had your faith."

James squinted toward the rising sun. A handbreadth above the horizon, it scattered droplets of gold onto the restless sea. *Did* he have faith? Though Thiago had been healed and had come to believe more firmly in God, James hadn't been sure either would happen. Did he truly believe that Hayden and Blake would be safe, or was he just reciting the expected platitude? Another trite proverb sat ready upon his lips—something about how Angeline could have faith too if she only believed—but it tumbled unspoken onto the sand. More proof that he wasn't a very good preacher at all.

"Thank you for working on our shelter." She peered behind him at the tilting stack of bamboo and fronds.

Running a hand through his hair, he gave a lopsided grin. "If that's what you call it. But yes, I'm trying. I may even erect a front wall today so you ladies can at least enjoy some privacy."

"Doctor, preacher, and home builder. Is there no end to your talents?"

He withheld a skeptical snort. He'd never had a woman look at him the way Angeline did. Other females had looked at him with interest, appreciation, fury, and even desire, but never with such admiration that his heart nearly burst. If he told her the truth—that he was good at none of those things—he feared the sparkle would fade from her eyes. And he didn't think he could bear to see it go. "At your lady's service." He gave a mock bow.

When he resumed his full height, her eyes were locked on his bare chest. She looked away and began fingering a wayward strand of hair. So accustomed to wearing minimal clothing in the sultry environment, he'd unwittingly forsook proper etiquette that morning. Still he found her innocence refreshing. And alluring.

"Sweet saints," she whispered then bit her lip.

"What did you say?"

"Nothing." Shielding her eyes from the sun, she returned her gaze to his. "I actually have a purpose for disturbing your work, James. To invite you to a picnic lunch." She gestured to her left. "Just beyond the cliffs. In an hour? Just the two of us?"

Heart leaping at her suggestion, he turned and grabbed his shirt from the sand and gave her a teasing smile. "Without a chaperone? I do hope you're not trying to seduce me?"

⤜⧼⧽⤛

Chastising herself, Angeline begged James's forgiveness and turned to leave. She truly had no idea how real ladies behaved. Maybe it was his bare chest that prompted her to ask such an improper thing. What was she thinking? Inviting a man to lunch! And without a proper escort? He must think her wanton.

His hand on her arm stopped her. His look of remorse stilled the pounding of her heart.

"Forgive me. My poor attempt at humor was completely un-warranted." He searched her eyes. "I would love to join you."

"Very well." Her insides unwound at his loving look. "On one condition."

"Anything."

She wanted to tell him—to insist—that he put on the shirt he held in his hand. His bare chest was driving her to distraction. Not because it was thick and corded with muscle. Not because it was tanned and lined in strength. But because it was James's. And he was so close. A sturdy rock of manhood—a cave into which she longed to crawl and never come out. And she hated feeling that way. Needing him made her vulnerable. Did all women suffer such uncontrollable longings during courtship? As if they couldn't get enough of their beau? As if they'd shrivel up and die without him?

When she didn't answer, he placed a finger beneath her chin and raised her gaze to his, one brow lifting. "Your condition, Miss?"

"Oh, yes." She attempted a smile. "That we don't discuss any of our problems."

He nodded his agreement.

And like a gentleman, he kept his word. For two hours Angeline and James—and Stowy—escaped the world with all its problems and stresses: the temple, the beasts, the visions, the disasters, the pirates. And most of all, Dodd. For two hours she sat on an old quilt in the sand and memorized every curve of James's mouth; the scar that angled down the right side of his lips; the flex of his jaw; every sparkle in his eyes; the way the wind played havoc with his hair, making it poke out all over; the sound of his voice that reminded her of the thunder of waves. And his laughter, which brought a lightness to her spirit she'd never known. After sharing some of their meal, Stowy curled up in James's lap, something he rarely did with anyone but her. Sweet saints, if the cat trusted this man so much, what reason did she have not to do the same?

She discovered they both enjoyed the writings of Emerson and Thoreau, the artwork of Frederic Edwin Church, the sound of a violin, and fruitcake. They spoke little of their past and shared dreams for their future. A future that was beginning to form out of the haze of Angeline's memories. Like the bright sun, it shoved aside the bitter cloud of her past and shaped her dreams into sparkling possibilities.

She could spend a lifetime on this blanket with this man on this beach. And die happy.

Finally he leaned toward her and planted a kiss on her lips. A soft, chaste kiss, his breath feathering her cheek, as if he touched precious porcelain. She drew in a breath of him and felt her pulse race, imagining what it would feel like to be loved tenderly and gently, not harsh and rough like an animal satisfying an impulse. Memories invaded, sullying the moment. Voices shouted insults in her mind. James cupped the back of her neck and ran a thumb over her cheek, luring her out of the darkness.

"Angeline, sweet, sweet, Angeline," he breathed over her lips before tasting her again. Angeline's world spun. What she wouldn't give to be pure and innocent for this man. To be the lady he believed she was. Perhaps she could wish her former life away, abandon all her bad memories to the past where they belonged.

James tasted of mango and salt and she pressed against him, wanting more and more, trusting him like she'd trusted no other. It began to rain. Small drops at first but then larger and larger, until the two separated, gathered their things, along with Stowy, and ran back to camp laughing like children.

Hours later as the sun sank behind the tips of the trees, Angeline sat on the beach, Stowy in her lap, studying the webs of foam each wave created upon the shore. Each one was so delicate, so beautiful, so unique, it would put the finest Chantilly lace to shame. Yet how many exquisite designs bubbled over the sand one minute and then were gone the next? If she hadn't been sitting here to observe, no one would have seen their beauty. How true of their own lives. Tossed upon the sand by God, some forming gorgeous patterns, others fading away too soon. But did anyone notice? Was something beautiful if no one ever saw it to proclaim it so? If it was swept away before anyone realized its value?

"May I join you?"

Startled, Angeline glanced up to see Hayden standing beside her, a friendly yet concerned smile on his face. "Of course."

He plopped to the sand and stretched out his legs, planting his hands behind him. For several minutes he stared at the sea, his jaw bunching then relaxing, then bunching again. No doubt, he was anxious about sneaking aboard the pirate ship in a few hours. Yet, why would he come to her and not his wife?

"Is there something I can do for you, Hayden?" She caressed Stowy's fur.

He glanced over his shoulder at camp, where some of the colonists were starting the evening fire and several others were cutting fruit for supper. "You and James have an understanding?" He faced her.

The topic took her by surprise. "We are courting." Curiosity caused her to search his expression. Why would Hayden concern himself with her and James's relationship? Especially in light of the danger he faced that night.

He blew out a heavy sigh and gazed at the horizon. "I don't know how to say this, but I feel I should discuss it with you before..."

"Before you risk your life tonight?"

"Indeed." He rubbed the stubble on his jaw. "I don't know what will happen, but I care deeply for both you and James. And, well, I suppose there is no delicate way to say this. Back in the States, I saw your likeness on a poster at the Norfolk sheriff's station." He stared at her. "You were wanted for murder."

Angeline's heart collapsed. Her blood turned to ice. She gazed out to sea, trying to force breath into her lungs, trying to put on an expression of shock, of indignation. Anything but reveal the terror gripping her.

"The name wasn't yours," he continued. "Clarissa somebody, but I'd know your face anywhere."

She dug her toes in the sand, staring at the wavelets stroking the shore, not finding them as beautiful as she had only moments before. "My face is a common one."

"Hardly."

She looked at him, at the way his lips curved in that alluring smile, and she knew why Magnolia was smitten with him.

Angeline gave a huff of resignation. "What do you wish to know?"

"What do I wish to know?" He gave a cynical chuckle. "Well, if you're going to marry James, I suppose I'd like to know what your real name is and whether you are, indeed, a murderer."

A crab skittered across the sand. She followed it with her gaze.

"Just tell me it isn't true," he continued. "Tell me it was a mistake and I'll never mention it again."

A torrent of emotions clogged Angeline's throat: fear, sorrow, anger. She opened her mouth to answer him, but nothing but a squeak emerged.

"Angeline. I know you. You aren't capable of murder. Tell me they had the wrong woman."

The crackle of a fire sounded in the distance, and she fully expected to see her clients appear to taunt her. She wanted to lie to Hayden. Wanted to shout that she had no idea what he was talking about. But it seemed that no matter how hard she tried, no matter that Dodd remained in a coma, her past would find a way to ruin her future.

"Zooks, Angeline. What happened?"

She closed her eyes, wishing the crashing waves would sweep over her and carry her away. "It's a long story, Hayden." Tugging on the chain around her neck, she pulled out her father's ring and rubbed it gently with her thumb. The ruby and topazes barely shimmered in the fading light. "It started when my father was murdered. Thrown out the window of his shipyard by some madman claiming ownership."

She expected more questions. She expected the typical expression of sympathy. What she didn't expect was to see Hayden's face turn a shade of white to match the sand.

"What was your father's name?"

"Frederick Paine. Why?"

Hayden seemed to be having trouble breathing. "And the man who fought him?"

"A Mr. Carson, I think. He took off afterward. We never saw him again. Why? What do you know of this?" She laid a hand on his sleeve. His arm trembled. "If you know something about my father, please tell me."

"I never met your father." Hayden stared at the sand, his shoulders taut. "But I know about the deal that sent him to his death. The felonious accord which made Mr. Carson believe he owned your father's shipyard."

Angeline's thoughts spun in a whirlwind. "How could you possibly know that?"

"Because I was the man who struck that bargain."

CHAPTER 29

W hat are you saying?" Leaning forward, Angeline palmed the sand and shoved to her feet, still not believing her ears. Stowy circled the hem of her skirts, howling in annoyance.

Hayden rose and brushed sand from his trousers. Guilt dripped from his expression.

"You murdered my father?" Blood boiled through Angeline, muddling her thoughts and inflaming her anger. "You murdered my father!" Hot tears spilled down her cheeks.

"Not directly." Agony stretched across Hayden's eyes. "I had no way of knowing Mr. Carson would react the way he did."

Raising her hand, Angeline slapped him across the cheek. Her hand stung, but it felt good. Hayden rubbed his jaw. She backed away and broke into sobs.

"I'm so sorry, Angeline. I was a swindler, a confidence man back in the States. I hurt a lot of people, God forgive me." He took a step toward her, holding out his hand.

She shoved it away. Then batted tears from her face. She would not let this man see her cry. "You swindled this Mr. Carson?"

"Yes, I sold him your father's shipyard."

"But it wasn't yours to sell."

"No." He lowered his chin.

"What did you think would happen?" Leaning over, she grabbed a handful of sand and tossed it at him. The grains struck him and slid down the fabric of his shirt. He never flinched. "What did you think!?" she shouted.

"I didn't." His eyes misted. "I had no way of knowing Carson would shove your dad out that third-story window." Wind tossed hair into his face and he snapped it away. "I'm not that man anymore."

Angeline didn't care. All that mattered was that he was responsible for her father's death. He was responsible for what she'd been forced to do afterward in order to survive! "Do you know what happened to me after my father's death? Do you?" She thrust her face into his. "I was an orphan. Went to live with my uncle. A terrible man." She turned her back to him. She wouldn't tell him anymore. Wouldn't give him the satisfaction of knowing the pain he had caused her. Instead she stood seething, longing for the pistol that used to sit in her belt.

"I'm so sorry, Angeline."

Turning, she charged him and pounded both fists on his chest, her only thought to make him suffer as he had made her. But her thrusts merely bounced off thick muscle. He grabbed her hands and forced her to stop. Tearing from him, she dropped to her knees, gasping for air. Stowy hissed at Hayden.

"Angeline." He took a step toward her.

She snapped her fiery eyes his way, feeling as though they could shoot darts at him if she so willed. "Don't come any closer."

"I hope you can forgive me."

She scooped up Stowy. "If you're truly sorry, then do me one small favor."

"Anything."

"You must not tell James. Not about the poster. Not about our talk."

He hesitated, drew in a deep breath, and glanced out to sea. "I make no promises."

Angeline stood and stiffened her spine. "I hate you, Hayden Gale. I will never forgive you. Ever."

Hayden slid into the dark water and dove beneath an incoming swell. Thank God the waves came in strong tonight. The thunderous sound would hopefully mask any splashes he and Blake made as they swam toward the pirate ship. Well past midnight, clouds covered a waning moon and a smattering of stars, keeping light at bay and the night reigning in darkness—another sign God was on their side. Well, of course the Almighty was on their side. Surely He wasn't on the pirates'? Hadn't they prayed with James, Eliza, and Magnolia before they'd left? If God could heal Thiago, certainly He could make their mission to steal gunpowder successful.

Cool water gushed around Hayden, gurgling and slushing past his ears. Saltwater filled his mouth. He spit it out. The scent of brine stung his nose. Every muscle was tight. Every nerve coiled. Every sense heightened. *Oh, God, please just get me back to Magnolia in one piece.* Not hanging from a yardarm.

He broke the surface and spotted Blake just ahead of him. Getting to the pirate ship shouldn't be a problem. Getting past the few pirates on board was another story. Hopefully it wouldn't be as difficult as his encounter with Angeline had been earlier that day. An encounter he couldn't shove from his mind, no matter the present danger.

He'd swindled many people in his past, made a thousand spurious deals that had relieved people of their fortunes and lined his own pockets. But he'd never hurt anyone he cared about.

Until now.

Not only hurt, not only stolen money from, but apparently his actions had destroyed her life, had possibly led her to murder and God knew what else.

Drawing in a deep breath, he dove beneath a roller, wishing the waves would wash him clean of his past. But he supposed God didn't work that way. God forgives, God redeems, but He doesn't always sweep away the consequences of one's bad choices. Like everyone in the colony, Hayden had hoped to escape the horrors of war by coming to Brazil. He had also hoped to escape his equally horrifying past. But it had found him anyway. First in the form of his father, and now in the form of precious Angeline.

He plunged upward through the surface, his eyes stinging from salt, his lungs gulping air, his heart heavy with guilt. He could do nothing but apologize to both God and man. God had already forgiven him. Hayden prayed Angeline would do the same someday. Water slapped him in the face like she had done earlier. He deserved that and more for what he'd done. Even still, he could not abide by her wishes and keep silent. James deserved to know the truth—whatever that truth was. Hayden could not allow one of his best friends to marry a murderer.

All such concerns fled him when he and Blake struck the side of the ship. He must focus on their mission or all would be lost. Waves lapped the wood and spread foamy claws upward toward a railing that disappeared into the thick black of night. The oaky smell of moist wood filled Hayden's lungs as Blake nodded and began climbing the rope ladder.

Captain Ricu was on board. At least they'd seen one of his men rowing him to the ship at nightfall. That was hours ago, and by now, the flamboyant captain was surely sound asleep in his cabin. The long days spent in the tunnels seemed to steal his ostentatious vitality. Most of the pirates ashore were asleep as well, save the few that guarded the camp. Since they were preventing the colonists from escaping by land, not by sea, it had been easy to slip into the water without drawing their attention.

Hayden gripped the thick line, propped his bare feet on the hull, and followed Blake. Coarse rope, which felt more like a dozen needles, burned his hands. The ship creaked and groaned beneath each incoming wave, mimicking the ache in his muscles. Above him, the night soon swallowed up Blake. Hayden continued until finally a hand gripped his arm and hauled him over the bulwarks. He landed like a wet fish on the foredeck. The *drip, drip* from his clothes and his heavy breath echoed like alarms over the ship.

Thankfully, the guttural snores of several men rose to drown out the sound—pirates, who with bottles clutched to their chests, lay in haphazard positions across the deck like marionettes whose strings had been severed. Even the watchmen, muskets strewn across their laps, slouched against masts and gun carriages as if God had poured a sleep potion on them from heaven.

Lifting a silent prayer of thanks, Hayden inched his way around prostrate forms, eyeing the pistols and swords strapped to their bodies. The colonists could sure use some weapons, but he dared not risk waking the sleeping miscreants. The gunpowder was far more important. Destroying the tunnels and—if what James said was true— keeping the final beast imprisoned was their top priority. Then perhaps Captain Ricu would give up his quest for gold and leave them alone. If not, they'd find another way to deal with him.

Hayden dropped down a hatch, ignoring the foul stench that bit his nose. He'd been on this ship twice before. Once to rescue Magnolia and the second time to deliver the treasure maps to the captain. Both times, he'd taken note of the layout—knew the ship's magazine must be located between the second deck and the hold. He only hoped it wasn't locked. Grabbing a lantern from a hook on the bulkhead, he led Blake into the bowels of the ship, past the wardroom and the pantry until they stood before a bolted door.

Apprehension stormed across Blake's gray eyes. He yanked a small ax from his belt and raised it above the iron lock. It would make noise. They both knew it would. What they didn't know was whether that noise would penetrate the pirates' blissful slumber. But they had no choice.

Blake slammed the ax down.

Clank!

The lock swung on its hinge but didn't break. Groaning inwardly, Hayden exchanged a look of frustration with his friend. They waited. The ship rolled over an incoming wave. Blake rubbed his sore leg. Wind whistled through the hallway, joining the creak and grate of aged wood. But no human sounds met their ears. The lantern sputtered, casting ghoulish shadows on the bulkhead. Blake raised the ax again.

Clank! Thud!

The lock snapped off and fell to the deck. Lifting the lantern, Hayden pushed the door open to reveal a dozen kegs of gunpowder, piles of muskets, pistols, grenades, cutlasses, and cannonballs. He exchanged a grin with Blake. Now the hard part began. Getting one of the heavy kegs up the ladder to the main deck, over the bulwarks, and into one of the cockboats tied to the ship without getting caught. Once in the boat, it would be a short trip down shore away from camp where they could hide the keg until they could formulate the best plan to put it to use.

Clipping the lantern on the deckhead, Hayden grabbed a pistol and shoved it in his belt then slid a handful of shot in his pocket. All these weapons. All this gunpowder. It seemed a shame to leave most of it behind.

"We could blow up the ship if we wanted," he said without thinking.

Loosening his tie, Blake ran the ends over the sweat on his neck. "Everyone on board would die."

They stood staring at each other, the possibility of enacting such a heinous task weighing heavy in the air between them. The deck tilted. The lantern swayed. A chill bit through Hayden's wet clothes.

Blake shook his head. "You don't have it in you either, Hayden. Not anymore."

Hayden's tight chest unwound. Before he'd come to know God, he wouldn't have hesitated to kill men who were intent on killing him. But something *had* changed within him in the past few months. Well, a lot had changed, if he was honest. But one thing he'd come to know with certainty—human life was precious. Every human life. Each person a unique masterpiece of the divine Creator.

Even pirates.

He released a breath and nodded at his friend while Blake snatched a couple of pistols and a sword and shoved them into his belt. Then together, they carried a keg of powder down the hall and up the ladder onto the main deck where a blast of wind flapped Hayden's damp trousers against his leg and sent ice up his spine.

Something didn't feel right. Yet when Hayden glanced around, the pirates remained sprawled in the same positions as before. A lantern swinging from the mainmast cast ribbons of dark and light over the deck as it screeched in harmony with the creak of wood. They set the keg down and glanced over the port railing at the dark shape of a boat thumping against the hull. Blake grabbed the rope dangling over the side and began tying it around the keg while Hayden kept watch.

Just a few minutes. That's all the time they needed in order to lower the keg to the boat and be on their way. Just a few more minutes and their mission would be completed. Hayden shook his head at how easy it had been. Thank God the pirates had grown overconfident and become complacent in their vigilance.

Blake finished tying the rope and tugged on it to test the knot.

Squatting, Hayden helped him lift the keg, his muscles straining as they set it atop the bulwarks. They were about to lower it over the side when boot steps clapped over the deck and a shadow emerged from the darkness. Lantern light glimmered off a jeweled waistcoat and winked at them from a gold ring in one ear.

"And where you think to go with that?"

Hayden's body turned to mud. And like mud, he wanted to spill to the deck, squeeze between the planks, and disappear. Instead he set down the keg, wondering if the despair in his own eyes matched the despair he saw in Blake's.

Captain Ricu graced them with one of his annoying, insolent belly laughs. "What be this? You think to make idiota out of Captain Armando Manuel Ricu?" He stomped his boot on the deck, jingling the bells that adorned it.

Hayden cursed himself silently. Why hadn't he heard the man coming? Rum and sour fish wafted beneath Hayden's nose. Why hadn't he *smelled* him?

Four pirates swarmed them, relieving them of their weapons and leveling pistols at their chests. Ricu planted fists at his waist and stared at them, though his expression was lost in the shadows. Probably for the best as Hayden could feel his anger from where he stood.

"I treat you well and this be how you repel me?"

Blake shifted the weight off his bad leg and huffed. "Repay. And we could have blown up your ship, Captain. And you, along with it."

"Instead you steal to blow up later."

"No," Hayden began. "We—"

"Enough!" Ricu stormed, swung about and charged through his sleeping men, kicking them as he went and shouting words in Portuguese.

Groaning and grunting, the pirates scrambled to rise, rubbing their eyes and standing at attention once they saw their angry captain.

Further Portuguese words were brandished about before Hayden and Blake were escorted back to shore, along with the captain and a few of his men. At least he didn't hang them from the yardarm or enact any other vicious pirate torture Hayden had read about. Such as the rosary of pain that made a man's eyes pop out or flogging with the "cat," a whip made from knotted strips of rope that ripped open a man's flesh. He suddenly wished he hadn't read any of those fanciful pirate tales as a kid. Trying to evict them from his mind, he glanced at Blake who sat beside him in the jostling boat. Stiff and stone-faced like a warrior, a tic in Blake's jaw was the only indication of his angst.

Whatever Captain Ricu had planned for them, it couldn't be good.

MaryLu Tyndall

Pirates jerked them from the boat and hauled them through tumbling waves onto dry sand. With a snap of his fingers, Ricu sent several of them marching toward the colonists' camp.

Hayden's heart stopped. Beside him, Blake's breath came hard and rapid.

Captain Ricu took up a pompous pace. "Since you not know to behave. Since I cannot trust you, I take what is most precious to you."

Hayden's mouth dried. He had nothing precious but Magnolia.

Within moments, women's screams pierced the night. Both he and Blake started forward, but the tips of two swords held them back.

"Now you listen. Now you behave." Ricu grinned.

"Please, Captain," Blake's voice came out in a desperate growl. "They had nothing to do with this. Punish us. Not them."

Heart in his throat, Hayden squinted into the darkness where the pirates took form, dragging two women across the sand, one with brown hair, one with flaxen.

"Leave them be!" Batting aside the blade and ignoring the pain slicing his hand, Hayden charged forward with one thought in mind: kill the man who handled his wife so harshly. But he only made it a step when something hard struck his head. He toppled to the sand, barely conscious.

Conscious enough to hear Magnolia scream and the captain's glum pronouncement:

"I take your wives prisoner aboard the *Espoliar*."

Chapter 30

"Y ou can't go." James clasped Angeline's hands. "The pirates may not allow you to return."

Violet eyes, moist with tears yet sparking with defiance, raised to his. "They are my friends. The only friends I've ever had." She swallowed as the rising sun highlighted the smattering of adorable freckles on her nose. "If Captain Ricu is allowing me to bring them food and see how they fare, how can I refuse?" She squeezed his hand then released it. "I *know* you understand."

Of course he understood. If Ricu would allow him to go, he'd row out to the *Espoliar* in a second. "I still can't believe you talked him into it." James had seen her speaking to the flamboyant pirate yesterday evening after supper. A brief conversation in which Angeline did most of the talking and Ricu did most of the staring, giving her a look as if he wished to swat her away like one of the sand fleas that inhabited the beach. By the time James was halfway there to rescue the foolish woman, Ricu had shrugged and walked away while Angeline turned to face James, a smug look on her face.

"I had merely to mention his lady's name and how he would wish someone to care for her should she find herself in such a predicament."

"You have that pirate wrapped around your finger." He eased a lock of her hair behind her ear, constantly amazed by this woman. "But what else would I expect?"

She smiled. "By a tenuous thread, I assure you."

"All the more reason not to deliver yourself into his hands," James growled. It had been two days since Eliza and Magnolia had been imprisoned aboard the ship, and everyone in camp was overwrought with worry. Each evening Blake and Hayden had returned bone-weary and bruised from the tunnels where Ricu had dragged them as part of their punishment. Unable to sleep or even to eat, both men spent the night pacing the beach in frustration while dipping their heads in secret plans to rescue their wives. Yet after contemplating a thousand scenarios, nothing seemed feasible. Nothing that wouldn't put their wives in more danger, and risk all the colonists' lives. The worst part— James knew from experience—was imagining what Captain Ricu and his men were doing to Magnolia and Eliza. Though Angeline tried to comfort them with hopeful words of Ricu's desire to change, Blake and Hayden suffered immensely, their haggard faces reflecting the torture they felt within. Captain Ricu was far smarter than James had given him credit for. Sure, he could have killed Hayden and Blake on the spot, but that might have caused the rest of the colonists to rise up in rebellion. This way, Ricu kept them all in check on the threat of hurting two of the colony's favored women.

A breeze tossed a curl across Angeline's shoulder as she squinted at the *Espoliar* rocking offshore, the golden sun rising behind its stark masts. "I will be all right, James. Don't worry."

Yet *she* was worried. He saw it in the tightness around her mouth, in the way she bit her bottom lip. "I can't lose you," he said.

"You won't." She tried to smile.

"You stand barely above five feet tall, and you forget you don't have your pistol anymore."

"I haven't forgotten." She frowned as if she truly did miss the weapon. "What good would it do against a dozen pirates, anyway?" She gave a little shrug.

"That is exactly what I am saying!" James said.

Which only made her smile all the more. She brushed sand from his shirt. "Is this our first squabble?"

"No."

She seemed to ponder that for a minute. "Indeed, I fear you are correct. We've had many before. Are we to spend our entire courtship quarreling?"

"Not if you stop being so stubborn."

"Hmm. I'm not sure that's possible."

"Something we agree on at last." He grinned.

She reached up to caress his jaw. "There are many others, I'm sure."

When she touched him like she was doing now, James believed he'd agree with anything she said. "We'll have a lifetime to discover our many areas of agreement." He placed his hand atop hers but suddenly frowned. "That is, if you don't go getting yourself killed by pirates."

She smiled. "I better go." Bending, she picked up the sack at her feet containing fruit, smoked fish, and a few of Eliza and Magnolia's personal items then headed toward the cockboat where Blake and Hayden waited to see her off.

James followed after her. *Mule-headed, reckless woman!* The frayed hem of her emerald skirt sashayed back and forth over the sand as she marched dauntless into unknown danger.

Courageous, beautiful woman.

Angling a wide circle around Hayden as if he had a disease, she stopped to speak to Blake before she allowed the pirates to assist her into the craft.

Captain Ricu appeared at the railing, doffing his red-feathered hat in his usual colorful greeting, but his eyes were on Angeline approaching in the boat.

"If he lays one finger on her!" James huffed and kicked the sand then glanced up at Hayden and Blake, their sullen gazes glued to the ship.

"Forgive me, I'm being thoughtless." When he should have been comforting his friends, he was the one demanding comfort. Once again, he'd failed as a preacher.

Blake slapped him on the back. "We will all feel better when Angeline returns with a good report."

If she returns. He watched as the pirates assisted her up the rope ladder and then over the railing, where she disappeared from sight. *Please, God, watch over her.*

⚜

Not since her father had been alive had anyone cared whether Angeline lived or died. James's raw emotion, so often worn on his sleeve—and one of the things she loved about him—had kept her warm all the way out to the ship. Kept her legs moving even now as Captain Ricu,

865

after sifting through the contents of her bag, escorted her below. The massive man smelled of port, gunpowder, and tobacco. He repeatedly glanced over his shoulder at her, licking his lips as one would when selecting a choice cut of meat for supper.

Angeline had met men like him—men far more prolific in stature than brains. Men who, decked in garish pretention, swaggered their authority about in order to mask a wavering confidence within. To say she was not frightened would be a lie. Her jittery stomach was evidence of that. But to say she couldn't handle herself with such men would also be a lie. She had proven that already with this particular man. But would the allure of his lady-love's approval continue to restrain his nefarious passions? That was the question that had her heart in a knot.

"You no bigger than sprite." He guffawed. "A bela sprite, I say."

"But I should warn you, Captain, this sprite has a vicious bite."

At that, he swung around, his frame filling the narrow hallway. Two lanterns creaked as they swayed from hooks on the walls, their shifting light barely chasing away the gloom. The pirate behind her bumped into her, but Angeline steadied her thrashing heart and stood her ground. Instead of striking her as she expected, Ricu laughed, a deep husky laugh that bounced over the bulkheads like thunder. "I bet you have bite, little one." He turned and continued down a ladder. Hoisting the sack over her shoulder, she tried her best to navigate the rungs as carefully as possible while holding her breath against a stink that would send even the staunchest sailor reeling. The last thing she wanted was to slip and tumble down on top of the man.

"Perhaps we try your bite soon." Ricu stopped at the bottom and held up his lantern. Maniacal threads of light twisted across his face as eyes as dark as onyx assessed her.

The pirate behind her chuckled.

Angeline resisted the urge to kick him in the groin. "Where are my friends?" she demanded.

Grunting, he jerked the lantern to his right. "Faro will show." Then turning to the rotund pirate behind him, who had more hair on his chin than his head, Ricu spouted off a string of Portuguese before climbing up the ladder with a groan as if every step caused him pain.

Down the hall, the pirate unlocked a door, shoved Angeline inside, and slammed it shut. A squeal of delight etched across Angeline's ears before arms surrounded her in a strong embrace. *Eliza.* Or at least Angeline thought it was Eliza in the darkness, for the woman could embrace like no other. She could also grip quite hard as she shook Angeline's shoulders. "What are you doing here?" Her tone had turned from delight to anger.

Finally her face came into focus as Angeline's eyes grew accustomed to the shadows. Muted light drifted in through a tiny porthole near the deckhead, offering the only reprieve from the gloom. A pile of sailcloth was stacked against the bulkhead on the left. Beside it, a chamber pot fumed from the corner. Atop the rickety table hooked to the wall sat an empty pewter plate and an old book. Two chairs framed it, providing the only place to sit, aside from the narrow cot on her right—the cot from which Magnolia now rose. The Southern belle flung an arm around Angeline's waist and squeezed. "How fares Hayden, Blake, and everyone else?" The woman's attempt to keep her tone light failed as desperation rang in her voice.

"Everyone is well. Tormented with worry, but well. How are you both?" Angeline squinted to see her friends in the shadows and, thankfully, saw no cuts or bruises, nor additional tears to their already tattered gowns. "The pirates haven't. . .they haven't. . ."

"No," Eliza said. "Not yet, anyway."

Magnolia hugged herself. "That beastly captain drags both of us to his cabin each night and then just sits there staring at us while he drinks his brandy."

Relief settled over Angeline. "That's good news. He's keeping you from the other pirates as well."

Eliza drew a ragged breath. "I fear one of these nights he will drink too much and forget about this woman you say he loves."

Angeline feared the same. The ship teetered over a swell, creaking in complaint. Balancing her feet on the deck, she flung the sack on the table. "I brought gifts." Opening the pouch, she pulled out the fruit and fish and set them on the plate, then reaching back into the sack, she withdrew a small wooden object and handed it to Magnolia. "Hayden said this would bring you comfort." Though Angeline couldn't imagine why. What woman preferred a carving of a toad over fresh underthings or soap or a hairbrush? But as soon as Magnolia saw it, she clutched it to her chest, her blue eyes pooling.

"He also said he loves you very much and bids you be strong."

Brushing aside a tear, Magnolia nodded, her face beaming with such intense emotion, Angeline looked away. That same emotion, a desperate longing, now burned in Eliza's eyes—so unusual for the stalwart woman—as her gaze shifted to the sack.

"And Blake sent this." Angeline pulled out a Georgia Army belt plate, which Eliza gobbled up in her hands as if it were made of gold. "Strange gifts, if you ask me."

"Not strange at all." Eliza pressed the belt plate to her chest. "This is Blake's most prized possession. I'm surprised he risked it falling into the pirates' hands."

"He told me to tell you that he would have sent his heart, but you are already in possession." At the time, Angeline had thought the phrase too sentimental and trite for the staunch colonel to say, but now as she repeated the words and saw their reaction on Eliza's face, she knew it had been the perfect message.

Eliza laughed and cried at the same time, and Angeline wondered if she'd ever share such an incredible bond with James.

"I can't believe Captain Ricu allowed you to come." Eliza finally gathered her emotions, still staring at the belt plate, but then her gaze snapped to Angeline. "You aren't a prisoner too, are you?"

"Possibly."

"You risked too much." Magnolia sat in one of the chairs, the toad still cradled in her hands.

"Not too much for my friends," Angeline replied. "Besides, Hayden and Blake would go utterly mad if they didn't hear word of your well-being."

"I fear I will go mad if I do not see my husband soon." Magnolia sighed. "Please tell us you bring word the pirates will release us soon."

Captain Ricu's voice bellowed from above decks, followed by the stomping of feet. Angeline bit her lip. "I wish I could, but I have no idea."

"It doesn't matter." Golden light from the window oscillated over Eliza with the sway of the ship. "God told me we will soon be returned to the colony."

Magnolia lowered her chin. "I wish I could believe that."

"I have faith for us both, Magnolia." Eliza knelt before her friend and gazed up at her. "We *will* get out of here."

Angeline wasn't so sure. How could God speak to people? He was way up in heaven and, obviously, completely unaware of what was happening here on earth. But it would do no good to shatter her friends' hopeful illusions.

Rising, Eliza faced Angeline. "But you. You shouldn't have come."

Angeline shrugged. "Even if they keep me here, I deserve it more than either of you."

"Why would you say such a thing?"

Unaccustomed to the wobbling deck, Angeline lowered onto the other chair. She was so tired of keeping secrets, pretending to be someone she was not. "You think you know me, but you don't. I've done terrible things."

"I doubt that," Eliza said.

"It's true."

"Whether it is or not, the past no longer matters." Magnolia reached for her across the table. "God has forgiven you."

Had He? Angeline hadn't asked Him for forgiveness. Mainly because she wasn't sure He would give it, but also because if she was honest, she was angry at God for what had happened to her. "Perhaps I haven't forgiven *Him*," she said. "He hasn't been very kind to me. Why did He allow my father to die? Allow me to become—" She stopped. "Allow all the horrid things that happened afterward."

"Did you ever ask Him?" Eliza said. "Did you ever seek His will during those difficult times?"

Angeline shook her head.

Eliza sank to the cot and stared at the belt plate. "I fear we are very much alike, Angeline. I spent most of my life making my own decisions, going my own way, thinking I didn't need God. I wanted to live my life without anyone telling me what to do. And I made such a mess of things. I caused myself and a lot of people tremendous pain."

Angeline studied her friend. Eliza caused people pain? Unlikely. At least not the enormous amount of pain Angeline had caused. Tugging her father's ring from beneath her bodice, she fingered the beautiful jewels. "I assumed God didn't care what happened to me. He wasn't there when I became an orphan, when my uncle tried to. . ."—she gazed at her friends, who both stared back with such loving eyes, she couldn't help but continue—"ravish me."

Magnolia raised a hand to her mouth. Eliza remained silent, listening.

Waves rustled against the hull.

"What happened?" Magnolia asked.

"I ended up begging on the street." Angeline hugged herself and stared at the stained deck. "I became a trollop." There, she'd finally said it. The words floated through air thick with stink and steam before the weight of their shame plunged them to the deck. Wind whistled against the window. The ship canted to the left. Angeline cursed herself for a fool. Why, oh why had she said anything? She could feel Magnolia and Eliza's eyes piercing her—eyes, no doubt, filled with disdain and disgust. She couldn't bear it another minute. Rising, she clutched her skirts and started for the door, intending to bang upon it until the pirates released her.

Magnolia grabbed her hand before she took a step. "God was there with you."

Eliza blocked Angeline's path. "There and loving you as He is now."

Overcome by the concern on their faces, tears filled Angeline's eyes. "With me? God was with me? Then why did He allow me to become. . .what I became?"

"You never asked Him for help," Eliza said. "God hated what your uncle did to you, but afterward, I know He was there waiting to love and help you. But it sounds like you ran away from Him instead. You wouldn't allow Him in your life. How can you blame Him now for the choices you made?"

Tugging from Magnolia's grip, Angeline swept past her friends.

"I don't mean to be cruel, Angeline," Eliza continued, spinning to face her. "Just honest. It will do no good for me to placate you with comforts or flatter you with kind words that don't get to the root of the problem. Life is cruel. Terrible things happen, but it's how we react that matters. It's who we run to for help that makes all the difference."

Like a sharp knife, the words sliced through Angeline's heart, leaving a winding trail of pain and shame. She backed away from her friends until she struck the hard bulkhead. Could her life have been different if she'd turned to God, begged for His help? Would He have answered her? Taken care of her?

The ship creaked and groaned, mimicking her tormented conscience. Eliza and Magnolia gazed at her with nothing but love and concern. Not disgust. Not repulsion. Not condemnation. Her throat burned. Her vision blurred. Shock sent her thoughts whirling. Shame for her own stupidity gutted her. She wobbled, and instantly her friends led her back to the chair.

Magnolia sat beside her. "Ask His forgiveness and start anew. I did. And it has changed everything."

Angeline couldn't argue with that. Just months ago, Magnolia had been nothing but a spoiled, vain, selfish lady. Yet, here she sat, imprisoned on a pirate ship, concerning herself with Angeline. Giving hardly a thought to her own predicament.

Maybe God could do that for Angeline. Change her. Make her new. Maybe He *had* been with her the whole time. A tiny spark of hope pushed away the blackness in her soul. . .like a match struck in a dark room. "You aren't shocked, appalled, disgusted?"

"Hardly," Eliza said. "We've all done horrible things."

"But this. . ."

"Is no worse than my selfishness." Magnolia rose. "Or my vanity, pride, or boorishness."

"Or my rebellion, stubbornness, and independence," Eliza added.

Angeline smiled and sobbed at the same time. "I'm so sorry." She wiped moisture from her face. "I came to comfort you, and here I speak only of my own problems."

"It's quite all right." Magnolia shrugged and shared a smile with Eliza. "What else have we to do?"

"Perhaps this is why God allowed us to be brought here," Eliza said. "Just to have this talk with you. In that case, it is worth it."

Angeline's throat clogged with emotion even as her heart seemed to swell. This was certainly not the reaction she'd expected from her friends—not the reaction she usually received from proper women. Would God equally surprise her with His response? Warm arms enveloped her as both Eliza and Magnolia pulled her into an embrace. All three ladies stood teetering with the rolling deck, crying and laughing and encouraging one another until the clank of lock and key jarred them from their camaraderie and the entrance of Captain Ricu separated them. With narrowed eyes and a grunt, he dragged Angeline from the cabin.

"Thank you for allowing me to visit my friends, Captain," Angeline remarked as he led her through the narrow hallway.

His only reply was another grunt.

"And I also thank you for not harming them. Your lady—*Senhorita* Abelena was it?—would be pleased."

He wheeled around, his coiled black mane swinging about him, his eyes darts in the dim lantern light. The hall closed in on Angeline, and for a moment she'd thought she'd lured the mad pirate out from hiding. But then his shoulders lowered and he breathed out a sigh.

"I run out of rum to keep men happy. Soon they will want their turn."

"Then release the women, Captain. Their husbands have suffered enough for their crimes."

"Humph." Turning, he continued up a ladder to the main deck where a blast of wind flapped Angeline's skirts and swept away the foul smell from below.

His gaze took in the open sea as if he longed to be as free from Brazil as some of the colonists were.

"You can't fool me, Captain," she said, risking his anger but sensing something in his eyes.

He snorted and faced her.

She pointed toward his chest. "There's a heart growing in there. You *are* changing." She leaned toward him and whispered, "But your secret is safe with me."

"Beware your words to me, bela sprite. I am still Captain Ricu, and I take what I want when I want!" He spat the words with venom, but there was no sting in his eyes as he shoved her toward his waiting men who assisted her into the boat below.

Somewhere between ship and sand, as the waves struck the small craft, showering her in mist, as the rising sun sprinkled her in gold dust, Angeline whispered her first prayer to God in years. Just a quick "hello" to see if He was listening. A tingling began deep within her. A burst of light. A flood of love raced through her veins, pumping them full of life. By the time she met Blake, Hayden, and James ashore, she could hardly think, could hardly form a coherent thought.

No sooner had she reassured them of their wives' safety than Ricu and his men hauled them off to dig in the tunnels. The rest of the day went by in a blur as Angeline's mind and heart whirled with thoughts of God, of being loved by her Creator. Excusing herself from supper, she retired early. But she couldn't find sleep. How could anyone sleep with such a glorious feeling bubbling up inside? All warmth and love and peace and protection. Angels' songs called to her in the night, celebrating, rejoicing, inviting her to a feast.

It was the voice of her heavenly Father welcoming her home.

Tears dampening her cheeks like the water dampened her bare toes, she strolled among the waves till well past midnight, one minute begging for forgiveness, the next laughing and singing, and the next dancing through the lacy foam, until, exhausted, she finally dropped to the sand and fell deep asleep.

She dreamed she was a princess captured by an evil magician who had imprisoned her in a dark dungeon for years and years. But one day a prince came. White-robed, with gleaming sword in hand, He stormed the fortress, fought for her, and loosed the shackles that bound her hands and feet, drawing her from the dungeon into the light. She shrank back, ashamed of the filth that covered her. The prince drew her close. She resisted. How could she allow someone so clean and beautiful to touch her grime and muck? He persisted, and finally she fell into His embrace. Instantly, the dirt cracked as if made of dried clay and fell off her, piece by piece, until she stood wearing the white robe of a princess.

A light pierced her eyelids, flooding them with gold.

She slowly opened her eyes to see the edge of the sun arc above the sea. She was clean. Clean at last! She chuckled. All these years, she'd never wanted to trust anyone, never wanted anyone to rescue her. But as it turned out, she needed God to sweep in and save her most of all. And He *had* rescued her. In every possible way.

Rising to sit, she drew a deep breath of the salty air and allowed the gentle breeze to finger through her hair. She'd never felt so free, so light, so loved. *Thank You, Father. Thank You!*

No more bad memories, no more guilt. No more lies. She must tell James. Regardless of the consequences, she could not continue their courtship without telling him the truth. He was a man of God, after all. Surely he would understand.

873

CHAPTER 31

James lifted the basket toward Angeline. She dropped an orange inside. He'd been thrilled when he'd spotted her climbing over the railing of the ship yesterday. He'd been more thrilled to find her unharmed when she returned to shore, bearing a good report from Eliza and Magnolia. And he'd been equally thrilled when she'd invited him to accompany her this morning to scavenge for fruit. She rarely enlisted his help for much of anything, especially something as easy as picking fruit. Which could only mean that she enjoyed his company and she was serious about their courtship. Maybe this time she wouldn't change her mind and push him away. The thought put a smile on his face as he watched her scour the low-hanging branches. Rays of morning sun cut through the canopy and formed ribbons of shimmering ruby in her hair as her graceful arms reached to pick a mango. Standing on tiptoe like a ballerina, she cast an alluring smile at him over her shoulder.

Yet there was something even more alluring about her today. A lightness to her step, an unusual joy on her face. Was there ever a more innocent and chaste lady? She was the perfect woman for him. And he thanked God every day for allowing him to court her, to hopefully marry her one day. Soon, if he had his way of things.

"When you were on the ship, did Captain Ricu say anything about Eliza and Magnolia's release?" He raised his voice above a particularly loud burst of squawking coming from the canopy.

"No, but I do have a feeling it will be soon." She glanced up at a pair of blue and green macaws who seemed to be scolding them for trespassing. Stowy leapt on the tree trunk beside her and started toward them.

"I hope you're right." James pointed at a papaya hanging from a high branch to their right. "I'll get this one." He plucked the fruit, dropping it in the basket, then met her gaze. A shadow crossed her violet eyes, a momentary hesitation before she smiled and continued onward.

Perhaps she thought about the pirate gold and the fourth beast and what would happen to them should it be released. Something James never ceased to fret over. Though he'd recently tried interpreting more of the Hebrew book, his progress was slow. Ever since Ricu had taken Eliza and Magnolia aboard his ship, James had trouble keeping focused. And Blake and Hayden had been so consumed with getting their wives back unscathed, they'd all but forgotten why they'd gone after the gunpowder in the first place.

Or perhaps the beasts, the angelic battle, the prison alcoves, and fire lake were all just silly myths from an ancient book and none of it was real. He ran his hand through his hair and sighed. On days like today, when he hadn't seen a vision in a week, when the sun was shining and the birds were singing and his heart burst with love for Angeline, it was easy to entertain a smidgeon of doubt about the supernatural war they found themselves entangled in. Perhaps the disasters were just that, disasters. Perhaps Graves had been murdered by a *bandido*. Perhaps the visions were caused by bad water, as Hayden had inferred.

But James knew that wasn't true.

Still, he didn't want to think about it now. For the moment, he was strolling through a lush jungle with the woman he loved, serenaded by an orchestra of birds and breathing air fragranced with sweet orchids. He would allow himself this bit of pleasure.

The gurgle of water drew them to a brook tumbling playfully over rocks. Setting the basket down, he squatted and cupped water to his mouth. Fresh and cool, it soothed his throat as he splashed some on the back of his neck. Angeline knelt beside him and did the same then flicked droplets at his shirt, giggling.

He cocked a brow and shook his wet hand in her direction. Drops sparkled like diamonds in her hair and on her skin, making her look even more angelic—if possible. She feigned indignation and sprayed him again. They continued for several minutes, laughing and showering each other until water dribbled from their chins and hair. An odd, wonderful feeling bloomed within James and began to swell through every inch of him. Something he had never felt before—happiness. Not only happiness at the moment but hope for many more happy moments with this precious woman.

Stowy jumped onto the pebbly bank and began batting at tiny bugs floating in the stream.

"I'm glad you invited me to come along. I was so worried about you yesterday." James kissed the water from her lips, drawing in a deep breath of her coconut scent. Circling a hand around her back, he pressed in for more when she nudged him away. Her sad smile dissipated the gaiety of the moment like the water drying on her skin. "I need to speak to you about something, James."

"Sounds serious."

"It is." She flattened her lips, those luscious lips he'd just kissed and longed to do so again.

He sat back on a rock, leveling his elbows atop his knees. "Very well." The look on her face caused his gut to clench as she picked up Stowy and stroked the cat's fur.

"It's something about my past that you should know before. . ." —she glanced at the stream—"before we continue courting."

Relief washed over him. Whatever sin she'd committed, it couldn't be worse than what he'd done. Perhaps she had lied, cheated, even stole something. Though he doubted such an angel could even do that. "Whatever it is—"

"Let me tell you, please." She drew a deep breath and bit her lip. "There's no polite way to say this, James." Her eyes misted, and she glanced down.

James reached for her hand, hating to see her so distraught. "There's no need to tell me."

"Yes, there is." She met his gaze, wiped a tear from her cheek, and swallowed hard. "I was a prostitute."

The word spun gibberish in James's ear before the breeze carried it away. "If that was meant as a joke, I don't find it amusing in the least."

Yet he found no teasing, no humor, in her eyes—eyes that had dried to a hard sheen.

He stared at her, unable to process what she'd just said. It bounced around in his head like some intoxicated balloon.

"It was only for a short while, a little over a year," she continued, looking away. "I was cast out on the street. I had no food, no home, no means of support. I would have died, James." She searched his eyes, pain and hope screaming from her own.

But he had gone numb. Finally the balloon struck the tip of his reason and popped. Jerking away from her, he punched to his feet, his heart imploding. Shock became anger. Anger became disgust. All three stormed through him like the horsemen of the apocalypse, trampling everything in their path. His reason, his sympathy. . .

His love.

Releasing Stowy, Angeline slowly stood, fear appearing on her face for the first time.

James wiped the back of his hand over his lips and spit. He'd kissed her! A tramp! "I thought you were a lady." His voice came out strangled. "I thought you were pure and innocent."

Pain scoured her eyes. "Are any of us really innocent, James? Are you?"

"I never sold my virtue to strangers for money. I never sold my soul to the devil!"

Feminine laughter drew his gaze over Angeline's shoulder to Tabitha, sashaying about the clearing, her lips upturned in a coy smile. *Of all the times for a vision!* Ignoring her, he glanced back at Angeline, whose expression had sunk into that look that had become so familiar to James during the war. The same look that had appeared on many a soldier's face when James had told them they wouldn't make it through the night.

"Is that what you think of me?" Angeline asked, her voice barely a whisper. "That I am allied with Satan?"

"What am I to think? You led me to believe. . .you accepted my courtship, knowing what you were. . ."

"What I *was*, yes. And what I am no longer." Strength permeated her trembling voice, and James looked away, unable to bear the sight of her—the thought of her with another man.

Many men.

"I'm sorry to have bothered you, Mr. Callaway." Her voice came out wooden. Turning, she started to leave. He gripped her wrist. She winced and tugged from him, tearing her sleeve, exposing the scar on her arm.

"This scar. It's a knife wound." He grabbed her again. "Who did this to you?"

"A man."

"What man?"

She met his gaze. "One of my clients, if you must know. Turns out he preferred to slice women rather than enjoy them." Her breath came heavy. Her lip trembled, but she stood her ground.

He wanted to feel sorry for her, wanted to consider how horrible her life had been, but he was too angry. Everything was starting to make sense. Her aversion to being touched, the pistol she used to carry around, the distance she kept. It wasn't because she was chaste and timid around men. It was quite the opposite. He felt sick to his stomach.

And to make matters worse, she merely stood there with shoulders drawn back and chin stiff. Not dissolving in shame, not begging his forgiveness, and not even lashing at him in anger. Which only increased his fury.

How could she have deceived him? How could she have allowed their courtship? Heat raged through him, tightening his jaw and forming sweat on his neck. He'd come to Brazil to escape women like her, to start a new society without the immorality and decay they caused. And then he fell in love with the only prostitute on the journey! What was wrong with him? "Do you know what women like you have done to me?" He tightened his grip. "Ruined me! Tore my life from me. Made me a failure." And caused his father's death. But he wouldn't tell her that.

She raised her chin. "It seems to me, Doctor, that you give a great deal of power to women who, in your assessment, possess none at all."

Tabitha giggled. "Oh, touché, my dear. She's good, James. I must say, I'm growing quite fond of her."

"Shut up!" James shouted at the insidious vision.

"I'd be happy to if you'd kindly release me." Angeline yanked from his grasp. Stowy circled her skirts, looking as if he would pounce on James.

"I wasn't talking to you." James let go of her wrist, his frustration at the boiling point. He waved a hand at her. "Go."

⊰❖⊱

Angeline glanced around the clearing, wondering who else was present, then took a step back from James, rubbing her wrist. Inside, a storm of agony raged. Outside, she maintained control. She'd learned that useful skill during her time working in a brothel. She'd also learned how to deal with enraged men. She should leave as he'd ordered. Yet he looked so distraught, so lost. And all because of her lies.

James took up a pace. "I trusted you. You knew how I felt about immoral women."

"Which is why I didn't tell you until now." She drew a breath for strength. "And I am no longer immoral. I am forgiven. As a man of God you should know that and forgive me too."

"Don't you dare"—he pointed a finger at her—"Don't you speak of God to me." His bronze eyes hardened. "Women like you know nothing of God. Women like you lure men to their deaths."

Angeline's heart crumbled to dust. She had expected shock, perhaps a bit of disgust, but she hadn't expected hatred. *Oh, Father, help me. Please help me cope with this pain,* she breathed a silent prayer as all her dreams of happiness shriveled beneath the rage spewing from James's lips. . .from his eyes.

"I will lure you no further, sir." She took another step back, intending to leave, when he grabbed her shoulders and shoved his mouth onto hers. Forcing her body against his, he clutched bunches of her hair and kissed her rough and angry, not loving and gentle as before. Agony screamed within his groans. She shoved her hands against his chest, trying to free herself, but he was too strong.

He withdrew, his breath stinging her face. "Is that the way you like it, Angeline? Is this what your clients did to you?" His voice bit like a viper.

He released her and stepped back, shame flooding his eyes before he turned and wiped his lips as if her taste was poison.

Angeline couldn't breathe. Couldn't feel her legs, her arms. Darting to the water, she scooped up Stowy and stumbled from the clearing, tears finally pouring down her cheeks.

❦

James stayed in the clearing until the sun set. Ignoring the taunts flung his way from Tabitha and Abigail, he dropped to the sandy dirt and stared at the water flowing past, dashing over rocks and plummeting into troughs, sparkling when the sun alighted on it and turning ashen when clouds hovered overhead. On and on it flowed, no matter the obstacle, no matter whether the sun shone or gloom set in. Much like life. Or was it? For he felt as if the obstacle before him was much too large for him to ever get past.

He stayed in the clearing because he couldn't move. Whether it was rage or fear or despair that kept his legs locked, he didn't know. Perhaps it was shame. Shame for the way he'd treated Angeline. Shame for the things he'd said. For the way he'd forced his kiss on her. The thought of her allowing men to grope her, touch her—bed her—had ignited a rage in him he could not control. Something dark and evil had come over him, shoving aside all decency. But he wouldn't blame some unseen force. He wouldn't blame anyone but himself.

Once again he'd been played a fool by a beautiful woman. Once again, he'd given his heart only to have the vixen tear it to shreds and destroy his life in the process.

A chill came over him as the sun sank behind the trees and shadows crept through the jungle, stealing the light. Finally he rose and trudged back to the beach. But instead of joining the others, he borrowed some rum from one of the colonists and made his way beyond the cliffs to a private section of beach. Hours later when the night was spent and the sky spun around him, he toppled backward in the sand. The last thing he heard before he drifted into a welcome oblivion was the eerie howl of a wolf.

He was on a ship. The smell of salt and fish swirled about him as he balanced on the swaying deck. There was peace out at sea. In the purl of the waves, the creak of the ship, the endless horizon, the snap of sails that sped the ship on its course far away—far away from all life's problems. James allowed that peace to roll over him as sunlight stroked his eyelids with warmth.

But then it was gone. The light, the warmth. Even the scent of the sea had turned putrid, metallic. He opened his eyes, gripped the railing, and glanced over endless swells of dark red—*blood* red. Panic sent his thoughts spinning. He barreled down the foredeck ladder. "Is anyone here? Hello!" But the ship was empty. Only a single rat scampered across the deck and disappeared below. A grating sound drew his gaze to the ship's wheel spinning in its casing as if directed by some maniacal sailor.

James sped to the railing again. Blood clawed the hull, maroon fingers reaching for him. His stomach convulsed and he wretched its contents into the sea. Hanging over the bulwarks, he gasped for air, his heart thumping in his chest. Lightning arched a white blade across the sky. In the distance, a gaping darkness loomed on the horizon. No, it wasn't darkness at all, but rather a complete absence of light. Like a hole in the universe that sucked everything, including the earth and sea, into its black void.

And the ship was heading straight for it.

Dashing onto the quarterdeck, James grabbed the gyrating wheel and struggled to keep it steady, but it leapt from his hands and spun wildly, first to the right and then to the left. A *meow* shot his gaze up to see Stowy perched atop the binnacle, wind tossing his black fur while his amber eyes stared off the bow.

A scream penetrated the rush of wind. James leaned over the starboard railing to see a small boat just ahead of the ship filled with people. Grabbing a telescope, he leveled it upon the craft. His heart sank. His friends. Blake, Eliza, Magnolia, Hayden, and Angeline sat in the dinghy, gripping the thwarts, fear blaring from their eyes. Blake and Hayden rowed and rowed, their faces sweaty and red, but the boat continued to drift toward the darkness. Angeline stared at James. Struggling to stand, Magnolia waved her arms. "Help us! Save us, James. Save us!"

Panic sent him racing across the deck, seeking another boat he could lower. There were none. He tried to stop the wheel again but to no avail. A rope. There must be a rope. He found one coiled by the foremast. But what could he do with a rope?

One thing he knew. If he didn't get to his friends in time, they'd fall off the edge of the earth and be swallowed up in darkness. And in that tiny boat, they would never survive.

"James!" Someone gripped his shoulder. "James, wake up!"

But he didn't want to wake up. He had to save his friends. He swatted away the offending hands and moaned, "Leave me alone."

"It's Blake. Get up." But it wasn't Blake's voice. It was Hayden's. James pried his eyes open, immediately sorry he did. Sunlight pierced straight through them and stabbed his brain with a dozen hot pokers. Pain radiated down his back into every limb. He blinked, and Hayden's face came into view.

"Get it together, man. We need you." Urgency branded Hayden's tone.

"Bother someone else. I was having a perfectly good nightmare."

Clutching his arm, Hayden pulled James to sit. His stomach did a flip, and something foul-tasting flooded his throat. "What on earth is the matter?"

"It's Blake. He's been attacked by a wolf."

CHAPTER 32

Blood bubbled from Blake's side where fangs had torn flesh and muscle from bone. Despite Angeline and Sarah's furious efforts to restrain the life-giving fluid, it dripped onto the pallet, sliding over bamboo and soaking into the sand beneath. James sped from the shelter and heaved into the bushes—only the third time since Hayden had woken him twenty minutes ago. Of all the nights to drink to excess. . .something he hadn't done since he'd recommitted his life to God.

Hayden slapped him on the back, not a friendly smack, but one that harbored a threat in its sting. "Get in there and do something. Now."

James glanced over his shoulder at the women hovering over Blake then at the crowd of worried colonists swarming the front of the makeshift clinic. Thiago, Delia and her children, even the Scotts and their slave, Mable. Others too, nearly the entire colony, save those men Ricu had dragged to the tunnels.

James faced the bushes again, air vacating his lungs until he could barely breathe. "We must get Eliza and Magnolia from the ship."

Clutching his shoulders, Hayden jerked him around. Dark strands of hair wavered over fierce green eyes that pierced James's very soul. "We can't. You have to do this. *You* have to save him."

Sarah approached and touched his arm. "You are the only one who can, James."

Angeline glanced up from where she pressed a bundle of rags to Blake's wound, her eyes hollow and distant. He stared at her, wondering how she could even look at him after the way he'd treated

883

her—wondering how he could even look at her. Yet, he couldn't seem to pull his gaze away. A spark of pleading penetrated the distance between them and went straight for his heart.

James rubbed the scar on his cheek and cursed under his breath. *NO! I can't do this, God. Why have You put me in this situation—again?* Visions of his father lying in a puddle of blood burst into James's mind, reminding him that no matter how much he'd wanted to save him, he'd been unable to move. Or even breathe. And his father had died in his arms. What would make this time any different? Lowering his chin, he squeezed his eyes shut, searching for another solution, someone who could perform the surgery, anyone with enough skills to follow his command. But there was no one. No one but him.

And he could not let his best friend die.

God, please don't let me fail. He drew a deep breath, opened his eyes, and lifted his hands before him. They trembled like leaves in a storm. His eyes met Hayden's.

"God can calm the storm," was all the man said before dragging James back to Blake's side.

James pressed a hand on his roiling stomach and stiffened his jaw. "I need boiling water, needle and sutures, clamps, a strong lantern, plenty of clean rags, and any alcohol you can find." He snapped stern eyes to Hayden. "Steal it from the pirates if you have to."

Hayden gave an approving nod and sped off.

From the outskirts of the shelter, Thiago crossed himself. "I hope Lobisón not bite him."

"Surely you don't believe that nonsense anymore," Sarah chastised him as she gathered a pile of clean rags. Without looking at James, Angeline found scissors, clamps, needles, and sutures and laid them all neatly on a tray.

Thiago lifted one shoulder. "I believe there is still evil in world, yes?"

"Indeed." James swallowed, trying to settle his nerves, still not looking at Blake's wound. Evil he could deal with. But blood?

"What can we do to help?" Mrs. Jenkins shouted.

Sarah exchanged a glance with James before turning to answer. "Pray."

"Now, if you please, I need room to operate without a dozen eyes upon me." Though the colonists were at least four yards away, James felt as though he stood in the center of a courtroom, surrounded by accusers. And he, on trial for his life. His pulse throbbed. Sweat slid down his chest.

The crowd retreated, but only inches, as Angeline placed the last instrument on the tray. Her hand quivered.

"Can you handle this?" James asked her.

Violet eyes assessed him. "Can *you*?"

He flattened his lips as Hayden returned with a bottle of rum. "The pirates left it on the beach."

Blake coughed. Blood trickled from his lips. At least he had lost consciousness. James couldn't be sure he wouldn't do the same. He released a ragged sigh, concentrating on the crash of waves, the soothing chorus of myriad birds, not on the hammer of his heart and the tremble in his hands.

"James." Angeline gazed up at him, her hands pressed on blood-drenched cloths. "I can't stop the bleeding. He's growing pale."

"Do something!" Hayden's shout stiffened every nerve. Bracing himself, James nodded for Angeline to remove the rags then lowered his gaze to the gaping wound. A mass of mangled flesh stared back at him. Broken ribs floated atop a pool of blood, where it appeared a pulmonary vein had been nicked. Blake didn't have much time before he bled out. *God in heaven, help me. I can't do this without You.*

Can a lady admire a man who broke her heart into a million pieces? A man who had insulted her in every way possible, who had *assaulted* her in body and soul? The answer, Angeline discovered, was yes. For she could not help but respect the man who, with erratic breathing, sweat streaming down his face, and quaking hands, had diligently worked for hours, sewing up the insides of a man he loved more than a brother—a man whom they all loved more than a brother.

While doing her best to quell the agony of her heart, she obeyed his every command, stood by his side, ignored her own queasiness, and watched him as he grimaced, winced, huffed, and concentrated harder than she'd seen anyone do. Sarah also assisted, while Hayden stood to the side, his face mottled in agony and fear one minute, while in the next, he bowed and whispered prayers to the Almighty.

They could not lose Blake. The colonel had been their leader since they'd begun this journey. The only man who could guide such a mishmash of grumbling, erratic, fanciful personalities. He was the strong warrior who had led armies on the battlefield to victory and who now refused to accept defeat for their decimated colony. They would fall apart without him. Eliza would fall apart. The poor woman—Angeline bit her lip—she had no idea that at this very moment her husband's life teetered on the cliff of eternity. Would their child be born without a father? *Oh, God, no. Please, no.*

James blinked back sweat from his eyes, and Angeline dabbed his brow. He didn't glance at her. Hadn't glanced at anyone for hours. He'd just kept his eyes locked on Blake's mauled flesh as if looking away for one second would break the trance that had come over him as soon as he picked up the first instrument. After that, he'd worked methodically and precisely, each movement the practiced step of an elegant dance. Every slice, every squeeze, every suture skilled and beautiful in its simplicity and grace, even amid the horror of nicked veins and a punctured liver. Tirelessly, Sarah held the lantern above Blake, keeping it steady against the occasional wind gusting through the shelter, ignoring the sweat dotting her neck and soaking the fringe of her collar.

Rays of sun reflected off crystals of sand and dappled the bamboo roof with light, hypnotizing Angeline as she tried to keep her focus should James need something. The metallic smell of blood mixed with sweat and alcohol threatened to turn her stomach inside out, but her silent vigilance of prayer kept her strong. Kept her hopeful.

Finally, James closed Blake's loosened skin, ordered her to pour alcohol over the needle and sutures, and then began sewing up his friend's side. His bronze eyes remained as hard as metal as he completed the work. Then grabbing the rum, he doused the wound, wrapped it tightly in clean rags, and stepped back. Finally his gaze lifted off Blake and scanned the three of them. Worry formed creases at the edges of his eyes.

Hayden stepped forward. Sarah set down the lantern and rubbed her arm. Angeline drew a stool over for James to sit, all of them breathless for a word of encouragement.

Whatever had held James's spine in place during the long

procedure suddenly liquefied and he dropped to the chair. He released a breath so deep, it seemed he'd been holding it the entire time. His shoulders slumped and what looked like tears glazed his eyes before he lowered his chin. Sniffing, he rubbed those eyes before glancing up again. "We wait now. If he doesn't get an infection, he will live."

Hayden gripped James's arm and shook him. "You did good, Doc. Real good."

"Wonderful," Sarah added. "God be praised."

"Thank you for all your help." James gave a sad smile. "All of you." His eyes landed on Angeline, but as if it the sight of her repulsed him, he lowered them to the dirt by his boots. Which was, no doubt, what he still thought of her.

Finally he struggled to stand. "Keep an eye on him. I'll return later." Then stretching his shoulders, he turned and walked away. Sarah began cleaning up bloody rags, but Angeline couldn't pull her gaze from James as he headed down the beach—the way the last vestiges of sunlight cut across the sharp angles of his back, his confident gait, the wind whipping his tawny hair into a frenzy, the way he dipped his head as if deep in thought. She should be angry at him. She *was* angry at him. But it didn't matter—he still held her shattered heart in his hands.

"What happened between you two?" Sarah dropped the scissors into a bucket of bloody water.

"Nothing. It doesn't matter." But it did matter, more than anything. She just couldn't talk about it or she feared she'd collapse into a puddle and melt into the sand to be lost forever. She busied herself helping Sarah while Hayden covered Blake with a tattered quilt and said a prayer over his friend.

When the mess had been cleaned and Sarah had taken the dirty instruments to the creek to clean, Angeline turned to go, but her gaze landed on Dodd, still unconscious in the corner. Oddly, she found no anger rising at the sight of him. No hatred, or fear. Only pity. Since Eliza and Magnolia had been taken aboard the pirate ship, Sarah and Mrs. Jenkins had been looking after him, trying to force broth down his throat as much as possible. Yet after eight days, the poor man grew thin and gaunt.

Kneeling by his side, Angeline dabbed a moist cloth over his face.

Once, she had been happy about his condition, had wished him dead. Now, she repented of that horrid desire and said a silent prayer for him. Besides, he could no longer cause her harm.

Dipping his hands in an incoming wave, James grabbed a fistful of sand and started to scrub blood off his skin. Astonishing. The sight of it no longer sent icicles up his spine. He shielded his eyes against the sun now dipping low over the mountains. He'd been operating on Blake nearly all day. *Operating.* Like he used to do on the battlefield. When he had saved lives. Some lives, at least. Hopefully, the one he'd sutured up today.

If not, he would never forgive himself.

He sat back and allowed the waves to wash over him, soaking through his trousers and rippling up his sides. Cupping a handful of the foamy saltwater, he splashed it over his face and neck. The cool liquid leeched the tension from his body and seemed to carry it out to sea with each receding swell. He drew a deep breath and bowed his head. *Thank You, Father. I know it was You who helped me today. No one else could have calmed me down like that.*

As soon as he'd picked up the scalpel, a cloud of peace had enveloped him. Like a warm cloak on a winter's day that shielded one from icy shards and brisk wind, it had permeated his skin, settled his nerves—and his soul—and suddenly he knew what he must do. And he had the confidence to do it, and do it well.

Why hadn't he ever thought of praying before? Back when the blood had overwhelmed him and the terrors had begun, back when his hands—and his body—had quivered at the mere mention of blood? Why had he not turned to God for strength then? All these wasted years he could have been saving lives. *Forgive me.*

He'd been too proud and too angry to ask for anyone's help. Especially God's. How foolish was that for a preacher? Snorting, he rubbed the back of his neck. Foamy waves lobbed a shell against his foot. He picked it up and flicked it between his fingers. For years he blamed his fear of blood on the war, on the horrors he'd witnessed.

A thought seared a trail through his conscience.

For years, he blamed his nefarious liaisons on the loose morals of the women he'd consorted with, never taking responsibility for his own actions, never asking God for the strength to resist them. Never leaning on the only One who could help him with his weaknesses. All his weaknesses.

Was he any better than the women he'd taken to bed? Hadn't he committed the same immoral act? Yet all this time he'd blamed them while holding himself innocent, believing his only sin was falling for their beguiling traps. Blaming them for destroying his life when it was his own weakness and lack of trust in God that had caused his undoing.

James tossed the shell into the sea and hung his head.

⸎

"He doesn't appear to be getting better." Hayden's voice startled Angeline as she sat tending Dodd. She glanced up, saw the hesitation in his eyes, and offered him a welcoming smile. Hayden had caused her father's death, sent her life spinning like a cyclone into the darkness. She should be furious with him—*had* been furious. But all that had changed when her Father in heaven forgave her and washed her clean.

"Poor fellow." He knelt beside her. "I wonder if he'll ever recover his senses."

She returned her gaze to Dodd. "He better do so soon. I doubt we can keep him fed enough much longer."

"I can't say I miss him very much," Hayden said. "Though I suppose that's not very kind."

"He was"—she bit her lip—"or rather *is* a hard man to like."

Silence, save for Dodd's shallow breathing and the wind whipping through the frond roof, settled on them both. Shifting across the sand, Angeline dampened her rag in a nearby bowl of water.

"No doubt, after our last discussion, you feel the same way about me." His voice lowered in shame.

She searched his green eyes, seeing only sorrow and remorse.

"What I did was reprehensible," he said. "Unforgiveable."

Angeline swallowed, allowing herself a moment to consider how different her life would have been had her father not been murdered. She would not have gone to live with her aunt and uncle. She would not have been forced onto the street, constantly on the run. She would not have become what she had become. And then James and she would still be together. Or would they? She wouldn't have come to Brazil at all. In truth, she would never have known him. And that thought hurt most of all. "I have discovered recently that nothing is unforgiveable." She smiled, dousing her few remaining coals of anger with undeserved grace—the undeserved grace God gave to her and that she must give to others.

"I don't know what to say." Hayden's brow wrinkled. "But—"

She placed a finger on his lips, praying he didn't misinterpret the intimate gesture. "Then say nothing more. What's done is done. You didn't murder my father directly. I don't think you would have done it if you had known." She drew a deep breath of the new life within her. "I forgive you."

A mixture of surprise and admiration rolled over his face. "You've changed, Angeline."

"Let's just say God and I had a long talk."

Hayden chuckled. "Indeed. He's been chatting with me lately, as well."

She wiped Dodd's face and neck as minutes passed by in silence. She felt Hayden tense beside her, knew he had more to say, but she didn't want to talk about her past anymore. Wasn't it enough that it had already ruined her future?

"That *was* you on the wanted poster then, wasn't it?" Hayden asked.

Releasing a sigh, she faced him. What difference did it make if she told him the truth now? She was done with lying. "Yes."

His lips grew tight, and he stared at Dodd. "Wanted for murder. Did you do it?"

"Yes." She gauged his reaction but he didn't flinch, hardly breathed. If only she could go back and change things, choose another action, lean on God for help instead of trying to do things herself.

Wind gusted through the shelter, stirring sand and flapping the coverlet on top of Dodd. "It was self-defense. My uncle attacked me. I grabbed a bookend from the table and struck his head." Memories flashed. The lust in the man's eyes, his rough hands grabbing her and forcing her against the wall. "I was just trying to get him off me."

Hayden was silent. Would he tell everyone? James? Her friends? She dreaded the looks they would give her. She dreaded the loathing that would follow. She had so wanted to remember the sweetness of their friendship when she was back in the States, not be haunted by their hatred. Waves sizzled ashore. A gull squawked overhead.

"No one need know," Hayden finally said, drawing her gaze. "I believe you, Angeline. I've come to know you. You aren't a murderer."

She laid a hand on his arm, hardly daring to believe. "Thank you, Hayden."

Placing a hand atop hers, he helped her to her feet. "We all came here for a new start. You deserve one like the rest of us. Now, go rest." He jerked his head toward the women's shelter down the beach. "It's been a long day. I'll take first watch over Blake."

⤜⟡⤛

Dodd listened to the sound of their footsteps shuffling away before he opened his eyes. He'd woken up several hours ago but had found himself too weak to move or even speak. Soon, he'd realized something must have happened to the colonel because he could hear James stitching him up. It must have been a serious wound from the sounds of things. Probably an injury from the windstorm, which was the last thing Dodd remembered. Regardless, Dodd had kept his peace. Then afterward, when Angeline had sat beside him and dabbed a cool cloth on his head, he'd thought to enjoy her sweet ministrations for a while before making himself known. But, oh, what a heavenly miracle had then occurred! The words he'd overheard passed through his mind, awakening memories that the woman's beauty must have forced him to forget. Angeline Moore was Clarissa Paine! The infamous woman who'd murdered her own uncle—bludgeoned him in his own house. Every law officer in Virginia had been put on alert, wanted posters had been handed out. Dodd couldn't imagine how he had missed it. Ah, sweet justice would finally be served. At least the kind of justice Dodd would choose to enact. Despite his weak condition, he lifted his lips in a devious grin.

CHAPTER 33

A burst of wind caught the crinkled pages of the Hebrew text and shuffled them across James's vision. With a huff, he shifted back to the end of the book and flattened the papers with his palm. An ache etched across his shoulders from leaning over the manuscript all day, and he sat up straight and attempted to stretch the kinks from his neck. Foam-capped rollers curled toward shore and spread creamy gauze over the sand, sending crabs skittering into their holes and the colony's children running in laughter. Ah, to be young and carefree again without a worry in the world. Without concern for food or shelter or pirates or invisible beasts who could plague the world with terror.

Which was why James had spent the past week studying the ancient Hebrew book, desperate to find a way to stop the pirates from releasing hell on earth. Yet he'd found nothing useful. Or perhaps he was missing something, some crucial piece of information that would make sense of it all.

Down shore, two men chopped wood while the women prepared supper around a blazing fire. The Scotts sat beneath a palm, looking quite peaked as Mable fanned them with a frond. Laughter drew James's gaze to Delia chasing her children through the tumbling waves. Beyond them, Thiago and Sarah held Lydia's hands as the child teetered along in her first attempts to walk. Children grew up fast. Too fast. Too soon they would have to face the hardships of life. The heartbreak.

Heartbreak. His eyes latched upon Angeline, hanging wet clothes with some of the other women, her hair ribbons of sparkling ruby in the waning sun. A viable pain seared his heart at the loss of her. He no longer blamed her for what she'd done—what she'd become. He understood. He forgave her. But he still couldn't bring himself to receive her back into his life. Or his heart. Though, in truth, he doubted he could ever banish her from that tender spot. Still, he had vowed to start over in Brazil, become a great preacher and spiritual guide to the colony.

And how could he do that married to a prostitute? Wouldn't that make him just as much of a failure as he'd always been?

He couldn't shake the images bombarding him day and night of her in other men's arms. Many other men. Of them groping her, fondling her, kissing her. . .and God knew what else. He'd wanted a pure woman, an innocent woman to make a fresh start with. A godly start.

Blake broke from the group of colonists and headed toward him. Holding his side, he moved slow and hesitant, pain lining his features. James shook his head. He'd commanded him to stay in bed and rest for at least another week, but the colonel wasn't accustomed to taking orders. Still, not a minute passed in which James didn't thank God for helping him save Blake's life. It was truly a miracle.

A miracle like Dodd waking up from a coma after eight days. The man's recovery was astounding. After eating every piece of fruit and fish in sight, he was back to his impertinent, greedy self. In fact, he'd even been strong enough to join the pirates at the temple today.

Thoughts of the ex-lawman vanished when the colonel stopped beside James, shifting weight off his bad leg and staring out to sea.

"Sit." Closing the book, James slid off the boulder and gestured for Blake to take his spot.

"Don't coddle me, Doctor." He grinned.

"That's an order, Colonel," James returned. "From someone who has had his hands inside your gut, I believe I have the right."

Blake pressed his side and eased himself to the rock. "If you'd stop reminding me, it might stop hurting."

"It will stop hurting when it heals, and it will heal when you rest."

"You sound as bad as Eli—" His gaze jerked to the pirate ship, anchored offshore, its stark masts golden columns in the setting sun.

"Blast it, I miss her."

James should say something here, quote some comforting scripture about how God would rescue her and all would be well. But James had learned two things in the past months: One, God's ways were often not what anyone would expect, and two, God needed no defending.

Blake stomped his boot in the sand, the leather soles sinking into the grains. "Would that those pirates would find their infernal gold and release Eliza and Magnolia. Yet if they *do* find the gold, they are likely to free the final beast." Blake squeezed the bridge of his nose and grimaced. He nodded toward the book in James's hands. "Have you discovered anything of value?"

James sighed and shook his head. "The beginning told how the beasts came to be imprisoned and how they can be freed. The middle consisted of nothing but poetry, songs of praise, and a tale of a mighty prince coming to rescue his people. I can't make sense of how it connects to the rest."

"And the end?"

"Talks about 'the six,' whoever or whatever that is," James said. "Something about the *six* being the only ones able to put the fallen angels back in chains."

"But who are these six? How are we to find them and what exactly can they do?"

"The book doesn't say. At least not yet, but I do have a few more pages to interpret."

Blake nodded. "Best get to it. I fear we don't have much time. I want my wife back. And I want this madness to end. I'm tired, Doc." His normally stormy gray eyes had turned dull as fog. "So tired."

"We all are. But we can't give up now."

Wincing, Blake rose to his feet and gripped James's shoulder in a brotherly squeeze just as shouts of glee and raucous laughter down shore caught their attention. The pirates, Captain Ricu in the lead, his red feather aflutter atop his hat, burst from the jungle, jugs of liquor in their hands. Songs in Portuguese filled the air as the band stomped across the sand to their side of the beach where the captain and three of his men began rowing one of their cockboats out to the *Espoliar*.

Dodd, Patrick, Moses, and three more colonists brought up the rear and headed toward them.

Acid welled in James's belly. Nothing good could come from the pirates' joyful mood.

Nothing good but gold. And lots of it, according to Dodd and Patrick—gold that filled the fourth alcove from floor to ceiling.

"Filled? The entire alcove?" James asked as the other colonists assembled around the two treasure hunters.

Dodd smiled and rubbed his hands together then winced at the cuts covering them. Shaking dirt from his hair and shirt, he glanced at Patrick, who remained as unsoiled and modish as one could in the middle of a jungle. He fingered his goatee. "Stuffed full. A veritable fortune! Just like the old pirate who gave me the map said."

"What of the chains?" Blake eyed the man with suspicion. "The shackles?"

"Don't worry about them." Dodd took a sip from a canteen one of the colonists handed him. "If they are there, they're buried. And probably lying in the dirt like the others. Nothing's there but gold, I assure you. No imaginary beasts that will destroy mankind." His chortle filled the air, drawing a few chuckles from the crowd, before he slid to sit on a stump, his breath coming hard and his face paling. Even in his weakened condition, his vulgar gaze searched the mob and latched upon Angeline, where it remained for far too long.

James's insides bunched in a knot. Hugging herself, Angeline turned and walked to the other side of the group where Dodd couldn't see her, causing James to wonder once again whether they had met in the States. The thought of the circumstances of that meeting made bile rise in his throat. He squelched the vision and focused on Patrick, who was continuing to prattle on about how rich they were all going to be.

Hayden crossed arms over his chest and snorted. "You are bigger fools than I thought if you think you'll see any of that gold."

Dodd and Patrick exchanged a knowing glance. "We shall see," Patrick said. His grin sent ice down James's spine. It seemed to have the same effect on Hayden as he studied his father with suspicion. Regardless, James had bigger problems than Patrick and Dodd's greed.

And from the look on Blake's face, he agreed.

Though James had entertained doubts—many doubts—along the way, and though everything within him wanted it to be false, he knew the fourth beast was still chained in that alcove. He wasn't sure how he knew, but he did. He also knew that the removal of the gold would no doubt aid in the monster's release. Especially if someone read the inscription above the tomb. In fact, now that James thought of it, the gold had probably been hidden there as bait for greedy men—just the type of men whose hearts were dark enough to free the fallen angel.

Everything he'd read in the Hebrew book, everything that had happened, finally started to make sense.

Dodd slowly stood, color returning to his face. "We start pulling out the gold first thing in the morning." He peered through the crowd looking for someone. James didn't need to turn around to know Angeline had slipped behind him. He could smell her coconut scent, feel her presence in the way his heart leapt, his throat burned, and every sense came alive.

"I don't care about the wretched gold!" Mr. Scott shouted. "My daughter is held captive by pirates! I want her back and I want to leave this loathsome jungle." Mrs. Scott clung to her husband, looking as though she'd aged a decade in the past few weeks. Poor woman. Mr. Scott was looking none too well himself, his lack of interest in gold speaking volumes as to his present discomfort.

Mumbles of assent bounced through the mob.

"The pirates won't keep us here any longer will they?" Mrs. Jenkins drew her daughter into her skirts.

Blake scanned the crowd. Though most wouldn't spot it, James knew his friend, could see the angst roll over his face. "I have no idea. But I urge you not to give up on our colony just yet."

"What colony?" Mr. Scott's ensuing chuckle was contagious.

"Oh, I almost forgot," Patrick's assured voice, along with his eyes, flew over the group—both finding a perch on his son, Hayden. "The pirates said they'd release your *wife*." He hissed the last word before turning to Blake. "And yours, Colonel. Right now, in fact." He flicked fingers in the direction of the ship. "Ricu feels you have learned your lesson and won't attempt any more tomfoolery."

Hayden needed no further impetus to take off in a spray of sand, parting the crowd with his exuberance. Blake, though equally exuberant, followed at a much slower pace. Within minutes the two ladies were rowed to shore and deposited in their husbands' arms. James turned away from their tender reunions, feeling his own eyes mist at the intensity of affection between husbands and wives. Unfortunately, those eyes landed on Angeline standing in the distance, staring at him. She tore her gaze away then strolled down the beach, her green skirts swaying in the breeze. At the very least, he owed her an apology for his cruel words and abominable behavior. But he couldn't face her. Not yet. And definitely not alone. Not until he had a better grip on his emotions and wouldn't fall prey to those pleading violet eyes of hers.

Besides, he had a far more pressing matter at hand. Somehow they had to stop the pirates from removing the gold and releasing the fourth beast. If they didn't, James feared all would be lost.

The moon floated atop the horizon, draping glittering silver over the sea. Her stomach a torrent of angst, Angeline had skipped supper and gone for a walk, in desperate need of some time alone—to think, to mourn, to pray. She'd hugged Eliza and Magnolia, laughing and crying for what seemed like hours before Blake and Hayden demanded their wives back. At least some good fortune had finally shone upon the colonists. Some sign that God had not forgotten them—that perhaps this whole nightmare would come to an end. Another sign was that the pirates had lessened their sentries around camp. No doubt they no longer cared if the colonists escaped to Rio, for by the time any of them made it, the pirates would have gathered their gold and sailed away. Which also meant that perhaps they didn't intend to murder them before they left.

Stowy nestled deeper against her chest. Running fingers through his soft fur, she thanked God for the stray cat who'd wandered into her life aboard the *New Hope*. Even back then, God had known she would need a comforting companion. Lifting her skirts, she dipped her toe in the bubbling foam of a wave, smiling when it tickled her skin. Wind pulled hair from her pins and tossed it behind her, and she drew a deep breath, filling her lungs with the salty, fresh smell. She'd grown to love Brazil, its creamy-sanded shores, emerald waters, verdant, steamy jungles, and high, lofty mountains. There was a wildness, a purity, that lured her heart away from the pretension and conventions of society. She could be happy here.

If only James would love her.

And if they could conquer these beasts.

But neither of those things was likely. Hence the reason for her walk. If they didn't find a way to restrain the fallen angelic monsters, things would get worse—far worse, according to James. If they *did* defeat them by the grace and wisdom of God, James would still not love her. And she couldn't live with that. At least not side by side with him in the same town, eating meals together, seeing him every day.

Either way, she would have to leave this beautiful place. Go back to a land where she was wanted for murder and had no way to support herself. But this time, God would be with her, though she supposed He'd always been. But this time, she would call upon Him, rely on Him, trust Him.

A shadow emerged from the sea like a mermaid coming ashore. Water dripped off his hat and coat as he headed toward her. The visions no longer startled her. In fact, whirling around, she hurried in the opposite direction, ignoring the man she recognized from her past, ignoring the lurid suggestions bubbling from his lips like the foam atop the waves. Laughter bellowed from down shore where a flickering fire and a bawdy ruckus told her the pirates were already deep in their cups celebrating their impending wealth.

The colonists still circled their own fire, partaking of their meager meal of roasted fish, coconuts, and mango mandioca pudding. Off to the side, James sat on a rock. Hayden held a lantern while he finished interpreting the book. As if that would do any good. Angeline quickly chastised herself for her lack of faith. She'd felt the love and power of God the past few days, she truly had. But she couldn't imagine what He expected any of them to do against such evil.

Oh, Lord, protect us all. Protect James.

"Come now, Angel, make ole Neal happy like you used to." Still dripping from the sea, the heinous man leapt in front of her.

Ignoring him, Angeline walked the other way. She wasn't ready to join the others. In fact, she must—no, she desperately *needed to*—put as much distance between her and James for the remainder of her time in Brazil.

Another shadow leapt out at her.

Not bothering to lift her gaze, she brushed past it. Sweet saints, was she to have no peace at all tonight?

"Now, that ain't very friendly." The voice halted her.

Dodd. She slowly turned to see his predatory smile gleaming in the moonlight. "I thought you were a vision." She lowered her shoulders. "But now I see you are only a nightmare."

"Ah. . ." He laid his hat over his chest. "The lady pains me greatly."

Stowy perked and stared at the man. "What is it you want?" She continued walking.

"Did you miss me while I was unconscious?" He slid beside her.

"No."

"Yet, I distinctly remember you caring for me, sitting by my side and washing my face." He caressed his own cheek and moaned in delight. "I can still feel your loving touch."

Angeline longed to slap the moan from his lips. "I suppose I might have." In fact, she could only remember one time she'd done so, and that was when she and Hayden had spoken about. . . she snapped her gaze back to Dodd's.

He grinned. "I see you remember." Jumping in front of her, he faced her and walked backward as she proceeded, skimming her with lurid eyes.

Swinging hair over her shoulder, Angeline stiffened her jaw. "What do you want?"

"It's simple, really. You see, I'm about to be a very wealthy man. Much wealthier than the good doctor."

"I care not for your financial standing." Stopping before she bumped into him, she stared out to sea, wishing more than anything for the kraken to emerge from the foamy waters and drag her down to the depths.

He grabbed her arm. "Hmm. I don't think you do. In fact, you're becoming quite the bore, Angeline. Playing the righteous prude does not become you." He released her and slid fingers up to her neck. "I much preferred the harlot."

Stowy hissed at him.

Frowning, he backed away.

Angeline lifted her chin. "The harlot is gone, sir. I am a new creature. I have been cleansed and forgiven by God."

His shoulders shook as laughter barreled from his mouth. "Well, I'll tell you what, then, *Clarissa.* Just for old times' sake and since I like you, I really do, I'll not tell a soul that you are a murderer as well as a prostitute if you give me just one night. Just one night with dear old Dodd. Is that too much to ask for?"

She felt Stowy tense in her arms, nails springing from his paws. Perhaps she should release him and allow him to gouge Dodd's eyes out. But that wouldn't be pleasing to God. "Are you so desperate and so pathetic a man that you have to threaten to ruin a woman's life for one night's pleasure?"

"Desperate, aye," he said. "Pathetic. . .well, why don't you let me show you just how pathetic I am?"

Angeline was suddenly glad she had skipped supper. "I wouldn't spend the night with you if you could make me queen of England."

Dodd's face fell. His eyes narrowed and the lines at the corners of his mouth became spears.

"You are too late, Dodd. James already knows." She wouldn't tell him just what he knew. "So you have no power over me."

"Whether that is true or not, you forget one thing, my dear." He slid fingers down his thick sideburns. "I am a lawman, bound by duty to bring murderers to justice. And if you don't give me what I want, that's just what I intend to do, bring you home and make you stand trial for murder."

CHAPTER 34

Thank you all for meeting this late." James circled the fire and tossed another log into the flames. Sparks leapt into the air, disappearing into the darkness where the moon seemed to absorb them in its advance across the sky. Snores rumbled over the thunder of waves from both pirate and colonist alike, ensuring James all but the six of them were asleep. For what he had to say was not for prying ears. Nor for the faint of heart.

"We have no choice." Blake's tone grew solemn. "We must do something."

Hayden led Magnolia to sit on a log. "Are you sure about this fourth beast?" He scratched the stubble on his chin. "I haven't seen many visions lately. None, in fact, last week."

"*I* have." Holding his side, Blake eased to sit beside his wife. "And my nightmares have increased."

Eliza glanced at Magnolia. "We saw many visions while on board the *Espoliar*. Aside from the rats, they were our constant companions."

Magnolia squeezed her husband's hand. "If Eliza hadn't been there, I would have gone mad."

"If we hadn't been together, we both would have," Eliza said.

"And you, James?" Blake asked. "Have you been spared these torturous apparitions now that your fear of blood is gone?"

James stared into the fire, wishing to God that were true, but lately he'd been seeing his father everywhere. . .chopping wood in the distance, walking down shore, dashing through the jungle. But every time James rushed to confront him, he disappeared. If only he could speak to him, tell him how sorry he was. Just once. "It was God who took my fear from me, and no, I have not been spared."

All eyes turned to Angeline as she lowered to a stump and adjusted her skirts around her feet. "I've seen many," she finally said. "Too many."

James scrubbed his face, battling the irresistible pull to look at her, not wanting to see the pain on her face that he heard in her voice, not wanting to see the sorrow and anger in her eyes every time she looked his way.

Wind sent the flames sputtering and brought a welcome chill to the sweat on the back of his neck.

Hayden snapped hair from his face. "So, what are we to do about this beast, Doc? I assume that's why you asked us to forego our sleep."

"Yes. I finished interpreting the book." Drawing a deep breath, James sat and leaned forward on his knees. "From what I have learned, I believe it is possible to send the freed beasts back to their chains and keep the fourth one from being released. The Hebrew text speaks over and over of the six." God help him. He had studied and prayed and studied and prayed, asking for wisdom to interpret the words correctly. If he was wrong—even in a verb tense or the meaning of a single word—it could mean their doom.

"The six?" Eliza fingered a locket around her neck, her voice tainted with the skepticism she so often tried to hide.

James stared at the sand by his boot and wondered how to continue, how to share what sounded like complete lunacy, but what he knew in his gut was the truth. Picking up the book, he opened it to where he'd placed a leaf as marker and began to read from his translation. " 'The six are known to the six, yet not known. Called from afar. A destiny from above. And only through them can evil be chained.' "

He glanced at his friends. All eyes were upon him, sparkling in the firelight. Some were narrowed in confusion, others wide beneath arched brows, while others shifted to stare at the dance of flames.

Magnolia scrunched her nose. "What does it mean, 'known. . .yet not known'? And who are these six?"

James drew a deep breath, hesitated, then decided he might as well just say it. "I believe *we* are the six."

Hayden chuckled. Eliza slipped her locket within her bodice and folded her hands together. James didn't look at Angeline, but he could feel her eyes on him.

"What makes you say that?" Blake asked, lines forming on his forehead.

A howl echoed from the jungle, deep and malevolent, setting James's nerves on end. As if they weren't already tight enough. "I've prayed and prayed about this. I know this sounds absurd, preposterous even. But hear me out. When we all came aboard the *New Hope* eight months ago, we were complete strangers to one another, correct?"

Blake nodded. Eliza shared a glance with Magnolia while Angeline lifted her gaze to Hayden, who was oddly staring at James. James shifted uncomfortably on his seat, hoping that the reason for Hayden's interest was not that he had known James from before. Closing the book, he set it down on the sand and continued. "Yet, somehow our lives are connected." He faced Eliza. "I saw your husband commit a horrible act on the battlefield." She swallowed and gave a slight nod. "An act that affected Blake greatly and changed his life." Releasing a sigh, the colonel swung an arm around his wife and drew her near.

"That's three of us who affected each other's lives before we even knew one another." James turned to Magnolia. "You told me that you knew Eliza before you boarded the *New Hope*."

"Yes"—she smiled at her friend—"we met at a party at Eliza's aunt and uncle's hotel."

"You introduced me to Stanton..." Eliza's voice trailed off, her eyes growing wide. "I would have never married him..."

Magnolia winced.

"I would never have run away from home, been disowned by my family." Eliza lowered her chin, and Blake brought her hand to his lips. She looked at him in horror. "Who knows, maybe Stanton would never have murdered your brother."

Blake eased a curl from her face. "What's done is done, love. It doesn't matter now."

Hayden's gaze shot to his wife. "And you were engaged to my father."

"I need no reminder of that huge mistake." Magnolia stuffed hair into her bun.

"But don't you see?" James stood, his blood pumping fast. "That links Hayden to Magnolia and Magnolia to Eliza and Blake to Eliza and me to Blake and Eliza." He dared a glance at Angeline. "But what I cannot determine is how you are connected in all this."

"I'm not." Angeline swept pointed eyes his way. "You of all people should know that a woman like me could never be used to defeat evil." Her sharp tone sliced through James's heart. Yet even as she said the words, her gaze brushed over Hayden before returning to the fire.

Withdrawing his arm from Magnolia, Hayden picked up a chip of wood and began fingering it. Seconds passed as another gust of wind kicked sparks from the fire into the night. "Angeline and I have only recently discovered a prior connection," Hayden finally said. "I swindled the man who murdered her father. Inadvertently causing her father's death, in fact." He tossed the wood in the fire as everyone stared at him in disbelief, eyes shifting from him to Angeline.

But she refused to look at any of them, her eyes downcast, her arms looped around her waist, her hair sparkling in red and gold like the fire itself.

"I didn't know what had transpired after I tricked the man." Hayden's tone weighed heavy with remorse. "I simply left town with my pockets full."

Angeline finally raised her gaze to Hayden's. The moisture covering her eyes threatened to undo James and send him dashing to her side. "You couldn't have known." She smiled and glanced over the group. "Hayden and I have made our peace."

Shoving down yet another burst of admiration for the lady, James tore his gaze away and instead focused on his growing excitement as the pieces of the puzzle were coming together. Yet at the same time, sorrow also consumed him at the horrible way each of his dear friends had affected the other ones. All except him. Aside from seeing Eliza's husband kill Blake's brother, James had no direct connection with any of them. Perhaps it was *he* who wasn't part of the six.

"Before you go thinking you are innocent, Doc..." Hayden shifted his boots in the sand. "You and I crossed paths once."

James studied his friend. He would have remembered a man like Hayden. "You must be mistaken."

"Nope. I snuck in the back of your church in Knoxville on a cold night in February. I didn't stay long. I needed to find some meaning to my life. I'd grown tired of swindling people, of searching for my father."

A burst of dread formed in James's gut, even as hope dared to spark. What had he preached that night? Had his words been a comfort to Hayden?

"You preached on how God was a father to the fatherless, a husband to widows. How He adopts us into His family so we are never alone. Your words really spoke to me that night, Doc. You have a gift. I left that church wanting to change my life and give God a chance."

James would have allowed his heart to lift at the great testimony except for the look of despair resident in Hayden's eyes. And the frown tugging at his lips.

"Until I saw you in a tavern later that night slobbering over some woman."

Night birds and insects buzzed from the jungle, making James hope that he'd heard the man wrong, but when all eyes snapped toward him, he knew he hadn't. A brick landed in his stomach. Closing his eyes, he prayed for the ground to open up and swallow him whole. Anything to avoid the looks of shock and disgust on the faces of those whom he'd come to love and admire. He shook his head and rubbed the back of his neck. He had so wanted to start anew, to be a good preacher and spiritual guide for the colony. But how could he do that when his friends knew the truth?

As if things weren't bad enough, Hayden continued. "I know you're not that man now, but when I saw your hypocrisy, I gave up on God, moved to Norfolk, and ended up achieving my greatest swindle. . .the one which caused the murder of Angeline's father."

Could things get any worse? Now James had indirectly caused Angeline's father's death! His heart became an anchor in his chest. He dared a glance her way, but she stared at the fire, a tear sliding down her cheek.

Behind him, angry waves tumbled ashore, thundering and frothing like his insides—like his mind. Here he'd thought he had no real connection with his friends, and it turned out he'd had the worst connection of all.

"I knew you, as well, before our trip." Angeline's honeyed voice brought James's gaze up to her. No, impossible. James couldn't take any more bad news. His body felt numb, his mind dazed. He merely stared at her, feeling as if it would be best if he just floated into the night sky alongside the sparks from the fire.

Her freckles tightened like they always did when she grew angry. "You were drunk, stumbling through the streets of Knoxville, blood splattered on your shirt, muttering something about your father."

The night his father had died. James lowered his chin, feeling the pain even now.

"I brought you to my room, cleaned you up, and took care of you."

James stared at her in shock. This woman—this trollop—had been the angel who had changed his life that horrid night over a year ago? The night he'd wanted to kill himself. If not for her, he might have succeeded. Vague memories like shadowy figures slipped in and out of his foggy mind. When he'd found his father shot in a tavern and James couldn't save him, his anger had gotten the best of him, and he'd drawn his sword on the man responsible—Tabitha's husband. They'd fought. James stared at the fire and rubbed the scar angling alongside his mouth where the man had sliced him, where the man had bested him and could have run him through, but he'd granted James mercy and ran off. Laden with guilt, and wishing the man had ended his life, James drank and drank and drank until he couldn't feel anything. But an angel had come to his rescue. Or at least he'd thought it was an angel. When he'd woken the next day, he was in a room above a tavern, the night's rent and a hot meal paid for. And his memories full of an auburn-haired woman ministering to him in the night, holding his head while he tossed his accounts, wiping his forehead, singing gently.

"You tended my wound. You knew all along where this scar came from."

"No. I only knew when it happened, not why or how."

And James wouldn't tell her now. Or any of them. He'd already brought more than enough shame on himself. Yet further memories of that night invaded as he stared at her in shock. "You spoke scripture to me."

She nodded. "I remembered a psalm from my childhood. My father's favorite, Psalm 23. It was the only thing I could think to do. You seemed so distraught. . .so. . . ."—pain misted her eyes—"so hopeless."

"That scripture, your kindness that night, it changed my life." James fought back the burning behind his eyes. "I made a decision to be a better man. To leave my home and start anew."

She blinked, her eyes shifting between his.

The fire crackled and spit like his conscience was doing. Though he'd bedded women without benefit of marriage, he'd thought her profession made her a worse sinner than he. He'd looked down on her, thought of her as too stained to become his wife. Yet, all along, she possessed the heart of an angel, while his was as black as coal.

Blake struggled to rise. "This is incredible. Unbelievable! Before we ever met, each of us affected the others. Our paths crossed in ways we could never have imagined, and the encounters changed each of our lives dramatically."

"For the worse," Hayden spat.

"No, you're looking at it all wrong," Blake continued. "Yes, our associations caused bad things to happen. But, don't you see? None of us would be here in Brazil at this time and place if we hadn't met before." The colonel scanned them, determination firing from his eyes. "If my brother hadn't died, I wouldn't have started this expedition. I would be home with Jerry. Angeline, if your father hadn't been murdered, you would have never ended up an orphan on the streets. You would have never met James. You wouldn't have joined this venture."

Angeline nodded. "Indeed. I'd be with my father."

"Magnolia." Blake spun to face her. "If Hayden's father hadn't stolen your family's money, you and your parents would still be on your plantation in Georgia, or at the very least, still in Roswell, living a good life. If you hadn't introduced Eliza to Stanton, she would have never run off with him and been disowned by her parents. She would have never become a nurse. She would have never been ostracized by the South and in need of a new start." He shifted his gaze to Hayden. "If you hadn't been disillusioned by James's hypocrisy—sorry James"— he added over his shoulder—"you wouldn't have swindled the man who caused Angeline's father's death. Then not only would she have never come to Brazil, but she would have never saved James that night, changed his outlook, his purpose to want a moral society, which eventually brought him here as well. All these chance meetings and events have led us to this exact moment. To this exact place."

Thoughts and memories spun a web in James's mind of impossible encounters, of strings of time and place and plans and devices that when looped together formed a perfect lattice of will and purpose. "Not known but known," he repeated the words from the book, his heart hammering. "That's us! Called from afar. A destiny from above. Six is the number of man. It makes sense now. God gave dominion of earth to man. Man handed earth's keys to Satan when Adam rebelled against God. God chooses to work through man to defeat evil on earth."

"I don't understand," Magnolia said.

"Never mind." James shoved a hand through his hair and took up a pace. "God knew this would happen. He knew the beasts would one day be released. Before we were even born, He chose us for this task, adjusted the course of each of our lives to bring us here to this place at this time for this purpose. Don't you see?" He glanced at his friends, their expressions frozen in shock and amazement.

"We are the six. God brought us here to defeat the evil beasts."

CHAPTER 35

Trying to settle her restless thoughts, Angeline made her way to the shelter she shared with the colony's women. She must remember to thank Hayden for not mentioning their other connection. Though it would bolster James's theory of the *six*'s prior associations—or not so much a theory anymore as incredible fact—it would do more harm than good to disclose that she was a murderer. After all, how much of her sordid past could her friends tolerate? They might even lock her up if they thought her capable of killing someone. She wouldn't blame them in the least. Of course they'd find out soon enough if Dodd followed through with his threat. She had resigned herself to that. And then she would leave this beautiful land, along with her only friends in the world. No, not her only friends. God loved her. He would always be with her. Even if she had to stand trial for murder.

Skirting around sleeping colonists, she was nearly at the entrance to the hut when footsteps sounded and a touch on her arm wheeled her around. She raised her hand, ready to strike.

"Whoa, whoa, it's only me," James whispered as he grabbed her wrist and lowered it. "Why so skittish?"

"Force of habit, I suppose," she breathed out then tried to see his expression in the darkness. Could he fathom what her life had been like working for Miss Lucia? The disgust and shame she faced each day, the constant fear, the customers who'd enjoyed beating her as much as they had using her body? It was why she'd always carried a pistol, until she lost it in the flood.

A cloud shifted, and moonlight revealed a spark of understanding in his eyes. Followed by sorrow—overwhelming sorrow. "Will you walk with me?" he asked.

A breeze showered her with his musky scent and tossed his hair in every direction, just like his touch and the kindness in his voice were doing to her thoughts. Jumbled and anxious, they churned with ideas of destiny, purpose, battles against evil, and now with her feelings for this man before her, who had the power to destroy her. Should she go with him? Allow him a doorway back into her heart?

Yet in the end, she knew she could not deny him. She nodded. They hadn't gone far before he spoke. "I am a buffoon." He stopped before the waves that spun arcs of silver filigree on the dark sand. Angeline's heart ceased beating.

"The hugest buffoon ever to live," he continued.

She shook her head, afraid to hear any more. Afraid her heart could not ride the wave of yet another crest of hope, only to be plunged to the depths of despair.

"I have misjudged you, Angeline."

Angeline's lungs beat against her chest. She sought his eyes in the darkness, but he lowered his gaze.

"I believed it was an angel who tended me that night." He took her hands in his, caressing her fingers. She withdrew, not ready to receive his touch, not ready to erase the hurt he'd caused her.

"I was right. It *was* an angel. It was you, Angeline, my angel." He released a heavy sigh. "I'm so sorry. Can you ever forgive me for the cruel things I said, for forcing my kiss on you? I behaved like a monster. A complete cad."

Yes, he had. And he had broken every piece of her heart. But at the moment, she found the memory fading beneath the soothing baritone of his voice, the brief look of love in his eyes afforded her by the shifting moonlight. Dare she hope?

"But I cannot erase my past," she said. "I was—"

"You *are* a proper lady." He leaned to gaze in her eyes. "With a good heart and a kind spirit and an honor and decency that I've come to realize far exceeds mine."

He shamed her with his praise, and she looked out to sea where the moon flung diamonds atop ebony waters. "You go too far."

"Not far enough. For years I've blamed my troubles, my sins on others, only to discover it was my own weakness, my own lack of faith, which caused my pain."

She smiled. "I have discovered the same."

He cupped her face and brushed fingers over her cheek. Warmth trickled in pleasurable eddies down to her toes.

He leaned to whisper in her ear. "Let us start fresh, you and I. Please, Angeline."

She closed her eyes, cherishing the feel of his breath on her neck. "Start afresh? We may not even survive tomorrow."

"Which is why I cannot wait another minute without begging your forgiveness." He raised her hands to his lips. "And without telling you that I'm absolutely mad about you. I love you, Angeline."

She tried to cling to the words spinning in her mind, but her anger kept them out of reach. "You hurt me, James." She tugged from his grip. "You hurt me badly."

"I know." His voice caught. "I'm so sorry. I never meant to."

"How can I trust you? How do I know my past won't cause you to hate me in the future?"

"Because God has shown me what a hypocrite I've been. My past is far worse than yours, my heart far darker." He took her hands again, holding on tight. "If there is to be any loathing of pasts, it will be me loathing mine."

Minutes passed in silence as his calloused fingers caressed hers. "I don't deserve your forgiveness or your love, Angeline. But I want you to know that you are the angel I've been seeking my entire life."

Could a heart leap beyond a body and soar into the skies? For that's what it felt her heart was doing at the moment. She was hardly an angel, but the way he was looking at her right then made her believe she *could* become one.

"I love you too, James. Perhaps from the very first time you pulled me from the sea."

He smiled. "May I erase my last foolish kiss with a new one?"

Tossing propriety to the salty breeze, Angeline flung her arms around his neck and drew him close. This time, his lips pressed tenderly on hers, caressing, exploring, delicate yet hungry. Waves crashed over their feet, soaking her hem and tickling her legs, but she didn't care. She felt like she was a thousand miles away, floating on a blissful cloud.

The bristle on his jaw scratched her cheek, delighting her even more. He ran fingers through her hair, gripping the strands hungrily as if he couldn't get enough of her.

"Ah, how touching." Dodd's voice etched an icy trail down Angeline. She shoved from James, her heart racing, her mind reeling.

His breath coming equally hard, James shielded her with his body and faced the intruder. "Have you no manners, Dodd?"

He snorted. "Why don't you ask the lady? She and I are *well* acquainted."

Not now, Dodd. For a few moments. . .a few brief, wonderful moments, Angeline had forgotten about Dodd and his threats. Passion bled from her body and dripped into the foam at her feet, replaced by a chill that threatened to bite her heart in two. It wouldn't take long for James to put the pieces together. Even now, as his gaze shifted between her and Dodd, she saw understanding tighten his features.

She might as well say the words that thundered silently between them. "Dodd was a client many years ago." Turning toward the ex-lawman, she stiffened her chin. "I told you James already knows." Yet, she was afraid to look at him now. Afraid to see his reaction to this new discovery. To her surprise, he took her hand in his. Tears flooded her eyes—tears of joy that quickly turned to pain when Dodd flung his next arrow.

"But does the preacher know that you're a murderer as well as a trollop?"

Her heart crumbled. Sweet saints, would the man never leave her be? James snapped his gaze to her, his eyebrows bent. She tried to tug her hand from his, but he wouldn't let go.

"It's true," she said, her voice trembling. "I'm sorry, but it's true."

James shook his head, still staring at her.

Dodd stuffed thumbs in his belt. "She killed her uncle, you know. Her own flesh and blood. What sort of woman does that?"

Confusion burned behind James's eyes. Should she try to explain what happened? Would it make a difference? "I went to live with my uncle and aunt after my father died. He abused me, beat me, barely gave me enough food or clothing. . .made me a slave in their home."

Dodd huffed, pulling out his pocket watch and snapping it open as if bored with the story.

"One night he forced himself on me." She swallowed down a burst of fear at the memory. "He shoved me against a wall in the library and told me if I didn't do what he said, he'd kill me. I couldn't let that happen. I was only eighteen. An innocent girl."

Dodd chuckled. Ignoring him, she continued. "I missed my father so much and hoped my uncle would love me as his own child." She wiped a wayward tear, hating her own weakness. "We struggled. I grabbed a bronze bookend and struck his head. I didn't mean to kill him." Her legs wobbled and James steadied her. "After that I ran away." She lowered her gaze, unable to bear his steely eyes anymore. "You know the rest."

"Lovely story, don't you think, Doc? I so adore the slight quaver in her voice, the tremble of her lips. It adds that extra tug on your heart. She's very good at what she does. Very good, indeed."

James released Angeline's hand. The loss of him, of his strength and warmth, crushed her to the bone. She gazed out to sea, feeling the lure of its peaceful depths.

Thunk! Snap!

She turned to find Dodd toppling backward, arms flailing and curses spewing from his mouth before he landed smack on his derrière in the sand. James shook his hand. Despite the circumstances, Angeline couldn't help the smile that curved her lips or the sense of satisfaction that welled in her belly. Or the thrill at seeing James defend her honor.

Dodd, however, was not of the same mind. Struggling to rise, he rubbed his jaw. "Fool! Before you make the wench any promises you can't keep, Doc, you should know that after I get my share of the gold, I'm taking her back to the States to stand trial for murder."

⁂

He'd left her. James had left her standing on the beach beneath an umbrella of moonlight, with but a kiss on her hand to seal his feelings. But at the moment, he had no idea just what those feelings were. Aside from his overwhelming love for her. *A murderer!* Despite the circumstances—horrific as they were—she still had taken a life. Self-defense, yes. But how could he come to terms with such a crime? Yet, indirectly, hadn't he done the same?

He needed to think. So after Dodd had scrambled back into the hole he'd crawled from, James had excused himself. He had too much to sort out. Too many fears and dreams and hopes and memories and shocking news cycloned in his head. Not to mention he must go over their plan to defeat the beasts tomorrow.

Defeat evil angelic generals. How ludicrous did that sound?

It was too much for one man to handle. Or at least for *him* to handle. So he'd left her there, hope lingering in her eyes and an unspoken plea upon her lips.

Now, hours later, after pacing and praying along the distant shore, peace still eluded him. Falling to the sand in a heap, he drifted into a fitful slumber. He was back on the ship, pitching and rising through a sea of blood. With each flap of white sail and each thrust of the bow, the mighty vessel advanced toward the black, broiling horizon. Shards of flames shot across the darkness, followed by deep growls, ominous and fierce. Stowy perched on the binnacle, his amber eyes latched on James. Ignoring the cat, he dashed to the starboard railing. Foamy blood thrashed the sides of the small dinghy where his friends sat, staring blankly at the gaping dark mouth just ahead. Somehow they kept pace with the ship, though they had no oars or sails.

James cupped his hands. "Ahoy there!" They turned as one and stared at him, fear sparking in their gazes. Fear that turned to pleading. Angeline waved. Hayden shook his head at James in disappointment. Magnolia cried out for help. Eliza clung to her husband who faced the darkness once again, his jaw a bone of defiance.

James spun around and searched the ship. He must help them! He needed rope. He needed to increase the ship's speed to draw closer. He gazed up at the sails, stark white against a blood moon. Making his way to the ratlines, he tripped on something. The cat sped by him, emitting an eerie meow.

"It wasn't your fault." The familiar voice came from behind.

James slowly turned. His legs turned to mush. He stumbled backward. The hard wood of the mainmast prevented his fall. "Father. What are you doing here?"

The man hadn't aged. No, of course he hadn't. He was dead. But he looked younger than he ever had. Gone were the lines of grief and tension from his face. Gone was the weariness in his eyes, the gray from his hair. He even seemed to stand a bit taller.

And he smiled now at James as he'd never done when he'd been alive—a smile of love and approval and forgiveness.

"Son, I've been sent to tell you something." He adjusted the white tie he always wore over his black frock. "Something important."

"But you can't be here. Not really." James swallowed. "This is nothing but a dream, a vision." He rubbed his eyes.

"Dreams have meanings, son."

The ship crested a scarlet wave, creaking and groaning on the ascent. James steadied his boots on the deck, drinking in the vision of a man he thought he'd never see again.

"My death was not your fault," his father repeated.

James looked away. "It *was* my fault, Father. I should have been the one at the tavern that night. I should have been the one to come to the aid of Mr. Reynolds. Not you. But I wasn't at the church when his message came." James swept guilty eyes toward his father. "Do you want to know where I was, while you were dying from a gunshot wound? While you were lying in a puddle of spit and ale and drowning in your own blood?"

The words bore no effect on his father's loving look.

Which only angered James. Anger at himself. "I was with a woman. Mrs. Tabitha Cullen, to be exact. The wife of the man who shot you."

"I know, son." His father smiled—not a smile of victory or sarcasm but one of forgiveness.

"How can you stand there and look at me like that? Don't you see? Tabitha's husband accused Mr. Reynolds of compromising his wife. But it was me who was with her. With her that very moment when you went to stop the brawl. It was me." James's insides twisted into a hopeless knot. He should toss himself overboard. A fitting punishment.

To drown in the blood that he had shed.

As soon as James had heard the news, he'd raced to the tavern, knelt before his father. There was already so much blood. James might have been able to save him, but the terrors had gripped him, and instead he'd sat frozen and watched his father die.

"I failed you, Father." Tears filled his eyes. "As I failed you my entire life."

"No, no, no." James's father laid a hand on his shoulder—a solid hand, a real hand—one that bore the gold ring with the cross in the center that he'd worn to his grave. "You were never a failure. 'Twas I who demanded too much. Expected more than any son could give. I am sorry, James. I finally know what grace is." He smiled, and there was such peace in his eyes, James longed to dive into them and be lost forever.

The sails thundered above. A roar brought both men's gazes to the blackness swallowing up the horizon. "Your friends need you, James," his father said. "Gather them aboard and fight the darkness. You have been chosen. You and you alone can lead them to victory."

Dread sent James's heart pounding. He rubbed the scar on his cheek. "Me? Why me?"

"Why not you?" His father stepped back and began to fade.

"Please don't go." James wiped a tear away.

"We will meet again." His father smiled. "You can do this, son. God is with you." He gave him one last approving nod before he turned, stepped off the railing of the ship, and disappeared into the mist.

Something bright appeared at the prow of the ship. A white figurehead in the shape of a lamb—a lamb with a lion's head and a sword in its grip. A glow beamed from within it, casting light upon the bloody sea. Why had James not seen it before?

A fiery arrow shot across the darkness as if the stars themselves were falling. Then another and another. Thunder roared as the ship sped toward the horizon, pitching and rolling and sending scarlet foam washing over the bow. Heart thrashing, James clutched a rope, tied it to the railing, and spied his friends now drifting just yards off the ship. He flung it toward them. Blake caught it, and within minutes his friends climbed over the bulwarks and joined him aboard. Their frightened gazes sped over one another and then to the black hole about to swallow them alive. With determined nods, they took one another's arms and formed a defiant line at the bow just as the ship broke into the darkness.

⌘

"Will you marry me?" It was James's voice. At least Angeline thought it was, though the words jumbled in the wind.

She turned to find him standing there looking like a schoolboy, his face hopeful, his eyes filled with love, his fingers twitching by his side.

By the looks of his wrinkled shirt and trousers, he had passed the night much like she had—restless and filled with nightmares.

"I beg your pardon?"

The rising sun sparkled off his wide grin as he took both her hands in his. "Will you marry me?"

She searched his eyes, firing with golden flecks of hope, and found no trace of betrayal, humor, or anger.

"You want to marry a murderess and a prostitute?" Squelching down the thrill blooming within, she had to be sure he knew what he was asking.

"No, I want to marry *you*, Angeline."

Emotion burned in her throat: hope and fear and excitement all jumbled together. "When you left last night. . ." She'd thought it was over between them. He'd accepted her past as a trollop, but a murderer? How could she expect a man of God to tolerate that?

"I'm sorry. I needed to think. Not about my love for you. About what Dodd said, yes, but also about my own life." He flattened his lips. "I had a dream about my father." His eyes grew glassy, and he gazed out to sea. "He always expected me to be perfect, and I always failed him."

"No—" she began, but he silenced her with a gentle finger to her lips.

"I've done bad things, Angeline. That night back in Knoxville, you saw me at my worst. Yet despite my own past, I still expected everyone around me to be perfect." He glanced at the jungle. "I wanted to create a moral utopia where nobody fell away from grace." He chuckled and shook his head. "But I have discovered recently that where imperfection lives, God's grace abounds."

A tear slipped down Angeline's face.

James continued to caress her fingers. "I have also discovered that none of us will ever be perfect. That's what grace is for. I will never create a perfect utopia here on earth. I will never be perfect, and you will never be perfect. But God covers all our imperfections if we merely turn to Him."

Angeline squeezed his hand as a laugh-cry emerged from her lips. She could hardly believe her ears. This was precisely what she had prayed for during the long night.

"So, will you marry this imperfect man who doesn't deserve you?"

He raised her hand and placed a gentle kiss on it.

She batted her tears away as reality set in. "You heard Dodd. He intends to take me back for trial."

"Then let him. I will go with you. As your husband."

She searched his eyes. "I can't ask you to do that."

"Then don't ask. Just answer me."

A giggle burst from her lips. "You're mad."

"Incredibly, wonderfully, and hopelessly."

"James, Angeline!" A call came from the camp.

James glanced over his shoulder to where Blake, Eliza, Magnolia, and Hayden prepared to head into the jungle. Eliza had woken Angeline before dawn to inform her of their plans. Though the scheme sounded crazy, Angeline agreed and had slipped down the beach to pray. Pray for James. Pray for protection. Pray for God to empower them. Yet she feared her faith was too small to be of any effect.

Down shore, a few colonists stirred from their sleep and began stoking the fire for breakfast. Though the pirates drank and sang well into the morning hours, their greed had woken them early to head to the temple. Along with Dodd and Patrick and a few other colonists they had dragged from their beds.

Blake gestured for Angeline and James to join them. He had thought it best not to tell the rest of the colonists their plans. No need to spread unnecessary alarm when there was nothing anyone else could do. But the six of them must leave soon before the others started to question.

James faced her, a questioning look on his face.

"I will give you my answer later." When her heart stopped flipping and bouncing through her chest like an acrobat and when her thoughts descended from the clouds onto reason. Then maybe she could think with her head and not her heart. And pray. Yes, she must find out what God wanted. A first for her. But a habit she intended to foster for the rest of her life.

"Very well." He extended his elbow as if they were going for a stroll in a garden. "Shall we go defeat some demonic beasts?"

CHAPTER 36

"I feel so helpless," Blake muttered as he trudged beside James through the jungle. "Not bringing anything with us but the shirts on our backs. No weapons—not that we have many—no clubs or spears or even iron skillets to slam over the fallen angels' heads." He gave a nervous laugh.

"The battle is not yours, but God's." James quoted from Second Chronicles. "We need only Him." Which is why he'd left the Hebrew book back on the beach. They didn't need it anymore. He'd read it over and over but still found no particular instructions for defeating the beasts, save commanding them back to their chains. At first he'd found that rather alarming, but then God had led him to the story in Second Chronicles where the Israelites faced a massive army of Moabites and Ammonites. Outnumbered and overwhelmed, the people trembled in fear. But God was with them.

"Ye shall not need to fight in this battle: set yourselves, stand ye still, and see the salvation of the LORD."

That verse had flown off the page and embedded itself in James's heart. And he knew that they had only to show up in the tunnels beneath the temple and God would do the rest. Yet now as they made their way through steamy leaves and branches and vines laden with all manner of skittering, crawling things, a small part of James began to skitter as well. Had he really heard from God? Had his father been correct when he'd told James he'd been chosen for this task? Or had it just been a silly dream?

Doubts saturated him, like the sweat trickling down his back. Tabitha sauntered out of the leaves on his left, Abigail on his right.

She winked at him, her dark lashes fanning her cheeks. "You haven't changed, James. I see the desire in your eyes." Tabitha sidled up to him, pressing her curves against his arm. Both ladies giggled. James turned to see if Blake noticed, but the colonel kept walking, face forward. Ignoring the women, James pressed on.

And nearly bumped into his father.

The man blocked the way with a body that looked more real than the trees. Yet the colonel strode right through him as if he wasn't there.

"Who do you think you are, boy?" His father clicked his tongue in disgust. "You're leading these people to their death. Just like you led me."

Guilt gripped James's heart, threatening to squeeze his remaining courage. He brushed past him. He appeared in front of him again, looking more like James remembered—tired, aged, and worn. "That wasn't me last night," he snarled. "That was just a foolish dream. I don't forgive you at all. You're nothing but a failure."

James halted, gut clenching. Those words were more what he'd expected to hear from his father.

"*Believe the truth, reject the lie,*" a voice within him whispered.

But what *was* the truth? The truth was God's Word: forgiveness, love, grace.

Clamping down his jaw, James charged forward. "I don't believe you. Leave me alone," he said as he passed right through his father.

That's when the wind picked up.

❧⁕☙

Blake glanced up to see patches of dark sky through the canopy. He'd grown accustomed to storms rising quickly in Brazil but not this quickly. Wind whipped leaves and dirt in his face. The wound in his side ached. Ignoring it, he shoved aside a swaying branch, drew Eliza close, and continued forward. They wouldn't allow a little storm to stop them.

But he would allow his brother.

The boy appeared ahead on the trail in his Confederate uniform, leaning against a giant fig tree, unaffected by the battering wind. A vision. Only a vision. Blake stiffened his jaw and proceeded, but the boy's call to him halted him in his tracks. How could he ignore his only brother? He missed him so.

Jerry lifted blue eyes—so like their mother's—to Blake. "Why did you marry the woman whose husband murdered me?" Those eyes, now burning with hate, shifted to Eliza. "Why?"

Blake's heart shriveled. Thunder shook the ground. Drawing a deep breath, he led Eliza forward.

"How could you?" His brother's voice haunted him. "Do I mean so little to you?"

Blake's breath clogged in his throat. Agony burned behind his eyes. But he kept going. *Father, help me. Please, help me.*

"I love you, Blake. Don't you love me?" Sobbing came from behind, and Blake turned and stared at the boy he would gladly have given his life to save. But it wasn't his brother. Jerry was dead and in heaven. This was a monster. No matter what form it took.

"Leave me alone!" He yelled above the rising tempest. Then drawing Eliza close, he lifted an arm to protect them from flying debris, and proceeded.

Lightning scored the sky.

❧

"Did you see something?" Eliza shouted over the wind. She'd felt her husband stiffen beside her several steps back, had witnessed him stop and stare at a tree, then stop again and shout something. Now, he gripped his stomach as though someone had stabbed him.

Another flash of lightning lit the darkening skies. Thunder roared. Eliza jumped and dodged a flying branch as she huddled beneath her husband's arm.

"It's nothing." Blake gave her a reassuring smile and kissed the top of her head. "I wish you didn't have to come along. Especially being with child. It isn't safe."

"I would be in more danger if I didn't come." She hoped her words reached his ears in the torrent of wind. His nod confirmed they had.

She glanced up to see how the others fared and wished she hadn't. Her father crossed the clearing up ahead, one hand behind his back, the other rubbing his chin. Turning, he started back the other way, deep in his musings, pacing as she had so often seen him do in his study back home. The sight of him stole Eliza's breath. He was young once again, strong, determined, so handsome in his suit of gray broadcloth, his

921

thin mustache and dark hair clipped to style, his regal stride. She knew he was a vision, she knew she should ignore him.

But she couldn't.

Finally his eyes met hers. "You left me. Disobedient girl! Left me all alone. Ran off with that Yankee! Broke my heart." Anger turned to despair.

Eliza reached out to him. He withdrew. Lines creased his skin as it folded and drooped. His dark hair shriveled and turned gray, falling out in clumps until all that remained were feeble wisps atop his head. His shoulders stooped, his eyes grew cloudy. And she turned away as she and Blake passed him by, unable to bear watching him age. Seeing the agony in his eyes. The loneliness she had caused. She tossed a hand to her mouth to subdue a sob.

"Resist it!" Blake shouted, squeezing her shoulder. "It isn't real."

Nodding, she drew a deep breath and faced her father, who now walked beside her. "Go away. I want nothing to do with you." It was the hardest thing she'd ever said, yet as soon as she spoke the words, hatred fired from her father's eyes before he became a dark mist and blew away in the wind.

The sky broke open, releasing an army of rain.

Droplets stung like pinpricks. Magnolia ducked beneath a banana tree. Stopping beside her, Hayden plucked a giant leaf and held it over her head. "We should keep going!" he yelled above the tapping of rain and roar of wind.

Oh, how she hated what the rain did to her hair! Matted it to her face like strands of oily rope, making her look like a wet cat. But why was she thinking of that now? She hadn't been overly concerned about her appearance in months. Still, she hated that Hayden saw her like this. Would he still love her looking so hideous? Taking the leaf from him, she shielded her face from his view and dashed onto the trail again. Up ahead she spotted the blurry shapes of Blake and Eliza.

And someone else.

Someone wearing a gray cloak and limping across the trail. Splashing through the growing puddles, Magnolia drew near, curious who the intruder was. Perhaps a colonist who had followed them? A gust of wind nearly knocked her down. Clutching her close, Hayden tried to use his body as a shield, but the tempest shoved them both to the side as if they weighed no more than a feather. Leaves and twigs struck them from all around. Batting them away Magnolia peered once more toward the strange person.

Gray, spindly hair flowed from beneath a hood covering the woman's head—a hood that stayed put, despite the tempest. A flash of white light blinded Magnolia. *Crack! Snap!* Magnolia followed Hayden's gaze above to see a wide branch cascading through the canopy, heading straight for Blake and Eliza.

Releasing Magnolia, Hayden charged forward and barreled into the couple. All three of them tumbled into the middle of a large fern as the branch struck the ground with a thunderous roar, flinging mud into the air.

The earth shook. The cloaked figure reappeared. With a long pointed fingernail, she slid the hood from her face. Rain pummeled skin, shriveled and blotched. Drooping, sunken eyes met Magnolia's. The skin beneath them hung in blue, veiny folds. Magnolia gasped. It was her! Her old self that appeared in her reflection.

She screamed. Wind whipped her skirts against her legs, stinging her skin. Rain slapped her face. And an overwhelming terror gripped her that she would never be beautiful again.

"The LORD seeth not as man seeth; for man looketh on the outward appearance, but the LORD looketh on the heart."

Yes. Yes. She closed her eyes and hunkered down against the wind. That was true. She knew that. And with God's help, her heart was getting better every day. Hadn't she noticed improvements in her reflection? It might take a lifetime, but she would end up looking like a princess in the end. Bracing against the buffeting wind, she drew a breath and stood. The old woman gave her a malicious grin. But Magnolia waved a hand at her. "Be gone. I'm beautiful in God's eyes."

The vision faded, but Magnolia couldn't help the tears flowing down her cheeks.

❦

Hayden darted to his wife and absorbed her in his arms. Sobbing, she buried her face in his shoulder. When he nudged her back to ensure she wasn't hurt, her sapphire eyes skittered over the jungle seeking something. Or someone. Wiping wet strands from her face, he kissed the droplets of rain from her eyes. "They aren't real!" he shouted. "I love you." Then dipping his head to brace against the wind, he led her forward. Water rose on the soggy ground, gripping their ankles and making it difficult to walk. A branch struck his shoulder. Pain throbbed across his back. Covering Magnolia with his arms, he continued.

A silver slipper appeared in his vision, enclosing a very delicate foot dangling from a tree limb. Hayden glanced up to see Miss Sybil Shilling, casually sitting atop a branch as if she were a little girl on a summer's day. Her satin gown with velvet trim fell in lavish folds over her legs, completely dry. Her hair, a bounty of chestnut curls, remained untouched by wind or rain. He remembered her well. He'd swindled her out of a dowry that would have provided the homely, bird-witted girl the only means of a good match.

Before she even opened his mouth, Hayden said, "I'm sorry, Sybil."

"You're sorry!" She leapt from the tree as if she were a monkey and landed before him. "I never married, you know. Old spinster Sybil, the joke of the town."

Magnolia stared at Hayden, but he knew she couldn't see the woman. All the more reason for him to ignore her as well, ignore the guilt that tore his gut, ignore the look of anguish on her face.

"You told me I was beautiful. You told me you loved me."

He had. He'd flattered her more than any of his other victims. Perhaps because he'd felt sorry for her. But in the end, he'd not only broken her heart, but her life as well. How could he have done such a thing? How could he have been such a monster?

"Forgive me." Halting, Hayden's legs gave out. He lowered his chin and fell to his knees in a puddle. A chill soaked into his trousers. And his heart.

Magnolia gripped his drenched shirt, forcing him up to face her. Water slid down her face, dripped from her lashes and chin, as her sodden curls lashed about her cheeks. "You aren't that man anymore!" She shouted, tugging on his shirt. "Do you hear me? You aren't him anymore!"

How did she know what he'd seen? But then again, she always knew when he was hurting. Drawing her close, he pressed her head against his chest and kissed her sopping hair. She was right. He *was* a new man in Christ. The old things had passed away. Strength returned to his legs. He stood. The vision of Sybil crumbled to dust and blew away in the wind.

Swoosh. Swoosh. Swoosh. The beat of many wings filled the air. Dark blotches covered the canopy, swooping, diving, screeching, and stealing what remained of the light.

Angeline rarely screamed. She'd seen too much horror, suffered too much at the hands of unscrupulous men to shriek like a fribble-hearted female at every frightening thing. But when the bats started diving for her, she screamed louder than she ever had. The hideous creatures' shrieks pierced through the rumble of the storm, sounding like tortured mice—murderous mice.

James grabbed a fallen branch and began swatting them away. A few fell into the puddles at her feet, twitching from their wounds. Bile rose in her throat, and she covered her head with her hands.

"They are trying to stop us!" Spinning to face their friends behind them, James cupped his hands over his mouth and shouted, "It's the beasts! They don't want us going to the temple! Keep moving. They can't harm us!"

In defiance of his words, lightning flashed, thunder blasted, and the rain thrashed down harder than ever. Wind shot droplets through the air like pellets, stinging Angeline's skin through her gown. Water gushed over the ground, picking up the dead bats and carrying them away as if they were leaves.

James pulled Angeline to her feet. Shielding her with his arms, he sloshed forward down the trail.

Above them, the bats disappeared into puffs of black smoke.

Which only made her heart beat faster. She knew they faced an unearthly evil. She'd just never witnessed it firsthand. Not like this.

James squeezed her. "It will be all right. Stay close."

The confidence in his voice, in the way he held himself, emboldened Angeline to ignore the dozens of customers who now assailed her at every turn, their eyes hungrily licking her, their mouths voicing obscenities.

"Whore! Trollop!" one shouted.

"Filthy slut!" another spat.

Covering her ears, she slogged through the rising water. Above her ankles now. *Oh, God, not another flood.*

"You think you're cleansed, eh? You think God forgave you?" Her uncle's wicked chortle echoed through the storm, transforming into thunder.

Halting, Angeline closed her eyes. She couldn't face the man she'd killed. She couldn't face the man whose assault had led her down the path to darkness. Not now. Wind whipped her blouse, her hair, branding her skin. Rain hammered her like punishment from God.

Branches, twigs, and leaves flew at them from all directions.

James covered her with his arms and led her onward, ducking and diving beneath the onslaught. The din of the storm grew louder. The force of the wind and rain more violent. Doubts rose within Angeline that she knew if she entertained, would surely send her running back to the beach. Sweet saints, how could they ever fight such power?

Yet James believed they could. She could feel his faith in the steel of his arms, the rock-determination of his body next to hers, in every confident breath he expelled. And it gave her strength to go on. On and on, head lowered, ramming into the wind, dodging wooden missiles and slogging through a river of water, until finally the crumbling walls of the temple appeared.

And a darkness invaded Angeline's soul. No. More than darkness. A heaviness weighted with despair and hopelessness.

She hated this temple.

James stopped to wait for the others and pressed her against the wall, shielding her with his body. There, battered by the elements and about to do battle with unimaginable evil, terror squeezed all hope from Angeline. Were they all about to die? What if these were her last moments with James? She couldn't bear the thought. There, barricaded by his strength and warmth, she knew there could be only one answer to his question. The answer God had reassured her was the right one during their trek there.

She lifted her gaze to his, but inches apart. "Yes."

"Yes?" His breath wafted on her cheek. His hair whipped his forehead. He searched her eyes before understanding widened his own. "Are you agreeing to marry me?"

She nodded, smiling.

He drew her to his chest. A rumble of joy burst from inside him, caressing her ear. Thunder cracked the sky. The ground shook. Water tugged at her gown. But Angeline didn't care.

Nudging her back, James cupped her face in his hands. "You have made me so very happy." He kissed her forehead, her nose, and proceeded down to her lips—would have kissed her as she so desperately wanted if someone hadn't coughed.

Hayden's hair flailed in the wind like sodden pieces of rope, but his grin and subsequent wink sent heat flooding Angeline's cheeks. She stepped back from James as the others approached. No time to celebrate.

Covered in scratches, their clothes torn, and with water dripping from their hair, the six of them looked as if they'd fought the kraken and lost. James turned and barreled through the wind and rain, leading them around the wall. The water hugged their ankles as, one by one, they slipped inside the broken gate.

No sooner had they entered the courtyard than the wind stopped, the rain ceased, and the water receded. The sky, however, remained black and ominous, still emitting its menacing growl. Dripping and panting, they stared at each other in numbed shock.

Blake's features tightened as he donned his warrior's mask. "Let's do this."

Trying to settle her beating heart, Angeline slipped her hand in James's as he ushered her onward, slogging in the mud past the gruesome obelisks and into the temple. Steam rose from the stagnant pond, and a glimmer drew her gaze to the gold moon and stars hanging above the altar. James led her into the tunnels, followed by Blake and Eliza, and finally Hayden and Magnolia. Angeline lifted up a silent prayer for God's protection and help. She knew her faith was weak, and she suspected Hayden and Eliza also struggled. Would God still honor their mission? Could He use such weak people to accomplish His will? If not, at least she would die trying to do the right thing. For the first time in her life. For the first time she would battle evil and fight for good. For the first time she believed in something larger than herself, believed in destiny and purpose, and that life had meaning.

MaryLu Tyndall

She only hoped that life would not end today.

A roar much like an approaching train blared through the narrow passageway. The ground shook. Torches fell from hooks on the walls and sputtered on the wet dirt. Darkness swamped them. Rocks pelted Angeline. Ducking, she covered her head with her hands. They were going to be buried alive.

CHAPTER 37

J ames covered Angeline with his body. The ground leapt like a wild pony. Sharp pebbles stabbed his back and arms. Pain lanced through him. Something large struck his head. Momentarily dazed, he shook it off and gathered his wits. *God, help us!*

"No weapon that is formed against thee shall prosper."

The silent words swept through him, sparking to life places shriveled in fear. God was with them, and He was more powerful than any beast. "Keep going!" James shouted over his shoulder. "They can't harm us."

Though the pain burning in his head spoke to the contrary. Though he couldn't see a thing but thick, inky blackness. Drawing Angeline close, he stumbled forward over the heaving ground, their bodies shoved into sharp stone on one side then slammed against barbed rock on the other. Bruises formed. Angeline moaned, and he wished more than anything he could shield her from all harm. Rocks tumbled over them. Sizzling heat belched up from below like dragon's breath. Gripping the wall for support, James shuffled forward on the pitching dirt. Knife-sharp rock sliced his hand with each jolt. If only he could see.

"My Word is a light."

Yes. James drew a deep breath. "Thy word is a lamp unto my feet," he repeated the scripture from Psalms. "And a light unto my path." Though the roar of the earthquake muffled his words, a glow appeared from above. A soft glow like the glimmer of predawn, dousing the tunnel in a golden hue just bright enough for him to make out their surroundings.

Thank You, Lord. Heart swelling with awe, James sped ahead. He'd been down these tunnels enough times to know his way, and the quicker he went, the sooner this mad quaking would stop. Or so he hoped. Still, no matter how tightly he held Angeline or how fast he went, their bodies flopped back and forth against razor walls like corn through a prickly sieve. The shaking forced them to their knees one minute then tossed them in the air the next. Dust filled James's lungs until he could barely breathe. Angeline moaned. Magnolia shrieked, only heightening James's fear for all the ladies, especially Eliza so far along with child. *Oh, God, are You sure we are the six?* It wasn't so much a prayer, but a doubt he realized he shouldn't have entertained. A doubt that whipped his fears as out of control as the ground was doing to his body.

Halfway down the second stairway, a dozen pirates appeared, torches in hand, the flames distorting the terror on their faces as they pushed past them, shouting, cursing, and scrambling on top of each other to get away from the mayhem. Four colonists—three farmers and the cooper—followed fast on their heels in much the same condition.

"Doc, Colonel!" Mr. Jenkins shouted as he passed. "The walls are caving in. Get out now!" The others nodded their agreement as they shoved by them.

Angeline trembled in James's arms. Dust filled the air. Bending over, she coughed. But they couldn't go back now. God had sent His light as confirmation they were doing the right thing. Hadn't He? Ah, why so many doubts? When James had been so full of faith just that morning. When all these troubles should prove they were in God's will. Why else would the enemy be coming so hard and fast against them?

James squeezed through the opening into the first chamber and turned to assist Angeline. A jolt caused him to lose his balance. They both went tumbling to the dirt, barely missing a row of sharp stalagmites. Flickering light from torches on the walls wove a kaleidoscope of devilish shapes over the craggy ceiling. Dizzy, James closed his eyes. The ground rattled beneath him. The foul stench of sulfur and death stole his breath. Coughing, he tried to rise, but nausea churned in his belly. He had to get up. He had to go on. His friends depended on him. God depended on him.

Yet fear kept him paralyzed. Fear of failure. Fear of dying. Of losing Angeline, losing his friends, people who counted on him. Heat enflamed him. Overwhelming heat, as if he'd been thrust into an oven. His skin prickled. Blood boiled through his veins. He looked at Angeline beside him. Like a wilted flower, she melted on the ground.

What was he doing? Who did he think he was? He'd failed at everything in his life, what made him think he could succeed in defeating such powerful beings?

Angeline's gaze locked upon his. She must have read his thoughts for she struggled to rise and tugged on his arm. "Get up, James! Get up. We need you!"

Her violet eyes sparked with life, determination, and something else. . .faith. In him?

Forcing himself up, he gathered her in his arms. "Thank you," he said as Blake and Eliza poked through the opening, followed by Hayden and Magnolia. Sweat matted hair to their heads and darkened their torn clothing. Scratches lined their arms and faces—faces stark with fear but also set with determination. All four of them swayed in his vision as if he'd had too much to drink. But it was the ground still moving beneath them, rising and falling like ocean swells. Blake gave him a nod of encouragement.

Rattling drew James's gaze to the broken irons at the bottom of the two empty alcoves. They leapt over the dirt with each thrust of the ground. But no. Not with each thrust. Their movements were driven and angry as if something. . .or someone. . .moved them. His throat closed.

A missile fired from above, spearing the dirt beside him. Then another and another. The stalactites loosened, one by one, and shot to the ground. Tucking Angeline beneath his arm, he ducked and dodged, making his way to the opening that led to the chamber below. Magnolia screamed.

"Run!" Blake yelled, shielding Eliza with his body as he stumbled forward. Spears rained down upon them like lightning rods.

A growl spun James around. A shard impaled Hayden's foot. He yanked it out. Blood squirted, which would normally have sent James cowering. He started for his friend, but Magnolia knelt and pressed her handkerchief over the wound.

931

The hail of spikes continued.

Eliza and Blake disappeared through the opening. James shoved Angeline through and then turned to help Magnolia and a limping Hayden before jumping in behind them. More darkness. The shaking increased. James felt as though he were trapped in the hold of a ship during a mighty squall. No, much worse than that, for at least the hull of the ship was made of wood not rock as sharp as spears. He groped to find Angeline but lost his footing and was thrown against his friends. They fell, tumbling downward, screaming, legs and arms reaching, bodies scraping against rock and one another until they barreled through a hole, like rag dolls, onto the dirt of the final chamber.

Torches danced on walls that were cracking and sliding as if made of dough. Their shifting flames flickered over a stack of gold coins and trinkets that filled the top of the fourth alcove and spread out to a circular wall of rock that kept the treasure at bay. If the treasure indeed filled the alcove all the way to the ground as Dodd had claimed, then it was enough gold to own the world—if one wanted such a thing. Which Captain Ricu apparently did as he clung to a boulder to keep his balance, while four pirates, along with Dodd, removed the final layer of rocks that kept the gold out of reach. Beside them lay a pile of empty burlap sacks. Shouts of glee drew James's gaze to Patrick, who, down on all fours, bracing against the quake, looked like a hunting dog about to be released from his leash. None of them noticed James and his friends.

Assisting Angeline to her feet, James started for Ricu. He had no idea what he would do, but he must stop him or anyone else from speaking the Latin phrase. Even though all of them seemed more interested in the gold at the moment. But he couldn't take that chance, not when the phrase was clearly seen etched in stone above the alcove. Etched in more than stone, from what James could tell. The phrase above this final tomb was ingrained with gold that now glittered in the torchlight, making it all the more visible. And desirable. Even if the pirates hauled off all the treasure, their greed would drive them to scrape every ounce from the wall as well.

The ground tilted, and James slipped. Captain Ricu turned. His eyes narrowed, and his shout brought the tips of several cutlasses oscillating before James and his friends. James retreated to stand beside Angeline.

Another jolt struck, and Ricu leaned against a boulder for support. Sweat and fright made the mighty pirate captain shrivel before their eyes. Still, his voice rang through the chamber like a gong. "Leave at once!"

The pirates advanced.

Sweat stung James's eyes. He wiped it with his sleeve as the shaking settled to a gentle sway. Surely the addle-brained pirate could see that the walls of the chamber were about to collapse. Did he put so little value on his own life and so much on the gold that he was willing to risk being buried alive just to possess it? Pain lowered James's gaze to a sword jabbing his chest. The tip sliced a trail over his skin with each roll of the ground. The rest of the pirates leveled their blades at his friends. Yet they all stood bravely. Even Magnolia, whose trembling lips were the only indication of her fear. Angeline slipped her hand in James's. They were all going to die. Either by the blade or by the quake. *God, why did You bring us here if we are to fail?*

But then he remembered. . .and he prayed. . .and he hoped. . .

"No weapon formed against us shall prosper." James spoke the words God had given him earlier.

The swords flew from the pirates' hands. They twirled through the air, round and round, glittering in the torchlight before landing in a heap of *clanks* and *clangs* in the far corner. The pirates stared at them, then back at James, then over to the blades again, fear screaming from their wide eyes.

"Well, I'll be. . ." Hayden exclaimed. Blake shouted an "Amen!" Eliza laughed with joy, and James squeezed Angeline's hand.

"How you do that?" Ricu's face grew pale beneath a sheen of sweat.

Clanking drew James's gaze to the broken irons in the empty third alcove. They rose and fell and leapt and plummeted as if they had a life of their own. The stink of rotted flesh and feces swept over him. It burned his throat and lungs and he doubled over, gasping for air. His friends did the same. Even the pirates and Dodd coughed and wheezed—all except Patrick who had risen to his feet and stared at them as if they were all mad.

Wave after wave of heat swamped them. Sweat streamed down James's back, gluing his shirt to his skin. Skin that felt as though it were being roasted alive. His friends withered beside him. A mighty roar echoed through the chamber. The room lurched as if a giant slammed against the walls. Stalactites fell from the sky, piercing one of the pirates through his chest. He dropped to the ground with a moan. Magnolia screamed. Eliza started toward him, but Blake held her back. It was too late anyway. The man's vacant eyes stared at the ceiling. The floor tilted left then right, tossing them back and forth like a seesaw. The boulder beside Ricu rolled on its side. He backed away, eyes bulging.

Dodd stumbled toward Blake. "Don't you see the gold?" he shouted, pointing toward the alcove. "I told you it was here!"

Ignoring the buffoon, James watched as Patrick and one of the pirates struggled to remove a loose rock in the middle of the wall surrounding the alcove. The ground jolted, aiding their efforts, and the stone slid to the side. Gold coins poured from the opening like water from a faucet. Laughing with glee, Patrick grabbed a sack and held it beneath the hole while another pirate scrambled to collect the coins on the ground—both seemingly oblivious to the fact that the cave was about to collapse. In fact, there wasn't a drop of sweat on Patrick, not on his skin nor dampening his clothes.

The ground stopped shaking. The rest of the pirates darted to the wall and yanked and pulled until another stone loosened, creating a bigger hole through which goblets and jewelry poured along with coins. Ricu smiled and ordered them to fill the sacks as fast as they could.

James started toward them, his plan to keep them focused on the gold and not the Latin phrase, but the earth jolted once more and sent him careening backward. Dirt began swirling in eddies across the ground. Whirling and spinning and rising until columns of dust cycloned all around them. The pirates ceased gathering gold. Everyone backed away as the shapes coiled in a mass of mud and rock, rising higher and higher until each one slowly coalesced into a human form. James's parents, the women who had caused his downfall, the soldiers he'd lost on the operating table. And many other people he'd never seen before, but from the looks on his friends' faces, they were people they each recognized. People who now began to berate them with insults and taunts and accusations. James ignored them, as did his friends. They knew how to deal with these lies. But Ricu, the pirates, and Dodd saw them as well, for they stared at them in horror, while Patrick continued gathering gold into sacks.

The broken irons in the third alcove clanked and rattled as if enraged. The swords in the corner leapt in the air. They turned and pointed at James and his friends, each tip aimed at their hearts. Blake leapt in front of Eliza, but she eased out to stand beside him and took his hand. Hayden and James exchanged a nervous glance. Magnolia's chest panted like a bellows.

Captain Ricu crossed himself. Dodd jumped behind a boulder, and the pirates crouched to the ground.

James swallowed. There was no place to hide. No place to run. His gaze locked on Angeline, who stood bravely by his side. She smiled. The blades shot through the air. Angeline closed her eyes. Magnolia shrieked. *Swoosh!* Air wafted against James's arm. A dozen clanks sounded behind him. No screams. No pain. He glanced at his friends. They examined themselves for wounds, but no blood appeared. Either the swords had missed or, miraculously, had gone through them without any damage. James couldn't help the chuckle that spilled from his lips. God was, indeed, with them. And by the looks of confidence on his friends' faces, they now believed the same.

The visions collapsed into piles of dirt on the ground.

"Meu Deus! Deus salve nos!" Ricu gazed up toward heaven in an appeal to a God James was sure he rarely addressed. "Hurry, take gold. We leave!" he ordered his men. Then withdrawing a handkerchief from his vest, he turned and watched the third alcove chains continue to dance, shaking his head in disbelief.

The poor man. If James didn't believe in the power of God, he'd assume he was fast becoming a madman at what he'd seen today.

The ground swayed. The heat and fetor rose. Halting his greedy harvest, Patrick grabbed one of the pirate's pistols, cocked it, and leveled it at Ricu's back.

"Captain Ricu, behind you!" Magnolia shouted. James shifted curious eyes her way. But, no doubt, she favored the flamboyant pirate over her ex-fiancé.

Ricu wheeled about, bells clanging and trinkets sparkling. "What be this?" He stared agape at the pistol then snapped his fingers toward his men. "Kill this man."

935

But the pirates only chortled and continued shoving gold into their sacks.

Patrick grinned. "I do apologize, Captain, but I'm afraid this *be* a mutiny."

Magnolia gasped. Angeline grew tense beside James.

"We not on ship, idiota. Cannot be mutiny."

"Well, perhaps a prelude to a mutiny, then." Patrick called one of the pirates to his side. "Relieve your captain of his weapons, and tie him up, if you please, Eduardo." He glanced around the chamber. "These crumbling walls give me an idea. We were simply going to kill you, dear Captain, but I believe I'll let the chamber do it for me."

James exchanged a glance with Blake that said he agreed they should stay out of it. They were here only to keep the fourth beast from being freed. Nothing more.

"What?" Captain Ricu's eyes sparked fire. "Branco, Faro!" he called to his men and spat a string of angry Portuguese.

"Sorry, Capitão." One of the men shrugged. "He offer larger cut of gold. How could we say no?"

Ricu growled, his eyes burning embers. "I am Captain Ricu, and I take what I—"

"Want when you want." Patrick waved the pistol in the air. "Yes, yes, we know, Captain, but I fear your reign of narcissism has come to an end."

"*Traidor desleal, patife!!*" Sweat streamed down Ricu's face. Plucking another handkerchief from his pocket, he wiped his forehead and neck as further Portuguese curses flew from his mouth. Finally he settled. His face grew tight. His hand inched toward the pistol stuffed in his belt.

"Ah, ah, ah, Captain." Patrick braced his feet on the rolling earth. "I *will* kill you. Don't think I won't. I'm giving you a choice here, Captain. I can shoot you dead on the spot, or I can tie you up and leave you here to take your chances with the"—he took in the walls where chips of dirt and rock started to break free—"crumbling earth."

Two pirates approached their captain and relieved him of his sword, knife, and two pistols before grabbing rope and turning him around to tie his hands. Ricu's face bloated as red as a beet. He cursed and spit and growled like an animal in a trap. A violent jolt struck the chamber, sending the men off balance. Ricu kicked behind him, striking one of the pirates' legs. He fell to the ground. Without glancing back, Ricu plowed toward the opening, stumbling over the teetering earth. Patrick fired. The shot cracked like a whip, echoing off walls. Ricu's terror-streaked eyes glanced over James before he disappeared through the opening.

Angeline's breath came hard beside James. Hair clung to her face and neck in sodden braids. Her skin was pink, her gown was damp with sweat, and she seemed to be fighting for every breath. He kissed her forehead. She wouldn't make it much longer. Neither would Eliza, who sat slumped across a boulder behind them, hand on her rounded belly. *God, please, help us.*

"I'll be all right, James," Angeline whispered with a nod. He smiled and wanted to tell her how proud he was of her, how much he loved her, but Patrick's sarcastic voice brought him around.

"Never fear." Patrick waved off Ricu with his smoking pistol. "We will kill him later. Now, get that gold! And you"—he leveled the weapon at James and his friends—"get out! Or I'll shoot all of you. I don't know what tricks you are playing. I don't know how you made those swords fly, but you won't make this pistol move before I shoot one of you through the heart." His hard gaze took them all in. "Why are you here, anyway? Want to steal the gold for yourselves?"

James braced himself on the quivering ground. Sulfur and gun smoke stung his nose. He wouldn't answer the man. Nor would he leave. Not when there was still a chance someone could read the Latin phrase. But his eyes betrayed him as they shifted above the alcove.

Patrick fingered his goatee and glanced up. Grabbing a torch, he leapt onto a boulder and held it toward the alcove. "Writing in Latin. How odd. What would Latin be doing beneath this old temple?"

Dodd finally emerged from behind a boulder, shook dust from his coat, and cast wary eyes over the scene.

The ground canted. The rock walls shook. But Patrick seemed unfazed. "My Latin is a little rusty, but I think I can manage it."

CHAPTER 38

"Hold hands!" James shouted. With Patrick about to speak the Latin phrase, James had no other choice. He must do the only thing he knew to do. His heart seized in his throat as Blake helped Eliza rise and the six of them formed a line with linked arms. "We command you beasts to return to your chains!" James shouted.

The quaking increased, tossing them over the ground. Larger rocks broke from the walls and ceiling and thundered to the dirt. An eerie *thwack* that sounded like the snap of a thousand whips sent a rod of steal down James's spine. A crack etched through the rock wall on their left as if an invisible hand drew a chaotic design. Frozen in place, James watched as water trickled from the cleft, slow at first like a lazy stream, then faster and faster until it gushed from the ever-widening fissure. Chunks of rock broke from the wall in the torrent that now surged into the room, cascading onto the floor, splattering mud into the air.

"What's happening?" Magnolia yelled.

Dodd leapt onto the boulder beside Patrick, but the man shoved him down, the first hint of fear appearing on his face. The pirates stopped their work.

"Why isn't it working?" Blake shouted. Eliza stood firm beside him. Hayden, Magnolia trembling in his arms, inched back toward the entrance.

The ground canted. Balancing himself, James shook his head. "I don't know! This is all the book said to do. Besides something about a prince."

"A prince?" Angeline stared down at the water swarming around her shoes. "What prince?"

"There was a story in the book about a prince who came to rescue his people, but his name was never mentioned." James had gone over it several times, praying for help with the interpretation, praying he hadn't missed something.

The water soon flooded the chamber floor and began to rise. "Hurry!" Patrick shouted at the pirates. "Fill the sacks, take the gold above and come back for more!" Snatching a pack of gold from one of the pirates, he sloshed through the water and disappeared through the entrance, only to return within seconds for another. The pirates followed suit. Dodd knelt to fill his own sack, water gushing around his knees.

James squeezed his eyes shut. Perhaps in all the mayhem no one would say the Latin phrase now, but they still needed to imprison the other three beasts. Terror like he'd never known drained the blood from his heart. Not terror of drowning or being buried alive, but terror of failing. Failing God, failing his friends. Hot water, brown with dirt, licked his ankles, seeped into his boots.

The ground tilted. Water sloshed left, then right, shoving them into the filthy mire. Shaking sludge from his hands, James rose and helped Angeline. Mud splattered her arms and neck and slid down her gown. She lifted her eyes to his, and for the first time he saw her confidence waning. *God help me. What do I do?* James had no idea. Panic fired idea after idea into his mind. None of them sticking. None of them making sense.

Patrick, Dodd, and the pirates continued to fill their sacks and carry them above. Instead of pouring out in a stream, the gold now only trickled from the holes with each leap of the ground. One of the pirates tried to pry loose another rock lower in the wall.

That's when the snakes appeared, dozens of them slithering through the muck. Magnolia screamed and leapt into Hayden's arms. Eliza scrambled to stand atop a boulder. Angeline buried her head in James's shirt. Reaching through the water, Dodd grabbed one of Ricu's swords and began hacking the reptiles. But still the snakes slithered around their trousers, around the women's skirts, slinking between their legs. One of the pirates leapt atop a pile of rocks and shot his pistol into the water.

"Behold, I give unto you power to tread on serpents and scorpions, and over all the power of the enemy: and nothing shall by any means hurt you."

The scripture blared in James's mind. "They can't hurt us. They aren't real!" he yelled as a jolt sent both water and snakes to the left, splashing against the wall, only to return and flood them once again. One of the slithering beasts coiled around James's leg. *It sure feels real! God, please help!* Terror choked him. He kicked the snake off. And the next one. And the next. His friends did the same.

The snakes were harmless, just as God had said. Another tremor struck. James caught his balance and steadied Angeline. Hayden lowered Magnolia to the water as the reptiles disappeared.

Eliza grabbed her wet skirts and waded toward James. Stark golden eyes met his. "The prince who rescued his people!" she shouted, kicking one of the remaining snakes away. The ground tilted, sending her tumbling back. Blake caught her and held fast. "The prince who rescued his people!" she repeated with more exuberance, nodding at James as if he knew the answer.

The answer Magnolia must have also just realized as she lifted wide eyes to James. "Of course!"

Angeline gripped James's arm. "You know. The prince who rescued his people!"

James's thoughts were as muddied as the water now clawing his knees, splashing on boulders and up the sides of the chamber. His dream of the blood ship played in his mind. He and his friends had linked arm in arm as the ship approached the darkness. But it wasn't completely dark. There had been the figure of light at the bow. The lion-lamb. *The Lion-Lamb!* The name lit the shadows of his mind like a flame in a dark tunnel. With a nod, they all joined arms again. James cleared his throat and shouted at the top of his lungs: "We command you to return to your chains in the name of Jesus!"

"In the name of Jesus," Angeline repeated, and each of them followed, ending with Blake who shouted, "In Jesus' name!" with vehemence.

Patrick faced them, gold coins spilling from his arms while laughter spilled from his lips. But his chuckle was soon muffled by a thunderous growl that sounded like a mortally wounded animal. A very large animal. A very angry animal. The force of it shoved James and his friends backward into the hot muck.

Water ceased pouring from the wall. The roar silenced. The ground became still. Chains in the empty alcove lifted in the air around the pole that stretched from top to bottom. The sound of rattling metal echoed through the chamber as the irons shook and trembled with such violence, it seemed they would burst. Then as if by invisible hands, the lock looped around the thick clasp and clanked shut.

No one uttered a word. Only the sound of breathing and the *drip*, *drop* of water filled the cave. All gazes remained on the lock. The third beast was imprisoned again. And James had no doubt the first two had also returned to their chains in the room above.

They had defeated the four demonic generals!

With God's help. In the name of His Son.

James glanced at his friends, all bloody, bruised, muddy, and sweaty. And they all began to laugh, to cry, to praise God!

Patrick, Dodd, and the pirates stood, mud dripping from their shirts, disbelief dripping from their expressions.

A snapping sound drew James's gaze to the chasm where the water had poured forth. The crack widened and jetted upward then spiked across the ceiling like lightning, etching a rut that grew larger with each turn and twist. Rocks chipped off walls and stalactites fell into the receding water. The earth jolted and the crevice expanded, arching down the opposite wall and jutting across the muddy ground. The floor split open. The remaining water poured down. Steam shot into the air.

"The room is collapsing!" Hayden shouted.

"Get out! Get out!" Blake yelled, holding his side and grabbing his wife.

They hurried back through the hole. Dodd brought up the rear, carrying two sacks of gold. Once back in the first chamber, James glanced at the alcoves. Chains hung suspended in air, locked tight. He smiled, longing to shout at the beasts, to tell them they could no longer hurt the colonists—that they couldn't send visions and nightmares and floods and snakes. But there was no time for gloating. The earth still shook like a carriage on hilly terrain as the walls around them crumbled.

Drawing Angeline near, James scanned the group, bouncing and jostling in his vision. "Where's Patrick?" he yelled. The celling of the first chamber began to crack. Halting, Hayden glanced back toward the opening. "Go ahead! I'll get him!" He started limping toward the lower chamber. James handed Angeline to her friends and insisted—against their protests—that they keep moving. Then turning, he followed Hayden. He wouldn't let his friend deal with Patrick alone. Or risk getting killed by staying too long.

"Father, please! Come with us!" Hayden shouted as he ducked to avoid falling rocks. "You'll be buried alive."

"Go on without me!" The imperious man pulled another empty sack from the pile, knelt at the base of the rock wall, and scooped gold into it.

The water was gone, replaced by a sea of mud sliding across the chamber with each leap of the earth. Some fell into the steamy fissure that grew wider with each passing minute. Balancing on the trembling ground, Patrick wiped a sleeve over his forehead and yanked a rather large goblet from the pile.

Perhaps they could hit him over the head with one of them and drag him above. But James doubted they had time. He must ensure the others made it safely to the surface. Yet how could they leave Patrick here? Hayden started for his father when a jet of steam shot from the crevice, forcing him back.

"Go on, Hayden. . .I'll be along." Patrick grinned. "And richer than you ever imagined."

The room split. Pebbles showered them from above. The rock wall shielding the gold shifted. Some of the rocks tumbled from the top into the mud beside Patrick. Another tremor struck. The wall teetered like a heap of pudding. Patrick gazed up in fear, started to leave, but it was too late. Raising his arms to cover his head, he crouched as an avalanche of rocks struck his shoulders and back and piled around his feet. Momentarily stunned, Patrick shook his head and raised his gaze as gold—finally freed from its barricade—showered over him. Ignoring the gashes on his arms and shoulders, he grabbed handfuls of the treasure and flung it in the air, laughing.

The chasm widened. Steam spit in his face. He screamed and fell backward. The ground opened up. Rocks and gold slid into the opening. Terror pinching his face, Patrick tried to move away from the growing fissure, but the weight of the rocks and gold surrounding his feet and legs kept him in place. Coins slid into the crevice as the mouth opened wider and wider, gobbling up the chamber.

"Father!" Hayden shouted, agony spiking his voice.

In that split second between time and eternity when life hangs between the living and the dead. . .Patrick's gaze met Hayden's. And for the first time since James had known them, a thread of affection spilled from father to son.

Hayden saw it too. He dashed toward his father.

But the ground widened, and the man slid into the steaming fissure, along with all his gold. His scream silenced within seconds.

Heat seared them as Hayden stood staring at flames leaping from the opening. No. Not flames anymore, but molten lava bubbling over the edge.

Clutching Hayden's arm, James hauled him back into the chamber above, angry when he saw his friends had waited. "Go!" he shouted. Magnolia grabbed her husband, and the two darted forward.

Elation, terror, and heartache battled in James's chest as he clutched Angeline to his side and followed the others through the tunnels. Was it his imagination or was the passageway narrowing with each step? Heat pursued them—heat that could turn them to ash in seconds. Heat and the roar of a mighty fire. He didn't look back. Didn't want to see what he assumed was a sea of flames chasing them up the shaft.

Ahead, Blake assisted the others through the final hole back into the temple. Turning, he reached down for Angeline and James. The ground trembled. The entrance crumbled, filling with dirt and stones. Heat scorched James's back. Angeline struggled through the opening. The bottoms of her muddy, seared shoes were the last thing he saw as the hole narrowed even more. He thrust his arm through, and Blake hauled him up. Rocks scored his skin.

A tremor struck the temple. Debris rained down on them. Something sharp speared James's shoulder. Pain radiated across his neck. The temple columns began to quiver like noodles. Water sloshed out of the steamy pond. The moon and stars dislodged from the wall above the altar and clanged to the ground.

"The temple's collapsing!" Hayden yelled as they all darted for the front.

"Where's Dodd?" Angeline shouted.

James glanced back toward the tunnel entrance. The opening was barely wide enough for a person to squeeze through.

"Get out!" He nudged her forward, grabbed a shovel one of the pirates must have left and dug around the entry. Steam poured from the shrinking hole. A mighty roar sounded. Dust erupted from the opening. The tunnels must have collapsed. No one could survive that. Hand covering his mouth and nose, James turned to leave, but Angeline darted past him. "There he is!"

A flash of light hair appeared among the rubble. Dodd's face, barely recognizable beneath the mud and blood, gazed up at them. "Help me!"

"Give me your hand!"

A sack of gold appeared instead. Disgusted, James shoved it back. "Your hand, man. Your hand!"

"Take the gold first." He breathed out. "I can't lift it."

"Leave it! Leave it, or you'll die."

Dodd closed his eyes. The entrance toppled in on him. Dirt and rocks filled the space where he'd just been. Dust filled the air.

Angeline coughed and batted it aside. "No!"

A hand burst through the rubble.

James grabbed it. Angeline clawed away the dirt. Groaning, James tugged with all his might. Dodd's shoulder appeared.

The ground shook. Temple walls cracked. The dirt loosened, and Dodd's other hand punched through the debris. Bracing her shoes on the wall around the entrance, Angeline pulled, she on one side, James on the other. Dodd's chest popped through. Finally his legs appeared. But his feet remained. Fire leapt up from below. Dodd screamed. James yanked him the rest of the way. Looping Dodd's arm over his shoulder, James hoisted him up and dashed toward the portico, whispering a prayer. Angeline ran at his side as they both dodged slabs of stone and tumbled down the stairs and across the courtyard. Obelisks fell left and right. Weaving around them, they burst through the gate into the arms of their friends at the edge of the jungle. All seven of them fell in a heap on the ground, covered in mud, blood spilling over face and arms, chests heaving.

But clinging to one another in victory.

The roar of a thousand cannons pummeled the sky. A plume of

flaming rock fired into the air above the temple. James shot to his feet and hauled the others up, ready to run. The wall surrounding the temple collapsed with a thunderous crash. The temple shook as if some giant child thought it nothing but a toy. Then it flattened as if that child stepped on it. Stones larger than a house folded inward and sank into the ground. A wave of dust blasted over them. James squeezed his eyes shut. Coughing, he clung to Angeline as they both fell to the dirt, gasping for air.

The shaking stopped. All grew quiet. Not a breeze stirred, not a bird sang. Afraid to open his eyes and discover he was dead, James sat there holding Angeline, listening to her breathe. He felt her move and push from him. Finally he opened his eyes. Ash and soot showered over them like snowflakes.

The temple was gone.

CHAPTER 39

"W"ilt thou, Angeline Moore, have this man to be thy wedded husband, to live together after God's ordinance..." Angeline smiled at James as he continued, half reading from the *Book of Common Prayer*, half gazing at her with his bronze eyes so full of love they seemed ready to burst. Was it proper—or even legal—for him to perform his own marriage ceremony? Angeline supposed if they were breaking some cardinal rule, God would make an exception in their case. For she wouldn't be able to stand another day—another night—without this man. Especially not the time it would take to travel to Rio de Janeiro to see a priest.

James took her right hand in his. Strong, bruised fingers intertwined with hers, the sensual action sending her breath spinning. A salty breeze tossed his hair over the collar of his shirt. The shirt that was missing two buttons and was singed in one spot where the heat from the tunnels had burned him. A badge of honor for his godly mission to restrain evil. One that he had accomplished with great courage and God's power. They all had, in fact. But James had been their leader. The prophet, the forerunner.

And she couldn't be more proud.

Nor could she be more excited that today he would become her husband. This preacher-doctor who looked more like a sailor stranded on an island than a groom. A sailor who had picked a fight with otherworldly beasts from the looks of the cuts and bruises on his face, neck, and arms. But as he stood there on the sandy beach beneath a bamboo arbor laden with orchids and red ferns, his hair and shirt

946

blowing in the wind, he was the most handsome man she'd ever seen. The thought that within minutes he would become her husband made a tingle spread clear down to her toes.

"I, James Callaway, take thee, Angeline Moore, to be my wedded wife, to have and to hold from this day forward, for better for worse, for richer for poorer, in sickness and in health, to love and to cherish, till death us do part, according to God's holy ordinance; and thereto I plight thee my troth."

Someone sniffed in the audience, and Angeline saw Magnolia lift a handkerchief to her eye. Beside the Southern belle stood all the people who mattered most in the world to Angeline: Hayden, Eliza, Blake, Sarah, and Thiago. Next to them, Moses shadowed Mable who perched beside the Scotts. In the distance, Captain Ricu watched along with a group of his pirates. Those who had sided with Patrick— apparently over half his crew—were conspicuously absent. They had been "reward their due" Ricu had explained when asked, and Angeline hadn't wanted to inquire what that meant.

Dodd, bandages on his feet and legs, sat on a boulder to the right. She smiled at Mr. Lewis, who sat beside him, having reappeared from the jungle yesterday, dazed and with no remembrance of the past two months. Had he turned into a man-wolf, this Lobisón, as Thiago still insisted, and then somehow changed back when the beasts were imprisoned? Angeline didn't know, nor did she want to think about it on such a glorious day.

The crash of waves and serenade of birds provided the music. An overskirt the ladies had woven from purple and pink flowers made up her wedding gown. Yet she might as well be wearing taffeta silk for the way James looked at her.

Shifting his stance he turned to Blake, who fumbled inside his waistcoat pocket for a ring. A band of gold? Yet what else could shimmer so beautifully in the afternoon sun?

"With this ring I thee wed, with my body I thee worship." James slid it on her finger and adored her with his eyes. "And with all my worldly goods I thee endow." His lips slanted. "As scant as they are."

Tears glazed her eyes. She smiled up at him. He brushed a thumb over her lips in such an intimate, caring gesture, her knees turned to mush.

"I now pronounce us man and wife, in the name of the Father, and of the Son, and of the Holy Ghost. Amen."

Cheers of joy filled the air. Yelps and whistles and a few Portuguese words emanated from the pirates as the colonists flooded the couple with congratulations.

But Angeline couldn't take her eyes off her husband.

Not during the excruciatingly long celebration that followed, not when they entered the private hut prepared for their honeymoon. And not even an hour later when, to the gentle lull of waves, James and she became one in flesh in the eyes of God.

Afterward, they held each other and talked and loved and prayed and spoke of their adventures, their God, their future, and their dreams. They were both still awake when the first blush of dawn creased the horizon. Pulling aside the canvas flap that faced their private beach, Angeline sat to watch the sun rise on a new day, happier than she'd ever been. James inched behind her, straddling her with his legs while encasing her with his arms. She leaned back on his chest and sighed, thanking God for cleansing her, for forgiving her, for loving her. And for making all her dreams come true. "I never want this night to end."

James nibbled on her ear. "We will have many more nights together. A lifetime."

She sighed as wind tossed her curls that smelled of coconut and orange blossoms over his face, tickling his skin. He twirled a finger around one of the delicate strands, longing to wrap his entire body in the silky web.

And remain there forever.

Last night, his eyes had been opened to what real love was. Not selfish pleasure, but giving everything of oneself. The melding of soul, spirit, and body in a love that was as close to perfection this side of heaven. No wonder God held marriage so sacred, so holy. It was a taste of paradise, of God's unconditional love, a bonding that was more spiritual than physical. And to dishonor it by using it only for one's pleasure, to fulfill a physical need, absent of real love, was to spit in the face of God Himself and His incredible gift to man. It was also to do great harm to one's own body and soul.

James hadn't understood that until now. But God had cleansed him. He had cleansed Angeline. And together throughout the night they had danced across the heavenly realms.

The golden arc of the sun peered over the horizon, curling ribbons of saffron and scarlet over sky and sea. Squeezing her against him, he trailed kisses up her neck, his body reacting in delight when she moaned.

"If you keep that up, Mr. Callaway, I fear we will never leave this hut."

"If that were to happen, Mrs. Callaway, I fear I will die a very happy man."

⚓

"Upon your honor, Captain Ricu, please assure me that you aren't kidnapping these people." Blake squinted into the sun and stared at the ostentatious pirate, his red plume fluttering in the wind, his Portuguese bark sending men to assist the colonists into two waiting boats. "I wouldn't want them pressed into piracy."

Ricu faced Blake. "Colonel, do I lie? I take them to Rio, of course! Though you give me good idea. I can always use more men." His eyes twinkled mischievously.

Angeline chuckled at the disconcerted look Blake exchanged with James.

"No fears," Ricu continued with a grin, sunlight winking off his silver tooth. "Your God has much power. More even than me." He chuckled as if that were beyond comprehension. "I no cross swords with Him. Deliver people safe."

"What of your gold, Captain?" Angeline asked. "And your lady?"

He waved a jeweled hand through the air. "Gold stay buried with monsters. I value life more than wealth. Wealth I find. Life, I have one." He shrugged. "Perhaps two. Besides"—he grew serious and leaned toward Blake and James, crossing himself—"I see much evil as I cross seas. And what I see in tunnels should not be free. Not for gold." He stood back and shouted an order to one of his crew. "And my lady? If she prefer gold over golden heart"—he laid his hand over his heart and winked at Angeline—"then she not the lady for me."

Angeline gave him a smile of approval as sobbing drew her gaze to Magnolia and her parents. Poor Mrs. Scott wilted like a sun-bleached

949

flower in her daughter's arms. Mr. Scott stood beside them, looking as if he attended a funeral. They had decided to leave with the rest of the colonists—first to Rio and then on a ship back to the States. Angeline couldn't blame them. The jungles of Brazil were no place for landed gentry so unaccustomed to discomfort.

An argument ensued that seemed to have something to do with Mable, but finally the slave slid behind Magnolia while Magnolia's father planted a kiss on his daughter's cheek and led his weeping wife to one of the boats.

Other tearful good-byes were performed in morbid playacts across the shore. Most of the colonists had opted to go home. Good food—anything but fish and fruit—a soft bed, new attire that wasn't stained and torn, a house that didn't blow away in the wind, libraries and plays and concerts, all the pleasures of society, lured them to abandon the fledgling colony for civilization. Even with James's assurance that there would be no more visions or disasters.

But Brazil had burrowed deep within Angeline's soul. It had changed her. Shown her that she was more than a comely face and figure to be used by men. It was here where she had met God and found her freedom. It was here where she had fallen in love. And it was here where her husband remained. She would stay with him, follow him wherever he went. Forever.

Her throat burned watching the mournful partings as the colonists settled, one by one, into the boats. She'd already hugged the ladies who had meant so much to her, who had treated her like one of them, and she'd bid farewell to all the men who were leaving. Except the one heading straight for her now.

James saw him too and slipped beside Angeline.

Dodd tugged off his hat and swept a hand through hair too long and unkempt for the civilization to which he headed. He wiggled his crooked nose and lowered his gaze. "I came to say good-bye."

Though his tone was penitent, the sound of his voice sent a spike of dread down Angeline's back. Surely he was up to something. Despite his recent promise that he wouldn't take her home to face charges. Perhaps he had changed his mind, saving the cruel announcement until the last minute when he would clap her in irons and haul her aboard the *Espoliar*. She could almost see his malicious grin of victory.

But when he raised his face, all she saw was remorse.

"Good-bye, Mr. Dodd." Angeline forced lightness into her tone, though her voice came out scratchy.

"I have no doubt you're not sorry to see me go," he said.

"I can't say that I am."

He smiled.

Hoping to discourage any last-minute change of heart, Angeline added, "I do thank you, however, for not turning me in."

Dodd's eyes shifted toward the sea, where incoming waves collapsed into bubbling foam. "You came back for me. Both of you." He glanced at James. "You saved me, after all I've done." He fumbled with his hat.

James held out his hand. "All is forgiven, Dodd."

Surprise creased Dodd's forehead as he gripped James's hand in a firm shake. "Doc, I saw some things back there in the tunnels...things I need to consider. Things that got me thinking there's more to life than gold."

James grinned. "Indeed, there is, Mr. Dodd."

Angeline spotted a light in Dodd's eyes she'd never seen before. Was it possible God could change even Dodd? Well, of course it was.

"I'm sorry you didn't get your gold," she said.

"Are you now?" He grinned. "Where do you think that wedding ring on your finger came from?" He winked, plopped his hat atop his head, then turned and leapt into one of the boats.

❦

Fourteen. Fourteen colonists. That was all that was left of New Hope. Yet, as James led them through the jungle to the spot where he hoped to reveal his plan, he couldn't help but feel that these fourteen souls— together with God—could accomplish miracles.

Would accomplish miracles.

His father's Bible tucked beneath his arm, he entered the rubble-filled clearing and was relieved to not feel the usual heaviness. Turning, he faced his friends. Blake stood behind Eliza, his arms circling her and resting atop her rounded belly as both their confused gazes assessed James. Hayden, his foot bound from his wound, assisted Magnolia over a pile of rocks before they both stopped and scanned the clearing with alarm. Angeline sidled up to James with a look that said, *I don't know what you're doing, but I believe in you.* It warmed him even more than the heat of the day. Moses, hand entwined with Mable's, sweat marring his forehead, approached the desolation with caution. Delia and her two children followed behind. And lastly, Thiago stepped beside Sarah, Lydia hoisted in his arms. As James's gaze took in the way Thiago looked at Sarah and Moses looked at Mable, he wondered if he might be officiating more marriage ceremonies in the near future.

The thought brought another smile to his face, which quickly flattened when all their questioning eyes latched upon him. He cleared his throat and ran a sleeve over his forehead. Why did it always seem hotter here where the temple had once stood? Gazing up at the wispy clouds floating across the sky, he listened to the chatter of wildlife and chirp of birds filling the air—life's constant lullaby.

"This is where we must build New Hope," he finally said.

Blake's forehead crinkled. "Here? Where the cannibals used to sacrifice"—he swallowed—"you mean on top of the tunnels?"

"Yes." James said. "I believe we must. I believe we have to." He gestured to a heap of remains where the temple had once stood. "I'm going to build a church here. A grand church with a steeple that rises high into the heavens."

Silence, save for the buzz of insects, met his declaration, yet when he faced his friends again, the skepticism on their faces gave way to understanding. And finally to nods of affirmation.

"I says it a good idea," Moses said.

Hayden gave a slanted grin as he scanned the area. "There's plenty of good farming land. Much of it already cleared."

"And it's close enough to the river," Eliza added.

"We build road to river. Good road," Thiago said, tickling Lydia who responded with a giggle.

Sarah shrugged. "If we must start over, this place is as good as any."

Angeline gazed up at James. "We must build a fountain in the middle of town. A glorious, sparkling fountain."

For her, he would build a lake.

Magnolia twirled a lock of hair and frowned. "But why here? Why this morbid spot? It still makes me tremble."

Lengthening his stance, James glanced over the ruins. "We must protect it. No one must ever dig beneath this land again. No one must ever come near those beasts." He hesitated, not wanting to sound like a madman, but yet needing to share what he believed God had told him. "We are the guardians of these fallen angelic generals. That is why we were sent to Brazil. Not only to confine them. . .but to keep them confined."

He half expected laughter, perhaps snorts of disbelief, but instead his friends stared into the clearing as if remembering the battle they'd so recently fought, remembering the horror of seeing such evil on the cusp of being released. Slowly, one by one, each determined gaze locked upon his.

Eliza smiled. "And we will teach our children to protect it, and they will teach theirs after them."

Blake gave an approving nod and drew his wife close.

"Indeed," James said, joy swelling within him. He raised the Bible in the air—the one his father had given him all those years ago. He'd not appreciated it back then. He'd not realized the power that existed in the Word of God. But he wouldn't make that mistake again. "So what do you say? Shall we build New Hope on this place? Shall we make it the Southern utopia we always dreamed of? Shall we put a church atop the gates of hell? A symbol of good triumphing over evil?"

"All in favor, say aye," Blake shouted.

"Ayes" fired into the air.

James turned to Angeline and nearly melted at the look of admiration in her eyes. He was no longer a failure. Not in her eyes. Or in the eyes of God. He had found his God-given purpose. And what a purpose it was! To protect the world from an evil that, if unleashed, would kill thousands, maybe more.

And to cherish and love this woman beside him with all of his heart, forever.

EPILOGUE

Present day

There is a quaint little town in Brazil called New Hope. Located just south of Rio de Janeiro and a short distance from the coast, it boasts close to thirty thousand inhabitants. Some are farmers, some tradesmen, some workers, some teachers, doctors, priests. At first glance, there is nothing special about the town. Yet if you decide to stay awhile, you might hear pockets of English spoken here and there instead of Portuguese. You might notice that grits, fried chicken, vinegar pie, and cornbread are found on restaurant menus, that the city seal has distinct markings of the US Confederate flag, and that once a year on the fourth of July, the local women get dressed up in hoop skirts for square dancing and singing. If you lend an ear during the celebration, you may even hear the familiar tune of "Dixie" floating on the city streets.

In the center of town sits a church made of stone—a church more than one hundred and fifty years old. Though its stone walls are chipped, and one of its wooden doors is rotting, its white steeple thrusts toward the heavens, strong and bright. Stained glass decorates the windows, and some say in certain light you can see scenes form in the colored glass, depicting an ancient battle between humans and angels, complete with floods and fire and lightning bolts. If you are ever cold, just slip inside that church and I guarantee, you'll be warm before you know it. What causes the heat when there is no electricity in the building, no one can explain to this day.

In front of the church stands a fountain with an angel carved in stone standing in its center, sword in hand. Water pours from the tip of the sword back into the fountain, where steam rises to meet the day. They say the fountain has curative properties, and you'll often see locals and visitors alike dipping their hands in the unusually warm pool.

If you're lucky, you'll meet the old pastor of the church, a man by the name of Aleixo Callaway. A tall man in his eighties with a shock of gray hair and bronze eyes that can see right through a person. The kindest man you'll ever meet. Honorable and wise, he is highly revered among the locals. In fact, it's on account of him that the city council hasn't torn down that old church and put up a new one. If you see him, ask him why. But make sure you have an hour to spare, for he loves to tell the tale of how his great-grandfather, along with five others, defeated four of the fiercest evil angels ever created, and entombed them beneath the church. It's his job to keep them there, he'll tell you. A job he'll pass down to his son Cristovao when Aleixo passes on.

A bunch of malarkey if you ask me.

But it sure makes for a good story.

Author's Historical Note

New Hope, of course, is a fictional town, but it may interest the reader to know there is a real city in Brazil called Americana, located in the Brazilian state of São Paulo, very near to where I positioned New Hope. The town was originally populated by American Confederates fleeing the South, desperate to preserve their Southern way of life. They came to be known as *Confederados*, and the town became thus popularly known as *Villa dos Americanos* (Town of the Americans).

Though the majority of the Confederates who sailed to Brazil eventually returned home to America, many thousands remained. Their unique influence and culture are still evident throughout the country today. These immigrants didn't just bring their Southern way of life, they brought new agricultural innovations and introduced the Georgia Rattlesnake watermelon, which flourished in Brazil. They also brought the buckboard wagon and Protestantism, as well as improvements in education and medicine.

If you happen to visit Americana, there is a small Confederate cemetery nearby in the city of Santa Bárbara named Campo. Take a stroll among the graves and view names such as Carlton, Cobb, Green, Moore, Smith, and tons more—all common names in Alabama, Georgia, and South Carolina in the nineteenth century. Inscribed on one of the headstones you'll see the words:

"Soldier rest! Thy warfare o'er. Sleep the sleep that knows no breaking. Days of toil or nights of waking."

Four times a year, a group of people gather at this cemetery and hold a service in a nearby chapel, where they sing Protestant revival hymns and gaze at an altar covered with three flags: Brazilian, Confederate, and American. Afterward they dress in costumes of nineteenth-century America and enjoy a huge meal of biscuits and gravy and Southern fried chicken. If you look real close, you'll see that some of the people have red hair, freckles, and blue eyes, and many of them speak in a quaint English dialect. An odd sight, indeed, in the middle of Brazil! Although these American descendants have been meeting for years, it wasn't until 1955 that this group of Confederados formally became the *Fraternidade Decendencia Americana* (American Descendants' Fraternity), dedicated to preserving both the history and the culture of their Southern descendants.

ABOUT THE AUTHOR

MaryLu Tyndall, a Christy Award Finalist and bestselling author of the Legacy of the King's Pirates series, is known for her adventurous historical romances filled with deep spiritual themes. She holds a degree in math and worked as a software engineer for fifteen years before testing the waters as a writer. MaryLu currently writes full-time and makes her home on the California coast with her husband, six kids, and four cats. Her passion is to write page-turning romantic adventures that not only entertain but open people's eyes to their God-given potential. MaryLu is a member of American Christian Fiction Writers and Romance Writers of America.